I0760466

THE COMPLETE SERIES

EVA CHASE

Their Dark Valkyrie: The Complete Series



First Digital Edition, 2021



Cover design: Bewitching Book Designs

Ebook ISBN: 978-1-989096-93-2

Hardcover ISBN: 978-1-989096-94-9

# CLAIMED BY GODS

THEIR DARK VALKYRIE - BOOK 1

# 1

*Aria*

I'd like to tell you that I died in epic fashion, guns blazing in the middle of a vast street brawl, or at least something scandalously hot, like falling off a balcony during the most incredible sex of my life. The truth? My death was cringingly mundane.

I hopped off my moped on the grungy Philly street and loped across the road to the doggy daycare where a client was waiting. The blazing July sun made the asphalt stink, and chances were ten to one the guys on the corner had crack and pistols underneath those baggy jerseys. It was hard to say which was more dangerous: the neighborhood or the package stashed in my shoulder bag. A well-paid courier doesn't ask what she's carrying; she just delivers the goods on time.

One of the toughs whose name I'd never had to learn stood behind the front desk, and Gene was leaning against the wall nearby. Oh joy. He straightened up and gave me a greasy smile as I tugged the taped-up parcel out of my bag.

"Ari. Always a pleasure."

"Wish I could say the same, Gene," I said brightly, handing the parcel over to the tough. He examined it with a brisk nod and reached under the desk to get my money. Whines and yips emanated from the inner room where their few doggy charges hung out, providing a front for whatever their real business was. I didn't ask questions about that stuff.

Gene blinked at me. I'd learned a long time ago that you could be as insultingly honest as you'd like as long as you made the words sound cheery enough. Brains like his just didn't know how to process both the meaning and the tone at the same time.

Unfortunately, the dimness of his brain also meant he never gave up on hitting on me, even though he was old enough to be my dad and so smarmy I doubt I'd have had the slightest interest when he'd been in his twenties either. He was also the cousin of one of my biggest clients, so I couldn't just stab him a few times to get the point across, as much as I'd sometimes wanted to.

Not fatally, of course. Just somewhere painful enough that message would stick.

Instead, when he sidled over to me and tried to put his arm around my waist, I had to simply dodge to the side, pasting a stiff smile on my face. My hand dropped to the pocket of my jeans, taking comfort in tracing the lump of the switchblade I *would* use if I absolutely had to.

"Aw, come on, honey," Gene said. "You can't come in here lookin' like that and deny a guy a little fun. I'd show you a good time."

I had on my jeans—fitted but not *that* tight—and a loose white T-shirt with a neckline that barely grazed my collarbone. No makeup, my shoulder-length blond hair rumpled from the moped ride. By *looking like that* he meant existing while young and female.

"I'm sure you would, Gene," I said, still smiling. "And I could show you my fist breaking your nose. But I think it's probably better if we avoid all that and just stay friends, huh?"

Gene put his puzzled face on again. He took another shuffle at me, and I raised that fist, arching an eyebrow.

"Three-time high school boxing champion," I added. "You really want to try me?" My voice was still sweet, but I let a hint of a glare harden my gaze.

Gene took me in and decided that backing off was in the best interest of maintaining his delusion that I'd be chomping at the bit for him any day now.

I'd never actually boxed in my life, but I'd landed enough effective punches that it didn't feel like a total lie.

The tough finally handed over my damn envelope. I flicked through the bills, tossed a "Thank you!" at him, and stuffed the money in my bag as I headed out the door.

It was a good payout, and I'd already done a decent run this week. I could pick up something for Petey this weekend. Not half the things I wanted to get him, since it had to be small enough that Mom wouldn't notice. A pack of those trading cards he was hooked on, and some snacks—maybe better shoes to replace the ratty sneakers she should have realized he'd grown out of? If I dirtied them up some first, she might not realize they were new…

Picturing my little brother's grinning face was the best antidote for Gene's unwelcome attention. A real smile crossed my face, but at the same time my heart squeezed.

Trading cards and shoes weren't enough. Nothing was going to be enough while Mom was… the way she was. If Petey's life there turned into even half the nightmare mine had been…

I shook those thoughts away. I was doing everything I could despite her. I wouldn't *let* anyone hurt him. And as soon as I'd saved up enough to get a nice house and the sharpest lawyer in the city, I'd fight until he could live under my roof instead.

The hooky beat of a pop song spilled from the open doorway of the mini-mart next door. A little sway crept into my stride as I made for my moped. Maybe I'd go dancing tonight, blow off some steam before I was pounding the street again. It'd been a while.

I wasn't looking left as I walked across, because it was a one-way street. But just as I hit the middle of the road, a yellow jeep came roaring around the corner, faster than any sane person should have been driving even going the right way.

The driver gave a shout. The tires screeched. I threw myself toward the opposite sidewalk.

Which might have saved me, if the guy behind the wheel hadn't been so high he decided to try to avoid me by veering in the same direction I was going.

The grill slammed into my side with a sickening crunch I heard as well as felt. Agony exploded all through my body. My legs crumpled. The corner of the bumper bashed my head with a skull-splitting *crack*.

The jumbled noises around me were swallowed up by a wave of pain. As my vision shrank to a pinhole and the light contracted with it, I had enough consciousness left to think, *Fucking jackass and his fucking jackass jeep*. And then, *Who's going to take care of Petey? He won't even know why I'm gone.*

A sharper, frantic jab of distress cut through the surging pain. But it wasn't enough to keep me there.

The wave crashed through me and over me and pulled me under, down into the dark where there was simply nothing.

---

Eyelids twitched.

*My* eyelids twitched.

Awareness crept through my body from there, sensation prickling through numbness across my cheeks and forehead, down my neck and over my chest and limbs.

I *had* limbs. I had a chest. A chest that was no longer a flaming mass of pain.

My head was still foggy. I blinked, and colors swam before my eyes. A chill tingled over my skin and my back felt weirdly heavy, but otherwise I didn't seem to be in bad shape. Had someone gotten me to a hospital? Maybe it was drugs making my mind and my vision so loopy.

I blinked again, and the colors merged into shapes. The shapes moved. Two of them, close by, came into focus.

Two men, both tall and muscular, though one was as beefy as anything with dark auburn hair and the other leanly slim, his hair pale red. And those perfectly chiseled faces, broad and square-jawed on one and gracefully angular on the other… If this was a hospital, it was more like the Hollywood movie set version.

Both of them were peering at me intently. Beefy took another step closer, holding out a white sheet as if to give it to me. To *me*? Because…

My awareness sharpened, my mind settling deeper into my body. Into my lightly chilled skin, which was chilled because I was wearing nothing over it. I was lying completely naked on some kind of padded surface in the middle of this big yellow room, with two strange men twice as big as me looming closer.

An icy jab of panic shot through my nerves. My arms and legs jerked as I got control of them through my daze. I scrambled against the floor, pushing myself away from the two men.

No, not just two. There were two others standing farther back, and a woman also, all of them watching me. The strange drag on my back made me wobble as I pulled my legs under me, bracing my hands and feet against the floor.

"Hey, there," Beefy said in a rumbling baritone, shaking the sheet as if to tempt me with it. As if I were a dog he was beckoning with a treat. "It's all right. No one here is going to hurt you."

Uh, yeah right. Because you could always trust *anyone* who made promises like that.

"What the fuck is going on?" I said, hunching lower to cover myself. "Where the hell am I?"

"Quite a different experience from the other ones, isn't she?" Slim glanced around at the others, his voice lightly amused. His gaze came back to me, and he cocked his head. "A little smaller than I realized she'd be. A regular pixie."

I had no clue what the hell he was talking about, but I knew I didn't like that comment. I gritted my teeth, the muscles in my shoulders flexing. "Just try me."

"And such spirit!" He grinned as if he expected me to join in the joke.

"Give her time to adjust," Beefy said. "We've got to let her get comfortable." He frowned, motioning with the sheet again. "Are you sure you don't want this?"

"I want you to tell me how I got here and what the fuck you think you're doing," I said.

My gaze darted past them and landed on a door at the far end of the room. I could make a run for it. They were stronger and bigger than me, sure, but I was fast. And they didn't seem to be expecting me to bolt, so I'd have surprise on my side.

"That's a little complicated," Slim said. "Why don't you relax and get your bearings for a minute, and then we can get into the nitty gritty details?"

A rough laugh burst out of my throat. Relax? Was he kidding?

I looked to the woman again—almost as tall as the guys and just as striking in looks, her face smooth as a supermodel's amid her waves of honey-brown hair. Who the hell *were* these people?

Would she help me, or was she planning on leaving me to the mercy of these men? Or on joining in with whatever they had planned?

She stared back at me, her mouth tightening. I thought I saw sympathy in her expression, but she didn't speak, didn't budge an inch.

I was on my own then.

The other guys were still hanging back near the room's big arched windows. Not too close to the door. Beefy took another step toward me.

How long until he forced the issue? I had to get out of here, and I had to go *now.* I shoved myself forward off the polished hardwood.

If my body had been working properly, that effort would have propelled me halfway across the room in just a few quick strides. But my shoulder blades twinged as if something had yanked on them and that weight on my back threw me to the side. What the hell was hanging off of me?

My shoulder glanced off the wall. Slim was in front of me in an instant, blocking the way. He was still fucking *smiling.*

My fist swung out, more out of instinct than because any part of me thought I had a chance in a hand to hand fight with him, and he outright laughed. I teetered backward and fumbled at my back in an attempt to detach whatever was dragging on me. My fingers brushed a softly rippled surface that my mind couldn't make any sense of.

Beefy closed in on me from the other side, brandishing that damned sheet. "Fuck off!" I said in what was practically a snarl. I dodged to the side, and Slim followed, his eyes sparkling with pleasure.

"Very different from the others," he murmured. "Good, good." He glanced over his shoulder. "Oh, nephew, I think you'd better mellow her out for a bit so we can give introductions another try later."

Mellow me out? One of the other guys, a little shorter than Beefy and Slim but still powerfully built, drifted across the room toward us. Beneath the fall of his shaggy white-blond hair, his eyes were crystal blue and weirdly dreamy. He met my eyes, but his expression didn't give any sign he'd noticed how freaked out I was. A shiver rippled through me.

No. I couldn't let them trap me here. I wouldn't let myself be helpless.

I hurled myself toward the door again, compensating better for the burden on my back now that I was getting used to it. Slim snatched out. But he didn't touch me—at least, not anything that should have been me. A jolt of sensation shot through me to my back, as if he'd grasped onto a limb I hadn't known I had. It jarred me to a stop.

My head spun. None of this made sense. "What the hell did you *do* to me?" I said, lashing out with another fist.

Slim sidestepped neatly, still holding onto that part of my body that shouldn't exist, that never had before. He gave me a smaller smile.

"We made you alive again, pixie," he said. "We made you a valkyrie."

He tugged that alien limb, and then I saw it at the corner of my eye: the unfurling of a huge silver-white feathered wing. A wing his fingers were curled around with a pressure I could feel along the length of it, all the way to where its flesh met my back.

A choked cry broke from my lips, and then the dreamy-eyed man filled my vision. His hands cupped my head. Before I had a chance to struggle, fluffy numbness enveloped my mind, washing the men and the room and all my frantic thoughts away into a warm bright void.

# 2

*Thor*

The girl slumped at Baldur's touch, her eyelids sliding shut and her head sagging. I pushed in to catch her before her body hit the floor.

She'd looked so tough a moment ago—small, yes, but wiry with muscle and blazing with rage—that the softness of her slack arms surprised me. I eased her down to the floor and draped the sheet I'd tried to offer her over her. She hadn't liked being naked in front of us. I'd been able to tell that much without her saying it.

Her wings were already shrinking with a faint rustling of the feathers, contracting back into her body where they'd stay until she urged them out again. If she ever got to that point. My mouth twisted as I brushed a lock of her dark blond hair away from her closed eyes.

She looked peaceful now, but she'd been terrified on top of furious a minute ago. *We* had terrified her. Why in Asgard's name hadn't I been prepared for that? Maybe the ones before had been the strange ones, holding still in their initial confusion, patient enough to hear our story and witness who and what we were.

But humans, all of them, were *my* charges more than that of any of the others here. I was the guardian of humankind. And the last five minutes had been a pretty epic failure of that duty.

Loki came up beside me, rubbing his narrow chin as he studied the girl. His eyes twinkled. "Well, I did promise something different, didn't I? She's a fighter, all right."

"A good one," I allowed. I'd been in enough battles to know experience and skill when I saw it, even in rough mortal form. "Which was promising to see. Of course, it'd have been better if she'd been aiming to fight our enemies and not *us*."

"I'm sure once we've established ourselves and our enemies properly, we can get her on the right track."

"Oh, you're sure, are you?" Hod said where he was standing with arms crossed near the windows. His expression was as dark as his short black hair. "Just like you were sure this 'brilliant' new idea of yours would go off without a hitch? From the moment she came to, it's looked like one giant hitch to me."

The light in Loki's eyes flared momentarily hotter, but he replied in his usual wry tone. "I'd imagine it didn't *look* like anything at all to you."

Hod's scowl deepened. After centuries of practice, he could aim his blind glower based on Loki's voice so accurately you'd almost believe he could see the trickster. "You know what I mean. Semantics don't change anything."

"If the success of every endeavor were judged by its first five minutes, civilization would be a terribly desolate affair," Loki said breezily.

"She's fine for the moment," Baldur said beside me, his voice as slow and melodic as always. As bright as his twin was dark. "I calmed her mind."

"Right." I pulled my thoughts away from my younger brothers

and our trickster companion, back to the matter at hand. "Let's find some way to make her more comfortable so she'll be in a better mood the second time she wakes up."

Freya ambled over and motioned with a graceful arm. "Bring her up to the usual bedroom. We should find her some clothes. Something to eat. And perhaps give her a little time on her own before she has to face the lot of you again?"

Loki chuckled, but he didn't argue. Hod looked happy enough to have the problem taken care of without him, and Baldur… Well, it was hard to tell what Baldur was thinking these days in general. Not a whole lot seemed to penetrate that dreamy glow around him. He didn't look bothered by the suggestion, anyway.

I eased my arms around the girl and lifted her. In sleep, she felt like barely anything. Keeping the sheet tucked around her, I rested her head and shoulders against my much wider shoulder and carried her to the stairs.

Freya followed me up. As I laid the girl on the bed in the room the other valkyries had used for the brief time they'd been with us, the goddess opened the wardrobe and considered its offerings. She took out a white silk blouse and a pair of gray linen slacks, folded them, and set them in a neat pile with various undergarments at the end of the bed. Then she stood and contemplated the girl.

"Do you think we should have listened to him?" I asked. She knew who I meant by *him.*

"Loki has gotten us out of trouble at least as often as he's gotten us into it," she said. "As… questionable as his methods may sometimes be. And it's true our first few tries didn't get us very far."

"Yes." My jaw tightened as I remembered the other young women who'd slept in that bed. Who'd been in our presence for just a few days and then…

We didn't even know for sure what had happened to them. They hadn't come back. That said enough right there.

"If that trickster has ever been loyal to anyone, it's Odin," Freya added. "He wants to find him as much as the rest of us do. I'm sure he wouldn't have suggested anything he suspected would hurt our cause, in any case."

"Point taken." After all the time I'd spent in Loki's presence, all the crazy exploits he'd gotten me wrapped up in over our long lifetimes, I still couldn't say I had any idea how that bizarre but clever mind of his worked. Norns knew I hadn't come up with any brilliant new plans on my end.

The goddess let out a sigh. I glanced over at her, focusing for a moment on her instead of our valkyrie. On the woman I could almost call my stepmother, except that the term felt a little ridiculous when I'd already been several centuries old at the time of the new marriage. Sometimes Odin hardly felt like he could be my father. When he wasn't there in the room with that vast presence of his, anyway.

I should extend some kind of courtesy. As sort-of family, and, well, fellow god stranded here on the human plane. I didn't dislike Freya. We just didn't have a whole lot in common.

"Are you holding up all right?" I said.

Freya's gaze slid to me with an amused twitch of her full lips, as if she could tell how much effort it'd taken me to pick what seemed like the best question. "As well as can be expected, I suppose. It's not as if I'm any stranger to your father's long rambles."

"It's never been quite like this, though."

"No, it hasn't." She shook her head and turned toward the door with a huff. "I'll get those refreshments for her, since apparently the other three in this house can't be bothered."

I didn't know what to do but stand there by the bed as I waited for Freya to come back. A furrow creased the girl's brow. Suddenly she didn't look so peaceful anymore. What else could I do for her that would make her feel safe when she woke up?

I moved the pile of clothes up the bed so she'd see them the moment she opened her eyes. That didn't seem like enough, but nothing else occurred to me.

Freya swept back in with a glass of water and a plate with an apple and crackers. "Just something to tide her over," she said when I raised my eyebrows. "Not everyone can eat a whole roast every hour like the insatiable Thor."

"I'll have you know the most roasts I've ever eaten in one day is five," I said. We wouldn't get into how many *other* things I might have eaten that same day. My stomach grumbled. Maybe I'd better put something in it to hold me over until dinner.

Freya let out a little laugh, and the girl stirred. Her lips parted with a murmured breath, her fingers curling into the pillow I'd rested her head on. The goddess and I both went still.

"We should leave her," Freya said under her breath. "I don't think she's going to be happy to see any of us quite yet."

And just leave the girl alone in this unfamiliar room in an unfamiliar house? My legs balked. But on the other hand, was seeing an unfamiliar person in that room really going to comfort her any?

"All right," I said. "But we've got to make sure we do right by this one."

"We *meant* to do right by all of them," Freya muttered as we slipped out, and a lump settled in my gut that had nothing to do with hunger.

# 3

*Aria*

Sunlight seeped through my eyelids. Time to wake up. I opened my eyes cautiously. My heart thudded with a sudden lurch that told me something was wrong.

That thought dredged up a wash of memories: the strange men around me and the glimpse of the wing—the screech of tires before that, the crunch and the pain—

None of that was here now. I tensed against the soft duvet that was cushioning my body but stayed still as I took in the room.

Blue wallpaper with a faint leaf pattern covered the walls. A big window stood across from the foot of the bed, closed, the gauzy curtains on either side drifting in a current that must have been thanks to an air conditioning system. A sheet was wrapped loosely around me, but the air against my face was cooler than made any sense for July.

If this even still was July. Who the hell knew with all the bizarre stuff I'd experienced in the last few hours… or days… or however long it'd been? Maybe I *had* gone dancing and someone had slipped me something awful that came with hallucinations?

But I was usually pretty careful about my drinks. And it wasn't like some wacko drug could explain what I was doing here, or where *here* was.

I pushed myself slowly into a sitting position. My pulse leapt for a second at the pull of the sheet against my shoulder, but the strange weight on my back was gone. I reached behind me to feel down my shoulder blade and found nothing but my regular bare skin. A breath rushed out of me.

Okay. So the wing, at least, has been a hallucination. Or something.

And the jeep hitting me? The agony and the bones I could swear I'd heard cracking?

I tested my arms and touched my ribs. Not even my skin was broken. Nothing hurt. Hell, I felt *better* than I did most days when I woke up, honestly.

There was also no sign of the row of tiny scabs I'd had on my wrist from a scuffle a week ago. I studied it, frowning. Maybe I had been out of it for longer than a day or two.

That idea made me edgy. My gaze fell on the clothes in a pile on the bed beside me. Preppy looking stuff, not what I'd have usually worn at all, but it beat going around naked. That part, and the sheet, had been real. The guys might very well be real too. Who knew when they might turn up again?

I pulled the clothes on quickly. The silky shirt was a bit baggy, but the pants fit without falling off my narrow hips, thank God. A light rose scent wafted off of them. That wasn't my usual style either, but I felt a hell of a lot better with that much less of my skin exposed.

What had happened to the clothes I'd been wearing when… when the jeep had hit me—or hadn't hit me—or whatever? What had happened to the things I'd been *carrying* in those clothes? My heartbeat stuttered again, and this time I couldn't find quick reassurance. I couldn't see anything in the room that belonged to me.

My fingers curled into my palms. My switchblade. I had to get it back. It was the only thing I had…

*You hold onto this, and you use it if you have to, Ari. For the times when I can't be here.*

I closed my eyes against the icy jolt and forced myself to breathe deep. In and out, until I felt a little steadier.

I'd get my knife back, and I'd deal with whoever had carted me off here. But first I needed to be prepared.

The view out the window showed me a three-story drop and a sprawling lawn with a border of trees. I couldn't see any neighbors, which meant it wasn't likely anyone out there could see me, and if I tried that jump—if the window would even open—I really would break all my bones.

Okay, so what did I have in here that I could use?

A glass of what looked like water and a plate with a Granny Smith apple and a stack of crackers sat on the bedside table. My eyes lingered on them. A pang crept up my throat, reminding me how dry my mouth was. My stomach was too tight with tension for me to want to put any food in it, though, even if I'd trusted this stuff. The people here could have put anything in it.

The bed's solid oak frame didn't offer much. Inside the matching massive wardrobe I found only more clothes, all in white and shades of gray.

The room had two doors—one, closed, beyond the enormous oak wardrobe, and another on the other side of the bed that was halfway open, revealing white tiles and the edge of a sink. I scooted across the bed and went into the bathroom.

My reflection in the mirror over the sink looked the same as usual. Maybe my gray eyes looked a little frantic, and the waves of my blond hair were particularly messy, but that was definitely still me: Aria Watson, twenty-two, short and scrappy and wingless.

I turned the tap and scooped a little water into my mouth with my hand. I trusted that stuff more than what was in the glass. Then I tried the mirror. It opened to a cabinet with a couple extra bars of soap, a dented tube of toothpaste, and a silver comb.

The comb's pointed handle looked like it could do some damage if used right. I grabbed the thing and tucked it into my right hip pocket.

A knock sounded on the other door, the one that must have led to the rest of the house. My shoulders stiffened. I drew the comb back out, wrapping my fingers around the teeth so I could stab with the pointy end if I needed to.

An elegant female voice carried through the door. "Hey in there. Would you mind if I came in? I'm thinking you must be rather confused. Any questions you have, I can do my best to answer."

A woman, not one of the men. The same woman I'd seen with them, who hadn't done a thing to help me? But then, maybe she hadn't had a choice with them around. Even if she was in on this scheme with them, I'd have a better chance of getting out of here if I figured out what was going on.

"Okay," I said tentatively. "But I definitely want those answers before anything else."

As I stepped back into the bedroom, the door eased open. It *was* the woman from before—the tall graceful figure with a cascade of honey-brown waves who looked as if she could have walked right out of a magazine fashion spread, Photoshopping still in place. Her perfectly fitted lilac sheath dress only amplified that impression.

She shut the door behind her and gave me a small smile that was a bit tight. Her gaze took in the comb clutched upside down in my hand, and one elegant eyebrow lifted.

"*That* isn't going to be necessary," she said.

"I'd like to take my time deciding that," I said. "And I'm staying over here. You can start explaining now."

She practically floated to the bed and set herself down gingerly on the edge, her body turned toward me. I backed up a step, but not too close to the wall. If it came down to a fight, I needed room to maneuver.

Not that this gal looked like much of a fighter. But you never knew. The prissy pretty ones could have cores of steel under all that polish.

"I'm sorry," she said. "The boys really made a hash of it, didn't they? You'd think after all the centuries they've lived, they'd have learned better manners."

*All the centuries*? "You're not really making things any less confusing," I said.

She inclined her head. "The most important fact is this: You died, and together we summoned your essence here and reformed you. With… a somewhat different constitution than you're used to. That's why you feel so strange. That's how you ended up here."

She stopped. I kept staring at her, waiting for her to follow that explanation up with something that sounded like part of reality, but apparently she was finished. Apparently *that* was supposed to explain everything.

A guffaw jolted out of me. "You're trying to tell me that you brought me back from the dead."

She looked back at me steadily. "It isn't that difficult a thing, when you're a god. Or a goddess, as the case may be."

Okay, I still didn't know how I'd gotten here or how the car crash I'd thought had ended me factored in, but clearly I was being held by a bunch of total psychotics. They thought they were *gods*? That couldn't be good. People deluded enough to think they were invincible were the most dangerous people out there.

But if I was going to get away from them, I'd have to play along for now.

"And what would a bunch of gods and goddesses want with me?" I asked.

The woman opened her mouth to answer, but at the same time the bedroom door whisked open. I flinched, my hand tightening around the comb.

The figure in the doorway was one of the men I'd seen when I'd first woken up: Slim. Still tall and lean as before, his amber eyes as bright as his light red hair. The green tunic he was wearing made his hair gleam even starker.

He grinned at the two of us, the smirk as sharp as the angles of his handsome face, but his voice came out warm and smooth. "I don't think you should be doing all the talking here, Freya. I know you'll just make the rest of us look bad."

She rolled her eyes. "I think the rest of you did an excellent job of that with no help from me."

He made a scoffing sound and focused on me, with a little dip of his head that was almost a bow. "My apologies for your unsettling awakening earlier. Loki, at your service."

The woman's name hadn't quite connected, but I knew that one without even having to think. "Loki… like the Norse god who was supposed to destroy the whole world?"

His eyes gleamed even brighter. He sure looked the part, as crazy as he might be.

"I don't think I can take quite that much credit," he said. "It really was a joint effort."

I didn't know whether it was the stress of the situation or the ridiculousness—well, probably both—but all at once laughter bubbled up from my chest, too fast for me to catch it. I clutched my comb-weapon and pressed my other hand over my mouth, but the giggles spilled out anyway.

The guy who thought he was Loki looked at the woman who was supposedly Freya and said mildly, "You know, I don't think she believes us."

Then he snapped his fingers, and a burst of fire leapt from his hand, wide as his head and licking all the way up to the ceiling. A waft of heat cut through the air-conditioned room to brush my face.

I stopped laughing.

"Nice little trick, isn't it?" he said. With another snap of his fingers, the flames disappeared. His slender pale hand looked unmarked, but the fire had left a faint yellow-brown scorch mark on the white ceiling plaster.

Freya glanced up at it and wrinkled her nose. "Was that really necessary?"

"It seemed the quickest way to cut to the chase," he said. "So what do you think, pixie? Good enough, or do you need a little more? I could do a little shapeshifting …"

He passed his hand in front of his face, and before my eyes his features shifted. His narrow jaw rounded, his angular features softened around the edges, and the pale red hair that had drifted over his high forehead spilled down to his shoulders in a cascade to rival Freya's. I'd swear even his eyelashes grew. In the space of a second, a lovely if shockingly tall woman was gazing back at me.

I blinked and blinked again. The bottom had dropped out of my stomach. This was insane. Impossible.

But also way too real.

The guy... who maybe was the Loki from the myths I'd read as a kid? Was I really going to go there? He waved his hand, and his face fell back into its previous sharply handsome state. "Convinced yet?" he asked me.

"I, um…" My hold on the comb had faltered. I adjusted my grip, keeping my body rigid to stop myself from shaking. I didn't know what was true, but I couldn't deny whatever was going on here, it was deeply fucked up.

I wasn't going to get out of it unless I kept my head.

I pulled my posture a little straighter, glancing from Loki to

Freya and back again. "I still want to know why either of you would have brought *me* here."

"Well, it's a bit of a long story," Loki said. "The gist of it is, we needed a valkyrie, and out of all the recently deceased young women in the area at the time we put out the call, you fit the profile the best. My profile, that is. The first few, we used different criteria, but those didn't work out all that well."

"A valkyrie," I repeated. He'd said that right before that other guy had knocked me out before. When I'd seen that wing…

The memory sent an uncomfortable shiver through my nerves.

"Yes, you know: Odin's champions, overseers of the battlefield, so on and so forth." He waved vaguely. "You see, we seem to have misplaced the Allfather, and having a valkyrie on hand ought to make tracking him down much easier."

I was already shaking my head. This was too much. "I don't know what you're talking about. I'm not a valkyrie, and I'm obviously not *dead*, and… This is crazy. Do you have any idea how crazy this is?"

"We brought you back," Loki said, so matter-of-factly it chilled me. "And we brought you back as a valkyrie. Quite a trick in itself. Your powers only manifest as you need them or call on them… It's easy enough to demonstrate."

He twitched his fingers, and a small knife appeared in his hand. Without missing a beat, he slashed it across his other palm. Blood welled up along the angry line, thick and a red so much darker than his hair. Freya grimaced and looked away.

And something stirred inside me.

My pulse thumped heavier, echoing through my head. A prickling raced through my muscles. Every nerve seemed to perk with a sudden awareness. The space between my shoulder blades quivered with a deepening itch.

"You can feel it, can't you?" Loki said. Both he and Freya were studying me now. "The call to battle. *Where blood is spilled, the valkyries fly.* All you have to do is open your wings."

"I—I don't have any wings," I said, but my voice sounded weak through the thumping of my heart.

He smiled. "Of course you do. You just have to let them out."

The itch on my back dug in even deeper. I sucked in a sharp breath. Wings. I couldn't have *wings.* Let them out? How—

In the back of my mind, without even meaning to, I pictured broad feathered wings like the one I'd caught a glimpse of before, spilling out from my skin. The itch between my shoulders burst with a jab of pain. Something—some part of *me* that I could feel echoing all through the rest of my body—stretched out against the thin fabric of the blouse, straining and unfurling and tearing right through.

I stumbled forward at the sudden weight and grabbed the bedframe to catch myself. The torn blouse hung from my chest, and from my back…

My throat tightened. I made myself glance back.

A huge wing, the feathers mingled white and pale silver, loomed over me.

My nerves jittered, and the wing twitched in response. Because my nerves ran through it too. Because it was part of me, just like the one I could feel weighing on the other side of my back.

I squeezed my eyes shut. The comb dropped from my fingers. "No. It can't—"

But it was. It was real. I could see them. I could *feel* them, not just on me but in me.

Loki's voice reached me, still smooth but gentler now. "You can send them away when you want to, too. They're yours. They follow your command. Just pull them back into yourself."

Yes. Get them away. Get them off of me. I clenched my teeth and willed that weight back into my body—let me absorb it, let them be *gone.*

The feel of the wings shrank until there was nothing left but a twinge on my back. Then that faded too. I opened my eyes with a gasp.

Freya had already opened the wardrobe. She pulled out another blouse, this one sleeveless and ivory, and offered it to me as she cut a glance toward Loki. "Let's try not to go through too many clothes all at once."

I accepted the shirt to replace the torn one drifting against my back. My fingers curled into the cool fabric. My hands were shaking. I bent to grab the comb off the floor, as if it could do much for me now.

Gods. Valkyries. And I was somehow mixed up in this all the way down to my bones.

I swallowed thickly and looked up at the god and goddess who'd just witnessed my transformation.

"Can you start over from the beginning? With the long version, this time."

# 4

*Aria*

As I stepped into the big room where I'd first woken up, I took in all the details I'd been too overwhelmed to notice before: the speckled gold pattern overlaid on the lighter yellow of the wallpaper, the two sofas and scattered armchairs with ornately carved teak frames. A bunch of lilies sat in a porcelain vase on one of the matching side tables, giving off a pungent perfume.

I never liked lilies. They made me think of funerals. At Francis's—

I cut off that thought before it could send me into the downward spiral of memory and meandered as if at random to one of the chairs. It wasn't really at random. I'd picked the chair closest to the far doorway. The one that, if I'd read the layout of this building well, should put me in the right direction to reach the front entrance.

The teeth of the comb bit into my palm as I sat on the firm cushions. I kept my fingers wrapped tightly around it. The people who'd brought me here might not be people at all—might be actual gods, or something like it—but even if that was true, that didn't mean I was safe here. Or that I wanted to stick around.

Freya and Loki had called the others in the house to join us. The five of them settled into seats they'd pushed into a semi-circle facing me, Loki in the middle. The man with the shaggy white-blond hair who'd knocked me out with his touch sat at his left, next to the guy who'd hung back during that first encounter.

The two of them were like a study in opposites but somehow eerily similar at the same time. The second guy had his black hair cropped short, and his dark green eyes were narrowed while his neighbor's bright blue ones drifted as dreamily as before. They were both a little shorter than Loki, with boyishly smooth faces and enough muscle to fill out their T-shirts, but the same features and build that looked soft on the dreamy guy had turned hard on the dark-haired one. He couldn't even be bothered to look right at me.

They were both striking-looking in their own ways, that was for sure. Apparently being a god meant divinely good looks. Which was true for the guy at Loki's right, too—the incredibly beefy guy with a dark auburn ponytail who'd tried to tame me with a sheet. When I looked at him, he gave me a smile that was slightly grim, but his broad, square-jawed face still couldn't have been easier on the eyes.

I had no idea who light-and-dark pair might be, but given the company, I could make a stab at naming Mr. Muscles there.

"Let me guess," I said, pulling my legs up onto the chair—better if they thought I was getting comfortable. "You must be Thor."

The grim smile stretched into a wide grin. "Very good," he said in his mellow baritone. "You catch on quick. Do you mind telling us your name?"

They didn't know? I remembered what Loki said about me just fitting certain criteria. I guessed my name hadn't gone into that evaluation.

For a second, my chest clenched, as if my name was something I should hold onto. But I couldn't see how it really mattered. "Aria Watson," I said. "Ari, preferably."

"Nice to meet you, Ari," Thor said. For a god with a reputation for going around smashing things up with a giant hammer, he seemed pretty chill. The welcoming vibe he gave off made me start to relax despite myself.

My gaze darted back to the other side of the room. "And you two are…?"

"Allow me to introduce the opposite twins," Loki said with a flourish of his hand toward the pair. "Baldur and Hod."

"Hello," the dreamy pale guy said. His voice was melodic but kind of distant at the same time.

His dark… *twin?* shot a scowl Loki's way and then turned his narrowed eyes toward me. "Good to see you've settled down," he muttered.

Hod had some kind of stick up his ass, apparently. He couldn't really be blaming me for freaking out, could he? Or was he peeved I hadn't recognized them? Well, excuse me for not having read up on my Norse mythology in ten plus years. I'd had bigger things on my mind.

The name Baldur did sound kind of familiar, like he should be important. Hadn't there been some retro game Francis had raved about that was Baldur something? That probably had barely anything to do with the actual mythology… if the actual mythology even had anything to do with the supposed gods and goddess sitting across from me.

"So," I said, focusing back on Loki, since he seemed to be the biggest talker in the bunch. "You said you'd explain everything. What I'm doing here. What *you're* all doing here. From the beginning."

"Yes. Well." He smiled crookedly and ran a hand through his

pale red hair. "You know who we are. How familiar are you with the stories that get told about us?"

"A bit," I said. "It came up in school when I was pretty little. I probably read some books from the library or something. But I'm no expert."

"All right. A relative blank slate." His amber eyes glinted. "The basic stories are mostly true. They also happened a long time ago. Since then we've been a lot less busy. So now and then, we pass the time by coming down to Earth and seeing what we can do for you lovely mortals."

"Or seeing what catastrophes you can create," Hod put in.

Loki ignored him. "We came down from Asgard—our home realm—on one of those ventures some time ago, the five of us here and Odin. Odin as in the Allfather, my blood-sworn brother, her husband"—he jabbed his thumb toward Freya—"and literal father to the rest of this lot. We're really the only ones who've kept together all that much. I'm not sure where in the nine realms Heimdall and Frigg and the rest of them are getting their itches scratched these days."

"Somewhere they don't have to listen to you blather on?" Thor suggested, but his voice was amused and the look he gave Loki almost fond. He turned to me. "The important part is, Odin has a thirst for knowledge that's never satisfied. He goes off on rambles all the time. So, he took off, and we didn't think anything of it. Until year after year passed without any sign of him."

Freya had folded her graceful hands in her lap. She looked up from them now. "He's been gone nearly twice as long as his longest 'ramble' before," she said.

I glanced from one to the next, trying to judge their reactions. "Okay," I said. "That sounds like reason to worry. But he's, like, a *god*, right? A pretty powerful one, if the stories are even mostly true. What kind of trouble could he have gotten into?"

Loki lifted his angular shoulder in a shrug. "There are beings of power in the realms other than gods. The Norns know even gods can turn on each other. And we aren't simply worried about him out of the goodness in our hearts, though we have plenty of that."

Hod snorted. Loki raised an eyebrow at him, but the sullen god didn't speak.

Baldur had looked toward his darker twin too. "Brother," he said in his lilting voice, gently chiding.

Hod's stance stiffened. He waved dismissively. "Go on, trickster."

So Loki did. "We're somewhat restricted in our powers while we exist on the mortal plane here in Midgard. The longer we remain here, the more those powers diminish. But Odin is the only one who can call up the bridge that will lead us back to Asgard. Once, there were paths to the land of the gods here and there from the other realms, but after Ragnarok he closed them all off."

"Got it," I said. "You need Odin back to let you all go home, because you don't feel godly enough here anymore."

Thor guffawed and clapped the arm of his chair. "There's one way of putting it."

Loki spread his hands as if to say, *What of it?*

I shifted in my seat. "But what the hell do you need *me* for? You're gods. What could anyone do that you can't?"

"Ah, you see, we do have a few gaps in our range of talents," Loki said. "And sadly, we never bothered to fit Odin with a tracking device. But we did discover that between the four of us with blood ties, we can bring about the valkyrie summoning. As a valkyrie, you have a different connection to Odin. In some ways a more direct one. And other special abilities that will serve the search well."

"So, I just have to find Odin and that's all there is to it?"

"We'll need to train you in your powers first," Thor said. "But they'll come naturally to you, so that won't take long."

"And what happens after I find him?" Could I just waltz back into my regular life? Preferably without wings that wanted to sprout out of my back every time someone got a papercut around me?

"Let's not get ahead of ourselves yet," Loki said.

Oh, no, I wasn't letting them dodge that question. Or— "You've mentioned a couple times that there were other valkyries before me," I said. "If we've got this special connection to Odin, shouldn't they have found him already? What happened to them?"

Loki, Thor, and Freya exchanged a glance. Hod glowered at the floor, his mouth tense. Even Baldur's dreamy aura seemed to dim slightly.

"We're not totally sure," Thor said. "They went looking, and they haven't come back."

"Our best guess would be that they were caught up in whatever caught the Allfather as well," Loki said. "Which only lends proof to the possibility that he *is* caught and hasn't simply lost track of time. But you're better equipped than any of them were."

Hod muttered something and shook his head. Baldur cast another tender glance toward his brother, but his fingers flexed against the arms of his chair. "We must give it a chance," he said.

"Give *what* a chance?" I said, my fingers tightening around the comb. "What's so special about me?"

The corner of Loki's thin lips curled higher. "My companions here felt that an ideal valkyrie would be a young lady pure of heart and noble of deed. It's my opinion that pure-hearted noble-doers are also pushovers. Seeing as their approach wasn't working out, I suggested we look for someone more resourceful. Perhaps even cutthroat. Not afraid to get her hands dirty if survival required it. Wouldn't you say that you fit the bill?"

My shoulders tensed. How much did he know? Had he seen, somehow, exactly what I'd needed to survive?

Loki looked mildly back at me. They hadn't even known my name—that meant they didn't know any details, right? Just the gist of it?

I wet my lips. "I've survived a lot, if that's what you mean, yeah."

"Well, there you go. The others didn't have the smarts to fend for themselves properly. I can tell you'll do just fine."

"You've already admitted you don't know what happened to the other ones," I said. "So you have no idea what I'll even have to do. And I still want to know what happens if it is all fine and I get Odin back here for you."

Freya leaned forward. "I suppose you'd return to Asgard with us," she said. "Make a life for yourself there."

"I had a life here."

"As a mortal human," Loki said. "You're less mortal and not at all human now. That isn't your world anymore."

I bristled inside. He didn't get to decide that. It was the only world I'd ever had, even if it was often a shitty one. I had people there who needed me. I had to get back to Petey before too long.

But I could feel their intentions dragging on me as they looked back at me, like those wings had dragged on my back. They didn't care. They just wanted me to be their tool, for them to use to get what they wanted. What did they care what happened to me after? If I even made it through what the girls they'd summoned before me hadn't.

They could stick that plan where the sun didn't shine.

I tested my grip on the comb and the angle of my feet against the chair's cushion. "Let me think about it," I said.

Then I hurled myself over the arm of the chair toward the door.

# 5

*Loki*

She certainly was a slippery one, this new girl. One second sitting there casual as can be, the next leaping for the door as if Fenrir himself were at her heels. I had to admire her wits—and guts—even as I darted across the room to block her way. She was going to have to learn soon enough that she couldn't outrun us.

Our pixie skidded to a halt when I appeared in front of the door. Her gray eyes flashed. She swiveled in a blink and bolted for the nearest window, her tangled blond waves flying out around her shoulders.

I glanced toward Thor. He was already moving to intercept her. We made a good team when the situation called for it, despite our many differences.

But this girl—Aria, she'd said her name was—wasn't an enemy. We needed to subdue her *gently*. Without her getting hurt in the process.

She fumbled with the window, but the frame stuck. Thor reached for her. "Ari—"

She flung herself away from him, ducking under his massive arm and scrambling toward the other doorway. I might appreciate her perseverance, but this chase was getting a tad tiresome.

"Ari," I said calmly, my steps gliding across the floor several feet at a time. "Can I recommend less running, more talking?"

"There's nothing left to talk about," she said. She spun when I cut her off from the door and took off for the first door again.

All right, enough of this. "Hod," I said, clapping my hands. "Do us a favor and work a little of that wintery magic on our guest? It's difficult to have a conversation like this."

The dark twin glared in my general direction, but then his head turned as he followed the sound of the girl's footsteps. He swept his hand forward.

Ari jarred to a halt halfway across the room. She stared down at her legs, which had frozen in place amid a patch of conjured shadow. A frustrated sound burst from her lips. She looked around at all of us, her expression fierce. That damned comb was still clutched in her right hand, as if she could do the slightest bit of damage to any of us with that.

But this was what we'd asked for when we'd called into the void for a human spirit to shape into a valkyrie: a fighter. A survivor. Whatever she'd been through, no doubt she'd made it this far by *not* trusting anyone.

She was going to be perfect for this task, if I could just convince her to work with us instead of against us.

Her chin came up as I walked over to her. She stared back at me defiantly. "I don't want to be here. I don't want to be part of this… rescue operation, or whatever the fuck it is."

So much fire, even utterly helpless as she was now. I came to a stop a couple of feet away. A different person I might have extended a hand to, used touch to solidify the emotional connection I needed to make. But I'd seen how this girl reacted when anyone even got close to her. She'd been harmed by contact like that more than she'd been comforted.

I could adjust my usual strategies. A trickster was nothing if not adaptable.

Thor was lumbering over to join us. I waved him back, my gaze staying focused on Ari. A muscle in her jaw twitched, and she clenched it tighter. She was frightened under the defiance.

"Ari," I said, low and soft and most importantly, honest. "I understand. We've whisked you away from everything familiar, and now we're making demands and setting restrictions… Of course you don't want any part in that. *I* don't want to be doing this either. But it's the best idea we've come up with, and I swear we'll do whatever we can to ease your way—and it's better than being dead, isn't it? Because that was your alternative. The life you had is gone either way." I snapped my fingers. "Like that. Would you really rather you weren't here at all?"

Ari's shoulders started to come down. The angry flush faded from her face. She hadn't thought it through before, had she? We'd told her she'd died, but how could a mortal mind wrap itself around that possibility when as far as she could tell she was still perfectly alive?

"I was really dead?" she said. "Completely, not just… dy*ing*, or in a coma, or something?"

I nodded. "The magic we used to summon you could only latch on to a spirit already—if recently—detached from its former body. We rescued you from the void, pixie."

That muscle twitched again, but it wasn't fear this time. "I'm not a pixie," she spat out.

I let myself smile. "You haven't met any pixies if you take that as an insult. They're small, sure, but most of the ones I've known were tougher than I am."

With luck, she'd prove to be too. I needed her to be. The others had been hesitant enough about going along with my plan. If this situation went haywire, I wasn't going to convince them of anything else for another century or two.

If it went well, then maybe I'd get a little less grousing the next time I made a totally logical and insightful observation.

Ari didn't seem to know quite what to make of my response. She sucked her lower lip under her teeth. And abruptly I found myself noticing that along with being stubborn and bold and quick, she was rather pretty in her pixie-ish way. As if that observation helped us any at the moment.

"You're gods," she said finally. "Can't you do something about the whole dying thing? Bring me back to life as a human again?"

"Baldur might have, if he'd been there before you completely kicked the bucket," I said, nodding to the pale twin. "But he wasn't. And now that's done. We can't just flip a switch and send you back."

"So it's being dead or being trapped here."

"You're not exactly trapped," I said. "You'll have plenty of freedom—when we know you aren't going to run off and cause all sorts of chaos in the mortal world. We've given you a gift, really. We just want to be sure you're going to use it… responsibly."

She wrinkled her nose at me, but her gaze had turned thoughtful. Her jaw worked. And I made an educated stab in the dark. Cutthroat or not, almost every human had a soft spot for someone other than themselves.

"There are people back in that world you're worried about, aren't there?" I said. "People you care about? If you were dead, you really would be gone from their lives. Like this, you could at least keep watch from time to time. See them again. It might not be the same, but it's more than you'd have otherwise."

She was quiet for a moment, locked in that awkward stance with her legs mid-stride. "All right," she said. "I'll see what I can do to help you with this Odin thing if you'll teach me how to use these powers you gave me. And if you can get something for me."

Still making demands, huh? I managed not to chuckle, since she'd probably bristle at that. "What is it you want, pixie?"

She grimaced at the nickname, but not as sharply as before. "When I died, I was carrying some stuff on me. I had a switchblade in the right hip pocket of my jeans. About four inches long folded, with a marbled dark blue handle. I want it back. *It* didn't die, so you can do that much, right?"

"I can," I said. It shouldn't even be that difficult, I didn't think. "I'll go get it right now. But I'll need to touch you. Hod, I think you can unfreeze her now."

She stiffened up even as Hod flicked his hand to dismiss the chilly shadow that had held her in place. But she stayed there, braced, as I shifted a little closer. Just close enough that I could rest my hand gently on the bare side of her shoulder.

The energy of her spirit tingled against my fingers. I absorbed the feel of it, the rush and the flow, the distinctive pattern that was hers alone. Then I stepped away from her and slipped out the door.

Outside, hot muggy air washed over me. I set off, letting the power imbued in my shoes of flight carry me. My strides stretched farther and farther until I was taking miles with every step—invisible to the mortal eyes I flew past, of course. On and on I soared through a blur of scenery until I'd traced the fading trail Ari's spirit had left to its source.

I came to a stop under the dim buzzing lights of a morgue. A rather unpleasant one even as morgues went. The air stunk with disinfectant and an underlying odor of rot, and the steel doors lined along one wall were smudged. I could tell which one our valkyrie's former body lay in; I could see in my mind's eye the mash of skull and brain and hair, the splintered bones. I didn't need to *really* see that.

Her belongings. They'd stripped off the clothes and tossed them in a basket—here. And there was her precious switchblade. An interesting personal effect. I supposed it fit the girl.

I fished it out of the bloody fabric and washed it and my hands at the sink. The stench of death crept deeper into my lungs, and a shudder passed through me. Ugh. She had better give me plenty of credit for this.

I raced back the way I'd come, the knife nestled against my palm. When I strode back into our country house's living room, I found everyone arranged much as they had been in the beginning—Ari back in her chair, my godly companions scattered across the seats around her. No one was talking. They all appeared to have been waiting for me.

What a useless lot they were sometimes. I shook my head at them with a grin and held out my hand to Ari, brandishing the switchblade. Her face brightened. She snatched it from me and tucked it close to her chest.

Humans were such strange beings. I couldn't recall seeing a mortal that attached to a piece of weaponry since King Arthur and his legendary sword.

"There you have it," I said. "Do we have a deal?"

"I already said I'd try to help, didn't I?" she said, and paused. "There is something else that occurred to me."

I flopped back into my previous seat, stretching out my legs, only a tad winded from that lope across the country. "By all means, share your concerns."

She hesitated again. Then she said, "What would you do with me if I refused to follow your orders? If I told you to forget it, not a chance?"

Oh. She hadn't failed to think that aspect through. I waited, but none of the others spoke up. Thor looked at his hands, folding them in front of him. They'd decided explaining this aspect was my job too. It figured, didn't it? Make Loki do the dirty work. That was how it always went.

I sighed. "We aren't cruel, Ari. We gave you this new life—we're not in any hurry to end it. If you decided you were going to do nothing more than sit around the house all day, then so be it. But we can't risk you endangering anyone else. You're our responsibility. If we felt you were making yourself a risk to mortal society—or anyone else—we would have to return you to the state in which we found you."

"Dead," she said, holding my gaze.

"Yes."

"I guess you haven't given me much choice then, have you?" she said, with a little smile so jagged it cut right through my chest.

I'd picked her. This was my doing. And now there was one more person who'd be pissed off if it turned out I'd been wrong.

# 6

*Aria*

For such a large house, the kitchen was awfully cozy. Just big enough for a countertop and the usual appliances—retro-looking enough that I suspected they were older than me, and possibly older than Mom on top of that—and a four-seater table tucked away in the corner.

I kind of liked it. I felt a lot more secure tucked away there, eating the sandwich I'd thrown together out of the wide assortment of options in the fridge and cupboard, than I would have at the vast dining table I'd caught a glimpse of on the way down the hall.

I'd planned to get started on this whole becoming super-powerful being right away, but the second I'd stood up again after my most recent escape attempt, a wave of dizziness had washed over me alongside a stomach gurgle loud enough that Loki had grinned. So I was going to stock up on energy and gather my strength before I took anything else on. I guessed it made sense that dying and being reborn and all that running around would have taken its toll.

Reborn as a *valkyrie*. My skin still crawled, remembering the alien weight of those wings. Could I actually fly with them? The idea made me shiver in a weird blend of anticipation and horror. My fingers squeezed around the handle of my switchblade, which I was still holding beneath the table. My borrowed slacks had pockets, but the warm plastic in my hand made me feel more grounded.

This whole situation was so crazy. Gods. Magic powers. Coming back from the dead. But I'd seen the proof with my own eyes. I *remembered* dying. I didn't know how anyone could have faked that or the stunts those gods had pulled. Those long minutes while my legs had been locked in place, prickling with the cold of the shadowy vise around them...

That was over now. No point in thinking about it. I had to focus on what was ahead. I'd learn whatever powers this weird collective could supposedly teach me, and then maybe I'd be in a position to slip their magical safeguards and actually get out of here.

From what I'd gathered, I'd lost less than a day. Petey wouldn't be worried about not seeing me or any gifts from me, not yet. Sometimes I'd had to go a whole week before I could safely drop in, and I'd just secreted him away for part of his lunch hour at the elementary school a few days ago.

Unless... What if the police had reported my death to Mom by now? What if she'd told Petey?

The image of his sweet and way-too-innocent little face swam up in my mind. The squeeze of his six-year-old's arms when he'd hugged me that last time. The excited sweep of his hands as he'd told me about the castle he'd built in class.

And also the holes forming at the toes of his shoes, because Mom couldn't bother to pick him up new ones. The shadow that had crossed his expression when he'd mentioned her and Ivan, her current guy.

*You could keep watch*, Loki had said. I was going to do a hell of a lot more than that. I could keep out of the rest of the "mortal" world—good riddance to most of it anyway—but I couldn't abandon my little brother. No way, no how.

I had to get back to him as soon as I could, just to let him know that I was okay—and that I'd never stop looking after him.

I took another bite of ham, lettuce, and mayo on rye, and Thor ambled into the kitchen. The gods had been giving me some space since our big talk, but I guessed his stomach had gotten the better of him too. He leaned over to peer into the fridge and pulled out a plate with a couple of leftover drumsticks, so big they had to be turkey or goose.

"Mind if I join you?" he asked.

I shrugged. "It's your house." Or was it? How exactly did real estate work when you were a divine immortal being?

In any case, it was more his than it was mine.

He sat down across from me and dug right into his meal, which as far as I could tell was a mid-morning "snack." In the time it took me to finish the last quarter of my sandwich, he'd cleaned one bone and pretty much finished the other, plowing through the meat with an occasional smack of his lips and a pleased gleam in his warm brown eyes.

"A body that big needs a lot of fuel to keep it running, huh?" I said.

Thor looked up from the bone he'd just inhaled one last fragment of meat off of. He blinked at me. Then a deep chuckle rolled from his lungs. "What can I say? Big guy, big appetite."

"Hmm," I said. "I could have polished two of those off."

He raised his eyebrows. "Oh, yeah?"

I jabbed my pointer finger at him. "Don't make any comments about me being a pixie or whatever either. I could drink you under the table too."

At that claim, he let out a full belly laugh, so powerful it rattled the table his legs had barely fit underneath. "Now *that* I would really like to see. I haven't even met another god who could out-drink me, unless it's Loki winning by trickery."

"Maybe later," I said, brushing the crumbs off my hands. "I'm thinking valkyrie lessons will probably sink in better if I'm sober."

"You can start with me if you'd like," he said. "Since I'm already here and all."

Out of my five saviors-slash-captors, I had to say Thor made me feel most at ease. Maybe because it seemed like there wasn't a whole lot of him that wasn't right there for me to see. He definitely didn't strike me as a schemer like Loki. And who knew what was going on in the heads of the others.

Thor, I got the impression, said what he meant, and if you didn't like it, well, maybe he'd convince you with that mythical hammer of his I figured had to be around here somewhere.

"All right," I said, getting up and sliding my switchblade into my pocket. "What part of valkyrie-ing are you an expert in?"

He chuckled again. "Come on. It's too hot to be running around outside, so we'd better use the great room."

The great room turned out to be a room even more vast than the living room we'd assembled in earlier. A huge brick fireplace dominated one wall, but the burnt logs in it looked old. An assortment of chairs, sofas, and tables had been pushed to the walls. Thor stepped into the middle of the empty space and wiped his hands together. I had the feeling he used this room for activities along the lines of what we were about to do fairly frequently.

"It was usually Odin who picked and created the valkyries," Thor said. "But we each have our own sort of connection to him and qualities we share that we were able to pass on to you." He gave me a broad smile. "I gave you lightning."

"Lightning?" I looked down at my arms. I hadn't felt all that zappy so far.

"Strong reflexes," he said. "Speed and power. You were

obviously pretty tough before, but now you are even more." He grinned.

"Hmm." I flexed my muscles. Did they have more juice than I was used to?

"Your powers will only fully activate when they're triggered—or if you consciously call on them," Thor said. "Otherwise we'd all go around smashing every glass we picked up and stomping holes in the floor accidentally."

I cocked my head at him. "Somehow I think you're speaking from personal experience there."

He laughed. "Maybe. Let's just say it's useful to be somewhat normal when normal is all you need. But I can help you get a sense of the strength you can call on, so you know how to reach for it. I'll just need to provoke it a little…"

He took a sudden step toward me and swung his fist at my head. My pulse jumped, and I ducked. He hadn't punched that hard, I could tell from the breeze of his arm passing over my head, but he wasn't going completely easy on me. His other fist was flying toward me an instant later.

I scrambled backward across the smooth hardwood floor, and Thor followed. He was still smiling, but the glint in his eyes was so eager it was almost terrifying. He *could* pummel me into a pulp if he wanted to—I had no doubt about that.

The thought sent a jolt of panic through my chest that seemed to splinter there, tingling through all my nerves. I wove and dodged, but each movement smoothed out, coming faster and easier. The frantic beat of my heart settled into a sharp but steady drumming. I slipped out of Thor's range with a speed that took my breath away.

Lightning. That was what this felt like, all right. Electricity dancing through my veins.

"You can feel it now, can't you?" Thor said, sounding not even slightly out of breath. This whole exercise was no effort for him at all. "Get a little creative. Play around with it. You can do more than you might think."

He ducked his head in an unexpected charge, and I leapt out of the way. The push of my legs propelled me up over him. I found myself spinning past him and landing with a thump in a crouch behind him. The impact barely rattled my bones. A startled laugh spilled from my lips.

I was a fucking superhero now. Just try to let anyone stop me when I got the hang of this upgraded body.

Thor upped his game now that I was finding my feet. He moved faster, swung harder, and tried to trip me up with slashes of his feet as well as his fists. I kept darting out of the way even more quickly, the air whistling in my ears.

We circled the room at least a dozen times. I rebounded off the walls, vaulted from the furniture. Each move came even more effortlessly.

A prickling burn was spreading through my muscles, but it was a *good* burn. Like I was pushing them to a limit they'd always wanted to reach. I didn't know how long we'd been at this, but I felt like I could keep going for hours.

An impulse gripped me to push *him* harder. Why did I have to be always on the defensive here? Anyone smart knew you didn't go starting fights you didn't need to get into—but they also knew to go for the gut if the fight came to you.

I dodged another punch and sprang forward instead of backward. My fist swiped at Thor's well-packed belly. His arm slammed down to block me. My knuckles smacked his gut for just an instant before his block sent me tumbling to the side.

My enhanced reflexes kept me on my feet, just barely. The side of my arm throbbed just above my elbow where he'd hit me. I dropped into a crouch, holding that arm carefully, ready for him to come at me again.

But Thor's hands had dropped to his sides. He did come, but it was carefully, his mouth twisted with concern. His voice was ragged.

"Shit. I didn't mean to— You surprised me, and I couldn't catch my reaction in time. Are you all right?"

It was weird seeing the man who'd been so joyfully throwing punches at me a moment ago suddenly so subdued and worried. I straightened up, offering my arm for him to inspect. "You didn't get me that hard. It'll probably bruise, but I'll live."

He touched my arm gingerly, eyeing the red blotch where his block had made contact. "I could ask Baldur to heal it. I shouldn't have hurt you at all."

His obvious sense of guilt sent a twinge through me. When had *anyone* in my life ever been this concerned about how they might have hurt me? And he hadn't even, not really.

I forced my voice out, keeping it as casual as I could, with a wry smile for good measure. "It's fine. My fault for taking you by surprise. The bruise will be a reminder that next time I try, I just need to be faster."

Thor peered into my eyes as if making sure I was serious. His stance relaxed. He threw back his head with a laugh. "You are something, Aria Watson. There aren't many gods who could have landed a punch at me, you know? I guess I'd better watch myself."

He met my eyes again with a warm grin and a glint in his gaze as if he really were impressed. Impressed with *me*. He'd kept a little distance between us, but he was close enough that I could feel the warmth of his whole body. Smell him, tangy and heady like some fine, ancient liquor. What the hell did Norse gods drink? Mead?

Thor's broad hand was still cupping my elbow, his fingers curled gently against my bare skin. My sense of that touch quivered up my arm and down low in my belly. All at once I found myself wondering whether his skin would taste like he smelled. What it would be like to be touched like that, while he looked at me like that, in all sorts of other places.

The clearing of a throat on the other side of the room broke the moment. I jerked away from Thor and spun around to see Freya standing by the doorway. Her expression was amused.

"Managed to bash her up already, did you?" she said. "We've been hearing you thundering around for over an hour. Maybe it's time for a little break, or we'll wear our valkyrie right out." Her gaze focused on me. "What do you say to a little stroll while you catch your breath?"

Ah, yeah, a little breath catching sounded about right. Because no way should I have been entertaining the thoughts I'd just had, not even for a second.

"I'll finish beating you up later," I told Thor, and tried to ignore the eager leap of my pulse as his chuckle followed me out the door.

# 7

*Aria*

When Freya had said a little stroll, she meant outside the house. The stark sunlight should have washed out someone with a fair complexion like hers, but it just made her hair shine like pale bronze and highlighted the rosy flush in her cheeks. I couldn't remember a whole lot about her from my childhood reading, but I was going to go out on a limb here and say whatever she was the goddess of, beauty had to be on the list somewhere.

I guessed she hadn't had a big role to play in summoning me here, seeing as valkyrie-me looked the same all-right-but-hardly-spectacular as the regular me had.

A narrow path where the bare dirt was packed hard cut across the lawn and into a stretch of meadows between scattered trees. Freya's white sandals skimmed over the ground, making barely a sound compared to the tap of my sneakers. Other than the breeze rustling the trees and lifting the summer heat a bit, that was the only noise around us. I still hadn't made out any neighboring buildings.

"Where are we, anyway?" I asked, right before an unnerving idea hit me. "Are we still on the… the 'mortal plane' or whatever you guys call it?"

A smile curved Freya's lips. "Yes, this is Midgard," she said. "We *can't* leave, at least not back to Asgard, without Odin. We're in the Hudson Valley, not too far from New York City. Some of the boys like to soak in the big city atmosphere while we're here."

I wasn't sure what "not too far" meant in godly terms, but I couldn't be all that far from home then. Once I got away from here, the question would just be how to get to someplace with proper transportation to get me the rest of the way to Philly.

The big brick house was hidden by the trees now. If I made a run for it here, Loki and the others wouldn't be around to stop me. Of course, I didn't know what powers Freya might have. And I didn't even know what direction I'd want to run in.

Just bolting hadn't worked out so well for me before. I was going to be smarter about my escape next time. Think it through. Be prepared for anything.

Freya glanced over at me. "Is that where you were living? New York?"

I blinked at her. They really didn't know much about me, did they? "No," I said. "Philadelphia. I've been to the Big Apple a couple times, but… I like Philly better." More compact. Less snooty, at least if you didn't go too far out into the suburbs. And familiar as the back of my hand.

Freya hummed to herself. "I'm sure we've been through there at least once or twice. At this point, we've been through pretty much everywhere." She laughed briefly. "And you have family there? Friends?"

"Some." Not any that really mattered other than Petey. Not any I wanted to talk to her about.

"And what exactly did you occupy yourself with out there that made Loki think you were the type to get your hands dirty?"

Her expression had turned a little sly. Of course this "stroll" wasn't just to give me a break in my training. She wanted something from me too. To know just how big a mess the girl they'd picked up almost at random was. My hackles rose, but I kept my voice calm.

"I left home when I was seventeen. Been looking after myself for the last five years. When you're starting with nothing, you do what you have to. I work for criminals. I've bent the law. I've stolen when it was either that or starve—or when I saw someone who really didn't deserve what they had. I've hurt people when it was either that or get hurt."

Because I hadn't done enough of that when it really would have made a difference. A painful jab ran through my gut.

"A survivor," Freya said.

I didn't like her flippant tone. What the hell would a goddess know about needing to survive?

"More than that," I said. "I was doing pretty well, the last few years. I've got an apartment that's all mine, no roommates needed. Clients I can count on as far as anyone can count on a criminal. It was a life." I wasn't going to tell her about Petey.

"But one of these criminals killed you?"

"No," I muttered, kicking at a stray pebble. My lightning-forged muscles sent it flying straight across the meadow. "Some asshole junkie in a jeep killed me."

"Ah." Her brow furrowed. "I may have experienced plenty of the modern age, but I do still find humankind's motorized vehicles rather disturbing."

"Well, they're particularly 'disturbing' when they're bearing down on you at a hundred miles an hour." I hoped that idiot driver had gotten bashed up bad in the crash. Lost his license. Some sort of karma.

Freya switched gears on me. "Seventeen is rather young to be leaving your home, isn't it?"

"Yes," I said stiffly. "But I had good reasons." Reasons I *definitely* wasn't getting into with her. Echoes of shouting and funerals and the ghost of unwanted hands traveling over my skin washed over me just with that quick mention. I shoved all those memories way, way back in my mind where they belonged and hopefully would stay for the rest of eternity.

I was going to save Petey from all that—from all the shit I'd been through under Mom's roof.

Restlessness rippled through me. I found myself looking into the distance again. Wondering how far in the distance I could find a real road where I might be able to hitch a ride before anyone caught up with me. Yeah, right.

When I yanked my gaze back, Freya was watching me with a tense little smile. A prickle ran down my back. Did she know what I'd been thinking?

Maybe she'd brought me on this walk out here just to test me—to see whether I'd try to run again. To make sure I really was committed now.

But look, here I still was. She couldn't complain about that. Now maybe she'd cough up a little more information about this bizarre little family of hers. The better I understood where they stood with each other, the easier I'd be able to work my way out of this crazy situation.

"So you're Odin's wife," I said. "And the other gods… are his sons?"

"Other than Loki," she said with an arch of her eyebrow. "He's no relation to any of them, as much as he might enjoy playing otherwise. He and Odin swore an oath to each other, a very long time ago. We've been stuck with him since then."

"Blood brothers," I said, remembering how Loki had put it.

"Yes. Thor and the twins are Odin's sons, from before our partnering." She exhaled softly. "Many things have changed in our realm since the days when humankind honored us."

Hold on. "Baldur and Hod really are twins?" I said. "I thought Loki was making a joke."

She laughed. "Understandable, but no. Non-identical, clearly, but born together all the same. Day and night. Summer and winter. And yet inseparable, other than…" Her voice trailed off, and she shut her mouth.

"Other than?" I prompted.

"Nothing. I lost my train of thought." She waved dismissively.

Ah ha. There were things the gods didn't want to talk about too. But I couldn't see pressing directly getting me any further.

"They get along, then?" I said. "Hod struck me as a little, um, grouchy."

Freya's smile came back. "He is that. But their bond is something else. And as their older brother Thor naturally keeps an eye on both of them, never mind they've been grown adults for innumerable years."

A close-knit family. Loki on the outside, but he was also clearly the sharpest of the bunch, so I couldn't see him as a weak spot.

Our path had taken us in a wavering circle. The house came back into view up ahead, the old bricks dark against the bright green foliage all around them. If I couldn't find a weak point among the gods, maybe their home had one. From this angle I could see the front and back porches and windows rambling all up the side I was facing. A couple of those were close enough to jump from… Even the third-floor ones might work if I could use these wings to fly. My back itched at the idea.

I didn't like the feel of them, but if that was what it took, I'd do it. I just needed to learn how first. I'd find out what the other three gods had to teach me, and then I'd be ready.

"Thank you for the walk," I said, tucking my hair back behind my ears as we reached the front of the house. "I think it was good to clear my head. Now I guess I'd better get on with this training I'm supposed to do."

"Thank you for the company," Freya said smoothly, as if she hadn't been using it as an excuse to pump me for information and who knew what else.

When we stepped inside, a lilting melody was carrying faintly down the stairs. Like a violin, maybe, but lower. And vaguely familiar.

Freya tipped her chin toward the stairs. "That'll be Baldur. You could go see him next."

Baldur. The dreamy bright god who'd knocked me unconscious with his touch—but in about as peaceful a way as anyone could ask for. I wasn't sure what to make of Loki yet, and Hod definitely didn't like me. I might as well find out what was going on behind those slightly dazed if gorgeous eyes, and what he'd contributed to my valkyrie-ness.

The song petered out as I reached the top of the stairs. Whatever piece it had been, the one he started playing next was even more familiar: the swelling notes of "Amazing Grace." I'd taken singing classes for a little while when I was a kid during one of Mom's rare generous phases. I'd sung that piece for my first and only recital.

The lyrics tickled at the base of my throat as I came up on the closed door the music was seeping through. As I eased it open, I couldn't help letting my voice slip out softly in time with the instrument.

"Through many dangers, toils and snare, we have already come. T'was grace that brought us safe thus far, and grace will lead us home."

Hell yes, I could use some of that kind of grace right now.

# 8

*Baldur*

The bow moved over the strings as smoothly as if it had a mind of its own—as if it were playing the music of its own accord, and my hand was simply coasting along with it. The low rich notes of the viola filled the room. I wasn't even paying attention to what song I moved to next, just letting instinct carry me. Losing myself in that world made of warmth and music. The only world where everything always felt perfectly at peace.

A voice wove through the melody. Raw but sweet, wavering on a note here or there but mostly hitting just the right cadence. My eyes popped open.

The young woman who was our new valkyrie had just slipped into the room. She froze, her mouth snapping shut, when my gaze met hers. I eased the bow to a stop.

"You have a good voice. It seems your parents named you well."

Aria's mouth twitched. She looked as though she wasn't sure whether she should smile. "My voice isn't half as good as you play," she said. "Is it normal for Norse gods to learn Christian hymns?"

"Is that what that song was? I have to admit I don't always take note of the source. I hear music I like, and I store it away up here." I tapped my head lightly.

"You must have quite a collection now."

After all the time of my existence, she meant. A quiver ran through my thoughts. I looked away, breathing in, settling into the warm glow the song had left behind that matched the sunlight streaming through the window of the music room. There was nothing distressing here. And the past wasn't worth thinking about, now that it was past.

When I turned back to Aria, she was watching me warily. "I didn't mean to interrupt," she said. "I thought maybe you could start your part of the whole valkyrie training thing."

"Of course," I said. Good that she was willing; good that she was eager. I smiled. "You want to understand what you are now as much as possible. I'll help in every way I can."

I stood up and set the viola in its place against the wall amid our collection of instruments. I'd dabbled in a variety over the eras, but the viola was one I kept coming back to. Nothing else could quite match the depth and purity of its sound. I trailed my fingers over the smooth wood affectionately.

"What exactly is it that you're going to teach me?" Aria said. "I'm still not totally sure how you all fit in."

I nodded. Some confusion was understandable, but I should do what I could to soothe it. My gaze slid back to her. "It will take time to absorb everything. I'm sorry your arrival was so difficult for you. We've tried to welcome our valkyries as gently as possible, but it's such a complicated situation. If there had been a way, I'd have wanted your permission first."

She did smile back then, a little wryly. "Well, it's done now, right? And I can't say I'd rather I was back to being dead. So I guess it worked out okay."

She *was* different from the other ones. I hadn't been sure of

Loki's reasoning when he'd made his case for a new strategy, but I could see the benefit of it in her now. The others—they'd agreed to help out of the goodness of their hearts, which they'd had plenty of. It'd been goodness they'd turned to when their fears or uncertainties had crept up. But goodness was soft and hazy.

The determination in Aria was something flexible but so much stronger, like the robust tension of a good bow. She wanted to learn because it was a challenge she looked forward to defeating, not just because she felt obligated to follow some vague idea of rightness. She was going to *enjoy* coming into her powers, not simply accept them as a duty.

That kind of light could sustain you so much longer, through so much more.

She'd bounced back quickly from the frantic girl she'd been this morning. It soothed *me*, seeing that.

"What do you know about valkyries?" I asked her.

"Other than what you guys have told me so far—that they've got something to do with Odin, and you've got to use someone dead to make one?" She shrugged. "Not much. They're warriors, right? That's why I needed some of Thor's strength in the mix?"

"In a way," I said. "But a valkyrie's position is something more sacred than that. In the old times, you and your sisters would have watched over the battles on Midgard and decided which side emerged victorious. Chosen which of the fallen deserved to ascend to Odin's great hall, Valhalla. Justice and mercy."

Her eyebrows lifted. "Sounds like a big responsibility."

There really wasn't much that fazed this one, was there? I felt myself relax even more into the conversation. I was giving her something she wanted. There was no discomfort here.

"Yes," I said. "Although you wouldn't have shouldered it alone. There would have been dozens of you, observing and considering."

"But now you're stuck with just me. After the trouble the ones before me apparently had, you didn't think a squadron might be a good idea?"

"Ah," I said, with a wave of my hand as if I could brush both of us past that point. "It takes a lot of energy for us to summon even one valkyrie. We do the best we can. Now, I can show you—"

"What happened to the other ones?" Aria broke in.

I cocked my head. "The previous three we summoned disappeared in their search. Loki mentioned that, didn't he?"

She folded her wiry arms over her chest. "I don't mean the ones you summoned. I mean all those dozens of valkyries Odin had before, off in Valhalla or wherever. If they're so attuned to him, why aren't they already looking? Why'd you need to make your own?"

Before. Another quiver ran through my consciousness, but only along the surface. Easier to sweep aside.

"It's been a long time since those days," I said. "Things have changed. Your wars have gotten so much larger. The old ways no longer made sense. Odin released the valkyries from their duties and the powers that came with them."

"Oh. That sucks all around, doesn't it?" Aria dragged in a breath. "All right. So what's next, teacher? How do justice and mercy fit in for me?"

Yes, back to the real matter at hand. "When making their judgments, valkyries needed to see inside the warriors they were judging," I said. "To sense their motives and emotions. Like shining a light on their souls."

"Got it," she said. "And you're the god of light."

Another smile stretched across my face. Yes. We all had our place—and she was finding her place among us already, wasn't she?

"Something like that," I said. "And you have that ability too. If you learn the right focus, you can sense what others are feeling—the harmony or lack thereof in their spirit—even from a distance."

"Like over a battlefield."

"Exactly. Although we hope it won't come to that. But it should help you, if you encounter anyone during your search for Odin, to decide whether they're a threat or a potential ally."

I glanced around, considering how we might best practice this skill, and the sound of a car engine drifted in from outside. I couldn't have asked for better timing. Beckoning Aria to follow me, I walked over to the window.

A small truck had just pulled up at the end of our drive. A young man hopped out of the back with a cooler and a couple of boxes of groceries. A middle-aged woman climbed out of the front passenger seat and hauled out a bag of gardening equipment. The gray-haired man who'd been driving followed the younger man over to the house.

"Our mortal maintenance crew," I said to Aria as she joined me. She peered down through the glass. "They bring supplies from town and keep up the property so we don't need to worry much about it ourselves."

"You're not worried they'll see something godly?" Aria asked.

"Loki makes sure they see nothing that would disturb them."

She made a skeptical sound. "I get the impression he'd probably have fun disturbing them, really."

I had to laugh at that. "You might be right. But he manages to keep that part of his nature in check. We all want to keep the harmony here."

"Especially when you don't know how much longer it'll be before you can get home."

She knew how to cut straight through to the heart of the matter too, didn't she? I closed my eyes for a moment, soaking in the sunlight and the familiar scents of the instruments and old paper scores.

"Yes," I said. "There's that. But it won't hurt them at all for you to try your sensitivity on them. Watch the woman from here, see if you can reach out to her with your mind. Almost as if you're going to caress her head with your thoughts. See what impressions come back to you then."

Aria leaned toward the windowpane, the errant blond waves of her hair nearly brushing the glass. Her eyes narrowed.

As she focused on the gardener, I found myself focusing more intently on our valkyrie. On the rise and fall of her chest, so close to mine, as her breaths evened out in concentration. On the light that lit in those gray eyes, the smile that started to curl her lips, when she must have caught what she was looking for.

I could get my own sense of *her* emotions, looking at her. There was that determination I hadn't needed any godly power at all to read. Beneath it, a growing sense of satisfaction—with the abilities she was discovering, I assumed. She wasn't *happy* here exactly, but I didn't think we could have expected that much yet. Content was a victory in itself.

And then, even deeper beneath that, I tasted a small but vivid pulse of love. Someone or something she held in her heart, so tightly and fiercely I had the urge to unravel it, to delve into every crinkle of that sensation. When was the last time I'd immersed myself in an emotion that strong? My pulse stuttered, half eager, half fearful.

Aria turned her head, and I jerked my awareness back to the surface. Her eyes were outright glinting now.

"I could feel it," she said. "When I reached out, like you said. Not a lot, but— She's a little worried. I think she has a pet at home that's sick. But she likes being out in the sun, working with her hands, seeing that the plants are growing well. She wants to do a good job even though she knows she's not being supervised closely."

Aria grinned at me triumphantly when she finished. I hadn't reached out to the gardener myself to compare my impressions, but everything she'd said felt right with what I knew of the woman.

I nodded encouragingly. "Try our delivery boy next, then."

I pointed to the young man who'd clambered back into the bed of the truck. He was sorting through a few boxes still sitting there, the sun bringing out a sheen in his dark brown hair. Aria leaned forward again, watching him. This time she spoke as she reached her awareness.

"He wishes he was back home," she said in a distant voice, with me and also with him. "There was something happening in town today that he's missing, and he's kind of peeved about that. But he's also intimidated by the house. He wants to make sure he hasn't forgotten anything he was supposed to bring in—so he doesn't get in trouble, I guess?" She glanced at me, coming back. "Has he gotten in trouble before?"

"Not that I can recall," I said. "As I mentioned, we try to keep harmony around here. No ill feelings. But mortal emotions aren't very often rational."

"Whereas godly emotions are?" Aria said, sounding amused. She peered up at me. "And what would I see if I reached out to *you*, god of light?"

I felt her attention on me like the flicker of heat from a flame. Seeping through the calm glow on the surface down toward a deeper space where things I didn't want to look at closely started to stir in response.

My chest hitched. I stepped to the side, breaking her focus. "I think you've proven you've caught on fast," I said. "Maybe we can find a crowd to test those abilities out on next time. You're already well on your way."

Her brow knit as her gaze followed me, but she didn't push the matter. She did turn back to the window. "A little more practice couldn't hurt, right?" she said. "I wonder what's going on in that other guy's head."

As she bent forward, I stayed where I was, the brief jitter of my nerves settling with that distance.

This one was different, all right. Maybe in some ways I'd rather she wasn't.

# 9

*Aria*

I left the music room with a weird twist in my gut. I'd learned what I needed to from Baldur. He'd been nice enough about it. But I couldn't shake the feeling that something had shifted while I'd been with him, something that had made his enthusiasm for the whole teaching thing dry up. He'd wanted me to leave at the end.

It shouldn't have mattered to me. I just couldn't help wondering what mystery lay behind those dreamy blue eyes. Because there was *something* more to him than rainbows and sunlight.

Curiosity killed the cat. Keep your eyes on the prize. Sayings I should keep in mind. Whatever was going on with any of these guys—gods—it had nothing to do with me.

I'd only taken two steps down the hall when Loki peeled himself off the wall he'd been leaning against near the staircase. "I take it you've been making the rounds," he said in his smooth wry voice.

"That's what I'm supposed to be doing, right?" I said. "Getting up to speed on this valkyrie gig, so I can find your missing Allfather?"

The slim god grinned. "And with such enthusiasm. I'm just offended you haven't shown any interest in seeing what I can teach you yet. Unless you were simply saving the best for last."

He didn't sound offended even a little bit. I rolled my eyes. "You just weren't conveniently available."

"Here I am now." He spread his arms as if offering himself. "Shall we?"

I didn't like showing any weakness, but I hesitated despite myself. Loki was a trickster. The other gods even called him that. I might have held my own with some of the toughest criminals in Philly, but none of them had divine cleverness on their side. Not to mention it was his fault more than any of the others I was stuck here.

And on top of that, now that I wasn't in escape mode, it was hard not to notice just how freakishly attractive all of the gods were. With the others, I could distract myself. But Loki—quick-tongued and full of sly humor along with the power that practically radiated from that leanly muscled frame—was exactly my type. Exactly the type I'd have steered clear of to jump some other guy's bones when I had that itch, because I only wanted someone I could forget about the next day.

Loki was doubly dangerous just because of the urge that lit up in me at the spark in his eyes—the urge to surprise him, to impress him, to beat him at his games… and we wouldn't get into all the things certain parts of me would have liked to do after that.

But I didn't really have a whole lot of choice about spending time around him, so I'd just have to keep reminding myself of the whole evil trickster god angle.

While I was coming to that conclusion, Loki's expression softened, which somehow managed to make his angular face even more attractive.

"Perhaps we didn't get off on the best of feet," he said, his tone turning self-deprecating. "My fault, mainly, as so much always is. Are there any other cutting instruments I can retrieve to help make it up to you?"

I looked at him, a bit of the focus Baldur had taught me tingling at the back of my skull. It was harder getting a read on a god than a mortal. I'd barely felt anything from Baldur before he'd broken the connection. Loki gave me a faint impression that was fiery and yet cool at the same time—and a sense of genuine apology. I was pretty sure he *would* have gone running back to Philly to grab a butter knife out of my kitchen drawer or the scissors from Mom's bathroom cabinet if I'd asked him to.

I was kind of tempted to make him do it, just for the hell of it. But what if that made me more indebted to him? Nope, safer to stick to the essentials.

"I think I'm good in the cutting department," I said. "If you're ready to teach, then teach. What valkyrie skills have you got up your sleeve?"

The sly light in his amber eyes flickered brighter. "All the best ones, pixie. Come with me. I'm going to teach you how to fly."

A shiver of excitement raced through my chest as I followed him to the end of the hall. I was going to *fly*, like a fucking bird. But the excitement came with a knot in my stomach at the thought of calling those heavy wings out of my back.

Loki popped open the dormer window there and eased it up high enough for us to climb out onto the roof. Hot air and the tarry smell of baking shingles wafted through the opening. He swept his arm with a hint of a bow to let me go ahead of him. "Ladies first."

"I wouldn't say I'm a 'lady,'" I said. "But I'll take it anyway."

I clambered out onto the slanted roof, setting my feet carefully as I found my balance. The warm breeze licked through my hair. We were three stories up, with a view over the lawn and the tree-lined meadows. The sun was dropping low in the sky, making the trees' shadows stretch across the grass.

That was a long drop below us if I lost my footing. But maybe valkyries didn't break that easily. I wasn't especially keen to find out.

Loki slipped through the opening as if his much taller body fit as well as mine had, with a casual, confident grace. I jerked my gaze away before I started admiring him or anything stupid like that and looked out over the lawn. The maintenance people had driven off in their truck a few minutes ago. No one else around. Quite the pocket of privacy the gods had found here.

"So, I guess if I'm going to fly I'll need those wings." I rolled my shoulders, the sleeveless shirt Freya had picked out for me shifting with them. It had a racerback, leaving my shoulder blades bare. I might be able to unfurl my new appendages without ruining any more clothing.

My back had already stiffened at the thought of encouraging my wings to emerge. The last time I'd already been stirred up by the sight of Loki's blood. Now I had to totally calmly just *decide* to do it.

Loki was studying me. "You don't like them," he said.

It was hard to argue when he put it that plainly. "Nope," I said. "Not exactly the most comfortable feeling, having two strange—and huge… things sprouting out of your body that aren't supposed to be there."

"You're thinking about it wrong," he said, leaning his elbow onto the top of the dormer. "I can take on forms with all sorts of bits and pieces I'm not used to: wings, tails, hooves, breasts." He arched his eyebrows. "But I don't see them as foreign parts I'm stuck with. They're more like different facets of my own body that I'm bringing to the surface. And that's what your wings are. They *are* meant to be there now. They're yours. Own them. Embrace them."

I dragged in a breath. Maybe he had a point. I was going to have to get used to the wings if I was going to *use* them—to get out of here, to get to Petey, and to get through who knew what else lay ahead of me. The thought of them lurking under my skin still made me feel itchy, though.

"Bring them out slowly," Loki suggested. "Take your time absorbing the feeling, getting to know them. I can help you adjust your stance so you can hold them more easily."

He stepped toward me, and my body tensed at the sudden movement. His hand paused half a foot from my shoulder. Again, he seemed to study me.

"If it's all right with you that I help?" he said.

I swallowed thickly. While the trickster god might not have Baldur's ability to read emotions, he clearly didn't miss much. The thought that he might be able to guess the deeper sources of my discomfort made the itch turn into an uneasy prickling. But this was why he was here. To teach. To help me figure out this valkyrie thing.

People who just wanted to shove you around—or worse—didn't generally ask for permission first.

"Okay," I said. "Slow and steady. Let's do this."

Loki let just his fingertips rest on my back where my wings would emerge, his touch so light I barely felt it. "Picture them, as you did before," he said softly. "Easing out from inside you, stretching up bit by bit…"

I needed those wings. I needed to fly. I took another deep breath and brought up the memory of the wings emerging. The itch dug into my back. Dug in and closed around the ridges of cartilage waiting to burst out.

Yes. Out you come. Easy now.

I nudged them with my mind, a push and a tug. A burning sensation trickled across my shoulder blades. Then they were rising, spreading over me, inch by feathered inch, their weight pressing down on me more with each passing second.

"There," Loki murmured. "These are yours—just as much as

those pixie arms and legs are. Your muscles. Your bones. Your nerves. Straighten your back, here." He pressed my spine. "And round your shoulders just slightly—yes."

As I adjusted my stance to his instructions, the weight of the wings melted across my back. Still there, but not quite as intrusive.

"Flex them," he said, stepping back to give me room. "Try them out, just standing here. Feel how much a part of you they are."

I focused on the wings, and they responded. They unfurled wider over me with a sensation as if I were stretching my arms over my head.

My muscles. My nerves.

I curled the tips in again with a tentative flap, and the feathers stirred the breeze. The movement of the air tingled down through the wings. It quivered right through the rest of my body in a way that wasn't exactly unpleasant.

My wings. *Mine*. And they were going to take me home.

"So how do we get from this to flying?" I asked.

Loki grinned. "At some point you just have to take a leap."

He sprang into the air—and stayed there, hovering just beyond the edge of the roof. I eyed him.

"How do you do that?"

"Magic!" he said with a snap of his fingers, and chuckled. "Somewhat literally. I happen to be in a possession of a pair of highly supernaturally charged shoes."

"Hmm. Maybe I could just borrow those."

"You could try. Unfortunately for you, they're tuned only to work on my feet. Of course, you could simply make use of those glorious wings of yours already. Come on." His tone turned into a challenge. "Bet you can't catch me."

"We'll see about that," I muttered. The drop from the edge of the roof still looked awfully far. My heart thumped faster as I tested my wings. They caught against the air with each flap, almost lifting me off the shingles already.

Good, sturdy wings. They'd carry me. I just had to take that leap of faith…

I pushed myself forward, over the eavestrough, out into the open air. My body plummeted with a lurch of my gut. A yelp broke from my throat. My arms flailed out, and my wings flailed too—flailed and swept against the air, cutting off my fall. I swooped upward, the wind rushing past me.

A giggle tumbled from my throat. I was flying. Really, truly flying.

As I lost momentum, I flapped my wings again, a little frantically and then with more confidence. Glide upward. Bank left. Some instinct deep inside me knew the right ways to move. I propelled myself back to where Loki was waiting.

"Well, look at you," he said. "What do you think?"

"I think," I said a little breathlessly, "I can go a hell of a lot higher than this."

I stretched my wings farther, pushing myself up toward the sky. A stronger wind buffeted me, and I soared on it, its warm fingers teasing across my wings. The waning sunlight streaked over my skin, the fresh country air filled my lungs, and for an instant, I felt invincible. I could go anywhere. Do anything.

I dove and swooped upward again, and the exhilaration made me giddy. I laughed, reveling in the sensation. Loki strode after me, walking on the air. When our gazes met, he was beaming at me, as if he was as pleased as I was with this new discovery.

"That's my girl," he said.

His voice was pleased, maybe even proud, but the words brought my mind back to earth. I *wasn't* his. I wouldn't let myself be. The only person I belonged to was me, no matter who had brought me back into this altered—and really kind of amazing—body.

I flapped my wings faster to send myself speeding up even

higher into the sky. Up and up, until the air pressure started to lift and a strange sensation filled my ears.

Loki ascended with me. When I stopped, hovering with steady sweeps of my wings, he brandished his arm toward the landscape around us.

"I've passed on more than the power of transformation to you," he said. "You'll find your valkyrie senses are much more honed than you're used to. When you need to soar over battles, it helps to be able to zoom in on the details as you make your choices. Your eyes are sharper than a hawk's, your ears keener than a wolf's."

"Like yours?" I said.

He chuckled. "Oh, no one can beat mine. Take a look. See what you can see."

I hadn't had the opportunity to stretch my sight before. As I peered down over the world, distant shapes and colors came into sharper relief when I focused on them. There was the Hudson River snaking along to my left. That sprawling patch of gray off in the distance—in the space of a breath, my vision narrowed in on shining skyscrapers with glinting windows. New York City. Could I even hear the distant honking of its cars? No, that had to be someplace closer. There. My eyes narrowed in again on a farmstead to the west where someone was honking at a cow that had wandered onto the road, miles from here.

If New York was over there, that meant that Philadelphia would be… this way. I spun around as if simply enjoying the movement, but at the same time I noted the direction relative to the house for later use. My home city was too far for even these honed eyes to make out, but I could almost feel its hum. All those human lives my valkyrie senses were created to be attuned to.

"The whole world, opened up to you," Loki said. "Spectacular, isn't it?"

"Yes," I had to admit. My gaze roved across the fields, my ears perked. More cars wove along other roads around us. A plow rumbled across a field. Things I could see without any special focus. I frowned. "Don't we have to worry about regular people seeing *us*?"

Loki gave me a crooked smile. "You're part of the godly realm now, pixie. No mortal can see you unless you make a conscious effort to let them."

That was useful to know. I could fly anywhere then.

Bringing my attention back to my new body, I swooped and soared in another wide circle, swaying with the wind. Oh, this was spectacular, absolutely. I still wasn't sold on the whole wings thing while I was on the ground, but up here… Yeah, I'd keep them.

The shadows of the trees were stretching all the way to the house now. A low rolling voice carried up to us from an open window.

"Loki! Get your ass down here for dinner. And ask Ari to please come too."

Loki motioned to me, still smiling. "Best not to get between Thor and his preferred dinner time. He's not the most pleasant company if you leave him hungry. Besides, I think you've come an awfully long way in one day."

"I have," I agreed as I soared with him toward the house. And I was going to go a whole lot farther the first moment I had the chance.

Tonight, if the gods slept, I could slip out of here without anyone noticing I'd left.

# 10

*Aria*

The pillow on my bed was so downy I almost wanted to burrow my head in it and give in to sleep. But my thoughts were still rattling through my head, keeping me way too alert, my body tensing and then relaxing at each creak of the house. I'd said I was exhausted from all the training I'd done today and headed up to the bedroom after dinner. Night had fallen outside the window now, stars showing against the deep black of the sky that I never really got in the city with the constant haze of streetlamps. I'd stopped hearing any sounds of movement an hour ago.

It seemed the gods did sleep. Which meant it was time for me to get moving.

I eased off of the bed and padded across the floor to the bedroom door. The hinges squeaked softly as I opened it. I winced and froze, but no one stirred in the rooms around and beneath me.

Had they really trusted me to just stay put? Maybe I'd put on a good enough show of enthusiasm today that they'd believed I'd bought into their whole plan completely. Not that I was going to assume as much and get careless. I had my own plans, my excuses all lined up.

I slipped down the hall to the dormer window that led onto the roof. The pane hissed open. I squeezed out into the warm night air.

Crickets were chirping somewhere below. Tiny glints of fireflies darted across the lawn, which was faintly lit by the light near-full moon. It was kind of pretty, if I'd come out here to admire the view. I crept away from the window across the pliant shingles and bowed my head.

The prickling, burning sensation of my emerging wings still made my nerves twitch, but I was getting used to it. Especially when I spread them and felt the air wafting against their feathers, the memory of how it had felt to soar up toward the sky that afternoon washing over me. My pulse gave a giddy leap.

I was going to feel that sensation again in a moment. And with luck I'd be seeing Petey not too long after that.

I sprang off the rooftop into the air with a flap of my wings. They caught the air before I even started to fall. I swept up over the house, inhaling sharply, the breeze streaking over my skin and ruffling my clothes.

For the first few minutes, I just glided around the house and yard, waiting to see what would happen. If the gods had some kind of safeguard in place, I could still play innocent, say I'd had trouble sleeping and wanted to practice my flying a little more. If I hadn't actually left the property, they couldn't accuse me of trying to flee.

But no one emerged from the house to see what I was doing. There was no sign that anyone had even noticed. I wet my lips. Could it really be this easy?

They might have ways of finding me after they woke up. I didn't know what all magic they were capable of. But maybe it wouldn't even come to that. I wasn't completely sure yet what I was going to do after I saw Petey. I could always sneak back here and go to bed as if I'd never left, and they wouldn't even know I'd gone. No point in trying to make a real run for it until I was sure I knew all the tricks I needed to evade them.

I took one last turn around the house, and then I banked to the right, pointing myself to the southwest. With a couple flaps of my wings, I was soaring toward home.

The wind raced over me, warbling in my ears. The landscape spilled out below me like I'd only seen before in aerial photographs. I grinned, reveling in the freedom.

And then a blob of shadow appeared in front of me, smacking into my body.

Cold tendrils wrapped around my limbs and my wings, weighing down on them. I yelped and struggled, but they resisted my efforts. The shadowy menace dragged me back down to earth.

Down to a field beyond the house where a dark-haired, dark-eyed god had his face tipped up to watch me fall.

The shadow didn't hurt me. It deposited me on the ground feet first with just a faint thump. But the cool clinging of its tendrils was making me shudder. I squirmed against it, trying to break free.

"Get this thing off me!"

"I don't think that you're in a position to make demands, valkyrie," Hod said in his flat voice. "I'll let you go when you tell me where *you* were going."

Would he even then? Somehow I doubted it. I forced my body to stop moving in the tangle of shadow and stared back at him through the thin moonlight. He was turned toward me, but like before, his gaze didn't quite meet mine. As if he thought I wasn't even worthy of that much acknowledgment.

"Don't lie," he added. "I know you were going *somewhere*. I waited to make sure you were leaving before I stopped you."

"Not much for sleeping, huh?" I said.

His gaze shifted, but it only seemed to move from my cheek to my forehead. "I'm the god of darkness," he said. "This is when I'm most awake."

"So you get to be the watchdog. Lucky you."

He ignored my jab. "Where were you going, valkyrie? If you'd like, we could take this discussion back to the house with the others. I'm sure Thor would be in an *excellent* mood woken up in the middle of sleeping off that dinner."

I let out a breath. I couldn't think of any lie that he'd believe that would go over better than the truth. "I was going home. Just to see how things are. I was going to come back."

"Sure you were," Hod said. "What exactly were you planning to do out there? Showing off how your new powers could help the criminals you've been hanging out with? Maybe stealing a thing or two?"

I bristled. Obviously Freya had reported our conversation to the others. And not in the most flattering terms.

"No," I snapped. "I'll be happy never to see the assholes I worked for again, and what the hell would I want to steal? I just want to make sure my little brother is okay. That's all. Sorry for having someone I can't just up and leave without even saying goodbye."

Hod blinked slowly. "Your little brother," he repeated.

"Yeah." My anger died down as I thought about Petey. "He's only six. And I'm basically the only person he can count on. He *needs* me. If he's heard I'm dead…" My throat choked up. I swallowed hard and managed to finish, a little raggedly. "I just need a few minutes with him. With all the stuff you guys want me to do for *you*, is that really too much to ask?"

The god was silent for a moment. I couldn't read the expression on his chiseled face, but at least he didn't look definitely pissed off anymore. His gaze slid farther to the side.

"No, it isn't," he said. "If that's really all this is about, you can go. But I'm coming with you."

He motioned, and the shadow that had clutched me released, slipping away from my skin. I rubbed my arms as if I could wipe the feeling of those cool tendrils from my memory. My body had tensed at the idea of having company for my visit. I didn't have much choice, though, clearly.

"Can you even fly?" I asked. "How do you figure you're going to keep up?"

His mouth slanted with a thin smile. "I'll manage. Lead the way."

I hopped off the ground with a tentative sweep of my wings, thinking I was going to have to go low and slow the whole way to the city. Beneath me, Hod made a tugging gesture toward him. The darkness of the night congealed around his feet into a thicker patch of shadow like the one he'd caught me with. He knelt on it, and it eased up into the air like some kind of bizarro flying carpet.

"Okay," I said, "I'll give you props for that. It's a pretty cool power. Is that what you're going to teach me in my valkyrie lessons?"

He grimaced. "No. Are we going, or did you change your mind?"

"Just trying to make conversation. Come on."

If he was going to be like that, I didn't really want to talk to him anyway. I soared up into the air with a few beats of my wings and pushed on toward Philly, not bothering to check whether Hod could keep up. He was a god. I shouldn't have to be holding back for him.

I sped across the landscape as fast as my wings would carry me, dipping down occasionally to check the highway signs and make sure I was on the right track. At maximum velocity, I could soar faster than the cars and trucks roaring along below me. When I bothered to glance back, Hod was keeping pace, perched securely on that patch of shadow, the wind only lightly ruffling his short black hair. He didn't look at me but somewhere farther in the distance.

Definitely not the friendly type. I guessed the other three had gotten all the charisma.

A familiar skyline came into view up ahead, and relief swelled in my chest. Part of me hadn't been convinced I'd even make it here until this moment. I flapped my wings even harder, putting in one last burst of speed to carry me the rest of the way home.

The scruffy-looking street outside Mom's scruffy-looking house was quiet as I dropped down onto the neighbor's roof. An old clunker sputtered past, and then the only noise was the faint rustle of the breeze through old Mrs. Jackman's laundry on the line out back. It had to be after midnight now.

Hod came to a stop beside me. He drifted over as I edged along the roof to where I could see Petey's window. His room was dark, but he'd left the curtains open, the window a few inches ajar. Like always.

Past evenings when I'd paid a stealthy visit, I'd scrambled onto the fence next door and then clambered the rest of the way using the ridge in the siding. Today I could be a little more graceful. I leapt with a stretch of my wings and glided onto that ridge, catching the window ledge with my hands.

Petey was asleep. I'd known he probably would be, but a twinge of disappointment ran through me anyway. His pale little face was slack, mushed against his pillow, his golden curls spilling every which way. His hand was clenched in a fist around the edge of his sheet.

It'd be mean to wake him up. He didn't look sad, at least. No sign that he'd been crying. I'd only had fake ID on me when I'd been dropping off that package—the coroner or whoever might not even have figured out my real name.

I'd rather Petey never had to know exactly what had happened to me. As long as I could keep dropping in like I always had, he didn't have to know.

I wasn't going to wake him up, but I could leave him a sign that I'd been here. That I was thinking about him, always.

Hod had dipped down beside me on his flying shadow. "Where are you going now?" he said sharply when I left the window.

I shot him a glower. "To the corner store. To buy him a chocolate bar so he knows I came." I paused. "Well, to steal a chocolate bar, unless you happen to have some cash on you. When you summoned me, you guys didn't bother to summon the money I had on me when I died."

Hod made a face, but he fished in his pocket, produced a wallet, and offered me a five-dollar bill.

"Thanks!" I said brightly. "Are you babysitting me all the way to the store, too?"

"You haven't convinced me yet that you don't need the babysitting," he muttered. "You did try to take off on us *twice* this morning. How short do you think our memories are?"

I kept my voice sweet. "Well, you all did kind of materialize me out of some deathly void without any warning or explanation. Next time that happens, I'll be a little more chill about it, I promise."

Loki had told me I was invisible to mortals, but I didn't totally believe it until I walked into the 24-hour shop a few blocks over and the lady working nights didn't even look up from the magazine she was reading behind the counter. I waved my wings in the air. Not a blink. Ha! Now if only the gods couldn't see me unless I wanted them to—then everything would have been a whole lot easier.

I grabbed a 3 Musketeers bar out of the row of boxes under the counter and tucked the five-dollar bill in its place. Payment and a tip.

Hod skulked after me the whole way back to Mom's house. I flapped back up to Petey's window and pushed it farther open with a creak of the frame. The screen had gotten torn years ago and Mom had never bothered to replace it, which had always suited me just fine. If she'd known how often I'd come in and out through this window over the last few years, she probably would have padlocked it shut.

Petey was so out he didn't even stir. I tiptoed over and tucked the chocolate bar under the end of his pillow. It'd been his favorite kind for the last two years, and I always joked with him that he and I were the two musketeers. "Two is all we need!" He'd know who had left it, no question.

Back at the window, I sat down on the ledge. I didn't really want to leave. Not right away. My brother's body hunched, small and fragile, under the blanket. The rasps of his sleeping breath washed over me.

"Are we done here?" Hod said where he was hovering outside.

"Give me a second," I said. "You're lucky I'm not asking to stay the whole night. Just look at him."

"I *can't*, even if I wanted to."

It took a second for me to process those words. My head jerked around. Hod gazed steadily back at me—except not into my eyes. Somewhere in the vicinity of my nose. Close, but not quite.

As if he couldn't quite pinpoint where my eyes even were.

I could have smacked myself. "You're blind."

"And you're not as observant as you'd like to think," Hod replied, but there wasn't much of an edge to the words. And it was a fair point.

"In my defense, I've been a little distracted in the last twenty-four hours," I said, and paused. "How did you follow me on the way out here? How did you even know I was leaving the house?"

He might have heard the window or me on the roof if his ears were good, but he'd said he'd waited until I left the property. I'd already been up in the air then.

Hod's lips twisted into something that wasn't quite a smile. "We brought you back to 'life'," he said. "We made you a valkyrie. That left a connection. If I concentrate, I can tell where you are. Any of the four of us could."

Oh. That made my whole escape plan a lot trickier. I wanted to ask whether distance affected this connection thingy, but that would only raise his suspicions. I could find a subtler way to figure that out later.

The god of darkness, always in the dark. Or *did* it look dark, if you simply couldn't see at all? Somehow I didn't get the feeling he wanted me prying into the intricacies of his blindness either.

I turned back to the bedroom. A murmur escaped Petey's mouth. He tucked his arm a little closer to his face. An ache spread through my chest, up to my throat.

I did have to go. But I'd be back. I swore it to any gods that actually existed, if there were more than the five I'd met so far.

My wings fluttered to hold me in place as I eased the window back to its previous position. Just in case Mom happened to be paying extra attention this morning. I pressed my fingers to my lips and then to the window as if Petey would feel that kiss on his forehead where I'd have wanted to press it.

A car engine growled down the street. A patchy red Chevy parked in front of the house, and a bulky figure swayed out of the passenger seat with a wave to whoever was driving. My shoulders stiffened.

Hod had turned toward the sound. "Who's that?" he asked.

"My mother's current boyfriend," I said. "Stoned to the eyeballs, it looks like."

Even as I was saying that, I realized I was wrong. His movements were clumsy, but in a jerky way. Twitchy. He looked *high*, not stoned. And high on something that wasn't treating him well.

It'd been a couple months since I'd last seen Ivan in person. How much had his habits changed since then?

He rattled the doorknob for a moment before he managed to get the key to work. Then he stomped inside. I held there for a minute, my wings flapping steadily in time with the too-loud thump of my heart. There wasn't anything I could do about that asshole.

I pushed my wings a little higher—and Ivan's voice bellowed through the house, raw and furious. "*Pete!*"

I flinched. Petey's bedroom door slammed open. My little brother woke with a jerk, pushing upright on the bed, his head listing as he dragged himself out of sleep.

"Where the hell did you put my controller, you little shit," Ivan roared. He barged through the room, flinging the blanket back on Petey's bed, swiping the toys off his play table in the corner. A Lego structure smashed on the floor.

"What?" Petey said, his voice wobbling. "I didn't take anything."

"You're always fiddling around with it," Ivan said. "It must have been you. Cough it up."

Petey cringed back on his bed, hugging his knees. "I really don't know. I didn't touch it today. I promise."

"Don't you fucking lie to me, you pathetic waste of space."

Ivan loomed over Petey, one bulging arm raised. A cry caught in my throat. I threw myself back at the window.

My fingers had just closed around the pane to yank it up when Ivan stepped back. His hand dropped to his side, his chest heaving with ragged breaths.

"Don't you dare mess with my stuff again," he growled, and thundered back out of the room.

A tear was streaking down Petey's cheek. He stifled a sob and heaved his blanket tight around him.

"Petey," I said, but he couldn't hear me either. Fuck, how did this visibility thing even work? I was supposed to be able to let him see me if I wanted to—

I braced my arms to shove at the window pane, and a hand closed around my forearm.

"No," Hod said.

I glared back at him, even though I knew those fathomless dark green eyes couldn't see my expression. "You heard what just happened even if you couldn't see it. He's terrified."

"I can hear that it's over," Hod said. "And I don't think appearing before your brother as a winged magical being is going to put his mind at ease."

"Would you let me do it even if it would?" I asked.

He didn't answer that. "You have to let him go. You're not part of his world anymore. There's nothing you can really do for him." He hesitated. His voice thawed, just a little. "You showed him you care. That has to be enough."

As if on cue, Petey shifted his pillow and uncovered the chocolate bar. He snatched it up, a brilliant smile crossing his face. His gaze darted to the window, as if he were looking right at me. But he couldn't see *me.*

And yet he was beaming at me.

My heart squeezed, and Hod's grip tightened. I couldn't fight him. I already knew that.

At least, not like this.

I let him pull me back from the window. With a wrenching in my chest, I swept up into the sky.

The gods needed me right now. They wanted me to fulfill their mission. Fine. I'd track down Odin for them, and then they wouldn't need their valkyrie anymore. Maybe they'd be distracted enough that I could get away completely. Maybe they wouldn't even care at that point.

Either way, I was coming back here as soon as I could. And next time I'd do more than leave a chocolate bar.

# 11

*Hod*

I might not ever have seen a dawn, but I knew when it came. I could feel the moment the first rays of the sun seeped over the horizon like a faint but rising energy jittering over my skin, breaking through the stillness that had been the night.

No matter how many times I experienced that sensation, it always set my nerves a little on edge for the first few minutes. A vibration carried through the walls from the ceiling, a stirring in the bedroom above the study—Baldur's. My twin brother had been sleeping restlessly again, tossing and turning.

Nightmares, maybe. I didn't like to think about what those nightmares might contain. Whether I might feature in them, and how.

The chaos of the human world always agitated his mind, even if he didn't complain about it. We'd been here too long. He needed the calm of Asgard.

A knock sounded on the study's half open door.

"Hod?" our new valkyrie said.

I turned in my chair to face her automatically, directing my eyes as well as I could to where I could sense her face was. It wasn't too hard to estimate from the direction and volume of her voice, from the soft sounds any body makes as it moves: the rustle of clothing, the rising and falling of breath. I'd formed a mental construct of her already from our earlier interactions—short and wiry and deft but forceful in action.

She'd contracted her wings. The soft murmur of those feathers would have been impossible to miss.

"Shouldn't you be in bed?" I said. We'd only returned a few hours ago from the reckless jaunt across the country I'd let her talk me into. I could get by on a nap or two throughout the day, but mortals—or those recently mortal—generally seemed to require more.

She shrugged, another rustle. It was a different shirt from yesterday, not the silvery hiss of silk but a somewhat coarser rasp I'd guess was cotton. "I got a little sleep. My mind decided I'm done." She paused. "You still need to teach me whatever it is you brought to making me a valkyrie."

"So you came for your lesson?"

"It seems like it's about time. Everyone else managed to fit theirs in yesterday."

She was shifting from her wary tone to the brasher one I was becoming equally used to. I'd have thought our valkyrie had only two modes if I hadn't heard her voice soft with affection at her little brother's window last night.

I was already regretting the decision to let her go see him. She hadn't been up to anything nefarious, that much was true—this time. But her ties to her old life clearly remained tight, and venturing back into it had only strengthened them. I didn't believe she was eager to learn so she could fulfill our mission. Loki had chosen her because she was like him—a sly one, a schemer. No doubt from the moment I'd sent her back toward this house last night she'd been forming new plans of her own.

That damned choked sound she'd made when she'd mentioned her brother had swayed my resolve for one imprudent moment.

She took a step closer, swiveling to take in the room. "What are you doing in here anyway? You can't read all these books, right?"

I propped one elbow against the desk and the other on the back of my chair. "I can in a way." With the right supernatural compulsion, I could make the ink murmur its words to me. "We all find ways of adapting."

She hummed to herself. "I'm going to guess that's not what you're going to teach me, though."

"No." I *was* going to have to teach her, regardless of her motives for asking, but that didn't mean now was an ideal time for it. "I think it would be better if you were fully rested first. What I have to show you is… more discomforting than what you'll have learned from the others." Which was why I hadn't rushed in to provide my part earlier.

"Well, now you've really piqued my curiosity. I'm definitely not getting back to sleep with that idea in my head. Might as well get it over with!"

She wasn't going to give up. Why was I wasting my time arguing? If she wanted to learn so badly, let her find out for herself.

I pushed myself to my feet. "If you insist."

Just the thinnest warmth was starting to creep through the window. A row of small potted ferns sat along the sill. I let my fingers come to rest on the delicate fronds of the nearest one and motioned for the valkyrie to join me.

"You've talked with the others about the traditional duties of the valkyries," I said.

She nodded, a whisper of her hair, as she came up beside me.

She was close enough now that I could smell her as well as hear her: clean and hot and ever so slightly sharp, the way fire smelled beneath the smoke. Had that come with her transformation into a valkyrie, or had it always been her natural scent?

"The basics," she said. "Watch the battles, choose the winners, send the deserving up to Valhalla. That about covers it, right?"

"It does. But only on the surface level. You don't just choose the winners—you choose the losers as well. And what happens to the losers in a war? What happens to those deserving before they ascend?"

"They die," she said. "Obviously."

"And when a valkyrie chooses, sometimes she's the one who takes that life." I stroked my hand over the fern. It tickled my fingertips. "Your new senses will allow you to feel the hum of life inside a body. You gather it in your grasp and then you ease it all the way out. There's a darkness in you that can swallow it whole."

The living energy in the fern quivered at my touch. I curled my fingers as if I were physically gathering it against my palm. The fronds trembled and turned dry against my hand. The warmth of that energy cooled as it congealed. I closed my hand into a fist—and it was gone. The fern was nothing more than a limp husk. Nausea unfurled in my gut.

Loki's plan still seemed like another of his harebrained risks as likely to blow up in our faces as get us where we needed to go. But, by the Allfather, wherever he was, I hoped this valkyrie would be the last one we needed. If only so I never had to carry out this tutorial again.

"I could do that?" Ari said. She sounded unnerved. Good.

"You wouldn't be a valkyrie if you couldn't. This is the lesson. Now it's your turn."

She shifted, reaching toward one of the other ferns. After a moment of silence, she said, "I don't think I feel what you were talking about."

"I can help," I said briskly. This was what I was here for. I'd just have to get it over with.

I set my hand over her smaller one, the smooth skin of her knuckles brushing my palm. The darkness in me reached out to the sliver of the void running through her being. Teased it closer to the surface of her awareness. Set the plant's energy thrumming in contrast.

Ari sucked in a breath. "Oh."

I eased back, letting her instincts guide the process from there. Somewhere inside her, she already knew what to do.

A shiver ran through her body. Her hand clenched. I let mine slide to the fern beneath. It had crumpled like the one I'd killed.

"And that works on anything living?" she said. "Just like that?"

"Any life can be snuffed out. Or cast from its body toward Valhalla, although those doors aren't open to mortal souls any longer."

"Got it." She let out a jagged chuckle. "Now that's an ability I wish I'd had on call last night!"

I tensed. My fingers leapt to close around her wrist, yanking her so she faced me. "*Never* treat the taking of a life lightly. In a battle where someone has to die, you make that choice. That's the only time you do. You can't go stealing away lives out of nowhere."

"Okay, okay," she said. "It was a joke. A bad one, obviously." The strands of her hair murmured as she cocked her head. "And a sore spot for you."

"Not one that's any of your business."

"That doesn't mean I can't be curious."

"It means I've got nothing to say about it," I said. My lungs had already started to constrict. "Drop it, valkyrie. And don't joke like that again."

"Fine. I'm sorry."

She was silent then, for a moment that stretched into another and then another. I realized I was still holding onto her wrist and released it. Ari inhaled slowly, but still she didn't speak. Her silence niggled at me.

"What's the matter, valkyrie?" I asked. Let her spit out whatever her complaint was. She thought I was being too harsh? She didn't like having her questions cut off? Let her try me. I could remind her what her place was here. That she hadn't been owed a place here at all.

The shape of her voice suggested a grimace. "What makes you think there's something wrong?"

"You got quiet," I retorted. "Normally you're as bad as Loki, the way you go on."

She exhaled. "I was just wondering why you don't really look at me. Not *look at me* look at me—I know you can't see. But I've watched you with the other gods. You can at least make it seem as if you're meeting their eyes. But you don't with me. Like I'm so much beneath you, you can't be bothered."

The anger I'd been stoking faltered. That wasn't at all what I'd expected. She hadn't said how that impression affected her, but her discomfort was threaded through her voice.

"It's not you," I said. "Well, it is, but it's only that I'm not as familiar with you. I've had hundreds of years to build a model of each of them in my head, to fine tune it. I have less experience to draw on with you. I have to approximate more."

Her posture unclenched. I hadn't realized how much I'd unsettled her. "Well," she said, "it seems like there's an easy way we could fix that."

Her hand closed around mine and drew it to her face. She rested my palm lightly against her cheek. My fingertips brushed the scattered waves of her hair. Her eyelashes grazed the pad of my thumb when she blinked. And just like that, the construction of her in my head reconfigured itself in infinitely more detail. Detail that included the soft warmth of her skin against mine. The way her breath tingled over the inside of my wrist. All the life in *her* sang beneath that surface.

A pang shot through me in response.

"Wonderful," I said in a voice I could already tell was too curt, aiming my blank gaze at where I now knew her eyes to be. "Familiarity increased. Lesson concluded. Just hope you never need to use that one."

"That's it?" she said.

I nodded to the door, that motion just as curt. "You can go."

It was an order, not an offer. She made a brief disgruntled sound, but she went. I waited until I was sure she'd left the hall, and then I went out after her. An uneasy energy stirred through my body and gnawed at the dull ache that pang had left behind.

I knew the house well enough after all this time that I could move through it without hesitation. My model of it was near-perfect. The creak of the floor and the vibrations that ran through the boards told me when a piece of furniture might have changed position, though they rarely did. Nothing hindered me on my way to Loki's bedroom door.

The sounds of motion on the other side told me he was up. I strode inside, greeted by his huff.

"Just because you can't *see* doesn't mean a person can't still want a little privacy," he said, his voice momentarily muffled by the shirt he was pulling on.

I snorted. "You're the last one to ever think of anyone else's privacy, aren't you? I just wanted to tell you that your valkyrie has all her training. So let's get on with things."

Loki chuckled. "What a hurry you're in all of a sudden."

"We all want to get back to Asgard," I said. That was the only thing I wanted right now. Baldur was becoming more detached with each week longer we were trapped here. Back in those even more familiar halls, we could all stop this constant fretting. And we could get away from mortals and valkyries and the lot of them.

Away from the strange sense of longing this valkyrie in particular had somehow managed to provoke in me.

"Hmm," Loki said, in that way he had as if he knew far more than he ought to. "While she's coming along well, I don't think it'd be fair to throw her into the fray quite yet. But I might have just the thing for a final test."

# 12

*Aria*

It was already late in the day when we reached our destination: a small, faded-looking industrial city somewhere in the north end of Michigan. Shadows clung to the vacant factories with boarded up windows we passed. We walked through the streets, invisible to mortal eyes, but the truth was in this part of town there wasn't much of anyone around to see us.

I peered through the gap where one warehouse's front door sagged on its hinges. The dwindling sunlight didn't penetrate the interior at all. A smell like grease and chalk mixed together hung in the air, and traffic rumbled along the highway a few blocks over. When I extended my senses, the mass of human lives—all that living energy I could steal into the shadow inside me if I got close enough—hummed around me at a distance.

A cheerful scene, this was not.

"What are we looking for?" I asked. All Loki had said about this trip so far was that we needed to wait until it started to get dark before we could take much action. I'd dozed as much as I could to prepare for this apparent test, and then trained a little more: sparring with Thor, testing the limits of my wings on my own. Not knowing what the test *was*, it was hard to know how to prepare.

"It's come to my attention that a warg has been roaming around this bit of Midgard," Loki said. He brushed a rotting cardboard box aside with his foot, his lips curling in distaste. "You'll track it down, corner it, and overpower it. If you can manage that, I think you're ready for whatever might await you when you go looking for Odin."

"Great," I said. "Wonderful. What the hell is a warg?"

"And why didn't you mention to the rest of us that one was causing trouble?" Hod demanded from where he was stalking along at the edge of our group.

"A warg is a monster that looks a lot like one of your wolves," Thor said to me. He'd kept close beside me since we'd entered the city, his bulky body like a shield. "But bigger, faster, fiercer, and smarter."

"Oh. Well, that sounds like fun." I bet I didn't get to keep him as my shield when I went after this one.

"And I didn't mention it because it only recently started causing enough trouble for us to bother interfering," Loki said. "Mortal eyes see only a stray dog. It's broken into a few stores and apartments scrounging for food. Nothing too horrifying. But it seems to be developing an interest in fresh meat. It savaged a little girl last night. And I'd hate to think what may have been happening to the pet population in the area."

My back had gone rigid. A little girl. I guessed one life didn't mean much to the gods who'd watched billions come and go, but that was all I needed to hear to consider this more than just a test.

"All right. Let me at it."

"Patience, pixie," Loki said. "I don't want us spending all night on a tracking mission. I'll get you close enough that you should be able to follow the trail fairly quickly."

"One can't help wondering when it was you found the time to be keeping an eye on this creature," Freya said from where she was strolling along behind us. Even though she hadn't been part of my training directly, she'd scoffed at the idea that we leave her behind. *It's my husband she'll be looking for. I'd like to have some say in whether she's ready.*

"Oh, I'm capable of keeping track of all sorts of things with very little effort," Loki said loftily.

"And you have an affinity for wolves, after all," Baldur remarked in his airy way.

The trickster god cut his gaze toward Baldur, his shoulders tensing, but the god of light barely seemed to notice his apprehension, so I doubted he'd meant to cause it. "Yes," Loki said. "There is that."

Was that one of the shapes Loki could shift into? It would suit him. I was going to ask, but then he stopped by a wide alley that stretched between two brick factory buildings and raised his chin toward it. "That way," he said. "You take the lead now. Let's see how much you've learned, pixie."

Oh, I'd show them, all right. Honestly, I was a little curious to find out myself. This was my first chance to try out these skills on an actual menace.

I wanted to get on with the whole finding Odin thing, but I wasn't going to be any good to Petey if I died all over again in the process. So I couldn't exactly argue with the gods' wariness to throw me straight into whatever had swallowed up the other valkyries they'd sent looking.

I edged down the alley, tucking my hand into my pocket and drawing out my switchblade. I didn't know how much good that four-inch blade would do against a warg, but it was more likely to do damage than my bare hands were. And the warmed plastic against my palm steadied me.

Maybe I hadn't been able to use this weapon to protect myself as much as I should have, back when it had really mattered, but I could make it count now.

As I scanned the alley, my heightened senses directed my attention. My gaze caught on a tuft of coarse fur clinging to the corner of a brick. At shoulder height, where some massive furred body must have brushed against these walls. A murky, musky smell crept into my nose.

I swallowed hard and kept going. My five spectators trailed along behind me, giving me a ten-foot lead and total silence.

The alley split like the head of a T, left and right. I glanced in each direction, watching, listening, tasting the air. Only a hint of a breeze stirred the muggy atmosphere, but I caught a hint of that murky scent from the right—where my perked ears also picked up a panted breath from somewhere far down that dirty concrete path through this industrial maze.

I skirted a dumpster that looked like it hadn't been used in years but still gave off a stale stink and picked my way between the buildings. Disintegrating shreds of wood and warped bits of metal scattered the cracked cement. The factories and warehouses loomed on either side, cutting off the sun completely. Only a narrow line of gray-blue sky showed above me.

Another rough breath led me around a second turn. The smell got thicker in my oversensitive nose.

Up ahead, a few hulking metal machines had been put out to pasture in a concrete yard surrounded by a chain-link fence. Something had torn a gash in that fence near the alley—a gash as tall as I was and twice as wide.

The shadow beneath one of the machines shifted. It wasn't all shadow. A huge dark shape was slumped there. Taking its rest before its nighttime prowl?

My mouth went dry. My fingers tightened around the handle of my switchblade. I eased through the gash in the fence, not even daring to look back and confirm the gods were still following me. My gaze never left the beast cloaked in the shadow.

I couldn't tell what the machine casting the shadow might have been meant for. It was a jumbled structure of rusted metal panels, looping tubes, and cylinders that might have spun once but now were locked in place with grit and their own share of rust. The contraption farther beyond it looked like a massive sewing machine, taller than me, with a steel "needle" as thick as my wrist.

The form in the shadow had to be at least twice as large as I was. My sharpened eyes could only just make out the tips of its thick pelt along the edge of its body. How the hell was I supposed to "overpower" that thing?

What did I have that it didn't? My wings. I extended them with a swift unfurling, ignoring the biting burn that came with pushing them out so quickly. I could always fly out of reach if I needed to. Herd it from above. *Corner it*, Loki said. And then… trap it somehow?

Or kill it, using the power Hod showed me this morning?

It'd been attacking kids. A monster like that needed to be put down—if I could pull that skill off when it was a huge, fast creature and not just a plant sitting still in a pot.

I was only halfway to the shadow when the monster lifted its head: an immense, wolfish head with pointed ears and a glint of teeth along its muzzle. It growled low in its throat.

And then it charged.

I leapt out of the way with a heave of my legs and a flap of my wings, only my enhanced valkyrie strength pushing me far enough to dodge the swipe of the warg's claws. It spun on me and lunged again. I fluttered higher into the air with a lurch of my heart. Its jaws snapped shut just below my heel.

Fuck. If I'd had any doubts about whether this thing needed to be destroyed, they'd vanished now. The question wasn't so much whether I was going to kill it as how I was going to while making sure it didn't devour me.

The beast circled the yard beneath me as I swept higher still, pulling myself well out of range to gather my thoughts. I had strength and speed, flight and heightened senses. And the ability to sense emotions, intentions—Baldur's gift.

Dragging in a breath, I focused on the monster. On the pulse of vicious energy inside its head.

It had sensed what I was here to do. It planned to end me before I ended it. Even now, it was gathering itself for a jump at me.

I could read that: what move it would make next. If I could feel that out, I could stay one step ahead of it and dive for its weak spots the first chance I got.

Which meant I had to get closer again.

I flitted out of the way of its leap and then dropped back to the ground. The warg whirled, bounding left and then right, a feint and a jab. But I'd seen that coming. I rolled out of the way, stabbing out with my switchblade. The blade sank into the flesh just behind the creature's foreleg before I yanked my weapon back.

The warg snarled and whipped toward me. Blood dappled the pavement. My pulse beat fast and hard through my veins. I just had to keep this up, had to keep weakening it, until I got a bigger opening. I could do this. For myself. For Petey. For the little girl this monster had hurt.

It sprang at me with a gnash of its teeth, just at the moment I'd felt to expect it. I dodged and slashed out at its other side. The beast swung around so quickly my knuckles brushed its side before I could pull myself away. My eyes connected with the warg's for a single instant. For long enough to take in their flat yellow sheen—and a cold gleam of intelligence shining behind them.

As if there were a human being behind that monstrous face, staring back at me.

My stomach flipped. My wings flapped instinctively,

propelling me up and away. At the same moment, another darkly furred body hurtled at me from the top of one of the abandoned machines.

A gasp jolted out of me, and then clawed feet were slamming me into the concrete. I thrashed and rolled, squirming away just as teeth grazed my cheek, digging my heels into a furry gut and heaving back against it with all the strength Thor had passed on to me. Pain lanced down my face with a wet chill, but the warg on me stumbled back just far enough for me to scramble out from under it. Right into the lunge of a third.

Three of them. There were three of them.

I spun around, swaying as I caught my balance, my palm gone clammy against the handle of my switchblade. My fist smacked my latest attacker's muzzle to the side, but only by a few inches. And the other two were closing around me again.

I couldn't do this. Couldn't take on all of them. I'd needed all my strength and concentration just to fight the first. I threw myself up toward the sky, spreading my wings—and a monstrous jaw clamped hard around one wing tip.

Teeth raked through feathers and flesh, dragging me back to earth. Pain splintered through those unfamiliar nerves and into my back. I cried out, panicked adrenaline shooting through my body, and slashed out with my hand with all the desperate force I could summon.

A crackle of lightning seared down my arm and along the blade, blasting into the monster's side and sending it flying across the yard. Its body smashed into one of the machines and crumpled to the ground, motionless.

What the *fuck* had that been? I didn't have time to ask, to experiment. Another warg was barreling into me. I stumbled to the side, hissing at the slice of its claws through my calf. My hand waved the switchblade wildly, but wherever I'd summoned that lightning from, I didn't know how to call it up again.

I was not going to die here. Not again. I *was not.* It just wasn't an option.

I swept my leg around, slamming it heel first into an incoming warg's snout. My valkyrie strength sang through my muscles, seeming to blaze hotter with the blood pulsing from my wounds and my enemies'.

The warg snapped at me again, and I dove right under its jaws with a speed I wouldn't have believed anyone could be capable of a couple days ago. My blade cut across the beast's throat.

Not deeply enough. More blood pattered down on me, but the creature staggered to the side, still growling. Where the hell was the other one?

Before I could whirl to check, the one I'd wounded was charging at me. A haze of pain emanated from its head. I'd weakened it. I had to take the advantage while I had it.

I leapt aside and heaved at the beast's shoulder with all my might. It staggered and sprawled on its side. I sprang onto it, willing all the strength in my body to weigh it down as I jammed the tip of my blade against the softest part of the creature's throat.

The flickering life energy of the monster washed over me, heavier and brighter than both Hod's ferns and the people in the city around us but with the same heady tingling. It flailed its limbs, and I slammed my elbow into the joint of its foreleg with a force that made the bone snap. Then, with a ragged breath, I dug my fingers into the coarse fur and hauled at that energy with the darkness already unfurling in my chest.

The warg's eyes rolled back, but the light didn't entirely fade from them. The one I could see slid to meet my eyes. Suddenly I was sure, down to my bones, this was the same one I'd locked eyes with before. The first one I'd tangled with. That sense of cold but clear intelligence washed over me again—thoughts as sharp and certain as the ones in my own head. A consciousness on par with mine, that I was about to extinguish forever.

A shiver ran down my spine. My grip on the creature's ruff and its life wavered, just for an instant.

The monster sensed that split-second of hesitation and bucked with a gnash of its jaws.

My body jolted. I slid and almost tumbled from my hold. My hand whipped back just a hair from disappearing into that maw. My other hand clenched its fur with renewed determination. With one last, frantic yank, I wrenched the life from the warg's body.

The dark space inside me swallowed that energy whole. The creature beneath me slumped. My body slumped too, a sob hitching from my throat.

The third warg had wheeled and fled. I saw a flash of its tail as it raced down an alley on the opposite side of the yard, and then I was alone there with the bodies of the two I'd killed.

Two monsters. But the ache spreading from beneath my ribs wasn't victorious at all.

# 13

*Aria*

The gods were still arguing around me when we reached the house in the middle of the night.

"The point is you told her there was one," Thor said with a sweeping gesture of his broad arm, his voice not much more than a growl. "You purposely left her underprepared. We were supposed to be testing her, not throwing her to the wolves—literally."

"And we did test her," Loki said evenly. "She proved she could handle herself even if the odds shifted even more against her. Even if her enemies multiplied or came on her unexpectedly. From what I saw, it was the wolves that got thrown."

"Just like always," Hod muttered. "You set up some precarious scheme and then act as if it wasn't just dumb luck it worked out in your favor."

Loki shook his head. "If our valkyrie should be offended by anything, it's your apparent lack of faith in her."

"What's done is done," Baldur said. He gave me a warm if slightly distant smile. I thought it had gotten a little thinner as the arguing had continued. "Let's not dwell on it. Why don't we focus on the good that's come of this? Aria succeeded—very well. We should celebrate that victory."

I didn't feel much like celebrating. All but the worst of the wounds the wargs had left me with had closed up of their own accord, another surprise valkyrie ability, and Baldur's gentle touch had washed away the rest along with any lingering pain, but I was still wiped out. My body was ready to collapse into bed… and my head was still cluttered with too many jostling thoughts for me to think I'd actually fall asleep.

Freya slipped in beside me and tucked her hand around my elbow. "I think what our valkyrie needs is a little time away from the lot of you," she said, sweetly but firmly. "It's been a long, tense night, Ari. A walk will help you wind down."

I was too distracted by the jumble in my head to protest when she guided me away from the others, across the lawn toward the same path we'd strolled along earlier. When my mind caught up, apprehension prickled over my skin. Was she going to pump me for more information? Make sure my motives had been pure or who knew what else?

I was trying to figure out the smoothest way to extricate myself when she glided to a stop just beyond the first cluster of trees and turned to face me. Her deep blue eyes peered into mine, but her gaze was soft rather than sharp.

"That was hard for you," she said. "And not just physically."

Emotion swelled inside me: relief that someone at least partly understood, panic that she'd decide it made me unworthy somehow. What would they do with me if they didn't think I could complete this quest for them after all?

I grappled for words. "I've never killed something like that before. Something… The wargs aren't just animals, are they? Not regular ones. It felt almost like I was killing a person."

Freya's mouth twisted. My sense of her mental state was faint and vague, but the concerned vibe I did pick up felt nothing but genuine. Was she actually *worried* about me? And if she was, was it for my sake, or for how it would affect their plans?

"They're beasts," she said. "Vicious, driven by animal-like instincts to dominate and devour. But yes, they can think more than the beasts you're used to. That doesn't mean they should get to live doing whatever they please."

"No." But it also didn't mean I was going to feel ecstatic about having to be the one to cut those thoughts off permanently.

"You'll need to be prepared," she said. "If enemies of Asgard have captured Odin, they'll be monsters of a similar sort. Even closer to human, most likely. But they've already cut down three before you. They won't show *you* any mercy."

"Oh, I'm not going to be merciful when someone's coming for my throat. No guilt over that, believe me." Just a vaguely unsettled feeling I hadn't been able to shake yet.

A feeling that had dislodged a whole bunch of other uncomfortable thoughts. Freya started walking again, at a more leisurely pace, and a question that had been nagging at me for a while now tumbled out.

"Can you—can the gods die? You call us 'mortals,' but… I don't remember my mythology all that well, but I know there were prophecies about deaths and all that."

"We can," Freya said. "Most of us did, during Ragnarok, although I can't say it was much more pleasant for those who simply witnessed the entire thing. But those who died returned to life in the aftermath of the destruction."

"So even if you die, you come back," I said.

"Well, we aren't entirely sure what would happen if any of us were pushed to the brink again. We knew Ragnarok was coming. It was meant to be. What's to follow has never been clear." She rubbed her mouth. "Some of us might have vanished already. There are others of Asgard we haven't spoken to in centuries."

The next question I was almost afraid to ask, but I had to.

"Are you sure *Odin* hasn't been cut down like those other valkyries were? That wherever he is, whatever's happened to him, he's still alive?"

*That you're not searching for someone who can no longer be found?*

Freya's jaw tightened a little, but her voice stayed mild. "I would know. If his essence had departed the realms… I would know. As would the others, I expect, maybe even more sharply than I would."

Okay. That explanation sounded like new-age blathering to me, but it wasn't as if I didn't know that the gods had senses beyond what I'd been used to. I could take her word for it.

"So you're stuck here just waiting for him." I tried to imagine it —the existence of a god. What my existence would theoretically look like, if I managed not to get myself killed on this mission of theirs. "Does it get… *boring*, being around this long? What do you even *do*? I mean, when you don't have a valkyrie around to put through the paces."

Freya laughed. Her amusement felt genuine too. "Oh, I'm sure we all have our moments of boredom. But humans provide endless new entertainment and drama, and this is just one of the nine realms. We all have our pet subjects. Baldur follows music; Thor enjoys sports. Norns know what mischief Loki is occupying himself with at any given time. Hod collects all the latest manuscripts on philosophy and scientific inquiry—a strange combination, I'd say, but he doesn't ask my opinion."

I kind of wanted to bristle at the idea of people like me being around just for the entertainment of a bunch of gods, but then, maybe it wasn't that different from watching reality TV? If we did it to ourselves, I couldn't really get mad at them over it.

"What about you?" I asked.

"Oh…" Her gaze turned distant. "It's always interesting to see the directions fashion rambles off in and returns to. But mostly my expertise is love. Romantic and motherly. I intervene on occasion, when a misunderstanding seems a little too tragic or when I can help a child come to be." Her smile came back, a little bittersweet this time. "I just have to be careful not to get *too* invested. I'm not a meddler on Loki's scale."

It didn't really seem right that the goddess of love should have a husband who apparently wandered off doing who knew what for ages at a time. How lonely must she get? I had enough sense of self-preservation not to ask that out loud, but I couldn't help prodding a bit. "I guess it's hard without Odin here."

"Well, it's not as if I hadn't seen what he was like before we forged that connection." She glanced at me. "Before you think I'm all soft-bellied sap, I should mention my other specialty is war. It was skirmishes and battles that Odin and I first bonded over. Believe me, if I could be the one taking the risks we're asking you to, leaping into the fray to find him, I'd charge forth without a second's hesitation. I wish I could."

As she said it, I saw the steel in her under that dolled-up exterior. She meant *that*, unquestionably. She didn't like having to ask me to go in her place.

I'd already had every intention of surviving for my own benefit, but I felt compelled to say, to show her the steel I had too, "I'm not going to get caught like the valkyries before. I'll figure out what happened to him, and I'll make it back. You can count on that much."

"You know, after tonight's performance, I think perhaps I can." She stopped again and touched the side of my arm. "Thank you for doing what I can't. I'm sorry you didn't have more of a choice in the matter. You seem more settled now. Would you like to get back to the house? If you're hungry, we may be able to scrounge up a few bits of food Thor hasn't already devoured."

"I think I need to sleep more than I need to eat right now." I had to fight to suppress a yawn.

We headed back to the house in a weird sort of companionable silence. Weird because I couldn't remember the last time I'd just walked in silence with someone and not felt like I needed to be totally on guard.

Freya wasn't all that bad, really. I was pretty sure I wasn't ever going to need to stab her, in any case.

A flicker of movement beyond the house's roof caught my gaze. A dark flutter against the equally dark treetops. I narrowed my eyes, calling on my valkyrie senses. The details of branches and leaves sharpened to reveal a shape swooping from one perch to another. A hawk.

Another dropped down out of the night sky to join it. I frowned. Hawks were daytime birds, weren't they? What were two of them doing suddenly hanging out around the gods' house in the middle of the night? And the energy I sensed in them had a deliberateness to it that sent an uneasy prickling down my back. It set off a deeper tremor in my gut, something hotly insistent. An instinct I didn't know how to read.

"What?" Freya asked, taking in my expression.

"There are two hawks in that tree," I said, nodding to it. "Something about them doesn't feel right. Like they're watching the house." And like they should mean something to me. I just didn't know what.

Freya's expression hardened. In that moment, she looked every inch the war goddess. "You've been tested enough today," she said. "When you get inside, tell Loki I could use a hand. Then go enjoy that bed of yours. You've earned it."

"What are you going to do about them?" I asked.

The corner of her lips curled upward. "I can be very charming when I want to be. And once they're charmed down here, I'm sure our trickster can determine what tricks they're up to. If it's anything all that exciting, you'll hear about it in the morning."

# 14

*Thor*

I was on my third slice of breakfast ham when Loki sauntered into the kitchen. Somehow, even when he was doing something as innocent as pouring himself a cup of coffee, he always managed to look as if he were up to no good. I supposed I should just be glad that in recent memory he'd always been scheming on our side.

"Did you glean anything else from that hawk?" I asked.

"Nothing more than confirming what I'd already seen," Loki said. "It had a tang of rot on it, even though the bird itself was lively enough, and a shiver of unfriendly magic. Neither of which I like, but neither of which is all that catastrophic at this point."

"No creatures like that ever came around here before."

"No," Loki said. "I do have to wonder if that little battle last night caught someone's attention."

I looked up from my ham. "Like who?"

He gave me a narrowly amused look. "If I knew that, I'd already be knocking on their door, not discussing it with you."

"But you think they might be after Ari."

"Or interested in her, at least. She did surprise even us, after all."

Her blast of lightning. The last three valkyries hadn't displayed that talent. I'd had no idea I could pass on my affinity for the stuff that literally, but clearly I had. And with a similar lack of control. She'd used it on instinct, the same way the battle rage came over me.

Baldur drifted into the kitchen with a gentle nod to both of us on his way to the fridge to retrieve a hard-boiled egg. I nodded in return and refocused on Loki. "And you haven't had any thoughts on how *that* could have happened?"

Loki spread his hands. "No more than you. Perhaps you always passed on a spark, and none of the others ever had enough spirit for it to really take light. She does have rather a lot of fire."

"Yes," Baldur said in his light voice, joining me at the table. "She's been quite impressive."

"She has," I agreed. If I hadn't been so worried about Ari's fate last night, I might have enjoyed being awed by how quickly she'd gotten comfortable with her new strength and speed. I'd have taken her as a fighting partner any day. Holding her own against not one but *three* wargs…

A little of yesterday's anger tickled up with that memory.

"Your theory seems to have been right," Baldur added, smiling at Loki. "Perhaps character isn't half so important as determination and adaptability."

"I think Ari has plenty of character too," I said. "And I'll give Loki more credit when he proves he's not going to kill her before she gets a chance to do what we've been training her for."

Loki waved off my complaint as he took a gulp of his coffee. He always drank it fast and scalding hot. "Stop your fretting. She was fine. And if she hadn't been, the five of us were right there. I'd like to think at least one of us would have been quick enough to intervene if she'd looked as though she needed it."

Had he been thinking that the whole time we'd been watching? I probably would have jumped in if I'd seen one of the monsters about to land a fatal blow, but I'd have done it expecting Loki to chide me afterward for ruining the test.

I scowled at myself. I'd accepted what I'd thought were his rules too quickly, hadn't I? He might have a faster wit, but he wasn't any more in charge around here than the rest of us were.

If Hod had been here, he'd have some dark comment at the ready to match my mood. But the god of night usually slept not long after dawn. We wouldn't see him for at least a couple hours.

"I still say it was a dirty trick."

Loki grinned. "And I'd say there's no such thing as a clean one. Do you think our enemies are going to play fair? If they had, those pure-of-heart girls we summoned would have fared much better."

He was right. That didn't mean I had to like it. "Oh, shut up," I muttered.

"You all should shut up," Freya declared, sweeping into the room. The scent of honeysuckles trailed after her like it always did when she'd been exercising her powers. Charming that wretched hawk down—some task for a love goddess.

"And why exactly is that?" Loki asked, cocking his head.

"Still having the same stupid argument." Freya gestured toward the hall. "If you're so worried about the girl, why don't you pay a little more attention to what she's going through *now* instead of what she's already been through and come out the other side of. The lot of you didn't have the faintest idea how unsettled she was *after* she survived last night, did you?"

I blinked. "Of course she was a little shaken. But once Baldur looked after her wounds…"

"She seemed to prefer time to process on her own," Baldur said. "I gave her that space."

"Because that's all she's used to, not because that's what's good for her!" Freya sighed and shook her head. "It's amazing you men manage to get anything done, I swear. Three days ago she was a regular human being, and the next thing she knows she's fighting deadly monsters she wouldn't have thought belonged anywhere other than myths. I had a talk with her last night, but I think she's still struggling. She's already up, you know. She's been sitting on the roof for the last hour just watching the sky."

Oh. I'd assumed I hadn't seen Ari because she was still sleeping. Even Loki looked mildly chagrined, though I wasn't convinced he'd completely missed everything Freya had mentioned. Maybe he simply hadn't thought it worth bothering with. Who knew with the Mischief Maker?

If anyone here knew how to deal with the aftermath of a battle, it was me. I pushed back my chair. "I'll go see what she needs."

Freya crossed her arms. "Just keep in mind she probably needs a *subtle* touch, Thunderer."

"I can be subtle," I retorted. But the truth was, subtlety wasn't exactly my strong point. I paused in the hall, considering my possible tactics. Then I hustled up the stairs to retrieve something from my room before I headed out the door.

It was another fine summer day—finer than the last few, really. The humidity had died down, leaving a heat that was more crisp than suffocating. Birds were chirping and fluttering between the trees. All except the one the hawks had been perched in last night, I couldn't help noticing. That didn't bode well.

I circled the house, tapping my thigh with a solid thunk of the object I was carrying. It grounded me, reminded me of my strengths. I might not be a smooth talker like Loki or filled with gentle light like Baldur, but I'd spent enough time around our valkyrie to have a decent idea where to start if she needed steadying.

Ari was where Freya had said she'd be, perched by the edge of the roof outside the third-floor dormer. Her blond waves were swept back from her face, and she had her head tipped back to soak up the sun. It was hard to judge her expression at that distance.

"Hey, Ari!" I hollered. "You look like you could use something to do."

Her gaze darted down. A grin flashed across her face when she saw me. "What did you have in mind?" she shouted back.

I shrugged. "Come down, and I'll show you."

She stood up, and her wings unfurled from her back with a rush of rustling feathers, no hesitation now. As casual as could be, she stepped off the end of the roof. Her wings caught the air just enough to turn what should have been a fall into a swift glide. She landed in front of me with a thump of her feet and an arch of her eyebrows.

"Here I am. Show away."

I'd agreed that she'd been impressive last night, but that was nothing compared to seeing her standing here, so sure in her new body and abilities. The sunlight played over her hair and brought a fiery glint into her gray eyes, and a sensation that was more than just awe twinged below my gut. Part of me—the part most aware of how long it'd been since I'd last gotten laid—started picturing what it'd be like to feel that body under mine.

I reined that part in. I'd come out here to reassure her—in my own way—not to put a move on her. Not that I suspected Ari would welcome those sorts of advances anyway. Nothing would kill the trust I thought I'd earned faster than treating her like a conquest rather than the fellow warrior she was.

Her expression was cocky as ever, but I thought I saw a shadow of the uncertainty Freya had hinted at pass through her eyes before I answered. She might be a warrior, but this was still a strange new world for her. One with dangers she'd never imagined. Both out there and possibly within herself.

What always made me feel better in the face of unknown dangers was showing myself how easily I could crush them, at least the outside ones.

"I thought you might enjoy a little target practice, of a sort," I said, and hefted the weapon I'd been carrying at my side. "How would you like to give Mjolnir a try?"

Ari's eyes widened as she took in the broad gleaming shape. "Your hammer. Isn't it enchanted or something? *Can* I even use it?"

"There's no magic on it that says who can or can't do what with it," I said. "But it is magic. Always hits its mark. Always comes right back to you. Very satisfying to play with."

That eager gleam came back into her eyes. Oh, yes, I'd picked the right offering. "Okay," she said. "You first. I want to see what I have to beat."

I guffawed and rolled my shoulder. "Let's see. The end of that low branch there on the elm." I pointed, flipped the hammer by its short handle—showing off, maybe a little—and hurled it.

Mjolnir streaked through the air and smashed into the end of the branch with a burst of splintered wood and shredded leaves. The breeze warbled around the hammer as it flew back to smack into my waiting palm. A wash of satisfaction passed through me.

"I try not to destroy anything *too* large," I said. "Or Freya gets a little testy about the landscaping."

Ari laughed. "I bet. Give me a try."

I passed the hammer to her with only a little twinge as it left my grasp. It was true that anyone *could* use Mjolnir, but it felt almost like a part of me. I didn't lend it easily.

Ari's much smaller hand closer around the handle. The muscles in her arm flexed as she tested its weight. She scanned the yard and nodded to an old fence post that had long since lost the rest of the fence. "That's coming down."

She wound back and threw, gritting her teeth at the effort. Mjolnir spun, shining, and bashed the post into a shower of woodchips. Ari clapped her hands with a cry of triumph and remembered to reach out for the hammer's return at the last second. Its momentum tugged her toward me, but she just laughed again.

"All right, that is kind of fun. You want another turn?"

"Why not?"

She handed the hammer to me, and I took aim at an abandoned squirrel nest near the top of an oak. Mjolnir sent down a rain of dry leaves and twigs.

I offered the hammer back to Ari. She set her sights on a rock about as high as my knee and twice the width of my leg, protruding from the grass in the meadow beyond the trees.

"Let's see just how accurate this thing is," she said, and whipped it forward.

Mjolnir flashed, and the rock exploded with a cracking loud enough to scatter the nearby birds. Ari gave a breathless cheer as the hammer soared back to her hands. She looked down at it as if examining the grooves in the well-worn metal. That shadow crossed her expression again.

"It seems almost wrong to enjoy destroying something that much," she said.

A knot formed in my gut. So she'd already gotten there. It'd taken a long time before I'd ever been able to put that vague discomfort into words.

"It was only a rock," I said. "And it's practice for going up against the things that would destroy us if we let them."

"True." She raised her head. "I guess you've fought a lot of battles with this."

"It wasn't made just for bashing branches," I agreed, studying her face.

"How many people—and monsters, or whatever—do you figure you've killed?"

What was she looking for from me? I wished I had Baldur's skill at sensing emotion, figuring out the perfect reassurance. The best I could do was be straight-forward and honest, which was what I was best at anyway.

"No one in a good long while," I said. "But before that? More than a few. Always to protect my people and yours. It's what I do." I paused. "The wargs last night—those were your first kills."

She shrugged. "I mean, other than spiders or whatever. But I guess that's what I do now too. As a valkyrie. *Something* got the ones you sent before. Something is holding Odin. If it's me or them…"

"You'll do what you have to do," I supplied. "But that doesn't mean you have to enjoy it all the way through. I'm not going to lie. When I'm caught up in the battle rage, knowing I'm defending those who need me, it can be pretty exhilarating. I like that feeling when I'm in the moment—that power. But after the battles are over, I can't say I ever look back on those times fondly."

Sometimes I even wished the rage wasn't quite so all-consuming. But maybe I wouldn't be the defender I was without it. I wasn't going to try to sacrifice that power just to find out.

Ari glanced at me. Whatever she'd been looking for, I got the sense she'd found it.

"I saw someone die in front of me, a long time ago," she said. "Someone who probably wouldn't have, if *I'd* done what I should have done then. It was awful."

She might have meant to say more, but her voice choked up. She smiled tightly and handed Mjolnir back to me. I took it from her slim fingers, and without thinking let myself wrap my other hand around hers. *A long time ago.* How old could she have been then? But I could see the guilt twisted through her as plainly as if it'd been a rope bound around her body. I didn't know the exact right words to loosen it, but I could try.

"I'm sure you did everything you knew how to back then. Just like you fought with everything you had last night. No matter what happens, you're not going to let us down, Ari. Just being here is more than we should have asked of you. And I can already tell you're going to do so much more."

Her fingers curled around my palm, soft but strong, and

squeezed back. Then she pulled her hand away with her more usual smile, the pain I'd glimpsed disappearing back behind that fiercely unshakeable expression I was used to.

"And when I get back, I still have to make good on that promise to drink you under the table," she said. "So let's get on with this. No one can argue whether I'm ready to go for Odin now, right? Just point me in the right direction, and I'll find your Allfather."

# 15

*Aria*

We were supposed to gather in the living room, but I caught Hod in the upstairs hall after the others had already gone down. I took a breath to say his name, and he stopped just at that, his head turning toward me. His dark green eyes settled on my face, almost as if he really were meeting my gaze now. I wasn't sure if I'd have been able to tell he couldn't see me if I hadn't known to look for the subtlest signs.

"I wanted to talk to you, just for a minute, before we do this," I said.

"What's on your mind, valkyrie?" he said in that flat voice of his. As if I really believed he was that dispassionate after the emotion I'd seen in him the other day in the study. "Having cold feet?"

I grimaced at him, even though he couldn't see that either. "No. I just wanted to ask…" I paused. He might not be dispassionate, but that didn't mean he'd be compassionate either. I couldn't think of any better way to put this. "The last three valkyries didn't come back. I plan on making this time different, but if I can't—if something happens, and I don't make it—would you check on my brother? At least once?"

He knew where Petey lived. As far as I could tell, he was the only one who even knew Petey existed. The dark god had been *at least* compassionate enough not to rat on me to the others about my sneaky late-night trip.

Surprise flickered across Hod's chiseled face. "I'm not going to *intervene*," he started.

"I know," I said, cutting him off. "I get it. But the idea was that after all this is over, I'd get to watch over him a little. I'll feel better knowing that someone will be there, whatever way you can be."

I intended to do a lot more than just watch if I had the chance, but we didn't need to get into that.

Hod turned his face away from me, his eyes going even more distant than they'd looked before. "What are you worried will happen to him?" he asked. "That man who was yelling at him—has he hurt your brother before?"

"No," I said, "but that doesn't mean— There are tons of things, okay? All kinds of awful things that already happen or could." Memories flickered up from my own childhood: Mom's hoarse ranting, insults that cut deep, the slam of a door, a hungry gnawing in my belly. And the worst of them, the one thing I hoped more than anything Petey never had to experience: the creak of a bedroom door in the middle of the night, the weight of a body that wouldn't take no for an answer.

My skin crawled. I pushed those memories back down where I kept them bottled. "And I couldn't fix most of those things even when I was alive, not properly. He just shouldn't be alone. Okay?"

My throat had gotten tight. Hod slid his blind gaze toward me again. "All right," he said gruffly. "He won't be."

Relief rushed through me. "Thank you," I said. "Really. It means a lot to me."

"I know," Hod said. "That's why I agreed. Now go on. Valhalla is waiting for you."

I was pretty sure Valhalla had no interest in me at all. The gods had made it clear I wasn't a typical upstandingly moral specimen who should have *deserved* all the powers I'd gotten. But oh well. The Hall of Heroes would just have to deal with me sullying up the place a little on my way through.

When we reached the huge living room where I'd first arrived in the house, the other gods were ready. They'd cleared a span of the hardwood floor. Loki motioned me into the middle of that space, and the five divine figures formed a circle around me.

"Unlike us, normally a valkyrie would be able to find her way straight back to Valhalla in Asgard from the human realm without any help at all," the trickster god said. "Lucky for you, it's tied to your nature, no bridges or paths required."

"But I can't take any of you with me?" I said. That would have made this quest a hell of a lot easier.

"Unfortunately not," Loki said, his tone turning wry. "Unless, I suppose, you harvested our souls as chosen warriors, but that skill was only meant for human mortals, and it would require our dying to test it out. So we're not especially keen to give it a shot, seeing as failure may be permanent."

"Fair enough. So, how do I make this happen?"

"Since *you've* never been there before, the matter is a little muddied. So we'll stick with what's worked before. We'll all picture the great hall in our minds. You use your special valkyrie sensitivities to absorb that sense of it. That should trigger a recognition inside you to open up the way. All you have to do then is follow it."

"And then once I'm up there, I'll see some sign of where Odin's gotten to?"

Loki nodded. "Your valkyrie nature is bound to him just as it is to Valhalla. Once you're there in his hall, you should feel a sort of call leading you to the right door to whatever realm he's in. Go through, observe enough that you can give us a decent sense of where that is, but get out of there as soon as you're in any danger. Which may be quite quickly, given the disappearance of the others, so be on guard from the start."

"Bring a weapon," Thor put in. "The hall is full of them. You'll have your pick."

"And then to get back here…?" I said.

"Picture this house and open one of the Midgard doors," Baldur said in a bright tone that smoothed a few of the jitters out of my nerves. "It will take you straight back to us." He sounded as if he were sure I'd make it that far.

I dragged in a breath. It was one thing to find I'd been turned into some kind of mythical being with wings sprouting out of my back. Now I was about to leave Earth—or at least the human part of it—behind completely, to leap off into who-knew-what. My hand dropped to my pocket to trace the line of my switchblade.

I'd just have to be ready for anything.

"Good luck," Freya said, her voice wry, but when I glanced at her she smiled with a lot more warmth. Of course she did. They all wanted me to succeed. This was the whole reason they'd summoned me in the first place.

Lucky for them, I was just as keen on getting this job done as they were. They had their home and someone they cared about on the line, and so did I. It didn't really matter that mine were totally different, did it?

I squared my shoulders and drew my back up straight. "All right. Let's do this."

In their circle around me, the gods closed their eyes, remembering Odin's hall behind those eyelids. I took another breath and closed mine too so I could focus completely on the impressions they gave off beyond sight, beyond sound.

A sense of warmth and a sharper flickering heat washed over

me, and an image formed in my own mind of a great hearth. Joyous shouts, an atmosphere buzzing with mead and good humor. Brilliant light reflecting off gold on the walls. A huge expanse full of boisterous companionship and—

A thread of connection twanged deep inside me like a string on a guitar. I was meant to be there. That place was meant for me. My pulse stuttered, but I grasped hold of the thread without hesitation. Grasped and yanked myself forward along it.

My body shook, and the air warbled around me. The bottom of my stomach dropped out. Then I was stumbling onto my hands and knees on a polished oak floor.

Bright light shone all around me. The floor was smooth and dry, but a faintly alcoholic odor wafted off it. All that mead, absorbed from thousands of spills, I guessed.

I eased myself upright. The shakiness seeped out of my body, leaving only a weirdly comforting feeling as if I'd finally gotten home, even though I'd never been in this place before.

Valhalla had changed a lot since the memories the gods had used to guide me here. The huge hearth still lay at the far end, but no fire roared in it now. Rows of long oak tables filled the space beneath the high arched ceiling, but the benches all stood empty. The whole place was silent except for the whisper of my feet over the floor as I moved. The gold plating on the walls still gleamed brightly, but even it looked kind of melancholy.

No more honorable warriors. No more valkyries. No more anyone, from the looks of it. I rubbed my arms, chilled by the vast emptiness even though the air was warm.

The weapons Thor had mentioned were mounted on the lower walls—spears and swords and axes of all sizes, some tarnished, some glinting as if freshly polished. As I studied them, something balked inside me.

Those weren't my kinds of weapons. I wouldn't feel comfortable with any of them in my hands. Not like I would with my switchblade. It'd been enough when I'd taken on the wargs.

Loki had picked me for this job because he wanted someone different, someone who didn't fit the usual valkyrie mode. So I should keep being that. I palmed my switchblade from my pocket and swiveled on my feet.

Light spilled not just through the many windows but also a wide door opposite the hearth. The rest of Asgard, the world of the gods, must wait out there. Curiosity tickled at me, but that wasn't what I was here for. I was here to find Odin.

My gaze fell on an immense gold throne next to the hearth. I'd never met the ancient god who was lord of the valkyries, but I could almost picture him sitting there, leaning forward as he took in the crowd with a knowing smile on his weathered face, silver glinting amid the brown of his hair and beard.

The image sent another twang through me, softer but deeper than the call of Valhalla. Odin was out there, somewhere beyond these walls. I was meant to be his champion.

I followed that tug down the hall all the way to the throne and hearth. Standing at the edge of the huge fireplace, I could make out a doorway beyond the dead embers. I picked my way through the ashes and pushed it open.

My breath caught. On the other side, a branching path spilled out over a chasm so deep the bottom was swallowed in shadows. The silence in the dim light felt even more ominous than in the hall behind me.

I eased forward to the start of the path and realized it was branching in a more literal way. The surface of the path was roughly ridged like bark. The whole thing was an enormous tree laid on its side, its branches splitting off into the thicker darkness.

The trembling thread inside me urged me onward. One of those branches led to Odin.

I treaded carefully onto the trunk, not letting myself look into the chasm. The main path, at least, was several feet wide. I stayed in the middle and watched my balance. My wings might save me if I toppled over the edge, but who knew in this crazy place? I unfurled them over me.

One, two, three, four branches passed before the call to Odin tugged me to one on the left. The branch was only a few feet wide, the chasm even darker as I ventured across it. A door came into focus at the end. I would have been relieved if I hadn't been so uncertain about what might be waiting beyond it. But I wasn't exactly sad to leave behind this creepy place.

I flicked out my blade and braced myself with my other hand on the doorknob. Slowly, I turned it, all my heightened senses on alert.

Nothing showed itself on the other side of the door except a darkness so thick it was solid black. I didn't have any choice. I had to go through.

Folding my wings close to my back, I stepped over the threshold.

The blackness hit my body like the cold smack of an ocean wave, and then I was through. My feet hit rough rocky ground. Cool damp air closed around me along with a thinner darkness broken by a faint gleam of light far ahead of me. A putrid smell like rotting meat reached my nose.

I registered that in the first split-second, and then a mass of figures jumped at me from all sides.

My street-honed instincts might have been all that saved me. I ducked and rolled in an instant, lashing out with my knife and my foot at the same time. Bodies collided over me with hoarse breaths and jabbing elbows and a blade slicing through my shoulder to the bone. The jolt of pain flared through all my senses.

There was no room for fair play in a brawl. It was me or them. I shoved myself up with my wings, my knee ramming into what felt like a groin, switchblade whipping through the air, fingers jabbing where I thought I caught a glimpse of eyes. Go for the soft bits. Hit wherever you can cause the most pain.

My knife struck its mark, hot blood spurting over my hand. I flung myself away as some kind of spiked club slammed into my gut. Fresh pain of my own sparked all through my abdomen. A grunt burst from my lips. Another attacker flung itself at me, and another.

I spun and kicked and jabbed, pulling on all the god-given strength I had in me. My elbow smashed into something round—a skull?—with a sickening crunch. A sharp edge scraped across my shin. My leg wobbled, and I heaved myself away again, toward the light. They were coming at me too fast for me to get a real hold on any of them, to wrench away one or another's life with the darkness inside me as well as my blade. If I could at least see…

The putrid smell thickened. In the dim light, my frantic gaze caught on a row of symbols cut into the rock wall, twisted lines melded together into deformed shapes. Then it found two bodies slumped by the wall up ahead—not attackers I'd taken down. Human corpses that looked as if they'd just been tossed there haphazardly, the red ring around one's neck suggesting she'd been strangled. My stomach lurched just as shrieks that sounded equally human echoed from around the bend where the light was.

I didn't have time to decide whether continuing that way was the best idea. My attackers hurtled after me, shouting in a language I didn't recognize but could grasp the shape of: They were calling for help.

I dodged, but one had already smashed one of my wings with his club, clinging on for another blow. A second rammed his head at my already bleeding gut. I cried out as the first wrenched at my wing, but I managed to stumble far enough that the blow to my stomach only clipped my side. A ram of my knee cracked that figure's collarbone.

Five more attackers came running from around the bend, all of them like the ones I was still struggling with: limp black hair plastered against sallow skin, eyes so pale the irises blended into the whites, bodies short and stout in stained tunics and short pants.

Pain was already radiating through every part of my body. Odin was somewhere here, but I couldn't get to him. I didn't even know if I could fend off the attackers already on me.

Valhalla. I had to get back to Valhalla.

I punched at the guy on my wing right through the flesh and feathers, sending more agony splintering through its surface but knocking him off into the wall at the same time. My switchblade slashed across another's face. I hurled myself backward, away from them and the others rushing to join the skirmish, as fast as I could.

Valhalla. Valhalla. Through the haze in my head I focused on my memory of that lonely gold-drenched hall. The thread of it vibrated inside me. I clung on and hauled with all my might.

The caves and my attackers warbled away. I sprawled out of the darkness onto the polished floor. Blood streaked the floorboards as I shoved myself into a sitting position. Pain seared deeper into my gut. Cuts throbbed on every limb. I didn't think I could count on my valkyrie skills to heal me from injuries quite this deep.

I stared at the arched ceiling. Valhalla wasn't good enough. I didn't just need to be here. I needed to be home.

Midgard. Baldur had said something about doors.

My ankle wobbled under me when I tried to push myself onto my feet. Sprained, at least. I dragged myself closer to the walls.

There. Doors, a few of them, scattered between the windows and the weapons. If I could just make it to the nearest one…

I propelled my battered body along, gritting my teeth against the stabs of agony, ignoring the trail of blood I was leaving in my wake. I'd said I'd make it back. I'd said it, and I was damn well going to do it. No pack of shrimpy soulless demons was going to get the better of Ari Watson.

I had to grope upward two times before my fingers closed around the doorknob. They clutched it and wrenched.

The door flew open into a vast blank space as bright and blue as the summer sky. I closed my eyes, thought of the soft green lawn outside the gods' house, and shoved myself over the threshold.

My body thumped into the grass, which wasn't quite as soft as I'd been hoping. A strangled sound shot up my throat. I rolled over, and then I couldn't seem to move at all. Pain weighed me down like a heap of boulders. I was buried in it.

"Ari!" someone shouted. Thor, I thought. Footsteps thumped across the yard. I frowned up at the stark blue sky.

"They didn't get me," I announced raggedly to whoever happened to be listening. "I didn't let them get me."

Then darkness swam up over my vision, and I tumbled down into a void inside my head.

# 16

*Aria*

Baldur's gentle hands lingered on my stomach. His godly magic had repaired my wounds while I'd been out of it, but prickles of pain remained here and there. I had the feeling I'd taken some damage that couldn't be patched up that easily, even by him. His softly handsome face was briefly solemn as he concentrated.

Where he touched me, I could feel a glimmer of what had to be his life energy, warm and bright as sunlit gold. Just as the gods' emotions were almost undetectable to my new senses, I'd never noticed any of their living essences before, even though I could pick up on people from miles away. Even close like this, the hungry void in me didn't stir at all. Apparently no valkyrie could claim a god's life. I'd just have to hope I didn't meet any I had a reason to fear.

Really, all I could do was lie back on my bed where I'd woken up an hour or so ago and let Baldur do his thing. And, you know, try not to think about the fact that I was lying half-naked on a bed with one of the most gorgeous men I'd ever known putting his hands all over me. I wasn't usually guy-crazy, not even a little, but everyone has their limits.

Baldur leaned closer to inspect my shoulder, bringing warmth and a scent like a breeze through spring fields. I studied the ceiling, but I got a twinge down low anyway.

Okay, as soon as I was done with the whole valkyrie-on-a-mission thing, I had a few things of my own to take care of. Number one: going to see Petey again. Number two: getting this damn itch scratched with the nearest halfway decent non-godly man.

A little voice in the back of my head reminded me of all those myths about gods cavorting with mortals. It wasn't impossible that one of the four here might be up for a hook-up. I just had trouble seeing that as a good idea. I was tied to them enough without making things that much more complicated.

Anyway, before I worried about *any* of that, we had other problems to take care of.

"So, what happens now?" I asked. "Those… people, or whatever they were, that attacked me—what are we going to do about them?"

"Dark elves," Baldur said helpfully. "From what you said, you found yourself in Nidavillir, their realm."

Elves, huh? I'd have expected those to be smaller and pointier eared, but what did I know?

"Okay, dark elves. They've got to have Odin if my sense of him led me there, right? And from the way they came at me, they must have been guarding that entrance. I guess we know what happened to the other valkyries. I also saw those dead humans there—it sounded like the dark elves were hurting other people too, torturing them or something. We're going to go after them, aren't we?" Pay them back for all the shit they'd put me and who knew who else through.

Baldur nodded, straightening up. "We now have a much better

sense of direction. We can't reach Nidavillir through Asgard as you did, but the lower realms connect in other ways. There should be a few entrances we can access from Midgard. For now we'll keep watch for dark elves coming and going in your world, and in time they should lead us to one of those."

*In time.* I grimaced. I'd like to bash around those bastards with Thor's hammer right now—or watch him do it, which would also be acceptable. They'd practically killed me all over again. If I hadn't been able to tell that from the agony I'd been in stumbling back here, I'd have known for sure from the look on Thor's face when I'd woken up. He hadn't been sure I *would* wake up.

He'd been worried about me. Possibly they all had. Even Hod had looked a little relieved when I'd started talking, although he might just be glad he didn't have to fulfill the promise he'd made me.

"I can help with that," I said, squirming into a sitting position. My body felt stiff, like I'd overdone it with a workout a day ago, but the last of the sharper pains were gone. "How do we find dark elves?"

"Hey." Baldur's lips curved with a smile. "You did what we asked of you, even though it was clearly a difficult fight. You've earned some rest, Aria."

I didn't feel like resting. Every time I closed my eyes, I saw those sprawled human corpses in the cave, heard those desperate shrieks. Whatever the dark elves were doing, I didn't think Odin was the only one in trouble.

"How am I supposed to rest with those freaks running around in *my* world?" I asked. "We've got to stop them."

"We will," Baldur said. "We'll take every step we can. You've already played the most important part you could."

He hardly even sounded fazed. He'd just found out that the leader of the gods, his father, was being held captive by a bunch of weirdo elves that were going around trying to slaughter anyone who interfered, and he might as well have been talking about a day at the beach. I frowned, studying his face as he stood up beside the bed.

"Are you really that calm all the time?" I said. "Doesn't *anything* bother you?"

I thought I caught the slightest twitch of a muscle in his temple. Enough to make me want to peel back that dreamy exterior and find out just what made up the man underneath. I *knew* there was more to him than he showed.

Then Baldur shrugged and gave me that same sunny smile. "This is just my nature. No matter what happens, the sun shines down on us. We'll find our way through. I trust in that, so no, I don't worry."

"Oh, yeah? You weren't even worried when everyone was *dying* and the world seemed like it was going to hell during Ragnarok?" I was improvising a little, but I'd gotten the gist of it from what the other gods had told me.

The light god's dreamy expression definitely shifted then. Just for a second, a brief tightening, but his voice came out a little strained too.

"I wasn't there for Ragnarok. I couldn't feel anything about it."

He glided out of the room as if he were a beam of light before I could ask him anything more about that. I blinked at the doorway he'd disappeared through. Guilt pinched my stomach for provoking that reaction, but it was followed by a deeper pinch of curiosity.

He hadn't been there? Then where the hell had he been?

Somewhere he wasn't too happy remembering, from the looks of things.

Well, that was another mystery for another day, if he ever wanted to speak to me again. Today, I had some dark elves to take on. No way was I going to be able to relax just lying here in bed waiting for someone else to get things done.

I eased myself gingerly to the edge of the mattress and found that when I stood up I only felt as if plywood splinters were jabbing through my muscles, not whole knives or anything. I'd experienced worse. Being hit by a speeding jeep put a lot of things in perspective.

By the time I'd made it to the hall, the splinters were more like sandpaper grit. A steady improvement. Voices carried from the second floor. I shuffled down as quickly as I could manage.

When I pushed open the door to the study, Loki, Thor, Hod, and Freya all fell silent where they were gathered together by the desk. Thor opened his mouth, probably to ask whether I really should be walking around, so I jumped right in.

"Okay," I said. "I'm back in one piece. Where are we looking for these dark elves?"

---

The piney scent of the nearby forest hung in the air even on the downtown strip of the West Virginia city I was checking out. This high in the mountains, it was even a tiny bit cool as summer went. Goosebumps rose on my arms when the evening breeze tickled past me.

I should have brought a jacket. Of course, that would only have gotten in the way of my wings if I needed them.

The gods had said there'd been dark elf activity in this area decades ago. They weren't sure if any had been around since, but it was one place to start. I guessed they were checking out other potential leads while I poked around here.

I let my eyes sharpen as I scanned the road. Nothing had jumped out at me so far, but halfway down the main street, my gaze caught on a poster taped to a telephone pole with a photo and the word MISSING in large font across the top. I crossed the street to take a closer look.

The photo was of a middle-aged woman who looked like she'd

had more hard times than easy ones. Her brown hair was scraggly and the teeth behind her smile crooked. Apparently she'd been last seen a couple towns over nearly a year ago. From the yellowing of the paper, I guessed it had been there quite a while too.

I breathed in deeply, testing the air the way I had periodically since I'd gotten here. A couple times, I'd thought I'd picked up a hint of that rotten smell I'd noticed in the cave, but as soon as I'd tried to follow it, it had vanished into the breeze. Maybe it'd just been my imagination. Or a butcher shop's trash bin. Hod had said that scent wasn't anything they usually associated with dark elves anyway.

As I continued past the shops and restaurants, a twisted shadow on the side of one building snagged my attention. I hustled closer and frowned. Three jagged lines, twined together, had been carved into one of the bricks on… I stepped back and checked the sign. It was a backpacker's hostel.

An uneasy prickle ran over my skin when I dropped my gaze back to the symbol. I hadn't had time to commit them to memory very solidly, but I was pretty sure I'd seen a marking like that on the wall of the dark elves' cave. Or at least one a lot like it.

But then, even if it had been made by dark elves, there was no way of telling how long ago or whether they'd been here since. The edges of the carving were worn down by the weather. It wasn't recent.

The prickling sensation stayed with me the rest of the way down the main street. I glanced over my shoulder abruptly a few times, but I didn't catch any movements that looked suspicious. My fingers curled around my switchblade, closed but ready if I needed it.

Around a corner in the fringes of the downtown strip, I spotted another of those symbols, this one with four lines instead of three. I paused, cocking my head as I studied it. Nothing about it meant anything to me, other than that association with the dark elves. But I didn't like it.

That one was on a small charity building. Soup kitchen and beds for the "needy." I bit my lip. No, I didn't like this at all.

Something rustled at the edges of my hearing. I stiffened, my hackles rising. The sound stopped too.

Carefully, I walked on, setting my feet as quietly as I could. Cars and other pedestrians passed me, but the street wasn't all that busy on a weekday in this nowhere town. In the gaps in between, I kept my ears perked.

There wasn't much, but the rustling reached me twice more, ever so faintly, only for an instant. That was enough.

Someone—or some*thing*—was stalking me.

# 17

*Loki*

I slunk from shadow to shadow, my wolfish shape blending into the dark patches with a mix of stealth and magic. I only caught glimpses of Ari now and then in the gaps between the buildings, but I didn't need more than that. My raised ears could pick up the soft rasp of her shoes against the pavement, even the murmur of her breath.

I did like the glimpses I caught, though. Our valkyrie was certainly coming into her own. She moved down the sidewalk with a bold but not reckless confidence it was hard not to admire.

Every time I saw it, I remembered that first moment she'd reappeared on the lawn yesterday afternoon. Battered and bleeding, she'd managed to pull herself all the way back to us—and to crow about her victory before those injuries had completely caught up with her. Then back on her feet, chomping at the bit to get moving the very next day…

I'd forgotten mortals could possess that kind of strength and fire. I didn't see it very often even among the gods. It made me want to push her even farther to find her limits and to hide her away so no one could ever batter that spirit right out of her, both at the same time.

That was all right. I was used to having complicated impulses. We'd see which one won out.

Ari's pixie frame ducked down an alley between a clothing store and a bank. Had she seen something down this way? I went still, tasting the air through my fangs. Nothing unexpected reached me. I pulled back behind a dumpster before she emerged into the longer alley I'd been loping along.

Her shoes scuffed against the damp concrete as if she were heading in the opposite direction. I waited several seconds before slipping out from my shelter to keep pace.

I'd only taken two steps when she whirled and sprang toward me with a burst of supernatural speed.

Her switchblade flashed. Her eyes widened at the sight of me. I reared back a moment before she reached me, returning to my usual form so she didn't try to kill me like the smallish warg she'd probably taken me for.

"Imagine running into you here," I said. "What a lovely coincidence."

Ari's legs had locked. Her eyes narrowed. "Coincidence my ass. What the hell are you doing here?"

I gestured lazily with one hand. "Oh, taking the lay of the land, investigating various avenues."

She crossed her arms. "*I* was supposed to be the one investigating this town. You could have told me you were coming along. But you didn't want me to know. You were following me. You *still* don't think I can handle myself after yesterday?"

Her voice was tart, but under the snark I thought I detected a note of hurt. I hadn't realized I might wound more than her pride. And even the pride, she'd rightly earned.

My mind tripped through a hundred possible excuses to settle on the right one. "Not at all, pixie. Believe me, there's little I'm surer of at this point than your capabilities." The truth of that statement sank in as I said it. I really hadn't been worried about her, had I? I'd told myself that was why I was keeping an eye on her, but really…

I gave her a self-deprecating grin. A little more honesty couldn't hurt. "I was actually rather curious to see what other tricks you might pull out of your metaphorical hat. Watching you is leagues more entertaining than spending time with any of those lunks whose company I've already kept for eons."

Ari kept frowning, but her shoulders came down. "You aren't supposed to be entertaining yourself," she said. "We're supposed to be tracking down those dark elves."

"I'm very skilled at multitasking," I said. At her skeptical look, I nodded to the alley. "They've been here more recently than we were already aware. I've picked up traces of their passage. Not in the last few years, though, and I don't think for very long. The signs would suggest they came and went from west of here."

"Oh. Did you see any more of their symbols?"

I raised my eyebrows. "Symbols?"

She studied me for a second. When she seemed to come to the conclusion that I honestly didn't know what she was talking about, a triumphant glint lit in her eyes. "Come on," she said. "Apparently it's a good thing you weren't investigating on your own."

I followed her back onto the street and down the block. The passers-by drifted around us, not seeing us but instinctively making room. I'd have loved to see their expressions if they'd gotten to witness our valkyrie in her full winged glory. My gaze lingered on the taut muscles of her back, the smooth skin that hid those wings at the moment.

Mostly smooth. Baldur had healed her wounds from her two battles with us, but she'd come to us with other scars already in place. A thin curving one veered from the peak of her left shoulder down the back of her arm halfway to her elbow, like a path just waiting to be traced.

"There." Ari pointed to a brick in the side of a dreary-looking building. Some sort of symbol had indeed been carved there: four lines twisting around each other in a barbed tangle. My brow furrowed.

"What makes you think this has anything to do with the dark elves?"

"I told you I saw markings on the walls of that cave. I'm pretty sure this was one of them. Or at least it looks a lot like them." She paused, glancing up at me. "You haven't seen anything like this before."

I shook my head. "I'm familiar with the language of the dark elves, spoken and written, but this is something else. If you saw it in their domain, though… It's been a long time since we've crossed paths with them. If they're up to something nefarious, as all evidence indicates they are, I wouldn't put it past them to have developed some new visual code precisely to avoid our notice."

Which was not an encouraging sign at all. This building had nothing to do with Odin. What other schemes were the cave-dwellers up to that they were working so hard to hide from us?

Perhaps taking Odin hadn't been the point. Perhaps he'd merely been a casualty of a larger plot—one he'd stumbled onto?

"It's a charity for the homeless," Ari said, tipping her head toward the building. "I saw another symbol on the hostel a couple streets over. No others so far."

I turned that information over in my head. "Ports for people far from home or without a home at all. People unlikely to be quickly missed."

Ari's jaw tightened. "That's what I thought too. But what would they want with people anyway? Why would they be hurting—killing—humans? Do they have something against *us*?"

She still said "us" so easily, as if she weren't so much more than mortal now. Bristling as if she were preparing to defend the entire human race.

"I don't know," I said. "It's not their standard modus operandi. But whatever ghastly business they're into, we'll uncover it and put a stop to it—you can be sure of that."

She nodded, turning on her heel, and her gaze jerked to the side. I'd caught a flicker of dark movement by one of the roofs too. "What was that?" Ari muttered, and before I had a chance to answer, she was already dashing toward it.

"Whoa there." I caught her by the waist—not roughly, but with just enough force to stop her. She'd put so much energy into her dash that the interrupted momentum sent her stumbling back against me. Her shoulders collided with my chest. My arm instinctively eased around her, my head dipping next to hers. "Always in such a rush, pixie."

She shoved out of the loose embrace and spun around with a ragged breath, still close enough that its warmth grazed my throat. Behind the already fading flash of panic in her dilated eyes, there was a shadow of desire. The sight of it went straight to my cock.

Our valkyrie didn't like to be held, but some part of her craved my touch.

"Why did you stop me?" she demanded.

I reined in my own cravings, the ones I'd been trying to ignore now stirring more insistently inside me. "You're quick to race in, no fearful hesitation," I said. "It's commendable. No one would ever mistake you for a coward. But sometimes slow and careful gets the job done better."

"I can be *careful*," she bit out. Her eyes were still stormy. She closed them for a second, swallowing audibly. "Maybe I'm a little wound up because of what I saw in those caves. Thinking about what those *things* might be doing to people—people who have no one to fight for them…" She looked at me again. "But you said you believed I can handle myself. I'm not going to do anything stupid."

"I know," I said. "I do." Faced with that unwavering gaze, I was run through with a piercing sensation from gut to breastbone.

I'd brought her to this place, in more ways than one. I'd ripped her out of the blank peace of death to fight battles for gods she hadn't even known existed. More than anyone, I should know the strain of being forced to play by rules I hadn't agreed to. Perhaps I owed her a little more.

"If I interfere, it's not about you," I said. "It's about me, and how much is riding on us finding Odin. Getting back to Asgard."

"What do you mean?"

I sighed. "My powers are fading faster than the others' are. And every attempt we make at finding the Allfather that fails, you can be sure they're more and more inclined to blame me. I'd rather not deal with that. All right? If I micromanage, you can attribute it to that. It's certainly no failing on your part."

Ari wet her lips, holding my gaze. "Why would they blame *you*? You picked me, but the other valkyries—"

I shrugged, letting a smile creep across my face. "What can I say? I'm a trouble-maker. So it's easy to blame all possible trouble in the world on me."

Her expression tensed for a moment, as if she could relate to that idea more than I would have guessed. "So you picked another trouble-maker to have on your side."

My smile grew. "I suppose you could look at it that way. Although we'll have to see whether you decide to be on my side after all."

She looked as if she might have had some snappy answer to that remark, but at the same moment, the dark flicker we'd seen earlier solidified into a bird. A raven. Which glided down from the rooftop it had hopped along and shifted into the shape of a young woman, her hair and eyes and the loose dress she wore as dark as her former feathers. None of the mortals blinked as she ambled toward us. They couldn't see her either.

Well, well, well. What a surprise, and yet perfectly fitting.

Ari's knife hand came up, her shoulders braced. I touched one lightly. "It's all right. At least, no immediate threat. She ought to be a friend."

The valkyrie stayed tensed. It would seem she didn't entirely trust *me* to have an accurate take on any given threat.

"Loki," the woman said in a voice that was sweet but slightly hoarse. "I've been looking for you."

"I'm not generally all that difficult to find if you're really trying," I said. "Assuming I don't mind you finding me. I almost didn't recognize you, Muninn. It's been a long time."

The raven woman gave me a smile that recalled the angles of her beak. How many decades—or maybe even centuries—had it been since Odin had returned from one of his wanderings without his usual feathered companions? He'd never bothered to explain why they'd parted ways, beyond "It was time for them to seek something more," in his typical cryptic manner. What had his former pets been up to since then?

"It has been a while," Muninn agreed. No doubt she knew the exact date and time we'd last been in each other's company. I'd never seen her shift into human form before now, but it didn't surprise me that she could. We all changed with the tides of time—and Odin's ravens had been human enough in their affect.

"Allow me to introduce Muninn," I said to Ari with a sweep of my arm. "Mistress of memory and once one of Odin's regular companions." It certainly was interesting that she'd resurfaced now. I looked back to the raven woman. "Was there any particular reason you were looking for me?"

She'd cocked her head in eerily bird-like fashion at Ari. "You got yourself a valkyrie," she said. "Fascinating."

Ari bristled, but I knew she didn't need any help from me here. "About as fascinating as a raven that can turn into a woman, I guess," she said.

Muninn simply blinked at her. "I'd imagine you're here for the same reason I am." She turned back to me. "I had a sense something unpleasant had happened to Odin. I've searched for him across Midgard but found no trace. Asgard is closed to me without his help, but he hasn't heeded my call. All of which I find rather concerning. Don't you?"

"We do," I said. "He isn't in Asgard; I can confirm that much. I don't suppose you've gleaned any clues as to his whereabouts?"

"Not so far," she said. "But I wanted to offer my help, if you're searching as well. We always did find that two heads were better than one." She smiled faintly at her halfhearted joke.

"Where is Huginn these days?" I asked. Her partner, the raven of thought, had been gone just as long.

She shook her head. "He went off on his own adventures. Eager to spread his wings, you might say. We haven't spoken in a long time."

Her demeanor suggested nothing but concern and a little wistfulness, and Odin's ravens had been nothing but loyal in the centuries they had been in our midst. I never trusted anyone or anything completely, but we might as well make use of her offer.

"What have you seen of the dark elves?" I asked, and gestured to the carving on the wall. "Or symbols of theirs like these, here in Midgard? They seem to be tangled up in the matter somehow."

"I saw those marks in their caves, too," Ari put in.

Muninn frowned, studying the marks. "The dark elves hadn't caught my attention, but I can think of a few places we should explore."

# 18

*Aria*

"You saw dark elves around this end of town recently?" Hod asked as we walked through a shabby neighborhood on the outskirts of Pittsburgh.

Muninn, who was leading the way, nodded. With her sharply pointed chin, the movement reminded me even more of the raven I'd watched her transform into and out of a few times now. It was more unsettling than Loki's various shifts. At least he still moved completely like a man when he looked like one.

"I don't remember exactly when," she said, her voice a weird mixture of rough and chirpy. "But it was in the last year. And those symbols you've pointed out—I came back yesterday to make sure they were the same ones. That's what I can show you now."

Thor swung his hammer in an easy arc at his side. He'd detached it from his belt the second we'd arrived by our various magical or winged means. "If there are any dirt-eaters here now, they'll regret sticking around."

Loki cut a glance toward the brawny god. "If there are any here now, we want to *capture* them so we can question them about the entrance to their realm. Not bash their heads in, satisfying as that might be."

He said it lightly, like he said just about everything, but the memory of yesterday's conversation lingered in my mind: his seriousness when he'd admitted how much finding Odin mattered to him. It'd disappeared behind his usual joking façade a moment later, but the emotion in his words had resonated right through my heart. Remembering, I had the urge to step closer to him.

Or maybe that was just a baser part of me, remembering the feel of his arm around my body.

"We don't know yet how involved the dark elves might be in Odin's disappearance," Baldur pointed out, bringing me back to the present.

"They tore up Ari," Thor grumbled. "They're up to no good one way or another. That's all I need to know."

"I think this may be one rare case where you can't find the good in a situation," Freya said, raising an eyebrow at the god of light.

Baldur chuckled in his dreamy way. "Finding out what they know about Odin would be good, regardless."

"*If* we find them," I said. So far I hadn't seen any sign of anything supernatural in this rundown suburb. It was the middle of the day, but the clouds that had covered the sky this morning had dimmed the sun so much it felt like dusk. No sign of rain yet, though. Just muggy heat so thick you could practically carve it.

"We're almost there." Muninn picked up her pace, her steps springy as she crossed the street. Halfway down the next block, she veered toward a bungalow that was even shabbier than its neighbors. The glass in one window had been broken, only shards poking from the frame. Half of one of the concrete front steps had crumbled.

Five twisted lines marked the house's cinderblock base.

Muninn nudged the door, and it swung open with a squeal of

its hinges. My skin prickled. I already didn't like the vibe of this place. It reminded me too much of houses and apartments I'd passed through during my first couple years on the street, before I'd gotten enough of a foothold to steer clear completely.

The room on the other side confirmed my suspicions. On the cracked linoleum floor between the scruffy armchairs, multicolored vials lay in a heap. A yellowed syringe sat on some smudged newspapers. The stink of old urine, chemical-laced smoke, and mildew assaulted me. I wrinkled my nose, edging around a frayed blanket stained with who-knew-what.

"Crack house," I said to the gods who'd filed in behind me. Hod was grimacing, and even Baldur looked a little ill. If I hadn't already been sure the dark elves were targeting the people least likely to be noticed missing, I would be now.

Freya edged farther into the room and toed a crumpled take-out box. "It doesn't look as if *anyone* has been here in quite some time," she said. "Look at the dust."

She was right. A thin layer of dust had collected on all the furniture, even the floor, disturbed only now by our feet.

"That's weird," I said, looking around. "The place is still open. There's even—" I prodded a deflated baggie with my toe. "They didn't completely finish their drugs. But it doesn't look like there was a raid either." I'd witnessed one of those, briefly, during a mad scramble out a window and down a fire escape. This place was a mess, but it was a mess that was orderly by druggie standards, not the total chaos of a bunch of police officers having barged through. The house should have been boarded up if it'd been identified.

"What do you think that means?" Thor asked, coming up beside me.

"I don't know." I swiped my hand across my mouth, not wanting to say what I was thinking. But what was the point in denying it? "Maybe *all* of the people who were using this place were taken away, just not by cops."

Thor let out a growl. "Are you *sure* I can't bash at least a few of them?" he said to Loki.

The trickster god was eyeing the room with vague curiosity. "As much as I respect those who live along the fringes of society, this looks like the home of the absolute dregs," he said. "I'm not sure whatever the dark elves did to them was any worse than they were doing to themselves." His voice was matter-of-fact, but the usual gleam in his eyes had dimmed. He wasn't anywhere near as unaffected as he was pretending.

"That doesn't mean they deserved it," Thor snapped. His face flushed red.

Loki shot him a mild glance. "Of course not," he said. "I'm just pointing out that you might want to moderate your fury, or you'll run out before we're even halfway to the bottom of this."

Thor muttered something that sounded insulting under his breath, but he let go of the argument.

"Well, there's clearly no one here, human or elf, now," Hod said. "If there's nothing else useful to do in this place, can we move on?"

Loki strode into the rooms that branched off from the first. "No secret elfy entrances, no more symbols, no clues that I can see," he announced as he returned.

"I'd hardly call that a thorough job," Thor said. He marched past the trickster god to make a check of his own.

Freya waved her hand in front of her nose. "While he's doing that, can the rest of us leave?"

"There's another spot," Muninn assured us, her eyes darting downward apologetically. "Closer to where I saw the elves themselves before. I hope we'll find out more there."

After we'd been waiting on the tiny patchy lawn for a few minutes, Thor stomped back out, his expression grim.

"This way!" Muninn said, darting on down the street.

I fell into step beside the thunder god as we all trailed after her.

I'd never seen him this upset before. And it was over a bunch of junkies.

But if I'd had just a little less luck in those first years after I left home, I could have ended up in their place. They were still people. People the dark elves were going to have to learn to steer clear of.

"You really care about them," I said. "Everyone the dark elves might have hurt. Don't you?"

Thor heaved a breath and looked at me. His face still had that angry flush. "I'm the god of men. I'm supposed to protect your entire realm. I can't do much about what you do to each other, as much as it pains me sometimes, but I should at least be able to stop other beings from preying on you. How long has this been going on without my even noticing?"

He wasn't just angry with the elves. He was angry with himself. The most powerful man I'd ever met felt powerless right now.

A little ache ran through me. I had the urge to take his hand, whatever comfort that was going to give him.

Oh, why the hell not? It didn't have to mean much. He'd been there for me, and I didn't doubt he would be again—as long as we had the same goals, at least.

I reached for his hand and slipped my fingers between his much thicker ones, giving them a quick squeeze. A twitch passed through Thor's muscles. A hint of the bright golden energy I'd felt from Baldur yesterday tingled over my skin. I guessed that was just what the life of a god felt like.

Thor squeezed my hand back, as gently as I suspected he was capable of, which was still pretty firmly. My heart jumped at the brief sensation of being pinned in place but steadied out the instant he relaxed his grip.

"Ari," he said, so low and tender my pulse thumped for a totally different reason.

"Here!" Muninn called out from ahead of us. "This is the other place."

Thor's jaw tensed. I let my hand slide from his as he hurried to join Muninn. Whatever he'd been going to say, he could say it later. Right now, I was really hoping he'd get to bash some dark elf skulls after all.

The building Muninn pointed to was an elementary school. My hackles went up as we approached. Were these assholes taking *kids*? Hell yes, skulls definitely needed to be broken then.

I saw the symbol right away, scratched into the concrete frame around the main doors. This one looked more recent to my eyes than the others had, which I guessed fit what the raven woman had said about the dark elves being here not long ago.

It was a Saturday, so the building was dark. Loki motioned toward the lock, and the doors eased open. We all tramped inside.

Our feet echoed loudly in the empty hall. Every school smelled the same, didn't it? Like photocopied paper and cheap glue.

A lump filled the bottom of my throat. It was too long since I'd seen Petey, since I'd really talked to him. I wanted the dark elves dealt with, but he came first. The next time I could slip away for a few hours, I was out of here.

Freya peered into one of the classrooms we passed. "I suppose we should search the entire building for any signs?"

"Or we follow this." Hod stopped, rubbing his shoe against the floor with a rasp. A fine gray grit dappled the floor in a faint splotch. The kind of grit that might be left from someone passing by who'd been wandering in caves not long ago.

Thor strode forward. "There's more this way," he said.

We hustled after him around a bend in the hall and through a set of double doors that opened into a gymnasium. This part of the school smelled like old sweaty socks. I swiveled in the dim light, searching the floor and then the walls. "Why would they come in—"

The bleachers next to us erupted with a flurry of movement. Pale-faced black-haired forms hurled themselves toward us with glints of blades. A yelp of warning, too late, broke from my throat.

Thor roared and swung his hammer. I fumbled for my switchblade. One of the dark elves slammed into me, knocking me to the floor. I jerked to the side as he stabbed at my chest. Wings. I needed my wings.

They erupted from my back with a force that shoved me, swaying, back onto my feet. Two more of the dark elves sprang at me. They were all around us, a wave of them, filling the air with the scent of damp mossy rock.

And blood. I leapt into the air, managing to kick off the elf that wrenched at one of my wings, and caught sight of Muninn ducking with a thin cry as an attacker sliced his knife across her arm. Thor pummeled several with his hammer, but another threw herself at his shoulders, sinking her knife into the muscles there. Streaks of red splattered the gym floor.

Baldur pushed back a few with a brilliant burst of light. Hod was whipping shadow around him, but not quickly enough to stop a dark elf that ducked under them and jabbed at his calf. Loki had shifted into his wolfish form. He snarled and lunged at the nearest attackers, but a gleam of blood already smeared his dark gray fur. A golden falcon soared down to claw at another elf that stabbed at him. Was that Freya?

The power and skill the gods were fighting with took my breath away. But there were too many of the dark elves, another darting in as soon as one fell back, swarming the bunch of us in a raging mass.

I swooped down, kneeing the one clinging to Thor's back in the face, lashing out with my switchblade at the clump that had surrounded Muninn. In the instant they fell back, she sprang into the air with a burst of feathers, raven again. Behind me, someone let out a hiss of pain. The elves raised their voices in a battle cry as if they were already victorious.

No. I couldn't let this happen. I was a fucking valkyrie. The one real purpose I had was turning the tide of a battle. And I needed a tide that was going to sweep these miscreants all the way back to the wretched caves where they belonged.

Another dark elf flung himself at me, and as I dodged him, a second flung himself off another's back to ram his knife at my head. I elbowed him away only fast enough to stop the knife from outright entering my skull. It scraped across my scalp, his knuckles colliding with my forehead in a burst of pain.

I tried to summon the blast of lightning I'd flung at the warg a few days ago, but my body wouldn't comply. Apparently I needed to be panicked completely out of my mind for that to activate. But I had other methods of destruction.

The flame of darkness inside me unwound through my body as I spun around. It yawned with an unsettling hunger that I was more than happy to give into. I swept out my arms, slicing one elf across the gut and digging my fingers into another's lank hair.

The pulse of the creature's life energy beat against my palm—and flowed up into it. The darkness loomed and swallowed, and the dark elf collapsed. I'd taken his life in the space of a second.

A painful exhilaration filled my chest. An attacker raked her dagger across my wing, but I battered her aside with a punch and wrenched myself back out of the fray. But only for an instant. I dove, smacking my palm against the scalp of an elf breaking through Baldur's golden shield. Snatching at another who was ramming his blade at Hod's side. The darkness inside me opened its maw wider, inhaling one life and another.

I couldn't reach them all, but I reached enough to shift the tide. As one, two, three more bodies fell in my wake, Thor let out another roar and charged through the mass of attackers. His hammer toppled at least half a dozen more. Loki leapt into the space he'd opened up, tearing throats open with his wolfish claws and teeth.

Another cry went up among the elves, but this one sounded

desperate. In a blink, those still standing bolted for the bleachers. Thor barreled after them, his face nearly as deep a red as his hair, his eyes wide with fury. His hammer slammed through several more. Loki pounced on another with a rake of his jaws. Muninn shot down from above and jabbed her beak into a fleeing elf's neck.

"Baldur!" Freya called. She was standing with Hod, who'd fallen to his knees. Blood was soaking down the dark god's slacks from a wound at his waist.

"No," he gritted out. "I'm fine."

She merely scoffed. His bright twin rushed to his side. I sank to the ground myself, the throbbing of my own injuries catching up with me. A sharp ache dug into my temple. My scored wing crackled with pain.

Fallen dark elves sprawled all around us, none of them moving. Thor came to a stop, his chest heaving, the flush starting to fade from his face. "I don't know where the rest of them disappeared to," he growled.

We hadn't managed to catch any to question. We'd been too busy not dying. But Loki just grimaced, swiping a hand at his own wounds. "For now, I'll say good riddance."

We'd won the battle. And now we knew a little more. It wasn't just Odin the dark elves had a beef with, clearly. They'd have happily killed all of us—and they'd come way too close for comfort.

# 19

*Aria*

When I woke up from the nap Baldur had induced while I healed, the sky outside my bedroom window was dim but not dark. Pale pink streaked across the clouds from the setting sun. I focused on that pretty color for a moment as echoes of the battle with the dark elves rose in the back of my head. The blood. The battering. The heady sensation of the life energy I'd wrenched from their bodies.

My stomach rolled. I shook the memories away. Like Thor had said when we'd talked about fighting, I'd been defending myself and people who needed it. One slip, and it'd have been my life destroyed all over again. It wasn't as if I'd *wanted* all that violence.

Right now, there was only one person I wanted to be thinking about. One person I should be thinking about.

I crawled out of bed, testing my limbs to make sure they were all back in working order. If I'd felt like I was recovering from an intense workout after my first confrontation with the dark elves, now I was coming out of a rotten flu as well. I grimaced at the burn in my muscles and went out into the hall.

It was still early enough that I could make it home before Petey's bedtime. I had to actually talk to him this time. Let him know I was here, that I was still looking out for him. I sure as hell couldn't go into another battle without doing that.

No voices sounded from below. The house was still and silent, only one light on downstairs—in the kitchen. A thick savory smell greeted me when I walked in. A note was lying on the table.

*Dear pixie,*

*Thor insists we let you keep sleeping, and I have a feeling I'll end up with his hammer in my head if I argue any more. We're checking a possible lead. There's stew in the fridge if you're hungry, and Hod is probably in the study being grim if you have any use for him. I promise we'll save some dark elves for your blade.*

He hadn't signed it, but the spiky handwriting would have told me Loki had left it if the nickname and the jaunty tone hadn't.

I might have been annoyed, but their leaving without me had made my life that much easier. I had only one god to worry about, and conveniently the one I had some hope of making a case with. I yanked open the fridge, bypassed the stew—as good as it smelled—for a more portable bun I stuffed a few slices of ham in, and headed for the study.

"Yes?" Hod said when I knocked on the door. I pushed it open to find him sitting at the desk where he'd been the last time I'd visited him in here, only this time he had a book open in front of him. His hand lay flat against it, but as far as I could tell it didn't have any braille. He'd been using that magical way of reading he'd hinted at before, I guessed.

His unseeing gaze had lifted toward me. "What is it, valkyrie?" he asked.

Of course he knew it was me. No one else was here. For all I knew, he could tell from the sound of my breath or the rustle of my clothes. Not much seemed to get past him, regardless of his blindness.

"I thought I should give you a heads up," I said, "so you don't have to chase me down again. I'm going to see my brother. I won't be gone too long."

Hod frowned. "I don't think—"

"I'm going," I said firmly. "I did everything you all have asked me to do—and more—and now I'm going to do something for me. Unless you want to fight about it."

I wasn't sure how much of a fight I could really make against a fully-fledged god. Hod didn't look particularly worried. He sighed and rubbed his temple, scattering the fall of his short black hair along his forehead.

"All right," he said. "But you're not going alone."

I bristled as he stood up. "You still don't trust me?"

He managed to give me a glower. "Mostly I don't trust the dark elves and whoever they might be allied with. But no, I don't entirely trust you either. The whole reason Loki picked you is because you look out for yourself first. Or am I wrong and you're actually selflessly devoted to making the world a better place?"

Now I was *really* bristling. "You don't have to be an asshole about it," I said. But there wasn't a whole lot else I could say. The truth was I'd already planned on breaking at least one rule in the next couple hours. And it wasn't like I had any intention of sticking around and doing my divine duty after we got this whole dark elf problem sorted out.

That wasn't selfishness, though. I was thinking of Petey at least as much as myself.

"Are we going or not?" was all Hod said.

I muttered something highly insulting under my breath and marched to the front door, trying to pretend I didn't feel him following behind me.

On the front lawn, I tugged forth my wings. They sprang from my back with hardly a prickle now, as easily as my knife from the switchblade handle. Like they were becoming even more a part of me instead of some alien appendages tacked on.

I didn't totally like that idea, but there was no denying they were useful. With a few quick flaps, I was soaring toward Philly. Hod careened along behind me on his shadowy magic carpet.

I wanted to lose myself in the rush of the wind and the flow of the landscape beneath me, but anxiety had balled tight in my gut. I'd gotten too distracted by the dark elves and the horrors I'd witnessed in their realm. It didn't matter how many people they might be preying on—Petey had to come first. He needed me more than anyone. I'd promised him I'd be there for him.

But for now, he was still dozens of miles distant. There wasn't much to distract me except the god of darkness skimming along beside me.

"Why did they leave you behind anyway?" I called over to him.

Hod kept his face turned forward, as if he were navigating by sight. "I was the most injured in the skirmish this afternoon. They assumed I needed the most rest."

The same reasoning they'd used with me. I guessed I couldn't be too offended if they'd treated one of their fellow gods the same way.

"Are you *sure* you should be flying all this way, then?" I asked. "I'm telling you, I'll be perfectly fine on my own."

He shifted his eyes toward me then, the green even darker in the deepening evening. "That didn't work back at the house," he said. "It's not going to work here."

I shrugged with the sweep of my wings as if it didn't make that much difference to me. "Well, you can't blame a girl for trying." Another, more unnerving question nibbled at me. "Do you really think we need to worry about the dark elves out here?"

"What do you mean?"

"You're the one who mentioned them, and they did hit us pretty hard today. If we hadn't all been together…" I paused. "Loki said you all can still die. And that you don't know if you'd come back again if you do."

Hod made a dismissive sound. "Loki says a lot of things. I'll admit those things are true, but we're a lot more resilient than any mortal. The dirt-eaters had the upper hand, briefly, because they caught us by surprise and we weren't expecting an assault. We won't make that mistake again."

That didn't mean they couldn't surprise us in some other way. But I shook off that uneasy itch, pushing my wings faster as Philly's city lights came into view up ahead. The sense of home loosened the clenching in my gut a little. My valkyrie senses could even pick up the hum of all those human lives ahead of us, breathing and eating and laughing and all the things humans were supposed to do.

I could still do all those things as a valkyrie. Just not with other human beings, if the gods had their way.

I glided over the rooftops until I reached Mom's street. Then I swooped down in a perfect arc to land on Petey's windowsill.

He was crouched on the bedroom floor, making gruff voices for his action figures as they waged war across his thready rug. His head didn't even twitch when I settled on the ledge by the half-open window.

I just sat there for a few minutes, watching my little brother at play. His gray-blue eyes were bright but distant as he focused on his imaginary world. Whatever story he'd cooked up, it involved half the contents of his toy bin—although he didn't exactly have a huge number of playthings anyway. A lock of over-long blond hair fell into his face, and my fingers itched with the urge to brush it back.

This part was going to require some quick thinking—and acting. I didn't glance over at Hod, but I could feel him hovering a few feet away, waiting. I wasn't getting him to leave, even for a minute. That was obvious. So I'd just have to count on my speed and his sense of discretion.

Petey made one of his superheroes blast off into the air. I

gripped the window ledge and focused all my attention on my body: the muggy but cooling evening air against my skin, the flaky paint beneath my palms. At the same time, I yanked my wings back into my body.

"Valkyrie!" Hod said, and I knew I'd done it. I shoved myself through the window's opening an instant before his grasping hand whipped through the air behind me, just missing my arm.

My feet thumped on the floor, and I winced. But I was in, breathing the sour scent of the sheets Mom never bothered to wash in the warm room. Petey spun around. A grin leapt across his face, so joyful it made every painful moment of the last week completely worth it.

"Ari!" he whispered, knowing he had to stay quiet even in his excitement. He sprang off the floor and threw his arms around me, pressing his face into my shoulder as I crouched into the hug. The sweet smell of childish skin replaced the room's less pleasant odors.

My pulse hitched. Petey's embrace felt different from usual—more desperate.

"Hey," I said softly, running my hand over his rumpled hair. "Is something the matter?"

"Mom said I wasn't ever going to see you again," he mumbled into my shirt. "I *knew* she couldn't be right."

Those two sentences told me all I needed to know. Mom had found out about my death—and she'd decided she could cut deeper by making Petey think I'd abandoned him than by telling him the truth.

I hugged my little brother tighter. Too bad for her I had ways of coming back and proving her wrong.

Knuckles rapped against the window. When Petey didn't flinch, I realized only I could hear them. As I'd hoped, Hod was staying unperceivable. He couldn't come in here and drag me away from Petey without causing a whole lot more distress.

The god of darkness could be cold, but he was also logical. And his sense of logic should be telling him letting me play normal with Petey for a few minutes would do less harm than trying to intervene.

"Valkyrie, get out of there," Hod growled, but I ignored him. I squeezed Petey once more and kissed his cheek. As I eased back, the collar of his shoulder slipped to the side and revealed a mottled purple-and-brown mark just above his collarbone.

My pulse stuttered. "Petey, what happened to you?"

My brother's eyes went wide. "It's nothing," he said quickly. "I tripped and fell."

A twist of rage and guilt wound around my stomach. "Let me see," I said, keeping my voice gentle.

Petey stiffened, but he held still while I shifted his shirt even more to the side. His narrow shoulder—goddamnit, why didn't Mom give him more to eat?—held not one but four splotchy bruises, like fat splayed fingers. Tripped and fell, my ass. My own fingers clenched around the fabric of his shirt, careful not to brush the tender skin.

"Ivan or Mom?" I said, already pretty sure of the answer. Mom dealt in neglect and willful obliviousness, with a side of emotional torture. She'd only raised her hand at me once, and that had been the day I'd left. But she had a taste for violent men that even seeing her first son dead hadn't cured her of.

Petey's his lower lip wobbled. I forced my hand to relax and patted his arm. "It's okay, buddy. You can tell me. I won't get you in any trouble."

"I knocked his favorite mug off the counter, and it broke," he mumbled. "It was an accident."

"Of course it was. He's just… He's just a big bully." I swallowed all the coarser names I'd like to have called him and tugged Petey to me again. The darkness that had stirred in the battle with the elves this morning was churning in my belly. Somehow it made me feel both queasy and invincible at the same time.

I didn't want my little brother seeing those feelings in me. Didn't want him catching even a glimpse of what his Ari was capable of now.

"I can't stay," I said. He was used to that. "I just had to see you. I'll *always* be around, watching out for you, even if you don't see me for a while. Okay? And next time I'll bring a pack of those cards."

I waggled my eyebrows at him, and his smile came back. He couldn't feel it—the fury radiating through my veins. I ruffled his hair one last time and straightened up.

"I love you, Ari," he said in his innocent six-year-old way.

"I love you too, kid," I said, but my throat tightened. He hardly knew who I was anymore. *I* hardly knew that.

But I knew what I could do, and I knew exactly who I had to do it to.

By the time I pushed myself back out through the window, my body was shaking. Hod clamped his hand around my forearm, and the effort I'd been making to keep myself visible dissolved.

"What in Hel's name was that?" he snapped.

"Get off me!" I shoved him away, jerking my arm out of his grasp, and dove with my wings surging out over my back. I could hear the TV going in the basement. Ivan would be down there in his stupid little man cave. Pathetic fucking man who'd smack around a little kid. My anger seared through me, burning dark and deep. The rest of the world around me faded amid that roar.

He was never going to touch my brother again.

"Ari!"

Hod tackled me from behind as a wall of his shadowy magic slammed into me from the other side. We both crashed into the lawn, just a few feet from the basement window I'd been aiming for. I hissed and lashed out at him with elbows and knees, but the dark god pressed me into the earth with his hands and tendrils of shadow.

"Let me *go*," I said, outright flailing now. "He deserves it. He deserves every bit of hell I can rain down on him. Fucking bastard."

"Ari." Hod's voice was low but strained. "This isn't your place. You can't just go around killing random people because you're angry."

"He's not a random person. He's the asshole who hurt my little brother. Get the fuck off me!"

"I'm not going to," Hod said. "Not until I know you're listening. And I've got more power in one hand than you've got in your whole body, valkyrie, so don't try me."

I gritted my teeth. "I *have* to do this. You don't understand."

Hod's eyes gazed down at me, flat and yet fathomless at the same time. "Then why don't you tell me about it?"

I dragged in a breath—every muscle quaking at the sensation of being pinned down, all that fury and pain and guilt writhing inside me—and burst into tears.

Hod flinched and leapt back. The shadows clinging to my legs loosened. I slapped my hands to my face, but they couldn't hold in the tears or the sob that wrenched up my throat. Fuck, fuck, fuck. Get a hold of yourself, Ari.

I swallowed hard and swiped at my eyes. A few tears streaked down my cheeks, but I managed to inhale without a hitch. Hod stood braced between me and the basement window, his eyes wary, his mouth twisted. Lord only knew what he was thinking now.

When he spoke, his voice was still strained, but there was a softness to it I'd never heard before. "Go ahead and tell me. I'm all ears."

The corner of my mouth twitched despite myself. My fury had spent itself with the tears. Now all I felt was an aching emptiness inside.

Had I really wanted to be a killer? I didn't know. But then, I already was one.

I'd never killed a human being before, though.

I wet my lips and drew up my knees, resting my hands on them. My gaze stayed on my dirt streaked fingers as I found the words. "It's not a very exciting story. I had a crappy mom. She liked to date crappy guys. My older brother tried to protect me, but he was practically still a kid himself."

"Your *older* brother," Hod repeated.

"Francis." It'd been years since I'd said that name out loud. It made my mouth turn dry. "He gave me that switchblade. Told me it was his way of being with me, if he ever wasn't there, if I needed it. But even when things got really bad— I didn't use it when I should have. I *gave in*. Such a fucking coward. When Francis found out, he attacked the guy. The guy attacked back, slammed his head into the corner of the kitchen counter."

I sucked in another breath. "Second-degree murder, they called it."

That was one memory I'd never be able to shake. I didn't want to. Francis deserved better than being forgotten, even that last gut-piercing moment when I'd stood over his crumpled body seeing the blood pooling beneath his pale hair, with tears blurring my vision and a shriek in my throat.

"The man who did all this," Hod said. "He's in prison now?"

He didn't ask what I'd given in to. What Francis had found out. I hadn't known I could feel as grateful as I did right then. The memories of those awful nights, pressed into my lumpy mattress, willing my mind away while that bastard grunted and pawed at me and more… I would have left *those* behind forever if I could. They wrenched at me too much even when I didn't look at them directly.

"Yeah," I said. "At least five more years before he's got a chance at parole. But Ivan could turn out just as bad. I can't let anything happen to Petey. I can't just let things *happen*, let him get hurt because I didn't try to stop it."

My voice had gone ragged again. I shut up. We stayed there through a long stretch of silence.

"I do understand," Hod said abruptly.

My gaze jerked up to his face. He was frowning, his head bowed.

"What do you mean?" I said. How could a god have any fucking idea—

"I know what it's like," he said, "to feel like you killed someone you love." He laughed roughly. "I know it better than I'd wish on anyone. At least you— How old were you, Ari?"

My fingers dropped to the grass, twisting into the strands. "Twelve. But it doesn't matter. I still should have done more."

"You can't, though," Hod said. "It's already over. All you've got left is the rubble in the aftermath."

He said it with a hollowness that resonated with the empty ache inside me. I wanted to argue, but that statement was true, wasn't it? Even if I stole Ivan's life from his body, it wouldn't change a damned thing about what I'd done or hadn't done ten years ago.

Hod held out his hand to help me up. I hesitated and took it. His grip loosened when I was on my feet, but he eased a step closer, raising his other hand cautiously. My breath caught as he rested it on my hair just above my ear. Not close enough to be an embrace, but maybe as close as I could have accepted right now anyway. Part of me wanted to lean into him and part wanted to run away, so I just stayed where I was, in between. Held but not quite held.

"You won't let him down," the dark god said quietly. "I can tell. There'll be a way. It's just not this."

My throat choked up all over again. I blinked hard. I still didn't let myself step right to him, but I leaned my head into his touch, just a little. Taking the comfort he was trying to offer just for a moment.

The energy that whispered beneath the dark god's skin was the same golden warmth as Baldur's and Thor's had been. In that way, he and his twin were completely the same.

"I want to believe that," I said.

"Stranger things have come true for you in the last week, haven't they?"

I looked up at Hod even though I couldn't exactly meet his gaze. His mouth had quirked with a bittersweet smile.

"Come on," he said. "You're not killing anyone tonight. Let's get home."

# 20

*Baldur*

Loki had the laptop open on the dining room table, chuckling to himself as his long fingers clattered over the keys. The rest of us peered at the screen from our cluster around him. Windows of text and images flew by on the screen.

"Gods using computers," Aria said. "I'm not sure this is a good mix."

Her tone was teasing, but when I glanced at her, her face looked drawn. Was she worried about the laptop or something else? An echoing worry stirred inside my chest.

"It's an *excellent* mix," Loki declared. "My new electronically inclined friend—the one who gave me this computer, not the computer itself, as much as I adore it—set me up with some picture recognition software. In theory, it should seek out matches for those symbols the dark elves are using through all the public photographs on the internet. We'll be able to see if there's anywhere they're particularly condensed."

"And if there is, that should be where their gate from Midgard to Nidavellir is," Thor filled in.

"Exactly! No need for us to run all over the world to find it. Although I won't fault Muninn for keeping up her search that way."

"It'll only work if they were careless enough to leave signs that obvious," Hod said.

Loki waved him off. "Oh, take your gloom and doom someplace else, nephew. I have internet access. Soon I will rule the world!"

He winked at Aria, and she smiled, but there was tension in her expression that I couldn't help seeing. It sent a shiver through my nerves.

"Any tools we can use to get us closer to Odin are a blessing," I said. "I'm sure it'll come up with something useful."

"There," Loki said. "The god of light has spoken. No further argument necessary."

"Let us know when you've solved all our problems, then," my twin muttered. He turned to go, hesitated, and lifted his eyes in my direction with a motion of his hand to follow him.

I walked with him out into the hall and up the stairs. His hand skimmed the banister, a barely necessary point of orientation. His movements looked a little stiff, though.

"Are you still in pain from yesterday's attack?" I asked. "If you need me to work more healing—"

Hod shook his head with a jerk. "I'm not asking for anything from you. Everything is perfectly healed. You don't have to worry about that."

He led the way into the study and stopped by the desk. For a moment, he just stood there, bracing his hand against the wooden surface.

"Brother," I started.

He swiveled abruptly to face me. "We've never talked about it," he said. "What happened—the mistletoe, Loki's ploy… Not really."

A chill so strong and swift I couldn't displace it swept through me. "Because we didn't need to," I said, pushing warmth into my voice and trying to let it warm the rest of me. "I know it wasn't your fault. I know you never would have meant to. There's nothing more to be said."

"There is," Hod insisted. "Allfather help me, brother, I don't know if I ever even apologized. It was so long, in between, and then after we were just glad Ragnarok was over, and I never wanted to press you. I never wanted to remind you of what you must have been through. But I know it can't have been easy for you."

"Hod," I said. "It's done. I don't think about it, ever." I didn't let myself. "You can absolve yourself."

"Can I? It was my hand. It was my doing as much as his. I know he likes to blame everything on the damned prophecies, but you never deserved a fate like that. You—"

"It's *done*," I snapped. The words crackled from my mouth as if the ice inside me had mixed with my voice. "We're in the light now. Let us stay there."

Hod winced, his whole body going rigid. A sharper agony wrenched through me. I was supposed to be here to keep the peace, to bring joy, not lose my temper when he was obviously only trying to help, as unwanted as that help was.

"Baldur," he said roughly.

I touched his arm before he could go on, summoning all the warmth and light I had in me. Letting it wash over those prickling reminders of the past and melt them away. I might have said it badly, but what I'd said to him was true. We had to focus on what we had now, where we were, and all that was good about it.

"There's nothing to apologize for," I said, "because there's nothing to forgive. We had our roles to play, and we did, and everything happened as it was supposed to happen. I promise you, I don't bear a single shred of resentment." That much, at least, was also true. "Let's think about what's ahead of us, not what's behind."

Hod paused and then nodded. "I shouldn't have disturbed you. You're right."

He sat down at the desk. I glanced around at the rows of books ranging from old to new across the shelves, and a quiver of that chill stirred inside me again. "Be peaceful," I said to my brother, and went out to chase a little more peace for myself.

The music room was my surest route. As I headed toward it, the creak of the stairs drew my attention.

Aria was climbing up from below. That discomforting aura still hung around her. My heart squeezed.

I wasn't sure I'd been able to comfort my brother all that much, but I could offer more to our valkyrie. I should, or I'd be failing her too.

I waited for her to reach me. She gave me a questioning look with a raise of her eyebrows. I nodded toward one of the doorways down the hall.

"Would you join me in the music room? I feel that perhaps we could use something to clear our heads for the challenges still ahead of us."

She inhaled sharply, and for a second I thought she was going to refuse. Then she shrugged. "Sure," she said. "It definitely can't hurt."

She trailed behind me into the room. Simply stepping inside sent a wash of calm through me. I breathed in the scents of fine wood and polished metal, and everything inside me stilled.

Yes, this was what I needed. I couldn't ease the chaos going on around us unless my own spirit was easy. And if I could make Aria's spirit rest easier too, then at least I'd have accomplished something fruitful today.

Aria cocked her head as she considered the rows of instruments. "I don't know how to play anything. I don't even know that I'm *that* great a singer, but if you really want the company…"

"You enjoy it, don't you?" I said. I'd felt the pleasure of it in her when she'd sung briefly along with my viola the other day. "That matters more than skill."

She snorted. "I guess that depends on who's listening. But okay. I don't know if we know many of the same songs, though. How up are you on the latest pop charts?"

I chuckled. Just talking with her was already setting me more at ease, before I'd even picked up an instrument. She always seemed so… impervious.

"Not the most recent ones, perhaps," I said. "But I am intrigued by current music as much as by the classics. I may just be a few decades out of date still. Whenever we travel down to Midgard, I've always got a lot of catching up to do."

"A few decades. Let's see. Why don't you tell me what music *you* like from the most modern eras you've caught up to, and we'll figure out where I can fit in."

I considered my most recent dabbling. "I have become rather fond of Liza Wang and Ahmed Rushdi, but I suppose English songs are a better bet?" Her puzzled look was enough of an answer. "I have found much to appreciate in the works of Elvis Presley, and Stevie Wonder, and The Beatles."

Aria laughed. "Seriously? All right. I can work with that." She cracked her knuckles. "I had at least three music teachers in school who were Beatles maniacs. Let's medley that up. Do you know 'Ob la di, ob la da'?"

I picked the acoustic guitar off the wall. "Well enough to manage the tune."

A glow came into Aria's face as we launched into the song, matching the glow that spread through my chest as my hands moved over the strings. There was something so pure and joyful about calling forth a beautiful melody from such a simple object. If she didn't hit every note perfectly, it didn't matter. Her voice wove through the sounds of the guitar from that song into "Can't Buy Me Love" and "Hard Day's Night."

I started picking songs somewhat at random, just to see where we could match. If she didn't pick up the thread partway through the first verse, I simply switched again. Aria grinned, caught up in the challenge.

Without thinking about it, I shifted from the more energetic songs into softer tunes. My thumb strummed the opening chords to "You've Got To Hide Your Love Away," and Aria's mouth twisted.

Her voice spilled out as sweet as before, but lower, with a slight tremble as she reached the chorus. No, this exercise had gone in completely the wrong direction.

I stilled my hand against the strings, and her voice faded out. She shook her head, running her fingers back through the messy waves of her hair.

"Sorry, we can try again."

"You were fine," I said. "You were great." Perhaps right now I needed to take a direct approach. The subtle one clearly hadn't worked well enough. "Whatever's wrong, Aria, you're with us now. We have hundreds of years of experience tackling whatever the realms throw at us. We'll see this through. It'll be all right."

She looked at me from behind her hand. "You can't know that," she said. "You don't even know what's bothering me. What if it isn't all right? Not every problem gets fixed, you know."

"Then you set those concerns aside and find other things to take joy in," I said. "Why dwell on what you can't change?"

"Because you don't know whether you can or not?" she said with a swing of her arm. "Anyway, it's not as if you can just ignore everything that makes you upset, bury it forever."

I blinked at her. That was the only thing you *could* do, often enough. "Why not?"

"Because… because it's still there. And you'd know it's still there, even if you're not letting yourself think about it. Even if you're distracting yourself and acting like there's only the good stuff. I've tried it. It never works for very long."

Something tightened around my chest, not exactly painful but not comforting either. The comment that tumbled out wasn't one I might have said otherwise. "If you bury it deep enough, it can be gone for centuries."

Her gaze focused on me. I made myself look back at her, even though the sensation inside me had tightened even more. "It's not really gone in that case, though, is it?" she said quietly.

"It may as well be," I said. "If it never comes back up. In which case, what does it matter, if everyone's happier that way?"

"I guess I'm just not that good at burying things."

I set down the guitar beside my stool and stood up. "Then let me help you."

She held herself in place as I stepped closer to her. I raised my hands to either side of her face, just barely grazing her cheeks with my knuckles. She could sense my surface emotions just as I could sense hers. I thought of the last few days, of everything I'd seen of her, and let admiration flow from me to her.

"You found us a way back to the Allfather," I said. "You've fought for yourself and for the rest of us. You have wings to soar on and strength no mortal can match."

The corner of her lips quirked up. "I've nearly gotten myself killed twice," she said wryly. "I *did* get myself killed a couple days before that. I'm sneaky and selfish when I need to be, and if you'd met me before I became a valkyrie, you wouldn't have been complimenting me at all."

"I don't know about that," I said. "But you are a valkyrie now, even if you've been sneaky, even if you've been selfish. Because of that, really, since Loki was doing the picking. It's part of your strength."

"Right. One off-key mortal note in a symphony of godliness."

The metaphor brought a smile to my face. None of my godly companions would have made that comparison. She fit here more than she realized—more than maybe I'd realized until just now. She was a part of our harmony, twining through all our disparate melodies. I wouldn't have wanted to let that go, no matter how many other emotions she stirred up in me that I might have wished to keep buried deeper.

I opened my mouth to tell her at least part of that, and her gaze twitched away from me. Her brow furrowed.

"Aria?" I said.

"There's something—" She cut herself off, her eyes going even more distant. Her attention had shifted to something beyond this room, something I couldn't detect. In some ways, her valkyrie senses were sharper than mine.

She glanced at me briefly. "Thank you," she said. "For trying. There's something I just need to—to check." Without another word, she slipped out of the room.

# 21

*Aria*

For the first minute after I left the music room and crept down through the house, I started to think I'd imagined hearing… whatever I'd even heard. The noise had been so faint, right at the edges of what my newly honed ears could pick up—but something about it had pricked at the hairs on the back of my neck. That seemed worth investigating even if I couldn't explain why.

There it was again. I froze on the bottom step, straining my ears. The sound was barely a whisper. A shiver passed through me anyway. I needed to find it—to find out what it meant.

Loki, Thor, and Freya were still chatting in the dining room around the computer. I assumed Hod was off in his study again, his favorite spot to hole up. No one came after me when I eased open the front door. Either they were too occupied to notice me leaving, or at this point they all trusted me to at least come back.

I palmed my switchblade and flicked it open, scanning the lawn. Nothing looked out of the ordinary. If the sound had really been all that threatening, Loki at least should have noticed, right?

His senses had to be even more finely tuned than mine. He was the one who'd given me that power.

I wavered, debating whether I should go ahead on my own or get back-up first, and the breeze carried the sound to me a little more clearly. It was laughter. Childish laughter from somewhere distant.

It sounded almost like *Petey*.

My shoulders tensed. That didn't make any sense. No one except the gods even knew I was here, and none of them except Hod knew Petey existed. As gentle as he'd been with me in the end last night, I didn't for a second believe the god of darkness would have brought my brother out here for a surprise visit.

I stalked across the trimmed grass through the warming mid-morning sunlight. How far away could this kid be? I skirted a couple of the trees at the edges of the main property and veered off the path when the laughter reached me again, still faint, but getting louder. I was closer.

I'd walked another few minutes when something stirred in the shadow of an old elm tree on the other side of the overgrown field I'd just reached. The laughter spilled out from there. It sounded even more familiar now. Nerves twitching, I pushed on, the long grass hissing against my pants. The plastic handle of my switchblade was dampening with sweat against my palm. But if it was a kid, I didn't want to hurt him.

"Who's there?" I called out. "Over by the tree. Can you move where I can see you?"

I was about ten steps away when the figure sidled to the edge of the shadow. Not right into the light, but close enough that I could see her features. Lank black hair, sallow skin, eerily pale eyes. A dark elf.

My legs locked. My head whipped around, but I didn't see any others of her kind nearby.

"What do you want?" I said. Was there any chance this one actually wanted to help us?

The crooked grin she gave me turned that possibility into dust. She opened her mouth and let out another peal of that laughter. Bright and high like a little boy's. The hairs on my neck stood straight up.

It *was* Petey's laugh. She was imitating it somehow, note for note.

"Ari," she said, in Petey's voice. "You wouldn't let anything bad happen to me, would you?"

My knife hand shot up, but I held myself still, as much as I wanted to charge at her.

"What did you do to him? What the fuck is this about?"

The dark elf ducked her head almost bashfully. When she spoke again, it was in a dull rasp of a voice that sounded nothing like my little brother at all.

"We haven't done anything to him... yet. If you want him to stay safe, you'll leave us alone."

I stared at her. My mind was still struggling to catch up through my initial burst of panicked anger.

How had they even figured out about Petey? Had they gotten lucky, just happened to see me head out there last night? It wasn't as if any of them could have followed me, keeping up with my wings on those stumpy little legs.

But it didn't really matter, did it? They did know, and they'd gotten close enough to him to learn the sound of his voice. They'd been willing to attack gods, to target the homeless and school children... I didn't for a second believe they'd hesitate to hurt Petey if they thought it would get them what they wanted.

"Okay," I said. "Fine. You do whatever the hell you want, and I won't say boo. Just stay away from my brother."

She held my gaze with her unearthly eyes. "You're the one who needs to stay away. Stay away from the gods you've been helping.

Don't say a word of this or anything else about us to them. Go, now, and don't come back."

"*What*?" I sputtered.

She folded her arms over her chest. "We're watching. We'll know. If you set foot near that house or the gods in it again…" She bared her teeth. Jagged teeth like splintered rock.

My heart thumped. Leave the gods. It was because of them I was still around at all, not to mention I had them to thank for my powers… but I'd always intended to leave, however I could, when they'd found Odin. I was staying here on Midgard, end of story.

Bowing to her threat felt different, though. Like running away with my tail between my legs. I didn't fight battles I didn't think I could win, but I wasn't a coward either.

I didn't have much choice, did I? I'd thought it myself just yesterday: Petey came before everyone else. The dark elves could be tearing down the whole rest of the world, and it was Petey I had to protect first. I'd promised him. Just yesterday, with that trusting little face gazing up at me…

That jab of guilt in my gut—I had to bury it, for him. Bury it way deep down like Baldur had said. Bury myself way deep down where the gods couldn't or at least wouldn't be bothered to track me down.

They didn't really need me now anyway, did they? I'd pointed them at Odin's kidnappers. That was all they'd really expected of their shady valkyrie. They'd kept trying to get me to stay back at the house. Even they couldn't claim I was letting them down somehow.

The memory of yesterday's battle flashed behind my eyes. The darkness churning inside me, the lives it had sucked away. The exhilaration in those moments…

My chest clenched tight. One more thing to bury. For Petey. Everything, always for Petey.

"All right," I said. "I'm going. Don't you dare even touch him, or you'd better believe you'll regret it." I flipped the switchblade back into its handle with a little more force than was necessary.

The dark elf didn't look intimidated. She just watched me with those peeled grape eyes as I unfurled the wings from my back. I shoved off the ground, away from her, away from the gods' house.

I had to be fast, this first stretch. I didn't know how far their senses could follow me with that faint connection between us. Once I had enough distance, I could go to Petey…

My wings kept beating at the air in a swift steady rhythm, but the bottom of my stomach dropped out.

I couldn't go to Petey. That was the first place Hod would look for me, whether he could sense me or not. The dark elves weren't going to care whether I *wanted* the gods coming to me or not. They'd just see that I was talking with them again.

I propelled myself through the air even faster, the landscape below me blurring, the wind stinging my eyes. Just go. Far, far away, where they'd never think to look. Bury myself for real. Until it didn't matter anymore, until they'd won their way back to Asgard and everything in my life could go back to being—well, as normal as it could be.

---

The last of the fading sunlight burned the sky orange-brown along the horizon. The ache spreading through my wings dug a little deeper. Each flap felt more ragged.

I'd been flying for hours. I had no idea where I even was anymore, other than I'd left New York and Philly far behind. No gods had caught up with me, so I guessed I'd done all right. But my wings were about ready to collapse. It was time to come to earth.

A hum of human energy called to me from just up ahead, where city lights gleamed. The pulse of all those living bodies breathing, eating, dancing…

Yes. That's what I wanted. That was the perfect way to bury the hollow that had been spreading through my abdomen since I'd set off on this flight. One night of just pretending to be the girl I'd been a couple weeks ago—or someone even more free than her.

I dipped lower and lower as I skimmed over the suburbs and into the city proper. My feet touched the sidewalk beneath a sign lit with neon lights, and my wings folded into my back with a sound like a sigh. I walked straight into the club.

Inside, the warm air washed over me with the tang of alcohol. Strobe lights rippled over the crowd of undulating bodies. I snatched a shot off the tray of a server weaving past me and threw it back in one gulp. The sour liquid seared down my throat.

The server looked around, trying to see who'd snatched the glass. It looked like I'd be drinking free this one night. A smile stretched across my face with the tingling buzz of the alcohol. I lifted another glass and leapt on into the crowd.

The bodies parted in my wake like they never had when I'd just been another solid form in the sea. I spun and bobbed in time with the pounding music. My hair whipped against my face; my arms swayed in the air.

One song bled into another and then another. My wings had been tired, but the rest of me was ready to let loose. I grabbed a third shot, which was strong enough that it made me wince on the way down, and threw myself harder into the music. By my fourth, my head was starting to fizz. That was good. A fizzing head couldn't think about all the assorted people I'd left behind.

It wasn't quite the same, dancing like this. I liked not having to worry about some random dude grinding up against me, but at the same time, I missed the actual feeling of contact. Knocking elbows accidentally. Brushing past my fellow human beings to make room. Knowing I was there, part of the crowd, one of them.

But I wasn't one of them. Not anymore. I never would be again.

All right! Time for another shot. I snatched up a blue one this time and drained it. The glass slipped from my fingers and shattered on the floor. I stared at it for a moment, and then I stomped on the shards, letting their crinkling sound blend into the music.

I whirled one way and shimmied another, my fellow dancers shifting away whenever I came near them. The pulse in my head was almost as loud as the music. I swayed and spun—and faltered when my gaze caught on a tall lean figure slinking through the sea of bodies, straight toward me. As if he knew exactly where I was.

Because he did. The multicolored lights dappled Loki's pale red hair and paler skin. He raised an eyebrow as he reached me, his lips forming their usual sly grin.

# 22

*Aria*

Loki didn't say anything at first. He moved with the music, with a grace that shouldn't have surprised me but did here in the midst of all those mortals, sidling closer to me and then easing a little farther away. That eyebrow stayed arched as if challenging me to keep up with him.

I started to dance again in defiance of the heavy thump in my chest. Stepping even faster, whirling even tighter, hitting every beat as if I knew them by heart. Loki matched me move for move, every motion so fluid it was hard to tear my gaze away. I wanted to reach up and run my hands up the lean muscles I could see beneath his tunic, the way I might have in a different club on a different day, if a regular guy I liked the look of that much had looked at me that way.

Loki's eyes never left mine, flickering with their amber light even here. He eased closer, setting a cautious hand on my waist as we dipped together. A flush spread over my skin at the contact. He bent his head close beside mine—close enough that suddenly I couldn't smell anything except the hot spicy-sweet smell of his body, ginger and cardamom and a dash of honey. Good enough to eat.

"If you wanted to dance, there wasn't need to cross half the country, pixie," he said by my ear. "I can even vouch for a few of the clubs right by us in Manhattan."

"Maybe I wanted a bigger change of scenery," I said.

"Hmm. I almost feel as if you were trying to escape *us*. But why could you possibly want to do that?"

A jolt of panic broke through the haze in my head. The dark elves. Would they see us even here? Would they punish me for being found?

My body went still. I pulled back far enough to meet his gaze. "Could anyone know you're here? Not just these people." I waved my hand toward the crowd. "Dark elves, or—or whatever."

Loki had stopped when I had. He stayed close, his hand still resting on my side. His eyes narrowed. "No one, human or dirt-eater or otherwise, could have followed me. What happened, Ari? Why did you run?"

My throat tightened. But I had to tell him now, didn't I? He'd found me. I didn't have any excuse I could make up that I was sure would be good enough to get him to leave without me.

"A dark elf came by the house," I said, as steadily as I could manage. "I have a little brother back in Philly. They figured that out somehow. She said they'd hurt him—kill him—if I helped you at all again. She said they'd be watching to make sure I didn't even go anywhere near you."

Loki's jaw tightened. "Petey," he said, and then at my expression, "Hod told us about your little trips when we realized you'd disappeared. He went out there to look for you. You don't have to worry about that, pixie. When I don't want to be seen, I'm not seen. Although at the time it was mostly you I didn't want to tip off."

A little of the pressure inside me eased off. My buzz crept back in, relaxing me just enough for curiosity to take hold. "How did you find me?" I asked.

He shrugged as if it'd been no big thing. "Instinct. We all called you to us when we summoned you, but I was the one who found you that first time. I know you down to the quiver of your spirit." His lips curled up. "You could almost say we're soulmates, if you believe in that sort of garbage."

I couldn't help rolling my eyes at him, despite the wash of deeper heat those words sent through me. "The one of a gazillion soulmates who happened to die at just the right time?"

His smile turned sharper. "There, you see. You understand me exactly. Although a 'gazillion' may be a slight exaggeration."

He leaned in again, his breath grazing my cheek, and my heart skipped a beat. The throng was still dancing away all around us, but I didn't care about anything outside this little pocket of space that held him and me and the question hanging over us.

"Now that I've found you," he murmured, "how do I convince you to come back?"

"Do you need to convince me?" I asked with more bravado than I felt. "I'm surprised you haven't already thrown me over your shoulder and carted me off."

He chuckled. "Come on now. You should be able to tell that's not my style. Just be glad it wasn't Thor who tracked you down."

"I can't go back," I said. "Not while the dark elves are watching Petey."

"I can make sure they never know you're with us," Loki said. "I'm not known as the master of disguise for nothing. You—and he—would be safe in my hands."

I made a skeptical sound. He touched my cheek with his other hand, easing back. His eyes searched mine. "I know how much you must care about him. I can see it. I've been there. Odin isn't even my brother by birth, but I gave up so much for his damned—" He cut himself off with a little shake of his head. "If there's one thing you believe, believe that we'll protect your brother. May I never return to Asgard if I'm lying."

His last words carried a crackle of energy as if they'd magically bound him to that oath. I hesitated, wanting to believe him, and yet…

"It's safer if I don't go back at all. You don't even need me. What does it matter where I am?"

"You're our valkyrie," Loki said. "You're our responsibility. And we might not *need* you at this exact moment, but you can hardly deny you've helped."

The memories I'd tried to bury stirred in the back of my head. Baldur was wrong. It wasn't that simple to get away from them.

"By killing people," I said.

"Well, I'd hardly call dark elves *people*, but…" Loki cocked his head. "Is that what's bothering you? You were only trying to make sure they didn't kill us."

I wet my lips. The hollow sensation in my gut came back, so deep and empty even the music pounding around us couldn't touch it. A truth I had managed to bury, so far I hadn't even known it was there, tickled up into my head.

"It isn't just them I've wanted to kill. I don't know if Hod told you everything—if he told you that he had to stop me from going after my mom's boyfriend last night."

"Because he'd hurt your brother."

So, Hod had spilled the beans about that too. I nodded. "I would have done it. Even if he'd been lying there helpless and asleep… I think I would have *liked* doing it. It felt almost *good*, taking life from those dark elves."

Loki brushed his fingers over my hair. The tender gesture wrenched at my heart. I wanted to lean into it, and at the same time I wanted to pull away, because he couldn't mean it. He shouldn't mean it, not for me.

"Ari, you're a valkyrie now," he said. "You're meant to dispense justice by shifting the tide of war."

"That doesn't mean I should have *fun* with it," I blurted out, my buzz loosening my tongue. "There've been so many times, so many people I might have wanted to get out of my way, when I never could— What if it's not just to turn the tide that I'll want to do it?" I swallowed hard. "Maybe someone like me isn't meant to have that kind of power. Maybe there's a good reason all those valkyries Odin used to summon were pure of heart and whatever."

Loki shook his head, his smile somehow grim and amused at the same time. "You know who you're talking to, don't you? Hello, I once orchestrated the end of the world. You're not going to convince me that you're somehow such a wretched soul you don't deserve the gifts you've received."

"That—that's different," I said, but my protest sounded weak even to me.

Loki leaned close again, his face just a hair's breadth from mine, bringing that spicy sweet scent with him. For a second, I thought he was going to kiss me. My pulse stuttered way too eagerly.

But he just spoke, the air from his lips moving against my cheek. "It should be comforting, pixie. No matter how bad you are, no matter how bad you get, you can never be the worst there is. I've already got that title in the bag."

His tone was light, flippant even, but a splinter of pain echoed from him into me at the same moment. The trickster god cared so much more than he liked to admit. Somehow that tugged at me even more than the closeness of his lips.

"Come back with me," he went on. "Come back with me and smash those bastard cave-dwellers right out of your realm. We won't let them lay one finger on your brother. Take all that darkness in you and rain it down on them."

I shivered. The words resonated more deeply than *I* liked to admit. My hands clenched. My tongue slipped away from me again.

"I'm scared," I said, so quietly I wasn't sure he'd even hear me. I wasn't sure I wanted him to. "I'm scared of myself, like this—of what I could do." To anyone, whether they deserved it or not. Of having to decide whether they did deserve it.

Of everything that came with being a fucking valkyrie, really.

"Good," Loki said, his voice nothing but warmth now. "*That*, not any 'goodness of heart,' is what makes the difference between you and someone unworthy. And think about it, Ari. If you're afraid, imagine how afraid the dark elves must be of you and what you can do, to make a threat like they did."

He sounded almost awed with that last remark. He saw me, he saw every dark place in me, and he was *awed.*

I was still a little dizzy with the shots I'd inhaled, and the warmth and the awe wrapped around me with an urge I couldn't quite bring myself to deny. I grasped the front of Loki's shirt with both hands and tipped my head that last tiny distance to catch his mouth with mine.

The god drew in a startled breath, and then he was kissing me back, hard and hungry. His thumb traced an arcing line across my side. Everywhere our bodies touched, heat tingled through my nerves as if he'd literally set me on fire. But what an intoxicating fire it was.

I let myself sink into him, into the hot heady sensation of his lips meeting mine, where nothing else mattered just for a moment. If he was going to give, then I'd take everything I could get.

He kissed me again, and the electricity of it set me alight like a sparkler. A whimper crept from my throat when his mouth trailed away from mine, charting a scorching path along my jaw.

"Tell me you'll come back," he murmured beside my ear. "I'm not going to drag you. I want you to want to. We can make those bastards pay, Ari."

Yes, yes, yes. Fuck it. Who was I to argue with a god? My grip on his shirt tightened.

"I'll come," I said. "But first, I want to dance."

He chuckled and nipped my earlobe, already swaying with the beat of the music. The swivel of his hips by mine sent a fresh wave of fire through me. I gave myself over to it. If I burned, then I fucking burned.

---

Only the thinnest of dawn light was drifting through my bedroom window. I blinked at it blearily and rubbed my eyes.

My bedroom window—my bedroom in the gods' house. A now-familiar sheet was pulled up to my shoulders; my head rested on the downy pillow. A faint ache nibbled at my temple, but it wasn't that bad, really, considering how many shots I'd done in fairly quick succession. Six of them: five before Loki had shown up at the club and one after we'd started dancing again, before we'd gone back to kissing…

My heart flipped over. That was the last thing I remembered: his lips searing against mine. Had I—had *we*—?

I shifted under the sheet and felt the fabric of my clothes shift with me. The same clothes I'd been wearing last night: one of those racerback tanks and jeans. Nothing seemed out of place.

A strange mix of relief and disappointment came over me. I really preferred to be fully conscious when I got it on with anyone. And my first time with a *god*? Yeah, I'd like to remember that.

But I'd wanted him, I'd pretty much thrown myself at him, and clearly he hadn't wanted me quite as much.

Well, what had I expected? He *was* a god.

I sat up, kicking back the sheet, and the door eased open. Loki slipped inside, shut the door behind him, and ambled over to perch on the edge of the bed. His amber eyes gleamed in the faint light. Somehow that was enough to make me lose my breath.

Damn, I definitely needed to get laid somehow or other sometime soon, or I was going to turn into a total imbecile.

"Sleep well?" he asked.

"It seems that way." My gaze darted back toward the window. "Did you make sure no one could see me coming back with you?"

"The day a dark elf can see through one of my illusions is the day I curl up and die of shame," Loki said. "And I spoke to Hod while you were sleeping. He checked on your brother while he was looking for you. The boy hasn't been harmed. Hod headed back out there to keep watch for the dark elves—well, 'watching' in a metaphorical sense, at least."

I let out my breath. "I'm sure he appreciated that order," I said sarcastically.

"I didn't order him, actually, as much as I might have enjoyed doing so. He volunteered."

A pang of startled gratitude shot through me. The god of darkness had been kind enough after I'd dragged him out there the other night, but I wouldn't have expected him to go out of his way for me. Hod must have cared even more than he'd let show.

I swallowed my surprise and looked up at Loki. It figured that even first thing in the morning after running all over the country, he still looked brightly magnificent. I had to stop noticing that.

"Well, I'm back here now. I still don't know what exactly you think I'm going to do now that I'm here that'll be so helpful."

Loki smiled. "Oh, I'm sure we'll find some way to keep you busy."

His tone was jaunty, but his eyes were searching, as if he were waiting for something from me he hadn't gotten yet. I groped for the right words.

"About last night..."

"It was quite a night," he offered, his smile stretching a little farther, when I faltered.

Just spit it out, Ari. My hands balled in the sheets. "I don't actually remember the trip home, but obviously I slept alone." A question without actually asking the question.

"Yes," Loki said. "Well. In my experience across the ages, drunks make lousy bed partners."

My back tensed. A flood of heat that wasn't at all pleasant coursed through my cheeks. "I'm sorry for making a pass, then. You don't have to worry about it happening again."

"Ari." Loki sighed and motioned to me. "Come here?"

My body balked, but the unexpected earnestness in those amber eyes melted some of my defenses. I scooted a little closer. Loki glanced at the foot of space I'd left between us with a faintly amused expression and then raised his head to meet my gaze.

"I regret that you were drunk," he said. "I don't regret anything about you being you. Make all the passes you want. Just make them while sober is all I'm asking. I have self-restraint, but I can't say I enjoy employing it all that much."

Oh. *Oh*. The heat that had surfaced in my face seeped down through the rest of my body, pooling low in my belly. The words tumbled out. "I'm sober now."

Loki grinned in that way that turned my whole body into a knot of want. "Yes, you do appear to be."

I shifted closer to him, my hand brushing his thigh. He touched my cheek and teased his fingers into my hair. My breath caught.

"This could still be a bad idea," I felt the need to point out.

Loki's smile widened. "My favorite kind."

And then our mouths collided.

I hadn't imagined the heat of his kisses in the club. That hot tingling spread through my nerves again, licking through every part of my body. The trickster god parted my lips with a skillful flick of his tongue that sent a bolt of need through me.

I pressed closer to him as our tongues twined, straddling his lap. Loki eased me into place with an encouraging sound and a hand on my hip. I arched against him. My breath stuttered at the feel of him hard beneath the fly of his slacks, aligned perfectly with my core. I wanted to do so much more than kiss this time.

Loki slid his hands up under my tank top, spreading that fiery tingling in their wake. His lips broke from mine just long enough to yank the top off of me. Then our mouths locked together again, trading air and heat as he made quick work of my bra.

He cupped my breasts, swiveling his palms to draw my nipples tighter with a shiver of the hottest of sparks. I moaned into his mouth. His slender fingers teased over the peaks and under the swell of them as if exploring every curve.

His lips and tongue teased over my jaw and down my neck. I wrenched at his tunic, and he helped me tug it off. We pressed together skin to skin, wave after wave of divine fiery warmth washing through me as he grazed his teeth against my throat. I ran my hands over the lean muscles I'd only caught a hint of before, firm and smooth and rippling at my touch.

With a slight heave, Loki tipped us over on the bed, his hips still between my legs. His weight shifted against me, and a spark of emotion that was more panic than pleasure shot through my chest. My pulse lurched.

Clamping down on that reaction, I gave his shoulder a light shove. When he eased back, I shoved again, harder. He let me flip him over with a flash of a grin before he reclaimed my mouth.

I rocked against him, able to lose myself in sensation now that I was on top and at least that little bit in control. My sex pressed against the bulge of his erection, and he groaned, kissing me even harder.

"Ari," he murmured, nipping my lower lip. Almost pleading. As if he wanted this even more than I did. He gripped my hips, bucking to meet me, and I moaned too.

I fumbled with his fly and yanked at his slacks. Apparently gods wore boxers. I tugged those down too, and his cock sprang free. Tall and slender like the man, and so hard it was fucking glorious. I licked my lips without thinking. My throat tightened—I didn't do blow jobs, there was no way that would end well—but I almost wanted to try, seeing him.

I settled for stroking the silky skin of his erection as I unzipped my jeans. Loki pushed himself up on one elbow and drew my mouth back to his. We kissed between pants for breath, getting sloppier by the moment. When I'd kicked my jeans aside, he slid his hand down my body to dip between my legs.

His fingers glided over my damp panties, and bliss flared even hotter through my core. My grip on his cock tightened. Loki gave another groan. His fingers leapt up to hook around the side of my panties. With one swift jerk, the fabric snapped.

Fuck me. I rubbed myself against his cock, my clit quivering. A whimper slipped out of me as he dipped his index finger right inside me. Our kisses were outright frantic now. But I hadn't lost my head completely.

"Do we need—" I started, and gave a rough laugh at the absurdity of the question. "Can valkyries get pregnant?"

Loki matched my laugh with a breathless chuckle of his own. "Not without a whole 'nother level of magic, pixie. You're safe from bearing any shifty trickster babies."

"In that case…"

I eased the head of his cock right down to my slit. He slid his fingers out to clutch my thigh as I lowered myself onto him. With a little arch of his hips, he filled me all the way. The head of his cock hit just the right place inside me to leave me trembling with desire.

We set a rhythm that was almost frenzied, me riding him and him rising to meet me, every pulse like a shot of blissful fire through my veins. His hands were everywhere, tracing flames everywhere they touched: caressing my breasts, stroking my ribs, angling my hips so I could take him even deeper.

Blazing pleasure spiraled up from my core through my chest. I tipped my head back, pumping harder, chasing my release. His thumb teased across my clit, over and over, and then pressed harder. And I exploded.

The flare of ecstasy rocked my body and seared through my vision. I shuddered over Loki with a cry. He kept his hand on my clit, pounding into me with a shaky sigh, and I came all over again alongside the hot gush of his release. In that instant, my body was nothing but heat and pleasure, and I believed I could burn my way through anything—and anyone.

# 23

*Aria*

We sprawled on the bed, Loki on his back and me tucked against him, his thumb stroking idly up and down my back. Just when I was wondering if that was it, if he'd gotten what he'd come for and was done now, he dipped his head to seek out my lips. The kiss wasn't as desperate as the ones before, but it still sent a lick of fire through me.

Maybe I'd better be clear about *my* expectations here.

I took a moment to catch my breath and then said, "Just so you know, I'm not looking for any kind of—I don't know—commitment or anything like that. I don't really do that anyway."

Loki guffawed and tickled the top of my head with a gentle sweep of his fingers. "So, what you're saying is, hold off on any professions of undying love?"

My gaze jerked up. "Were you planning on making one?"

His lips had curled with amusement. "That's not really my style either, pixie. I have, as you mortals put it, 'gotten around,' even more than the myths would indicate. I'm not going to assume I own you just because we enjoyed each other's company. You go chasing whoever else you take a mind to chase." His eyebrow lifted. "Perhaps I could even join you with another conquest sometime."

Two guys at the same time? Two *gods*? Because that was what my mind shot straight to: Thor's strong hands, Baldur's gentle touch, Hod's intense presence. I'd never tried a threesome before—it was a whole lot easier feeling in control with only one partner to keep track of—but the idea felt suddenly appealing. Maybe because one of those partners would potentially be the smoking hot god lying right next to me.

"Have you done that before?" I asked.

Loki waved his hand breezily. "I've done just about everything." He fell silent for a moment and then started grazing his fingertips over my hair again. "Although to tell you the truth, I haven't done much of anything in a while. It all got rather mundane. I'd forgotten how stimulating it can feel, being with someone who can keep me on my toes."

"Stimulating, huh?" I muttered.

"Were you not stimulated?" he teased. His tone turned a little more serious. "I'd never rein you in, Ari. I mean that. But just so you know where I stand, I do also hope we enjoy ourselves like this again."

"Hmm," I said noncommittally. The truth was that just the fleeting touch of his hand against my head, the warmth of his body aligned with mine, was enough that I was tempted to jump him again right now. But I wasn't sure admitting that was such a great idea. Loki was "stimulating" as fuck, but he was also a trickster through and through. There were reasons I'd tried to ignore my attraction.

We were here now though, so it seemed reasonably safe to tuck my head under his chin and drink in the spicy-sweet smell of his skin. A quiver of his living energy ran under it, that faint pulsing my valkyrie senses were finely tuned to.

Just like the other gods, his energy was brighter than any human or elf I'd run into. Bright and intense—but oddly not quite as warm as what I'd felt from all the others. When I focused on it, I could feel a sharp cool tang amid the brightness. More like bronze than gold. I frowned.

"You've gone pensive, pixie," Loki said. "What's on your mind?"

"Your… life essence or whatever. The other gods feel pretty much the same, but yours is a little different. I guess it's because they're all brothers?"

His hand stilled against my hair. Just for a second, but long enough that I knew not to believe his casual tone when he answered.

"No, it'd be because I'm not a god."

I pulled back to stare at him. "Ha ha, very funny."

No," he said smoothly. "It's true. You obviously aren't up on your mythology at all. Thor and Baldur and Hod are all Aesir, the rightful inhabitants of Asgard. I'm an interloping giant who just managed to make good with the guy in charge. Of course, I'm perfectly happy to accept the title of god when people feel like offering it."

"Oh." I guessed that explained a little more why there was that friction between him and the others that I'd noticed from time to time. You'd think they'd have gotten over it after all this time together.

"Are you deeply offended?" Loki asked. "You thought you'd landed a god but it turns out not quite?"

I rolled my eyes. "I don't give a shit what you call yourself. I just didn't realize."

"Good then," he said in that same a-little-too-casual tone. Then a more natural lilt came into his voice. "All different beings have their own sorts of energy. I'd imagine Freya comes across a little differently from the boys' club too—she's Vanir, not Aesir, although search me what separates the two. Humans are another thing altogether. As are valkyries."

He dipped his head, his lips brushing my temple. The fleeting kiss sent a fresh tingling through me, but my mind was already spinning off in another direction. "And dark elves would be something else too," I said.

"Well, yes. I supposed that factor would be helpful if we didn't have to be close to pick up on that energy in the first place."

I pushed myself upright. "I don't have to be close. I'm supposed to be able to home in on the energy of a battle from just about anywhere."

An eager gleam lit in Loki's eyes. "Where are you going with this?"

My heartbeat raced faster. "I don't think I could take in the whole country, let alone the whole world, from here—but I could fly around—I could feel out where there are a bunch of dark elves all in the same place, emerging and disappearing. Like they were coming and going from this realm."

"Through the gate!" Loki scrambled off the bed and threw on his clothes in an impressive display of chaotic grace. "You can rest your wings. I can run through the sky faster than they'll take you anyway. With the amount of activity the cave-dwellers have got going on this side of the ocean, I don't think we'll need to cover the entire world. We can scour the country in an hour."

I grabbed my own clothes. My excitement mingled with trepidation. What if it didn't work, and I sent him running all over the place for nothing?

But this was what I'd come back for. I'd come back to try. And also possibly for super-hot not-quite-a-god sex.

"You going to carry me around?" I said, pulling on my

borrowed linen pants. I really needed to find myself some new jeans.

"This isn't the time to worry about your dignity," the trickster said. "We can make it a piggyback ride. Come on. If we're quick, we can be back with good news before the rest of these slugs even go down for breakfast."

I hurried after him to the dormer window. My legs balked as he pushed it open. "If the dark elves see me…"

He beckoned me after him. "The illusion I put on you will stick until I take it off. No one will notice you're with me unless I let them."

"Okay, okay." I clambered out after him. He scooped me up and settled me against his back exactly like he'd said, piggyback style. I draped my arms across his shoulders and braced my knees against his waist, and he sprang out into the air.

This was how he'd caught up with me at that club so quickly, I realized as he darted higher toward the sky. He hadn't been right behind me; he'd just been able to cross that distance so much faster than I had.

In the space of a couple of breaths, he'd already strode high enough up that the entire state sprawled beneath us. On our earlier travels, he must have held back so the rest of us could keep up.

"Anything around here?" he asked.

"First I have to figure out what I'm even looking for," I said. I'd been too busy avoiding getting killed by the dark elves—or worrying about getting Petey killed—to have paid much attention to the unique qualities of their energy. But as I breathed in, dragging up those memories, I found I could almost taste it anyway. Slower in its pulsing and a little thicker than human energy, slightly oily. I grimaced and cast out my senses.

Life thrummed all across the landscape below: scraps of it in the smaller towns, a boisterous burst from New York City up ahead, and everything in between. I caught a hint of that oilier energy here and there, but when I trained my focus on it, it either faded into the mass of human life or gave me the impression of nothing more than one or two figures. No larger fluctuations.

"I don't think the gate's here," I said.

"Then onward!"

Loki raced forward through the sky, miles falling away behind us with each stride. We fell into a pattern: He paused, I reached out my senses, we moved on. Sometimes I didn't sense any dark elves at all; others there were only a few, like before. My hopes started to sink. Maybe they'd found some way to disguise their presence from my valkyrie awareness.

Loki stopped yet again, and I opened myself up to the energy humming below us. A town here, a city there, more cities dotted across the hilly landscape—and a patch of oily energy.

I tensed against Loki's back. He touched my calf where it rested against his thigh. "Here?"

"Wait." Just a bunch of dark elves wasn't enough. What mattered was what they were doing.

As I concentrated hard on that patch of lives, three of them winked out, one after the other, as if they'd died. A minute later, five new ones appeared seemingly out of nothingness. A smile stretched across my face.

Not out of nothingness. Out of their passage between their realm and ours.

"There," I said, pointing as I honed my focus even more closely. We were so high up that the cluster of buildings I was pointing at on the side of one of the lonelier hills looked like a tiny blotch.

Loki cackled to himself. "We've got them now."

I laughed too as he spun toward home, relief coursing through me. He'd strode past a few states when his head twitched to the side. "Look who's here."

He glided to a stop. A black feathered shape swooped over to join us. With a shiver of the air, Muninn transformed into her human body, other than two much larger black wings she flapped to keep herself level with us.

"Where are you coming from, Loki?" she asked, looking only at him. "You look awfully pleased. Did you learn something?"

"Only the exact location of the dark elves' gate," Loki said with a grin. "We'll have Odin back by dinnertime."

Her eyes widened. "Where is it?"

"Back hills of Kentucky. I'm about to round up the gang for a closer investigation. I assume you'll join us?"

"Of course," she said.

I adjusted my position against Loki's back, and her gaze never left his face. Understanding hit me. She couldn't even see me. Loki's illusion hid me from her, too.

"I may have a few weapons I can bring to the battle," the raven woman went on with a dark glint in her eyes. "Let me retrieve them and I'll meet up with you as soon as I can."

Loki bobbed his head to her, and she contracted back into her raven form. With a few swift flaps of her wings, she'd soared away from us.

As Loki set off again, an uneasy sensation settled in my gut. "So, we're going straight to that gate—to go through it, to fight the dark elves and get Odin back?" I said.

"That seems the obvious course of action," Loki agreed. "What's the matter, pixie?"

"Your illusion can stop them from seeing me. But if I'm fighting with you, if I'm killing them like a valkyrie—they'll know I'm there."

And then they'd come after Petey like they'd threatened.

"You don't have to make this your fight too," Loki said.

He meant that, just like the others had meant it when they'd said I could hang back before. But it didn't feel like the right answer any more than it had then.

"Even if you get Odin, it's not like you'll have stopped the dark elves from being in Midgard, right?"

"That's true. We can't exactly justify—or carry out—a total extermination. We might be able to banish them from this realm if we can find evidence of their exact crimes, and once we have Odin's powers with us again…"

"But that will take time," I filled in. "Even if they don't know for sure I helped you again, for all I know they'd kill Petey just out of spite."

Loki was silent for a moment. "I won't deny that's possible, Ari," he said.

I let out a pained breath. "Then what am I supposed to do? As long as they know where to find him, they could hurt him whenever they wanted. They might have *already* hurt him for all I know."

"No," Loki said firmly, cutting off my spiral of panic. "Hod is guarding him. He can take on plenty of dark elves himself—and if they'd made an attempt, he'd have sounded the alarm."

Right. I sucked in a breath. I owed the blind god a whole lot of thanks the next time I saw him. But still…

"I can't expect you all to keep protecting Petey forever," I said. "Or even for very much longer. You'll all have to be there to fight the dark elves off at the gate, won't you? And then you'll be going back to Asgard."

"And so will you," Loki said gently, as if I needed the reminder. But even if I could have evaded the gods somehow, convinced them to let me stay here in the human realm, I couldn't protect Petey from the dark elves' vengeance all on my own either. That knowledge sank like a boulder in my gut.

"I can't leave him there," I said. "He'll never really be safe." He never had been, even when it had just been my mom and her revolving door of asshole boyfriends. And I couldn't very well take Petey with me anywhere, could I?

I swallowed hard. Loki touched my leg again as we glided down over the house. "I think you already have your answer. We'll move your brother somewhere the dark elves won't be able to find him. And then you can show those dirt-eaters what a valkyrie's real rage can look like."

# 24

*Hod*

Ari's hair rustled as she bowed her head. Across the street, three sets of footsteps went up the front walk of a house. The sun was warm, baking the shingles of the roof we were perched on, and the breeze brought the bright scent of daffodils from the garden below, but none of that shifted the cool shadow that hung over the valkyrie.

A childish voice carried up to us. "What are we doing here?"

"We're meeting your new family," Baldur said with his calm warmth.

Ari let out a shuddering breath. "Is this really the only way we could have done this?" she said quietly.

I knew she already knew the answer to that. "If I'd left his memories, he would have slipped up. Said something that tipped people off that the story we gave them wasn't right. He could have ended up back with your mother. Even an adult who knows the full gravity of a situation has trouble living a conscious lie."

"Yeah." She drew her legs up in front of her. The feathers of her wings, still spread at her back, fluttered faintly in the breeze. "I always thought someday I'd have a proper job, a house, everything set up so I could challenge Mom for custody and win…"

"You couldn't have given him that, not the way you are now."

"Not as a valkyrie. I know." She exhaled raggedly. "I just keep reminding myself that this is better than if I'd just died and not been here at all to do at least this much for him."

The emotion in those words brought a little ache into my chest. I'd known Ari loved her brother from the first moment she'd talked about him, but love could so often be possessive, even selfish. Instead of clinging to him, she'd given up her place in his life for his own good.

"You're doing the right thing," I said. "You're looking after him the best way you could have. He's lucky he had a sister like you."

Her next breath sounded choked. Her hand whispered across her cheeks. Swiping away tears, I realized. The ache inside me bit deeper. The urge to take her in my arms had been growing in me since the first moment we'd laid out this plan to her, to pull her to me like I hadn't dared to the other night—but I'd been able to tell then that she wouldn't have wanted that. How could I say now was any different? The last thing I wanted was to remind her of the man who'd hurt her.

So I stayed where I was.

The three figures across the street had reached the house's front door. One of them—probably Loki—knocked. A moment later, the door opened.

"Oh," the woman who'd answered it said a little breathlessly. "You're here. Hello. It's so good to meet you."

"May we come in?" Loki said in a voice as smooth as usual but higher pitched. The trickster had transformed himself into a refined lady for this role—supposedly a social worker from the local child services agency. We'd picked out a family waiting for a foster child that had seemed like the best possible fit for Ari's brother, and Loki had doctored all the necessary records. Baldur was coming along as his assistant, to conduct good vibes and ease the transition.

My job, as always, had been spreading the darkness. I'd wiped every identifying memory from the little boy's head. I'd wiped all memory of him from all the minds in the city that held it: the mother who'd left him to be assaulted, the boyfriend who'd done the assaulting, the dark elves who'd been lurking in threat, the teachers and friends who might have asked after him. None of them would think to look for him now.

I couldn't have reached every single dark elf who might have been in on that threat, but we'd whisked him away to a city in Canada where Loki's computer hadn't found any signs of their activity. The chances of them stumbling on him by accident and recognizing him were slim.

He was safe. And he had no idea he'd ever had a sister, let alone one who'd been willing to sacrifice so much for him.

"I'm fine," Ari said abruptly. Her voice didn't sound teary anymore.

"I know you are," I said, because I had the feeling that was what she needed to hear. And I didn't really doubt that she would be fine. She was awfully resilient in all sorts of ways, this valkyrie of ours.

The door to the house opened and closed again. Only two sets of footsteps descended the walk. And then they must have made themselves unperceivable to mortal eyes again, because a moment later Loki had glided up to meet us.

"Everything's in order," he said. "He seemed to warm up to the foster parents right away." There was a murmur of cloth I realized was his hand squeezing Ari's shoulder. "You won this battle, pixie."

She shifted, leaning into his touch. Just for a second, but it was enough to turn the ache in my chest into a sliver of jealousy. When had the two of them gotten so familiar?

"I want to stay a little longer," Ari said. "Then we can go kick those dark elf asses."

Loki chuckled. "We'll go finish preparing for *that* battle."

"Are you coming, brother?" Baldur asked.

I shook my head. "I'll return with the valkyrie."

When they'd left, Ari eased her legs down again and leaned back on her hands with a soft creak of the roof. "You don't have to stay," she said. "I didn't go through all this just to screw it up acting stupid now. I just… want to be near him a little more."

"I'm not worried about you doing anything rash," I said. "Do you *want* to be alone?"

She paused. "No," she admitted. "Not really."

We sat for a stretch in silence. Every slight movement she made sent a reverberation through me. I had to say something more.

"I'm sorry."

Her head jerked around with a hiss of her hair. "For what?"

"For suggesting you were selfish. And for— I've been hard on you since the start. I can admit I misjudged you. Loki made a good choice this once, picking you."

She was quiet so long I thought I might have inadvertently offended her more. Then she said, in a tone that suggested a smile, "Okay. Apology accepted. And it's a good thing you feel that way, because it seems like you all are stuck with me now."

"Is that a bad thing?" I asked.

"No, maybe not. I mean, considering the alternatives… Thank you, for being there for Petey and for making this work."

"I know how much it mattered to you. You haven't really left him alone."

"Yeah." She rubbed her hand across her mouth. "Now that you know all my tragic secrets, do you figure someday you'll tell me your sob story? It seems only fair."

The corner of my mouth twitched up even as my gut twisted. "I don't know. Not right now. Maybe someday."

"Well, whenever you're ready, I'm prepared to rage on your behalf."

I snorted, but the words brought back the earlier ache. I had a feeling she would rage, if I let her. But I hadn't even let myself, not ever.

There was something relieving about knowing I'd have someone who'd shout alongside me if I ever felt the need to, though.

Without letting myself second-guess the moment, I slid my hand across the shingles until my fingers brushed Ari's. I gripped them gently. She didn't pull away.

"Someday," she repeated, and hesitated. "I slept with Loki."

A prickling sensation shot through me from head to toe. My back tensed, but I managed to keep my hold on her hand loose and my voice even. "Why are you telling me?"

"Well, I'm sure you'd have figured it out before very long anyway. And I kind of wondered if it'd matter to you."

"It isn't really my business," I said, wondering how much of my reaction she'd already been able to read. "If you want to be with him that way, I'm not going to judge." Not her, anyway. Him, I could fantasize about strangling a little more often than usual.

She hummed to herself. "The other thing is, it's not just about him. I feel connected to the four of you. I thought maybe it would go away once I scratched that itch… but if anything I feel it more now. With all of you."

"We summoned you," I said, but I didn't think that covered the feelings she was talking about. The truth was, more and more, I'd been sensing something similar. "In a strange way, I think maybe we all needed you. Or someone like you."

"Strange, huh?"

"Well, I mean…" I wasn't sure I could talk my way out of that one. I settled on the truth. "You're not what we thought we needed in a valkyrie. Clearly we were wrong. It's been a long time, just the five of us and Odin when he's between wanderings. I'm not sure that's been good for anyone."

"So, you're glad I blew in here and shook things up?"

"I'd say so."

"Good." She let out a shaky laugh. "You know, I've slept with a fair number of guys in the last five years. But you're the first person I've let myself cry in front of since I was twelve. So… you can decide whether one counts any less than the other."

I turned my head toward her. I couldn't see her, no, but the shape of her couldn't have been any sharper in my mind. The ache spread to the edges of my ribs, but it wasn't exactly painful in that moment.

Perhaps I'd been something she needed, too. Something she still needed.

I raised my hand to touch her cheek. She set her hand over my fingers, squeezing them. Then she tilted her head and pressed a soft kiss to my palm.

My pulse jittered at the bolt of sensation that shot down my arm, and I moved without any more thinking. My fingers slid into the waves of her hair as I pulled her into a real kiss.

It'd been a long time since I'd kissed anyone. Passionate dalliances weren't really my domain. But my mouth seemed to know exactly how to move against Ari's to send a tremor of pleasure through my body and draw a pleased murmur from her throat.

She kissed me back, her hand coming to rest on my neck. The shadows in me stirred in harmony with the dark power contained in her spirit, but she wasn't all dark. Not by a longshot. A brilliance like the sun twined through that darkness, all the warmth and vigor she could bring to bear too. Our dark valkyrie was full of light.

When her mouth slipped away from mine, it was only so she could rest her head on my shoulder. She grasped my hand again, tightly.

"I guess we'd better get going. That battle isn't going to fight itself."

"No, as convenient as that would be."

"The rest… We can figure that all out afterward, right?"

She said it easily, but she tensed a little against me at the same time, as if she was uncertain of my answer. As if the wrong answer would hurt.

I had power here too.

I squeezed her hand back, my voice dropping low. "I'm not going anywhere."

It seemed that was the right answer. Her body relaxed. She pushed herself to her feet and turned toward her brother's new home again.

"Be happy, Petey," she said, and blew a kiss toward the house. Then she spun around.

"Let's fly."

# 25

*Aria*

We came to a stop, hovering a few miles from the town that held the dark elves' gate—if it could even be called a town. I could make out only a few dozen wooden buildings, all of them in pretty bad repair. A couple of roofs were caved in, others sagging. Weeds were sprouting up all through the gravel road.

The short, stout figures of the dark elves moved between the buildings here and there, but I didn't see any people. Couldn't taste anything but that sluggish oily energy the elves gave off.

"I don't think anyone human has lived there for a long time," I said.

"A ghost town," Thor said, smacking his hammer against his palm in anticipation. "As good a place for the gate as any."

"I don't see any gate," Muninn said, cocking her head in that bird-like way she had.

"It's there." Freya pointed to a patch of trees on the hillside. Her mouth twisted. "I can feel the chill of the caves even from here."

Loki spun his curved dagger in the air with a sharp grin. "Then into the chill we'll go."

I had my switchblade at the ready, but it was mostly my valkyrie life-taking ability I'd be relying on. Hod had already gathered more shadows to curl around his lean arms and solid chest. Baldur stood ready on the glowing patch of magic that had carried him here, an opposite match for his twin like always.

"Getting to the gate should be the easier part," Freya reminded us. The goddess of love and war looked as stunningly beautiful as ever, but a fierce light gleamed in her eyes that I wouldn't have wanted to go up against. She was carrying a short sword, though I knew it was her magic she planned to do most of her fighting with. "Inside the caves, we'll be more vulnerable. We plow through them as quickly as we can, find our way to Odin, and get out. No stopping for any fancy business."

She didn't look at anyone in particular, but Loki pressed his hand to his breastbone in mock dismay. "No need to doubt me. I shall make my kills clean and swift."

"Are we all ready?" Thor asked in his low voice.

I dragged in a breath and nodded with the others. I still didn't know what the dark elves had meant by the markings they'd left across the country, but I didn't need to. They'd kidnapped the father of the gods, they'd threatened my little brother, and they'd nearly killed me the first chance they had. No, I wasn't going to feel the slightest twinge of conscience over battering our way through them today.

"Baldur?" Freya said.

The bright god raised his hands. His muscular shoulders flexed. "On your command."

We dove down toward the ghost town so fast the wind shrieked in my ears. A shriek rang out below us too as the illusion that had hidden us fell away and a dark elf spotted us.

"Now!" Freya cried.

Baldur heaved his arms forward with all his might, and a searing wave of light swept out ahead of our charge. It hissed through every building, every body, knocking the dark elves flat on their backs with their eyes scorched black. A more fitting color for their personalities, really.

We plummeted past them and raced through the trees where Freya had sensed the gate. The opening was nothing but a wide crack in the rocky mountainside, but an eerie energy emanated from it over my skin. What lay on the other side wasn't earthly at all.

We ran into it without hesitation, Freya and Thor at the lead. I plunged into crashing black darkness that spat me out into a dim, damp cave like the one Valhalla's doorway had led me to.

Thor was already barreling ahead, roaring with anger and swinging his hammer. Sharp slices of Freya's magic hummed through the air. The few dark elves who'd been near the gate when they'd emerged lay crumpled by the walls.

I raced after them alongside the others. Our force burst from the passage into a wider cavern.

A horde of dark elves rushed to meet us, teeth bared and knives hissing. Baldur whipped more streaks of light at them, but his power seemed dampened here, their resistance stronger. Thor's hammer sang through the air. With every crash of it, more elves poured in. Loki lashed out with his dagger, quick and sharp as he'd promised, flames licking over his other hand.

Where the hell was Odin in this place? Several openings branched off from the larger cave, all of them equally shadowed. I swooped over the elvish army, snatching up shudders of life energy through my fingertips with each flap of my wings, but an uneasy stirring rose up from my gut. We were lost. Something was missing.

I couldn't have explained the sensation, but I couldn't shake it either.

Then Muninn cried out where she'd soared in a circle around

the outskirts of the room. She pointed with her knife. "This way! The Allfather is this way!"

The gods pushed together in one mass, bashing and blazing a path to the passage she'd pointed to. A dark elf sliced through one of Hod's shadows, but I caught his hair and his life with one hand. Hod aimed another wallop of darkness at an elf that threw herself at my wings. I dove past him with a grateful brush of his shoulder, just in time to see a swarm of our attackers all launch themselves at Thor.

He heaved his hammer toward them, but blood gleamed where blades sank into his thigh, his back. I threw myself forward, snatching at the elves his swing couldn't reach. My arm collided with his brawny body, but one attacker crumpled before he could jab his knife even deeper. The other I kicked away into the next arc of Thor's weapon.

The thunder god caught my gaze for one warm instant. Electricity crackled in his eyes, his face flushed with the heat of the battle, but he offered a quick nod of appreciation despite that.

I didn't have time to enjoy that brief moment of thanks. As we pressed on into the narrower passage, the elves came at us at a furious pace. I could barely get a strong enough hold to tear a life away. For several pulse-thumping minutes, I resorted mostly to stabs of my switchblade and the impact of my elbows and knees. It didn't matter whether they lived or died as long as I kept them off of us.

A dank smell closed in around us, with just a thread of that rot I'd smelled in the caves before. We took another turn, and another, Muninn calling out the way, but the uneasy feeling sank deeper inside me. We *were* missing something. I was sure of it. But damned if I knew what.

Maybe that impression was just some sly magic of the elves. None of the gods seemed to have noticed anything wrong.

We spilled out into another larger cavern, and the raven woman let out a victory cry. There he sat: the Allfather, the tall bearded figure I'd glimpsed in a memory that couldn't be mine as I'd gazed at his throne in Valhalla. But it wasn't a throne the dark elves had given him. Chains twisted all around his body, binding him to the spear of stone he was braced against. His head hung low, bruised and bloodied. I didn't think he was even conscious.

Freya's voice pealed out, ragged and furious. She swept forward, her sword gleaming alongside the slashes of her magic. Thor charged after her. He slammed his hammer against the side of the rock where one of the chains crossed it, and both stone and metal shattered.

Loki darted in to catch Odin as the Allfather sagged forward with the slipping of his bonds. The trickster waved off Thor, making a motion as if to indicate the brawnier god should keep swinging his hammer instead. Baldur slipped through the chaos to support his father's weight on the other side. A healing glow seeped from him into the slumped figure as we reversed the direction of our assault.

My heart thumped frantic but almost giddy. All we needed was to get out. Back out into the sun and fresh air. I could almost taste it ahead of us.

Finding Odin had renewed all the gods' spirits. Loki's flames sizzled through the dark elves and Hod's shadows whipped after them, toppling our attackers in every direction. They pushed forward with a fresh burst of speed, and I found myself bringing up the rear of our battalion. I jabbed my blade and snatched out at flickers of life as the remaining dark elves charged after us.

We'd just broken back out into the first massive cavern, only it and one more tunnel between us and the brighter realm ahead, when a peal of laughter pierced through the grunts and clangs of the battle. My body went rigid, my wings stuttering in mid-flap.

It was Petey's laughter.

The sound that should have been joyful was chilling here. It echoed off the cavern walls, rising and expanding as another elf must have taken up the sound, and another, and another. Suddenly it seemed as if Petey's laughter was ringing out at me from all sides, from hundreds of mouths.

They were reminding me of their threat. Reminding me of what they'd do to him if they found him. Hod had promised he'd wiped the memories of all the dark elves who'd been watching nearby, but obviously there were plenty of others who knew.

Panic clutched my chest. I kicked out at a dark elf that grabbed at my ankle, but the motion felt sluggish, as if I were moving through water.

They were going to come for him. They were going to come for Petey and wrench him with those groping hands and gnashing teeth. How could I think, how could I fight—?

My frantic gaze darted across the room and connected with Loki's. His arm was still braced around Odin, his dagger slashing at the attackers around him, but he met my eyes and mouthed two words.

*They lie.*

He couldn't know that. He couldn't know anything about what was happening to Petey right now or would happen later. But resolve rose up inside me, breaking through the panic.

I knew. I knew the gods had done everything they could for Petey, that they'd continue watching out for him after we escaped here. I trusted that if anything could keep him safe, it was the plan we'd already put in place.

And to make sure of that, we *had* to escape.

I let out a cry of my own, rough with fury. My valkyrie power surged through my veins. There was nothing scary about it now. It was pure strength, resonating through me.

At a lash of my knife hand, lightning streaked through several elvish bodies, toppling them. I dove from side to side, severing a throat with a jerk of my blade, letting the coiled darkness inside me swallow life from another attacker. My wings beat the air with a rush of energy. My body moved faster than it ever had before, the enchanted hammer sparked through the air, Loki's flames danced—and the dark elves fell back around us. They stumbled to a stop amid the littered bodies and let us go.

Thor pummeled his way through another surge of attackers on our way down the last cave. Freya took a blow to her face that split her perfect lips. But we made it. We heaved ourselves forward with a final burst of might and spilled into the gate, through the blackness beyond, and out onto soft grass beneath warm sunlight.

# 26

*Aria*

Odin staggered as his feet hit the softer ground. All of the gods pulled close in an instant. Muninn grasped the Allfather's arm, looking up at him with hopeful eyes. Loki gave him a fond but careful slap on the back.

"Take us home, brother. Before those cave-dwellers decide to tear after us out here."

The Allfather nodded without a word. He straightened up and raised his arms toward the sky. Light seared up toward the clouds from his hands like a wide blazing rainbow. It burned sharper and clearer until I had no doubt it would hold my feet.

Thor made a triumphant sound and marched forward. Loki and Baldur followed, still offering Odin their support, with Freya and Muninn staying close on either side of him. The Allfather's steps grew steadier as he started to ascend the glowing bridge.

I glanced back toward the gate, but I didn't see any sign that the dark elves had followed us. My body shivered, shedding the tension of the battle.

We'd won. We'd rescued Odin, and maybe soon he'd be able to tell us what else his enemies had been planning and why they'd imprisoned him, and then we could win against them all over again. But even though most of me suddenly felt ten times lighter, my heart beat in my chest with a heavy thud.

That was all true, but I was also leaving my real home behind. Maybe there wasn't that much I'd miss about it, maybe there wasn't much room for me there now, but it had at least been *mine*.

Petey was here, with the new family we'd secreted him away to. My last glimpse of him, his little blond hair disappearing through the doorway of that house, rose up behind my eyes, and a lump filled my throat. I could go to him instead. I could be there, somehow or other…

No. My hands clenched at my sides. We'd gotten Odin back from the dark elves, but they were still here. They still remembered me and Petey. I couldn't put him back in danger.

Hod had started after the others, but he paused and turned back toward me. "Valkyrie?" he said.

His attention no longer felt like a demand. I knew I had to go, at least for now. Exhaling, I set one foot and then the other on the glittering arch. But that didn't feel quite right either.

If I was going as a valkyrie, I might as well fly like one.

I pushed a little into the air and flapped after the others. Hod walked on with a small but soft smile. Seeing it, even the pressure in my chest eased a little.

I was finding a place among gods and giants, a place that maybe I'd be able to call mine eventually. There was plenty to look forward to ahead of me.

The landscape beneath us turned hazy and then faded away into pure blue sky. A golden arc came into view up ahead. Everyone picked up their pace at the sight of it. *Asgard*, I thought, with a tingle of anticipation.

We emerged from beneath the arc into a vast square laid with marble tiles. A gleaming stone building that must have stretched as long as a football field loomed at our right—Valhalla, I guessed. Somehow it didn't command quite the same awe in me from the outside as it had when I'd walked through its dining hall, but it was impressive all the same.

Smaller—but not exactly tiny—stone structures stood farther in the distance, beyond an epic fountain with a dozen cascades of shimmering water gurgling down it. A warm breeze ruffled the feathers on my wings, smelling warm and sweet as honey.

"Oh!" Thor said, stretching his arms. "It's good to be back."

"Everything looks in order," Baldur said with a smile.

"Not much likely to happen to it when no one can get in," Loki pointed out. "But it is good to see Ari didn't throw any wild parties while she had the place to herself." He aimed a wink at me.

"We'll have to choose a house for you," Freya said, looking at me as she brushed her hand across her husband's temple. "No need for you to hang out in that empty war hall. There are quite a few places available—we'll take a little tour and you can pick your favorite."

"That sounds… that sounds really good," I said, and found myself beaming back at her.

Odin's head had twitched to the side at my voice. Thor took his arm with a warm grin at me.

"You haven't gotten to properly meet your newest valkyrie yet, Odin. She's already done you proud."

The Allfather listed a little to the side as he swiveled to face me. Before I'd thought one of his eyes was swollen shut, but I realized it was sealed with a gouge of a scar. An old one from the looks of it, not anything I guessed the dark elves had done to him considering that no one else had commented on it.

His other eye traveled over me with only a vague focus. His shoulders were still stooped. A prickle of the uneasiness I'd felt in the caves crept through me again. He'd been battered by the elves, but shouldn't he be recovering now that he was home too? He was a god like the others. Baldur had lent him healing energy.

"It's because of her that we found you," Hod was saying at Odin's other side. "We sent her up to Valhalla, and she followed Yggdrasil's path to determine who was holding you."

The prickle deepened with a chill that seeped right through my skin. Yes. I'd followed Odin's call to that other doorway to the caves. I'd been able to sense him out there, the god of all valkyries.

I couldn't sense anything like that now, even though he was standing just five feet away from me.

Loki had sauntered over to us. His gaze traveled from me to Odin, and a shadow flickered through his eyes. He turned on his heel.

"Where has that raven gotten to?"

Muninn must have slipped away while everyone was reveling in their relief at being home. But I didn't really care about her. What mattered was the god in front of me.

I stepped closer to Odin and rested my hand over his. Warmth thrummed across his skin, but my valkyrie senses reached deeper. A pulse of energy met my search: a thin, cool energy that made me shiver.

It didn't feel like the warm glow the other gods carried. It barely even felt *alive.*

I wrenched my hand back. "This isn't Odin."

Everyone in the courtyard stiffened. Freya frowned and touched Odin's shoulder gently. "Dearest?"

"Father? Did the dark elves do something to you?" Baldur asked, his smooth face creasing with worry.

Odin started to shake. His hair crumbled, and then his skull, and on and on, his entire form disintegrating into a pile of ash. In the space of a breath, the figure we'd thought was the Allfather was gone.

Freya shrieked and pressed her hand to her mouth. Her other

hand closed tight around her sword. Thor let out a growl and raised his hammer, searching the courtyard for an enemy to pummel. Loki's gaze skimmed across the grounds more calmly, but his mouth had set into a hard flat line.

"Only Odin can open the bridge to Asgard," he said. "So if that's not Odin… where in the nine realms are we?"

# BOUND TO GODS

THEIR DARK VALKYRIE - BOOK 2

# 1

*Aria*

You'd think the realm of the gods would be a glorious place, right? All warmth and sunlight and beauty. But as I wandered across the vast vacant courtyard at the edge of Asgard, the gold-gilded stone walls of Valhalla looming at my right and the marble tiles ringing out with my and my companions' footsteps, I wasn't sure I'd ever been anywhere that felt quite this desolate or haunted before. A cool breeze tickled over my bare arms, raising goosebumps.

Of course, maybe the *actual* Asgard would have met my expectations. This was a fake one that I'd been brought to by a fake Odin, along with the four gods who'd summoned me to be their Valkyrie, and Odin's wife, the goddess Freya. All of whom looked just as unsettled by the fake-Odin's recent crumbling-into-dust routine as I was.

"The details all look right," Freya said. She swept her honey-brown waves back behind her shoulders as she took in the space.

Her normally smooth forehead was creased with worry. "How could anyone have recreated Asgard this well?"

"*Have* they even recreated all of it?" asked Loki. The trickster's amber eyes flashed. "If you'll all excuse me for a moment…"

He sprang off the ground, his magical shoes allowing him to walk as if flying. In an instant, his tall lanky form had sped away from us into the distance where a whole city of smaller—but still pretty epic—stone halls stood. His pale red hair whipped like a flame in the wind he'd stirred up. He paused so far down one of the marble walkways that I could barely make out his green tunic against the trees beyond him. Then he spun and whisked back to us, his angular face set with a frown.

"Well?" Thor said in a growl of a baritone. He was still testing the weight of Mjolnir, his godly hammer, in his hand as if looking for something—or someone—to smash with it. The muscles in his beefy arms flexed. "What did you find?"

"It appears to be a rather thorough replica," Loki said. "All the halls, the orchard and the Norns' forest beyond… Someone has gone to a lot of trouble at our expense. I'd almost be flattered if it wasn't a very thorough *prison*."

My arms itched to hug myself, but I kept them stiff at my sides. "Is there any way out with the bridge gone?" The rainbow bridge fake-Odin had called up, to lead us who-knew-where that wasn't actually Asgard. My throat tightened.

I'd only left the world I'd grown up in, the human realm the gods called Midgard, because there wasn't much of a place for me there anymore. Technically, I'd already died there. The gods had called me back into being as a valkyrie after I'd been crushed by a speeding druggie-driven jeep. But I'd been starting to find a sort of home among the gods as they'd taught me to use the valkyrie powers they'd given me… and as they'd started to mean more to me than almost anyone back home, all of them, in their own ways.

*Almost* anyone. I'd left behind my little brother, who I'd nearly died all over again protecting. Petey didn't remember me anymore, a fact that sat in my gut like a hard peach pit I'd accidentally swallowed. Hod, god of cold and darkness, had wiped his mind and wiped the memories of him from everyone who'd known him except for me. After our enemies had threatened him to get to me, it'd been the only solution we could see to keep him safe.

I'd come to Asgard with the promise I'd still get to watch over Petey from afar. If he'd been in danger again I could have intervened. Not while I was shut up in some shiny prison, though.

"If it were the real Asgard, there'd be other doorways," Loki said. "But somehow I doubt that whoever arranged for us to end up here plans on letting us waltz right back out."

"Not after they've gone to this much trouble," Freya murmured in agreement.

Thor set his strong hand on my shoulder. "There'll be a way out, Ari. If we can't find one waiting for us, we'll just have to bash our way out."

The trickster raised an eyebrow at him. "I'm sure you'd enjoy that too, Thunderer."

"Where's the raven woman?" Hod asked. "I haven't heard her among us since before that false Allfather fell." He trained his dark green eyes toward the others with his usual intensity, but he couldn't see them any more than he could have seen Muninn, Odin's raven of memory, who'd helped us with the rescue. Supposedly helped us, anyway.

"I haven't seen her since just after we arrived," Baldur said, his voice as dreamily bright as his shaggy white-blond hair. Despite being twins, he and Hod were a study in opposites. Both were strikingly good-looking, like all the gods seemed to be, with a boyishness to their faces and a height that didn't quite reach Loki's or Thor's, but that was as far as the resemblance went. Baldur was brawny and soft and glowing with the light he ruled over. Hod was lean and hard and shadowy.

Their personalities had plenty of contrast too. Baldur smiled gently as he took in the courtyard. "Perhaps she's searching for answers as we are."

Hod made a skeptical sound. "Maybe she *has* the answers, and she has no intention of sharing them. She's the one who led us to Odin in the dark elves' caves, isn't she? She was *his* raven. How could she not have known something was wrong?"

His blind glower was as dark as his short black hair, but I knew there was more to him than grim snarkiness. Hod kept his tender side tightly under wraps. I'd gotten close enough to see it—and to get a taste of just how tender he could be.

"None of us knew," Loki pointed out. "I'm his sworn blood-brother. The three of you are his sons. Freya's his wife. All of us should have realized. But only Ari did." He cocked his head at me. "Interesting. What was it that tipped you off, pixie?"

The memory sent a shiver through me. "When you sent me to find Odin before, through Valhalla and Yggdrasil, I felt a pull to him." That was why they'd been conjuring valkyries—the three before me who'd failed as well as me. Apparently Odin had dismissed all the woman warriors he'd brought into his service a long time ago, but the gods had used their own ties to him to pass that bond on to me as if he'd resurrected me himself. "I didn't feel any sense of connection with this one. Not even in the caves. I just didn't realize what was missing right away."

"Hmm." The trickster spun on his heel. "I don't like this at all. Well, let's take a closer look around and see if we can't discover the raven's hiding place. We can give our valkyrie a little tour along the way."

"A tour of an Asgard that isn't really Asgard?" I said as the rest of us fell into step around Loki.

"It does look an awful lot like the real thing," Thor said beside me. He pointed toward one of the nearest halls, with a roof thatched with silver reeds. "I'd almost think that was my hall, my home… if I hadn't just watched my father crumple into a pile of dirt." The growl came back into his voice on the last few words.

Right. This trap must be just as painful for the gods as it was for me—maybe even more. They'd been waiting decades to get back home, wondering why Odin hadn't returned from his travels on Midgard, unable to find him themselves. For just a moment they'd have thought they were finally back, and now they didn't even know where they were.

I did hug myself then. Nothing about this sat right. I had wings ready to sprout from my back, my switchblade in my pocket, and god-given strength, speed, and sharpened senses at my disposal—and I could do nothing with any of those things to make this situation better.

"Muninn!" Freya called out in her sweetly measured voice. "Come back to us. We should talk this over."

From the way her elegant hand rested on the hilt of the sword at her side, I wouldn't have blamed the raven woman for not believing that the goddess of love and war only wanted to talk.

"That great wall you can thank me for," Loki said, only a little tension in his jaunty tone as he pointed to the high stone wall that lay beyond the halls. "At least, if it were the real one, you could have. A little wagering, a little magic, and we got the whole thing for free."

Thor raised an eyebrow. "I seem to remember it being a little more complicated than that."

"You all almost paid our giant builder with my hand in marriage," Freya said archly. "An offer that got made a lot more often than I can say I appreciated."

"Ah, but you made such a lovely lure, dear goddess." Loki winked at her. "I never let you be bound to any dastardly giants, did I?"

"A little less bragging about past exploits and a little more finding our way out of this mess?" Hod suggested.

"I don't see why we can't do both. Why, look, this is a spitting image of my own hall, and—"

Loki's voice cut off with a muffled yelp. He looked down at the marble tile he'd just stubbed his toe on. A crack ran down the middle of it, one side raised higher than the other. The trickster's eyebrows drew together as he knit his brow.

A deeper shiver ran through me. When Loki let his concern show, you knew something was really wrong. "What is it?" I said.

"This cracked stone." He prodded the marble edge as we all came to a stop around him. "It plagued me for ages… until one of the craftsmen finally replaced it. The cracked one hasn't been there in at least a century."

"In the real Asgard," Thor said.

Baldur turned, his dreamy gaze focusing a little more closely on our surroundings. "I hadn't thought about it," he said in his melodic voice, "but that tall pine at the edge of the orchard—it was cut down not long before we left for Midgard last time."

I shifted my weight from one foot to the other. "What does that *mean*?"

Hod's expression had gone slack with understanding. "This Asgard isn't an exact replica of the current realm. It has bits and pieces from different times. Features we were more likely to remember even after they changed?"

"The memories that stood out the most," Loki said with a nod. "And who do we know who deals in memories?"

Freya's fingers tightened around the sword hilt. "The raven."

Loki's eyes lit with a frenetic gleam. "It all makes sense. How convincing this place is—how convincing that Odin was. How we were all fooled except for Ari." He nodded to me. "You have no experience with any part of Asgard outside of Valhalla to draw on. No recollections of being in Odin's presence. So the illusion couldn't catch hold quite as well."

"Illusion?" I said. This place felt awfully solid to be just a hallucination or something.

Loki took a step ahead of us, weaving his hands through the air with a flourish. "An illusion constructed out of our memories. Muninn didn't just lead us into this prison. She created it."

# 2

*Baldur*

"You're trying to tell me that little raven built this entire place?" Thor said to Loki with a sweep of his arm.

I followed his gesture, taking in the false Asgard again. This time I breathed a little deeper, opened my senses to it a little more freely so I could pick up the emotions floating around me. Tension radiated off my companions, which was why I'd tamped down my sensitivity in the first place. But getting out of here was more important than avoiding some immediate discomfort.

"I'm saying that's what the evidence suggests," the trickster replied. "I've seen her do it before—conjure objects or scenes out of memories she's gathered. Odin had her show me things a few times that way. Never anything on close to this scale before…"

He shook his head in awed disbelief at our surroundings. "This must be taking all her energy and concentration to maintain. And she'll be feeding off the memories she's gleaning from our minds right now."

Memories. A dark quiver ran through my thoughts like a sliver of ice. The last thing I wanted to do was dwell in the past. If Loki was right… what else might Muninn conjure out of our histories?

I didn't let myself glance at Hod, but my twin was there at the edge of my vision, with a shadowy scowl. So many things we'd put to rest between us… and now the raven might stir them up all over again. I didn't want to think about how much more pain she could cause him as well.

Instead, I trained my attention on the buildings around us, the courtyard we'd left behind, the distant trees. The whole sprawling realm. If Muninn was creating this out of her mind, then perhaps I could reach *her* emotions through it. Catch some impression that would help us navigate her prison.

Now that I was paying more attention instead of shutting off the negative vibes around me, a faint current of prickling resentment touched me along with the breeze. An anxious twitch. If that was her, she wasn't feeling very happy at the moment either. If there was some way to connect with her, to appeal to whatever good nature she had, was there any chance that we could sway her actions?

None of the impressions gave me the slightest opening. I didn't know how to extend my hand to a place born out of a person. What could I say to her when I had no idea where that anxiety or resentment might come from?

When I brought my focus back to my companions, Aria was watching me, her gray eyes clouded with concern. "Did you sense anything from her?" she asked.

When we'd summoned our valkyrie from her death, my contribution had been to bestow her with the same sensitivity to people's inner life—what the valkyries in olden times would have used to decide which of the warriors on the battlefield deserved to ascend to Valhalla. But that talent wouldn't be as strong for her, and she didn't have much practice using it yet.

"I think so," I said. "Nothing very clear—nothing we can use."

"Why would Odin's raven have shut us away in some false realm?" Freya said. "Surely she wasn't… *helping* the dark elves in whatever they've done with him? If he's even with them at all."

"He is," Aria said. "Or at least he was. I felt his presence clearly from their realm when I first went looking for him."

"She's hardly Odin's raven anymore," Loki said. "I haven't seen her with him in at least a couple centuries. He never did say how they came to part ways. I'm developing the sneaking suspicion it wasn't the friendliest of leave-takings."

"But to turn completely against him, and all of us…" I couldn't imagine any being's loyalties shifting so completely.

Muninn and Huginn, her partner and the raven of thought, had been constant fixtures at my father's side for ages, expanding his wisdom with their own travels. They might have been birds in form, for all Muninn now seemed able to transform into a womanly shape, but their minds had been as deep and sharp as any lesser god's. What could possibly have happened to turn her into an enemy?

The question made me want to shutter my mind all over again, but I knew that wouldn't protect me from the darkness lurking here. Not when it was lurking all around us as well as inside me.

My hands clenched at my sides for a second before I forced them to release. I needed to be out of this false place. We all did. The uncomfortable possibilities were wearing at the fragile harmony we'd managed to keep for so long—and the hard-won harmony within my own mind. So many horrible uncertainties looming over us… How long could we all stay strong?

"We have to assume she was working with the dark elves," Hod said. My brother's mouth set in a grim line. "She led us astray in their caves—they were holding her false Odin. She couldn't have pulled that off unless they were in on the plan. And then she tricked us into coming into this prison where we can't stop whatever else they have planned."

"That still doesn't answer why she would throw her lot in with them," Thor grumbled. "She was the one who approached *you*, wasn't she?" He eyed Loki.

"She was," Loki said. "After we'd already determined the dark elves were involved and taken up the search. I'd expect she wanted to know how close we'd gotten and to steer us wrong if she could. She was allied with them before we ever encountered her."

Aria sucked in a breath. "That ambush in the school—she brought us to that town, saying she'd seen the dark elves' markings. Pretending she was helping us track them down. She led us right to the school. She was fighting with us against them, but I guess that was just for show. That was a fucking trap too. She arranged that attack with them."

My back stiffened remembering that battle, the blasts of light I'd used to fell our attackers, the blood spilling under Thor's hammer. The blows Hod had taken, so vicious he'd been left on his knees at the end. The dark elves had meant to kill us if they could that day.

Muninn didn't just want us imprisoned, then. She'd have happily seen us dead.

Loki tapped his forefinger against his lips. "An excellent observation, pixie. She tried to have us slaughtered, and when that didn't work and your insight helped us find the gate, she must have realized there was no more diverting us—unless she gave us what we were after."

"Odin," Hod said with a grimace.

"Or some semblance of him. Enough of one that we'd follow him into her prison." The trickster let out a huff, glancing around the place again. "It is a rather *boring* one once you get used to it. Nothing but stillness and a landscape we've seen a million times."

"Odin save us from whatever you'd find more interesting, Sly One," Freya said with a roll of her eyes.

"This might not be all there is to it," Hod muttered. "Who says she's done with us at this?"

"She'll have to be done with us if we break our way out," Aria said. She raised her chin, determination brightening her gaze.

I could feel the turmoil churning inside our valkyrie's mind without any effort at all: uncertainty at what this unfamiliar place might hold, a sharp pang of worry for the brother she'd left behind, frustration at feeling helpless. But she wasn't letting those emotions bury her. Watching her, I summoned my own resolve. I could hold steady too. Not just for me, but for her as well. We were the ones who'd brought her here, who'd promised her we'd keep her safe.

I couldn't let my fears for myself stop me from protecting this young woman who'd come into our lives like a burst of light and fire.

"Why don't we take a fuller lay of the land, like we already started to?" I said. "There may be clues we can find that will speed up our escape. There might even be others she's trapped here." We hadn't seen the other inhabitants of the real Asgard often in the last several centuries. So many of us had wandered off in various directions now that we had little to occupy ourselves with here, with the great war done. But to know it wasn't just the six of us here alone would set my mind a little more at ease.

"We'll have to be careful that anyone we meet is real and not conjured," Hod said.

"All the same, we may as well have a look." Thor strode forward toward his great hall just up ahead. "Let's see how well she's constructed the inside of my home."

We followed him along the path. He flipped his hammer in his hand in a gesture that looked almost playful, but the light in his eyes was fierce. The Thunderer didn't take well to being caged.

The sky overhead shone clear and blue, but with a false perfection that pressed down on me. My gaze slipped across the city toward the square contained deeper along its paths. The square where—

I clamped down on those thoughts before they could become fully conscious. A chill shuddered through my body all the same. Those were the last memories I wanted the raven scooping up and putting to her use.

The past was the past. It didn't matter anymore. It *shouldn't.*

Aria had fallen into step beside me. She glanced up at the shudder I hadn't quite contained. "Baldur?" she said softly.

The concern in her voice, despite all the fears she was facing herself, squeezed my heart.

"We'll get out," I said, as much for myself as for her. "Nothing's ever been able to trap the gods permanently yet."

She gave me that look as if she were trying to sense my own emotions, the ones stirring farther under the surface. The look that made some part of me tense and giddy at the same time, both reveling in her attention and fleeing it. It might be a wonderful thing to be known by a woman with a spirit like hers, but I kept certain things locked away for a reason.

I didn't ever want her to regret knowing me. That consideration came first.

She slipped her hand around mine, almost hesitantly, as if she thought I might pull away. The contact sent a warm tingle up my arm. I'd touched her before—to heal her wounds, mostly—but this overture felt more personal, more intimate. I gently twined my fingers with hers, and her smile, crooked but brilliant, almost made me forget where we were.

Then she raised her voice, sweet even if it was a bit thin, and started to sing.

It was one of the Beatles songs we'd played together a few days ago, her lending vocals to my guitar. A steady melody to match the resolute march of our feet. The lyrics were mostly nonsense, but the rhythm buoyed my spirits the way music always did. I couldn't lose myself in this, but I could wrap the tune around me like a shield.

I let my own voice roll out to join hers. Loki glanced back at us with an amused smirk. Hod shook his head, but a hint of a smile touched his lips. For a few minutes, our singing filled the empty space around us, as if to tell Muninn that no matter where she'd taken us, no matter what she had in store, we would not be shaken.

We ran out of lyrics just as we reached the door to Thor's hall. The thunder god shoved it open, and we all trailed in behind him, Aria and I at the back of the group. Her thumb skimmed the side of my hand, and suddenly I was thinking of how good it might feel if it traveled farther. If I took her right into my arms and lost myself in her brilliant defiance.

"I actually feel better now," she said with a halting laugh. "Too bad you don't have all your instruments here."

"I'd rather listen to your voice anyway," I said honestly.

Her cheeks turned faintly pink. She gripped my hand tighter—and then dropped it at something she saw through one of the arched stone doorways in the hall. She spoke louder to address all of us. "Hey—do you think it's safe to stop for lunch?"

Thor's grand dining table was laid with bread and cheese and steaming drumsticks, jugs of mead and bowls of fruit. My mouth watered as the scents filled my nose. Odd that I hadn't noticed the smell until just a minute ago. That fact made my steps slow.

Thor advanced right up to the table and set down his hands on its end with a thud. "One way to find out," he said. "The raven had better not be spoiling my reputation for hospitality."

"Nephew," Loki said with a note of exasperation, but the thunder god had already snatched up one of the drumsticks.

He raised it to his mouth, and the second his teeth touched it, ready to tear into the gleaming flesh, the meat and bone disintegrated the way my father had in the courtyard. One second solid, the next a pile of dust. Thor grimaced and wiped his streaked fingers on his shirt.

Aria's face had fallen. She scooped a plum out of the fruit bowl, turned it in her hand, and tried it. It crumbled against her lips as the drumstick had.

"Not much of a lunch to be had here," Loki said.

Aria swiped her hand across her mouth. The tension she'd found a brief release from had tightened her features again.

"Does that mean all the food in this place is garbage?" she said. "There's nothing at all here to eat?"

I hadn't felt all that hungry before, but at that question, a jab shot through my gut.

Had Muninn sent us here not just to stop us from finding Odin, but to starve us as well? The violent death she'd tried to arrange for us hadn't worked. This one would come on slower… but we couldn't fight our way out of it.

# 3

*Aria*

The ashy texture stayed on my fingers even after I tried to rub it off. My stomach hadn't twinged until I'd seen the food, but now it had tied into a huge knot. If Muninn hadn't conjured a single thing we could actually eat, we wouldn't last long in this place, would we?

The alarm that had been blaring in my head since we'd first realized this wasn't Asgard, that had only quieted momentarily when I'd distracted myself singing with Baldur, rang through my nerves again. I spun around, itching to release my wings, as if they'd help anything.

"Is anyone here?" I asked Thor.

He shook his head from where he was standing in the doorway. I'd seen his broad face both jovial and ferocious, but the morose look he had on now was something new. A few dark auburn strands had slipped free from his short ponytail. They shifted against his square jaw as he worked it.

"We'll figure out something. We'll get out of here before it matters, Ari," he said.

Something about the way he said my name made me wonder if I was the one who had to worry the most. The gods had at least some immortality on their side. Thor could put away a whole roast cow in one sitting, I'd bet, but how often did they *need* to eat?

Probably a lot less often than I did.

The itching dug deeper. A way out. We had to get *out*.

My mind leapt to the only place in the real Asgard I'd ever seen: the inside of Odin's abandoned hall of warriors, Valhalla. At the back of its huge hearth lay a doorway that lead onto the branching path of Yggdrasil, the tree that connected Asgard to all the other realms. A thin hope wound through my chest. I grasped onto it.

"What about Yggdrasil?" I said. "We should see what Muninn's done with that, right? Maybe there's some way we can use it, or your memories of it, to leave."

"It might be overly optimistic to anticipate a loophole that large," Loki said, "but it can't hurt to take a look. All part of the grand tour."

He said it with his usual flippant tone and a flash of a grin, but he hung back to wait for me as the others headed down the hall. His hand came to rest lightly on my back between my shoulder blades, as if he knew the itch I was feeling.

Loki's touch could be hot enough to spark flames under my skin—I'd gotten to experience that sensation to great effect a few mornings ago when we'd ended up in bed together—but he knew how to be careful too. The gentleness in that brush of his fingertips managed to heat me up anyway.

In theory, that hook-up had been a casual one-time thing. In practice… if I didn't die of starvation in here, I wasn't sure I was going to be able to stop myself from going back for seconds. The trickster had already made it clear he was up for another round.

I just had to remember that no matter how appealing his

company could be, he *was* also a trickster. I got the impression none of the other gods trusted him completely, and they'd known him a lot longer than I had.

We hustled back across the courtyard we'd arrived in to the gilded hall at the other side. Stepping through Valhalla's broad doors, I felt abruptly more grounded, more present, than I had before.

Because Muninn had been able to draw on my memories as well as those of the gods when constructing the inside. The vacant tables, the spears and swords hung on the walls, the glitter of gold all around, the lingering smell of mead—it was all the way I'd seen it when I'd first arrived here using my valkyrie powers. If I'd been a proper valkyrie, back in the old days, I guessed this would have been my home.

*Everything* was the same, including the huge golden throne at the far end of the hall and the gaping fireplace beside it. I jogged past the tables to that and came to a halt.

There was no door in the back of the hearth the way there should have been. Not even the faintest hint of one. I ducked and crunched over the strewn coals anyway to shove at the scorched stone back, but the bricks didn't budge.

"She didn't even want to pretend to leave a way open," Hod said. "I wonder if we could have made use of it if she had."

"Move, Ari," Thor said, his voice lower than usual. I clambered out and stepped back against one of the wooden benches.

"We don't need a doorway to get through." The thunder god's brown eyes flashed. His lips pulling back over clenched teeth, he heaved his arm and hurled his hammer at the fireplace.

Mjolnir slammed into the stones. They shattered with an ear-splitting crash. The hammer rebounded into Thor's hand, its metal surface gleaming. My heart leapt at the sight of the gaping blackness beyond the hole he'd broken open—for the two seconds before the stones jumped from the floor of the hearth and smoothed back into place.

"Damn it!" Thor growled out a few more curses in a language that wasn't English and whipped Mjolnir forward with so much force my hair fluttered in the stirred breeze. The entire hearth burst in a shower of clattering stone shards. They jittered on the floor as soon as they'd hit it and sprang back up before the hammer's handle had even found Thor's palm.

Thor whirled around. "Muninn!" he bellowed. "Come and face us! This is a coward's war you're waging." He flung the hammer at the tables. They smashed with a rain of splinters and melded back into place just as the hearth had. A growl escaped Thor's throat. He hauled his hammer arm back again, the red flush of battle rage spreading from his cheeks down his neck.

"Don't," I said, even though my chest had clenched in sympathy. There were a lot of things I'd have liked to smash right now too. "Don't let her goad you into wasting energy."

"Don't tell me what I can't do," Thor roared, spinning toward me.

I flinched at the fury in his voice, the wildness in his eyes—and his expression immediately faltered. His arm came down, the hammer dangling at his side. The fiery rage faded from his eyes as they softened.

"Ari. I'm sorry. I didn't—"

"It's okay," I said. I knew he hadn't planned to attack me. His regret at that brief outburst showed as clearly as it had when he'd blocked one of my strikes a little too hard in our sparring. I forced my fingers to unclench from the side of the bench where they'd clamped themselves and stepped toward him. "We're all frustrated. But obviously I was wrong. There's no way out in here."

He looked down at the hammer. "If I could just…"

Loki squeezed the broader god's shoulder. "I'm afraid we're not going to batter our way out of this one, old friend. At least not quite like that."

Thor made a vague grumbling sound. There was still something haunted in his gaze when he met my eyes again.

I pushed myself forward toward the entrance. "Let's go, then. If that didn't work, then we try something else." As long as we kept trying, then I didn't have to think about what would happen if nothing worked.

The sun, if it even was the real sun, beamed down on us as we came out of the hall. Freya shielded her eyes, peering up at it. The vast sky didn't hold a single cloud.

"A prison without a ceiling," she said. "And all of us with the power to propel ourselves into flight. That seems a careless choice, don't you think?"

Loki's sly grin returned. "Shall we test the boundaries of this Asgard?"

"Not all of us," she suggested. "But those who come to flying most naturally?"

She tugged her falcon cloak from the folds of her dress and flung it around her shoulders, contracting into the shape of a bird of prey as it hit her skin. Loki hopped into the air and glanced back at me.

"Are you coming, pixie?"

I hunched my shoulders, and my wings sprouted with the usual prickly burning through my back. The racerback tank I'd chosen exactly for that reason gave them free rein to unfurl. The silver-white feathers glinted at the edges of my vision.

A week or two ago, the weight of those appendages on my wiry frame had felt oppressive. Now, with a single flap and the rush of air over them, they sent a giddy tremor through me. They gave me more freedom, not less. Even if they also represented what I was now and therefore all the things I'd lost to become a valkyrie. My life, to begin with. A future in the world of fellow human beings. Petey.

No, I wasn't thinking about that now. I hadn't completely lost Petey, not unless I let Muninn and her prison win.

Loki loped up toward the sky, heading toward the high walls he'd said his wager had helped build. Freya-as-falcon swooped after him. I sprang into the air, and my wings swept me on upward. The cooler wind buffeted my face when I turned it toward the sun.

Maybe it could be this simple. Just fly out into whatever realm Muninn had constructed her cage of memories in. Shatter the illusion by breaking through its outer limits.

I soared higher, as if I could dive into the fathomless blue overhead like an ocean. The wind washed over me with the smells of metal and stone and the apple orchard to the south and… a faint aftertaste of ash that lingered on my tongue.

Ash?

Before I could wonder much about that, Loki gave a shout. The trickster had stopped against what looked like the open expanse of the sky. But as I drew up beside him with a few more flaps of my wings, I felt it too. An invisible pressure holding us down.

I strained my wings, but I couldn't propel myself any higher. Scowling at the air above us, I swung a punch at it. The impact sent a spear of pain radiating down my arm as if I'd hit my funny bone hard.

Okay, not doing that again.

Freya's falcon was circling beside us, unable to go any higher either. "Not that I have much hope," Loki said, and beckoned me to follow him gliding farther across the city. Here and there, we tried to fly higher, only to be pressed back down. My skin started to crawl at the sensation of that vague unseen ceiling.

We really were trapped in here, as utterly as we could be.

I gritted my teeth against my nerves. My gaze slid down, skimming across the town. Before my eyes, the buildings, the courtyard, the square closer to the orchard—they all wavered. Just for an instant, as if something darker had rippled through them.

My body froze except for the sweep of my wings keeping me aloft.

"Did you see that?" I said.

Loki tipped his head to one side. "See what?"

"Asgard." I motioned to the city. "For a second, it was like something flickered past the illusion. Maybe the place we really are?"

Loki considered the ground below. His eyes narrowed. "I've got the sharpest eyesight of all of us, and nothing like that has caught my attention." His gaze came back to me. "You don't have solid memories of the city to make the illusion completely real to you. Just like you didn't with Odin. You may be our key to finding our way through this prison, pixie."

Wonderful. Five divine beings around me, and *I* was the one who held the key. "No pressure or anything, right?"

He chuckled and held out his hand. "I think we can at least say the sky is not our escape route. Let's rejoin the others."

Freya darted down with us as we descended. Thor, Hod, and Baldur were waiting in the courtyard near the fountain. The goddess flew straight to join them, but Loki brought us down to earth at the edge of the marble-tiled space.

My feet hit the ground, and I willed my wings back into my body. I might take a weird sort of comfort in them now, but what I'd said to Thor about conserving energy applied to all of us.

"Ari," Loki said, and I turned. "Do you remember why I called you a pixie when we first met?"

I raised my eyebrows at him. "Because I'm small and I've got wings?"

He grinned. "Well, there's that, and there's also that pixies have more fight in every bit of their little bodies than any other being

I've ever met. You don't want to tangle with a pixie. And you've already proven that no one should want to tangle with you."

He brushed his lithe fingers over my hair, sending a pleasurable shiver through me despite the tension balled in my stomach. When his head dipped, mine tilted automatically to meet his kiss. In the moment when his lips found mine, his fiery heat coursing over me, my nerves rang with all the power my new body contained, the power he and the other gods had given me. I didn't care that they might be watching. If anything happened between me and any of the others—and I'd already shared a kiss with Hod—it wasn't going to be under the pretense that they were my one and only.

Loki didn't linger in the kiss. He pulled back with a smaller smile that felt more private, more personal somehow. Then he swiveled toward the others with a graceful sweep of his arm. "No blasting out, no blasting off, but I think we may have the kernel of our answer. If we simply—"

I caught a flash of darkness at the corner of my vision. My head snapped around.

With a chorus of snarls, a pack of enormous monstrous wolves lunged across the courtyard's marble tiles toward us.

# 4

*Aria*

The nearest wolfish creature slammed into me before I had time to react, shoving me away from Loki and pinning me to the ground with a gnash of teeth and a scraping of claws. The smack of my spine against the hard tiles shocked a cry from my throat. Pain seared across my chest with the slash of its claws.

I lashed out with all my god-given strength, ramming a knee into the beast's gut, whacking my forearm as hard as I could into its throat. Spittle dribbled onto me as its jaws lunged closer. I punched it in the muzzle. A sputter of the lightning I'd been able to intermittently summon sparked from my hand.

The monster flinched, relaxing its hold just long enough for me to heave it off me and scramble away. Blood dribbled down my shirt from where its claws had raked across my collarbone. The burn of that wound faded away behind the rush of adrenalin and the thudding of my pulse.

Wargs. That was what the gods called these over-sized, overly vicious wolves that held an almost human intelligence in their yellow eyes. I'd tangled with three of them in an abandoned factory yard a week ago, a battle that had ended with my first real kill and left me shaken. It might be my memory Muninn had stolen the creatures from.

Stolen them and multiplied them. As I urged my wings to release from my back and yanked my switchblade from my jeans pocket, I counted ten wargs facing off against me and my godly companions. Freya was swinging her sword at one's snapping jaws, Hod tangling another with thick strands of shadow. Baldur blasted one back with a surge of light he propelled from his hands. Loki flung a ball of fire into the face of another while Thor barged into the pack's midst with a roar, his hammer cracking ribs here, a skull there.

When Mjolnir bashed the one warg's skull, the creature didn't simply fall. It crumbled into dust like so many things in this fake Asgard.

I lifted off the ground with a sweep of my wings, just in time to escape the snap of the warg that had already tackled me once. It growled and tried to leap after me. The dust of the one Thor had killed didn't rise again like the rubble of the fireplace or the splinters of Valhalla's table. I guessed the raven woman didn't have enough power to keep illusions that acted like living, moving beings going forever.

The warg sprang at me again, its glinting claws swiping just below my feet. If it'd been a real living being, I would have felt the stirring of its life energy inside its body. I'd have been able to open up the shadows inside my valkyrie body and claim that life like valkyries once did as they decided the winners and losers on a battlefield. But the monster beneath me radiated nothing but hollowness. Just a construct, like Loki had said. A puppet, with Muninn pulling the strings somewhere hidden.

A puppet that had left me battered and bleeding. I gritted my teeth and dove. It wasn't really alive, so I didn't need to feel the slightest twinge of conscience over slaughtering it.

The warg twisted around, but I was too fast. I stabbed my blade straight down into the top of its head. A choked whine broke from its mouth, and then it was disintegrating like its companion.

I whipped my knife hand up and whirled around. Another warg was barreling toward me. I dodged, not quite fast enough to escape its maw. Its teeth sank into the edge of my wing and tore. That pain seared sharp through my nerves. I gasped as I wrenched my wing free.

I aimed a kick at the monster, slamming my heel into its cheek. The monster reeled to the side, right into the fiery slash of Loki's dagger. He wrenched the curved blade deeper into the creature's chest, and it crumpled into another heap of dust.

The trickster wiped his hands with a grimace and raised his head. The polished tiles of the courtyard were strewn with more piles of dust. Freya was just lifting her sword from the warg she must have taken down, sweat-damp tendrils of hair clinging to the sides of her smooth face. Thor walloped the last of the pack with his hammer, sending the beast skidding into the base of the fountain, where it crumbled too.

We stood there in the stillness, no sound but the rasp of our breaths, waiting to see if the battle was really over. Thor glanced at me and made a strangled sound. He strode over, his gaze fixed on the gashes across my collarbone.

"The raven is going to pay for that," he growled.

Now that the rush from the fight was fading, the throbbing of the wounds prickled deeper. I clenched my jaw against the pain. Baldur came up beside Thor, and I stepped toward him, knowing what he was offering without him needing to say a word. He'd healed my wounds enough times in the last couple weeks. It was basically becoming a hobby for him.

The god of light gave me a soft smile and laid his hand over the wounds. His power washed over me with a flood of warmth and an itchy tingling where the skin was knitting back together. When he lowered his arm, nothing remained of the cuts except dark pink lines like scars, but even those would fade in a few days. Unfortunately, I'd had to learn that from experience.

The neckline of my tank top was ripped, and the white fabric streaked with blood. Not much I could do about that without a convenient wardrobe on hand. I wet my lips. Construct or not, that thing could have killed me if I'd reacted any slower, if it'd caught my stomach instead of my chest. It looked like the raven woman wasn't content to just let me starve to death.

The wargs had attacked us right after I'd told Loki I'd seen her illusion waver. Right after he'd reminded me that I could be a real threat. My fingers tightened around the handle of my switchblade.

My older brother Francis had given me that weapon when I was just a kid, to protect myself against the monsters in our life back then—the ones in human form. Back then, I'd failed to protect myself with it. I'd failed to protect him when maybe I could have saved his life.

I wasn't going to fail the gods who'd given *me* a new life. I sure as hell wasn't going to fail Petey. I'd promised to be there for him, whether he remembered that promise or not. If the raven thought she was going to break me, she had another thing coming.

"Muninn!" I shouted, swiveling to take in the city beyond the courtyard. "Stealing from my head now? What else did you see? What exactly have I done to deserve the way you're trying to beat us down here, huh? I've never hurt anyone except people already trying to hurt me. What's your excuse, you asshole?"

"Ari," Baldur said softly, but I ignored him. This wasn't the right time for peace-making.

We needed to tear her down. Was there any way to weaken her concentration? If I could shake her, that might shake the whole illusion around us. Open up a way for us to escape.

I pictured the woman I'd met when she'd approached Loki and me offering her help. Slim with big dark eyes and mussed but glossy black hair. The little bird-ish quirks she kept even in human form, in the cock of her head and the slight hoarseness to her voice. What would rattle her? She hadn't cared about Thor calling her a coward. But she'd once been the Allfather's constant companion while he oversaw all of Asgard—the real thing. She'd flown through every realm, gathering memories from all over.

"Is this all you do now?" I called out, turning again. "Rule over a little jail for six people? No time to stretch your wings, to pay attention to anything else. Who put you up to this—the dark elves? Why did you let them stick you with such a shitty job?"

Loki sounded as if he'd smothered a chuckle. And a dark flicker caught my eye near the hall opposite Valhalla. A movement like the flap of a wing.

My pulse stuttered with a sudden certainty. She was here. She was right in here with us, lurking behind her constructs. She probably had to be to keep them going—close enough to steal the memories she needed from our heads.

I jogged up the path to the hall, scanning the stone walls, the thatched roof, the solid oak door. "You know I'm right. I bet you can see that too. I don't know what happened between you and Odin, why you're doing this, but you *know* it has nothing to do with me. This is just cruelty. Are you a monster like those wargs you sent at us, Muninn? Are you—"

Another flash of dark feathers shimmered against the pale stones. I threw myself toward it. My hand closed around nothing but air. Then, with a creaking groan, the entire front wall of the building tipped toward me.

I stumbled backward with a yelp, throwing up my arms. The wings I hadn't retracted yet arced over me too. They might have been the only thing that saved me.

The stones pummeled me, and I fell to my hands and knees.

The feathered appendages protruding from my back took the worst of the battering. An ache spread through them, but my more fragile head and ribs just pressed against the ground, unbashed.

"Ari!" someone shouted. There was a grunt and a thud as Thor must have started clearing the rubble. I tested my wings against the stones that had buried them and winced.

One of those stones was heaved off me, and I managed to shove another to the side. My wings retracted with a pained tremor. I kicked at the rocks on my legs.

An arm wrapped around my shoulders, helping to tug me free from the rest of the rubble. Hod's arm. I crawled out into the press of his embrace, the salty and faintly smoky smell of him surrounding me.

"I'm okay," I mumbled against his shirt.

He let out a shaky laugh. "Half of a damned building just fell on you, valkyrie, and that's all you've got to say for yourself?" He pulled back, his blind gaze managing to settle on mine as if he were looking back at me, his fingers tracing down the sides of my face. My breath hitched when his thumb brushed a scrape on my cheek. His jaw clenched. "You *are* hurt."

"I've been worse," I said. "Next time she'll have to try throwing the whole building at me." When his expression didn't shift, I added, "You want to kiss it better?"

"Ari," he muttered, but the glimmer that lit in his eyes and the sudden flush of heat between us suggested that yeah, maybe he did. And I would have been perfectly okay with that. But he straightened up instead, helping me to my feet with him. The others had gathered around us. I suspected Hod wasn't quite the exhibitionist Loki liked to be.

The trickster gave us an amused look, but there was a serious note in his jaunty voice. "What was that about, pixie? Did you see something else we couldn't? Because whatever happened there, the raven obviously wasn't pleased with you."

"I saw *her*," I said, brushing grit from my arms. My legs felt a bit wobbly, but my valkyrie strength was already steadying me despite the various bruises forming on my limbs. "She's here with us. Listening to everything we say." I raised my chin. "Which means she can get to us, but it should also mean we can get to her."

# 5

*Hod*

I stepped away from the rubble of the collapsed hall—one that in the real Asgard had been Bragi's, if my mental map of the city hadn't failed me—and almost tripped over a chunk of stone. I'd rushed toward the crash and Ari's cry so quickly I hadn't taken the time to chart out the lay of the land with the senses I did have at my disposal. Now it was a maze of uncertain obstructions. It was a miracle I'd managed to make it to her without falling on my face in the first place.

Ari's hand caught mine, though I'd already found my balance. I couldn't say I minded the warmth of her fingers curling around mine, but at the same time the reason she'd reached for me sent a wash of shame through me.

We were the gods here. We should be shielding her, not the other way around.

I should at least manage to stay on my feet without her help.

I squeezed her hand, letting myself revel for a few moments in the gentle strength of her grip, and let go. Not without a pang of loss, even though she was still right beside me.

There was something developing between us, something we hadn't had much chance to talk about what with the battle with the dark elves and now this. I wasn't sure I'd want to tell her just how much I hoped it *could* be just yet. She'd been happy for a little time with me, when we'd sat together and kissed as she'd steeled herself to leave her brother behind. She deserved to be happy. I never wanted anything I felt to turn into another burden for her.

"Hmm," Loki was saying. I stiffened automatically at the mischief in his tone. You never knew what schemes the trickster was going to come up with when he started sounding like that. His clothes rustled as he swung around. "I think I'd like to take a look at the site of our missing bridge."

"What, you think *you're* going to summon it now?" I said, testing my feet against the ground. Another hunk of stone lay to my left. Pebbles scattered under the sole of my right shoe. "Even if this isn't the real Asgard, I doubt Muninn is going to let you play Allfather." As much as Loki would probably enjoy lording that role over all of us.

"I may have a plan," he said in his sly way. Not telling us what that plan *was*, of course. That would spoil his bizarre version of fun. "Come on. We'll all want to be ready if it works."

Feet rasped against the ground as the others moved to follow him. My body balked. "Ari saw the raven *here*. Don't you think we should investigate that sighting first?"

"I'm not sure you're the best person to be making decisions based on sight, dear nephew," Loki called what sounded like over his shoulder.

My teeth gritted. Before I could snap out another retort, Ari leaned closer to me, a warmth and a whiff of her sweetly sharp scent. "Let's just see what he's got in mind," she said. "I doubt Muninn stuck around here after she tossed that wall on me anyway.

I know you and Loki don't really get along, but from the stories I keep hearing, it sounds like he is pretty good at figuring his way out of sticky situations."

"He is, when it suits him," I muttered, but I started to move. After a couple steps, I stubbed my toe on another errant stone and winced.

"Do you want me to—" Ari started.

"No," I said quickly, before she could offer to act as guide. I'd lived in Asgard for centuries upon centuries, even if it'd been a while since I'd been back there. I wasn't going to be led around this facsimile of my home like an invalid.

I summoned a swath of shadow to me, forming it into a narrow chilly length in my hands. Like a cane. Still not ideal, still not how I wanted our valkyrie seeing me—this reminder of what I lacked—but at least it would let me avoid any further obstacles Muninn threw in our path without assistance.

The others' footsteps had already moved away from us. I swept the cane of shadows over the ground as I strode after them, stepping around the rubble it caught on. The breeze was washing away the dust of the collapse, leaving only the crisp meadow-like smell that was far too much like my real home.

Because the raven had stolen it out of my memories of home, of course.

"So, you can see more than the others?" I said to Ari, still a warm whisper of fabric beside me. "Past Muninn's construction?"

"Just a little so far, here and there," she said. "When she's distracted, maybe? I haven't figured out a definite pattern, but that was what I was trying to do back there. To break her focus and see if I could get another glimpse."

"Don't ignore your other senses, then," I said. "Listen, smell, taste, touch… She's using them all to build this place, but that means every aspect can falter. We need all the clues we can get."

"You're right. I wasn't even thinking of that." She paused. "Have you smelled anything that's kind of ashy? Or is that something you'd expect to smell around here that maybe the others would be remembering?"

Ash in Asgard? "There might sometimes have been a bit of wood-smoke scent in the air from the hearths," I said. "Not often while it was warm like this, though."

She brushed her hair back from her face with a rustle of those soft waves. "Not wood-smoke. There's something a little more… chemical-y to it? That's why it didn't seem to fit. But I've only noticed it once, and then it faded. I don't know if it means anything."

"We'll have to keep it in mind," I said. "Unless the great Loki has already solved all our problems and we're about to walk right out of here."

"You never know," Ari said, but her tone was teasing. She fell silent for a moment, her shoes tapping against the smooth marble stones. "Do you two just get on each other's nerves, or is there a bunch of history I don't know there?"

"History," I said. "A lot of it." Not any I wanted to think about, even though it was hanging over me with every second we spent in this place. Normally Asgard didn't make me think about those times unless I let my mind go there, but with the city turned into a prison, it was hard to avoid the most negative associations.

"More tragedies you don't want to share with me yet?" Ari prodded. She kept her voice gentle, but she couldn't completely disguise the note of disappointment. She'd ended up sharing an awful lot of her painful history with me in the last week. The things she'd been through… I shuddered to remember them in the little detail she'd offered. It'd been easy enough to fill in the blanks.

I wished I could show her the same vulnerability in turn, but I wasn't solely the victim in my history. The parts that closed my throat and weighed down my tongue were laced with guilt.

Would she talk to me like this, touch me like she had a moment ago, if she knew the whole story? I wasn't sure it cast me in that much a better light than it did Loki. I'd prefer it if I never had to find out.

"It's long and complicated," I said. "And I don't think getting into it would be very productive toward getting out of here. It's just hard not to be reminded."

"Well, I don't know what happened, but you've stuck it out with him this long. Maybe you can cut Loki a little slack at least until we are out of here?" She bumped her elbow gently against mine.

It was hard to argue with that. Not that I'd wanted to spend all my days since Ragnarok with the Sly One around, but he and the Allfather had their seemingly unshakeable bond that I'd never understood, and Thor considered him an ideal partner for adventuring more than an annoyance most of the time, so by falling in with them, Baldur and I had fallen in with Loki too.

If he was so sly, so clever, why hadn't the trickster spotted *this* trick before it'd trapped us? I'd like to hear him explain that.

But because Ari had asked me to, I held my tongue as we joined the others where they'd stopped at the far end of the courtyard, where the rainbow bridge had set us down. I might not have ever seen the gleaming colors others had described to me in the past, but when it was here, its magic gave off a faint vibration, left a taste like sugary sap in the air. I discerned nothing of it now. The bridge had disappeared the moment we'd stepped off it with the false Odin.

I sensed Baldur's presence near me, like the warmth of sunlight on skin. I shifted a little closer. My twin had at least as many horrible memories that could be dredged up here as I did, and in them he was definitely a victim. He'd retreated so far into that dreamily peaceful state since we'd come back after Ragnarok, as if living in that haze was the only thing that let him keep the harmony he was always chasing. How long could he hold onto it here, shoved so far out of his comfort zone?

Norns willing, we'd never have to find out.

"How are you holding up?" I asked him quietly.

"Well enough," he said serenely, but I thought I heard a slight stiffness in his voice that wasn't usually there. "Hopeful that whatever experiment the trickster has thought up will get us somewhere."

Ahead of us, Loki clapped his hands. "Oh, Muninn!" he called out in a singsong voice. "You can hear me, can't you? Our little raven voyeur. Take a little trip with me, will you?"

What in Hel's name was the trickster up to? I shifted on my feet, drinking in the air, taking in the sounds of the false realm around us.

Loki's voice carried on, at a steady lulling pace, almost hypnotizing. "Think of all those times you crossed Bifrost with Odin. Perched on his cloaked shoulder or soaring in the air beside him. His feet thumping across that shimmering surface. The colors blazing beneath you, red and yellow and blue and everything between. The clouds parting into mist that tickled against your feathers. The green sprawl of Midgard's lands spreading out ahead of you."

A quiver crept over my skin. My breath caught. He was trying to draw the memory out of *her*, to cajole her into adding an exit to our prison by getting her to focus on the bridge. And it was working. The air vibrated with more power, an echo of the rainbow bridge's magic. Was it starting to form before the others' eyes even now? Ari stirred beside me as if in anticipation.

"Maybe Heimdall was there to offer you a wave and a few words in that gravelly voice, in that watchtower of his poised on Asgard's edge," Loki went on. "Or maybe it was just you and your partner in flight and your master, climbing that brilliant arc and—"

The quiver of magic snapped away in an instant, like a door slamming shut. A fierce wind blasted into us, sending us stumbling apart. It whirled around and wrenched me straight off the ground.

"No!" I shouted, but the wind ate my words too. It flung me through space I couldn't feel other than the lash of air against my skin and clothes, and threw me down on hard cold ground. As quickly as the wind had risen up, it slipped away, leaving me in silence.

Total silence. Not a voice, not a breath, not a rustle of clothing except my own. I swallowed, the sound of that action enormous in my ears. "Ari? Baldur? Thor?"

My voice rang out unanswered. Wherever the raven had tossed me, it was away from the others.

An edge of icy fear jabbed through my gut. If she'd done this to me, what had she done to my twin? To our valkyrie?

# 6

*Aria*

The world spun around me, the ground tipping. The marble slabs from the ground flew up between me and my companions. I tried to throw myself at a gap between them, and a burst of wind shoved me back.

I tipped head over heels and sprawled on the ground… which was not the ground anymore. My hands pressed against fine-grained wooden boards as I shoved myself upright. My heart lurched.

The courtyard we'd been standing in, the shimmer of the bridge starting to form, the gods and goddess I'd been standing with—they were all gone. But the place I'd found myself in wasn't exactly new. It was the only place in Asgard I'd been at all familiar with before today.

The gold, weapon-lined walls of Valhalla rose around me. A vacant bench stood at a thick oak table just a few feet from where I was sitting. The high ceiling glinted overhead. The cloying smell of alcohol and manly musk tickled my nose.

I scrambled all the way onto my feet. The wooden floor thumped under them as I jogged to the nearest side door between the mounted swords and spears. I gripped the handle and wrenched at it, but it didn't budge.

Shit. I pushed on to the next, and then next, all the way down to the broad door at the opposite end of the room from Odin's throne. When I reached it, my palms were stinging from heaving at so many. I still gave that one a good yank.

It didn't move an inch. The smack of my shoulder didn't move it either. I glared at it, rubbing the side of my arm.

Muninn had locked me in here, away from the gods. What had she done with them? And why had she put me here?

No, I didn't need to ask that. She'd tossed me into the place I had the clearest memories of so that she could build her construct on a stable foundation. All the better to trap me with. She didn't want there to be any chance that I'd see through this illusion to her or wherever we really were.

Voices echoed behind me. I spun around. At the sight that met me, I jerked backward, bracing myself against the door with a hiccup of my pulse.

The once-empty tables had filled with figures. Men in battle armor, metal or leather, muscles bulging as they grabbed mugs of mead or snatched hunks of meat off the roasts now sitting on platters between them. They packed every bench throughout the long hall. Here one rose his mug in a toast. There another threw back his head with a bellow of a laugh.

They weren't modern warriors. From their clothes, the ruddy tint to many of the heads of hair, the thick beards most of them were sporting, I had to guess these were Viking warriors from ancient times. The snippets of shouted conversation I caught were in a language I didn't know. They looked like they were having a good time, though. And the smell of the roasts made my mouth water.

That meat would probably disintegrate into dust if *I* tried to eat it, wouldn't it? These men, they were part of the illusion too. Not from my memories, but I guessed from that of the Asgardians here with me. Muninn obviously had no problem stitching constructs together from several different sources.

A figure in a white dress laid over with silver armor wove between two of the tables near me. A woman. My gaze followed her, startled. Her long blond hair tumbled down her back and her face was soft with youth, but muscles flexed in her own arms as she handed out more mugs to the assembled warriors.

There were others like her, more women in dressed-up armor, circulating through the room. A few wore battle helmets and most, I noticed, carried swords or daggers strapped to their belts. Warrior women.

Valkyries. A rush of understanding filled me. These were the original valkyries, the ones Odin had summoned way back when. The ones who'd flown into battle to harvest the souls of worthy men to bring them back here. I hadn't realized they'd acted as waitresses in between those times. I couldn't say I was sorry I'd missed that part of the gig.

I eased toward them, tensed to leap back if any of the conjured people showed any sign of aggression. But they kept eating and drinking and serving the tables as if I wasn't there. Gradually, my shoulders came down. I ambled down the aisles, glancing over the faces, trying to ignore the growing pang in my stomach.

Why had Muninn constructed all of them? They weren't trying to hurt me. She could have just left me in this place alone if she'd only wanted to imprison me. I didn't get it. But then, the raven woman had always seemed pretty kooky. Maybe this was for her entertainment.

A low, rolling chuckle carried from the head of the room, and my feet froze in place. Muninn had conjured one more figure. A tall, broad-shouldered man with a travel-worn cloak and a chestnut beard flecked with silver, one eye lost behind the gouge of a scar, was leaning back in the throne I'd only ever seen empty before.

Odin. I'd imagined him there when I'd first come to Valhalla on my own, a picture drawn by instinct. I'd thought I was walking across the bridge with him just a couple hours ago. But this… this wasn't the real Allfather, not any more than these were real warriors around me or this the real Valhalla, but he was as close to the real one as I'd gotten. Not a shuffling wounded puppet like the one who'd led us here. A vibrant reflection of the god from his actual life.

I edged closer, dodging a warrior who tipped back on his bench as he pounded the table in amusement. Odin's one light brown eye roved over the assembly. His lips were curled in a smile I could only call satisfied.

Two wolves sprawled on the floor by the foot of the throne. Not huge monstrous ones like the wargs, but regular sized, one gray and one black. Their ears stayed perked, but their heads rested languidly on their forepaws. Their gazes didn't twitch toward me either as I passed the last row of tables.

A raven perched on Odin's shoulder, its head bobbing as it leaned close to its master. Muninn or the other raven Loki had mentioned to her—of thought, he'd said? I couldn't remember that one's name.

If that was Muninn, was it the real one? Incorporating herself into this tableau while she spied on me?

My legs balked for a second. Then I marched right up to the throne and swiped my hand at Odin's shoulder.

My fingers collided with a feathered body. The raven squawked indignantly as I smacked it forward. With a ruffling of feathers, it hopped back to its perch. Odin didn't stir from his contemplation of his warriors.

All just part of the illusion, then. I frowned, following Odin's gaze over the crowded hall. Okay, I'd gotten to see the party. Now how the hell was I going to get out of here?

Somehow the throng of great warriors looked different from over here. Their faces seemed more shadowed. Before all the voices had sounded pleased or triumphant.

Now… Now an angry shout reached my ears. At a nearby table, one of the men had yanked another to his feet by the front of his shirt. The second man punched the first in the face, so hard blood spurted from the guy's nose.

In his throne beside me, Odin laughed. The sound rolled over me, setting the hairs on my arms on end.

Over there, some brawny guy had his face so deep in his mug he was practically snorkeling in his mead. When he raised his head, his cheeks were flushed. He swayed a little in his seat. He slammed his mug against the table and bellowed at a passing valkyrie to bring him more.

A platter clanged on the floor. A row of warriors on one bench jostled with each other as they fought over the choicest bits of meat on a goose they'd just been brought. Over here, a man grabbed a sword off the wall and jabbed it at one of his companions. They dodged back and forth in a dance of sword play, their blades clattering together. But they weren't just playing around. Their mouths twisted with hostility.

Even the gold on the walls looked tarnished now, dented here and there from a bash of a blade. One warrior flung another against the wall, and the building shuddered. A few golden flakes tumbled down from the ceiling like glittering snow.

"Bravo!" Odin called from his throne. "Let the feasting continue!" The set of his mouth looked uncomfortably like a smirk now.

Why had the scene changed? Had this really been what Valhalla was like back then? It didn't fit with what the other gods had told me. Why would the valkyries have brought back assholes instead of honorable warriors? Why would Odin have cheered them on when they squabbled? What would be the point of Valhalla if it was like this?

I paused, glancing at Odin's shoulders again. At the single raven on one, the other one bare.

Maybe these weren't memories from any of the gods. Muninn would have spent tons of time in this hall with Odin, wouldn't she? It'd be in her memories she was least likely to picture herself there rather than just what she'd seen around her.

And apparently what she'd seen had looked to her like a bunch of drunkards waging little wars against each other, with Odin egging them on. She clearly wasn't an Odin fan these days. It could be her memories had gotten skewed. Whatever the case, she'd wanted to show this to me. To give me her side of the story? Was this supposed to convince me that throwing us into this prison was justified?

"Are you trying to prove to me that Odin deserves whatever you're doing to him?" I called up toward the rafters. "It's a little hard to assume your take on things is unbiased. And he let all of these people go, didn't he? He sent off the warriors and the valkyries to finish their lives... after-lives... however they wanted. Even if you don't like how he ran the hall, he stopped it."

No answer. Not even a hint that she'd heard me.

The men having the fight by the wall spun around each other. The bigger one shoved the lankier one into the wall again. More gold flakes fluttered down. I traced their path backwards, up through the air toward the arched ceiling. A sliver of sunlight shone through the gold thatch.

An idea prickled through the back of my mind. Loki had been able to shift Muninn's thoughts enough to get her to picture the rainbow bridge, to bring it partly into being, and that was something she hadn't been meaning to think about at all. If I could work with the impressions she was already giving me, maybe I could trick her into giving me what I needed.

I flexed my shoulders, urging my valkyrie wings out from my back. They spread out on either side of me, heavy and solid. Mine. I flapped them to lift just a few feet off the ground.

"I get the picture," I said, pitching my voice over the din of the crowd. "Valhalla was a shitty place. The warriors were pricks. Odin was a bigger prick. The gold was dulling. The mead going sour. The ceiling starting to crumble."

I swept up a little higher, gliding over the warriors. More of them were fighting now, this one tossing mead in that one's face, another clambering right up on the table to kick at his neighbor's head. Real nice, guys. Keeping it classy. I'd known gangsters back in my first life whose company I'd have preferred.

Or were they just responding to Muninn's thoughts as she responded to what I was saying?

"Those weapons look ready to fall off the walls," I said. "I'm just waiting for one of those benches to crack right open. Odin would probably laugh at that, right? At least until that pretty throne of his toppled right over. Or will the roof fall in on his head? It's awfully wobbly. Barely holding together at all. He's lucky it hasn't already crashed down."

As I said the last few words, I shot up toward the ceiling with a few swift beats of my wings, as fast as they could carry me. At the last second, I spun backward and aimed my legs at the layers of golden straw with a massive kick.

My feet burst through the ceiling, so fragile in Muninn's mind. I flapped my wings and soared up through the hole I'd made, out toward the freedom of the bright blue sky with a gust of fresh air filling my lungs, and—

The walls below me toppled completely. A force walloped me

from behind. I whirled, my head dizzy, and a sensation twanged faintly in my chest. From my heart.

One of the gods who'd made me—one of them was close. If I could just hold on to that feeling, maybe I could…

I focused all my attention on that pale tug. My body whipped around again, and I tumbled forward onto hard-packed earth.

# 7

*Aria*

I leapt back up, tensed and wary, my feet braced against the earth. I'd landed in a meadow, grass sprouting here and there from the dry ground, with a hall nearly as large as Valhalla in front of me. No gold on this one, though, just stone.

No one else was around. It was just me and the warm breeze and a whiff of apple blossoms from somewhere nearby. I guessed I hadn't managed to make it to the god I'd sensed after all. Where the hell had Muninn sent me now, and why?

Voices filtered through the hall's wide door. Hoots and laughter—and a pained shout. My wings snapped open from where they'd folded against my back in my fall. Before I could take a step toward the hall, the door burst open with so much force it smacked the stone wall beside its frame.

Loki bolted out, his hair flying back from his forehead in a pale red flame, his strides lengthening as his shoes of flight lifted him off the ground. Oh. I guessed I'd found my way in the right direction after all. I moved to hurry after him, and a horde of figures charged out of the hall.

These men weren't human warriors like in Valhalla. They might be constructs with no real life energy for me to sense, but something about their bearing, the power in their movements, told me they were gods.

Loki was already outpacing them. Then a shining silver shape whipped through their midst and slammed into his back. With a gasped curse, he toppled to the ground.

The silver shape flew back into the hall. I froze for a second, staring. Had that been *Thor's* hammer? Why would he be attacking Loki? Or was that just what Muninn wanted me to think?

The mass of other gods descended on the fallen trickster. "You're not getting out of this, Sly One," a swarthy man growled. Another yanked Loki's arms behind his back at an angle that made Loki wince. His eyes blazed. He managed to kick one god in the gut and another in the groin before one of them heaved up his legs too.

"Muninn!" Loki rasped out. "Once was fucking enough. When I get my hands on you, I'm going to wring that feathered neck until—"

Yet another god shoved his meaty hand over the trickster's mouth. They hauled him toward the hall.

No. My body lurched into action. I sprang into the air, throwing myself at the closest of the gods tormenting the flailing Loki. "Let him go, you assholes! Let him *go*!"

My elbow jabbed the god in the eye while I aimed a kick at his ribs. He grunted, his hold loosening. I spun around to tackle the god beside him, and a huge fist connected with my temple.

I'd faced off against godly strength before, the times Thor and I had sparred while he was teaching me to use the strength and speed he'd given me. But he'd been holding back then, not really trying to hurt me. A valkyrie was no real match for a god. And this one hadn't held back at all.

Pain splintered through my skull. I reeled backward, my wings jerking, and landed in a heap on my hands and knees. My vision stuttered as I blinked. I shoved myself back to my feet, toward the throng. They were just constructs. I should be able to stop them. I couldn't just sit here while they manhandled Loki.

My head was still throbbing. I staggered before I found my balance.

"*Ari.*"

My legs locked at the urgency in Loki's ragged voice. My gaze found his through the crowd of gods around him. His mouth was free, but they held his arms and legs as tightly as before. He'd gone limp in his attackers' grasp. The blaze in his eyes had simmered down to a smolder that sent a twisting sensation through my gut.

I couldn't normally use the sensitivity to emotions that Baldur had given me all that well on the gods, but right now I barely needed it to read the trickster's expression. There was anger there still, but also resignation… and shame.

"Leave it," he said. "They'll be done with me soon. You might keep that switchblade of yours ready, though."

The gods marched back to the hall, carrying him between them. He stayed silent in their grasp as they pushed inside. The door thumped shut behind them.

What the hell was going on? Was *this* from someone's memories—Loki's, I'd have to guess? Or was Muninn stitching together bits and pieces into a horrible new scenario like she had with the wargs?

He'd wanted me to have my switchblade ready. I rubbed the tender spot on my temple where that god had punched me and pulled the knife from my pocket.

More bellows—some that sounded angry, and then others of amusement—carried through the building's door. I shifted my weight from one foot to the other, debating whether I should charge in there despite what Loki had said. He couldn't know exactly what Muninn had planned any more than I did. Although I wasn't sure there was any situation I could get him out of if he couldn't himself. It just didn't feel right to simply wait out whatever awful things they might be doing to him. They hadn't looked like they only wanted a polite chat.

I'd just gathered my resolve and started toward the hall when the door flew open again. Loki strode out, a wave of godly laughter ringing after him. I bristled, but none of the other gods appeared at the doorway.

The trickster was shadowing his mouth with one hand. He held the other out to me with a beckoning twitch of his fingers. His smoldering eyes didn't quite meet my gaze.

"What?" I said. "What did they do to you? Are you okay?"

He didn't speak, just made another twitching gesture with his fingers. Right, the switchblade. I frowned as I handed it over.

Loki's hand dipped for just an instant as he spun away from me, and I caught a glimpse of what he'd been trying to hide. Thick black lines zigzagged across his clamped lips, piercing the skin above and below with angry pink wounds. A choked sound escaped me.

Loki jerked the blade across his face. Bits of a black material that looked like leather rained down as he coughed and spat. The fragments disintegrated into dust when they hit the ground.

The trickster turned back to me, rubbing his mouth. I braced myself, but when he lowered his arm, his face looked the same as it always had. Because he'd healed already or because he'd shifted his features to hide the wounds? I'd seen him transform his face into that of a woman's before. I'd seen him morph into a wolf. He clearly didn't like that I'd seen him in this state at all.

He thrust the folded switchblade toward me. The second my fingers closed around it, he started walking. "Come on, let's get away from this wretched place."

I had to speed-walk to keep up with him. We skirted the hall and ventured into a thick stretch of forest, all pines and aspen, behind it. I contracted my wings to avoid the branches.

When the trees had closed in between us and the hall, Loki's pace slowed. He still hadn't looked directly at me since he'd come out.

"What was that all about?" I said quietly. "They… They *sewed* your mouth shut. Muninn must have some kind of sick mind to—"

"Don't blame her for that part," Loki broke in in a sharply flippant tone. "Other than her role in recreating it. These are memories, pixie, remember? You're getting a real introduction to the world of the gods."

My stomach clenched. "Then that really happened. They really — Thor helped them, didn't he? That was his hammer that stopped you from getting away."

"We all do things we're not especially proud of when caught up in the fervor of a crowd, hmm?"

"But *why*? Why would they do that to anyone? That's just…" My hands balled at my sides with the urge to go back and pummel all of those assholes into dust. Of course, what would probably happen was I'd end up with very sore knuckles and who knew what else.

Loki let out a weary chuckle and stopped. He propped himself against the trunk of a pine and finally met my eyes, a little of their usual mischievous glint coming back. "Well, you see, I made a wager."

"You what?"

He gestured vaguely toward the city we'd left behind. "I saw an excellent opportunity to win the gods a multitude of weapons. Some of the dark elves are quite skilled with their forges, you know. I had one set of brothers fashion Odin's great spear and a ship for Freya's brother Freyr, and then wagered with a different set of craftsmen that they couldn't produce better. And of course they couldn't resist trying. One of the lovely items they produced was Mjolnir."

"I don't really see how bringing the gods a bunch of gifts would have ended up with them attacking you," I said.

Loki's lips curled into a smile. "Well, the wager was for my head, if I lost."

My eyebrows jumped up. "Your *head*?" I was starting to understand all the comments the others had made about the trickster getting into as much trouble as he got out of.

"It had to be something they didn't think they could get anywhere else," he said breezily. "I'd thought the gods would decide in my favor, considering the massive favor I'd done *them*, but, well… The trouble for the dark elves was, I hadn't put my neck on offer, and there was no way for Brokk to take my head without damaging that. So, in the end he settled on the payment you noted." He flicked his fingers toward his mouth.

The story still didn't sit quite right with me. I studied his expression, which was so casual now. "Why wouldn't the gods have decided for you? Why would they have helped the dark elf do that instead of letting you escape if you could? They looked…"

They'd looked almost as if they were *enjoying* carting him off to his doom.

Loki shrugged. "You remember where we are, and what I told you that I'm not, don't you?"

"You aren't exactly a god because you weren't originally from Asgard," I said. "Technically you're a giant. But you're Odin's blood brother. You lived here with the rest of the gods—how long?"

His gaze slid away from me again, with a hint of melancholy he couldn't quite disguise. "It doesn't matter how long. The Aesir have very particular ideas about giants."

"So, they don't like you just because you're not one of them." My mind tripped back to schoolyard taunts, little scuffles in the hallways, with kids who'd made fun of the holes and stains on my clothes, my bluntly chopped hair, before I'd had the wherewithal to at least make myself look as if I fit in. As if that small agony was anything compared to the torment I'd just witnessed. I knew the flavor of it, though. I knew how deep the unfairness of it could sting.

"That's the gist of it," Loki agreed. "The gods and the giants have been at each other's throats rather a lot. I haven't got much love for the people of my birth either, I must admit. For the most part they're a violent boorish lot best left to stew in their own brutality."

"But *you're* not some violent brute," I said. "Anyone with half a brain can see that."

"Why thank you for saying so. But prejudice isn't always so easily dismissed, now is it? And… well, let's just say they have plenty of other reasons to not always feel completely friendly toward me. It's a complicated situation."

That was what Hod had said too. But Hod hadn't made any secret that he blamed a lot of those complications on Loki. I'd never heard Loki criticize any of the gods by name other than teasingly. How much were all those grumblings of Hod's justified, and how much was it simple prejudice?

My jaw set, a quiver of anger running through me. Loki caught my eye and laughed.

"You look so fierce on my behalf. No need to go off avenging me, pixie. It's all a long time in the past now."

Hod had been bickering with him just this morning. Freya had made her comments… My throat tightened.

"Is it?" I asked.

Something new lit in Loki's gaze as he looked back at me, bright but deep behind those amber eyes. He eased himself off the tree. His hand came to my cheek as he bent to kiss me.

It wasn't like the kisses we'd shared before, that instant sear of flames. His mouth moved softly against mine as if we were kindling a fire between us bit by bit, urging it from that first small spark. As if he *needed* my presence, my touch, to bring that flame to life. A swell of yearning filled my chest, and I kissed him back harder.

With a hungry noise, he looped his arm around my waist and tugged me closer. I gripped his neck, my fingers tangling in the silky strands of hair that fell there. Light seemed to flare at the edges of my eyelids.

This must be what it'd be like to stand in the white-hot center of a blaze like the eye of a storm, encased in brilliance and heat but not burned.

The trickster pulled back sooner than I'd have wanted him to, his head staying bowed over mine. My heart thumped out of kilter. "Loki..."

"I know," he said with a flash of a smile, and straightened up. "No commitments, no proclamations. There are simply moments I can't resist you."

I didn't like the impression I got that he'd just retreated from me. Those words weren't what I'd been going to say. But I had no clue what I *had* wanted to tell him, so I shut my mouth. And opened it again. When I wet my lips, the spicy sweet taste of him lingered on my tongue.

"What do we do now?" I made myself say. "I guess we should look for the others?"

"Or an exit," Loki said. "And there doesn't appear to be one here." His smile turned sharp. "Let's see what else the raven has in store for us in this grand adventure."

# 8

*Loki*

"Muninn really did quite an excellent job with this place," I said as we ambled through the forest that bordered our false-Asgard's city. "I suppose it's not surprising, given that she had so many extensive sets of memories to work with. Still, as much as I'd like to smash this construct to the ground and be done with it, I have to give her points for skill."

Ari made a noncommittal sound. She'd drawn in her wings, but the tension showed in her back and shoulders. She was prepared to whip them out the moment she felt we needed to flee. A couple weeks ago she'd held them like they were a burden and now she was relying on them like any other part of her.

She was truly rising to her role as valkyrie. The valkyrie I'd chosen. Even through the whirl of emotions I was trying to smother, I could feel a flash of pride at that.

"So, this really is what Asgard is like?" she said. "Other than little details that have changed since the memories Muninn is using?"

I dragged in a breath of the piney air, warm but with a thread of autumn coolness to it. The raven wasn't worrying too much about keeping her seasons consistent. The rustle of the dried needles under our feet, the slant of the sun between the trees—everything about the illusion rang true. I might have taken this walk a hundred times.

"If I hadn't seen everything I've already seen, I'd believe this *was* Asgard," I said. "When we get to the real thing, you'll find it very familiar. But thankfully with much less sudden emergences of horrifying past events." I winked at her, as if I were joking. As if I couldn't still feel the sting of that leather string around my lips and the sharper jab of all that godly laughter while Brokk had sewn it in.

"And I guess the other gods aren't around very much?" she said. "You said before that you haven't seen a bunch of them in a long time."

I nodded. "The world moved on without us, and some of us took it harder than others. A lot of the lesser gods simply slipped away. Maybe they found some lovely hut on a tropical beach and are living a life of relaxation. Others went off on whatever quests they could make up and never returned. Many of the Vanir returned to their original home—Freyr may still be there. I haven't paid a call in ages. Not that he's likely to celebrate a visit from me."

I gave Ari a grin, but she fixed me with those damned gray eyes that I was learning didn't miss very much. They shouldn't, with the talents we'd given her when we'd brought her back from the dead in the guise of a valkyrie. But her street-honed instincts clearly took those basic skills to a higher level than the three women we'd sent questing for Odin before her.

Of course, that was why she'd survived and they, as far as we knew, hadn't.

"Well, good riddance to them, if the rest of them were like that." She motioned toward the hall we'd left far behind. A hot prickle of shame ran down my back at the reminder of the scene she'd witnessed before the sewing. Not my most impressive moment, being hauled off by those louts. I'd like to wring Muninn's neck just for dropping Ari there right at that moment.

Our valkyrie hadn't hesitated, though. At least twenty gods around me, and Ari had launched herself at them as if she meant to take them all on in one go, just to free me. It had bothered her that much, seeing the way they were roughing me up, that she'd risked her life trying to stop them.

Literally risked her life, because illusions or not, I'd seen how hard that one punch had hit her. Norns only knew what Muninn might have allowed her creations to do to our valkyrie if she'd kept up the fight. All the fight *I'd* had in me had drained away in that moment, seeing her crumpled on the ground the second before she'd moved again.

A few minutes of embarrassed agony while the damned dark elf stitched my lips was an easy trade for keeping her safe. I'd endured the gods' unruly tempers enough times. She shouldn't have to suffer in my place.

"They had their moments, even the ones I didn't care for much," I said. "I found my ways of getting along with them."

"I guess there must have been something you liked about this place if you stayed here even when they treated you like that, instead of going home."

"Good food, comfortable lodgings, a temperate climate—what's not to love." I shook my head with a bemused smile. She didn't know what she was talking about when she called the realm of the giants my *home*. "You have to remember that my alternative was a rather barren land full of aggressive idiots whose preferred pastime was finding someone's head they could bash in. As you might imagine, I didn't get along with my neighbors there very well either."

"No, I guess not," she muttered, and kicked at a fallen twig. "I just can't… Even *Thor* was ready to hurt you."

She was still stuck on that memory, was she? I supposed it was easier for me to set it aside when I had so many to compete with it.

"None of them meant to do any permanent harm," I said, letting my voice fall into a reassuring tone. "They were simply making sure I fulfilled my wager." Even if it'd been their damned fault I'd lost it in the first place. Odin had done the final judging. "And Thor hadn't known me all that long at that time. Once we'd set out on a few quests of our own, tackled monsters and giant kings and wedding gowns—now that's a story I'll have to share in great detail some time—we developed a much better comradery. You've seen how we are now. No ill-feeling there."

"Hod seems to have some," Ari said quietly.

The twinge of anxiety I'd managed to shove low in my gut jangled through my nerves again. The less we talked about *that* the better. If Muninn hadn't already added it to her schedule of horrors to inflict on us, I'd rather it stayed off.

"And he's welcome to it," I said lightly. "All that glowering keeps him occupied. I expect he'd get very bored if he ever gave it up."

"But—"

"Ari." I stopped and turned to her, setting my hands on her narrow shoulders. A few strands of her dark blond hair drifted across her forehead, and I couldn't resist the impulse to brush them away from her eyes. Perhaps partly because of the heat that sparked in her gaze at my touch. I couldn't imagine ever getting bored of seeing that. Her passion was a gift in all its forms.

"You don't have to worry about me," I said. "I've taken care of myself for longer than you can conceive of. I was happy with the way things were, other than Odin's mysterious absence, and I'm even happier now that you've joined us. The past is just the past, no matter what Muninn tries to make of it."

Ari studied my face as if she were trying to read a deeper truth behind my words. I let only warmth and good humor show in the smile. The rest wasn't hers to carry anyway.

She bobbed up on her toes, pressing a kiss to my lips that I hadn't seen coming. A pleasant shiver passed through my pulse as I leaned in. Oh, yes, I'd chosen well when I'd set my sights on this soul.

I teased my tongue along the seam of her mouth, and her lips parted with an eager sound. Our tongues twined together hotly. She leaned into me, her small curves flush against my chest. I might have taken a few moments in this lull to discover what other sounds I could encourage out of her with the graze of my hands and the flick of my tongue, but just then an irritated yet still elegantly feminine voice traveled through the trees.

"Oh, damn it."

I raised my head, and Ari sank back down on her heels. "I think we may have discovered our missing goddess," I said.

Ari swiveled, hope lighting her face. She was as keen to be done with this place as I was. What memories was she afraid Muninn would conjure? I knew I'd only caught the barest hints of them, she kept them locked up so well.

We hurried through the forest to where it thinned at the edge of Asgard's orchard. In the midst of the gnarled apple trees, Freya was pacing. Her golden hair spilled to shadow her face as she stared at her hands. Her mouth was twisted at a fraught angle.

"Not again," she muttered, and then raised her voice. "Raven, stop this *right now*!"

"I don't think she's likely to listen to you," I said, ambling over. "If anything, she's glad you're distressed." I cocked my head, considering her hands, which looked as smooth and slim as ever. "What exactly is the problem?"

"Don't pretend you can't see it," Freya snapped at me. "It was your fault the first time. I'm shriveling up all over again. Turning old."

I arched an eyebrow, taking in her perfectly youthful face, and laughed. "No, you're not, oh goddess of beauty. She's playing more memory tricks on you. You're still yourself, as you were when we arrived here. She can't actually change our own forms."

"But..." Freya thrust her hands farther out in front of her as if the distance would give her better perspective. The only line on her lovely face was the furrow down the middle of her brow. Muninn hadn't managed to make her look old, but she had made the goddess look rather ridiculous. I couldn't say I minded this trick all that much.

"He's right," Ari said, pushing past me. She grasped Freya's hands. "I promise you look exactly the same as when I first met you. Don't let the raven mess with your head."

The grip of Ari's fingers against her own must have broken the illusion. The goddess let out a sigh of relief. She patted her face in turn. "What a wretched trick that was."

What a vain woman stood before me. Was that really the *worst* situation she'd ever encountered in her long life? I'd like to see her trade for some of mine.

"So, that was the worst thing you could imagine, dear Freya," I teased. "The most horrifying memory Muninn could pluck from your mind was the time you started to age?"

She grimaced at me. "If I remember correctly, none of the gods was all that pleased about the situation. No thanks to you."

Ari glanced my way. "How did you make the gods get old?"

I waved my hand. "Another long story. Once upon a time we required the apples of a special tree in this orchard to maintain our youth. Through a total accident, the goddess who picked those apples was kidnapped. With a little quick thinking and quick flying, I retrieved her and all was well."

"I'm not sure how purposely leading her beyond Asgard's walls was an *accident*," Freya said.

"I couldn't have known what the eagle wanted with her," I

protested. "Perhaps he was simply looking to have a chat."

Ari swiveled on her heel, taking in the orchard. "Do you still need to eat those apples to stop you from getting old… and dying, I guess?"

"No, thank Asgard," I said. "Our rebirth after Ragnarok removed them as a necessity. As I'm sure Freya has been deeply appreciative of, so that she never needs to worry about so much as a gray hair or a wrinkle."

"Oh, shut up," Freya said. "What's worse—to be upset at losing one's youth or to take glee in seeing it happen to others?"

The retort rankled. I hadn't been gleeful. It was good for the soul to find humor in dire circumstances, not that she'd know much about that. What *had* Odin seen in her to make her his second wife, anyway? Had she addled his brains with beauty and superficial charms?

"I was too busy risking my life fixing the problem to be taking much glee," I said with a roll of my eyes, keeping my tone light. "I don't recall you contributing much to the effort other than handing over the use of your falcon cloak. I suppose all the rest of your energy was needed to mourn your beauty."

Freya's jaw clenched. "You should have mourned it too, I think. Without that beauty, how would you ever have been able to come up with so many schemes around marrying me off to this creature or that one?"

"Oh, there were plenty of pretty faces around Asgard. I suppose I could have offered up your daughter."

I knew my tongue had flown too fast from the shadow that crossed the goddess's face. Not that her kind had ever shown consideration to *my* children.

She raised her hand to point an accusing finger at me, and the ground shook with thundering footsteps. I spun around to see none other than Thrym himself, once king of the giants, barreling toward us through the trees.

# 9

*Aria*

The entire orchard trembled as the massive figure barged toward us. Tall as Loki and nearly as brawny as Thor, the huge man toppled one tree with one swipe of his bulging arm and wrenched another up by its roots with a roar. Swaths of leather hung across his scarred body. A dented iron crown sat haphazardly on his wiry brown hair.

"Oh, perfect," Freya said, backing up to the thicker shelter of the forest. "Now you've brought the king of the giants to life. Just what we needed."

Loki snorted. "*I* brought him to life? I don't recall sending out any invitations."

"You brought up all your schemes, all the ways you used me in your wagers. It seems to me the biggest wager was against him. Where do you think the raven of memory got *this* idea?"

"Ah, I believe you were the one who started venting about my scheming and the various wagers I can assure you I never initiated.

Well, at least not the ones involving your hand in marriage, as in-demand as that boon was."

The raging giant tore up another tree and hurled it in our direction. I scrambled backward and ducked behind a pine. "Um, would you two mind settling this argument later and dealing with the giant king who's looking to smash us to pieces now?"

"With pleasure," Loki said, drawing his dagger from his belt with a flash of metallic light. "I have plenty of practice cleaning up the messes the goddess gets into." He beamed at Freya.

"That *I* get into?" Freya sputtered. "If I tried to count the number of times your supposed cleverness put us on the edge of disaster—"

"You don't need to. Continue contemplating your restored beauty and I'll take on the giant."

The giant in question stomped closer. I unfurled my wings, tuning out the rest of their conversation. I, at least, was going to do something to make sure Muninn's latest creation didn't batter us to smithereens. Maybe the hulking giant didn't look all that threatening to the gods, but I sure as hell didn't want to just sit around and wait for him to attempt to crush me.

I flicked out my switchblade and launched myself into the air. The arching branches all around made it hard to get much of an advantage in the air. The giant had almost reached the forest now, a trail of destruction strewn through the orchard behind him. I couldn't match him hand-to-hand, that much was obvious. But if I could find a weak spot like I had with the ceiling in Valhalla… A strike in the right place, and he should crumble into dust like the wargs, like the gods who'd grabbed Loki would have if I'd gotten in a good enough hit.

The eyes, maybe? If I could get close enough to his face to pull that off. The thought of going in there ready to stab that almost human figure in the most vicious of ways made my stomach lurch.

Just a construct out of memories, I reminded myself. Like target practice. Nothing real. No life lost.

Not that I could claim my hands were clean of actual killing after all the dark elves we'd had to slaughter fighting our way to what we'd thought was Odin. That bridge had already been crossed.

Switchblade at the ready, I glided closer to the giant. He snapped a huge branch off one of the apple trees and swung it in front of him like a club. His ruddy eyes focused on me.

"I won't be embarrassed like this!" he snarled. "You'll bring her to me, or you'll all fall."

I had no idea what he was talking about, but he didn't seem interested in bringing me up to speed. Before I'd had a chance to do anything at all, he heaved the branch toward me. I vaulted off a nearby trunk higher into the air, flipping over a tree top. My wings caught me over his head.

The giant slashed upward with the branch faster than I'd expected given his bulk. I shoved myself to the side with a flap of my wings, but the jagged end slammed into my ribs.

I tumbled into another tree with a hiss of pain. My chest throbbed all across my left side. More bruises to add to my growing collection.

Back in the forest, Loki swore. "Ari!" Freya called out. Splintered wood crackled underfoot as they both charged into the orchard.

I tossed myself out of the way of another swing of the giant's makeshift club, gritting my teeth against the burning in my ribs. My switchblade. My hands were empty. It must have fallen from my grasp when the branch walloped me.

My heart skipped with a sharper panic than even the giant had provoked. That knife was the only thing I had left of Francis. I couldn't lose it here. Muninn's world of illusions might swallow it right up if I didn't get it back quickly.

I scrambled down from the tree I'd landed in. The giant gave another roar. Then Freya leapt between me and that hulking form, her sword gleaming in the sunlight.

"It's me you wanted, isn't it, Thrym?" she said, settling into a fighting stance. "Why don't you come and get me?"

"I demand Freya as my bride!" the giant king bellowed. "A fair trade, the goddess for the god's hammer. I *will* have my price."

She grinned fiercely, her beauty turned blazing. "Here I am. So sad that so many of you forget I'm the goddess of war as much as the goddess of love. And I know exactly which side of me you deserve. Don't you dare lay one more finger on our valkyrie."

The anger in those words sent an ache through my chest. She wasn't just defending herself but me too. I'd better get on with helping her do it.

I cast around on the ground, searching for my knife. The thud of metal hitting wood rang out behind me. Then a sizzle and a bellow that sounded more pained than furious.

"Oh, and here I thought flames made a lovely addition to your weapon of choice," Loki's flippant voice rang out. "Look at that branch with its merry blaze."

A glint of blue caught my eye. There! I lunged for the switchblade, almost nicking my fingers in my haste to snatch it up. A pang shot through my ribs, but I ignored it. My hand clamped tight around the plastic handle. I spun around to join the battle.

There wasn't much left to join. Freya was slashing at the giant king from one side and Loki taunting him with jabs of his dagger and flashes of fire on the other. One giant, even a king, obviously wasn't much of a match for two powerful gods. And Loki could say whatever he wanted about his heritage, but watching him there, his face glowing with power as he distracted the giant long enough for Freya to whip her blade across the back of the brute's knees, he couldn't have looked more different from the man they were fighting.

That hulking monster was a giant. Loki might have been one once, not that it sounded as if he'd ever really belonged with them, but after all that time among the gods, I couldn't see him as anything but a god himself.

The slice of Freya's sword made the giant topple to his knees with a groan. Freya stepped closer, and at the same moment the hulk snatched a pointed spear of broken wood off the ground and thrust it toward her.

I yelped a warning and hurtled myself forward with my enhanced valkyrie muscles. My outstretched heel smashed into the giant's wrist. His fingers twitched, dropping the spear. Then he was sweeping that hand toward me. I threw myself into the air. He grabbed my ankle, wrenching me backward—and Freya brought her sword to his neck.

"This is as close to me as you're ever going to get," she said, and severed his throat with one swift strike.

No blood streamed down. The giant collapsed completely deflating with a puff of that awful dust.

Freya stood over him, panting. Dirt had streaked her arms and the side of one cheek, but it didn't dull her beauty. I wasn't sure how anyone could forget she was the goddess of war once they'd seen her like that even once.

No wonder Odin had wanted her to be his queen.

"Thanks," I said, coming back to earth with a flap of my wings. I stuffed my switchblade into my pocket. "I didn't know it mattered to you much if I got tossed around."

I'd meant it as a joke, but the words came out a little flat. Freya glanced at me.

"You are *our* valkyrie," she said. "All of ours, even if I didn't have a direct hand in summoning you. If it wasn't for you, we wouldn't be any closer to finding my husband. You've fought for me a lot more than I've fought for you already." The corner of her lips curved up. "And it is nice to have a break from the constant manly posturing. I really didn't want to lose the first chance at proper female companionship I've had in a century or two."

I hadn't really had friends even when I was alive. Too hard to trust anyone that much. No time to devote to them, when it all went to looking after Petey and making more money so I could do the first part even better. It was kind of hard to wrap my head around the idea that a goddess might want my "companionship." I wasn't sure exactly what we were going to talk about once we were done with the basic "explain to me how the hell this or that godly thing works" topics, but I wasn't going to argue with her. Not when she still had that sword in her hand, anyway.

Loki ambled over to join us, swiping the sweat from his high forehead with the sleeve of his tunic. "Well," he said, "we can't say the raven isn't keeping us on our toes. If I ever complained that our lives weren't exciting enough, I apologize tenfold."

Freya raised her eyebrows at him and sheathed her sword. Loki's smile turned sheepish. "Also I apologize for implying you couldn't fight your own battles, dear goddess. Possibly I've underestimated you every now and then."

"Possibly?" Freya said.

"Definitely. I start to think I should have brought the real you with me down to retrieve Thor's hammer rather than Thor in that dress. Although of course then we'd all have been denied the impressive spectacle of the dress, so…"

Freya laughed. "No, I think you made the right choice there. I wouldn't have missed that sight for anything."

Whatever tension had formed between them before dissolved into the air. I sucked in a breath, and the trees around me wavered.

I froze, studying them. Perking my ears, tasting the breeze, like Hod had suggested. A streak of gray shimmered between two of the trees and disappeared. That ashy taste tickled over my tongue again.

"It's happening again," I said. "The false Asgard is wavering. More than before. Maybe—"

I didn't get the chance to make any suggestions. The ground tipped up, folding the trees down on me, and the smack of a trunk sent me tumbling out of the orchard toward wherever Muninn wanted me next.

# 10

*Aria*

Darkness whipped around me. I flung out my arms and released my wings, trying to catch hold of something. A faint sensation tugged at my heart—one of the gods, one of my sort-of creators, someplace nearby. I threw myself toward that impression with all the strength in my body.

I collided with a solid form all lean muscles and smoky scent. *Hod*, I had time to recognize, and then Muninn's constructed world tipped me over again. Both of us fell, sprawling, onto a carpeted floor.

I scrambled off the god, mindful of my knees and elbows. He sat up with a dazed expression, rubbing the back of his head where it'd smacked the floor. "Ari?" he said. His fingers grazed my skin as he found my wrist and clasped it. "Are you okay?"

"Slightly more bashed up than the last time we talked, but still breathing," I said. The fall had woken up the ache in my ribs. And other smaller aches from earlier today that I didn't really want to count. As glad as I was to see Hod safe and relatively unharmed, I wouldn't mind bumping into Baldur for a little of that healing touch sometime soon. "Where did she send you?"

"Better we don't talk about that," he said grimly.

I'd seen how much the memories Muninn stirred up had affected even unflappable Loki. For now, I wasn't going to push.

I pulled myself into a crouch so I'd be ready to move fast if the situation called for it, but nothing in the room around us looked like a threat. The pale blue carpet was soft under my feet. A twin bed, neatly made with a spaceship-print comforter, stood at our right, a maple dresser and kid-sized chair-and-table set at our left. The window over the table was open, curtain drifting beside it. The breeze carried in the smell of a freshly mown lawn.

"Have you seen any of the others?" Hod asked.

I nodded. "I was on my own at first, and then I ended up with Loki and Freya."

"But no sign of Baldur?"

Oh. Of course he was more worried about his twin brother than anyone else. "No," I said. I wanted to say that I was sure Baldur could withstand whatever Muninn threw at him, but honestly, it was hard to tell what was really going on beneath the light god's bright surface. Sometimes I got the impression he was amping up the shine to deflect anyone from looking underneath.

"She hasn't hit anyone with anything we can't handle yet," I settled on, and frowned at the room around us. "I don't know what she's up to now. I'm pretty sure we're not in Asgard anymore."

"Not from how it feels to me," Hod said. "I'd imagine this is someplace on Midgard. Do you recognize it?"

I shook my head. "I've never been here before." The only kid's bedrooms I'd ever been in were the ones in my mom's house, and neither mine nor Francis's nor Petey's had ever looked this tidy. The carpet in mine had been so patchy you could practically play checkers on it. There'd been water stains on all of the ceilings from the leaks during bad storms, and a hint of mildew smell that had never quite left because of them. "This is definitely not from *my* memories."

Hod's brow furrowed. His head turned as if he were taking in the room, but I knew he couldn't see it.

"How much can you even tell about where we are?" I asked with honest curiosity.

"From the way the air moves, I can get a sense of the size of the space, where the large objects are. And touch can fill in a lot." He patted the side of the bed. "From the furnishings, I'm assuming bedroom? Not very large. Clean." He paused, his chest expanding with a slow inhale. "Something about it smells familiar. Maybe *I've* been here."

"Do you make a habit of dropping in on random kids?" I said, and tensed as the door eased open. A small figure stopped on the threshold at the sight of us. My heart flipped over.

Oh. Not a random kid at all.

Petey's thin eyebrows drew together as he contemplated us with his wide gray-blue eyes. Every part of him was exactly as I'd have remembered him, from the mussed golden-blond curls to those skinny legs—legs that poked from beneath shorts starting to fray along the hems. No need to ask whose head Muninn had pulled this part of the illusion from.

Because it had to be an illusion. Petey wasn't really here. But that didn't stop every particle of my body from aching to go to him.

I could go to him, couldn't I? It couldn't hurt the real Petey to give this one a hug, to tell him once more how much I loved him, that I was coming back for him.

Before I'd even finished thinking that thought, I was already moving. Onto my feet, stepping toward my little brother, my arms outstretched. Hod sucked in a breath behind me.

"Ari—"

Oh, God, he wasn't going to be a wet blanket about even this pretend reunion, was he? I ignored him and reached to brush a stray curl from Petey's eyes.

Petey flinched, jerking away from me. He stared up at me with stiffened shoulders. "Who are you?" he said in a quavering voice. "What are you doing in my room?"

The words hit me like a slap across my face. I froze. "It's me, Petey. It's Ari."

He drew back a step. "I don't know you. You're not supposed to be in my room. Mom says no one's allowed to go in there unless they ask me first."

My chest clenched up so tight I could barely breathe. "I just wanted to see you," I said. "You *do* know me. Ari. Your sister. I've been there since you were born."

"You're a stranger. I'm not supposed to talk to strangers."

"Ari." Hod had gotten up behind me. He set his hand on my shoulder, his grip firm but not hard. "This is his bedroom in his foster parents' home. Loki and I came to see it before we dropped him off, that last morning. We should go. She's just trying to hurt you. Don't let her."

"But…" My eyes had gone hot. Petey was still staring at me, his little body rigid. His chin wobbled. As if he was terrified of *me.* "Can't you make him remember? You shadowed the memories over —you must be able to bring them back. It won't count. It's not really him."

"It's not really him," Hod agreed. "And I can't work any magic on him. He's acting the way Muninn wants him to. You let him go once. You can do it again."

I hadn't had to stand there faced with Petey's bewildered gaze before. "Petey, please." I took another step toward him, searching his expression for any hint of recognition. He cringed backward, stumbling right out into the hall.

"Mom!" he cried out in a thin voice. "Mom, help me! There's a stranger—"

A shudder ran through my body. I closed my eyes, set my jaw, and shoved the bedroom door closed.

Footsteps pattered away on the other side. The fake Petey running to his false mother? I threw my shoulders back against the door, my head bowed, my breaths harsh in my throat.

Hod moved toward me, but I held up my hand to stop him. My fingers curled into my palm. I pushed myself off the door, spinning around, glaring into the corners of the room as if I might spot the raven there.

"That was sick, Muninn," I said. "Just *sick*. I don't know why you turned against Odin, but if you think you're somehow the good guy here, you're delusional. You don't just *use* a little kid— Do you have any idea— So Odin seemed a little heartless sometimes? You just proved you're a fucking monster!"

She didn't answer. I hadn't really thought she would. With a strangled sound, I hurled my fist at the wall. It dented the plaster with a satisfying thud and an equally satisfying jab of pain through my knuckles.

"Ari," Hod said, sounding more urgent now.

I leapt away from him, battering the opposite wall with my foot, slamming my heel down on the seat of the chair so the wood cracked. "This is all fake. This is all fake, and garbage, and— I didn't spend years clawing my way out of my mom's house just so you could shut me up in this stupid prison. Let us *out*!"

I took another swing at the wall and then swooped up on my wings and kicked the damned ceiling. Plaster dust sprinkled down. I whirled around, chest heaving, choking on a sob.

Hod stood by the bed, his mouth set in a pained line. Just waiting for me to finish my tantrum. Because what else could anyone call this? What the fuck was I actually accomplishing with all this flailing?

My shoulders sagged. The anger inside me dimmed, but that just left more room for the anguish.

"Are you done, valkyrie?" the god of darkness asked, but his tone was soft, not disapproving.

"I just wanted… I just wanted to hold him one more time."

My voice petered out. I eased forward and leaned my head against Hod's chest. He swallowed audibly. His arms came around me, hugging me to him.

"I know," he said.

"Even if he wasn't real…"

"I know."

I relaxed into his warmth, thinner than Loki's but steadier. He hadn't said much, but just that acknowledgment eased the worst of the pain. Enough that I managed to say, "Well, we're alone now, but I'm not sure there's any way you could kiss this better."

A chuckle broke from Hod's throat. His hands came up to cup my face and gently tilted it back. A hungrier darkness filled his unseeing green eyes. "I could try," he said in a low voice that sent an eager shiver through me.

A different sort of shadow flickered at the edge of my vision. My head snapped around, trying to track it. There. A flutter of wings in the ripple of the curtain.

This time I didn't hesitate. I launched myself away from Hod toward that glimpse of the raven. My snatching hands brushed through a sensation like ruffled feathers—and the room and the god spun away from me.

The world blurred around me. The ground tipped. I tripped over my feet and fell to my knees, which at this point had to be the most bruised part of me.

No carpet this time. Plain wooden boards. A wide-open living room, shelves lined with books along one wall on either side of a stone fireplace. A ceiling fan stirred the humid air overhead. I was surrounded by two empty armchairs and an oversized sofa where two figures sat nestled against each other. A haziness clung to the edges of the space, as if this was more a dream than a physical place. Not that the places I'd been in before here had been real either.

"You could go," the man said. His voice was as thin as his tall frame, his shoulders hunched. His hair fell sleek and white around his slightly pointed ears. A jagged scar cut across the left side of his face. The other side was lined with age. "I know it wasn't easy before. It can't be easy doing it again. I can manage on my own. I doubt Death will let me lose my way."

"No," the woman curled against him said hoarsely. She raised her head from where she'd had her face pressed against his chest, her glossy black hair spilling over her narrow shoulder blades, and I realized it was Muninn. The same loose black dress, the same darkly intent eyes as when I'd first met her.

When was this? *Who* was this? I had the feeling I'd stumbled into one of the raven woman's memories somehow. Had she meant me to? This felt more personal than anything I could imagine she'd have wanted me to see.

"I'm not losing one moment with you," she said, her fingers tangled in the man's shirt. "If I could, I'd conjure more."

He nuzzled her face. "We had plenty. More than I ever had the slightest hope I'd get. You've gotten no shortage of memories out of this, Miss Raven. Don't hold on too hard."

"No such thing," she muttered. Her head bent close to his again. She pressed a kiss to his lips, and his eyelids slid closed as he kissed her back. My face flushed.

No, I wasn't meant to be watching this at all. But it meant something that I'd managed to tumble from the memories she'd constructed for us into hers, didn't it? There had to be something here I could use.

I'd only started to turn when the scene around me collapsed in on me with a wash of darkness like vast wings battering me. I had just enough time to gulp a breath before Muninn hurled me empty-handed out of her memory.

# 11

*Thor*

I couldn't really explain how it happened. The moment anything that felt like a threat came at me, something in my mind and body shifted. The battle fury shunted logic and every other practical consideration to the back of my head. A wave of power rushed through my limbs. With my pulse pounding like a drumbeat in my ears, my feet battered the ground and my hand swung Mjolnir with no thought except how to most quickly connect each killing blow.

Topple them all. Topple them fast. Let the blood flow until not one of them could lay a finger on me and mine.

That was simply my nature. I worked the way I worked, and it had served us well through enough battles across the ages, when we'd had plenty of battles to fight.

The sad thing was, I couldn't say for sure which battle it was I was re-fighting at this moment. One of Muninn's twists of the landscape had tossed me into a field with a vast array of giants already charging toward me, their teeth bared with war cries and weapons raised. I'd hurled myself forward, hammer at the ready, the second my feet had steadied on the ground.

We'd fought a lot of battles against giants. I couldn't remember any particular one where I'd been on my own, but then, Muninn didn't seem to be aiming for accuracy. Mostly she seemed to be aiming to destroy us.

She could forget about that. I'd bash every one of these giant skulls five times over and still be ready to fight my way back to Ari and the others. One little raven wasn't getting the best of me.

My muscles heaved as I whirled this way and that, slamming the dark-elf-made hammer into a forehead here, a jaw there. Whipping it through a whole line of my enemies, tumbling them like dominos, before it flew back to my hand. If there'd been more of a gap in the fighting, I might have paused to call a clap of thunder and lightning down, but this fray never let up.

The giants might not be taking it easy on me, but this was a cleaner battle than any I'd fought in reality. With each battering, the bodies burst into more dust, until it coated the grass all around. Better than the blood that usually splattered me and my surroundings in the middle of a clash like this. I couldn't say I missed the metallic stink of gore in the air, the flavor of it creeping into my mouth.

But somehow, without the spurts of blood and the strewn bodies, the roar of the battle fury dulled. I kept fighting, kept bashing the giants that ran at me two or three at a time, because if I hadn't I'd have ended up with a spear in the gut or a club to the head.

I swung left and veered right, trying to summon more of the fervor with the momentum. It didn't work. A weight settled in my gut as I sent the next body flying with a streak of dust.

All these people I'd once killed. All the lives I'd extinguished. They weren't anything more than dust now out there in the real world too. I'd snuffed them out in one thump of my heart, with hardly a thought to any one of them.

The weight in my gut turned queasy. But what could I do but keep fighting until I smashed them all to pieces?

I lashed out to topple a giant who'd rushed up behind me, and realized I was no longer alone.

Ari had dropped down at the edge of the field. She staggered and caught her balance. My gut clenched tighter as she lifted her head to take in the view.

The view of me burying Mjolnir in this giant's head. Slamming it straight into that one's face. More dust rained down, with a faintly sour smell.

I swung faster, harder, my pulse kicking up a notch. The giants might go for her next. They weren't real. If they'd ever been alive, that was a long time ago. I couldn't stop until I'd destroyed them all. Until I'd conquered this damned memory Muninn had thrust me into.

The fiery rage shot back through my veins. A roar rang from my lungs. I hit and kicked and threw in an endless storm of motion as the swarm barreled toward me, sweat trickling down my back. The bodies and shouts blended into a blur. My hammer pummeled flesh and bone until it collided only with empty air.

I swayed to a halt. Were the giants really all gone? Nothing lay around me on the plain except the strewn dust.

My hammer hand dropped to my side. A tremor ran through my muscles. The queasy sensation coiled around my stomach.

Ari was staring. She eased to the edge of the field, clutching her switchblade, her wings unfurled high. The breath she drew in was shaky. Was that *horror* on her face?

"I would have helped," she said. "But I didn't— I couldn't figure out if I might just end up getting in the way. I guess you had it under control."

Her tone turned a bit wry on the last sentence. It prickled at me. Before I could decide how to answer her, another swarm of giants appeared on the horizon. My heart plummeted. Not again. Did the raven really think she could topple me this way?

Ari jerked straighter, her muscles tensing. By Hel, no, I didn't want her in the fray with me, seeing that fury even closer up. Risking the smack of my hammer if my aim didn't fly true, the sear of my lightning.

"Back," I said roughly, waving at her. "Keep away. This is my battle."

Muninn, send her somewhere else. There had to be somewhere better than here. Not that the raven was interested in bettering our situation. If I could fight my way through this scene straight to her, shatter her and her prison… Not that I seemed to have gotten much closer to her so far.

"I can fight," Ari said.

"I don't want you to," I snapped. The giants were almost on me. With gritted teeth, I heaved myself away from her to meet their charge.

It was a smaller group this time. With two stomps of my feet, I sent lightning streaking from the sky into their tightest cluster. I crushed the others even faster than the ones before, my lungs starting to burn with the strain, but the battle fury racing through my brain never quite drowned out my awareness of Ari somewhere behind me. Ari still watching Thor the destroyer.

Often I took pride in that role. But she hadn't seen much else from me in the last two weeks, had she? Teaching her how to pummel her enemies. Burning off frustration by battering the grounds around our Midgard house with my hammer. Destroying all those dark elves who'd swarmed against us.

Or maybe it was simply that having those outside eyes on me was stirring up a twinge of guilt that had always been there but I usually managed to keep buried.

I hesitated a second before I bashed my hammer into the skull of my last attacker. Twisted with rage, that giant's face that didn't look so different than my own probably did. *Brutes*, Loki liked to call them. What would anyone call me?

The body fell with a thump and deflated into a heap of dust. I scanned the field. Nothing else stirred for now.

"Thor?" Ari said. Tentative now. My fingers tightened around Mjolnir's handle.

"How did you end up here?" I asked without turning.

"I don't know," she said. "I seem to be able to kind of reach out toward you all if I come close to you while Muninn is tossing us around. But I haven't figured out how to use that to any real advantage yet. I guess we're always better off together rather than apart. More chances to pick apart her illusions."

Her footsteps rustled across the grass into the drifts of dust. The dust from the bodies I'd toppled, which had felt far too solid as illusions went. My stomach churned. I swiveled around then, pointing in a different direction. "Let's see if we can find a way to toss ourselves out of this place, then."

Ari held still until I reached her and fell into step beside me. I shifted a little to the right to give her more space, but I couldn't help watching her from the corner of my eye.

She flicked her switchblade closed and shoved it in her pocket, her head low. Her wings retracted. In the space of a few seconds, she looked like an ordinary young woman, albeit a determined and sharply pretty one. Even my nausea couldn't stop the current of desire that crept up from low in my belly.

"Are we okay?" she said after a minute, her voice still tentative.

My head snapped around. "What?"

"I just mean… you seem upset. Maybe with me. I don't know. The stuff Muninn's been throwing at us, the tricks she's pulling—I don't know what she could have shown you. I'd like to know we're still all right."

She glanced up at me, worry and confusion shimmering in her eyes. If my stomach had been tight before, it twisted into one massive knot now. She thought I might have some kind of problem with *her*. Shit.

I stopped dead in my tracks, turning to face her. "We're all right," I said. "We're absolutely all right. I'm sorry, Ari. You didn't do anything wrong. This is the first I've seen of you since we got thrown apart in the courtyard. I—I'm glad to see you, just to know you're okay."

She folded her arms over her chest and raised her chin, more of her usual energy coming back. "Then what *are* you upset about? Because something's obviously jerking your chain. Was it something about that battle? Bad memories?"

"Not exactly. I…" I let out a breath in a rush. "I don't want that, the way you saw me out there—the way you've already seen me more times than I'd like—to be the way you think about me. I fight because I need to, and maybe I can find enjoyment in it while I'm in the middle of it, but I don't revel in the killing. I don't seek it out."

Maybe that wasn't entirely true. There had been times, long before Ragnarok, when I'd gone journeying with Loki or one or another of my brothers knowing we'd probably come to blows with someone. But always someone who deserved it. And I hadn't felt that urge to seek out a fight in a long time.

Not since I'd watched my home and all the people in it consumed in a searing blaze no hammer could defend against.

"Hey." Ari touched my arm. Warmth blossomed under her fingers. "I'm not anyone to judge. How many lives did I whisk away when we took on the dark elves?"

"It isn't the same," I protested. "You don't get lost in it." *You don't wonder whether you really do have control or whether the fury is driving you.*

Her mouth twisted. "I know what it's like to get caught up in emotion. To want to hurt someone so badly you forget everything else in that moment. I don't like it either."

I frowned. My hand moved of its own accord, stroking over her hair. "I'm sure if you've ever felt that way about anyone, they deserved it," I said fiercely.

She closed her eyes, her expression relaxing at my touch. As if she welcomed it every bit as much as I'd wanted to offer it. Skies above, could I be that lucky?

"And the horde you were just tackling didn't deserve it?" she asked.

I wet my lips. "I was defending myself. So, I suppose they did. I don't even remember what we would have been fighting over in whatever memory Muninn pulled them from."

"What's there to feel guilty about then?"

I paused. The answer stuck in my throat. "Sometimes, I regret… We always talked about the giants as our enemy, you know. I didn't even trust Loki for the longest time. But the truth is, my mother was a giantess."

Ari's eyebrows rose as she met my eyes again. "Odin and all his many travels," she said, sounding only amused.

"Basically," I said, a little of my shame at the admission fading. "But he took me back to Asgard as his own, and I always acted as if I were only his. For all I know, I've killed cousins or uncles or who knows what relatives on the battlefield. I never stopped to ask."

"They didn't ask you either," Ari pointed out.

"You don't think there's something twisted about that?"

She shrugged. "I don't think blood means very much. My dad took off before I was old enough to remember him. My mom spent more time cutting me down than taking care of me. I'd sooner help a stranger than her. Being born isn't a promise to anyone."

"But you also wouldn't beat any of them into a bloody pulp."

"I might have been tempted recently," she muttered. She grasped my hand where it was still resting against her hair, curling her fingers around mine. "You want to know how I think about you, Thor? I see strength and devotion and a huge heart that can't stand the thought of anyone under your protection, which is basically all of humankind, getting hurt." She grinned. "Oh, and let's not forget an enormous appetite and the most enthusiastic laugh I've ever heard."

I could almost see my reflection glinting back at me in her gray eyes. I didn't need any of Baldur's special senses to know she was telling the truth. The tension that had been wound through my gut subsided.

Ari's head twitched to the side. Her eyes narrowed. "What?" I said. Even as the words left my lips, I caught a hint of something. A dark shimmer, a brief movement, there beyond the stretch of grass and then gone.

"The real world broke through again," Ari said, turning with her hand still clasped around mine. "I saw a little more this time. It was dark, but there was a reddish light, and for a second I felt so hot…" She looked back at me, but her gaze was distant. "It happened when Loki and Freya were talking too."

"I caught a glimpse of something too," I said. "Just now. But only a glimmer."

A smile leapt to Ari's face. "You did? Then the effect is getting stronger. We're getting closer to breaking through. It seems almost like… When it happened before, Loki was apologizing to Freya for not recognizing how great a warrior she is. And just now, I made you think about yourself, about all those battles, a little differently, maybe?" She studied my face.

"You did," I said. "You think that's what caused the break?"

"I don't know. But maybe, when we change our minds about something, or realize we were looking at them the wrong way in the past… That could shake up Muninn's construct, right? Anything that shakes up our memories and the way we think about them should, since she's using those memories as her foundation for this whole place. A little more of that and we'll crack the entire thing apart."

My spirits rose. "We can hope."

"Yeah, we can. Don't let her wear you down, okay?"

She slipped her arms around me, and I bent into her embrace. A smell like clover tickled off her soft hair over a scent like a just-lit flame. Every nerve in my body thrummed with the closeness of her.

When she drew back, her cheek grazed mine. My breath caught. She hesitated there, her lips just inches from mine. Heat rose in the space between us.

"Thor," she said quietly.

"Ari." My voice came out raw. "You and Loki…" The memory of him kissing her in the courtyard jabbed at me.

"…understand very well that I'm not looking to get tied down at the moment," she filled in. Her breath tickled over my jaw. "Which is a good thing, because I don't know if I could be happy just picking one of you. Unless you don't want—"

"To Hel with that," I said, and drew her lips to mine.

She kissed just as sweet as she smelled, the joy of our minor victory rippling between us. I ran my fingers deeper into her hair, and a pleased murmur escaped her. Her body melted into me as if she needed the strength she'd talked about—my strength—to get her through this, if only just in this moment.

The feel of her warm and eager against me almost made me lose my head in a very different way. But it also reminded me that we weren't anywhere near through this prison yet. Reluctantly, I eased back from her. She beamed up at me. The sight of the flush in her cheeks, the rosiness of her lips after that kiss, sent a bolt of lust right to my groin. It took all my self-control not to pull her right back to me.

"Still a lot farther to go," I said.

"Yeah." She turned, her hand on my arm, and her eyes widened. Her jaw went slack and then snapped shut. "I see—"

I leaned forward to try to make out what she'd deciphered, and an invisible force thrust up between us, ripping Ari away from me. With a shout, I snatched after her. My fingers closed only around empty air.

# 12

*Aria*

The world spiraled around me. I tried to shove myself back toward Thor. The wind whipped my body forward, and between the flashes of grass and stone, my gaze caught on a hunched figure behind the thick bars of a cage, a ring of fire licking all around it. The figure raised his head just slightly, showing a silver-flecked beard and one scarred-over eye—*Odin*. A twang ran through my chest: the connection I'd felt when I was searching for him before. That was the real god. But where was he? I had to catch every clue I could…

The smell of ash and something pungently bitter clogged my nose and mouth, and then I was wrenched away from there too. My groping hand closed around solid flesh. I clung on, but the wrist slipped from my grasp.

My ears popped. I fell on my ass on marble tiles that were so familiar their hard surface was almost a relief. I was back in the Asgard we'd first entered. The massive stone halls loomed around me, hot summer sun streaking between them. In front of me, a huge group of gods—constructs, I had to assume—had gathered in a circle in a smaller courtyard with buildings tight around it. They whooped and hollered at whatever they were watching.

I pushed myself to my feet, catching my balance against the side of the hall I'd landed next to. I hadn't completely lost Thor. He was just straightening up where he must have landed outside the neighboring buildings. His gaze fell on the crowd before it found me. He stiffened, his usually ruddy complexion paling.

What? My head jerked back around to search the crowd, but I was too short to see over the tops of most of the gods' heads. All I knew was that whatever they were doing, it was making them laugh and chatter amongst themselves. It sounded pretty good-humored. But obviously Thor saw something I didn't.

Or remembered something I couldn't have.

I scrambled onto a ledge on the side of the building for a better look. Clinging to the cool stones, I turned toward the crowd again, and froze.

Baldur was standing in a cleared space in the middle of the ring of gods. Distress, a sharper emotion than I'd ever seen from him before, was etched all across his face. One of the gods at the edge of the ring chucked a knife at him, another a stone, another what looked like a carrot. He batted them away with bursts of light from his skin, his mouth twisting tighter.

What the fuck were they doing? Why were they pelting Baldur, of all people, like that? Hell, they looked *happy* about it, smiles stretching across all those faces, the laughter I'd heard before carrying through the gathering. Like it was a friendly game, all in good sport. Couldn't they see he hated it?

No, they couldn't see anything. They were just constructs. I had to remember that. Constructs Muninn had built and guided like puppets.

But something about this must have come from a memory. It didn't make sense.

I braced myself against the wall to release my wings, but before I could leap off to fly to Baldur, a dark-haired form shoved through the crowd.

"Baldur!" Hod called out.

His twin brother turned. A flash of—was that *panic*?—crossed Baldur's face before his expression settled into one of relief.

Hod hooked his arm around Baldur's and cleared a path with lashes of shadow as he led the light god out of the ring. I watched them go until a flicker in the open space drew my gaze back. My mouth fell open.

Baldur had reappeared in the middle of the ring. But—

My gaze darted back and forth. There were two Baldurs now. The one standing with Hod at the fringes of the crowd, shaking his head with a smile that still looked a bit pained at whatever his brother was saying, and the one who'd appeared out of nowhere in the midst of the other gods.

The new one stood there with arms spread as if welcoming the projectiles, totally serene. I didn't see any magical glow around him, but when more of the gods took up the "game," tossing a plate, a potato, a spear, every object simply bounced off his body and dropped to the ground.

Huh. This just got weirder and weirder.

Maybe sometime long ago Baldur really had stood there and been pelted, for whatever crazy reason. Someone clearly remembered that.

Thor must have spotted his brothers—half brothers, given what he'd told me about his mother? He was striding around the outer edge of the ring to join them. I hopped down from my ledge and hurried after him. There was only one place I was getting any answers. It was a good sign, wasn't it, that almost all of us had found each other again? We had a better chance of breaking down Muninn's prison the more of our minds we could put together. At least, I hoped so.

"—not going to come to that," Hod was saying in a rough voice when I reached them. "Let's just go. We don't have to put up with her torture."

"I don't think leaving will be enough," Baldur said, his usual melodic lilt eerily subdued. "I can feel it. The things they're throwing at that memory of me. I can feel all of it."

If I'd thought Thor had gone pale before, it was nothing compared to the sallow shade Hod's face turned at that information. His hands clenched.

"Then we'll find the other constructs she's conjured up and stop them before it gets to that point."

"Gets to what point?" I asked, studying their expressions in turn. "What the hell is going on over there?"

Hod's dark eyes veered toward my voice automatically, and somehow even more color managed to drain from his face. "If we get on with this, you won't ever have to find out, valkyrie," he said, and strode forward, a stick of shadow darting across the ground in front of him. "Has anyone seen Loki yet? One or another of him must be around here somewhere."

"I'll turn him up if he's here," Thor rumbled, and set off in the opposite direction to cover more of the courtyard. Baldur trailed behind his twin. His apprehension quavered so close to the surface that I could sense it where I normally only felt that dreamy calm from him.

I hurried after them, slowing when I caught up with Baldur. "What's the matter? Why were they doing that to you? It really happened, didn't it?"

"It did," he said, his gaze still following his brother. "Hod's right. It'd be better if we simply stop it and don't have to relive the whole event."

"Why?" The other version of him, the remembered one, hadn't looked disturbed at all. He'd seemed to be welcoming the onslaught. "I don't get it. Did everyone just go bonkers one day, or was—"

"Aria." His voice stayed soft, but there was a note of steel in it. "I don't want to go there. Leave it. *Please.*"

I'd started to bristle, but the anguish in that last word wrenched at my heart. My mouth snapped shut. "I'm sorry," I said after a moment. "I'll try to help. What exactly are we looking for?"

Baldur glanced down at me then. Some emotion I couldn't read shimmered in his bright blue eyes. He set his hand on my arm and squeezed gently. The touch flooded me with a sudden warmth. For fuck's sake, every one of these gods was way too appealing. I'd just been kissing Thor, and tempting Hod into another kiss before that, and Loki, well… And now one possibly-only-friendly gesture from Baldur had set me alight.

Scratching that itch with Loki the other morning definitely hadn't sated my hunger. I didn't think it'd even taken the edge off. If anything, part of me wanted to find out what it could be like with each of the others even more now. As if this were even close to the time or place for that.

"Loki should be around here somewhere," Baldur said. "Possibly two of him as you can see two of me. And there may be another Hod. The more of them we can spot, the better."

"On it." I gave him a little salute and pushed myself off the ground with a flap of my wings. They did come in handy at times like this.

Someone in the crowd chucked an axe at the memory-Baldur. It glanced off his skin, and the gods all cheered. I grimaced at them, not that they seemed to be able to see me, and soared over the ring.

Freya's bright head came into view. She hustled over to Hod where he was circling the crowd. Her expression was already tensed. They all knew what was happening here, or about to happen. All of them except me. Whatever it was, it was clearly going to be awful.

I wheeled, and a shock of pale red hair gleamed between the shadows of the buildings. Loki sauntered out of a side path at the other side of the courtyard. He took in the scene, and his lips pressed flat.

When even he couldn't find anything amusing in a situation, you knew it was really bad.

"Hod!" I called with a gesture toward the trickster, and then remembered the blind god wouldn't be able to see my pointing arm. But Thor had heard me too. He hustled around the crowd to join Loki, and the two of them hurried to where the other three had stopped. I dove down, my feet touching the ground just as all five of the gods met up.

"You haven't found the spot yet?" Loki was saying.

Hod had bristled. "After all this time, with all the activity, it's hard to mark it exactly."

"Well, come on then. Obviously I have to do everything around here."

Loki stalked off around the ring, and the rest of us hurried after him. His gaze twitched from side to side. Then his shoulders tensed, and he sped up to a lope.

I saw why a second later. The sun caught on another head of pale red hair, this one partway through the crowd. The second Loki. I propelled myself off the ground with my wings for a better view.

Not just a second Loki. Another Hod, as youthful as always but with hair falling a little longer around his face, stood next to him. The memory-Loki was guiding him forward with a hand on his elbow. The memory-Hod was clutching a small branch, a few leaves as dark green as his eyes still clinging to it. The tip had been carved to a point.

The real Loki cursed and shoved his way into the crowd, but the other him and the other Hod had just reached the inner edge of the ring. That Loki bent close to Hod's ear as if to murmur something to him. He drew back the other god's hand, the one that held the branch, and gave a brisk nod.

My Loki lunged forward, grabbing the other Loki by the arm. The other Hod had already flung the branch forward. It spun through the air. The memory-Baldur turned to face his brother, and the branch struck him right over the heart.

Struck him and stabbed into his chest, blood welling up all around it.

A choked sound broke from my throat. I dove down, but Baldur's legs were already sagging. The god of light collapsed on the ground. Blood pulsed from the wound to pool on the marble tiles. Slowing as his heart stopped.

I hit the ground so hard I fell to my knees. They smacked the hard stone, but I hardly felt the impact. Baldur's head lolled. His bright blue eyes were glazed. My stomach heaved.

The crowd around us had gone quiet. A wail cut through the stunned silence. More and more voices joined it, with gasps and sobs, in a vast chorus of mourning.

I'd only dragged in one ragged breath, and the wails cut off as quickly as they'd risen up. I lifted my head. The crowd had disappeared. There was no one left but the real gods and the Baldur from their memories, lying there in that pool of his blood. Looking very, very dead.

He couldn't really have— I dropped my face into my hands, my heart thudding painfully hard. That sense I'd had that he was hiding something. The conversations about burying unpleasant memories so deep you never had to face them. That comment he'd made, with such a strange note in his voice it'd stuck with me: *I wasn't there for Ragnarok.*

Because he'd died before it ever happened.

Died… because Hod had thrown some special branch at him. Because Loki had guided the god of darkness there.

My gaze jerked up. The real Loki, my Loki, was standing in the courtyard where he'd tried to stop his old self. A shadow had dulled his normally brilliant eyes. His jaw worked.

A thump at the edge of the courtyard drew both our attentions. The real Baldur had turned away, his hand braced against the front of one of the halls as if holding his body up. His shoulders shook and tensed and shook again.

*I can feel it*, he'd said just a few minutes ago. *I can feel all of it*. What was he feeling now? Was he dying like his counterpart? I pushed myself off the ground.

Hod spun toward Loki, his face even harder than usual.

Loki spread his hands. "I tried," he said. "I tried to stop it."

"Not that there would have been anything to stop if you hadn't done it in the first place," the dark god spat out.

My legs wobbled. "Would someone please tell me what the hell just happened?" I said. "Is Baldur okay? Why was *anyone* throwing anything at him? How could that little branch…"

"I'll be—I'll be all right," Baldur forced out, but his voice was weak and ragged. Hod glanced toward him, shifting and then tensing as if he wanted to go to his twin but didn't at the same time.

Thor stepped toward me. He set a steadying hand on my back. "A long time ago—not that long before Ragnarok—Baldur and his mother, the goddess Frigg, started having dreams about him dying. Frigg was so worried for him she went around the realms asking every object to vow it would never hurt him. But she passed over the mistletoe. She said it seemed too young and meek to hurt anyone."

The initial scene made a little more sense, knowing that. "So everyone figured they'd test out those vows?" I said. From what I'd seen, it'd worked. Nothing had hurt Baldur in the slightest.

"Like a game," Loki said in an edged voice. "A stupid, careless game. Let's pretend to kill the god so recently terrified of dying."

"Better than actually killing him," Freya said.

"I didn't, did I?" the trickster said, whirling around. "I brought the mistletoe. I offered it to Hod. It seems to me he willingly took it. He wanted to join in, and I let him."

"You knew it might really hurt him," Hod snapped back. "Who sharpened its end into a spear? You didn't tell me what I was holding."

"You didn't ask. Did you even really want to know?"

An angry flush swept across Hod's pale face. "You can't be suggesting I was hoping for that outcome."

"How should I know?" Loki demanded. "The bitterness was wafting off you like the stink of a skunk. It was a stupid game played by stupid gods trying not to see the world was on the verge of collapsing, and I gave you the means to open their eyes."

"You killed him," Hod said. "You killed him with my hand, and for that they killed me too, and you went off merrily free. And we all know how you repaid the rest of Asgard."

Loki waved a hand at him. "Look at you even now. What matters to you more: having a go at me, or looking after your beloved brother?"

"You…" The word came out strangled. Hod threw himself at the trickster.

"Stop!" I cried out. Thor caught his brother by the shoulder. He glowered at Loki.

Loki looked from the two of them to the shaking Baldur and then to Freya, who was watching the scene with accusing eyes. He turned to me. There was a wildness in his movements, in his face, that I'd never seen before, desperate and vicious. I took a step back.

"It really happened like that, didn't it?" I said. "You really killed him." Not a trick. Not a little trouble he could talk his way back out of. Cold, deliberate murder. And he was defending it even now.

My stomach lurched again. Loki's expression shuttered.

"Fine," he said. "This is the way it always is, the way it always was. As if you had the slightest idea… Enjoy your high horses in your glass houses."

He spun on his heel and swept away on his shoes of flight. Hod looked as if he might try to chase him, but he moved instead to his twin. Freya caught Thor's gaze and shook her head as if to say, *What a shame, but what else could we expect?*

My gut was still knotted. I swayed back another step, and found myself flipping backward out of the courtyard, into the darkness of Muninn's mind.

# 13

*Aria*

I stumbled straight into a room I guessed was a study. A big oak desk stood at one end, surrounded by bookshelves. At the other, where I was now standing, two old-fashioned maroon armchairs faced each other with a little bow-legged table between them. My sneakers sank into the rich pile of the rug beneath them. A slight smoky smell hung in the air, but this time it was wood smoke, not the chemical ash I'd noticed before. From the fireplace in the corner, I guessed.

Whose memory was this? The furniture looked human-made, not the grand scale I'd seen on Asgard, but it was smaller and cozier than the study in the gods' Midgard home that seemed to be mostly Hod's domain. I'd never been in a house other than that one that even had a study.

I turned to try the door and found the wall where there should be one was solid, nothing but yellow-gold rose-print wallpaper. A claustrophobic itch crawled across my shoulders despite the room's cozy warmth.

A black shape fluttered past me. I jerked around to see a raven land on the top of one of the arm chairs. It cocked its head at me in a much too familiar gesture. Then, with a twitch of its body, the bird transformed into a woman.

Muninn settled into the seat of the chair, the skirt of her loose black dress tucked under her slim palm legs, her dark eyes watching me as intently as when she'd been in raven form. My pulse hiccupped. This whole time, she'd been hiding away from us, casting me off again every time I caught a glimpse—or bringing buildings down on me. What did it mean that she was revealing herself now?

"Valkyrie," she said in her sweetly hoarse voice. "Why don't you sit down?"

"Well, for starters, after everything you've thrown at me so far, I feel safer on my feet," I said.

She blinked at me as if she didn't totally understand what I was referring to. She might have looked like a person right now, and she was definitely as smart and aware as any human being I'd met, but from what I'd seen of her so far, her mind was as much raven as it was human. I wasn't sure how much concepts like fair play or compassion applied where she was concerned.

"I promise no harm will come to you in this room," she said. "And that I will not send you out of it until we're finished speaking."

The words rang with a magical force that sent an eerie tingling over my skin. I'd spent enough time in the company of gods to believe she was bound to that vow.

As much as all the things Baldur's mother had begged had been bound to their vow? My stomach clenched all over again, remembering the scene she'd torn me out of. But my body was still mottled with aches and pains, my legs a little wobbly. Sitting, if I had that promise, might not be such a bad thing.

I sank into the other chair, my gaze never leaving the raven woman. She flicked her sleek black hair back from her face with a fluttery gesture and considered me in return.

"Would you like something to eat?" she asked.

Despite all the tension in me and the horror of what I'd just witnessed, a pang shot through me. I licked my lips. "Something I *can* actually eat?"

"Of course. I'm not that horrible a host." She motioned to the table, and a silver plate appeared. It held a dinner roll stuffed with cheese and sliced meat, a bunch of grapes, and a raspberry tart.

Saliva sprang into my mouth as the bready scent reached my nose. I managed not to snatch up the sandwich but to grasp it firmly and raise it calmly to my mouth. I braced myself as I bit down—and my teeth sank into real bread, real cheddar, real ham.

In a matter of minutes, I'd gulped the whole thing down, the grapes and the tart too. Who knew when Muninn might decide to take them away? I couldn't help licking the last crumbs from my fingers, since I couldn't count on her being this generous again. Somewhere in there a glass of water had appeared on the table too. I grabbed in and drained it.

Muninn sat quietly, watching me, through the meal. When I finished, wiping my mouth with the back of my hand, she gave me a small smile.

"Refreshed?" she said.

"Yes." I hesitated. "Why did you give me that? Why am I here?"

She shrugged. "I simply wanted to talk. You've seen a lot since you arrived here. What the gods of Asgard are capable of. How they make their fun. How they settle their grievances. Not quite as pretty a picture as I'd guess they painted you of the place, is it?"

"They hadn't told me all that much about it," I said honestly. Had she tossed us into those memories for that reason too? Not just to torment each of us with glimpses of the past, theoretical or actual, but to put on some sort of demonstration? Just like she'd tried to paint Valhalla in the negative light of her memories. My hands clenched in my lap.

"I can't imagine you're very impressed either way," she said. "And there's so much more I could show you. Ages and ages of petty in-fighting and prejudice, callousness and violence. That's what the gods are made of, it seems."

"All of that was a long time ago," I said. "They haven't acted anything like that in the time I've been with them."

"Other than just now, when I *made* them remember their past?" Muninn leaned forward. "They've put on a little show for you. For their precious valkyrie and her precious mission to find Odin. They don't give a damn about you, any more than Loki gave a damn about Baldur's life, any more than Thor gave a damn about the endless lives he slaughtered, any more than Odin gave a damn whether his warriors were really all that worthy."

"Is that why you're putting us through all this? Because you don't like things they've done? It's kind of the pot calling the kettle black to accuse *them* of being cruel. How many times could any of us have been killed by the stuff you created in there?"

The raven woman didn't look fazed by my accusation. "If you had just sat tight, accepted the realm I'd given you, I wouldn't have needed to do anything at all. But you were trying to break out. Measures require countermeasures."

I had the feeling I wasn't going to convince her of my point of view any time soon. "Okay," I said. "Fine. That still doesn't answer why I'm here." Or why she'd shut us in this prison in the first place, not that I expected her to tell me about that.

Her smile came back. "I'm hoping you'll see reason," she said. "You've made your feelings about the holding cell I've created very clear. And it's true, I have no real dispute with you. You simply happened to be in poor company. So I wanted to make you an offer."

My body stiffened against the chair's soft padding. "What kind of offer?" I pressed when she paused.

"Leave them," she said, her eyes intent on me. "Let them deal with their memories alone. They suffer nothing but what they brought on themselves anyway. What I do isn't easy on my own. I could use a valkyrie on my side. They don't deserve your loyalty."

I caught a laugh. "And *you* do?"

"I would earn it. I don't expect something for nothing as they so often do. You'd have your freedom too. You wouldn't serve me—we'd be allies. Equals."

"Do you really think after all the times you lied to us, all the danger you've put us in, that I could ever trust you?"

She blinked, more slowly this time. "I can admit that you shouldn't have taken their punishment with them. You can escape it now. If you choose to return to them… I do what I have to in order to keep the holding cell stable. I can't promise anything about what you might see from your own mind."

My thoughts tripped back to Petey in his new home. A shiver ran down my spine. "If you use my brother again—"

Her eyebrows lifted. "Which one? There are so many things I've seen in your memories that you might want to avoid."

I swallowed hard. This was an offer, sure. It was also a threat. Just thinking about all the things from my past she might decide to dredge up if I refused chilled me down to the bone.

I didn't have to find out what else she'd put me through. I could accept her offer. Leave the gods and goddess behind. See what awaited me outside this room that I had to assume wasn't Muninn's real surroundings either. Maybe I'd have better opportunities to get the others free from the outside.

Or was I just thinking that to justify sparing myself?

I shifted in the chair, resisting the urge to draw my knees up in front of me like a child. "How would it work? This alliance? How could I know I could trust you to keep your word?" *How are you planning on making sure I keep mine?*

Muninn spread her dainty hands. "A simple vow should cover all concerns. On both sides. We'll both want some security in the deal, I assume." Her eyes glinted as if she'd read my thoughts as well as my memories.

If I took a vow of loyalty, I'd be stuck with her. And it would probably stop me from doing anything to help the gods she was against. I sucked in my lower lip.

Every part of me balked at the idea of wading back into those memories—both mine and those of the gods. I didn't know what to think of Loki or Hod after the scene I'd witnessed. What other secrets did Thor and Freya and even Baldur have that I might not have realized yet? They'd all hidden a lot from me, hadn't they?

But even as my anxiety gnawed at me to cut myself loose, other sorts of memories surfaced. Hod sitting with me on the roof across from Petey's foster family's house as I said my good-byes, offering words to steady me, taking me in his arms when I'd reached out to him. Baldur healing the many wounds I'd taken with his normally unshakeable smile. Freya talking through my discomfort with me, sharing her own frustration that she couldn't do more for her husband. Thor lending me his hammer so I could burn off some of my tension, kissing me just now with such unexpected vulnerability.

And Loki. My trickster. My stomach knotted all over again remembering the way he'd talked to Hod, the way he'd defended how he'd guided Baldur's death. How could that be the same man who'd brushed aside the way the gods had tormented him before, who'd reassured me that *I* didn't need to be angry on his behalf?

I'd known he might be dangerous. Was that his nature, like the fire he could conjure? Simmering hot below the surface until a sharp gust sent him flaring, burning everyone around him?

I didn't have all the answers yet. I'd barely had a chance to ask the questions. Muninn had suggested that the gods had expected a lot from me without giving anything in return, but they'd given me a lot. I wouldn't be alive at all if not for them. I wouldn't have these powers. They'd been there with me, supporting me, every step of this journey until now.

No. I couldn't abandon them. Hell, even the thought of what they might be going through right now made my heart ache.

"Thanks for the offer," I said, standing up, "but I'm going to have to say no thanks. So, go ahead and do whatever you've got to do. I'm with them."

Muninn's gaze followed me as she stayed put in her chair. Her jaw tightened. "Have you really thought this through?"

What did it matter to her that much anyway? In there, I was just one more person for her to torment, wasn't I? I couldn't see how she'd need a helper that much, one she couldn't just find somewhere else among the dark elves or whoever.

I paused. It wasn't really about how I could help her out here, was it? It was about how I might hurt her in there.

"You're right," I said. "I hadn't thought it all the way through. You don't even really want an alliance with me, do you? You're just worried about me being in your little 'holding cell' because I don't share that many memories with the others. It's too easy for me to see through your constructs when I'm with them. Too easy for me to shake up their memories with an outside perspective."

"You don't know anything," she said, her tone turning haughty. Her chin rose.

"I know I'm going to shatter this prison," I shot back. "I know you know it too, or you wouldn't be scared enough of me to try to wine and dine me. Maybe I should be the one making you offers. Let us out now, and we won't—"

She made a strangled sound and thrust out her hands. "Have the world you want then. It'll only get worse."

I stumbled backward—and out through an open door that hadn't been there an instant before.

# 14

*Baldur*

I tried to hold on. With every shred of strength I had in me, I tried. But the darkness swelled from right inside me, blotting out the courtyard and the wall I'd been braced against and my fellow gods. Blotting out *me.* I was nothing more than a thought in an infinite void, a dark cold expanse that went on and on and yet closed around me so tightly I struggled to breathe.

Silence echoed in my ears. No taste met my tongue, no scent reached my nose. No sensation touched me at all except frigid nothingness.

My mind shuddered. I had the impulse to close the eyes I could no longer feel, as if I could shut out the darkness with more darkness. Maybe they were already closed. I tried to grope and flail, but I couldn't tell if I was even moving. A shudder rattled through my thoughts.

Not this again. By all that was sacred, *no.*

It would be over. I grasped on to that fact the moment it rose up in my mind. This wasn't forever. It was only a trick of Muninn's.

She was emulating the cold dark of death I'd lingered in for years and years that seemed like an eternity, when I'd thought it might be an eternity after all. I'd had no idea, that first time, that I'd be reborn. For all I'd known, I was destined to drift in that chilling nothingness until my thoughts completely disintegrated and—

No. It wasn't doing me any good remembering that fear. I had to fight this. Muninn wanted to destroy us, and I couldn't let her.

If only she hadn't chosen her weapon so well.

Focus on what came after. Focus on the warmth and the light. Light to burn away the darkness she'd summoned. I tightened my hold on my thoughts and turned them in that direction.

It *had* been warm and light, that moment when I'd opened my eyes to a field on the edge of Asgard, tall grass hissing around me in a late spring breeze, the sun beaming overhead. With all that sensation around me all at once after so long in the void, I hadn't known how to process it. I just lay there for what felt like hours, soaking it in, my thoughts settling behind a fog of calm I summoned with the light. I needed that fog to drown out everything before: the cold and the dark and the nothingness.

Maybe it hadn't been all that long, though. When I'd stood up in the field, other gods and goddesses all around me were just finding their feet too. We turned, taking in each other and the halls of our great city, tall and shining, beyond the grass. A few of the others had started to laugh in pure delight. Tears streamed down one goddess's face past her brilliant smile. I'd smiled back automatically. I didn't know what they'd been through, but I could understand their joy.

I'd turned again and found myself face to face with Hod.

The last time I'd faced him—*no.* I cut off that thought, that memory, and the flare of darkness that clung onto it.

"Brother," he'd said roughly.

I couldn't say how he'd recognized me. We'd been by each other's side so often from the moment we were born, he probably could have read my presence in the rhythm of my breath, in the shift of my weight against the ground. He'd told me once that he could feel the light in me even if he couldn't see it.

I opened my arms, and he stepped into them. We'd never hugged all that much even as children, but that moment had seemed like the time for it. He'd squeezed me hard and stepped back, tension still strung all through his body.

"Brother, I—"

I cut him off instinctively, my mind sinking deeper into that fog of light. "It's good to be back, isn't it?" I teased my fingertips over the blades of grass. "It's wonderful."

He swallowed with a bob of his throat. "Yes. Yes, it is. Everything feels as it was. Does it look the same?"

I considered the city again. Was the gleam slightly more muted? I didn't know if I could trust my memories from before the void. It had crept through every part of me. Tarnished every image I'd ever held.

A cold shiver ran through me. I sank deep into the haze.

"As magnificent as it ever was." I beckoned him with a brush of my fingers against his sleeve. "Let's go home."

We hadn't made it all the way to the city in that first go. We'd only taken a few steps when a tall imposing figure moved to join us.

Our father, the Allfather, had been reborn with his travel-worn cloak draped across his shoulders and his dented broad-brimmed hat still shading his single bright eye and the scar of the other. He looked as if he hadn't so much come back from the dead as from a ramble around Midgard.

"My sons," he'd said in his low voice. He clapped Hod on the shoulder and pulled me into a brief but tight embrace. "It's been too long."

His gaze traveled across the field and paused on Frigg, our mother. She was watching us from where she'd hesitated in the middle of the crowd of reborn Aesir. Something in Odin's face darkened.

I didn't understand it then, didn't let myself focus on it long enough to ask, but later I learned their marriage had started to splinter not long after my death. He'd blamed her for the vows, for the game that had followed them and its tragic end. More, it'd seemed, than he blamed Loki, which had never made a lot of sense to me in the fleeting moments I'd let myself consider it. But my father's deeper thoughts were often mysterious.

He prodded my side then, firmly but not hard enough to hurt. "The vows that were made on your mother's behalf won't apply to you in your rebirth," he said, his tone going a bit gruff. "Don't tempt fate by pretending invulnerability."

"Of course not," I said.

I'd seen my own wife then: the lovely Nanna. She darted through the grass to join us and linked her arm around mine, tipping her head against my shoulder with a sigh that was almost a sob. Even as I raised my hand that first time to draw her closer to me, the fog I'd wrapped around myself crept into the space between us.

No matter how much light I summoned to cloud out the past, I knew I wasn't the god she'd married. I'd left too much behind in the darkness of the void. Not many marriages of Asgard had survived the first century after Ragnarok, but ours had crumbled faster than most.

In the present, in Muninn's false-void, I shivered. There wasn't much warmth in the memory of our falling apart. If I stayed there, the raven won. I cast my mind further forward instead.

The only figure of real importance I hadn't seen in the field that day was Loki himself. It was only some time later he'd come to me as I'd taken a stroll through the orchard. Another bright spring day, but I couldn't say whether it'd been just a few weeks after our reawakening or the next year. The days had blurred together with the haze around my thoughts.

"Oh, Light One," he'd said in his jaunty tone, falling into step beside me. But he'd kept a cautious distance between us, his head dipping somewhat deferentially. "I hope there aren't any hard feelings—bygones left to be bygones and all that? I've never borne *you* any animosity. The circumstances being what they were—making the best of a bad situation…"

"I hold no grudges," I told him. I didn't want to feel anything, didn't want to think anything about the time before the field at all.

He'd given me his brightest grin, brilliant enough to rival a blazing fire, and we'd never spoken of it again. You could say a lot of things about the trickster, but one thing he knew how to be without flaw was circumspect, if he felt he owed you that much.

That memory sent me sliding back into the dark of the present. The sharp words thrown back and forth between my brother and Loki as I'd spiraled into this place. I tried to squeeze those images out of my mind.

The cold squeezed tighter around me at the same time. Darkness choked the throat I couldn't otherwise feel. A jolt of panic scattered my thoughts.

Light. I needed light. That was the only way I could fight this.

Normally I could will a warm glow out of myself simply by wanting to. Light clung to me and wound through me the way shadows came to Hod. I willed a burst of brightness into the space around me, as if I didn't already know how that would end.

The light and the warmth vanished into the void, swallowed up the second they left me as if they'd never been there. The chill seeped even deeper.

I propelled more light out and felt it leached away from me before I caught control of myself. There was no point in feeding brightness to the dark. I had to pull back inside myself, hold on to the light I could find there. Just staying sane would be a victory. Muninn could wound me, but only as deeply as I let her.

There'd been so much light in my life, even in the years waiting for Odin's return on Midgard. Loki, eyes always gleaming with mischief, hair shining like fire, beaming as he made his sly jokes. Thor's jovial voice as he roared with laughter and passed on a plate of food while we sat by the crackling hearth. The walks I'd taken with Freya through the countryside, both of us quiet in a mutual understanding that we wanted company, not conversation.

And Hod, who dwelled in his own darkness so much that even a glimpse of light from him could fill a room. The times he'd stopped by the music room and leaned back to listen to me play, a rare smile crossing his face… I treasured every memory like that.

I'd seen his smile more in the last couple weeks, when he watched Aria. Our valkyrie lit something in my brother without even realizing it. But then, she had almost as much fire in her as Loki did. My memories of her glinted in my mind: her lilting voice as she'd sung along with my guitar, her grin warm or fierce depending on the situation in front of us.

Maybe not fire. Her strength and brightness were like she was made of steel forged out of sunlight.

Even as I thought that, the memory I'd been hiding myself in dimmed. A wash of cold crept through it, dulling Ari's shine. I whipped my thoughts from her to Hod, to Loki, to our other companions, but the darkness chased after me.

That had happened before too. The void had crept inside me until it'd filled every crevice in my head, tainted even my fondest memories.

I couldn't let that happen. I couldn't fall into that endless pit again. I'd left too much behind the first time. What would be left of me if I lost myself a second time? The others, all of them—they needed me in this battle.

The panic shivered through me. I tried to twist and pin down my thoughts, but they flitted every which way, fleeing the fingers of cold. I hadn't been ready for this.

I hadn't let myself be, I'd been so afraid to even consider it might happen.

A different memory rose up, one not bright or warm but tinged with regret. Hod had come to me wanting to talk about that moment in the courtyard, about what I might have gone through afterward, just a few days ago. I'd turned him away. I'd told him there was no need. I'd snapped at him to stop.

I'd been wrong. How had I ever convinced myself that I'd somehow made my peace with the past? I simply hadn't dwelled in it and had called that peace enough. But now that I was forced to dwell in it again, I didn't have the slightest idea how to fend it off. I had nothing but the panic and the dread rising up beneath it.

Just breathe. I clung onto that idea as closely as I could. Just breathe with the lungs I couldn't feel, the air I couldn't taste. In and out. Think of nothing but that. I *had* to hold on as long as I could. Eventually this would be over. Eventually Muninn would decide I'd had enough. Maybe I couldn't fight, but I could endure.

Let me not have lost too much by the time she gave in. And if I ever got another chance to talk, to push aside the haze and tackle the truth with someone who cared—skies above, let me not waste it.

# 15

*Aria*

I should have known I'd end up somewhere bad after Muninn's warning, after the anger on her face. But somehow I wasn't prepared to find myself skidding to a stop in the living room of my old house, with the sour smell seeping from the stained carpet and the sofa cushions sagging in the dim light that made it past the blinds. Every muscle in my body tensed instinctively, even though I was alone in the room.

Alone for that brief moment. I spun around, and Mom appeared in the doorway to the kitchen, her expression taut as a wrung towel.

She jabbed a finger at me. "Don't give me that look. As if you deserve half the time and energy I already give to you. Why don't you stay in your room where I don't have to see that pinched face of yours? You don't like dinner? Get a job and buy it yourself."

It was a patchwork of rants from across my childhood. Lord only knew which dinner I'd complained about—a lot of the time she'd just tossed a few pieces of bread and some margarine on the table and told Francis and me to go at it. By the time I was thirteen, a year after his death, I *had* started picking up odd jobs to keep me out of the house and put a little more food in my belly. She'd been making that suggestion since I was something like five, if she bothered to answer a complaint at all instead of just rolling her eyes and turning her back on me.

"Why don't *you* get a job?" I snapped back now before I had a chance to think better of engaging. My nerves jittered. Who else was going to appear? That hair-cut—lank, shoulder-length, and bleached a yellower blonde—that was circa the Trevor years. An icier shudder ran through me.

"Don't you talk to me like that, you little bitch!" Mom screeched. I was already diving for the door at the other end of the room. I dashed through the mudroom that was more of a trash bin, out to the backyard where the rusted swing set left by the house's former owners was creaking.

If I got far enough away, would Muninn just throw me back here? Might as well find out. I'd rather be running than waiting around for the real horror show to start. What I really needed was to find at least one of the other gods. The raven woman had all but confirmed it with her reactions. When we were together, challenging the memories, her prison got so much shakier.

I scrambled over the dented chain-link fence and dashed down the neighbor's driveway. The growl of a familiar engine, the one that had taught me to burrow myself deep under my covers if I heard it arriving late at night—as if that would protect me any—carried down the street.

My heart stuttered. I threw myself in the opposite direction.

I was stronger than that now. If he came at me, if Muninn forced the issue, I'd slit his fucking throat. The thought was sickening and satisfying at the same time.

I rounded the corner, past the laundromat and off-brand burger place. How far was she going to let me run? Maybe I'd just make for the park. Have a nice little jog to stretch my legs while I figured my way out of this.

I veered toward the next street, and Loki came stumbling out of an alley to my left. He managed to right himself with such assured grace you'd almost have thought he tossed himself around like that on purpose.

His bright gaze snagged on mine. "There you are. Do you have any idea how difficult it is to track you through this memory maze?"

I slowed as I turned to face him, but I took one step back and another. A different sort of tension had wound around my gut. While I'd wanted to find one of the gods, I wasn't sure I was ready to face this one. Loki looked a lot calmer than the last time I'd seen him, but the image of his vicious expression, the cutting edge to his words, lingered way too clearly. How could we fight together if I couldn't trust him not to stab me in the back?

"From what I remember, you were the one who ran off on us," I said.

He grimaced. "Somehow I doubt I'd have made the situation any better if I'd stayed. I thought I was ready, even if she dredged that up, but… Ari, it wasn't the way it looked."

"You didn't set up Hod to murder his own brother?"

"I—" He cut himself off with a rough sigh. "It's complicated. I'm just asking you not to judge from that one moment when the entire picture is so much larger."

"Complicated," I repeated. "I can't really think of any complications that would make doing that okay. You know, Hod said the same thing, and I was starting to think he was just excusing away hating you for no good reason. But seeing that, I'm surprised he can even stand to be around you."

Loki winced. He held out his hand to me. "Pixie…"

The cajoling note in his voice wrenched at me, too hard. I wasn't here for him to sweet talk me into sympathy. I didn't trust myself not to be swayed when I shouldn't be. He was too damned slick.

"Don't," I said. "Don't call me nicknames, don't act like I'm on your side here. If you want to help find a way to break this place down, great. Let's stick to that. I want to get out of here, not talk about ways to justify murder."

I spun around. Loki hurried after me.

And the vision of my childhood neighborhood split apart with a thunderclap.

I spun faster, my ears ringing, as darkness closed in around me. My pulse thumped. I waited for the dark to spill me out into some new memory… but it didn't.

My sense of my body stilled, and then started to fade. I was floating there in the black and the cold. What the fuck kind of torture was this?

I flipped around, as much as I still could move with my skin and the muscles beneath it going numb. A thread of sensation ran through my chest. One of my gods, one of the other gods who'd helped form me as a valkyrie, was somewhere close. Not Loki this time, I didn't think.

A pang of relief reverberated through me. I snatched out toward that impression, latching on and dragging myself toward it with all the strength I had in my body. The cold bit right down to my bones, and a gasp escaped me. I flung myself faster.

My hand closed around an elbow. Firm but cold skin. My fingers skidded up it over a well-muscled arm. I tugged myself closer, and a scent like a fresh spring breeze washed over me.

Baldur. What the hell was this place he'd gotten himself into? I still couldn't see him, couldn't see anything but the awful endless dark, but I held on. I tipped my head into the nook of his shoulder, and he shifted toward me as if he'd only just noticed I was there. His arm slid around my waist. Cold. Way too cold.

I hooked my own arm around him, pressing myself against him

all the way along his body. Trying to share whatever heat I still had left in my body with him. Could he literally freeze to death in this place? Everything I'd seen suggested Muninn would be pleased if her torture ended up killing us. Less hassle for her then.

"Aria," Baldur murmured, breaking through the dull silence around us. His lips brushed my forehead as he spoke. "You shouldn't be here."

"And you should be?" I said. I could feel his heart thumping in his chest now. Warmth started to flow beneath his skin where it touched mine. It had to be his memory. How could we break out of it?

I hugged him closer. "I *am* here. I'm right here with you. I don't know how you got this memory, but it's different now. You're not alone."

"I died," he said raggedly, as if the words had torn through something on the way out. "This is where you go when you die."

A realm of cold and darkness and nothing else. Oh, God. It was horrible enough for me, and I didn't thrive on light the way Baldur did. No wonder he hadn't wanted to talk about where he'd been during Ragnarok.

What did you say to someone who'd died and lingered there so long and now was having to relive that torture all over again? What could possibly convince him this hadn't been the torment it felt like? Anything I could have said caught in my throat. I opened my mouth, closed it again, and forced myself to go on.

"You survived it once. You'll survive it again. Like me. Shit happens, and we just keep going. And this time, you've got me for company. It's already warmer like that, right? All you need to do is bring the light."

He stirred against me, the flex of his muscles sending a much more enjoyable shiver through me. "I tried, but I lose it. It slips away from me."

"All right." I bowed my head back against his chest. "Then I'll just stay here in the dark with you until we make it through." And hope that would be enough.

His hand closed against my back. His head dipped down over mine, and this time when his lips brushed against my hair, the gesture felt purposeful. It felt like a kiss. My heart skipped. "Baldur…"

He sucked in a breath. I opened my eyes to a faint glow emanating from his form. He was visible now against the dark, hazing the black like one of those translucent jellyfish soaring through the depths of the ocean. Of course, I wouldn't have wanted a jellyfish to hold me like this.

Something I'd said must have gotten through. We were getting somewhere. The chilly darkness still clutched us tightly, but it was no longer complete.

"There you go," I said, looking up at him with a smile. "You found the light."

"You found me," he said, smiling back, but his expression was more tense, more present, than I was used to. The dreaminess had fallen away. "Thank you."

"I'm not sure I really did all that much," I said. "It's not exactly a painful trial to give you a hug."

He chuckled. His fingers stroked over my hair and down my back, drawing a trail of warmth through me. "That's not— I'm glad you've been with us, you know. I don't think I ever said that to you, even though I've been thinking it. *You* have a light you bring to our lives that we've needed."

I didn't feel all that brilliant, but if the god of light said it, I guessed he should know what he was talking about. And— "Hod said something like that too."

"Did he?" The soft smile came back. His eyes, even brighter than the rest of him, searched mine. "You feel close to him. And Loki too."

"Well, I did, anyway." That flippancy seemed out of place in the moment. I didn't know what he was looking for in me. Something he needed, to break the rest of the way through this illusion? Honesty had seemed to work best before. "I like all of you. I want all of you." A flush spread up my neck saying it that openly, but it was true. "Is that a problem?"

For a second, he didn't seem to know what to say. He cupped my face, lowering his so his nose grazed mine. "Aria… I've kept my distance from the rest of the world for so long. I don't know how to be what you need. But I wish I could be it. So much."

Longing rang through his words. It called up a matching desire in me. Fuck Muninn. Fuck her stupid prison. Let her see how little I cared about *her* and her machinations. Maybe I could be the one to shatter this place. This man in front of me—he mattered. And she'd tried to break him all over again.

"You're always thinking about that, aren't you?" I said softly. "What other people need. How you can make things easier for them. Keeping us all in harmony. Maybe you should think about what *you* need, what you want, for a change."

"What I want," he murmured. He tipped up my chin, and his mouth found mine.

If Loki brought fire to his kiss, Baldur brought the summer sun. Gentle heat radiated through me, stirring up a hotter desire low in my belly. I kissed him back with all the longing I had in me, pouring that heat back into him. No chill Muninn sent could cut through this.

Baldur's breath stuttered as his mouth shifted against mine, tipping to find a deeper angle. My hands slid down to explore the panes of his muscular chest through his shirt. His fingers teased into my hair, their touch sending quivers of delight through my nerves. I kissed him harder. Drowning in the brightness of him was the most amazing thing I could imagine in that moment.

"Aria." My name came out like a sigh. His mouth traveled away from mine, charting a heated course along my jaw and down the side of my neck. One hand dropped to my waist and started to ease its way up, closer and closer to the curves of my breasts.

I arched into him with a whimper. The darkness was falling back all around us as his glow expanded. A little more, and we might be free, at least of this one place, completely. But even as the movement of his lips left me burning with need, a different sort of chill shot through my nerves.

We were going fast. This was getting dangerous. How far did I want this to go? I wanted him—oh, fuck, yes, I did—but the shadows of memories Muninn had brought far too close to the surface nagged at the edges of my mind.

I must have tensed a little, because Baldur paused. He drew back just a few inches, watching my expression. Hunger still shone in his bright blue eyes, but he said, "You know you don't have to—"

The darkness flung itself at us, battering our embrace. In a blink, it tore Baldur from my arms.

# 16

*Aria*

A fierce resolve rang through me. I was *not* letting Muninn dictate all the terms here. I'd figured her out, at least in part. We'd warmed her darkness. I could fight back.

Focusing all my energy on Baldur, I threw myself back toward him. My hand caught his ankle. We flipped through the air together and landed in a heap next to each other on cool marble tiles. The impact sent a splinter of pain through my already raw knees. The fabric of my jeans ripped, baring the scraped skin.

I rolled over. We were back in the Asgard I knew, on the main path that led between the halls, the courtyard with its fountain gleaming in the distance. Gleaming under moonlight. Muninn had brought night down over us, a dark stillness that barely unnerved me after the pitch black we'd just tumbled out of.

And she hadn't gotten her way completely. Baldur was sitting up next to me, his white-blond hair swaying as he shook his head. I'd managed to keep us together, whichever of us she'd meant to send here. I didn't see anything threatening yet, but at this point I knew better than to trust that impression.

Baldur turned to me, and his bright blue eyes widened. It was the first time he'd been able to see me properly since I'd first caught hold of him in that vast nothingness.

"You're hurt," he said. "Let me—"

Rather than keep talking, he simply scooted closer, setting his hand on the side of my knee. Even though the raw skin there was still stinging, his touch sent a flare of heat up my inner thigh.

"I can't do anything about the tear in your jeans," he said, the rough note in his voice suggesting he wasn't totally unaffected either.

"I'll take whatever you can offer," I said, and almost bit my tongue.

Baldur gave me a slow smile that looked unexpectedly wicked for a moment, but it vanished as soon as he turned back to the task at hand. With a brush of his fingers, the scrapes on my knees sealed. He took my arm, grimacing at the sight of the bruises there.

"I've been building a collection," I said.

He gave a short soft laugh. "It certainly looks like it. I can mend them at least partly."

His hand slid up my arm, more warmth flooding me with it, and not just the healing kind. I resisted the urge to nibble at my lip —the lips he'd been kissing just a few minutes ago. When he'd finished with both, his gaze came back to my face.

"Is there anywhere else?"

Fuck me, was there anywhere else I wanted him to touch? Yes and no. How about everywhere?

The thought sent another nervous jitter through me. My fingers curled against the marble tiles. Before I could figure out how I was going to answer, a muffled groan reached my ears. My head jerked around.

"There's someone else here."

We scrambled up. The city had fallen silent again, but I set off in the direction the sound had come from. Who was Muninn tormenting here—and what if they'd already been badly hurt? Baldur hurried along beside me, his steps only slowing as we ducked down a narrower passage between two closely spaced halls.

"This is…"

We both came to a halt at the end of the passage. It was the way to the secondary courtyard where we'd last found ourselves in Asgard. The courtyard where Loki had guided Hod to throw the mistletoe spear and kill Baldur in their shared memories.

The moon was low enough that only a little of its light touched the courtyard. Enough to see Baldur's corpse lying there as it had in the daylight scene. Hod was crouched next to the body, his head bowed. Dark bits scattered the marble tiles beside him. It took me a second to realize they were the snapped pieces of the mistletoe branch.

Baldur had stiffened. As I glanced over at him, he squared his shoulders. With careful steps, he crossed the courtyard to his twin.

"Brother," he said gently. "What are you doing here?"

Hod lifted his head a few inches. His gaze flicked from Baldur to me where I was coming up behind the other god. I thought his posture tensed even more than it already was. He looked to his twin again.

"The raven put me here—what do you think? Where better?"

Baldur sat down beside him, close enough that if he'd extended his leg completely he could have nudged his own corpse with his foot. "I don't see anything holding you here."

"Oh, I tried to leave. Trust me. That didn't go so well."

The strain in his voice made my heart ache. I wavered, standing a few feet away, not sure this was my moment to intrude on. It wasn't as if I had anywhere else to go, though. Maybe I'd see a chance to weaken Muninn's prison more.

"Are you all right?" Hod added, his gaze still on his twin. "I can't imagine, going through all that again… I know you don't like to talk about it, but I also know it still haunts you, the first time."

Baldur's face fell. "I've tried to set it behind me, to not let what I felt then affect anyone else now. I'm sorry if I—"

"Oh, by the Allfather, I'm not saying that you did anything wrong. Just… We've been together since the womb, Baldur. I know when something's off. And it's been off from the first moment we found our way back to Asgard." His mouth tightened. "You live like there's ten layers of gauze between you and the rest of the world—like if you soften every possible blow in advance, nothing ever has to hurt. No one who's really all right has to put that much effort into staying that way."

Baldur wet his lips and looked at his hands resting on his knees.

"Finding the truth in the memories," I said quietly. "Changing the way you all remember what happened… It's wearing away at the prison. It's helping us get out."

I knew what Hod meant about the layers of protection the light god seemed to have swathed around him. That dreaminess I'd noticed from the first moment I'd seen him, that he carried almost like a suit of armor. But right then, as he inhaled shakily, something in the way he held himself changed. His spine straightened; his jaw firmed. As if he'd willfully sloughed off a few of those layers of armor.

He'd heard me, and he was coming through to fight in his own way.

"You're right," Baldur said. "It was… Death broke me. It broke me and then broke the pieces it'd made of me all over again, and somehow they came back together when we woke up in that field in the aftermath, but I've never felt as if they quite fit the way they're meant to anymore. I suppose I've spent a long time trying to avoid acknowledging just how wrong I came back out, hoping it might turn right if I just kept up a good face for long enough."

"I'm sorry," Hod said hoarsely. "By the nine realms, I'm sorry."

Baldur clasped his shoulder. "I never—"

The corpse shuddered. Baldur's voice cut off with a hitch. The form of his previous self, tunic stiff with dried blood, heaved itself onto its knees. Blood flecked the dead god's lips and teeth too. The corpse's eyes were clouded over, an icier blue than Baldur's real ones had ever been, but they focused on Hod. Words rattled from its throat. "Do you think sorry is enough, brother?"

Oh, God, what horror had the raven come up with now? The actual brothers threw themselves to their feet, stumbling backward to where I stood. Hod stared blindly toward the corpse, his muscles rigid from head to toe. The thing heaved onto its feet and swayed. A putrid sour smell like decaying meat rolled off it, making me choke.

"Draug," Baldur murmured, his expression tight.

"What?" I said, taking another step back when the corpse lurched toward us.

"Something like your idea of zombies," Hod said with a rasp. "The dead come back to life. Bloated and rotting and looking to pass on that death."

His hand balled into a fist, but I knew just looking at him that he'd never hit that thing, no matter that it obviously wasn't his brother in any way now. The real Baldur had never risen from the dead like that, clearly. Muninn was mixing memories again, merging that death with monsters the gods had dealt with.

The creature raised its arm. It was clutching the mistletoe spear, reformed, the pointed end stained dark red and aimed at Hod. "You struck me down, you stole my life and my light, and you want to say you're *sorry*?" the draug warbled.

Hod flinched. Baldur gripped his forearm. "That's not me," the light god said. "Those aren't my thoughts. I—" His jaw clenched. "Maybe I hide that from myself too. Maybe I've been angry at you. Maybe some part of me didn't want to talk to you because then you might have been freed from the pain too. But that wasn't fair of me.

I'm the god of justice, and I *know* you didn't deserve that. I know you never would have meant to hurt me."

"But I did," Hod said. "I *killed* you. It was my fault, at least as much as Loki's."

"All your fault," the draug gurgled. "All your—"

It lunged unexpectedly, swiping out with the mistletoe spear. I'd been right about Hod. His arm shot up, but only to block the blow. The spear tip sliced across his wrist, drawing a thin red line. Panic flashed across Baldur's face. He might have been able to stop it too, but God, how could anyone ask him to kill *himself* after all the horror he'd been through.

Desperation wrenched through me. The draug would kill Hod if it could. That was what Muninn wanted here.

It heaved forward with another lash, and I thrust my hands toward it. "*Stop!*"

Lightning crackled through my veins and burst from my palms. The corpse jerked and seized. It toppled over and hit the ground, disappearing into a puff of dust.

I lowered my arms, my body trembling. I really wished I had a little more control over when that happened, even though I was pretty happy with this outcome. I shot a glance toward the twins.

Baldur gave me a terse nod. A ragged sigh rushed out of Hod. He rubbed his face.

"That thing and what it said might not have been real," he said, "but you have to know it was my fault. Who else can you blame?"

The light god glanced at me and swallowed audibly. "If it'll take truth to beat Muninn's prison: How about myself?"

Hod's head jerked up. "What in Hel's name are you talking about?"

"I was there, wasn't I?" Baldur waved his hand toward the middle of the courtyard. "I let Mother collect those vows. I let them play that game—which was stupid; Loki was right about that. I flaunted the care and security I'd been given. If I'd been happy simply having it, if I'd shut down the idea of the game… I never would have been in a position where anyone could have hurt me. I can take responsibility for that."

Hod stared at his brother—as much as he could stare. A little of the tension left his shoulders. "So where do we go from there?" he asked.

Baldur dragged in a breath. "Well, I think first we need to get out of this prison. But then, after… I'd like to be able to talk to you about it more. Darkness is your forte. Maybe you'll be able to help me make more peace with what I went through. If you don't mind taking on some of that burden—"

"Of course not," Hod said quickly. "Anything I can do. It won't be a burden if it helps you heal."

A small but bright smile spread across Baldur's face. "Then I couldn't ask for anything else, brother," he said.

Hod smiled back—and the courtyard around us shimmered. It was working. I froze, my heart leaping as I searched for the chinks in Muninn's construct. We'd challenged the memories she was using again, shaken up her foundations. There had to be—

There. I caught a glimpse of gray rock through a gouge in the tiles. I leapt toward it, and the world tilted over again.

*No*. My arms darted out. I trained my mind on that image, that rock, the reddish glow and the ashen smell I'd caught before. That was the real world. That was the place we needed to reach.

The courtyard whirled away in a gust of fog. I half dashed, half skidded through it, my feet bumping over rough rock. A scene stretched out ahead of me, hazy around the edges like the moment I'd seen of Muninn and that man in what had seemed to be their home.

But this was no house. A dark cliff loomed over me, and a tall figure strode along several feet ahead of me, beside a river that glowed searing red. The figure wore a faded cloak and a broad-brimmed hat. A familiar twang ran through my chest.

"Odin!" I started to call, but the name snagged in my throat. As I'd opened my mouth, a flurry of men and monsters rained down on the god from the cliffside and from crevices in the ground beside it. He swept out his spear, but it was knocked from his grasp in an instant. He crumpled under the mass of attackers.

"There," Muninn's sweetly hoarse voice said, somewhere distant. "I delivered him. I fulfilled my end."

"You did," a man answered in a searing tone. "But are *you* really finished with him, raven?"

A force socked me in the gut, sending me flying back into the fog, and I lost her answer.

# 17

*Hod*

The warmth in my brother's voice melted some of my anguish. I smiled at him, sensing exactly where he stood from the gentle energy he carried with him everywhere. It seemed to wrap around me, quiet but reassuring. Were we really good? Better than we had been, at least?

Ari sucked in a startled breath. Her footsteps dashed across the tiles, and my head snapped around to follow them. The air rippled around us. I stepped forward instinctively. If she'd seen some sort of danger, I had to be there for her too.

For one instant, I thought I heard the rustling of a cloak, a rough cough I would have sworn was my father's. My breath caught. Then something struck me, walloping me off my feet.

"Hod!" Ari's voice called out from somewhere far away. Fear lanced through me. I reached after her, but I was sliding, tumbling, farther away.

I fought the wind, but no movement I made affected my direction. It blasted me so hard my ears rang. I careened through formless space until I jarred with a halt at the edge of a thin rug across a cool stone floor. My hand braced against the polished surface.

The raven's illusion had started to shatter. That must be it—I *had* gotten a glimpse of Odin, of some other place that wasn't part of her construct. Ari had been right. As we changed the way we thought about our memories, what we knew to be true about the past at all, Muninn's hold on us weakened.

And because we'd gotten close to breaking through, she'd tossed us away again.

At least I was gone from that awful courtyard. What worse was there she could throw at me?

It wasn't myself I should be worrying about now, I didn't think. What she'd put Baldur through—every part of me ached just remembering the way he'd talked about it. How broken he felt. How *wrong*. If she put him through that again, how much longer could he hold himself together?

Or maybe he was stronger than I was giving him credit for. Even as an ache rippled through me, a sense of relief flowed beneath it. I'd finally closed the distance that had grown between us. He was opening up to me. He was willing to ask for my help, even though those conversations would be even harder for him than for me. If I could pull him even a little out of the haze he'd been hiding in, all the torture I'd faced here would have been worth it.

Where had Muninn sent him now? What had she done with Ari?

The raven had already battered our valkyrie so much. I hadn't even had a chance to make sure *she* was all right, to ask what she'd been through. I'd been so lost in my own pain. But if Muninn had dredging up those memories for me and my twin, twisted them so cruelly… My stomach twisted at what she might have thrown at Ari.

I had to try to find my way back to her. She'd managed to find me before, using the connection between us. Whenever the prison faltered, it was because we were working together, finding those truths together.

I filled my lungs, getting a sense of my surroundings. A wide room, from the air currents drifting past me. A streak of warmth fell across one of my shoulders where sunlight must be spilling through a high window. A subdued murmuring carried through that window, along with the rasp of dragged logs.

My body tensed all over again. Ah. Muninn hadn't thrown me far in time from my last location. They were building Baldur's funeral pyre out there.

A wail rose up, petering out into sobbing. Nanna, Baldur's wife. I swallowed hard. I'd heard, after we'd all returned, that she'd thrown herself on his pyre to be burned up with him. You could almost say I'd killed two gods when I'd killed him.

Some *had* said that.

If this was that day, then I was in one of the lower chambers of my father's hall, one I'd never had reason to be in before then. The door behind me would be locked, until—

The bolt thudded over. The hinges squeaked faintly as the Allfather stepped inside with slow footfalls. Heavier than usual. I could feel the slump of his shoulders in the sound of his exhale.

Other footsteps slipped in behind him, so faint I might not have noticed them if I'd had all my senses to distract me. The second visitor stopped at the edge of the room and set the object he'd been holding against the wall with a soft thump.

"My son," Odin said.

"Father," I replied. Anticipation had clamped tight around my chest. I stayed turned away from him, turned toward the window and the sun. The first time, when this had really happened, I'd been standing facing him, hadn't I? But there was no need to recreate this memory perfectly. Would he say the exact same things, make the same excuses?

Part of me clenched with grim satisfaction at the idea of him having to speak to my back to deliver this message.

"You know, if it were simply my choice, we wouldn't be here," Odin said. His voice was strained but resigned. He'd already decided he had no choice. "But the balance is needed, now more than ever as summer fades from this realm. We need dark as well as light, but darkness when light is gone cannot be sustained."

"I know, Father," I said.

I didn't really. He'd been afraid of Ragnarok's approach; that much had become clear. But the balance hadn't made any difference to that war. It had come down on Asgard anyway. Had this one act really swayed anything that mattered?

I hadn't thought it through in much detail in the original moment. I'd been drowned in my own guilt and grief. His pronouncement had stung, but in some ways I'd welcomed it. Death was better than living on with the knowledge of what I'd done. I was accustomed to darkness. I could accept it.

Now, I could have tried for the door, tried to push past him, but I found I couldn't bring myself to move. What were the chances I'd make it that far before he and his companion stopped me anyway? Maybe his words would make more sense this time around.

"If we don't appease Asgard's sense of rightness a little longer, we could lose everything," my father went on as if I hadn't spoken. "That is the burden we bear."

He came forward to stand beside me where I was kneeling. His hand rested on my shoulder. "If I had known it would play out this way…"

Then what? He'd have done something differently? What *had* he seen, in all the travels he'd been on, in his visits to the Norns, in his searching visions? All of us knew that the Allfather saw more with his one eye than anyone else came close to with two. He'd sacrificed the other so that he could glimpse what lay beyond the world of the present.

"I would have liked to at least bear witness at the funeral," I said. "Pay my last regards." As if this conjured version of my father would give me any satisfaction there.

The stranger by the wall spoke up then as he hadn't in reality. His voice was a low rumble. "The blind god bearing witness? The murderer giving regards to his victim? What a joke."

"Quiet," Odin boomed. His grip on my shoulder tightened. "I think it is better for all of us if the deed is done before then," he said to me.

Better for *all* of us? A jolt of anger shot through me. I heaved myself to my feet and turned to face him after all.

"Why don't you just say it, Father?" I said. "Instead of talking about deeds and balance. You're going to kill me, like I killed Baldur. That's the plain fact of it. Shouldn't all this dancing around it be beneath you?"

With each sentence that spilled from my mouth, the anger inside me flared a little hotter. A good burning, with a sear of energy and conviction. So much more than I'd even realized I'd kept bottled up.

The Odin drawn from my memories was silent for a moment. Then he said, "Perhaps it is. I simply thought it might be kinder to you to avoid that much bluntness."

"Kinder to me?" A sharp laugh tumbled out. A starker searing blazed through me, so fast I didn't have time to examine it before the words burst from my mouth. "Tell me the truth, Father. If I'd been the one who'd died first—if it'd been me falling at Baldur's hand—would you have sacrificed him? Your light, your joy? Would our mother have even let you?"

The questions left an acid aftertaste on my tongue. Odin stood still and silent. Every moment he didn't speak turned any shame I might have felt at asking him back into anger.

"Are you just not sure?" I demanded. "Or is it that you know I won't like your answer if you tell the truth?"

The stranger by the wall started to laugh in a rolling cackle. Odin stirred. "What answer would you want me to give you, my son?" he said in a low voice. "What could I say that would satisfy you?"

Those words punctured the vicious swell inside me. It was my turn to hesitate. A tremor ran down through my gut.

How long had I wondered those things without saying them, without even really thinking them? The emotion in them felt very, very old. Bone-deep and woven through my veins.

How many times had I watched the other gods, including our parents, gravitate toward Baldur while leaving me alone? When had our mother ever gone on a quest to protect *me*, to ensure I'd never come to harm? It had all been for Baldur. Baldur the kind. Baldur the just. Baldur the bright.

Why wouldn't everyone prefer his company to the dark god who was most at home in the night?

Loki's cutting remarks in the courtyard came back to me. *The bitterness was wafting off you like the stink of a skunk.* Maybe it had been. Because this wrenching sensation inside me wasn't just guilt or grief. Some part of me had been desperately jealous of the love that had been extended to my brother, over and over, and not to me.

I gritted my teeth, but I couldn't stop that final question from rising up in my mind. Had I wanted to hurt Baldur, deep down? Wanted to let him fall, just once?

"I don't know," I said to my father. "I just— This isn't what I wanted. I know this isn't what I ever would have wanted."

"It's easier to make our choices again in hindsight," the Allfather said. "That doesn't mean you weren't true to yourself when you made them."

"He's my *brother*," I said, but the protest came out weak even to my own ears. Nanna's sobbing carried through the window, along with the fainter sounds of weeping from other gods. All that grief, I'd brought to this place. Because I'd resented how happy Baldur made them?

Odin clasped my shoulders again. He bowed his head close, brushing a dry kiss to my forehead like a blessing, the way he had all those centuries ago. "It's time. I swear that I will see you, after."

"Father…" I didn't know what else to say.

Odin stepped back, a whisper of his feet against the rug. The stranger lifted his club off the floor and approached with weightier steps. His clothes rustled as he raised his arms. I braced myself, my hands clenched at my sides.

Even if I was bitter, even if I'd been jealous, I could take my death with honor. I could accept the punishment I was due. I—

I wasn't really supposed to be here. I'd taken that punishment already, ages ago. This was Muninn's doing. If I got swept up in the memory, I could die here all over again. That was what she meant for me. She'd wanted me to get swept away until I forgot to defend myself.

The air shifted as my executioner swung his club. I dodged to the side, a split-second too late. The heavy shaft of wood missed bashing open my head, but it did clock me across the temple.

Pain exploded through my skull. I staggered backwards, reeling, and tipped over an edge in the floor into freefall.

# 18

*Aria*

This time Muninn's intent hurled me upward—up, up, into a darkness that spilled open to clear blue sky. As it spat me out, I whipped out my wings to catch myself on the breeze.

I whirled around. I was hovering over Asgard, the gleaming rooftops scattered below me, alone.

No, not alone. A brown feathered body soared past me. Freya's falcon, beating her wings hard as if her life depended on getting wherever she was going as quickly as possible.

I swooped after her, straining to keep up. "Freya!" I called. "What's happening? What's wrong?" Was this one of her memories now, a chase by a monster maybe? I didn't see anything flying after us.

The falcon didn't slow. "Freya!" I called again. What if it wasn't her after all but a construct of her? But when I stretched my senses, I could feel a tingle of her godly life energy even from a few feet behind her.

I flapped with a fresh burst of speed and shot past her. If she was caught up in a memory, maybe I could snap her out of it like Loki and I had before.

"Freya, can you at least give me a sign—"

The falcon banked at the sight of me. With a flutter, the goddess slipped out of the falcon cloak, draping it across her shoulders to keep her body in the air. She stared at me, her eyes slightly glazed as if she wasn't totally seeing me yet.

"My daughter," she murmured. "I have to find my daughter."

My heart squeezed. "Freya," I said, grasping her hand like I had when she'd thought she was slipping back into old age. "I don't know what happened before, but Muninn wants to hurt us. To break us down. If it freaks you out this much not being able to find your daughter, I don't think she'll ever let you. But you did find her eventually, right?" I had trouble believing Loki would have joked about bartering her off to giants otherwise, but then, I'd have had trouble believing he'd have orchestrated a murder too, so what did I know?

Freya's breaths smoothed out. She swiped her hand across her eyes. "So you bring me back to reality again, Ari," she said with a crooked smile.

"I've needed those reminders too," I said, thinking of the bedroom in Petey's foster home, Hod's strained voice.

"I just… I saw her. But you're right. This is what Muninn wants —us frantic rather than trying to work our way out." The goddess sighed. "Let's go down to earth. I'll think clearer there."

We had flown past the main city and the orchard now. Freya dipped down toward a glade in the thicker forest. We came down on the soft grass near a large stone well. Brown ridges jutted from the soil at the edge of the glade, but their shape and texture looked wrong for rocks. After a moment I realized they were enormous tree roots. But where was the tree?

"Those are the roots of Yggdrasil," Freya said with a tip of her head. "I suppose the raven decided no harm could come from us having access to them." She let her hand trail along the edge of the well. "This is where the Norns used to pass their time. They liked to water the tree, among other things."

Other things. "I've heard you and the others mention the Norns before," I said. "I've got no idea who they were."

"None of us really did," Freya said. "They just turned up in Asgard one day and settled down here, these three. Spinning prophecies. Some said they determined the future. I think they merely read the signs to see where it was leading." She paused. "Odin did too. We weren't married then, but I noticed he visited them often. He's always wanted to know all he can about what is and what will be."

"I guess that habit got him into a lot of trouble this time around."

"So it seems." She shook her head with a wry expression, her golden hair tumbling over her shoulders. "I wouldn't have stopped him from his wanderings, even if I could have, though. I miss him when he's away, but that thirst for knowledge is part of what makes him the man I love."

I thought of the Odin that Muninn had shown me in her tarnished Valhalla. He hadn't looked all that loveable then. But then, Freya could obviously be bloodthirsty too. That was why they got along.

"You've been together a long time?" I ventured.

"His relationship with the twins' mother fell apart not long after that scene you saw with the mistletoe and so on," she said. "I wouldn't have thought of anything happening between us, but after Ragnarok, when we all got our second chances… It seemed foolish to hold back from what might make us both happy."

She glanced at me sideways, with a teasing lift of her eyebrows. "I notice you're indulging in at least one godly dalliance of your own."

My face flushed. The worst part is, I didn't even know which god she was definitely talking about. Probably Loki. She'd definitely seen him kiss me.

"That's just—" I started, and didn't know how to finish that sentence. I had no idea what I was doing with any of them. Only that it felt good when I was doing it, and at the time that always seemed like enough. The thought of trying to define anything, put some sort of meaning on it, made my stomach twist.

"It's all right," Freya said. "You'll find no judgment here. I get the impression you're a woman who knows how to protect her own heart. I expect you can handle them."

*Them*. Okay, she'd definitely noticed something was up with the others. This seemed like a good time to change the subject.

"Muninn stayed with Odin for a while after Ragnarok, didn't she?" I said. "You must have gotten to know her pretty well back then. Maybe something you saw back then will give us more of an answer to escaping this place."

"I don't know if I would say I knew her well." Freya leaned back against the well, her expression going thoughtful. "She couldn't shapeshift back then, you know. She was always a raven. An extraordinarily intelligent and aware raven, but she could only speak to Odin, through a mental bond they had. I never spoke with her directly. From the way he talked about her, though, he thought of her as an old friend. I never got the impression he saw reason to doubt her loyalty."

"Did he ever say what happened right before she left? Where she'd gone? If there was anything—"

Before I could finish the thought or Freya could answer it, the walls of the well blasted apart. One of them knocked me back into the darkness that filled the gaps between Muninn's constructs. I sucked air into my lungs, trying to right myself, and only tumbled backward again. The wind whirled me around and then dropped me.

Muninn didn't want me asking those questions. Okay. I must be getting close to tearing this prison down.

I landed on a scuffed wooden floor, my hand shooting out to grip the banister instinctively. Freya was gone, off in some new nightmare of her own, no doubt. The dreary smell of my mother's house closed in around me. Tension clenched around my chest.

The upstairs hallway. I was in the upstairs hall, outside the bedrooms. Even as I realized that, steadying my feet on the floor, the creak of the stairs carried up from below. A heavier creak than my mother's steps would have made. Every muscle in my body clenched up.

"No!" I shouted at Muninn, wherever the hell she was. "Don't you dare."

Another creak. My heart lurched. I hurtled myself toward the wall at the end of the hallway with the burn of all my valkyrie strength.

"Let. Me. *Out.*"

I slammed into the wall fists first, and it cracked apart with a shower of dust. With a heave of my feet and a frantic flap of my wings, I propelled myself into the darkness on the other side.

Muninn's wind whipped around me, yanking me to the side. Not back there—no, I wouldn't let her. I beat my wings as hard as I could against it, groping for anything else I could hold on to. I'd beat her before. I could be stronger than her if I just pushed hard enough.

A forest spiraled by beneath me. The invisible force walloped me to the right. As my head spun, Asgard's halls flashed by. Was that Thor outside one? I reached toward him, but the wind snatched me back too fast, too strong.

I spun head over feet. "Ari!" Loki's voice called, there and then sucked away in the howl of air around me. I jerked up and plummeted, tripped down a set of steps—the ones from my old elementary school?—hurled myself upward again, and caught another impression of one of the gods. There. I wanted to go there. We'd fight her together. I was so done with being shoved around at the raven woman's whim.

My wings ached, but I flapped them even harder. The force dragged at them—and then snapped. I tumbled headlong into a dark room, landing on my ass.

A cold stone floor lay beneath me. A sliver of a moon gleamed beyond the window, and a massive bed stood just across from me. Three figures clustered to my right, huddled together by the back wall. And one form, pale and lean with short black hair mussed as if the wind had dropped him here not that long ago, bent over the bed.

Hod didn't seem to have noticed me. His hand drifted over the covers—over the body lying under them. A halting rattle of a breath carried from the pillow, followed by a faint groan. Hod's mouth tightened. He drew his fingers to his palm, and the sensation echoed in the shadows that lurked inside me as he pulled the last shreds of life into his own darkness.

The room had been quiet before, but now the hush was total. Hod straightened up, his hand falling to his side. His head turned toward his audience, and they pulled even farther back without a word. His lips curled into a grimace. He headed out the door, and the watching figures let out their breaths in one combined exhalation.

I pushed myself to my feet and hurried after him. I nearly collided with him in the hall outside, where he'd stopped, I guessed at the sound of my steps. He caught my elbow, steadying me.

"Ari?"

His voice was terse, but his grip on me trembled. I knew the dark god well enough to have noticed that he always got more prickly when he was trying to cover his own discomfort.

"The one and only," I said with a lot more cheer than I felt. Anything was better than my childhood memories, and at least I wasn't alone. We had a chance of escaping when we could work with each other. Muninn was jerking us around more and more. It must be getting harder for her to maintain any one illusion.

My gaze caught on an angry purple-red splotch on the side of Hod's forehead—the side that had been turned away from me before—and my body tensed. "What happened to you? Who did that?" Because I'd like to give them a matching bruise as payback.

Hod's hand rose to his temple as if he'd forgotten the injury. "It's nothing," he said, still terse. "I got careless. My skull is still intact, which is about as much as I could have asked for."

I wasn't so sure about that, but he clearly wasn't in the mood to discuss the trouble he'd encountered. I forced myself to look away, considering the hall. "What do you think we've gotten ourselves into this time?"

He shrugged. "If you saw me in there, it's already over."

I glanced back toward the bedroom. "You were taking that person's life." Person? These stone walls had an Asgardian vibe. "That *god's*?"

"Not everyone in Asgard looked after themselves so well after the rebirth," Hod said. "A few got to the point where what life they had left was barely life at all. They wanted their final end to be as peaceful and quiet as possible. So they'd call on me." He turned his face away. "This was *my* life, while Asgard was still active: called for duties no one wanted to even mention by the light of day."

Duties no one else could have done the same way, I wanted to point out. But I'd seen the way his audience had cringed away from him. I couldn't change his mind by lying.

"What now?" I said instead.

"I don't know. I suppose we wait and see what Muninn stirs up next."

Was she watching us now? Did she even realize where I'd gotten to in her ever-expanding prison? She must have to focus her attention on the others part of the time. I'd broken out of the last memory she'd tried to trap me in—I'd managed to find my way here to Hod.

"I think she's tiring out," I said. "She wants us anxious or upset all the time… It's easier to control us that way? So, maybe we'll have a better chance of breaking out completely if we're somewhere with happier memories. I haven't seen your hall yet. Why don't you invite me over?"

Something that sounded like a guffaw sputtered out of the dark god. "I don't know how happy that place is, but all right. Will you accompany me home, valkyrie?"

"It would be my pleasure," I said in a formal tone, and the corners of his mouth twitched upward.

We left that house behind and made our way to a smaller hall of stones that looked a slightly darker gray than the ones around them. A craftsman with a sense of humor or Hod's own choice? He nudged open the door and strode over the threshold, confidence drawing his posture even straighter in the familiar space.

"Here you have it," he said dryly. "Home sweet home."

# 19

*Aria*

My pulse thumped with curiosity as I peeked through the closest doorways of the dark god's house, finding a dining room and a parlor with a single chair and shelves upon shelves of books. So very Hod. Were his texts here written in whatever the Asgardian version of braille was, or did he have to use magic to read like he did with his collection back on Midgard? He trailed along behind me, but he didn't speak, letting me take it all in uninterrupted.

The lonely chair niggled at me. "You lived here alone?"

"Live, present tense, when we're back in the real Asgard," Hod said. "Does that surprise you?"

"I don't know. Maybe it was silly, but somehow I figured you and Baldur were pretty inseparable."

"Oh, he has his own hall, closer to the main courtyard. I'm told it has a beautiful view."

A strange edge had come into his voice. That talk with his twin had seemed to dull some of the guilt he'd been feeling, but not enough, apparently. Was that a point I could press to widen the gaps in Muninn's prison?

"We're going to get out of here, you know," I said. "And then you'll have all the rest of your godly lives to hash out anything else that needs hashing out. At least—"

I caught myself, realizing just in time that my own thoughts had started to veer in a guilty direction. Hod didn't need my pain layered on top of his own.

But clearly he knew *me* too well at this point. "At least I can talk to him?" he filled in quietly. "At least he's still here. At least he remembers who I am."

"It's stupid to compare," I said. "Let's just stick with, I know how shitty it feels when things aren't right with someone you care about that much."

"There might be some day, when all this is over, that you could talk to Petey again."

I stared at him. "You'd *let* me, Mr. Leave All Your Earthly Concerns Behind?"

Hod rubbed his mouth. "Maybe I've gotten a very thorough example of why trying to simply forget about old hurts isn't always the best course of action. And… even *I* know it's not right that he doesn't even remember you, all the things you did for him, when you could be a real part of his life." His voice dropped even lower. "I'm sorry I had to add to your pain."

My throat tightened so suddenly it took a moment before I could speak. "Hod… I'd have been in a lot more pain if I'd had to leave him with my mom. Or anywhere else the dark elves might find him. You were helping me."

"In a way." He leaned back against the door frame. "That's how I contribute, isn't it? Through darkness, through taking away, through death… Even *Loki* brings brightness rather than quashing it sometimes."

"Okay, now you're being ridiculous," I said. I'd have needed to argue with him even if I hadn't thought challenging all our takes on any given situation was the key to getting out of here. "You contribute a lot more than that. You've got all that knowledge from those books, and you're probably the closest thing this group has to a voice of reason, even if that's a little pessimistic sometimes, and… and sometimes what you take away is pain. You gave me the space to talk about things I didn't think I ever wanted to talk about with anyone. To let some of it out, knowing you were listening, knowing that it mattered to you. That meant a lot."

"You've only seen a small fraction of who I am, valkyrie," he said, but his voice had softened a little.

I made a scoffing sound. "I've seen enough. So you're not all shiny like Baldur and you don't have Thor's bravado or whatever. So what? You're *all* so different from each other… It's kind of hard to imagine you all not being together. Like you've got the perfect balance between the bunch of you."

Something about that comment made Hod wince. "Not quite perfect," he said. "There were all those fault lines we were trying not to let crack open. But with you being here—you've made it easier somehow. Stirred things up just enough to start clearing out the tensions, I suppose. It's hard to imagine *you* not being with us now."

A giddy warmth passed through me at that comment. I stepped closer to him, taking his hand.

"You know, I watched what happened in that courtyard, and I don't think you can be blamed for what happened. You didn't know. You thought you were just joining in with the rest of them. Loki—"

Hod shook his head with a jerk. "I'm not so sure about that," he said roughly. "Some of the things the raven has reminded me of… There were times I felt so *angry* at how the gods favored Baldur. I didn't have to throw the stick that hard. I could have asked what Loki was up to."

I squeezed his hand harder. "Do you really think you wanted him *dead*?"

The dark god paused. His jaw flexed. "No. Never that. But I might have wanted him to hurt just a little, just once. To have one thing go wrong."

Oh, my dear dark god.

"I don't know," I said. "That sounds pretty normal to me. I loved Francis with all my heart. But there were totally times when I resented all the things he got to do that I couldn't because he was older. And times, after the really bad stuff started… when I hated that I had to go through that and somehow he got off free. Emotions aren't fair. They just are. Does that mean it's my fault he died?"

My pulse hitched as I said it, as if I were half afraid Hod would say yes, it was. He brought his hand to my face, stroking his thumb across my cheek. "Of course not," he said firmly. "That's hardly the same, though. And I doubt *Baldur* ever feels jealous of anyone. The light in him just washes away anything like resentment."

"Didn't you hear him before? He's been angry too."

"Only briefly, and for justifiable reasons."

"Hmph." I tipped my head against Hod's chest. His fingers moved to my hair, sending pleasant shivers over my scalp with each caress. "I'd bet being good all the time is stressful in different ways. Can't you just believe you're good enough?"

"Can't you?" he shot back.

"I'm working on it," I said. "You have helped me in lots of ways, you know, despite all the grimness and skepticism. I think it says a lot that you could be so kind to someone you didn't trust at all to begin with."

Hod was silent for a moment. His hand stilled against my hair. "I don't think you can call those acts kindness, Ari," he said. "That was a man falling in love with you."

My breath stopped; my spine stiffened. I pulled back from Hod to stare into his face. His expression had already tensed.

"It's all right," he said raggedly, backing up a step. "I didn't expect the sentiment to be returned. If it's easier, you can pretend I never—"

An ache shot through my chest, even starker than my panic. I moved automatically, grabbing the front of his shirt and yanking him back to me. Bobbing up on my toes at the same moment to capture his mouth with mine.

With a stuttered breath, he was kissing me back. His lips had the same salty, softly smoky flavor as the scent that clung to him, and they moved against mine as if he knew exactly how to find the most sensitive angle. As if he'd charted every inch of me a hundred times instead of this only being our second kiss.

The sensation sent a quiver of joy through me, but the quiver turned into a tremor after just a few seconds. I clutched his shirt, trying to lose myself completely in the heat of his mouth, but I couldn't get control of my body.

Hod eased back, not so far this time. His forehead brushed mine. "Ari?" he said hoarsely.

I burrowed my face in his chest. "I'm sorry," I mumbled.

He paused. "Do you want to tell me about it?"

Just like that. Just like he'd asked when I'd randomly burst into tears on him outside my mother's house not that long ago. Simple and straight-forward and opening the door to anything I could have had to confess. No pushing, no pressure.

This was kindness, no matter how you looked at it. Did he really think it mattered why he offered it?

"I haven't let myself feel much about anyone other than Petey in a long time," I said, still talking to his shirt. "It was always safer to keep my distance. So much easier not to get hurt that way. I don't… I don't really know how to do it anymore. How to care about people. How to fall in love. But you all are so… I can't help caring. I can't help *wanting*. And it fucking terrifies me. So it's not you—it's not you at all. It's just me being a mess."

"You're not a mess," Hod said, outright fierce now. He tipped my head to press a kiss to my forehead that somehow felt as passionate as the meeting of our lips a few moments ago. "I'm not asking for anything. I don't expect anything from you. Whatever you want to give, whatever you can—"

His head jerked up. Before I could ask him what was wrong, I felt it too. A shift in the air around us, as if a breeze that shouldn't exist had passed straight through those stone walls. A breeze with a smell of chemical ash. Our talk had shaken something loose.

The breeze was coming from the doorway. We both dashed into the hall at the same time. The walls rippled before my eyes. I backed up and threw my shoulder at one, ready to grab Hod if the illusion broke completely.

My shoulder thumped against it with a spasm of pain. The wall didn't even crack. I frowned.

"Maybe we can get the memories to shift while her focus is shaky," I said. "Think of someplace else, someplace you'd rather be."

Hod's jaw set with concentration, and almost immediately the world whirled around us. The breeze that washed over me was sweet with the smell of spring grass, and when I blinked, I found we were standing in a spartan bedroom that held an ebony frame bed and a matching wardrobe, the plaster walls a light mint-green. I might have been confused if I hadn't recognized the view out the window.

"This is your bedroom in the house on Midgard?" I said.

A thin blush colored Hod's cheeks. "I wasn't really thinking," he said quickly. "It just happened to pop into my head."

I spun around and found myself faced with a blank wall where the exit should have been. "Muninn managed to steal the door." But I could get more of a running start at this one. I threw myself forward, fists slamming out.

My hands rammed into the wall. A gasp broke from my mouth at the impact, but it held. I swiveled, rubbing my knuckles.

Hod was already moving to the window. He jerked at the base and heaved again, but it didn't budge. The glass only rattled when he smacked his elbow against it.

"She lost some of her control over the construct, but she's got enough to keep us in here," I said. "Shit."

"We're getting closer," Hod said. "I could really sense the world outside that time. Have you found anything else that affects her focus?"

When had the prison shifted, either against Muninn's will or because she seemed frustrated with me before? Usually when we'd been talking, breaking down the memories the construct was based on. But also sometimes when I'd gotten too close to knowing more about her. And sometimes…

I stepped right up to Hod. "Let's see how closely she's watching."

I traced my hand up his chest to slip around his neck. Hod's distant eyes darkened with desire. He lowered his head, meeting me halfway in between.

As he kissed me, it was hard to remember I'd started this to try to shake up our prison. I didn't know what to do with all the things Hod had said, all the emotions churning inside me, but every inch of my skin ached with wanting.

One of his hands came to rest on my waist, the other sliding around my back to tug me a little closer. He kissed me again, shadows bleeding from his body to shimmer across mine. They licked the corner of my jaw, over my collarbone, across my ribs, sparking of bliss everywhere they touched.

I teased my tongue across his lips and they parted. The heat of his mouth soaked into mine. A pang shot straight through my core. Oh, hell. I couldn't walk away from this.

"I think her attention must be elsewhere," Hod murmured against my lips with another caress of shadow.

"Good," I said, my heart thumping. "Then we can do this."

I pulled him with me toward the bed, claiming another kiss as we went. He groaned. I clambered onto the mattress, up on my knees so we were almost the same height, and he slid his hands up under my tank top. His thumbs stroked the lower curve of my breasts and the shadows he brought caressed over the top. I wasn't sure whether he was directing them or they just came of their own accord until one whispered across my back—and flicked open the clasp of my bra.

"Hod," I said, momentarily startled.

"Do you mind?" he murmured. "I can call them back. My powers—when my feelings are this heightened—"

"No," I said with a quick shake of my head. "Don't stop. That was *hot*."

He chuckled. "Not something I've usually been accused of being."

"Not an accusation," I muttered in return. "Take a compliment." The last word cut off in a whimper as he cupped both my breasts, stroking my nipples into instant peaks.

I shoved my hands up under his shirt, eager to explore him skin to skin in turn. My touch drew a hungry sound from his lungs. He tipped me over on the bed, coming to rest beside me, his lips sliding down my neck.

Hod kissed my throat, my shoulder, my sternum, as if he were worshiping every part of me, leaving no inch of my skin unadored. Then his head dipped lower. His mouth closed over the tip of my breast, and I moaned, gripping his hair. His shadows teased over my lips, others tracing down my spine. I arched against him, wanting so much I couldn't find the words to say it.

He lifted his head for a second, and my pulse skipped with the thought that he was going to nudge me onto my back. But he just ducked lower, trailing kisses down the center of my chest to my belly. His shadows darted along the waist of my jeans as he flicked open the button. He tugged them down, his breath grazing hot against my panties.

His next kiss, right above them, was so tender that my throat choked up. I gripped his shoulder, tugging him back up, afraid of what might spill out of me if I let him keep going in that direction.

Hod came without complaint, tucking his arm around me and kissing me hard on the lips. My bare leg hooked over his thigh. Another groan escaped him, reverberating around my moan. His erection pressed against my core as he kissed me even harder. His shadows licked against me like an echo of a hundred tiny kisses, and the emotion I'd been trying to hold in tight spilled out anyway.

My chest hitched. Hod eased back from the kiss. He traced his hand down the side of my face and paused at the corner of my eye.

"Are you *crying*?" he said, his voice raw.

I sucked in a breath and just barely managed not to sob. "Good crying. Happy tears. I'm just… It's our thing, right? You've got to have me in tears at least once or it's not a full conversation."

"Ari…"

I tucked my head against his jaw. "I've never been with anyone and had it really mean anything before, okay?" Even that roll-around with Loki, as much as I'd enjoyed it, as many of my rules as I'd been breaking by going through with it, had been about scratching an itch, chasing desire, nothing all that much deeper.

No commitments. No proclamations.

But Hod had already made one.

His tone softened. "Ari. My valkyrie." His fingers slipped to my chin. He tipped it up so we were face to face, gaze to blind gaze. "I love you," he murmured, sounding a little choked himself.

I yanked his mouth back to mine. As our tongues tangled together, I wrenched at his slacks. He kicked them off, and I palmed his erection through his boxers. He held me tighter, pouring himself into the kiss. A wave of bliss coursed through me.

One of his shadows wriggled under my panties to lick against my clit. I gasped, gripped by a deeper need. "Please."

We fumbled our way out of our underclothes together. Then the smooth skin of his rigid cock was gliding against my clit. A wave of pleasure coursed through me. I hooked my leg back over his hip and urged him right into me.

A cry escaped me as he filled me. The giddy burn expanded from my core through every other nerve. Hod clasped my thigh, thrusting deeper as we fell into another kiss. We rocked against each other side by side. His shadows teased over my breasts, tingled against my clit. I whimpered, my teeth scraping his lip, and he bucked into me faster.

My head tilted back, my eyes rolling up. Hod took me deeper still, with a ripple of shadow all across the most sensitive points of my skin, and I came with a moan and a shudder. His breath turned ragged. He thrust with a few more erratic jerks of his hips and followed me into that final bliss.

# 20

*Aria*

I clung to Hod, reveling in his heat and his sweat-damp skin pressed against mine, until the afterglow started to fade. He kissed me, so sweetly it sent a fresh wave of longing through me. But I knew we didn't really have time to relish this moment. My gaze slipped to the window.

"I wish we really were back in this house," I said. "I wish…"

"A lot of things?" Hod suggested. His arms tightened around me for a moment. "Me too. But we'll get out of this. I can't imagine anyone keeping you caged for long, valkyrie."

I had to nuzzle him again, my mouth finding his for one last kiss. "Next time no crying, I promise," I said.

A smile crossed his face at the mention of a next time. Hod was always handsome, like all the gods were, but when he smiled… I couldn't look away.

I sat up and fumbled my bra back into place. My jeans and panties lay in a tangled heap near the foot of the bed. I squirmed into them with a glance around the room. "I'm not sure getting it on helped us much in the way of getting out of here, sadly."

Hod muffled a laugh with his hand. "Maybe if we tried again right now," he said with an uncharacteristically playful gleam in his eye.

I stuck my tongue out at him, even though he couldn't see it. "Don't get a one-track mind on me. Let me see—"

I hopped off the bed—and right through the floor.

Apparently our hook-up had affected Muninn's construct after all. The wooden boards gave way beneath me with a sigh. I plummeted down into darkness with barely time to let out a squeak.

My wings shot out from my back automatically. I whirled around, trying to grab hold of something, to fly back to Hod.

"There you are," Muninn's voice murmured as if inside my head. "Thought you could hide away? Here's something you should see."

An unseen force threw me against a stone wall. I slid to the ground in a low-ceilinged cave. The scent of rot filled my nose. I flinched, bracing myself against the rough stone.

I knew this place. It was Nidavillir, where I'd first come looking for Odin—the home of the dark elves.

The thought had only just crossed my mind when a woman tumbled into the cave through an opening I couldn't make out. The same opening I must have come through. She landed on her hands and knees, chestnut waves falling across her face, wings just like mine flexed above her back—and several dark elves hurtled out of the darkness to fall on her.

I clapped my hand over my mouth to cover a cry as one of their knives sank right into the other valkyrie's skull. Blood gushed out around it, painting her hair even darker. She crumpled to the ground. One of the dark elves spat on her before wheeling his short stout frame to stalk away.

"That's what happened to the others they sent," Muninn said. I had the impression she was perched just above me, even though there was nothing really there to perch on. "That's what your gods sent them *to*. Off to do the hard work for them, off to the slaughter."

"Only because the gods couldn't get to Asgard themselves," I said, closing my eyes against the sight of the murdered valkyrie. "They *would* have come themselves if they could." Freya's anguished voice rose up in my memory, talking about how much she wished she could go for her husband.

"And then they summoned you up." The raven woman's voice was disdainful. "And you followed the trail too well. If you'd just let it go, not tried quite so hard, I never would have needed to shut them away."

"Oh, so now this is *my* fault?" I shoved myself to my feet and spun on my heel, but I still couldn't see her. "You want to talk about taking responsibility for your own problems—how about you take responsibility for the shit you've thrown us into?"

"My offer still stands," Muninn said. "It won't for much longer. Do you really want to see how much worse this can get?"

"It'll only get worse for you, you—"

I raised my fist, and the force of her illusion smacked me across the head. I stumbled backward through the cave wall where I was whipped around and tossed to the side. My gaze leapt across the darkness, searching for some sign of Muninn.

A flicker of an image passed by my eyes. The raven woman hunched on a stone ledge, her head in her hands, her hair hanging lank through her fingers. A murmur slipped from her lips. "So damned tired of this."

My hand snatched out, and the image whisked away. I couldn't have said whether it was a glimpse of the present or the past. Whenever it had been, Muninn had been faltering. I felt her in that moment, her emotions radiating through the space around me. She was nearly exhausted.

A spark of triumph lit in my chest for about two seconds. Then I was hurled to the floor on the same stained carpet I'd found myself skidding onto what felt like days ago. The sour-stale odor of my mother's house wrapped around me, thicker this time. Thicker than I thought it'd ever actually been in reality.

Oh, no. We weren't doing this again. I sprang to my feet and heaved myself at the wall, meaning to break straight through it the way I had in the hall before.

My shoulder jarred against the solid plaster. I almost tripped over my feet landing back on the ground, holding my arm.

Muninn wasn't letting me go that easily this time. However exhausted she was, she'd been ready for that trick. But she couldn't be ready for everything. I just had to keep pushing.

The door. That was how I'd gotten out of this house the first time. I swung around toward it—and my mom appeared in the mudroom doorway. She planted her hands on her knobby hips.

"Sneaking out again? Can't be bothered to give your own family the time of day anymore, can you? I don't know how I raised such a selfish brat."

My chest clenched up. I didn't want to hear this. I *really* didn't want to find out what it might lead to. Jerking around in the opposite direction, I dashed for the other doorway.

She was already there in the kitchen, hunched over a chipped mug of coffee. "I'll do the laundry tomorrow," she muttered. "You can wear those pants another day. No one's going to be sniffing your ass."

I darted past her to the front hall. A different voice, a slightly flat tenor, carried from behind me. "Ari? Won't my favorite little lady spend some time with me?"

Trevor. I remembered those times way too well. The pat of his hand against the sofa cushion. The too-eager gleam in his eyes. The way he'd sit a little too close his knee pressed next to mine. The movies he'd pick—not porn or anything, but with more sex and violence than any other parental figure would let a nine-year-old watch.

I'd known from the first time he'd called me over that something wasn't quite right. He just hadn't shown me how wrong he could get until a year later. All I'd known then was that when I'd refuse, he'd vent to Mom, and Mom would lay into me even harder.

My pulse scattered. I ran toward the door—but there wasn't any door. Just one of those damned blank walls.

I didn't slow down. No, I sped up. I hurtled forward and rammed into that wall with a heave of my valkyrie strength.

My body slammed against it and toppled backward, pain radiating through my bones. My breath came out in a gasp.

"Ariiii."

The stairs. Maybe I could fly from a window. I swept around the bannister and charged up the creaking steps. Mom's bedroom. Muninn wouldn't be thinking about that. I'd barely ever gone in there.

I pivoted at the top of the stairs, leapt for her door, and Muninn's guiding force battered me across the head as if I'd been hit by a cast iron frying pan.

I fell, and fell, not onto the worn boards of the hall floor but into a thin mattress with a bulging spring by the small of my back. A scratchy wool blanket was pulled over my body up to my chin. The bedroom lay dark and silent around me. A cricket chirped outside.

A heavy footfall sounded on the stairs. One creak, and then another, and then another. Panic blared in my head. I moved to push myself off the bed and found myself paralyzed.

Just like I'd always been back then. Frozen with fear and dread, sweat beading on my forehead as my heart hammered at my ribs, listening to him climb those stairs. Only this time Muninn must have had a hand in this, pushing me down.

The blanket glued me to the mattress as if it were a layer of cement. A wave of fatigue trembled through it, but she held me there with all her strength. I'd be willing to bet she wasn't paying attention to anyone but me right now. She wanted her vengeance for the ways I'd challenged *her*.

*Do you really want to see how much worse this can get?*

I couldn't even open my mouth to curse at her. My jaw stayed clamped tight. Outside my bedroom door, the stairs stopped creaking. Trevor padded across the hall.

Fucking God, no no no *no*. I squeezed my muscles against the paralysis, but I couldn't budge an inch. More sweat trickled down the side of my face, leaving a chilly path in its wake. I willed my wings to emerge, to propel me off the mattress, but they stayed locked inside me. My lip pinched as my teeth bit down on it. The pain didn't jar me loose either.

The door eased open with a soft squeak. Trevor's broad, gut-heavy form stood silhouetted on the threshold. He stepped inside and closed the door behind him. Under his breath, he started to hum that damned song, that stupid fucking song about daisies and sugar that had been all over the radio for months and still made me want to vomit when I heard it.

Back then, I'd have squeezed my eyes shut. Pretended I was asleep, that I didn't know what he was doing, couldn't feel any of it, couldn't care. Maybe if I gave him nothing, he'd get bored of the groping and the rutting against my pajamas.

Except it hadn't worked. He'd gotten more creative as time went on. Oh, please, no, let this not be one of those times. Let this at least be early on, when it was easier to shut out.

He ambled across the room and stopped at the side of the bed, beaming down at me with that sickly crooked smile. This time, I glared back at him as if I could throw him out of the room with the power of my horror. My body cringed beneath the blanket.

He bent down to grasp the corner, and another figure emerged from the darkness right behind him. Hands clapped, and my mom's former boyfriend burst into flames.

The flare of the firelight glanced off Loki's light red hair and pale face. His amber eyes seemed to flare too as he watched Trevor crumble to the ground in a heap of dust. He kicked at the smoldering pile with a sneer. Then he turned to me. "I came as fast as I could. I'm sorry he got that far."

I snapped upright and in the process discovered that I could move again. A sound almost like a whine emerged from my throat as I scrambled off the bed, swiping at my arms as if the itch of the blanket and the memories that came with it might follow me. My shoulders were shaking.

"Ari…" Loki extended his hand and then paused with it halfway between us. Not knowing whether I'd want whatever comfort he was planning to offer, I guessed. I didn't know either. Another shudder wracked my body.

Control. I had to get control of myself. I still had to get *out* of here.

"Thank you," I managed to say, stiffly but steadily. "I… Thank you."

Loki nodded, his gaze fixed on mine. His hand still hovered in the air between us. He shifted his weight as if to move toward me, and the stairs creaked again.

I froze, my stomach flipping. Another creak, and another. He was coming *again*. Another Trevor. Fuck, no.

Panic took over. Before Muninn's invisible force could shove me back down on the bed, I bolted for the door.

# 21

*Loki*

Ari's distress radiated off her as if she were in full nuclear meltdown. I'd been able to feel it thrumming through the ever-shifting walls of Muninn's prison, growing sharper and more frenetic as I'd tried to follow our thread of connection to her. Now, watching her dash from the bedroom into the hall, it wracked my nerves.

So much pain contained in that small body. If she'd just talk to me, let me help her fight it…

I hurried after her. There was no way I was letting her out of my sight now. Muninn could throw a thousand walls up and I'd outpace them all to stay with our valkyrie. She'd needed me in there, and she'd need me again. Whether she liked that idea right now or not.

Ari swerved in the hall toward one of the other doorways, but as she ran for it, the floor dropped beneath her feet like a trap door opening. She dropped through it with a yelp. Cursing, I dove after her.

We landed in her kitchen, kitty-corner around the Formica table. On the other side of the room, a teenaged boy with a head of messy blond waves like Ari's was attempting to stare down a middle-aged guy who was a few inches taller and several wider, with a bald patch at the back of his head he'd inexpertly combed over.

It took me a second to recognize him in the glare of the kitchen's lights. Bald Spot was the man I'd just fried in Ari's old bedroom.

"You get out of this house, and don't you even *think* about coming around here again," the boy was saying, his voice ragged and his face flushed red. "If you ever touch her again—"

"You don't know what you're talking about, kid," the man said. "That girl makes up all kinds of crazy stories. Whatever she told you—"

Ari made a wounded sound. "No. Francis. *No*."

She shoved herself around the table and reached for the boy—for her older brother—but this once Muninn wasn't building with solid matter. Maybe she needed to preserve her energy, or maybe she saw it as a new form of torture. Ari's hand passed right through her brother's arm. He kept talking at a desperate pace as if he hadn't noticed her at all.

"She didn't tell me. I found proof. I know what you did, you sick fuck. So if you don't get the hell out of here, I'll—I'll call the police."

The man had tensed, but he kept his voice even. Even and dark. "You don't want to do that, Francis. Do you have any idea how they'll treat her if you feed them some story—"

"It can't be any worse than what you did to her," Francis snapped back.

Ari cried out and lunged at him again, but she caught hold of nothing but air. Her brother threw himself at the man with fist raised. The man dodged to the side, slamming out his arm to deflect the blow and shoving back at the same time.

Francis careened to the side, his head hitting the sharp corner of the counter with a fleshy crack. A sob broke from Ari's throat. She dropped with her brother as he collapsed, blood flowing from the wound on his head.

"Ari." I bent over her, touching her shoulders, but she smacked my hands away.

"Leave me alone. You don't— Francis…"

She pawed at his head as if she could heal the wound with strength of will alone. Muninn had let him turn solid now. Blood streaked across Ari's palms. My gut twisted, but for once in my long existence I hadn't the slightest idea what to say that might be welcome, that might soothe her anguish even a smidgeon.

He was lying there… lying there like Baldur had. Pale and bloody and totally innocent. I closed my eyes against the image.

By the Allfather, how could she have reacted in any other way to that scene in the courtyard? The crime I'd committed echoed one of the most horrifying moments of her life, only this time with me in the role of villain. I was lucky she was even tolerating me in the same room as her.

I might not ever be able to fix this. She might not ever forgive me for one act committed ages before she'd even been born.

That knowledge sank heavy in my chest. All right. That was a fact. But it was also a fact that I wasn't in the habit of giving up just because a situation looked dire. If there *was* a way to fix this, to repair the wreck I'd made of whatever we'd had, I'd damn well find it. Especially if in doing so I also struck a blow against this damned prison.

After a few minutes, Ari sat back on her heels with a stuttered sigh. She swiped at her face with the back of her hand.

"It's not him," she said to herself. "It's not him. It's Muninn's idea of torture. But she can't really hurt him." She raised her head and shouted at the ceiling. "I'm not falling for this!"

The body deflated with those words. In a matter of seconds,

there was nothing left of the supposed Francis except a smear of dust. Even the blood on Ari's hands crumbled into dust. She swiped them against her jeans and stood up.

"We've tired her out," she said to me. "She can't keep anything up very long anymore, not without all her concentration. And it's not worth it if it's not working. Not torturing us." She shot another glare at the ceiling with that comment, just as a woman appeared in the doorway.

Ari's mother. They weren't that close a match, but I could see Ari's heritage in the narrow gray eyes, the slant of the woman's nose. The corners of her mouth dug deep as it curved into a scowl.

"You had to go and ruin everything," she said, jabbing a finger at Ari. "We were fine. Just fine."

Ari's fingers clenched against the table-top. She took a step backward. "No, we weren't."

"You never could be satisfied with the way things were. Always had to make everything about you. As if any man would look at a scrawny thing like you and want *that*."

"Shut up."

"Francis would still be alive. I'd still have Trevor. We were making a real life for ourselves and you took it all away. If you'd just kept your stupid mouth shut—"

"I did, you fucking bitch!" Ari yelled.

Her mother froze, as if even this construct of Ari's memories didn't have a response to that. I was willing to bet Ari had never screamed like that at the real one, however much her mother had clearly deserved it. That moment's hesitation did give me an opening, though.

I held up my hand, a surge of heat racing through me. "Permission to light her up?"

Ari's jaw tightened, but her lips curled into a grim smile. She nodded with a short jerk of her head.

I snapped my fingers, and a spurt of fire shot up from the floor to engulf this figure of her mother.

Like the man upstairs, the construct crumbled before it even really started to burn. Not the most satisfying vengeance.

Ari sagged against the table, but her shoulders stayed tense. Her gaze lingered on the doorway. Braced for some new horror to emerge.

The moment stretched. Nothing else appeared. Muninn had switched to torturing my fellow gods for a bit, I had to guess. Or else she was even more tired than Ari had suggested—too tired to do more than hold these walls in place.

"You should never have had to see that again," I said into the silence. "Muninn deserves to have her head shoved up her ass and pulled right back out of her neck for putting you through it."

Ari's lips twitched at my creative imagery. She pushed away from the table. "Why are you here?"

"I'm trying to look after you, as difficult as you seem intent on making that task."

Her gaze snapped to meet mine. "Who says I need looking after?"

"I think we all do in this warped place, don't you?" I cocked my head. "It doesn't matter what you think of me, pixie. You're *my* valkyrie. I'm the one who dragged you into this mess—which has turned out to be a far bigger mess than I anticipated, unfortunately. So, even if you've decided to hate my guts, I'll still be here to burn up any assholes who need burning." I waggled my fingers in the air.

She let out her breath. "Yeah. They did need that."

Her head drooped again. I swallowed, but curiosity wriggled up my throat anyway. One of the milder of my many flaws.

"She really blamed you like that, didn't she? Your mother? Muninn didn't just make that up."

"My mom… lived in a reality where nothing much mattered except that nothing could ever be her fault." Ari lifted one shoulder and dropped it in a half-hearted shrug. "In a way she was right. If I hadn't been here, if I'd been better at hiding it, Francis wouldn't have died. Trevor wouldn't have gone to jail. Everyone would have been happier."

My jaw set against another flare of anger. "Everyone except you."

"Well, I didn't count, in her equation. I really didn't tell, you know. Two years, and it kept getting worse, but he'd always say, if I said anything, I'd be the one who got in trouble. I knew who my mom would believe. I knew Francis couldn't really do anything, not without ending up in the line of fire too…" Her voice wobbled.

"It isn't your fault," I said sharply. "Don't you dare take on one speck of the guilt that piece of human excrement should be carrying."

Her head jerked up again, her eyes startled. Did it really surprise her that I was angry about this? I didn't know every detail of what that bastard had done, but I'd seen enough in that scene and in every reaction Ari had when anyone got close to her…

"I could burn him up for real, you know," I said abruptly. "When we're out of here. An inexplicable case of spontaneous combustion. Really it'd be a kinder end than he deserves." But so very, very satisfying.

Ari's gaze stayed on my face for several seconds. "No," she said finally. "I don't think that would actually make things better." She looked away, braced against the edge of the table. "If I'd just fought back, if I'd screamed and hit or found some other way to show him he couldn't get away with it… But he could. He probably sized me up and knew I'd be too weak."

She sounded so defeated in that moment that my rage burned through me twice as hot. "You weren't *weak*," I said. "You were a child in a horrible situation. Trying to protect yourself and your brother like you always do. Taking it all on yourself so no one else had to be hurt. You were so fucking strong that even when the worst thing possible happened, you got through it, you kept going. You didn't let that despicable woman crush you. You didn't let the past break you."

"But maybe I did," Ari said. Her grip on the table tightened. "You don't know… It's been ten years since I last saw that asshole, and I still haven't managed to get him out of my head. I can't completely relax with anyone; I can't completely trust anyone. No commitments, no risk that I'll get hung up on the wrong guy, because it feels like it'd be so easy to end up trapped like that again."

"Ten years isn't that long after trauma like that," I said. The bitter weight I carried under my rage twinged in agreement. Centuries and centuries sometimes weren't enough.

She shook her head. "You don't even see it. You… You were the first person I've hooked up with who I knew I couldn't just walk away from the next morning. The first person in *ten years* where I didn't already have one foot out the door. And I fought it; I didn't want to take that chance, because I knew I wasn't going to want to walk away."

My heart squeezed. And then she'd ended up trapped in here with me, finding out just how wrong I could be. She'd given me that trust…

"So, why did you take the chance?" I asked quietly.

Her shoulders rose and fell. She glanced at me sideways. "I felt like you understood. You understood, and it didn't stop you from wanting me."

"It still doesn't," I said, not that hooking up was very high on my to-do list at the moment. I'd have been happy simply to have her welcome my embrace, to let me take a little of the burden she'd been carrying too long. "I've seen all that, I've heard everything you've said, and I still think you're one of the strongest human beings I've ever met, Ari. I wouldn't even recommend many gods take you on."

The edges of the room shimmered. I went still, watching from the corner of my eye. Muninn's constructs were becoming even more fallible. Maybe it wouldn't be long before we could shatter them completely.

"*I* don't understand," Ari said, turning to face me. "How could you have done that to Baldur? To *Hod*? You put both of them through so much shit—you murdered Baldur and made Hod feel like he was the murderer…"

My stomach clenched into a ball. I kept my voice even. "I never lied to you. I told you I was a villain. I'm sure the others told you plenty too. I am what I am, Ari."

Her gaze didn't waver. "If you're such a villain, then why are you trying so hard to help me? I have trouble believing it's just to get into my pants again."

"No one's ever that black and white. I'm allowed my finer moments."

"So, why didn't you make that one of your finer moments?" she demanded. "You had a choice, didn't you? Were you really just so pissed off at the stupid game that you thought murder was the answer?"

Despite my intentions, I bristled. "It was a lot more complicated than that. You saw one fragment of the history. I had my reasons."

"Then tell me them, instead of all this garbage about 'I am what I am'!"

My stomach clamped tighter. "That's the truth," I snapped.

"Is it?" she said. "Or is it just easier to avoid answering the question if you claim you're a bad guy and wash your hands of everything else?"

The accusation struck deeper than she could have realized it would. I managed to contain my flinch. If she'd known, if she'd had any idea…

But wasn't that just how she'd been arguing with me about her supposed weakness?

The walls around us wavered, more obviously this time. Ari's eyes widened. She pushed off the table, taking a step toward the cabinets. Then, with a heave, she threw herself forward with a smash of her fist.

The cabinets, the counter, the wall collapsed inward into darkness. Ari let out a cry of victory. She was just swiveling toward me when a gust of wind blasted up between us and tossed her right into that void.

# 22

*Aria*

Lord help me, I was so sick of being tossed around. As I spun into the blackness, I focused all that frustration on my memories of a sweet yet hoarse voice and a flutter of dark wings. Where was Muninn? Where was she, so I could punch her in her little raven face? She'd thought showing me all that history would wear me down? It'd only made me even more eager to tear her down—one feather at a time, if that was what it took. We were almost there. I *knew* her strength was flagging.

My wings flapped and banked. The darkness shifted around me, and I was back at the cage I'd seen Odin in before.

The Allfather was slumped against the iron bars, his head bent to the side and hat drooping low. His presence reverberated through me. The ring of fire continued licking at the base of the cage. A more muted reddish glow seeped over the rock all around—a cave. This was a cave somewhere.

I turned. A wall of thick liquid flowed past what I guessed was the cave's entrance, emanating a red-hot light like the stream where I'd seen him ambushed.

Like… magma? Were they keeping him in a *volcano*? After everything I'd seen in the last few weeks, it didn't seem impossible.

Muninn's voice drifted from deeper within the cave. "You never thought I was capable of something like this, did you? You never thought very much about me at all, except for what I could bring you. Did you even wonder where I was, all this time? Did you assume this place had killed me, not that it clearly mattered to you much?"

"I knew where you were, Muninn," Odin said, his voice low and rusty. "You didn't appear to want to be disturbed, so I let you be."

That sounded like a kind enough answer, but from Muninn's sharp inhale, it'd somehow made her angrier.

"I had a life," she said. "A life I could have had for all that time before. I used to think—"

"What?" Odin said after a moment, shifting against the bars. "What did you think, my raven?"

"I'm not *yours*," she spat out.

I edged away from them, away from the cage, toward the fall of magma. There was a small gap between the gush and the rock. If this was the entrance, if I could see more from here, maybe I'd have a better idea where we could find Odin… whenever we were able to really go looking for him again. If he was even still here.

My foot scraped the rough stone floor. A curse echoed through my head from some other place. Then a force battered my face with so much power I had to close my eyes and raise my hands to shield myself.

I stumbled backward and spun around, not wanting to accidentally take a dive into that searing waterfall. The uneven ground flipped up beneath me.

That next journey was nothing more than a brief lurch. I dropped my hands and found myself back in the front courtyard of Asgard, crouched on the marble tiles where we'd first arrived. From the slant of the sunlight and the deepening blue of the clear sky overhead, it was evening. The same time it'd have been if we'd never left this spot? I didn't have any clear sense of how much time had passed in Muninn's prison, traveling through all those years of memories.

The breeze licked over me with just a hint of a chill. I straightened up. The soft warbling of the water cascading from the central fountain was the only sound. Nothing and no one else stirred in the vast city of the gods, anywhere that I could see.

I hugged myself, wavering on my feet. Was Muninn just waiting to spring some new horror at me? Of course, if she'd wanted to horrify *me*, she wouldn't have sent me to a place I had no memories of. When I'd ended up back in some version of Asgard before, it'd always been to join one of the gods in a painful replay of the past. Was she so worn out she couldn't even bother to come up with a new torture for me?

Where were the other gods, then? Should I go exploring? Or try to bash my way out of this place into wherever they were?

I'd just made up my mind to at least peek into a few of the nearby buildings when the air shuddered. With a grunt, Thor came tumbling into the courtyard beyond the fountain as if out of nowhere.

He hit the tiles shoulder first, just barely protecting his head with the back of his arm. Mjolnir thumped against the tiles beside him. A pained sound escaped the thunder god as he rolled onto his back. I ran to him, my heart thudding faster when I saw how he staggered a little pulling himself onto his feet.

One side of his shirt was stained with blood. *His* blood, it had to be, because all the rest had turned into those smears of dust that marked my clothes too.

"Ari!" he said with that broad smile, even as he clamped his hand against his wound.

My breath hissed through my teeth. "Sit back down," I said, grabbing his other arm. "What the hell happened to you? Where did she send you?"

He didn't exactly listen to me, but he did lower himself onto the stone rim of the fountain, the water in the pool rippling with the impact of his brawny body. He glanced down at his bloody shirt and grimaced.

"Better idea," I said. "*Lie* down."

"I'm fine," he said stubbornly.

"You're about to refill the fountain with your blood," I shot back. "There's nothing dangerous here, not yet, anyway. And when something does show up, I have the feeling you'll be better at taking it on if you haven't been ignoring a mortal wound."

Thor frowned, his shoulders flexing. My throat tightened. "Please?" I said.

That one word softened his expression. He sighed, but he lay back on the rim. I peered over him, realized there was no way I was reaching the water by leaning, and hopped right into the pool.

Thor winced when I splashed a little water on his side to wash the wound.

"Can you get your shirt off without making it worse?" I asked.

He raised an eyebrow at me. "You want my shirt."

"So I can try to bandage you up!" I said, giving him a firm look.

He chuckled and wrenched at the fitted tee on the other side. With a quick yank of his muscled arm, the fabric split from hem to sleeve.

I helped him peel the shirt off, careful around the wound, which I could now see was a wide but shallow scrape across his lower ribs. The bleeding looked to be slowing. I tied together the pieces of shirt as well as I could and wrapped them around his torso with a thicker set of folds over the scrape.

Thor lay back down when I was done. I sat on the fountain rim by his head and squeezed as much water as I could out of my jeans.

"It was battles," Thor said, answering my earlier question about where he'd been. "Battles, battles, and more battles. I didn't realize I had so little variety in my life, but it seemed like that's all the raven could come up with out of my memories."

"And one of those battles got the better of you?"

"Not exactly." He paused. "I got tired of all the bashing and battering. Thought maybe I could try a different strategy. Why not? She was shifting the memories all around. Who was to say I couldn't? So I tried calling a halt to the battle to have a calm discussion about why exactly we were fighting. Because I've got to tell you, I didn't have any idea by that point."

I nudged his hammer, which he'd laid on the ground beside him, with my toe. "Thor the Thunderer gave diplomacy a shot. Not what she was probably expecting. And?"

He scowled. "They didn't even stop running at me. I waited to see if maybe, if I didn't even fight back, that might change something, but…" He motioned to his side. "So much for diplomacy."

"Well, it's not really your area anyway, right?"

He was silent for a longer moment this time. "I'd rather it was. But I guess this is what I am."

The comment echoed Loki's excuse so closely I had to restrain a cringe. But Thor had told me before how uncomfortable he felt realizing how much of his life had been made up of violence. He'd seemed to think I'd see him as some kind of beast because of it.

I let my fingers brush over his dark auburn hair, displacing the strands that had come free from his short ponytail. "That's just what she wants you to think," I said. "I'd like to see *her* give diplomacy a try."

He rumbled in agreement. "Should I be coming up with my last words?"

"No, I think you're going to survive. It looked worse than it was."

"Oh. Well, in that case."

He shoved himself upright, ignoring my squeak of protest. With a sweep of his arm, he scooted me into his embrace. He kissed my temple. "I'm glad you're all right, Ari. I kept thinking… You *are* all right, aren't you?"

I thought of all the horrors I'd been wrenched through, mine and others', in the last several hours, and my stomach knotted. But Thor hadn't been part of any of that agony. It felt like a relief to tip my head against his bare chest, soak up his body's heat, and say, "Yes. Yes, I am."

I didn't want to move. I wanted to stay there with his hand stroking up and down my back for a good long time. I was tired too. The smell of him, like warm tangy mead, teased around me. Without thinking, I found myself pressing a kiss to the bulge of his pecs just below his collarbone so I could taste it too.

Thor's fingers shifted against my back. "Ari," he said in a voice low with hunger—and a thud sounded behind us.

I leapt up, Thor heaving himself onto his feet almost as quickly. Freya was just straightening up where she'd fallen near the edge of the courtyard. Her golden hair was in disarray, but she somehow smoothed it perfectly into place with one brisk flick of her hands.

"Well," she said, with slight shudder. "This has been… something."

Baldur emerged from the air several feet away from her, managing to land on his feet. His youthful face looked weary, but less pained than when I'd found him in the darkness. I hoped Muninn hadn't found anything worse to torment him with.

His sweeping gaze caught on my hasty bandage around Thor's side in an instant. He strode toward his brother. "You're injured."

The thunder god waved him off. "Ari took care of it. I'll live."

"I might as well do what I can while we have a moment."

Baldur's bright blue eyes darted to me for a moment, looking me up and down as if to confirm I hadn't taken any new beatings since he'd last seen me.

"I'm okay," I said quickly. "Take care of him."

As Thor started grumbling something about not needing to be taken care of and Baldur knelt beside him, the air twanged again. Two more figures emerged at opposite ends of the courtyard almost simultaneously: Hod and Loki.

Hod caught himself with a knee and a hand on the tiles and scrambled up, summoning his shadowy cane with a flick of his hand.

"It's all right," I called to him. "So far everything's been calm here."

His shoulders relaxed at the sound of my voice. "I tried to catch you when you fell," he started.

"I know," I said before he could try to apologize. "She had a few more tricks up her sleeve."

Loki strolled toward us, taking in the courtyard with his amber gaze and a curious tilt of his head. "I wonder what tricks she has in store for us here. All six of us, back where we started. An interesting choice. Who got here first?"

"I did," I said. "And then Thor. It hasn't been that long, though. Maybe half an hour?" If I could rely on my sense of time at all. "I guess she's run out of horrible memories to throw us into. All that tossing us around really tired her out."

"We didn't break as easily as she was hoping," Hod said grimly.

"And it's easier to keep us all contained if we're in the same place?" Freya suggested.

"So she might hope," Loki said with a sly smile. "I'm all for disappointing her once again. Ari, you still seem to be the key to cracking through these constructs of hers."

He made a beckoning gesture, and I stiffened automatically. His expression darkened, just for a second.

Hod stepped toward me. "You don't get to order her around," he said. "And I'm not sure I'd trust any plans *you* come up with anyway."

Loki let out his breath in a huff. "Come on now. Do we really need to act as if the past really did just happen? We've coexisted peacefully for ages before now. Do I need to list all the impossible situations I've extracted us from before?"

"No," Hod said. "I let what happened go to keep the peace for too long. We're all thinking it. I'll say it. However we get out of here, after this, you're not welcome anywhere near the rest of us."

Loki's jaw worked, but he kept his tone glib. "I hardly think you can make that decision for the entire party. Declared yourself the voice of the group since you can't be the eyes, have you?"

"Loki," Baldur said, his voice melodic but steady. He left Thor, turning to face the trickster. "I think you've done enough."

My pulse skittered. This was starting to sound like more than just the bickering they'd done before. "Wait," I said. "None of this matters unless we do get out of this place. We get out, and then… and then anything you need to decide, you can decide it then." Fighting with each other was only going to serve Muninn's purposes.

Hod shrugged. "I've already said my piece."

"Well, fine," Loki said with a dismissive sweep of his hand. "As if the two of you didn't fall in with us in the first place because no one else could stand being around constant grimness and the perpetual daze. Thor and I will just have to go adventuring again."

He cast an expectant glance toward the thunder god. Thor shifted his weight. "When we do get home, I think I'll be happy to stick to feasting and drink for a good long while."

"I guess you'll have to enjoy those adventures on your own," Hod said. "Just don't bring them back here."

"*Here*?" Loki replied, his tone sharpening. "You mean this

prison we're still stuck in, which apparently you've all forgotten—except Ari, of course?"

"Anywhere," Hod snapped back.

"Okay, just *wait*," I said, stepping between them with my arms outstretched. "This is what Muninn wants. We have to work together, try to understand each other—it's by looking at the past in different ways that we've started to bring down her prison. We can talk this through."

A blaze had already lit in Loki's eyes. It seared through his voice. "It doesn't sound like we can. So you'll cast me out, finally, after all the ages, because of one act over a millennium ago? I suppose that's Asgardian justice for you."

"One act that left the two of them dead," Freya put in tentatively.

"Do you think I *enjoyed* that fact? Do you think I delighted in that outcome?"

"Yes," Hod said. "By all appearances you did."

"By all— You can't even *see*— You weren't even here to know —" Loki threw up his hands.

"Maybe you'd better go now," Baldur said softly. "When we break the prison, we'll all get out, either way."

A tremor ran through the trickster's body, so sharp I half expected him to explode into flame. His eyes narrowed.

"*No*." He spun around, jabbing his finger at one and then another of them. "No. I'm done. Let's have a real look at the past and see just how very different it is from the picture he painted for you. I've kept that bastard's secrets for his benefit and *yours* for long enough. Ragnarok was supposed to be the end. I was done with this fucking role. But you all just can't help shoving me back into it. So, here you go. I'll be your villain one more time."

"Loki," Thor said warily. "What are you ranting about now?"

"You'll see. Or hear, as the case may be." Loki shot a fiery look Hod's way. He motioned to the sky. "Play along with me, little raven. You wanted Odin to fall? Let him fall even farther. Let's have the tower. Let's have that night. You can see the memory. Isn't it juicy enough for you?"

For a few seconds, nothing happened. My heart pounded in my chest. I was just opening my mouth to try to salvage the mess we'd made of this meeting when the halls upended all around us. The tiles bucked up, throwing us toward the sky.

# 23

*Aria*

My wings shot from my back. I caught hold of Thor's hand, the closest of the gods. Then stone walls thudded into place all around the six of us.

We jolted to a stop on a woven rug in a cylindrical room. The ceiling rose to a peak overhead, crisscrossed with rafters and shadows. Windows ran in a circle all around the room. A tall wooden armchair that looked as if it'd sprouted right out of the floor stood in the center. There was no other furniture except a few small tables and bookshelves beneath the ring of windows. A cold night breeze rippled past us, carrying a scent like a coming storm.

Lightning crackled across the sky outside, followed by a distant rumble of thunder. The hairs on the back of my neck stood up. I didn't like the feeling of this at all.

Thor squeezed my hand. Baldur took a step toward the chair. He stared up at it, wide-eyed.

"This is my father's tower," he said. "The Allfather's high seat. I've never seen it."

"Because he never invites *anyone* up," Hod said from near my other side. "No one enters the tower except for Odin."

Thor bent close to me. "From that chair, through those windows, it's said he can see anywhere in the nine realms," he murmured.

"He never invited *you*," Loki said to Hod, that fiery heat still flaring in his eyes, crackling through his voice like the lightning outside. "No one sets foot in this room except the Allfather—and his closest collaborator."

"And that's you?" Freya crossed her arms over her chest, sounding skeptical.

"Do you really think Odin brought one of the treacherous jotun into Asgard, swore a blood-bond with me, just for fun? Surely you know him better than that."

"Why are we here?" Thor said. "What's so important that we had to see?"

Loki spun around. "You want to hold the Allfather up on a pedestal? You want to be horrified at the things I've done? Everything, all of it, was for *him*." He spat out the last word.

Freya's eyebrows drew together. "What in Hel's name are you talking about?"

"Let him tell you!"

Loki flung his arm toward a figure that had just stepped out of the shadows. Odin swept his broad-brimmed hat from his head and set it on top of one of the low bookcases. He ran his hand through his grizzled brown hair.

It wasn't the real Allfather. Even if I hadn't known he couldn't be here, that Muninn would never let him free from his cage just for this, my valkyrie nature didn't respond to this form's presence with the same tug of recognition.

No, this must be the Odin of Loki's memories.

And no one else but Loki had been here in those memories. Odin nodded to the trickster as if he'd expected to find him in the room, his gaze skimming right over the rest of us. "Oath-brother," he said in his low dry voice. "It's good to see you."

Loki's attention had completely shifted to the Allfather. He propped himself against one arm of the great chair. "Is it?" he said. "You didn't seem all that pleased with me when we last met down below." He gestured toward the city beyond the tower's windows.

"You know how it goes," Odin said. "We need a sense of order."

"While you're encouraging chaos behind their backs."

"Now wait a—" Thor growled, stepping forward, and Loki jerked up his hand to stop him. He was playing out the conversation of the past, I guessed, but this was still his present self, fully conscious of both us and Odin.

"You wanted answers," he snapped at the thunder god. "Watch and you'll get them."

I tugged at Thor's arm, even though a nervous ache was forming around my gut. "I think we need to see this," I murmured.

Thor drew back beside me, his mouth set tight. At my other side, Hod stood stiffly. His blind gaze was low, but I could tell that every particle of his attention was focused on the scene in front of us. Near the other side of the chair, Baldur and Freya stood silent and tensed.

The construct of the Allfather was shaking the dust from his cloak. "It's not chaos I've asked of you," he said. "Stir emotions. Spark passion. Start the flames burning."

Loki rolled his eyes at Odin. "You and your damned poetry. Spark a passionate desire to see my head on a pike is about the size of it."

Odin paused and turned fully toward the trickster. "Are you unhappy with your situation?" he asked. "When we met, when I offered you a place here in Asgard, you remember the oath you took."

"I swore my loyalty to you with my blood," Loki said. He ran his thumb across his slender palm. "You didn't tell me how much that loyalty would require."

"I haven't asked much of you before now, have I?" The Allfather arched one thick eyebrow. "You've had the run of the realm of the gods. You've gotten to play your games and work your tricks."

"While nearly every god and goddess out there still treats me like I'm an evil stowaway in their midst."

"And that's exactly why you're the one for this role."

Loki's hands clenched at his sides, the knuckles turning an even starker pale than the rest of his skin. "They already hate me, so why not let them hate me more? Brilliant logic, oh king of the gods."

"You can mock the logic, but it is sound." Odin looked him up and down. "I've not gotten the impression you even mind letting out the hostility I'm hearing right now, when the situation calls for it."

A rasp crept into Loki's voice. "I mind. I mind that I need to be angry at all. If I find ways to take a little joy in the dung-heap lot you've given me—"

"Loki." For the first time, Odin's full power thrummed through his words. Even now, even faced with just a memory, the trickster flinched. The ache in my gut dug deeper.

The Allfather straightened up even taller, looming beside his chair. "I asked this of you as one oath-brother to another. Do you think it doesn't pain me too? But what must be done… it must be done. I *need* you. I thought I could count on you. Was I wrong?"

Loki wet his lips. "No," he said, quieter now. "You weren't. I just don't understand. Why does any of this have to happen at all?"

"I've read the signs. Gleaned the omens. Unpuzzled the Norns tangled prophecies. This age is going to run itself down whether we like it or not. All we can do is end it well. A clean break. The realm cleansed in fire. I know you've got the spirit to lead that charge, don't you, trickster?" A dark gleam lit in the Allfather's one eye. "They need a villain. Who better could I have asked to play him?"

A chill ran down my back. Freya covered her mouth with a noise of shock. Thor's hand closed around mine so tight it almost hurt.

"And if I don't want to play that part?" Loki said.

"Then our fall may be that much more painful. Is that what you'd rather instead?" Odin's gaze didn't waver.

"I never wanted any of it!" Loki shouted, shoving himself off the side of the chair. "There wasn't really any choice, was there? Be your villain or be a villain by betraying my oath to you. Either way, the world falls apart and it's all my fault. While you stand there with your damned knowing smile…"

Odin didn't even stir at his rant. I suspected the Loki back then hadn't been quite that scathing. Faced with that unwavering calm, the trickster's rage deflated. He looked suddenly beaten in a way I'd never seen before. The sight tore at my heart.

"You'll stay the course?" Odin said.

Loki swiped his hand across his face. "You see everything, don't you?" he said. "Past, present, and future, from the mouths of the Norns, from your fragments of prophecies… Somehow I think you already knew I would."

"Good." Odin set his hand on Loki's shoulder. "All Asgard will thank you in the end."

He picked up his hat and vanished back into the shadows. Loki raised his head to watch the Allfather go.

"Funny," he said. "That particular end is taking an awfully long time coming."

I couldn't stand to hang back any longer. I pulled my hand from Thor's and hurried across the room to Loki. He turned at the sound of my feet, hope and apprehension both flashing through his expression—as if he thought I might shy away from him again at the last second. My lungs contracted. I slipped my arms around him, tipping my head against his lean chest.

"I'm sorry," I said.

"Whatever for, pixie?" Loki said in his more usual light tone. "For believing me when I asked you to? For drawing the intended conclusions from the information you had? I don't see any crime in that." But his hand quivered a little as it stroked over my hair. I had the feeling the confrontation had taken more out of him than he was willing to show.

"Loki," Hod said, his voice rough, and then didn't seem to know how to go on.

"I didn't really let myself wonder why he stayed so close with you, after everything," Baldur said. "I never… I never would have thought he'd have wanted…"

"I don't think he did want any of it," Loki said. "He just saw it as the lesser of two evils. Fortunately for him, he had someone to deliver those evils and deflect the blame."

"When I can talk to my father for real…" Thor said gruffly, and Loki nodded.

Freya made a startled sound. "The walls," she murmured.

I looked up. As I did, the window across from me quavered. A waft of that ashy smell drifted in, along with red-tinted darkness. The real world beyond the construct.

All the gods could see it. They turned toward it as I stepped from Loki. But before I'd reached that breach, it shimmered away again.

Thor smacked his hammer against the wall. The stones held. He frowned. "We're still just as trapped as ever."

Another spot on the wall twitched briefly open before my eyes. "No," I said. "We're not. She can shut us away in one place, but her prison is still breaking down. She's exhausted, and we keep changing our memories, and— If we could just wear them down a little more… We're almost out. I'd bet she can't do anything except hold this room in place as well as she can now, or she'd already have thrown us apart."

"What are you thinking, Ari?" Hod asked.

"I don't know. We get closer every time we shake up how we're thinking about the past. But I don't…"

I hesitated. There was another element to it. I'd seen it. Muninn hadn't opened up the floor in Hod's bedroom after we'd been together. The rush of emotion must have shaken her constructs too. Just like the illusion had fractured a sliver when I'd kissed Thor, when I'd started to get hot and heavy with Baldur. Because it focused us so completely on the sensations of the present? Because those feelings gnawed at Muninn's mind in some other way? I thought of the scene I'd witnessed, her curled up against the dying man.

There were people she'd cared for once. A man she'd loved.

But in the end it didn't really matter why. It only mattered that it worked. My heart started to beat faster.

We'd been through so much together. I shouldn't be afraid of this. I knew every man—every *god*—in this room. I knew they would never take anything except what I gave them freely. So why did the past hang over me like a goddamned anvil?

I dragged in a breath. We all had these stupid ideas about who we were, what we could and couldn't, do, weighing down on us, didn't we? I'd heard it from everyone around me in this room. Remembering that, an idea lit like a flame inside me. A flame that sent a flush of heat over my skin and a pulse of desire down through my belly.

"I need you," I said, looking to each of the gods in turn. "I need all of you."

The heat inside me carried through my words. Freya gave a soft cough. "I'll just be getting out of your way then."

Loki smirked as she slipped away into the darker side of the room, behind the chair. He stepped up beside me. Baldur and Thor joined him in a semi-circle around me, watching me with curious anticipation. Only Hod hung back, but just a little, his head cocked as if he were waiting to see where I was going with this.

Even though I'd already committed to this plan in my mind, I had to swallow before I spoke to make sure my voice didn't shake. "We aren't what anyone thought we were, are we? And we can show just how true that is."

"What did you have in mind, pixie?" Loki asked in a liquid murmur.

I balked, but only for a second. The second it took me to realize I knew exactly where to start. I grasped Baldur's hand and gave him a little tug to come even closer, holding his bright blue gaze so he'd see just how much I meant this.

"Baldur can be wicked."

Desire sparked in the light god's eyes. He bent to claim my mouth so swiftly I barely had time to breathe. His tongue teased my lips apart in an instant, his hand coming to my breast to pinch my nipple through my clothes. I gasped against his mouth as I arched into him. Urging, pleading with every movement for more.

He grazed his teeth down the side of my neck, offering shivers of pleasure with every nip, and I locked eyes with my trickster.

"Loki can be selfless," I murmured.

A grin stretched across his face. "Any time you like, my darling Ari."

As Baldur tugged up my shirt for better access to my breasts, Loki knelt before me. The light god rolled my other nipple, and Loki kissed the sensitive skin just below my belly button. He lingered there, flicking open the button of my jeans. A sudden flash of panic shot through me, but I shoved it down. I closed my eyes as he slid my jeans and panties down.

His lips charted a scorching path down my thigh and then up it again. By the time he reached the apex of my legs, I didn't have a shred of anything but wanting left in me. He brought his mouth right to my core, slicking his tongue over my clit, and I moaned.

It still wasn't enough. I looked to Thor through my haze of desire. His normally warm brown eyes were blazing as he gazed back at me. One of my hands was tangled in Baldur's shirt. The other I held out to the thunder god.

"Thor can be gentle."

He dropped his hammer on the floor and reached me in one quick stride. But when he rested his hand on my waist and brought his lips to mine, there was only tenderness in his touch. I lost myself in his kiss, in Baldur's strokes of my breasts, in Loki's hot mouth against my core. Bliss rippled through me from every direction.

When Thor raised his head to kiss my cheek, my temple, my gaze found Hod. And suddenly I wasn't sure what to say.

As if he'd sensed my dilemma, Hod smiled a little wryly. "Hod can bear witness," he said. "Without bitterness."

A sense of rightness settled in my chest. Then Baldur swept the peak of my breast into his mouth, testing it with his teeth, and Loki dipped a finger beneath the swipe of his tongue to hook up inside me, and Thor's large but careful hands caressed down my sides with the slightest shimmer of electricity. In that instant, I trembled with nothing but joy.

"And I am not a victim," I said, clutching Loki's silky hair, leaning into Thor's solid frame. "Not anymore. I take what I want."

And I wanted all of them. Oh, fucking yes. For the first time, the thought filled my mind without a hint of shame or fear. I gave myself over to it, to whatever would come next.

# 24

*Thor*

Ari moaned as she rocked in our joined embrace. I caught her mouth, keeping my kiss soft but sure. Her fiery sweet taste filled my senses. The feel of her naked skin against my bare chest misted my mind with a haze of lust, almost as potent as my battle rage. Lightning tickled through my veins, eager to spark from my fingers.

But I could hold my coarser urges in check. I *could* be the gentle lover she'd asked for from me. Baldur provoked a pleased cry from her with a squeeze of her breast, and I drew a whimper after it as I grazed my thumb over the other. When I trailed my mouth along the side of her jaw, she tipped her head to the side, offering better access to the pale line of her neck. Trusting me implicitly. My heart swelled at that gift.

Loki eased her thighs farther apart with a slick of his tongue I could hear. Ari gasped as he worked her over with hands and mouth. Her body started to tremble against mine. I held her, supporting her, drinking in the eager shivers with the press of my lips against the crook of her shoulder. She arched back with a clenching of the muscles all through her body. One hand clamped around my arm. I felt her release course through her.

The trickster kissed the side of her leg and straightened up with a sly smile. "And I ask nothing in return," he said.

He looked ready to step away, but Ari made a disgruntled sound and grasped the front of his shirt. She pulled him to her, into a kiss.

I'd come to women alongside Loki in the past, during our travels, but never for anything more than a quick roll in the hay. Ari was more than that—to all of us. But not even a flicker of jealousy rose in my chest. We'd all come together to bring her into our lives, and now she was a part of us just as we were a part of her. We were bound together in some strange way, both in battle and in desire. Watching Loki cup her face and kiss her back only made me wish I'd contributed just as much to her pleasure this time.

Maybe I could. When Ari let go of the trickster, she turned to me and tugged me into a kiss too. Her hand roamed over my chest, tracing heat everywhere it touched. My erection pulsed even harder in my pants. Damn, this woman was more intoxicating than any mead.

The valkyrie's hand slid all the way down to the waist of my pants. My breath hitched when she brushed her fingers over my groin. "I don't think we're done yet," she murmured, and kissed me again.

As my mouth melted against hers, she unfastened my belt. I couldn't hold back a groan. With a yank, she sent my jeans to my knees. Gentle. She wanted gentle. It should have been a challenge, but instead the thought sent a thrill of exhilaration through me. I could be the man she needed, even in this.

Baldur slid his arms around Ari's waist from behind. "Here," he said, with a smile that did look wicked, and hefted her onto the arm of Odin's high seat. The perfect height for her body to align with mine.

Ari grinned and wrapped her fingers around my straining cock. Hunger flooded my body. I kissed her tenderly but with all the longing I had in me, stroking her breasts, easing her hips a little closer to mine. Gently. Gently. Every soft movement, every second stretched out as I took my care with her, only made the heat of desire inside me flare brighter. Our tongues tangled, the faintest spark of electricity leaping between them, and she whimpered.

She was right. This was a part of me too: this passionate but steady man who had her quivering hungrily with just a brush of my fingertips. Right now, it was the only man I wanted to be.

Baldur knelt on the seat behind her. He nipped her shoulder as he gripped her ass, and Ari gasped into my mouth. Her body canted forward. She urged me to her, her hand still tight around my length, and rocked against the head of my cock.

Her frame was so small I had a moment's worry about whether I could give her what she was asking for without any pain, but her wetness slicked over me, her folds hot and ready, and skies above, there wasn't any bliss better than this.

I set one hand on her hips and let the other fall to the sensitive nub at her core. My thumb teased over it with another soft spark, earning me a moan from her. She arched toward me, and I sank into her, just the head. Her slick heat closed around me. I groaned into her hair.

"More," she said, gripping my shoulders. I let out a rough chuckle and shifted my hips. Inch by blissfully torturous inch, I slid deeper inside her. Then I eased back and plunged into her again. Ari gasped, clutching me tighter.

I found a rhythm, slowly building speed, penetrating her a little deeper with each thrust. Ari bucked to meet me. Her legs wrapped around my thighs and her mouth found mine again, our kisses ragged, broken by sounds of pleasure we couldn't contain.

I was bringing her that pleasure. I was sending her further into ecstasy with each measured roll of my hips. I sank into her all the way to the hilt, and she gave a cry that had nothing but joy in it.

"Next time I'll take the fierceness," she murmured against my shoulder. "I want every part of you."

The words sent a giddy tremor through me. I thrust faster, drinking in her scent, losing myself in the feel of her, and Ari came around me with a sharper cry. The clamp of her body around my cock stole the last of my control. My balls clenched, and I released my own ecstasy in a rush of crackling heat.

As the orgasm crashed through me like a wave, the walls around us toppled. The construct of the chair disintegrated into the air. I caught Ari against my body as we fell, slamming one arm out to deflect the impact. We pulled apart with a shared gasp.

"Well, well, well," Loki said, swiveling. "What have we here?"

The dark ragged walls of an immense cavern rose around us. Only a faint pulsing light gleamed over us from glowing patches of red in the ceiling high above. It all appeared to be a natural solid structure except for the wall to my right, where boulders jumbled against each other as if a landslide had covered the entrance.

Ari scrambled for her clothes. Her face was still flushed, but her eyes shone with determination rather than desire now. "We did it," she said. "We broke through."

I yanked up my pants and fastened my belt with a jerk. Mjolnir lay near my feet as if I'd set it down here and not in the room that had appeared as Odin's tower. I snatched it up with a preparatory swing.

"What is this place?"

"I smell ash," Hod said, his head cocked. "And sulfur."

"From that and the looks of the place, I'd say we've found ourselves in Muspelheim." Loki nodded to Ari. "The realm of fire. Not much lives here, at least not much we'd like to meet."

"This is the place I saw when I got into fragments of some of

Muninn's memories," the valkyrie said. She extended her wings from her back with a burst of wind. The silver-white feathers glinted starkly in the ruddy light. Her jaw tightened. "Odin was here then, and he's still here now. I can feel him. That way." She pointed to the rockslide wall.

Freya brandished her sword. "Let's go before Muninn and whoever else she has on her side realize we've escaped."

The thought of my father brought back the conversation Loki had shown us in Odin's tower. The way the Allfather had spoken to the trickster... Could he really have *wanted* Loki to do all the things he had? To bring down all of Asgard? And not just wanted that, but forced Loki to keep up the role despite his protests.

The scene had felt true, and its veracity left a queasy sensation in my gut. But we weren't going to find any answers until we had the real Odin with us again. No matter what he'd done in the past, Muninn and the dark elves needed to fall right now for their many crimes.

I gripped the handle of my hammer hard. "I can clear the way."

I charged at the wall, the ground shuddering beneath my feet, and flung Mjolnir with all my strength. The hammer slammed into the mass of rock and blasted straight through it. Chunks of stone rained down on the cavern floor, and more of that reddish light flowed in through the hole, beckoning us.

Mjolnir flew back to my hand. I whipped it out again, smashing more of the rubble into pebbles. The higher boulders tumbled down and cracked open on the ground. With one last hurl, I shattered a clear path through the avalanche.

We rushed forward, Ari and Freya with their blades at the ready, Hod's shadows snaking around him. The six of us burst out onto a rocky plain overlooking a thick river of magma. A mountain rose on the other side of it, blocking off most of our view. Heat wafted up, drawing a layer of fresh sweat across my skin, for much less pleasurable reasons. My muscles tensed as I scanned the landscape.

"Can you still sense Odin?" Baldur asked Ari.

She turned slowly, her wings fluttering as if testing the air. Her forehead furrowed.

"Somewhere that way," she said, motioning toward the mountain with a frown. "I saw… He was in a cave, behind a waterfall of magma. If we can find that…"

Loki was already springing into the air. He strode up toward the sky with swift steps that covered a vast stretch in an instant. I was ashamed to find that even now, after everything he'd shown us, suspicion jabbed my gut—that he might be running off on his own, abandoning us.

If that scene had been true, then he'd never really been against us at all. He'd let us hate him to spare us pain. And I'd never even seen it. I'd have to be a better friend now.

High above us, the trickster's eyes narrowed with a flash. He glided back down at full speed.

"I see the place," he called. "Just beyond that ridge. Are we ready to fight?"

Freya brandished her sword. "Never more."

Hod was already collecting his shadows into a plane beneath his feet. Beside him, Baldur gleamed with his bright magic. Ari stretched her wings in anticipation.

"Whatever they've got waiting for us, it can't be worse than what we've already beaten," she said. "We'll get to him this time."

All the battling I'd done in Muninn's prison had left me sore, but a surge of exhilaration ran through me. My fingers tightened around Mjolnir's handle. I had real enemies to fight here. Real enemies to *destroy* on our way to the Allfather. We would see him properly home this time.

For just a second, as the battle fury trickled through my thoughts, some part of me hesitated. A flicker of that more distant shame touched me. My gaze slid to Ari.

She smiled at me, her eyes as fierce and bright as the resolve inside me. Not a shred of fear or judgment in them.

"I think it's time to let that rage out," she said.

A different sort of pleasure rang through my nerves. Yes. I could be gentle, but I was a warrior too. And I'd never been more glad of that fact. Muninn and the rest would regret every bit of pain they'd dealt to me and mine.

With a battle cry, I leapt forward, letting the power of my fury carry me into the air after Loki.

# 25

*Aria*

The hot wind buffeted my wings as I propelled myself through the air. Who knew how much time we had, what other tricks Muninn and her allies might have planned? The sulfur stink filled my nose, but I kept my flaps strong and even. Rocky ground slipped by beneath me, but the dark craggy mountain ahead of us still seemed too far away.

"Is there anything I need to know about Muspelheim?" I called to the gods around me. For all my valkyrie powers, I was going to be the weakest link in this fight, and I was coming to it way too unprepared. I didn't want to make a mistake that screwed us over.

"There isn't much to the place beyond what you can see for yourself," Loki said, slowing his pace to fall in beside me. The wind rippled through his hair. He could have raced all the way to Odin's cage in a few minutes on his supernaturally enhanced shoes, I suspected, but trying to take on the rescue all by himself probably wasn't the wisest. "Harsh terrain, not much for sustenance. Home to rock dragons and stone spiders and not much else. Not anywhere we'd have thought to come looking."

"Why would the dark elves have brought Odin here?"

"So we wouldn't find him," Freya suggested. "You'd already tracked him to their realm. They knew we'd come there looking again."

"All the realms are connected by gates here and there," Hod said behind me. He'd be navigating from the sounds of the rest of our bodies in flight. "If they had a convenient gate, it wouldn't have taken much effort to send a force through it with him."

"I hate to think what they must have done to him that he couldn't escape, even when they had to move him to a new prison," Baldur said.

My memories of Odin, via Muninn's memories, trickled up through my mind. "I think they've had him a long time," I said. "You said he's been gone twice as long as ever before, right? That's, like, decades? When I saw him, from Muninn's eyes… he looked pretty beaten down."

"The Allfather can withstand more than any elf could deal out," Thor said gruffly, but his expression had darkened with worry.

Had Muninn known about the way the Allfather had used Loki, the destruction he'd encouraged behind the other gods' backs? She must have, with all the time she'd used to spend at Odin's side. One more reason for her to resent him. I wasn't sure how much I was looking forward to meeting the guy properly, after everything I'd seen.

But we needed Odin to get us out of here and to the real Asgard. That was all that mattered for now.

"This way," Loki called, swerving to the right. We veered after him, seconds before a spurt of fire speared up from the ground, close enough that my skin prickled with its heat.

I squeezed my fingers around the handle of my switchblade. It wasn't much of a weapon compared to swords or enchanted hammers or blasts of magic, but it was mine. It held all the love Francis had put into that gift. Even if I wasn't sure I could take on a rock dragon, whatever the hell that was, with it, it did sometimes come in handy for directing my sporadic bolts of lightning as well.

Another river of magma flowed around the side of the mountain through the same passage I guessed we'd fly through. The prickling of heat sank down to my bones. Was that the same spot where I'd seen Odin ambushed?

It had definitely been somewhere here, in the red glow of Muspelheim, not in Nidavellir's more cramped and shadowy caves. Muninn had led him *here* for his enemies to fall on him. So, transporting him here hadn't just been a last-ditch attempt to hide him. They had some kind of tie to this place too.

"We should fly high above that chasm," I hollered into the wind, pointing. "I don't think we want to find ourselves closed in."

Loki nodded without hesitation. As we all pulled higher from the ground, Baldur drew up beside me. He looked as if he were soaring along on a beam of light. Which possibly he was. He reached his hand out to me, and I caught it, twining my fingers with his for the few moments before I had to let go to keep my flight steady.

"I realized I should say thank you," he said, only loud enough for me, not the others, to hear. "Before we face whatever's waiting for us over there."

I glanced over at him, startled. "Thank me for what?"

He beamed back at me—the bright soft smile I was used to, not the slightly wicked one I'd learned I could tempt out with the right inspiration. It didn't look as dreamy as it used to, I noticed with a little relief. Muninn might have tortured him with his memories of his death, but he seemed to have come out of it stronger. Better able to face the reality in front of him without shying away from the shadows.

"You helped me find pieces of myself I didn't know were there," he said. "Maybe I've got a bit of darkness in me too. That's useful to know."

"More useful to me than you so far," I couldn't help responding. The memory of our encounter in Odin's tower flooded me with heat. I'd given myself over to pleasure like I'd never dared to before… and now I felt even more like myself. There were pieces of me that deserved more time in the open too, pieces *I'd* shied away from too long.

A hint of that wickedness crept into Baldur's expression. "I am hoping we'll have plenty of time to explore that side more," he said with a wider grin.

So was I. Oh, so was I.

"Ari, what else did you see in the scraps of memory you got from Muninn?" Thor called over. "What's waiting for us?"

"I don't know exactly," I said. "There were different bits that I think must have been from different times." I couldn't even say they were all from the week or two since the dark elves and whoever else must have moved Odin here from the elvish caves, if he'd been held here when they'd first captured him too. "He was trapped in a heavy-looking cage in that cave behind the magma flow. When I saw him there, he was alone or it was just Muninn there with him. It's possible they think he's hidden away well enough that they're not bothering to guard him."

At that moment, Loki pulled a little higher from where he was gliding along in the lead. His inhumanly sharp eyes narrowed. "Not anymore," he said. "There's your magma flow—and there's an army waiting for us around it."

I pushed myself faster to catch up with him, to see what he did. Beyond the tighter passage beside the mountain, the landscape opened up into a sprawl of plains and blood-red streams. A cliff stood farther back to our right, magma spilling in a churning torrent down its face. It flowed on into the river we'd been following at the cliff's base.

At first, the ground around that river looked as if a thick shadow was spread across it. Then the shadow twitched. I focused my own enhanced vision as intently as I could and caught the stirring of human-like forms.

"We can fly right over them," Thor said.

"But not over that dragon." Freya pointed with her sword.

A huge beast was unfurling its body by the edge of the cliff. Until it had moved, I'd have thought it was just part of the rock. Its stone-like scales shifted over its sinewy body, a reddish gleam showing along the seams. Another flew into view, heading toward us with wing-strokes so powerful they made the air warble. Two more joined it as the one on the cliff lifted into the air as well. The closest one opened its maw with a blech of flame I could feel even at a distance.

A shudder ran down my back. I couldn't fight those things, no.

Thor was already charging to meet them. He swung his brawny arm, sending his hammer flying. It struck the closest dragon across the skull. The creature flinched but pushed forward, faster, with a roar—right into a clot of shadow Hod had summoned. The streaks of darkness twisted around it, pinning its wings to its body, clamping around its jaws. It plummeted from the sky into the molten river below.

The other three dove at us. Freya sliced her sword through the air with a muttered magical line. Baldur hurled a streak of light in unison. Her conjured force and his brilliant magic struck the second dragon at the same time, cracking its belly open. Thor finished the job with a slam of his hammer right between its eyes.

Loki gave a shout, darting beneath a swipe of another dragon's claws. "Fire doesn't hurt these menaces," he said. "If someone could lend a hand..."

Hod threw a ball of shadow his way. Thor wheeled with his hammer. And the fourth dragon streaked up from below, straight for Freya.

She whipped around, but I could tell it wouldn't be fast enough. Not letting myself think, I threw myself forward, lashing out with my switchblade.

It glanced off the monster's side, and the dragon's barbed paw smacked into me, sending me spinning in the air. Pain jabbed down my side, but I'd distracted it enough for Freya to dodge. Thor rammed his hammer into the dragon's chest, and Baldur hurled another bolt of light at the other.

The two beasts whipped between us, one's tail slashing across Loki's chest, the other's jaws scraping across Hod's shoulder as he wrenched himself out of the way. *No.* I whirled around, and the gods lunged into fighting stances.

For an instant, all of us moving at the same time toward the same goal, a weird sense of power hummed through me, as if I could taste Hod's shadows, Baldur's light, Loki's fire, and Thor's brutal strength, lancing through my body and back to them.

I swept my arm in the hopes that the fickle lightning might streak from my hand. It didn't, but as the gods attacked too, magic exploded in the air all around us. Light streaked with fire whipped across one dragon's face. Mjolnir careened into the other dragon's belly with a stream of shadow that wrenched through the creature's scales. A bolt of flaming darkness seared down its maw, choking it as it started to fall. A ball of light slammed into the first dragon's jaw with the force of a hammer, splitting its head down the middle.

We all paused, a little stunned, as the dragons plummeted to their deaths. "What in Hel's name just happened there?" Thor demanded.

Loki regained his composure with a breathless chuckle. "I have no idea, but I'm thinking the time for sorting it out is *after* we've fought the rest of the battle, not before."

The army around the cliff looked as if it were swarming right into the rock. I shook off the hum still tingling through my limbs with renewed urgency. "There must be caves there leading up to the one Odin is trapped in," I said. "They're going to grab him." And do who knew what to him. Kill him, if they could, before we got to him? Drag him off someplace else so we'd have to go through this all over again trying to track him down?

Thor hurled himself forward with a roar that could have rivaled the dragons'. It reverberated through the air as we charged after him. We swooped down over the landscape toward the gap between the falling magma and the crevice I could now make out behind it. The twang of my connection to Odin rippled through me. He was still there—for now.

Spindly black shapes wriggled across the cliff-face. Creatures like enormous spiders, I saw as we flew near. They sprang off the rock at us as we raced toward the cave.

A yelp escaped me as one caught me, its wiry jointed legs clamping around my wings like a vise. I slammed my elbow into it, my knife into the huge faceted eye that stared blankly at me. Black liquid hissed up out of the wound, but its legs didn't budge. I was dropping out of the sky, falling way too fast toward that cracked stone ground—

A streak of flame blasted the creature right off me. Loki caught my hand, yanking me upright as I found my wings. "No ducking out of this one, pixie," he said in his teasing lilt. "Come on."

We hurtled after the others through the opening, into the cave. The battle was already raging. Mjolnir glinted in the hazy red light, and beams of Baldur's summoned light glanced off the jagged walls. I caught a gleam off the tarnished bars of a cage—Odin's cage—back in the depths of the cave. A horde of dark elves and other figures in sooty armor clogged the space between us and the Allfather.

But it was him—the real him. His presence echoed through me, yanking me onward with even more might.

I hit the ground with both feet and slashed out with my knife. The shadows inside me, the ones that could claim lives with the power Hod had given me, stirred eagerly surrounded by so many living, breathing foes with actual glimmers of life, not the hollow constructs I'd had to tackle in Muninn's prison.

I wrenched my hand across one warrior's head and slammed it into another's chest, snatching away the energy that sustained them like the valkyrie I was. In another age, it'd have been my duty to decide who lived and who fell, and which of the fallen ascended to the great hall of Valhalla.

All of these jerks could just forget about that.

As I rammed and wrenched my way through the crowd, that weird hum resonated through me again. The ripples of magic around me wavered and collided. Light and shadow and fire ricocheted off each other with twice their original force, blasting through the horde.

I caught sight of Thor's puzzled face in the fray, twisting with fury a second later. Mjolnir slammed through the crowd, sizzling with fiery light as it toppled every figure in its path.

A hoarse shout rang out somewhere in the depths of the cave. "Retreat! The word is to retreat! Leave him! We'll make good on this another day."

The horde surged away from us. A flutter of movement caught my eye. A black form swooped by along the ceiling of the cave. For the briefest moment, the raven's eye met mine. Then Muninn was bolting away with the rest of the army.

I soared after them, but the moment I reached the cage, my wings faltered. Something in my chest shivered and then stilled at the sight of Odin's hunched form.

His hand shot out to grip one of the bars. His head raised, just enough for the glint of his single eye to show beneath the wilted brim of his hat.

"Valkyrie," he rasped, with a voice that seemed to burrow right through me.

"It's him," I gasped out, unable to tear my gaze from him. "It's really Odin." I knew that down to the smallest bone in my body.

"Father," Thor said in a voice rough with horror. He bashed Mjolnir into the bars of the cage. They shook and cracked. With another heave, he'd battered the cage right open.

"Well," Loki said, weary but relieved, as Freya ducked in to throw her arms around her husband, "I have to say I've had quite enough of all this. What do you say we really go home this time?"

# 26

*Aria*

I woke up feeling as if I'd been asleep for days. For the first few minutes, I couldn't quite bring myself to even roll over. The plump mattress I was lying on, the soft blanket I was lying under, were just too damned comfortable. My muscles ached, but it was the dull ache of hard work now over with, not the sharp ache of fresh pains. I kind of liked the sensation.

My memories of the last short journey from Muspelheim were hazy. We'd helped Odin out of that cage, flown him up to the top of the cliff, and from there he'd managed to summon forth a shaky bridge up through the clouds that clotted the dark sky. As I'd realized we really were done, all the fighting was over, my eyelids had already been drooping. I had a vague recollection of an arm coming around my back to support some of my weight, eerily familiar stone halls coming into view around a marble-tiled courtyard… and after that I drew a blank.

So, where the hell was I? My heart lurched. I pushed back the blanket and sat up.

The bed was in a plain room, small but with a high ceiling. The stone-block walls told me it was probably one of the Asgardian halls. One of the real ones, that wouldn't upend me without warning. What looked like morning sunlight spilled across the smooth stone floor from a narrow window. A padded chair stood in one corner, and a low teak dresser sat against the opposite wall. No sound carried from outside the room.

I breathed in deep, and my heightened valkyrie senses caught a faint whiff of a tangy smoky smell. Oh. I was pretty sure I knew whose guest room I'd ended up in.

Cautiously, I slipped out of the bed and padded into the hall. A glance down it resonated with my memories. Yep, this was Hod's home.

I eased past a couple of doors to one that was only slightly ajar. Nudging it open, I found what had to be the master bedroom, twice as big as the one I'd left with a bed twice as large. Hod was sprawled on it, the blanket tangled around his waist, his lean chest and shoulders bare. In sleep, his face had softened. It was easier to see the resemblance to his twin now.

I hesitated, but the pang inside me pushed me onward. After everything I'd just been through, I didn't want to sit alone in one of his barely familiar rooms waiting for him to wake up.

After everything we'd been through together, I didn't think he'd mind the intrusion.

The door squeaked faintly as I ducked inside, but the dark god didn't stir. I clambered onto the bed and curled up next to him, inhaling his salty smoky smell up close now.

The mattress shifted with my movement, and Hod woke up with a backwards jerk, his body tensing.

Shit. "Hey, it's just me," I said, my face flaring. This wasn't the gentle morning welcome I'd been picturing.

Hod's shoulders had already come down. "My spare bed wasn't good enough for you, valkyrie?" he muttered, but he scooted closer at the same time, looping his arm around my waist to tug me to him, back to front. I smiled, nestling into his warmth. This was more like it.

"Sorry," I said. "I didn't mean to startle you."

"Not used to having anyone else in my bed," Hod said. He tucked his chin over my shoulder, his breath tickling over my hair.

"Is that something you'd like to change?" I murmured suggestively, and felt him smile.

He kissed the corner of my jaw, that tiny gesture sending a flare of heat through me. "I could get used to this, I think."

"We could try it a few times, just to be sure."

"Would *you* want to?"

I paused, reveling in how comfortable lying here with him was, how protected I felt tucked in against him. "Yeah. I think I would."

"I suppose your other suitors might take issue with you playing favorites," Hod said.

I rolled my eyes. "I didn't make any promises about this being the *only* bed I'd ever share."

"Huh. Next thing I know, you'll be wanting to invite them all over."

"That's a brilliant idea!" I said brightly. "There's room for more. Let me go get them right now."

"Don't you dare."

"You going to stop me?"

I made as if to squirm off the bed, biting back a giggle. Hod gave a low growl and grabbed me. He rolled on top of me, his head dipping down as if to claim a kiss, which was exactly what I'd been angling for, but the second I felt his weight pressing down on me, my body went rigid.

He pulled back in an instant. "Ari?"

My pulse had hiccupped, but it was already falling back into its usual steady rhythm. I dragged in a breath. "I'm okay. Just… got a little overconfident. I guess it'd be a little much to hope every bad reaction disappeared in an instant." I gave a little laugh. "Looks like we both still have crap to get over."

"Hmm." He sank back down beside me and stroked the back of his fingers down the side of my face. My throat tightened. I nudged myself closer to him again, turning toward him this time, and leaned my head against his chest.

"We've come a long way," he said after a moment. "Haven't we?"

"Yeah, I'd say we have."

"Then we'll just keep healing. Together." He brushed his thumb over my cheek. "No tears this time. That's a definite step in the right direction."

"Keep talking like that and they'll come," I grumbled.

He chuckled and tipped my chin up. This time when he moved to kiss me, no impulse ran through me except the urge to kiss him back.

The heat of his mouth radiated all the way through my body. I let myself linger there, trading breaths and the caress of our lips, until a sharper heat started to pool low in my belly. I slid my hand down Hod's chest—and the sense of a summons reverberated through my head as if someone had shouted my name.

I sat up, touching my forehead. The sensation came again, like an insistent tug. It echoed down through my chest to the place where I'd felt Odin's presence before.

"I think Odin is calling for me," I said. I wasn't sure I liked this new feature of being a valkyrie—the Allfather having a direct line to my brain.

Hod pushed himself upright beside me with a sigh. "I'd better come too, then. He wasn't in much of a state last night to discuss what he'd been through. Maybe now he can tell us more about who captured him and why."

I enjoyed the view as he pulled on more clothes, grimacing

when the call came again. "All right, all right," I said to Odin, who probably couldn't hear my answer anyway.

Hod led the way out into Asgard, his strides smooth and unguarded now that he could trust his home to stay as it was meant to. As we approached the huge hall at the far end of the city, the one with a higher tower rising from its rooftop, uneasiness coiled through my gut. I might not have really met the Allfather properly yet, but I'd seen an awful lot of Odin in the last day. And an awful lot of what I'd seen hadn't sat quite right.

"It has to be true, right?" I said. "What Loki showed us. Odin *told* Loki to make trouble, to push back against the gods…"

Hod was silent for a moment. "My father has always kept his own counsel," he said. "Or at least he did from his sons. But I know there was a lot he knew that gnawed at him—I've wondered how long he anticipated Ragnarok's coming. Whatever he did, whatever he asked Loki to do, it's because he thought it was best for all of us. I'm sure of that. Whether I agree with him that it was best…"

He couldn't seem to finish that sentence. No wonder. I couldn't imagine how much he was grappling with right now. It was his *father* he'd just had all these revelations about.

I found myself holding my breath as we pushed open the hall's front door. "In here," called the low dry voice that was somehow totally familiar even though I'd only heard it once in reality before this moment. After all, it was the same low dry voice that had commanded Loki to be his villain.

Odin sat in a tall, intricately carved chair in a room that felt like a miniature version of Valhalla. Spears and swords decorated the walls. The almost-throne was the only seat other than a few cushions in the corners. Baldur and Freya were poised at the Allfather's sides, Freya clasping her husband's hand and Baldur resting his fingers on his father's forearm.

They must have spent much of the night tending to the king of the gods, because years of fatigue and hurt had shed from

Odin's posture, from his face. He sat straight, his broad shoulders squared, and his single eye twinkled with more energy than I'd have thought he could ever be capable of again after seeing him in that cage. The authority of his presence filled the room. A tremor that was more apprehension than anticipation tickled down my back.

Loki and Thor stood a short distance away. The thunder god shot me a smile, and the trickster gave me a nod and a wink. We were all assembled now before the Allfather.

"My son and my unexpected valkyrie," Odin said in greeting. He leaned back in his chair. "I wanted you all here while we speak of the battle to come."

My heart sank, my worries about the god in front of me momentarily pushed aside. "Didn't we win that battle?" I said.

But even as the words came out, I was remembering the human bodies slumped in the dark elves' caves, the missing persons signs, the voice calling for yesterday's army to retreat, promising to fight to the end another day. The dark elves had been doing a lot more than keeping Odin captive. They'd kidnapped humans and killed them and who knew what else or why.

Of course it wasn't over. There was so much evil we hadn't even tackled yet.

Odin's mouth twitched slightly upward. "We won something," he said. "I am ever grateful for my freedom. I wish I could say it came with peace. But Surt has bigger plans than that."

The name meant nothing to me, but the gods around me stiffened, even Loki. "What does that bastard have to do with this?" he said.

"He's the one who ordered my capture," Odin said. "With the help of my former raven of memory, it seems." He rubbed his mouth.

"Um… Who is Surt?" I ventured.

"A giant who led an army into Asgard and set the city up in

flames," Freya said, her voice strained. "He killed my brother. He destroyed everything."

"But the city and we returned," Odin said, squeezing her hand. "And so did Surt. I shut him away in Muspelheim for his role in that uprising ages ago. It seems he's been stewing in his resentment of me and the rest of Asgard ever since."

"We stopped him," Thor said. "We retrieved you. What is there left that he can do?"

"Oh, there's plenty." The Allfather exhaled like a sigh. "Surt has been building his new army for a long time. He's allied with the dark elves and gathered the stragglers who've found their way into Muspelheim. But he knew that wasn't enough for his ultimate goal. So he's started summoning draugar to do his bidding too."

Hod set his hand on my shoulder, gripping tight. "The dead risen back to life," he said in a haunted tone.

Like that construct of Baldur rising up, lurching and rotten. A zombie. *Draug*, they'd called it. My stomach twisted.

The bodies I'd seen in the caves—the people they'd stolen—it all made a sudden sick kind of sense. They were building an army of the dead. Of *human* dead.

"And what does he mean to do with this horde of the undead?" Loki waved toward the doorway. "There's not that much in Asgard to claim these days."

"He'd be happy just to see our home torn from us," Odin said. "But that's not his only goal. It seems the balance of the nine realms has shifted. Many of them have become unstable. All except for Asgard, because of our power… and Midgard, at the center of it all. He plans to conquer the realm of humankind for his own purposes too."

A spear of ice jabbed through me at those words. This powerful giant wanted to conquer Midgard. And, what, set my former home up in flames? Turn it into a wasteland like the realm he ruled over now?

Petey was down there, with no one who knew anything to protect him…

My hands clenched. Each of the gods around me had glanced at me as if thinking the same thing.

I couldn't expect them to care about those lands half as much as I did, but I knew, with a faint whisper of hope under the balling of my gut, that they'd fight just as hard regardless. They'd stand by me, the four lovers who were connected to me in that strange balance of our own.

I stepped forward. "We have to stop him."

Odin bowed his head. "Yes," he said. "I agree. Which is why you're all here. We need to make our mark in this war *now*."

He really smiled then: a slow dark smile that curved his lips at a crooked angle. It sent a chill over my skin.

We'd come together. We'd saved Odin. But who was really more dangerous: the giant scheming in the realm of fire or the god we'd just rescued from him?

# FALLING FOR GODS

THEIR DARK VALKYRIE - BOOK 3

# 1

*Aria*

It was a little unsettling how distant the world of humans felt to me as I soared over the highway-split landscape. That world, the realm I was starting to think of as Midgard, had been my home for the twenty-two years I'd *been* a human. It'd been the only world I'd had any clue existed.

But anyone could have told you that I wasn't human anymore. The gigantic silver-white wings sprouting from my back were a pretty big tip-off. Also, the fact that I was flying through the air accompanied by five divine figures who'd never been human at all, who were coasting along in whichever way their godly magic allowed.

A month ago, I'd have been hustling through Philly's streets making a delivery for the gang that had most recently hired my courier services. Today I was on my way to seal a supernatural gateway that dark elves had been using to carry out horrible deeds on behalf of an evil giant.

All in a day's work for Asgard's only current valkyrie.

Even this high up, the summer wind was warm as it rippled over my wings and flicked a few strands of my rumpled blond hair across my cheek. The sun lit the fields below with a fierce glow and filled the air with the smell of baking grass. A trickle of sweat ran down the back of my neck. We'd decided to tackle the gate at midday because the dark elves, used to their dim caves in their own realm, weren't super keen on sunlight. At the moment, I wasn't feeling super keen on it myself.

The sights and smells of my former home sent my thoughts in other directions. What would Petey be up to today? Were his foster parents getting him out to the park or the swimming pool so he could enjoy the summer like he'd rarely gotten to under our mom's roof? Or maybe he was in school. I'd kind of lost track of the days of the week since the whole dying and valkyrie resurrection thing.

This was the first time I'd been back in Midgard since I'd left my little brother behind in the hopefully safe-keeping of his new foster family. The dark elves had threatened to kill him if I'd kept helping the gods around me. The elves had been killing people for who knew how long, dragging them off to the realm of fire where the giant Surt was transforming their bodies into draugar—ghoulishly bloated zombies.

My hands clenched at the memory of the bodies I'd seen in their caves, of the one elf's laughter when she'd talked about hurting Petey. If they laid one finger on him, I'd wring all of their stumpy little necks without a hint of regret.

Hod, the god of darkness, turned his dark green eyes toward me from where he was gliding along on a patch of shadow like some kind of bizarre flying carpet. He couldn't actually see me with his blind gaze, but it mustn't have been too hard for him to guess what I might be thinking about on our return to this place.

"The elves have no idea where your brother is now," he said. "And they haven't been taking children—kids wouldn't be much use for Surt's army."

"Small mercies," I muttered, but a twinge of emotion ran through my chest at his attempted reassurance. It wasn't like me to want to lean on anybody, but Hod had managed to uncover a softer side I hadn't realized I even had—one that left me in tears at inopportune moments, and one that now and then gave me the urge to hide away in his embrace. Maybe that wasn't so surprising when he'd been so clear about how deep his affections for me ran.

That thought sent a different sort of shiver through me, one both giddy and nervous. This wasn't a good time for me to get soft. We were embarking on the next phase of a realm-crossing war.

"We could always take a little detour on the way home," Loki said in his usual wry voice, shooting me a grin. The trickster was striding along on his enchanted shoes of flight, the wind whipping his light red hair back from his pale face like the flames he could summon with a snap of his fingers.

Would it be easier seeing Petey without being able to talk to him, to touch him, or simply holding on to my memories? Just a few days ago I'd come face to face with an illusion of him that had flinched away from me. It'd only been imaginary, a construct meant to break my will in the prison we'd found ourselves trapped in, but the moment had wrenched at me anyway.

My little brother was safer if I kept my distance. "When all the gates are sealed," I said. "When the dark elves can't get to him anymore."

"If you ever change your mind…" Loki said with a sweeping gesture. His amber eyes shone brighter. "This should be an interesting errand, in any case. It's difficult to believe that in all my time across the realms, I've never attempted to close off a gate between them."

"We made it through the gate easily enough before," Thor said, swinging the magical hammer he already had in his grasp. The brawny thunder god tipped his head to the fourth god with us: Hod's twin Baldur, light to the other's darkness. "One blast of

Baldur's powers should send any guards who braved the sun running."

The bright god smiled, looking more assured and less dreamy than he'd been most of the time I'd known him. "I'll clear the way." His tone sounded more present too. I'd been with him through some painful moments in the prison Odin's raven of memory had constructed, reliving the chilling void of his death, but he seemed to have come out of that torment stronger. More determined to face the horrors that might still lie ahead of us.

Almost from the start, I'd been drawn to all four of the gods who'd combined their powers to bring me back from the dead in valkyrie form. But I couldn't deny that this more confident Baldur made my pulse kick up even faster than before.

"Let's not assume this will be easy, boys," Freya said with an imperious flap of her falcon cloak. The goddess of love and war peered toward the horizon, a fierce light glowing from her beautiful face. The golden waves of her hair glittered like an exquisite battle helm. Then she winked at me. "As usual, I expect the two of us have to keep this bunch on track."

Thor gave a bellow of a laugh, tossing his hammer from one hand to the other as if it weighed nothing at all. "The cave-dwellers should be very familiar with Mjolnir by now. They'll run. Just watch."

His warm brown gaze slid to mine with a gentler smile that felt as if it were meant just for me. It brought back the heat of his tender caresses when we'd come together in epic fashion not that long ago. I couldn't help grinning back.

We might have a war ahead of us, but we were ready for it. Closing this gate was the first step toward seeing Petey safe for good and preventing the invasion Surt was planning. He and his army could forget about taking even one piece of my former realm—or the new home I'd started to find in Asgard, the realm of the gods.

The landscape below us was becoming uncomfortably familiar.

The gate we planned to shut was the one where we'd fought a battle with the dark elves last week—a battle in which we'd thought we were retrieving Odin from their clutches but instead had been led by a false version of him into that prison of memories. In those caves, I'd taken more lives with the dark power inside me, the one that valkyries had used to decide the fates of those on battlefields ages ago, than I'd have ever thought I'd be capable of.

They'd threatened my little brother. They'd killed who knew how many people for their master's army. I wasn't backing down until they were stopped for good.

The sagging wooden buildings around the gate looked even more decrepit than before. A handful of short dark-haired figures stood in a circle amid a patch of trees on the rocky hill at the edge of the ghost town. The oily energy the dark elves gave off made me shudder even from this distance.

Baldur raised his hands without waiting for an order. Light streamed from his skin and twined around his forearms and fingers. His gaze intent, he whipped the blaze forward.

With a high-pitched quavering, the wave of light crashed over the town and the gate beyond it. The guards around the gate toppled, their eyes searing pure black. No other figures stirred amid the buildings.

"Let's go, let's go," Loki said with a clap of his hands. He leapt down toward the trees. I swooped after him. The thick crack in the hillside came into view, like a black scar between the rocks and roots. That slick but sluggish energy wafted out of the gate from the realm it led into.

But we weren't looking to pay a visit this time. We wanted to make sure no one did, in either direction, ever again.

"See if you can work on it with those powers of yours," Loki said with a flippant gesture toward Hod. "The gate stinks of darkness."

Hod shot him a grimace, but only a faint one. They'd come to some kind of broader truce since our paths had tangled on our way through Muninn's prison.

The dark god leaned over to test his palms against the opening. The power he'd given me as part of my resurrection reverberated in time with the energy emanating from the gate.

"There's magic woven across it, but I don't think I can use that to completely cut them off," Hod said. "They're creatures of darkness too. A clot of shadow isn't going to stop them for long."

"Can we close it physically?" I asked. "Does it have to be magic? Why not just plug it up with a bunch of these rocks?" I nodded to the hillside.

Loki tapped his lips. "I think they'd need to be magically fused into place to be sure of holding, but that's still a start. Oh, Thunderer, how about lending a little of your storminess to the proceedings? A thunderclap should do nicely to reorganize the landscape in a fitting fashion."

Thor heaved back his arm to hurl his hammer at the rocky terrain above the gate.

Before he could let it fly, a surge of bodies burst from the opening.

Dozens of dark elves charged toward us, faster than I'd have thought those stocky legs could have carried anyone. Spears and swords flashed in their hands. Thor let out a roar and whipped his hammer forward anyway, right at the mass of our attackers.

Several of the dark elves fell, bashed aside by Mjolnir, but the ones on either side of its path sprang at us unfazed. A wavering orange light danced along the blades of their weapons. I tried to wrench one from the hands of a man who lunged at me, and it seared a throbbing line across my palm. I yelped, yanking myself away and into the air with my wings.

"They've got magic on their weapons," I shouted. Magic they'd never had when we'd fought them before—a fiery magic that reminded me of Surt's realm. Had he offered them extra power to battle us with?

It wasn't going to save them. The other gods had drawn back as I had, but only to momentarily regroup. Thor's hammer flew back into his grasp. A burst of fire flared in Loki's hands. Hod's shadows whirled up around him. In that instant, I could taste all of it: the crackle of lightning and the hiss of fire, the warble of the dark and the keening of the light, all rushing through me together. I snapped my switchblade open in my hand.

We lashed out in the same moment. As I hurtled forward, my breath rushed out alongside the gods'—and their powers blasted into the swarm of dark elves like a series of earth-shaking fireworks. Shadow and fire merged into a dark wash of flame that consumed several bodies in its path. With a boom, light splintered into a hundred lightning bolts, dropping every dark elf they touched. In an instant, nothing was left of our enemies except bodies strewn around the gate. There wasn't even one left for me to claim with my blade and my valkyrie pull.

I jerked to a stop, hovering just over the gate with a sweep of my wings. My heart skipped a beat. That merging of the gods' powers had happened before, hadn't it? When we'd rushed in to save the real Odin from Surt's cage. The fighting then had been so quick and brutal I hadn't stopped to think about it at the time, but I couldn't ignore it now. Something was going on, something that hadn't happened the first few times I'd fought beside the gods.

What the hell did it mean? And more importantly, could we use it again if we wanted to, to kick every dark elf ass to Kingdom Come?

# 2

*Baldur*

A rush of electricity sang through my veins as my hurled light melded around Thor's hammer. With a shriek, it exploded into a hail of lightning.

I glanced at my older brother, and he grinned back at me with his eyebrows raised. Neither of us knew what had just happened, but it had repelled the dark elves, so the "what" didn't really matter just yet.

"Wasn't that interesting?" Loki said, studying his hands. Before we could have a real conversation about that strange merging of our powers, another swarm of attackers burst from the gate.

Aria let out a cry and sprang forward. My pulse stuttered in fear for her as I leapt into the fray with the others. But our valkyrie could hold her own. A splinter of lightning sparked from the tip of her switchblade, and her other hand brushed one elf's forehead, yanking the life from him with her valkyrie powers.

The echo of my fellow gods' movements washed over me as I moved in turn. It wasn't just our magic that appeared to have merged. Without even trying, I found myself heaving forward a burst of power alongside Loki, Hod, and Thor, all of us together. Ari spun around with another slash of her knife at the same moment.

All the energy we cast out twined together and ripped through the charge of dark elves. Fiery light, shadowy sizzling bolts, and a flaming crash of thunder sent their bodies flying. Freya rushed in with a slash of her sword, but there was barely anyone left to duel.

A rush of exhilaration tickled up from my chest. I might not know what was happening, but it was clear we were connecting in some way we never had before. My brothers and the trickster were as invested in this fight as I was, and we would win it together.

A few of the elves managed to dodge to the side quickly enough to escape our magic. I lunged after one—and through the light shimmering in and around my body, a cold tendril unfurled. A dark icy finger like a strip of the void that had enclosed me in death, both centuries ago and just a few days ago in Muninn's prison. It snaked around my stomach.

My chest clenched, and my jaw tightened. I slammed my fist into the dark elf's head with an extra smash of light. The shiver of darkness inside me tugged at my gut, and I smacked him again, sending him reeling into a tree.

My lips twitched as he groaned. Yes, let him suffer a little before he died, after everything his people had—

I caught myself, snapping my fingers shut just a second shy of searing his skin with light that would have wounded but not ended his misery. A sharper rush of cold flooded me.

What was I doing? What was I *thinking*? Torturing this man wouldn't be justice.

I ended his life with a quick blast of light to his forehead, searing through his mind. My legs felt steady enough as I turned back to the others, but that slip of shadow had coiled even more insistently around my gut.

The void had crept into me while I'd floated there in that endless chilling nothingness. I'd felt it crawl down my throat and seep through my skin. Had some of it stayed with me when I'd come back into the light? I'd spent so long avoiding even thinking about my death and the torment that had come with it, I'd never looked inside myself for it all that closely. Perhaps it had been there all along, without the chance to awaken.

This might be the first battle I'd fought where I was fully present in over a thousand years.

The other dark elves around us had all fallen. Loki strode up to the ragged opening of the gate.

"Let's close this up before yet another assault comes our way," the trickster said. "All of our powers together should do the trick nicely, I'm starting to think."

I lifted my arms, summoning the glow coursing through my limbs back into my hands. Thor struck the rocks above the crevice with his hammer. They crackled and jittered with lightning as they tumbled across the opening.

Before they could fall through into the blackness beyond, Loki cast a wave of fire over them. Instinctively, I tossed a burst of light to meet his flames. Our combined powers fused the rocks between them and melted them into the edges of the crevice.

Hod released a flood of shadow over the molten mass, cooling it into a solid barrier that sealed the gate from top to bottom. The surface shone like obsidian.

Aria prodded the seal with her switchblade. The glossy mass resisted even the jab of the blade, not a scratch forming beneath it. Freya came up beside us and prodded the spot with a whirl of her magic as well.

She stepped back with a satisfied expression. "That feels as though it'll hold. Now what in Hel's name was happening between the rest of you?"

"I don't know," Hod said. "The last couple of times we've fought together, I've felt a sort of synchronicity—as if our movements and powers are flowing toward each other. I've never seen my shadows combine with anyone else's magic before."

"I can feel it too," Aria said. "Like a hum between all of us."

"Between you and the four of them," Freya said. "I haven't felt anything different."

The valkyrie nodded, her gray eyes sliding over us. "You didn't lend your powers to making me, right?" she said to the goddess. "They were the ones who summoned me. I'm a patchwork valkyrie made out of the pieces of your powers. Maybe that's got something to do with it?"

"It has to," Thor put in. "Odin may have a clearer idea. We can see what he makes of it."

He made a motion for us to take to the sky again. My body balked for a second before I called up the beam of light that would carry me onward.

The Allfather had stayed back, rather than join us on this mission, to continue recovering from his long imprisonment. We hadn't wanted to delay our efforts to contain the dark elves. Of course he'd want to hear our report and all that had happened. And well he should, as our leader. But I found I wasn't looking forward to that meeting at all.

---

You wouldn't have known Odin was at anything other than his best to see him now, poised on his throne in the meeting room of his great hall. He sat tall, his silvered brown beard trimmed down from its previous wild state, his single dark eye alert. His great gleaming spear leaned against the arm of the throne, ready, as if he might need to leap into battle in an instant.

The ruler of Asgard didn't believe in showing weakness.

"This effect you saw," he said, his penetrating gaze roving over each of the six of us in turn. "You've never experienced anything like that before?"

"Only today and briefly in the fight when we found you in Muspelheim," Thor said.

"It appears to be connected to our valkyrie," Loki said, resting a hand that looked unusually tentative on Aria's shoulder. "Or rather, that we have become increasingly connected through her. The process of summoning a valkyrie—each of us contributing some of our essence—it took a lot out of us, and most of what it took went into reforming her spirit as she is now. My best guess is that when she's fighting alongside us, something of that merging activates and allows our powers to work in greater harmony."

Harmony. Yes. That was the word for what I'd felt in those moments as we'd pushed back the dark elves together. I'd spent most of my existence striving for harmony, but I'd never had it come to me as deeply and fully as then. I'd found it thanks to Aria.

Her eyes caught mine from across the semi-circle we'd formed in the high-ceilinged room, and she shot me a little smile as if she were thinking the same thing. And I realized what I'd just thought wasn't entirely true. I'd experienced that exquisite harmony one other time—when Loki, Thor, and I had come together to demonstrate our desire for our valkyrie in every way we could.

A trickle of heat coursed over my skin. I'd much rather find the sensation again there than on the battlefield, given the choice.

"Aria isn't the first valkyrie you summoned," Odin said. "Did you see a similar effect with the ones previous?"

"The others… didn't remain with us for long enough for any connection to really gel," Hod said.

"We've been through much more with Ari," Thor said. "The bond between us—it goes beyond the hand we had in creating her new life." He cleared his throat, as if he weren't sure how much detail to go into there. "We've come to understand each other on every level: mentally, emotionally…"

*Physically*. The slight arch of the Allfather's eyebrow made me suspect that he'd guessed that aspect even if no one had outright told him. Very little escaped Odin. I couldn't read from his expression how he might feel about the idea that three of his sons and his brother by blood-oath might be centering their affections on the same non-godly woman.

Then Odin's gaze found me. "You haven't said much about the situation, my son," he said. "Do your impressions align with the others?"

"Yes," I said quickly. "The sense of harmony, the bond that's been forming—I'm sure it's all related." I paused, unsure how to continue. The mechanics of magic were far from my forte. And ever since Odin had returned to us, I'd found it hard to look him in the eye for very long and still remember how to use my tongue.

I'd have given anything to bring my father back to Asgard. A large part of me was overjoyed at our victory, ecstatic to see him sharp and determined as ever in his throne. We had been aimless for a long time without his guiding force, and now, with Surt preparing to invade both Asgard and Midgard, we needed that guidance more than ever.

But no matter how bright my happiness might be, a shadow lurked beneath it. I couldn't erase the memories Loki had shown us from my head—and I shouldn't want to.

My father had approved of my murder. He might even have encouraged it. He'd let me fall into the vast void that had wrenched me apart so thoroughly I couldn't imagine my spirit would ever heal completely, as part of some immense plan he'd never bothered to speak to me about, before or after.

No, he'd let me think any blame I could have assigned belonged with my twin, who had thrown the mistletoe spear that had struck me down, and Loki, who'd guided Hod's hand. Where was the justice in *that*?

I hadn't spoken to Odin of it. He'd been recovering, and I

wasn't certain Loki would even want me to reveal the secret he'd betrayed. But most of all, I hadn't known what to say that would express the tangled emotions inside me, or what Odin could possibly offer me in return that would tease them apart into some sort of peace.

As the Allfather turned back to the others, the tendril of darkness that had tugged at me earlier twisted around my gut and shot through the muscles of my legs. Before I could contain it, my heel jammed against the floor. A small crack spread across the smooth stone surface, spidering at its edges.

My heart lurched. I eased to the side, covering the mark with my foot. No one was looking at me. No one had seemed to notice.

I'd held the darkness inside me at bay for all those years by burying myself in a dreamy haze. I couldn't go back to that. I'd just have to quash it down with all the light I had in me. I'd survived this long. A sliver of the void couldn't overpower me.

"This is a new development, but a welcome one," Odin was saying. "Combining your powers around the valkyrie may be the key to defeating Surt quickly and decisively. We haven't located any of the other gates to Nidavellir yet, have we? Any spare time you have until we do, you should practice together, experiment. The more you can control this new skill, the more potent it will be."

A pleased smile slipped across his lips with those last words. The master planner had discovered a new strategy. I should have been happy too, but an uneasy shiver traveled through me.

# 3

*Aria*

Odin leaned back in his tall chair with a satisfied expression, as if he'd said everything he needed to and now we were all supposed to jump to do his bidding. His presumptuous attitude itched at me.

Who the hell was he to call all the shots here anyway? Okay, sure, the king of the gods, but he'd been stuck in some cage locked away from the rest of the world for decades. He hardly even knew that much about what had been happening around his capture, let alone anywhere else. The six of us had been working together—and working well—for weeks now. He'd only just joined the party.

And he hadn't bothered to ask *my* opinion about any of this.

"We can't count only on this special power, whatever exactly it is, right?" I said. "We have to find out exactly what Surt is doing right now, what plans he's making, so we can go in prepared."

Odin's one-eyed gaze settled on me with prickling intensity. It was hard to focus completely on that eye and not also the knot of scar where his other one had once been.

"I am keeping watch over Muspelheim from my high seat," he said.

"Great," I said. "Then you know how big this army of his is already? You've heard him talking about when he thinks he'll attack?"

The Allfather's mouth tightened. I got the impression he didn't appreciate getting this many questions thrown at him.

"The suggestion that my high seat allows me to 'see all' has been slightly overstated," he said. "I can look down over anywhere I please, but walls still restrict my view. Surt has kept his strategizing and his army mostly shut away."

As if I trusted this guy to tell us the full story even if he'd seen something useful. I set my hands on my hips. "We've got to get down there and take a closer look, then, don't we?" Get behind those walls if we could. Make sure there weren't things Odin was deciding not to tell us.

"Scouting out Muspelheim will not be an easy task. Surt has shut away the gates that allow access to all the other realms inside his fortress. Getting there is simple enough, but anyone who does would have to fight their way out."

"You've got your rainbow bridge magic for an instant transport out."

Odin chuckled at my phrasing, but his gaze didn't lighten. "Bifrost is a powerful tool, but not a subtle one. Surt would have his guards on anyone who used it the moment it appeared."

Okay, fair enough. But I'd make my way back to Asgard before without any bridge or gateway. That was the whole reason the gods had summoned a valkyrie to help them find Odin.

"*I* can go," I said. "My connection to Valhalla means I can will myself back there if I need to, no matter where I am. I've done it before."

Loki grinned. "That's the spirit. You'll be out-scheming us all soon enough, pixie."

Odin's expression shifted, a curious light coming into his eyes. Or maybe it was amused. I wasn't sure I liked it either way.

"An excellent point," he said. "All right then, my unexpected valkyrie. Are you proposing to set off on this scouting mission immediately?"

Across the room from me, Baldur was frowning. "She should get some rest first after the fighting today."

Odin's gaze didn't waver from me. I raised my chin. The question felt like a test—of how committed I was to this course of action, of whether I really had the guts to follow through. If I backed down even until tomorrow, I'd be giving the Allfather room to doubt me.

"I'm not that tired. I can make a quick initial sweep to give me an idea where I'd want to spend more time spying the next time around."

"I don't see how it could hurt anything," Freya said from where she'd come to stand beside her husband. She patted Odin's arm. "It *would* be good to have a clearer sense of our enemy."

Thor had turned to me, his forehead furrowed. "Are you sure this is a good idea, Ari? Surt will be watching for anyone from Asgard. It's been a long day already."

I shrugged, offering him a reassuring smile. "I'll sleep better tonight knowing what Surt and his minions are up to right now. If I start to get tired or I feel like I'm in danger, I'll just leap back to Valhalla. Nothing to worry about."

He gave me a look as if to say I should know he'd worry about me anyway, but his stance relaxed a smidge. "I'd feel better if I—or any of us—could go with you."

"That isn't possible though, right?"

Loki let out a huff of breath. "Sadly, it does sound as though the rest of us would be reliant on tangling with Surt directly to make our way home. Unfortunate, because I'd quite like a longer look for myself at that realm he's made his own. But I have every faith in your skills and judgment. If I can't go, you're my next choice out of all of us. I did lend you some of my wits, after all."

"I had plenty before you did any lending," I said, giving him a playful glower, and he laughed.

"Why do you think I picked you, pixie?"

Yes—I was Loki's valkyrie more than anyone else's. He was the one who'd insisted they try summoning a woman with a little more street smarts and a little less pureness of heart. If they'd stuck with the same criteria they'd used for their first three valkyries, my life would have ended with the impact of that idiot junkie's speeding jeep.

And the gods might never have found their way to Odin. I'd made that possible. I could make a difference here too. For them, and for Petey and everyone else Surt threatened.

"I can go by Yggdrasil, can't I?" I said, lifting my chin to indicate I was ready to get started. "I just need to know which branch to take."

Odin rose from his throne-like chair, gripping his silver spear like a walking stick. He'd left off his rumpled broad-brimmed hat, but somehow he looked even taller without it. He strode forward with his cloak rustling at his heels. "Come along then. I'll show you."

Loki brushed his fingers over my arm as I turned to follow the Allfather. Thor nodded to me, and Baldur aimed his bright smile my way. They drifted toward their own halls as we left Odin's, but Hod fell into step beside me.

"Did you think I needed an extra escort?" I asked the dark god with a raise of my eyebrow he couldn't see.

"I don't have anywhere better to be," he said casually. "Do you mind the company?"

Not when it was him, and not when my only other company was the ominous Odin. "I guess I can cope with a little hovering. As long as you're not planning on trying to convince me not to go."

Hod guffawed at that. "Oh, believe me, valkyrie, I know better than that by now."

It was only a short walk from Odin's hall down the marble-tiled path to the immense Valhalla, which once hundreds of reborn warriors and maybe as many valkyries had called home. We trailed along behind the Allfather, who walked briskly without a backward glance. The sun shone bright but not as starkly as it had down in Midgard, the breeze pleasantly warm and full of sweet flowery scent. It might have been a nice little stroll if I hadn't known I was on my way to a realm of barren rock and flowing magma.

Hod hesitated for a moment inside the great hall with its rows of long tables and its walls hung with gleaming weaponry. I guessed he hadn't come into this place often enough to have a solid sense of the layout. Shadows unfurled around him, testing the edges of the benches, as we made our way more slowly to the golden throne at the far end.

Odin stopped at the huge stone-lined hearth beside that throne. The back of the hearth gave way to a deep void I'd stepped into once before, when I'd traced Odin's kidnapping to the realm of the dark elves. I wasn't sure which I'd have looked forward to seeing less: those cramped dank caves or the searing heat of Surt's realm.

At least in the realm of fire, I had room to really fly.

As Hod and I reached the hearth, he touched my shoulder. When I turned toward him, he raised his hand to my cheek, his blind gaze knowing exactly where to find my eyes now.

"Look after yourself," he said. "I'll wait here for you until you get back."

A lump rose in my throat. Was he thinking about my last venture through Valhalla, when I'd dragged myself back to the gods bleeding and beaten? "I plan on making it back on my feet this time," I said.

"I'm glad to hear it." He dipped his head, and I bobbed on my toes to meet his kiss. His shadows wisped around me, holding me like an echo of his lean arms. In that moment, I wished I could just stay here with him and forget about Muspelheim and Surt and the rest—lose myself in the passion we'd sparked between us before.

Not just passion. He loved me. He'd told me so. That knowledge quivered in my chest, joyful and nervous at the same time. I wasn't sure I was equipped to properly handle my own heart yet, let alone anyone else's. But it felt like an honor to be given this much devotion from a man who'd endured so much.

I kissed him hard, wanting him to know how much even this gesture meant to me. Hod traced his thumb over my cheek and eased back, his pale cheeks faintly flushed. He kissed me once more on the forehead and sat down on the nearest bench to begin his vigil.

"Ready?" Odin said with just a hint of dryness. I had no idea what he thought of the intimacy he'd just seen, but I didn't really give a damn about his approval anyway. There didn't seem to be much point in hiding just how close all four of my gods and I had become.

"Let's go," I said, swiping my hands together.

The Allfather ducked into the cavern behind the fireplace, and I slipped after him. On the opposite side, the prone tree stretched out like a path of bark and branches into a thick nothingness.

The air was chillier here. A shiver crept over my bare arms as I padded after Odin along the trunk. With a twitch of my shoulders, I unfurled my wings from my back. If I knew one thing for sure, it was that I'd want to be prepared to fly the second I stepped through this gate.

"Why did you release all your warriors and valkyries anyway?" I asked, watching the sway of Odin's cloak ahead of me. "Baldur told me that you let them all leave a while ago. I guess there aren't even any of them left after all this time, wherever they went? But it'd be a lot easier with an army of our own."

Odin hummed to himself. "It was time to end that chapter," he said, as if that explained anything at all. He drew to a halt and pointed to a branch at his right. "That way will lead you to Muspelheim."

"Okay." I flexed my wings. "Any last-minute tips?"

I hadn't really expected any, but the Allfather gave me a foreboding look. "Stay wary. Move quickly. Don't let yourself become distracted from your task, or you may find you're the one caught."

All right then. All of that advice fell into the category of *No kidding*. I bobbed my head to him with a tense smile and started down the branch.

A cloying heat seeped from the patch of thicker darkness at its end with a whiff of sulfur. I braced myself and sprang through the gate.

I tumbled out into hot bitter-smelling air over a stretch of jagged rock. A cliff loomed near me, and a river of magma churned by several feet away, casting a reddish glow over the dark gray stone. A dim glimmer lit the dull sky, barely enough that you could call it sunlight.

With a flap of my wings, I whirled myself around—and caught sight of the dragon just opening its eyes where it was sprawled by the edge of the cliff. Its gaze turned toward me. Stone scales clinked as the creature lifted itself onto its taloned feet, its wings spreading with a warble of air.

I wasn't going to stick around to find out what that thing had in store for me. I took off toward the mountains on the other side of the river.

A searing gust of wind caught my feathers. I swooped into a crevice in the mountainside wide enough to fit me but not the dragon. A frustrated roar echoed through the air as it wheeled in the sky behind me.

I ventured along the crevice until it opened up around the side of the mountain. Peering out, I couldn't see any sign of the dragon nearby. With a triumphant grin, I scrambled out and soared onward.

I'd seen a pretty limited amount of Muspelheim during my last "visit." Just the cavern where Muninn had constructed her prison and the valley between it and the other cave where Surt's dark elf allies had locked away Odin. The realm around me appeared as vast as it was desolate. How was I going to find the giant?

When we'd been searching for the dark elves' gate before, I'd used the heightened senses the gods had given me to trace their oily energy. All living beings gave off some sort of tingling of life. It didn't look like there was much living anywhere here. If I found a whole bunch of people all together, that would probably be Surt's army. The other-than-undead part of it, anyway.

I reached out with my senses as I flew on, braced for any hint of those vibrations of life. A soft quavering touched me from somewhere to my right. I veered toward it, pushing my wings faster. Within a few minutes, the sensation had expanded into a faint ragged hum that grazed my skin.

A different feeling niggled at the back of my neck at the same time. I glanced behind me and then all around, but I didn't see anyone nearby. Maybe it was just my paranoia in this freaky place making me think someone—or something—must be watching me.

I glided over a groove in the landscape that looked like it might once have been an actual stream, now dried up. Farther along it, skeletal husks of trees that I suspected would have crumbled in a stiff breeze scattered its edge. The remains of some kind of forest? It was hard to believe any vegetation on that scale had ever grown here.

Not much could have grown here *now*, that was for sure. The heat squeezed tighter around me, my throat burning each time I took a deeper breath.

The hum of life ahead of me expanded. I soared over a stretch of jagged hills, and my gaze came to rest on an immense stone fortress on the other side of a great barren plain up ahead. Several wide towering buildings stood inside a wall that looked as if it'd been made by tossing boulders into place somewhat haphazardly. Magma flowed around those high but uneven walls like a pulsing glowing moat. Even as far away as I was, I could make out figures guarding the place from ledges along the wall and balconies on the jutting towers.

If that wasn't Surt's home, then I was the Queen of Portugal.

The nagging sense of being watched rippled down my back again. I jerked around, hoping to take my pursuer by surprise.

Nothing stirred amid the hills except a strip of frayed cloth the sluggish breeze couldn't tug away from the thorny leafless shrub that had snagged it. I studied the landscape for a minute longer and then moved on.

Instead of heading straight for the fortress, which seemed incredibly unwise, I circled around and flew along the line of low cliffs to the east. As I drew closer, more and more guards came into view along the walls. Others were sparring in the fortress's courtyard. Figures moved past the rough windows in the stone-slab walls.

Not all of them were dark elves. Several were either too tall or too light-haired to be those. And then there were the spidery creatures crawling across the sides of the buildings. I shuddered, remembering the one that had nearly crushed me between its knobby legs a few days ago.

Surt had gathered an army, all right. I wouldn't have believed that many people could live in this whole realm, it was so bleak. And those figures didn't move like the shuffling draugar I'd seen before.

Odin might be confident, but I wasn't so sure one special magic trick was going to be enough to bring this giant down.

I was just soaring closer, every sense perked, when a shadow swept over me. Another rock dragon was diving toward me from higher above. My nerves jumped, and I threw myself toward the shelter of the cliff.

There were no hiding places there, just sheer rock everywhere I looked. The dragon's talons raked the stone just inches from my shoulder with an ear-splitting screech. I yelped and reached out to Asgard, to the golden gleam of Valhalla.

The taste of stale mead ran over my tongue, and with a jolt, the bitter heat of Muspelheim fell away from me. I stumbled onto the worn floorboards of Valhalla. Hod was at my side, gripping my arm to steady me, before I could catch my balance myself.

"Are you all right?" he asked. "Did you discover anything?"

I rubbed the shoulder the dragon had nearly gouged. "Yes," I said. "And not anywhere near as much as I'd have liked to. If the seven of us are going to take down Surt's army, I think we're going to need a hell of a lot of training."

# 4

*Aria*

"Now!" Thor bellowed, and we all flung ourselves toward the targets. As my arm swung with my switchblade and my other hand shot out as if to wrench life from the wooden figure in front of me, four other pulses beat in unison with mine.

Loki's fire veered like the arc of my slash, streaming to speed Thor's hammer forward even faster. Bolts of light and shadow streaked around its trail and whipped apart again. Sparks and slivers of darkness exploded through the row of dummies. Before my feet had even touched the ground, our targets had crumpled into a heap of charred kindling. A thin smoky smell laced the warm air.

"Wow," I said, my chest heaving as I caught my breath. I wasn't just awed by the impact of our combined powers. Now that we were consciously trying to fight in unison, to bring out the connection that was growing between us, these merged attacks had come easier and easier. But with each practice strike, my awareness of the gods around me deepened. For a second or two, each time we hurled ourselves forward, it felt almost as if I was part of them and they were part of me.

Somehow that sensation was equally exhilarating and terrifying. I'd never felt so close to anyone in my life, not even my brothers. But in that moment, I wasn't just me anymore. If I let myself go even more than this, would I start to lose myself?

"One set left!" Freya called from the sidelines. She'd helped set up the targets in this field on the outskirts of the godly city. From the eager light in her midnight-blue eyes, I suspected she wished she could join in. Not that the goddess of war wasn't a formidable force without any mystical bonding going on.

The five of us stepped into a formation that was becoming automatic: me front and center, Loki and Thor to my left and right, Hod and Baldur just a step behind and between us. Thor raised his hammer, our signal to focus. We waited one beat to be sure we were all ready, and then we charged at our next set of targets.

I jabbed my switchblade into the straw chest of the dummy at the front with a satisfying crunch. A surge of energy washed over and through me as the gods hurled their magic forward. They were accomplishing a hell of a lot more than I was. For every one foe I might have been able to take down, their combined powers could have toppled fifty or more. But it didn't work if I wasn't fighting with them. We'd experimented with that.

When I'd stood on the sidelines with Freya and the four of them had tried to launch into battle in sync, their powers didn't just fail to intertwine. The sense that I was supposed to be out there with them had wrenched through me hard enough to make me stumble toward them, as if I'd been yanked.

Even now, as Thor chuckled at the ruin we'd left of the targets, that more intense awareness lingered. Baldur's contribution to my valkyrie transformation had been the ability to sense people's emotions—hopes and desires, regrets and guilt—which if I'd been a proper valkyrie I'd have used to decide which side on the battlefield deserved to win and who was worthy of being sent up to Valhalla on their death. I could read human beings pretty well, but the minds of the gods had been nearly impenetrable, even when I'd tried.

Now, though, as Loki shot me one of his sly grins, a jitter of restless tension reached me. And when Baldur's fingers grazed the small of my back in a brief but affectionate caress, along with the warm tingle of pleasure, a pang of distress echoed through me.

I turned to study the god of light. He smiled at me, his boyishly handsome face and shaggy white-blond hair as bright as ever. But that pang I'd just felt wasn't the only tremor of uneasiness that had reached me while I was near him this morning.

"Are you all right?" I asked, touching his arm.

Something flickered in Baldur's bright blue eyes, but his smile didn't falter. He took my hand in his with a gentle squeeze. "Never better," he said. "It's amazing how much more we all become when we can build off each other's power, isn't it?"

That wasn't really what I'd been asking him, but he did *sound* okay. Maybe that feeling of connection was unsettling him a little just like it was me, simply because it took some getting used to.

Loki brushed his hands together, scanning the mess we'd made with all the dummies we'd destroyed over the last few hours. "Odin will certainly be proud," he said. His wry voice had more of an edge to it than sounded completely comfortable.

The Allfather had requested that we take up this training, but he hadn't come out to observe any of it. Unless he was watching us from up in that high seat of his that apparently could give him a view over all of the nine realms. The thought made my skin crawl.

Who knew what he was doing while we were running around trying to prepare for war anyway? He'd told us what he wanted us to do, but not how he was going to fit into that strategy. He hadn't seemed all that concerned when I'd reported what I'd seen in Muspelheim, only nodded and gazed off in thought. He'd better not be planning to sit on his throne while we did all the fighting.

Of course, maybe not everyone here was looking forward to fighting next to Odin. It was hard not to think of the things Loki had shown us from his memories: the way the Allfather had used him as his villain and let him take on all the blame when Odin himself had ordered the trickster god to spread chaos in Asgard. The way Loki had pleaded in vain to be released from that duty. I didn't know how he'd managed to keep his peace with Odin for so long afterward, carrying that secret.

"It was good for us to practice," Hod said, swiping his hand through the sweat-damp fringe of his short black hair. "We'll fight together like this more effectively the more we've gotten used to the rhythm of it." *He* might have felt more at peace with Loki after those recent revelations, but I guessed it was going to take a while longer before he got out of the habit of arguing with the trickster on a regular basis.

"And it very effectively keeps us out of his hair, doesn't it?" Loki said in the same light but barbed tone.

Hod looked as if he were about to mutter something in return. I jumped in before he could.

"Are we ever going to talk to Odin about it?" I said. "About the things he asked Loki to do—about the fact that it seems like he *wanted* Ragnarok to happen? None of you knew about that before. We can't pretend it doesn't matter."

The five figures around me went stiff and silent in an instant. Thor rubbed his mouth. "We will speak with him about it. Of course we will. But now, with Surt posing such a huge threat—we have to stand together against him before we can sort things out between us in Asgard."

"He hasn't even been home for a week yet, after all that time imprisoned," Baldur added. "He'll be able to give us better answers when he's back to his usual self."

"It's going to be a hard conversation," Hod said. "It'll be better for *all* of us to have it when we don't have much more pressing troubles hanging over us. It's been centuries—a few more weeks can't hurt."

Loki's gaze had slid from one of the gods to the next as they'd given their excuses. His jaw tightened, his mouth twisting at a pained angle for just a second before he caught it but long enough to make my gut twist in response.

"You didn't seem to feel the past mattered so little just a few days ago, oh dark one," he said with a half-hearted smile, sounding only weary now. He shrugged. "And so it goes in Asgard."

Hod frowned at him. "I don't see *you* bringing it up with Odin."

"Because all the complaints I made before got me so far?" Loki waved him off. "He and I know where we stand with each other. If you're fine standing where you always have as well, that's your prerogative." He swiveled on his heel. "I meant to do some more scouting today. There must be at least a few more gateways between Nidavellir and Midgard. With a little luck, I'll track down another for us to seal."

"Hey." I caught his elbow before he could stalk away. The trickster paused and peered down at me, one eyebrow rising.

Loki knew how to put on his masks of indifference and carelessness so well, but I knew better than to believe this one. I'd seen firsthand what he'd endured to live here in Asgard, never accepted as an equal to the gods, never really trusted or respected. He'd accepted all that because of his blood-oath with Odin until he'd been pushed up to his breaking point, but even now, with the truth revealed, how much had changed for him?

I squeezed his arm. "I could come with you. We found that first gate together." *I* was still with him, even if a valkyrie's support didn't count half as much as the other gods'.

Loki's smile softened, and I caught a little more of the turmoil behind his amber gaze. "The offer is appreciated, pixie," he said. "But I think after all this group bonding, me, myself, and I is plenty of company."

"Okay." What I'd said didn't feel like enough. I reached up to grasp his tunic, and he bent his tall slim form to give me the kiss I'd been angling for. His lips lingered against mine for just long enough to leave my heart beating faster and my nerves singing for more.

"Perhaps we can enjoy each other's company tonight," he said with a wink when he eased back, sounding more like his usual breezy self.

"I could possibly be convinced," I said, unable to contain my smile, and he strode off chuckling.

Thor took in the field with its heaps of splintered and seared wood and straw. "I suppose we'd better get on with cleaning up this mess."

"Oh, you can bash it all into dust in a matter of minutes, can't you, Thunderer?" Freya said. "Ari, let's see what else we have around, before you lot resort to demolishing our forests."

She motioned for me to follow her, so I fell into step beside her as she headed toward the city in the direction of her hall. She'd housed half of the warriors who'd been honored in Asgard way back when, and I guessed they'd needed lots to keep them busy. That first batch of targets we'd brought over from her storage rooms.

The goddess tucked a stray golden wave behind her perfectly shaped ear. "I can't blame them, you know," she said. "For not knowing what to say to Odin? I'm not sure how to start to talk to him about the subject myself, and he's *my* husband. The way he perceives things, he may even have already gleaned the fact that we know."

"So why not just bring it up then?" I said. "*I* would, but, I mean, I wasn't even there when all that happened. I've got no idea about the details. It's not going to mean much coming from me. Do you think he's going to get angry?"

"I don't know. I think maybe..." She sighed. "There's a saying you mortals have about cans of worms? You bring up one thing and so many other concerns spring to the surface, and then you can't put any of them back. Odin rules Asgard. To challenge his judgment, the decisions he's made, it could rock the foundations of this place."

I kicked at a pebble lying on the tiled road we'd just stepped onto. "It seems to me those foundations are already pretty shaky. How do you build them up better if you pretend they're just fine?"

"It's more complicated than that," Freya said. "You *weren't* there. And there are so many things..."

She paused for long enough that I started to think we were done with the subject too. Then she said, "I have a daughter. Or maybe it's 'had' now. From my first marriage—Hnoss. After Ragnarok, when we were all reborn, she said to me that she thought Odin had more of a hand in events than he was letting on. She wanted me to ask him to—I don't know. Admit to us what his plans had been? Reassure us about the future? He and I had already been getting closer back then."

She dipped her head with a grimace. "I didn't believe her. I thought she was jealous of the closeness we'd developed, imagining the worst of him to excuse those hateful feelings. We argued so many times, and then she left. She couldn't stand to stay here while I stood by him. And she was right, this whole time. Maybe not in the anger she held toward him—that will depend on his reasons—but in her suspicions that I denied."

The regret in her voice made my stomach clench. If my mother had cared even a fraction that much about me or Petey...

"She must be in the nine realms somewhere, then, right?" I said.

"We'll find her. You can talk to her, tell her you're sorry. It doesn't have to be complicated. You've got to at least try."

Freya nodded. "I do. I just wish I knew where to start."

"We'll find her," I said again, firmly, even though I didn't have the slightest clue how I was going to fulfill that promise.

# 5

*Loki*

I shuddered as I came out of the tunnel, sending a quick lick of flame over me to burn away any cobwebs and other debris that might have attached to my body as I'd searched the abandoned mine. The late afternoon sun blazing between the tree branches overhead and the crisply green smells of the forest were a welcome relief. How the dark elves managed not to go completely mad living in dank spaces like that their entire existence, I didn't know.

Of course, given the sorts of adventures they'd been getting up to lately, one might make the argument that they *had* gone mad.

I'd had high hopes for this old mine. It was only miles from the town where I'd spotted dark elf activity in the past, where Ari and I had noted the symbols the dirt-eaters appeared to be marking on buildings that were a good source of prey. I had to imagine they weren't carting the vagabonds they captured all that far before hauling them into Nidavellir. There'd even been a few of those symbols etched on a weathered post outside the main tunnel.

Not a hint of them inside, though. Just like the other eight locations I'd already poked about in. All in all, this expedition had been a flop.

Nothing else in the area seemed promising. With a huff, I pushed off the ground and strode up into the air, toward the glittering arc of the rainbow bridge Odin had left open for our use.

The dark elves were sneaky. We knew that. Still, it was difficult to ignore the urge to set a thing or two aflame to vent my frustrations. Not least because I had so many things to be frustrated about. I'd hoped the journey down here would wear away those bitter feelings, but they lingered on.

Blasted Hod. Blasted Baldur and Thor and Freya too. They had the truth of things right in front of them, had seen it with their own eyes, and still they didn't dare question their king. Wasn't questioning all they'd done with me since the moment I'd set foot in Asgard? Over and over again, as if they never quite trusted any of my answers no matter how many I gave them.

The realm of humans fell away under my soaring feet. I passed through the clouds in the space of a few heartbeats. The softer warmth of Asgard settled around me with a hint of wildflowers, but it didn't soothe my irritation.

The scent tugged at my memories. A yearning I hadn't felt in decades, possibly centuries, rose up. Or perhaps it had been there all along, and I'd simply gotten so skilled at quashing it that I'd stopped noticing it.

As I crossed the last stretch of the bridge, I considered the city with its gleaming halls, so many of them vacant now. So many gods of Asgard who'd drifted away. Hadn't Thor and the rest ever thought to wonder why? *I'd* been glad enough to see most of them gone, but you'd think the others would have taken the time to wonder.

I veered to the left to skirt the edges of the city. Beyond a small span of forest lay an undulating field, the grass high enough to rustle against my calves as I stalked into it. Sprigs of clover and bluebells and dryas bloomed amid the thin strands.

On and on I walked, until the grass and the flowers thinned. Most of the vegetation gave way to bare earth mottled with stones, leading down to a desolate shore. Asgard's sea hissed over the pebbles.

The boulder stood there still, in the midst of that barren land. Claw marks too frantic and deep for time to have worn away decorated its lumpy surface. I rested my hand on the cool limestone and bowed my head.

I could still see the way my son had prowled around this boulder, hear the way he'd thrashed his wolfish body against the chains that bound him fast. Chains the dark elves had constructed for the gods with Odin's approval, if I recalled correctly. One more reason to want to bash the dirt-eaters' sallow skulls in.

*He's a danger*, the gods had all said. *A monster.* Fenrir had been no more monstrous than I was. Which perhaps wasn't saying much. But we'd both been shaped into our villainy by the Allfather in his supposed wisdom, hadn't we?

If I'd stood up to him more firmly then, might I have spared my son his fate, even if I couldn't have changed my own path? I hadn't thought so back then, but it was hard not to wonder at times like this.

Prod and jab the ones you dislike until they lash out exactly as you intended, and then act out your horrified surprise: That was the Asgardian way.

My fingers curled as if I could stroke my son's thick fur across the ages. The way he'd looked at me when I'd first discovered him here back then, so furious and yet so pleading… My hand balled into a fist.

There was nothing to be done about it now. That was why I hadn't let myself dwell on things like this. But the raven's prison had stirred up far too many memories and brought them into sharply vivid being. I'd lived through too much of my past all over again to keep it buried.

The memories must have wrapped me up more tightly than I'd realized, because when a holler of my name carried across the field and I raised my head, the sky above me had dimmed to a purple bruise. I pushed away from the boulder and turned around.

Thor was marching across the field toward me. He slowed to an amble when he saw he had my attention. His ever-present hammer swung from his belt. I'd gone centuries without thinking about how I'd won him that damned thing, and now I couldn't look at it without feeling the fresh sting of a leather thread sewn across my lips.

"Here you are, Sly One," Thor said as he reached me. He surveyed the landscape with a mildly puzzled expression. "What on earth are you doing all the way out here?"

I glanced at the boulder. "I felt the need to remember. The urge has passed."

Thor followed my gaze, and a shadow crossed his face. "It was a nasty trick," he said. "I should have said so then."

"Too late for that now," I said, but without any rancor. A little of the tension wound up inside me eased. It said something that Thor could stand here and make a comment like that when the beast my son had become had been the one to ravage his own father. How eagerly had Odin welcomed those teeth, the ones he'd planned for and directed there himself?

Not to mention the fact that the Thunderer had died in battle with another of my children, each of them slaying the other. My offspring had gotten around during that fraught occasion. If Thor could let bygones be bygones, I couldn't hold much resentment toward him.

"What brings *you* out this way, old friend?" I asked, motioning him back toward the city.

"Freya noticed you returning from Midgard, but didn't see where you'd gone," Thor said as we headed toward home together.

"I wondered if you'd discovered anything in your search down there."

"Alas, not today," I said. "There's altogether too much Midgard. I have a few thoughts on where to search next, though."

Thor nodded. "If anyone can out-wile Surt and his allies, it'll be you."

We walked on in companionable silence, over the field and through the strip of forest. Thor turned down the pathway, I assumed making for his hall, and I stayed with him on my way to mine. We'd only gone a little farther when he raised his hand to the opposite twins of light and dark, who were standing in one of the smaller courtyards. Standing and looking as if they'd been waiting for us.

"Trickster," Hod said in a flat voice, and turned his blind gaze toward Thor. "Where had he slunk off to?"

"You could ask *me* that question," I said, but a prickling sensation shot over my skin. Why would he be asking at all, and asking that way?

He thought I'd been up to some mischief—or worse.

Had Thor come looking for me just to hear my news, or had the other gods sent him off to bring me back, to ensure I was staying in line? His company might not have been so companionable after all. My hackles rose.

"All right," Hod said. "What have you been doing all this time?"

"I spent most of the time on Midgard, as I said I was going to, if you'd been listening, Blind One," I said, managing to keep my voice even. "I investigated several promising locations and determined none of them hold a gate to the dark elves' realm. Not the most thrilling report, but crossing possibilities off our list is better than nothing."

"Freya saw you returning hours ago."

"Yes," I said, and maybe my tone turned a little snippy then. "I needed some time to my thoughts, like anyone does. Do you expect a full accounting of those too?"

"It was a simple question," Hod said, as if he were offended by my taking offense. "You can keep your thoughts to yourself, thank you."

"Strange," I couldn't help saying. "After all the hesitation you expressed earlier about carrying out interrogations, you seem to have no trouble when it comes to me."

Even Baldur's normally placid expression tensed. He raised his hand. "I don't think my brother meant—"

"You don't need to make excuses for him," I said. "His tongue is in perfectly good working order even if his eyes aren't. If he wants to explain himself further, let him do it."

"Loki," Thor said. Was that a *warning* in his voice? I gritted my teeth against the acrid retorts I could have made. One might have slipped free anyway if light footsteps hadn't pattered along the path toward us right then.

"What's going on?" Ari asked, her gaze darting between our faces as she came to a stop at the edge of our cluster. "Did something happen? Has Surt—"

Her panic dampened the anger that had been flaring inside me. I grasped her shoulder gently. "Nothing's wrong. There's no news from Midgard. All seemed well enough when I was down there. We were just having a little chat about unrelated topics."

Hod shifted his weight, but presumably he didn't want to look like an ass in front of our valkyrie. I didn't know how she'd managed to gain that kind of power over Mr. Dark and Prickly, but by some sort of magic over the last few weeks, she'd softened him. He inclined his head when her eyes moved to him again.

"It's about time for dinner, isn't it?" Thor the Ever Hungry rumbled, and that was an easy subject to agree on.

"Are you offering to host?" I asked. "Or should I ask, does your pantry hold enough to satisfy more appetites beyond your own vast one?"

He chuckled and waved us on down the path. "I'm sure I can scrounge up a few scraps to satisfy the lot of you."

"I've got fresh plums I could bring," Baldur offered, and diverted to his own home to retrieve them.

Ari glanced up at me as we meandered along, a hint of worry lingering in her eyes. "You're sure everything is fine? I'd like to be kept in the loop here."

"I promise, anything that relates to our impending war, you'll hear about it as soon as anyone," I said. "Eager to smash some more dark elf skulls, are we, pixie?"

She made a face at me, but at the same time she hooked her hand around my arm. "I'll be glad when we don't need to smash anymore. I'm just looking forward to getting to that point."

"All in good time," I said. "I told you they were right to be afraid of you."

She looked as if she were going to grimace again, but her lips twitched into a smile so fierce it made my chest swell with affection to see it.

*My* valkyrie. And how well she'd done by us so far.

I only wished I could feel with confidence there was more than that one good thing in all of Asgard these days.

# 6

*Aria*

One thing I'd learned during my first venture into Valhalla, all by myself, was that I didn't need Odin's presence—or his permission—to go traveling down the branching path beyond the hearth. Without a hint of guilt, I slipped past the early morning sunlight drifting through the hall's windows and clambered through the opening at the back of the fireplace.

At the foot of Yggdrasil, the chillier air in the darkness there made me shiver. I focused on the rough but solid bark of the tree rather than the emptiness on either side of it, and set off. The branch Odin had pointed me to when I'd gone scouting in Muspelheim before was… this one.

I paused for just a moment at the base of the branch, willing my wings to emerge from my back. The straps of my racerback tank top twitched as the feathered edges brushed them. I touched my hair, making sure it was still tightly tucked into the ponytail I'd pulled it into. I didn't want there to be any chance of anything, including a stray hair, distracting me. My previous trip had made it clear that even a few seconds could make the difference between whether I returned or not.

Dragging in a breath that tingled through my lungs, I strode down the branch to the shadowy gateway at its end. Without giving myself a chance to consider any doubts, I plunged right through.

This time, I was ready for the rock dragon. The second I stumbled through into the hot sulfur-smelling air, I heaved myself back toward the cliff it had leapt at me from last time. A ragged protrusion offered a few ledges with a hint of shelter. I ducked under one and gripped the gritty rock, hugging the cliff-face as closely as I could.

There was a rasp and a warble of wind overhead as the dragon must have shifted from its perch. Its shadow swept over the barren plain below the cliff. But it didn't roar, and after a minute it wheeled around. The shadow disappeared as it settled back on the top of the cliff with a thump.

One hand and foot at a time, I eased myself down to the base of the cliff. Setting my shoes carefully to avoid any rattling of pebbles or stubbing of toes, I crept away, staying close enough to the cliff that the dragon shouldn't be able to see me unless it decided to do a second sweep.

By the time I reached a point where the cliff curved away from the area where I'd come out of the gate, sweat was trickling down my back. I hurried around the bend to where I'd be completely out of sight and then flapped my wings to send a cooling breeze over my skin, as much as it *could* cool me in this broiler of a realm.

There hadn't been any monstrous guards stationed between here and much closer to Surt's fortress last time, but I still kept my eyes peeled and ears perked as I lifted into the air and flew on toward the stone buildings I'd found the other day. I intended to get a better look at them this time—and to come back with some information we could actually use.

To show Odin that whatever information he was getting, staring down from his high seat, it wasn't enough.

I skirted the mountains I'd rambled through before and crossed the skeletal forest. The back of my neck itched more than once with the impression of being watched that was becoming annoyingly familiar. After whipping around a few times and not being able to spot any reason for worry, I resigned myself to just living with it.

If there was someone or something watching me, they hadn't bothered to attack me during my last trip or so far during this one. Maybe I was just picking up on the attention of some of the realm's more cautious inhabitants, ones who didn't want trouble any more than I did.

At the pointed hills I now knew Surt's fortress lay on the other side of, I took a diagonal route to my left. The uneven stone walls came into view just as I reached the low cliffs where the second dragon had come after me. Instead of venturing closer and risking drawing the attention of that beast or some other one, I glided onto a small protrusion and folded my wings against my back.

Loki had given me the sharpened senses the valkyries of the past would have used to scan battlefields and make their choices. I could put those to use here too.

I studied the shape of the fortress and every movement in and around it. As I intensified my gaze, more and more details came into focus across the distance. The guards by the walls were carrying weapons that reminded me of the ones the dark elves had come at us with the other day, the ones with the fiery burn. A sound reached my honed ears: a heavy clatter that made me think of a rockslide. It seemed to come from the direction of the fortress, but I couldn't make out its source.

I checked the top of the cliff for any sign of my draconic friend, and then I leapt to a ledge farther along, and then another, tipping my head to track the sound. It stopped for several minutes, so I stopped too. Then it came again, a little louder. Just over…

The acrid breeze tugged at my hair as I came to rest on a ledge even closer to the fortress. I braced my hands against the rough stone in case I needed to quickly spring away.

Just inside the fortress walls, at the edge of a lifeless courtyard, two figures emerged from a patch of darkness—a hole dug into the ground. They heaved a cart with them up a ramp set against the wall and dumped its contents over the top in a cascade of stones, some of them only pebbles, many as big as my head. A wide heap of rubble like that already rested against much of the outer side of that wall. They'd been excavating for a while.

Why? What else were they doing down in the tunnels they were digging? It had to be part of Surt's plan.

I was about to edge even closer when a dark shape dropped onto a spike of rock several feet away from me with a ruffle of black feathers. My body went rigid at the sight of the raven, my gaze twitching away from it and back. How had I not heard her sneaking up on me?

Muninn must be up to her old tricks again.

I tensed to lunge at her, and her form expanded, her feathers rippling away into strewn black hair and a loose black dress that made her pale limbs look gawkishly thin. The spear of stone she was perched on was barely wide enough for both of her human feet to fit on, but she managed to keep her balance there without any hint of a struggle. Her wide dark eyes were fixed on me.

"Hello, valkyrie," she said in her softly hoarse voice. "Has Odin sent you to play his raven now? His eyes and ears where he can't be?"

"Odin doesn't even know I'm here," I snapped. Maybe that hadn't been the smartest thing to admit, but I couldn't take the words back after they'd tumbled out. I adjusted my weight on the ledge. If I sprang fast enough, could I grab her and hope to hold her?

But even if I could, what would I do with her then? I could

transport myself back to Valhalla in an instant, but I couldn't take her with me. Maybe if she'd been dead and I'd summoned her like a warrior of old… but I'd never tried *that* before, so probably this wasn't the best time to experiment.

Odin's former raven of memory wasn't our greatest enemy here. I wanted to know what she might reveal about Surt more than I wanted her dead for the way she'd tortured us. Although if she happened to die after I found out something useful, I wasn't going to cry about it.

"What do you want?" I said. "Did you figure you'd harass me a little more before you sound the alarm?"

"No," Muninn said. "I don't think Surt needs to know about this. I don't belong to him, you know. I had no need for a new master."

"You're doing him an awful lot of favors for someone who's not working for him."

She shrugged, her dress moving in a way that recalled ruffled feathers. "We work together, when it suits me. It suited me to see Odin brought down. It suited me to try to stop you from freeing him. That's done now. I've never had any particular grudge against you personally. You didn't choose to be a part of this either, did you?"

The cock of her head and the gleam in her eyes were oddly sympathetic. A prickling spread along the base of my wings. I wanted to fly away from her, and I wanted to fly *at* her and smack that hint of a smile off her face, but I wasn't sure I'd like the results of either act.

"You haven't answered my first question," I said. "What do you want?"

"You've looked around here," she said. "You've seen the devastation. Muspelheim wasn't pretty even when I first found myself here, you know, but things have gotten worse. The heat rises;

the air grows drier; the magma flows faster. Barely anyone survives outside Surt's fortress."

"And they did before?" I said skeptically. I couldn't imagine this realm had ever been anyone's dream home.

"Some managed to make a bit of a life for themselves," Muninn said. Her gaze slipped away from me for a second, a shadow of melancholy passing over her face. Then her eyes jerked back to me. "No thanks to the gods."

"Do you really think letting this giant blaze his way across Asgard and Midgard is going to fix anything?"

"I don't know. It would at least be something different." She shifted closer to the cliffside on her precarious perch. "You're close with the gods who brought you to them. I saw that. But can you think beyond what they've told you? Can you consider that there may be other sides to the story?"

A sputter of a laugh escaped me. "Other sides? I don't think there's any way you can justify mass murder and the raising of those corpses into some kind of undead army."

"I'm not attempting to justify it," the raven woman said. "I simply mean to point out—have you heard the stories of the olden times? Did they tell you who crafted Thor's treasured hammer or Odin's great spear?"

I'd seen the end result of Loki's bargaining for those weapons in painful clarity in the memories she'd stirred up. "The dark elves," I said. "So what? That was ages ago, and it's not as if they did it out of the kindness of their hearts."

"They wanted to impress the gods. They often did. You'll find many of the treasures of Asgard came from them, sometimes freely given. Relations between the gods and the dark elves used to be those of tentative allies, and the elves were always more eager for that alliance. You might ask yourself why they turned in a different direction now. No one enters a war for the fun of it."

"If you know why they're doing this, why don't you just tell me?"

Her lips curled in a faint grimace. "Would you believe it from me? I think not. Better you seek the dark elves out yourselves, hear the tales from their own lips. I only have scraps as it is."

Go to the dark elves and have a little chat about why they'd tried to kill me, threatened to kill my little brother, and *had* killed who knew how many people? Sure, that sounded like it'd be a lovely visit.

But the raven woman's comments niggled at me. I hadn't heard the gods discuss why the dark elves might have allied with Surt. I'd just assumed there'd always been animosity between Asgard and Nidavellir. If Muninn was right…

"Why are you telling me any of this?" I asked abruptly. "What does it matter to you what I think?"

Muninn gave another of her dress-ruffling shrugs and started to straighten up. "All I've ever really wanted was for something to change. It doesn't matter to me that much how. Perhaps all it'll take is one new spark in the mix."

Before I could push for more answers, she leapt off the cliff, contracting back into her raven form in the same moment. She flapped away with a hoarse caw. I moved to spring after her, and the rattle of claws against rock drew my gaze upward.

The dragon was lounging along the cliff-top just a short distance farther along. If I took after Muninn now, it'd spot me for sure.

My hands clenched into fists, but that niggling of uncertainty dug right down to my heart. Maybe this wasn't the place I'd get the rest of the answers I needed. What else could my gods tell me that they hadn't yet?

# 7

*Aria*

"There are a bunch of buildings," I said, adding some shapes to the rough layout of Surt's fortress I'd drawn. The rough pencil rasped against the faded strip of paper that Baldur had scrounged up. The gods might have had a perfectly modern house down in Midgard, but up here they were still kind of stuck in the old ways. Maybe I'd have to encourage a little updating of supplies. "I'd guess the biggest one in the middle is the one Surt rules from, but I didn't actually see him, as far as I know."

"And where were these excavations you witnessed happening?" Loki said as he leaned against the table in Valhalla where I'd spread the paper.

"Over here." I tapped the spot by my sketched wall and added a dark circle there. "I've got no idea what they're doing down there other than clearing out a larger space."

"He needs somewhere to keep that army," Thor rumbled with a frown. "Perhaps he creates more room as he adds to their number."

"Odin might have seen something," I said. "Or he could look

from that high seat now and check things out. If he feels like telling us what he thinks is going on, that is." I still had my doubts about that. If he'd been able to watch the fortress at all, how could he have completely missed that activity? He'd probably just decided we didn't need to know about it.

Loki rubbed his narrow chin. "I do believe there's quite a network of existing underground tunnels throughout Muspelheim. Cooler and more protected than walking around in the open above ground."

"You speak from personal experience?" Hod asked, his tone dry. He was propped against the table opposite ours, since he couldn't see my drawing anyway.

"I have made a point of traveling nearly everywhere in the realms, both of my own accord and because the Allfather decided to drag me," the trickster said. "All the better for us."

"If we just attack his fortress, he could escape, then," I said. "Take off through the tunnels. We can't tear apart the whole realm, even with our combined power."

"Could we cut off the tunnels first, cause cave-ins or the like, before the main attack?" Baldur asked.

I blinked at him, startled to hear those words from him in that nonchalant tone. His tone was normal, but I couldn't remember hearing the god of light and harmony talking military strategy that blatantly before.

But then, he was also the god of justice. Sometimes justice required a sword.

"We'd need to know exactly where they all were," Loki said. "Leave one avenue open to him, and he'd slip through our fingers. He's proven himself awfully tricky for a giant. Not to mention the issue of the gates he's apparently built that fortress around. He could leap from there through any of them."

"He wouldn't be able to move an entire army through a gate at any speed," Hod said. "As long as we destroy his manpower, it doesn't matter that much how quickly we catch *him*."

"That's true," Thor said. "Cut off his might, and it's just a matter of tracking him down for the final blow."

Their comments stirred up my thoughts with the subject I hadn't yet mentioned. This was as good a time as any, wasn't it?

"Something else happened while I was in Muspelheim this morning," I said.

Hod's head snapped toward me in an instant.

Loki gave me an evaluating look. "Nothing too horrifying, I assume," he said lightly. "Seeing as you appear to have returned to us with all your parts intact. Why didn't you mention it earlier?"

I set down the pencil, fighting the urge to squirm in my discomfort. "I wasn't sure whether I should mention it at all. It was just— Muninn approached me. Just to talk."

Thor snorted. "That feathered fiend. She was looking to wrap you up in another tangle of memory, probably."

"That's what I thought at first," I said. "But the way she was talking… I'm not sure what her motives were. But that doesn't mean she didn't say anything useful. She brought up the dark elves and how they used to be kind of allies of Asgard. Now they've turned against you—they're helping a guy who wants to destroy you. Why would they do that?"

"The dark elves have always been shaky allies at best," Thor said.

"That's pretty different from becoming an outright enemy."

"They've had plenty of time for resentments to fester," Loki said. "But I take it you believe it would help us to know which specific resentments are afflicting them?"

"I've just been thinking…" I made a face at the attempt at a map I'd drawn. "They're doing a lot of work for Surt. He's got other people guarding his fortress, but the dark elves are the only ones we've seen gathering humans for his draugar army, right?"

"They've always lived the closest to Midgard of all the realms' dwellers other than us," Baldur said.

"So it makes sense then," I said. "We wanted to close off all their access points, but maybe that's not really practical, or effective. They know we're looking for them now. They'll be sneakier. What if we could figure out why they've turned against you… and turn them back?"

"Then Surt loses his army supplies and all the other work they may have been doing for him, just like that." Loki snapped his fingers, a smile stretching across his face. "A truly cunning plan, pixie. I applaud you."

My skin warmed at his praise, but Hod looked skeptical. "They've already gone this far," he said. "They've killed innocents and carted off their bodies to Surt. We've got no reason to think we've got anything we'd be willing to offer that would move them."

"It is difficult to appeal to someone's better nature if they don't appear to have one," Baldur put in.

"We should at least find that out, shouldn't we?" I said. "You don't know. I mean, come on, you all thought Loki had done horrible things for the sake of being evil, and it turned out he had other reasons. We obviously can't assume we know everything just from how it looks."

"A lesson you'd have thought this bunch would have learned by now," Loki said, a hint of acid in his tone.

The other three still hesitated. Thor ran a hand over his dark auburn hair. "That's a fair point. We don't know, so we should find out. It could be there's more to the situation than we realize."

Loki lifted his hands. "The voice of reason coming to us from the Thunderer! Who could have predicted that?"

Hod scowled at him, but he inclined his head in agreement. "All right. We'll be better off if we understand our enemies better. I won't argue against that."

"We might not even have to reach out to them at all," I said.

"We can start by discussing it with Odin and seeing what he knows—"

"Discussing what?" a low voice carried from down the hall.

I jerked around. The Allfather had just stepped into Valhalla, the peak of his broad-brimmed hat nearly brushing the doorframe overhead. He made his way toward us with steady steps, the base of his spear tapping along against the wooden floor in time. It touched the ground so lightly he couldn't have been using it for any support. The sound felt more like a warning than anything else.

"Aria had a thought about the dark elves," Baldur started, but I set my hand over his to stop him. It was my idea; I should be the one to try to convince Odin.

"We should find out why they're helping Surt with his war," I said. "And then we can either win them back to our side or convince them they're better off if they stay out of it. Either one would leave him without his main helpers."

Odin raised the eyebrow over his good eye. "And what inspired this line of thinking?"

I braced myself against the bench. "I spoke to Muninn. In Muspelheim. I think… if we found the right angle, we might even be able to win *her* back to our side." Even though the thought of fighting alongside her again made my skin crawl, I couldn't deny that she must have all kinds of useful inside info about our main enemy.

Odin let out a dismissive chuckle. "She's made her allegiances more than clear. As for the dark elves, they've been jealous of our power since the beginning. Now they've finally been given a way to act on those feelings. There's nothing more complicated to it than that, and nothing we could offer them except our defeat."

"I think the valkyrie's point has some merit," Loki said quietly. "They did fashion that spear of yours. They've given us enough gifts over the ages."

"I've seen no reason to think the dark elves might be swayed," Odin said firmly.

Frustration prickled up my back. "You've seen a lot with all the traveling around I've heard you do, and with that high seat of yours," I said. "Even *I* can tell that things are getting worse in the other realms. You told us yourself that only this one and Midgard have stayed balanced—that's why Surt wants them. Why haven't we done anything about *that*? Why are the realms failing at all?"

"A lot of questions from one only so recently with us," Odin said dryly, but his single-eyed gaze felt heavy on me. "All things run down eventually. You should know that as well as anyone, being so recently mortal."

The reminder of my death made my shoulders stiffen, but I pushed myself off the bench so I could at least come closer to meeting him face to face. "That's a bullshit answer. 'All things run down.' Sure, but Asgard isn't. Midgard isn't. So what's different with the others?"

"If Nidavellir is failing as well, that could have pushed the dark elves to take more drastic action," Hod said, tipping his head warily.

Odin made a sweeping gesture with his hand. "Our course is clear. Our enemies threaten us, and we must cut them off at the knees before they can. All this rambling only gives them more time to build their strength. Do you forget what they did to *me*?"

"Of course not," I said, struck by a sudden thought. "Why *did* they just keep you locked up? Why didn't they kill you while they had you? It seems like it would have made life a whole lot easier for them, if all they want is to destroy everyone here."

Odin's lips curled with what looked like disgust. "Surt was afraid that if he ended my life, I might be reborn in Asgard as before, outside his grasp, before he was ready to carry out the rest of his plans."

"Oh." I couldn't help asking, "Would you have been?"

"I don't know," the Allfather said darkly. "None of us knows our fate after this. Which is all the more reason we should follow the signs and recognize a day of reckoning is approaching, whether we like it or not."

"No," I said, taking a step toward him. Thor said my name like a plea and a warning combined, but I ignored him. They were too used to taking orders from Odin, but I didn't have that problem. "This is how you get your way with everything, isn't it? You act as if the future is set in stone, there's nothing anyone can do but accept the hand that's been dealt to us at face value and tackle it like that. Sounds like a really easy way to avoid responsibility for your choices to me."

"I only say what is," Odin said in a voice almost as thunderous as Thor's could be.

"Right," I said. "But you know what? If we'd thought like that when you were off in that cage of Surt's, you'd probably still be there, because we'd have given up and left you to the elves. So maybe that should be your hint that it's time to try a different way of looking at things. If you just—"

Odin cut me off with a smack of his spear against the floor. "I know what comes. We won't—"

A fierce cry and an ominous sounding thump carried through Valhalla's walls. My pulse hiccupped. All of us raced for the main doors in an instant, Loki speeding past the rest of us on his shoes of flight.

On the field that stretched between Valhalla and the forested fringe of the realm, Freya was flinging streaks of her magic, bright as her golden hair, at a group of lurching figures. As I pushed myself off the ground and flapped my wings to join the fight even faster, a putrid mildew-y stink filled my nose. The graying skin and bloated faces of her attackers confirmed my initial impression: They were draugar. Zombies who'd once been people like me.

My stomach lurched, but I whipped out my switchblade. They weren't human anymore. They weren't even really alive.

Loki gave a shout, and two of the undead forms burst into flames.

"We should come at them together!" Baldur called from somewhere at my other side.

A swatch of shadow had already toppled one of the others. Freya drew her sword and sliced the head off another. Jolted along by my surprise and fear, a bolt of lightning seared from my switchblade and blasted into the fifth. Thor's hammer smashed into the last of them a moment later.

I dropped to the ground near the scattered bodies, my chest heaving to catch my breath. Nothing else moved on the field beyond them.

Freya bent to tug something out of one of the fallen draugar's grasp. She held it up. It was a boxy metal device with an eerie red glow emanating from a sphere of glass at its center.

"I smelled them before I saw them," she said. "But it's a good thing I was nearby. This is dark elf work. There was one of the dirt-eaters with the pack of them, but he ran off as soon as he saw me coming." She turned the device in her hand. "If I'm getting the right sense of this, one push of this button and the contraption would explode. They were heading for Valhalla."

A chill crept up my spine. The rest of us had been in Valhalla—had they known that and meant to kill us? Or had they simply been trying to cut off one of our main avenues into Surt's world?

"How did they reach this realm in the first place?" Loki said. "Let's see if we can't scrounge up that dark elf to tell us."

He darted forward, and the rest of us hurried after him. We didn't end up going far. Several feet from the edge of the forest, he stopped by a scorch mark that had blackened a strip of grass. A smoky smell rose off it. He prodded the burnt area with his toe.

Hod came up beside him and inclined his head. "What's the

story of how Surt brought his army to Asgard during Ragnarok? Didn't he open a bridge of his own, one of fire?"

"He did," Thor said, his deep voice unusually subdued.

"Why did he only send seven people up here?" I said. "He couldn't really have thought he'd take us down with a little squad like that, could he?"

Odin's low voice carried from behind me. "It was a feint," he said. "He might have hoped they'd do some damage, but that wasn't the main purpose. The main purpose was testing how swiftly we'd react."

Loki grimaced. "And no doubt the dark elf that brought the draugar is reporting back to him right now."

"We fought them off," Baldur said, but with a hint of hesitation.

"You didn't use your combined power," Odin said. "The moment of a real fight, and you all reacted on your own."

"There was barely time," Hod started, and his father spun toward him with a singular glower.

"How much time do you expect Surt to give you? If we want to save this realm and Midgard, there's no more time for chatter. You should get back to your practice. We must be ready for our enemies." The Allfather cast one last look toward the scorch mark. "Foul giant."

I thought I saw Loki wince. But even I couldn't deny that we hadn't been completely ready for this tiny battle. I waved my switchblade with a crooked smile. "Time to bring out more targets?"

# 8

*Thor*

The sun had sunk almost to the distant treetops when I finished the last round of my patrol around the city. We couldn't know when Surt might make another attempt to breach our defenses. We had to be on guard now more than ever.

I found myself walking toward my father's hall rather than my own. All that time in Muninn's prison had brought up thoughts I hadn't considered in a long time. I'd tried to put them aside, but some of Odin's comments about Surt had stirred them up again. Maybe he could help set those thoughts to rest as well.

The hall was quiet, no one visible from the foyer. "Father?" I called out. He'd said he was going to survey the realms from his high seat—he might still be up there.

I swung my hammer as I waited to see if he'd come, taking reassurance from the heft of Mjolnir in my hand. It *was* strange to think I relied so much on this weapon the dark elves had crafted, when they'd been the ones most frequently toppled by it in the last few weeks. And now they were leaving bombs on our doorstep.

Maybe Ari was right—maybe we should dig deeper into why. It certainly couldn't hurt to know more.

That principle was why I was here right now.

My stomach grumbled, reminding me that it had been several hours since lunch and at least two since my ample mid-afternoon snack. I'd almost made up my mind to leave and stop by again after I'd refilled my stomach when a faint creaking drifted from deeper within the hall. Odin must be descending the ladder that led to his upper floor.

He appeared in the hallway a moment later, his weathered face weary but his posture still straight. His spear gleamed in his hand, not quite touching the floor as he strode toward me.

"You wanted to speak to me, my son?" he said, his tone unreadable.

"If I'm interrupting you…" I started.

He waved his hand dismissively before I could continue. "A small break will do me good. A bit of rest for this overworked eye." The arch of his eyebrow seemed to say that he didn't really think he needed rest at all. He motioned me toward one of the side rooms. "Did you uncover something in your rounds?"

"No," I said. "All looks normal, except for that burn where Surt's bridge must have touched our land."

Odin nodded. "I hadn't realized he might summon that type of fire on his own. With the chaos during Ragnarok, I never determined exactly how it had been formed—I assumed there was other effort involved."

My gut clenched at that idea. "Maybe there was again."

"I think not." The Allfather sat himself down on one of his fine wooden chairs and motioned me to another nearby. "I may not be able to watch everything at all times, but I haven't seen him associating with any allies of that stature. Only the dark elves and the riffraff he's gathered from Muspelheim. What matter did you wish to bring to my attention, then?"

"I only wondered..." I shifted on the chair, not sure how to proceed. "It may seem out of the blue, but I think it's time. We've never really talked about my mother."

Odin paused in the middle of adjusting his grip on the spear. He peered at me with his single brown eye for a long moment. "Did Muninn show you something distressing in that prison of hers?"

"No," I said. "I simply—I know she was a giantess. I have some kind of connection to Jotunheim. I thought, if I understood that better, perhaps it could help in defeating Surt." And in simply feeling more at peace with who *I* was, although I wasn't sure my father would see that as worthy reasoning. If Thor the Thunderer didn't know who he was by now, what could help me?

Odin let out a huff of breath. "There's nothing to be gained in speaking of her. It was a moment of ill-judgment on my part—although I have always been pleased with the result." He tipped his head to me. "I removed you from the giants' grasp the moment you were born. You are all mine and not at all theirs, down to your nature. I've had all the time in the world to observe it."

Those words didn't comfort me the way they might have once. I pushed onward. "There are still things I'd like to know. How did you come to, ah, meet her? What family was she of? Did—"

"Enough." Odin held up his hand, a definitive end to the conversation. He heaved himself back onto his feet. "You left that part of your life behind almost from the instant your life began. Leave it where it belongs. These are a people who can barely see two feet beyond their lusts and rages, other than those rare exceptions like Loki. We won't glean anything from them when they can barely glean anything of themselves. I should return to my searching."

He headed off toward the room that led to his high seat at a pace that offered no room for compromise. This was obviously a subject he had no intention of speaking on.

I frowned as I let him go. That remark about Loki brought back all the things the trickster had shown us in Muninn's construct of the room at the top of Odin's hall. The things my father had held his silence about for so very long. How many other secrets was he keeping?

But now didn't feel like the time for attempting to pry them loose. Not when Surt was sending his rotting army right to our back door. And I couldn't say Odin was wrong about the giants. By Hel, we'd been able to fool them into taking me for Freya with nothing but an ill-fitting dress and a veil that barely hid the battle fury in my eyes. By all evidence, most giants only saw what they wanted to see.

That fact settled deeper into my mind as I left the Allfather's hall. We'd deceived the giants so many times in the past. I wasn't sure we could trick Surt very easily—for him to have captured my father at all, he was clearly one of the sharper ones. But his kin back in Jotunheim… How might they play into this war?

Freya was just coming out of her hall a little farther into the city. She glanced at me and then past me to where I'd come from, and ambled over to join me.

"Did you talk to him?" she asked.

"Briefly," I said. "He was in a hurry to get back to his seat."

She hummed and sucked in her lower lip. "How did he seem to you?"

How could I answer that? The Allfather might have been my literal father, but his moods had always been nearly impenetrable to me. He kept his own counsel—that much had always been true.

"Concerned, but not overly so," I said, taking my best stab at answering. "A little tired. Impatient, but then, that's hardly unusual."

"He has all the patience in the world for his questing," she muttered, but there wasn't much rancor in her voice. "He's been quieter than usual even with me since we returned. I don't know how concerned *I* should be."

I didn't remember the goddess ever confiding that much to me before. Which suggested she was at least twice as worried as she was admitting.

"He's been through a lot," I said. "And there's a lot we still have to face. It'd be strange if he seemed completely normal."

"I know."

I hesitated and then offered the only comment I could think of that might make her feel better. "I'm concerned about him too. We're all keeping an eye on him."

"Some of us with different motives," she said with a hint of tartness. I wondered who she was talking about, but her expression had softened at the same time. "I suppose we'll see our way through this as we have so much else."

Before I could think of anything reasonably articulate to say in response, the smell of roasting meat wafted past my nose. An answering gurgle sounded in my belly. I was turning toward the scent before I'd even realized I was moving.

Freya laughed. "Let's see what we can ferret out for dinner, shall we?"

The savory smoky smell led us to Baldur's gleaming white hall. Around the back of it, we found him and Hod and Ari standing around a fire pit. A pig's carcass hung on a spit over the flames, its flesh browned and sizzling.

"It appears you have more than you can chew here," I said as I joined them.

Hod turned his head toward my voice. "Why am I not surprised that you showed up the moment the meal was ready?" he said with a smile.

"You know me too well."

"Just be sure you leave some for the rest of us."

"Ah, I don't believe I've ever downed more than half a roast pig in one meal."

I aimed a wink Ari's way. She grinned, but her expression looked a bit tight.

She'd taken on so much since we'd returned—and really before that too. All her solitary patrols of Muspelheim, having to contend with that raven woman and the other threats there on her own... I bristled instinctively, thinking about it.

Baldur moved to adjust the spit and check the meat, and I came to stand beside Ari, resting my hand on her shoulder with a gentle squeeze. She set her hand over mine. The simple sensation of her thumb tracing over the back of my hand sent a bolt of desire through me.

I kept those impulses in check, just enjoying the warmth of her touch. There'd be time to enjoy more with her, if she wanted, after other appetites were sated.

Hod had joined Baldur by the fire. He nudged his twin companionably as they discussed the state of the roast: Baldur going by sight and Hod by smell. Baldur's face lit up with a laugh.

When was the last time I'd seen them look so easy with each other? Definitely not since the mistletoe catastrophe. There'd always been a thread of tension between them from the moment of our rebirth. And if *I'd* picked up on it, then it hadn't been exactly subtle.

Now, despite this morning's attack, they appeared relaxed. Comfortable with each other.

My heart swelled with fondness. My brothers deserved that happiness after the struggles they'd been through.

Ari leaned over to kiss my knuckles. I couldn't resist drawing her chin up to kiss her properly. Her soft lips parted against mine, and right then I couldn't imagine how this place had felt complete without her.

She beamed at me, looking more relaxed herself at least for the moment, and went to grab the plates from the stone table nearby. "Isn't it about time we get carving that up? I'm starving."

"Let me," I said, moving forward. Baldur stepped aside with an amused expression and handed me the knife.

"Maybe you should take your portion last," he said teasingly. I couldn't remember the last time he'd poked fun either. Yes, we'd come through Muninn's tortures stronger.

"That's just asking him to eat everything that's left," Hod said with a laugh.

"We do need to keep our Thunderer well-fueled," Freya said, patting my arm.

I mock-glowered at them and dug the blade through the crackling skin. Juice seeped out to hiss in the fire, the sharper scent making my mouth water.

The pig tasted even better than it smelled, I discovered a few minutes later when I got to dig into the haunch I'd claimed. The flesh was just the right mix of chewy and tender, with a smoky flavor laced through the near-sweetness of the pork. I was about to go for a second helping when a tall slender figure with hair as bright as the flames in the fire pit emerged from the dusk.

"Well," Loki said, with a smile that looked as if it'd been cut into his face by a blunt knife. He came to a stop at the edge of our circle. "What a fine dinner I wasn't invited to."

Hod set down the plate he'd been holding. "Oh, don't sulk," he said mildly. "We are allowed to occasionally keep things in the family."

Loki's smile turned even stiffer. "The family," he repeated.

Ari swatted Hod's arm and motioned Loki over. "I don't think any formal invitations went out. Everyone just showed up."

"There's plenty more," I said, moving to the roast like I'd planned to anyway. The last thing we needed was the trickster in a mood. "I'll carve you a slice."

A minute later, Loki had a plate with a fine cut of pork on it. He considered it with a vaguely dissatisfied expression. I had no idea what the Sly One wanted now, so I just worked on chopping myself off the other haunch.

"After this morning's brief adventure, I think we need to talk strategy," Loki said. He started to pace around the fire pit. "Surt is getting bold. He must be close to ready to launch his full attack. Just barreling in there with our unified powers isn't likely to win the day."

"I assume you've come with your own ideas on that front," Freya said.

Loki gave her only the briefest nod of acknowledgment before barreling on with even more frenetic energy than he usually showed. "We need to step up our efforts to close off the gates to Midgard. Regardless of the dark elves' motives, which it may do us well to uncover, humankind is too vulnerable for them to have free access. Muninn may also be key, if we can contrive a way to capture *her*."

The beginnings of the idea that had been forming in my head earlier rose up. I lowered the carving knife. "There's also—When it comes to giants—"

Loki brushed me off with a flick of his hand. "Yes, yes, we know Surt is a giant. I have plenty of experience to draw on. We're well covered in that department."

"No," I said, a little more firmly. "I don't mean that. I was thinking about the time we faced Thrym and—"

"Come on now, Thunderer," Loki said. "This really isn't the time for reminiscing about past glories. If Surt was simply looking to marry Freya, we'd have a much easier situation on our hands. Now, when it comes to Muninn, she's clearly shown she's willing to talk to Ari…"

Hod jumped in to say that by no means should we be using our valkyrie as bait, and Ari argued that she could hold her own, and Freya wanted to return to the problem of sealing the gates on

Midgard. No one looked to me, standing there with my half-carved haunch. An itch of frustration ran over my skin.

Why should they look to me? I wasn't known for my scheming or my strategic prowess. They needed me to hurl my hammer on the battlefield in whatever direction they pointed me.

But there was an ache in my gut, a different sort of hunger than I'd ever felt before. What if I wanted to be more than that? Where in the realms did I even start?

# 9

*Aria*

I should have been able to sleep. I had the whole damned hall to myself—one that had previously belonged to some lesser goddess whose fate I hadn't really wanted to ask about—including the softest bed I'd ever had the pleasure of sleeping on. The night outside the window was still and quiet. Any chill it had brought, the blanket I was snuggled under protected me from.

But still, I'd been lying there for at least an hour with nothing to show for it but the groove I was probably wearing into the mattress with all my tossing and turning.

When we'd first gotten back to the real Asgard, there'd been a moment or two when I'd thought maybe I didn't need an actual building as a home of my own. What would be the point when I could just hop from one of my gods' beds to another depending on the night? But then as that first full night had gotten closer, I'd felt edgier and edgier about the idea of settling down to sleep the whole night next to anyone at all. Across all the one-night stands I'd had since I'd moved out of my mother's house, I'd never stuck around to cuddle.

What I had with the four gods who'd summoned me was different from that. I couldn't deny it. But it was also new and a little unsettling. To be practically *living* together… No. I didn't even know what to call this yet. I needed a place where I didn't have to think about it.

Which had worked out fine the first few nights, but now apparently I had too many other thoughts chasing each other around my mind.

I burrowed my head in the plump pillow and squeezed my eyes tighter shut, as if that would bring sleep on faster. After another couple minutes, I groaned and shoved myself into a sitting position. My jaw creaked with the size of my yawn. But still my head was buzzing with the memories of my latest trip to Muspelheim, the things Muninn had said, the attack by the draugar.

What if Surt sent a force like that into Midgard? We couldn't keep watch over that entire realm as well as Asgard. Muninn knew about Petey. She'd shown me his foster home in her prison, lifted from my and the gods' memories of the place. What if she pointed him there?

I rubbed my bleary eyes. Why would she do that? She had to know it'd only make me ten times more furious. If she'd wanted to threaten me, to hold his safety over my head, she could have done it this morning. I had to be here, and rested enough to fight properly, if I was actually going to protect my brother.

Maybe, as exhausted as I felt, it wasn't exhausted enough. I pulled on some clothes and walked down the hall, figuring I'd swoop around over the city for however long it took before I was barely keeping my wings unfurled. I slipped past the door—and froze on the first tile of the path outside.

Odin was stalking down Asgard's main throughway, his cloak swaying in his wake, his hat pulled low even though there was no sun to guard against. He was already most of the way to the rainbow bridge, well past my hall. Where the hell was he going at this time in the night that he couldn't just spy on from his high seat?

I hesitated for only a second longer, and then I darted after him, setting my feet softly on the stone tiles.

I stayed far behind Odin as I followed him, sticking to the deeper shadows around the buildings. When he strode onto the faint glimmer of his rainbow bridge, I waited until he'd just disappeared over the crest of it and leapt into the air with a light flap of my wings. By the time I'd glided over the bridge, he'd descended almost to the ground. He unfurled the last length of the bridge, which he'd contracted earlier so no dark elves could clamber up to Asgard that way, and set off across the tilled farmland where he'd set it down.

The rolling fields made it easy to keep an eye on his tall form even in the night. Wherever we'd ended up, it was warmer than it'd been in Asgard, the air sharp with heat despite the darkness. A half-moon shone starkly overhead. Only a faint breeze rustled the stalks of the plants below me. I flapped my wings cautiously, trying to make as little sound as possible. My valkyrie powers might make me invisible to any mortal unless I wanted to be seen, but I doubted that worked on the Allfather.

He paused once, and then again several minutes later, cocking his head as if listening for something. I couldn't hear anything other than the occasional rumble of a truck passing along the two-lane highway nearby. Both times he veered a little more to the right.

We passed a few houses that gave me the impression we were in some other country. I'd never seen any in that style back home. After a while, we crossed the highway and rambled over a couple of low hills. The vegetation turned scruffier, dry earth dotted with weeds and prickly shrubs.

At the top of the third hill, a dusty shack stood next to a

shriveled tree. Odin slowed. I eased down to the ground and crouched behind one of those thorny bushes to watch.

He paced around the shack and a little farther down the other side of the hill. Whatever he found there made him come to a halt. His head bowed in apparent contemplation. He rubbed his bearded chin. I thought I could make out a frown on his worn face.

My legs were starting to get stiff in their cramped position by the time he returned to the shack. He circled it once more, slowly, his single eye narrowed. He appeared to examine the tree in turn. Then, with a sigh I could hear even from my hiding place, he headed back the way he'd come.

I tensed behind the shield of my shrub, but Odin stalked down the hill a few dozen feet from where I was crouched without glancing my way. When he'd reached the bottom of the hill, I eased around the bush and crept up to the shack myself. What the hell had he been looking at?

It didn't take long to figure it out. Over the other side of the hill, the cracked earth was blackened with a scorch mark like we'd seen in the field in Asgard—the one Surt's bridge of fire had left behind. Had this been its starting point?

An uneasy shiver crawled over my skin. I rubbed my arms as I took to the air again. If Surt and his undead soldiers were lurking around here, I didn't want to be caught on my own.

How had Odin known about this place? Why had he come down just to look at it?

Somehow I had the feeling he wasn't going to answer those questions willingly. I'd bet he didn't plan to even mention this little trip to the rest of us tomorrow.

I had to fly a little faster than before to catch up with Odin. I wasn't sure enough of the path we'd taken to find my way back to the bridge on my own. He strode over the hills and across the farmers' fields at a swifter pace than before, now that I guessed he'd found what he'd been looking for. This time, he didn't stop to consider his direction at all.

When the sheen of the rainbow bridge came into sight up ahead, I eased up completely, dropping down onto the thick lower branch of a waxy-leafed tree. I might as well let him go on ahead of me before I followed, now that I knew my way home.

It was a good thing that I did. I'd just settled onto the branch when Odin jerked around. He peered back across the field. I went rigid, holding my muscles still and my breath in my chest, shadowed by the leaves around me. His gaze seemed to pass over the tree, but it didn't stop there. Finally, he started walking again.

What was he afraid of?

He reached the rainbow bridge and started up it, the base of it fading in his wake. Just a hint of it remained below the streak of clouds he disappeared into.

As soon as he was out of sight, I sprang into flight. The swoop of my wings brought me up to the bridge. I peeked cautiously through the haze of the clouds to see the Allfather's peaked hat just vanishing over the crest of the bridge.

I soared the rest of the way to Asgard, the cooler wind there buffeting my wings. Odin was out of sight by the time I reached the city. Back to his hall to get some sleep—or to spend more time spying on the world from that magical seat of his?

I'd hoped going out to fly would burn off some of my uneasy energy. Instead I'd ended up feeling even more wired than before. My pulse rattled through my veins as I headed down the street. I had too many questions jostling around with the worries in my head, and my mind was getting too foggy to sort them out.

My heart tugged me toward one of the other buildings along the main road. I hesitated outside the door to Thor's hall, but the longing inside me propelled me onward.

I didn't know where my place was here, now that Odin was back and calling so many of the shots. I had no idea what the future might hold for me or any of the gods I'd started to think of as mine. But the thunder god wasn't part of any of those conflicts. Thor came with no dark secrets, no furtive motives. He liked me, he wanted me, nothing more complicated about it than that.

It was easy to find his bedroom. The low rumble of his sleeping breath carried through the doorway. I slipped inside to find him sprawled on his back across a gigantic bed made to fit him. His brawny form almost filled the whole thing anyway, but that was fine. I didn't need much room.

I eased under the blanket and tucked myself in next to him, leaning my head against his shoulder. I hadn't meant to wake him up, but Thor shifted onto his side at my touch, his arm sliding around my waist.

"Ari?" he murmured sleepily.

I nestled closer to his muscled chest. A momentary panic clenched around my lungs—what was I doing here? Why had I given in to this impulse? What was he going to think it meant? But at the same time, the warmth of his body soothed my nerves.

This was Thor. He'd think it meant what I told him it meant.

And I needed this right now.

"I couldn't sleep," I said. "I just… I wanted to be somewhere I feel safe."

A pleased hum emanated from the thunder god's throat. He bent his head to kiss my forehead. "You'll always be safe here," he said.

I wasn't sure that was true, as much as he might have wanted it to be. At that moment, it felt as if it could be right, and that was enough. His hand stroked over my hair, and my eyelids drooped, and for the first time all night my body relaxed. In the temporary peace of Thor's arms, I drifted off to sleep.

# 10

*Aria*

I might have been nervous about falling asleep next to any of the gods, but there was something very appealing about waking up next to one of them.

I eased into awareness with Thor's tangy scent in my nose and those solid muscles pressed up against me. In my sleep, one of my legs had ended up tucked between his. Heat pooled between my thighs when I adjusted my position, and Thor let out a ragged breath. The evidence of his own arousal rested against my hip.

"Good morning," he said, his voice so thick with desire it sent an eager shiver down to my core.

"Very good," I said, and scooted up his body to capture his mouth with mine.

Thor kissed me back hungrily, but his hand stayed gentle as it skimmed down my back. It came to a stop at the waist of the jeans I hadn't bothered taking off when I'd crawled into bed with him. His thumb teased over the skin of my back with an electric tingle where my shirt had ridden up.

I traced my fingers up to his sculpted shoulders. My nipples hardened where they brushed against his chest through my shirt. I was just about to strip that shirt off so I could enjoy him skin to skin when a singsong voice called from outside.

"Oh, pixie! Ready for today's mission?"

From Loki's wry tone, I suspected he could guess that I wasn't particularly ready. But we *had* agreed last night that I'd help him track down another of the dark elves' gates today, and the sooner we got started on that, the safer Midgard would be. Protecting Petey was a heck of a lot more important than scratching this itch—as much as my body protested as I pulled away from Thor.

"Coming!" I hollered back.

The thunder god groaned as he sat up beside me. "Wretched giant," he muttered good-humoredly, but the words reminded me of Odin's remark about Surt yesterday. I hoped Loki's hearing wasn't quite good enough to have caught this one.

"You've survived how many eons without me around?" I said. "You can probably make it through a few hours more."

"That doesn't mean I *want* to," Thor said with a grin.

He looked so pleased with himself for that remark that I had to lean in for one more kiss. The sweep of his tongue over mine was a promise of more to come whenever we picked up where we'd left off.

Loki was standing on the tiled road outside the front door, his lips curled with amusement. "I apologize if I interrupted anything," he said, sounding not at all sorry.

"How did you even know where—" I started, and then remembered. I'd tried to take off on the gods once, after the dark elves had threatened Petey, and the trickster god had tracked me down without any trouble at all. He was the one who'd chosen me, who'd focused their powers when they'd summoned me and recreated me as a valkyrie, so the tie between the two of us ran even deeper than with the others.

Which wasn't really a bad thing. I couldn't think of anyone other than him more likely to get me out of a sticky situation, if I happened to find myself in another one I couldn't get out of on my own.

"I don't monitor you that closely," he said, motioning me along with me. "But you weren't at your own hall when I came calling there first."

"I had trouble sleeping," I said, as if he needed an explanation.

"And I'm sure joining the Thunderer in his bed was wonderfully restful."

I elbowed him in the arm, a little harder than I would have if he hadn't been an essentially immortal being. "It was, actually. A lot more than if I'd tried to snuggle up with *you*, I'm sure."

"Oh, I would have made sure you didn't regret that choice." His smile stretched wider as we headed down the road toward the bridge. He handed me a bundle of fabric. "I assume you haven't had breakfast yet."

The napkin fell open to reveal a roll filled with cheese. I dug into it, finishing it by the time we'd reached the glimmer of the rainbow. The pinch of hunger in my stomach subsided, but a different tightness gripped my gut. None of the other gods knew where Odin had gone last night, I didn't think. I wasn't sure what there was to tell yet, though. He hadn't done anything *wrong*.

"How are we going to do this?" I asked instead. The last time we'd gone searching for dark elves, I'd piggybacked Loki so he could speed us along while I used my valkyrie senses to search for the dark elves' distinctive oily energy. It wasn't the most dignified position, though.

"I suppose I could carry you over-the-threshold style," the trickster suggested with an arch of his eyebrows.

I wasn't sure that would be all that more dignified, and it'd definitely be more of a distraction. "Maybe we should stick with piggyback."

He chuckled. "Whatever suits you, pixie."

With his elbows hooked under my knees and my arms looped loosely around his shoulders, he leapt into the air. I'd forgotten how quickly he could move when he wasn't holding himself back for the rest of us. The wind warbled past us, tossing my hair. In just a few seconds, we'd crossed the rainbow bridge and were speeding through the sky above the Midgardian landscape that sprawled toward the haze of the horizon.

I let my awareness stretch out toward the streets and buildings we soared past. Flickers of energy touched my senses, most of it the soft brightness I felt from human beings. I caught one flash of something thicker, but only a single form. We were looking for somewhere that several dark elves had congregated around.

"I'm covering new territory, separate from the areas we perused last time," Loki said. "No point in retreading over old ground." It was the first time he'd spoken since we'd left Asgard. The muscles in his back shifted against my chest as he veered to avoid a looming mountain. Was he being quiet because of the exertion, or was something bothering him?

The sight of the land rushing away beneath us reminded me of last night's flight again. I rested my chin by the crook of Loki's neck, letting the spicy smell of him, like fire-warmed ginger and cardamom, wash over me. If anyone in Asgard knew better than to unquestioningly trust Odin's decisions, it was the god holding me.

"Do you really think that blocking the dark elves' gates is going to fix very much?" I asked.

He shrugged, shifting me closer to him as he did. "They're harming people. When it comes to that, you have to set down restraints, regardless of what their motives might be. I can't blame the gods for how they handled me after I completely committed to my role."

I didn't think I wanted to know what complete commitment

had involved. I hugged his shoulders a little tighter. "What did they do?"

"Oh, I was chained up to a rock in a rather dank cave with a snake dripping poison on my face. Not memories I like to dwell on."

I shuddered at even the vague picture his words drew up. The slight edge in his voice made me suddenly sure he'd *had* to dwell on those memories not that long ago.

"Muninn sent you back to that time, didn't she?"

"Briefly," he said. "I endured it then for Norns only know how long—a small second helping wasn't too heavy a burden." He gave my calf a light squeeze. "You don't need to worry about me, pixie. They did what they had to do. Just as we're doing what we have to do. What's driving the dark elves, we can sort out once they're no longer terrorizing the populace."

I did worry about him, whether he liked it or not. Especially when I knew how good the trickster was at hiding how deeply things affected him. I opened my mouth to say something along that line—and a trickle of viscous energy licked over me. I stiffened, and Loki glided to a half.

"Do you feel something?" he asked.

I focused all my attention on the direction that sensation had arrived from. We were poised over ruddy desert now. The impression of several pulses of dark elf life reached me from the base of a mesa to our left. As I traced them, a couple disappeared, and two new impressions emerged in their place. I swallowed hard.

"I think we've found our gate."

---

With Odin's blessing, the six of us were able to emerge from Asgard over the desert plain almost instantly from the rainbow bridge. We hovered above the dry earth and plateaus of reddish rock for a moment to get our bearings.

"So we just rush right in and blast them like before?" I asked. I agreed with everything Loki had said before, but at the same time the idea didn't sit completely right with me. The dark elves weren't going to be too keen on having any kind of conversation with us if we kept slaughtering them on sight.

Maybe they deserved it. On the other hand, that was probably how the gods had felt about Loki, and taking a heavy hand with him had led straight up to the end of the world, as far as I could tell.

"If they don't attack us, there won't be any need to blast anyone except the guards," Hod said beside me, but he turned his gaze my way. "Unless you've sensed something that suggests we should be more cautious in our approach?"

I couldn't offer anything except for my general sense that Odin knew a shitload more about this situation than he'd been sharing with us, but that wasn't concrete enough to hang a hat on. I wet my lips, willing the nervous patter of my pulse to even out. "No. Not so far."

"Let's move in then," Freya said, brandishing her sword with a gleam of her magic.

"When I give the battle cry, the five of us attack together," Thor reminded us. "We took them down last time without even knowing how to use our combined power. This time should be even easier."

I nodded. Baldur shot me a smile like a beam of light. "We've got this."

We swooped down toward the spot I'd indicated, the base of a ruddy mesa with a sprinkling of green on its high flat top. As we sped toward it, a dabbling of shadowed cave entrances came into view, along the ground and up to several feet higher. In the middle of them lay a craggy opening with that ominously deep blackness I'd felt from the gate on the other hillside.

If that wasn't enough to identify our target, several dark elves stood in the shadows of the rocky outcroppings around it. The daggers and spears clenched in their pale hands shimmered with the same fiery energy as those some of the elves who'd come at us last time had carried. Weapons charged with Surt's searing magic.

Thor bellowed, and I slashed my switchblade through the air. This time, none of that lightning I still didn't know how to consciously summon leapt from my fingers. But it didn't matter. I was flinging myself into the fight, and four heartbeats around me thumped in time with my intentions.

A swath of shadow-tangled fire crackled over the guards. Thor's hammer whirled into their midst trailing knives of light. The flames whipped faster as the hammer passed through them, and a dark blaze formed around Mjolnir itself. When the flaring of light and dark faded, the guards' bodies were scattered, smoking, across the dusty ground around the gate.

That small contingent hadn't stood a chance against all of us in sync.

We landed in a semi-circle, braced for a fresh wave of attack. I scanned the caves with my valkyrie sensitivity. "There are a few more here," I said. "It doesn't feel as if they're moving. I don't know what they're doing."

"Maybe lurking with more of those explosive contraptions," Thor muttered.

"All right then, dirt-eaters!" Loki called out in a tone that was somehow dark but jovial at the same time. "Show yourselves, and we won't be forced to burn you right out of your hidey-holes."

A shuffling sound reached my ears. We all turned toward it, and the shadow at Baldur's feet rippled. A clump of grass it touched shriveled. What the hell? My gaze jumped up and caught on the clenching of his hand. Was he okay?

I didn't have the chance to find out right then. Four rounded faces topped with black hair appeared at the entrance to one of the caves farther down the side of the mesa. All four of the dark elves had their hands raised in a gesture of appeasement.

"Please," the young man at the front said, his expression tight. "Just let us get back to Nidavellir before you close it up. That's all we want."

The woman just behind him snatched at his sleeve. "What? No. What's the point? We're better off staying here."

His eyes widened as he looked back at her. "But—it's home," he said quietly.

Her mouth opened and closed again. "Is anywhere really home now?"

She sounded so hopeless it wrenched at me. Freya clapped her hands. "Make up your minds what you want, or you won't be around long enough to get anything at all."

The man tugged at the woman's hand, and her head bowed. They and their two companions dashed through the gate's opening.

"They'll bring more guards!" Thor protested.

I readied my blade, but no one emerged from the darkness of the elves' realm. An uncomfortable ache crept through my chest.

Some of the dark elves were vicious. Some of them had delighted in hurting us. The woman who'd taunted me about Petey came to mind. But that bunch—they'd seemed so torn, so worn down...

My gaze slid toward Hod, who was still at my right. His mouth had curved into a frown.

"We sealed one before with our powers combined," Loki said, striding forward. "Let's see if we can conjure up the same effect again."

I shook off as much of the creeping dread as I could. "On Thor's cue?"

Thor raised his hammer, and his cry echoed through me and the others, shaking off most but not all of the heaviness that had settled around my heart.

# 11

*Hod*

My footsteps thudded dully across Valhalla's worn floorboards, as if they knew I wasn't meant to be there. I might be able to fend for myself as needed, even contribute to a larger battle, but no one would ever mistake me for a warrior. The lingering scent of now-stale mead made my nose itch. But this was the fastest way to get where I wanted to go.

There'd been plenty of drinking a couple hours ago. By the time we'd returned to Asgard, the spirit of victory had taken hold. We'd feasted and laughed, and if Ari had seemed a little more reticent than usual, I could have blamed it on the stress of the last few weeks.

I didn't actually believe that was all it had been, though. Since I'd turned in for the night, or at least attempted to, I'd had two voices cycling through my head. Our valkyrie's, saying, *We obviously can't assume we know everything just from how it looks.* And that of the dark elf woman hesitating by the gate: *Is anywhere really home now?*

Something wasn't right. Something more complex than the jealousy my father had blamed for the dark elves' betrayal. The sense of it gnawed at my bones.

I should have been able to go to Odin with that understanding. Should have been able to trust that his wisdom would guide us. But look where trusting him had gotten us so far. When was the last time he'd given us a straight answer? He'd been there to meet us when we'd stepped off the bridge with claps on our shoulders and that warm Allfatherly praise he could pull out when the situation called for it. Proud and benevolent.

What a crock. The bastard had ordered my death over a murder *he'd* all but orchestrated. To restore the fucking balance, to set the stage he wanted for Ragnarok—who in the realms knew? I doubted he'd ever own up to the truth.

I stopped at the smoky smell that clung to the hearth area and forced myself to exhale slowly. Forced my fingers to retract from where they'd started to dig into my palms.

That kind of anger wasn't going to serve me well. When this war was over, my father and I would hash out all of this, calmly but definitively. Odin wasn't going to listen to raging or ranting. I had to draw on the cool stillness of the shadows I carried with me.

Especially now. I traced my hand along the polished stones of the hearth and ducked beneath them. Cinders crunched under my boots. Silence closed in around me as my feet hit the rough bark of Yggdrasil's path.

What I was about to do might be foolhardy, but on the other hand it might very well be the least I could do. We needed answers. *I* needed answers. Who better than me to interact with the people who dwelled so much in darkness? Thor or Loki they'd have seen as an immediate threat. Baldur… I didn't think he'd have had any idea where to begin. And I wasn't going to ask any more of Ari, not when she'd already shouldered so many burdens that weren't meant to be hers.

She'd asked us to look beyond the obvious. I might not be able to see, but I could still do that much for the woman I loved.

I didn't need vision now. I was the Allfather's son, and his blood sang through my veins. The branches of the great tree resonated at different frequencies as I passed them, leaving a faint aftertaste on my tongue. A hint of grass and soil that was Midgard. The floral sweetness of Vanaheim, Freya's former home. A salty chill I knew was Niflheim, the realm of ice. And then a damp mossy impression that could belong only to Nidavellir, home of the dark elves.

I tested the branch with my feet and then walked cautiously along it. A quiver of energy emanated from the gate at its end. I paused there for a moment, dragging in a breath, gathering strands of shadow around me like a shield. Then I strode into the gate's embrace.

The air contracted around me, and a second later my boots hit uneven stone. A cool dampness congealed against my skin. Only the faintest current stirred the air around me. I reached out one hand, and it found a rough rocky wall just a couple of feet to my left.

The gate still quavered behind me. As long as I stayed where I was, I should be able to step right back into it when I needed to.

I wasn't alone. In the moment it took me to get my bearings, a shoe scuffed against the stone floor somewhere not far ahead of me. There was a faint rasp of breath. The air shifted minutely against my skin. They were gesturing to each other, I thought. Maybe still concealed in dark alcoves that would had hid them from anyone relying on sight.

The dark elves had fallen on Ari when she'd come this way looking for Odin. They'd slaughtered the three valkyries who'd come before her, from what she'd said of the vision Muninn had shown her as a threat. But attempting to kill a god was an entirely different matter. I might not have been able to offer much of an offensive on my own, but with my shadowy magic and the gate at my back, these mortal creatures weren't likely to hurt me either.

People, I reminded myself. Not creatures. They might have thrown themselves at us like animals more than once in the last few weeks, but they still had far more reason than a warg or a draug did. I wouldn't have come otherwise.

"What are you doing here, god of Asgard?" a sharp voice called out when I didn't move. "We have nothing of yours."

I turned my head toward the sound in as close a semblance of meeting the speaker's eyes as I could manage. "I'm not here to take or to attack," I said. "I'm here to learn. Who do you answer to? I'd like to speak to them."

Murmurs passed between the gate's guards—in the tongue of the dark elves, but I'd studied enough languages in my reading to recognize the words for *blind one*. They'd identified me. Good. That should work in my favor. Make me seem even less a reason for concern.

"Why should he come to you?" asked a different voice, this one female. "Maybe your friends are waiting on the other side of that gate to burst through."

"If we wanted to launch an assault, don't you think there'd be easier ways?" I said.

"You expect us to trust you an awful lot when you don't trust us at all," she retorted. The others muttered in agreement.

They might have a point. Simply arriving here braced for an attack wasn't all that great a show of good faith. My chest constricted, but I nodded. I'd come this far—I'd see my private mission through.

"I'll come with you to a meeting spot farther from the gate," I said. "But we will go slowly, and we will not go far. I'm already on your ground here."

More muttering, this round so low I couldn't make out the words at all. The man who'd spoken first let out a huff.

"Come," he said. "Then we'll see if the commander will meet you."

One of them touched my arm. I managed to detach it gently rather than yanking it away as I'd wanted to. "You walk," I said. "I can follow you well enough." I'd keep a better sense of space if I was navigating by my own powers.

I extended a length of shadow like a cane and treaded after the two guards who were leading me. My back prickled with the awareness of the few we were leaving behind. Technically I was now surrounded.

Between my free hand following the wall and the shadow cane testing the space around me, I formed a mental map in my head as I followed the scrape of the dark elves' feet. The tunnel curved to the left. We passed another cave opening at our right with a waft of slightly warmer air. After about five minutes, my guides stopped in a space that felt about the size of the dining room in my hall back in Asgard. My shadows flicked across walls sloping up toward a high ceiling.

"Wait here," the man said. The woman stayed, leaning against the wall with a rustle of her clothes, as he hustled off. I stood still and straight, fighting the impression that I might be making a horrendous mistake.

It seemed a long while that I waited. My mouth grew dry, my shoulders stiff from standing at attention. Then several sets of footsteps sounded in the passage where the guard had disappeared. The clink of metal reached my ears.

The commander had brought more guards. I had to hope they were intended for his protection and not to try to capture me.

They drew to a stop at the mouth of the passage. I suspected he hadn't even entered the room. His gravelly voice carried across the room to me.

"You wanted to speak to someone in charge. Here I am. I can't speak for all the dark elves, but I'm the best you're going to get. What do you want, god of darkness?"

I found I didn't know what to say other than the truth. Maybe Loki would have had some sly way of getting at the subject he wanted, but I didn't see much point in beating around the bush. Mostly I wanted to be done with this and gone from here, back to the open warmth and fresh winds of Asgard.

"I want to know why you've allied with Surt against us," I said. "Why you've been killing humans for him. Why you helped him capture Odin."

The commander let out a hoarse laugh. "And you figure I should tell you just because you asked?"

"I think something must have gone wrong. This kind of violence hasn't been the way of the dark elves in the past."

"'Gone wrong'," he repeated, with what sounded like a shake of his head. "And you have no idea. This is what it takes to bring you to our doorstep. What are you even offering if I tell you there is something wrong?"

"Perhaps we could help you set things right," I said. "In a way that doesn't require debasing yourself for that monster."

"Monster?" the commander scoffed. "The giant is the only one who's stood up to fight for our survival. While you and your fellow Asgardians lounge around enjoying your lovely city, forgetting the rest of us even exist."

My jaw clenched. "I'm here *now*. I'm listening now. Whether you take this chance is up to *you*. If the gods 'forget' you after this, you'll have no one to blame but yourself."

"Oh, so this is one more way to wash your hands of us, then? I'm not sure I even believe you don't know. Your great Odin was down here to witness the state of things for himself. And doesn't he see all when he looks down over the realms. But what has he ever cared for anyone but his own?"

The last words rang with bitterness so pungent it seemed to sear right through my skin. Right down to the smoldering anger I'd tamped down earlier. Before I'd thought through my response, it had already tumbled out.

"What makes you think he cares about even his own all that much?"

The commander paused for a moment. "Strange words from one of those who was very anxious to get him back."

He sounded skeptical, but there was something more open in his tone now. Something curious. I barreled onward.

"You know who I am, don't you? You know my story. You know who ordered my first death. I saved him, yes. That doesn't mean I'd defend his every action. I'm here *because* I don't trust every act he takes. Whatever's happened, whatever he might know about your complaints, he hasn't shared that with the rest of us. I swear to you, I want to know even if he doesn't."

Silence hung between us. When the commander spoke again, his voice was raw.

"I still say you're hundreds of years too late. That's how long it's been since the caves started collapsing. Should I tell you how much smaller our realm has become as the rock grows more brittle? How many have died with the ceiling of their homes crashing down over their heads? How the gardens we once maintained have begun to shrivel with rot? What it's like to hear the sobbing of children who are hungry or ill or homeless every day of your life?"

A wave of horror rolled over me. "I didn't know," I said.

"Of course you didn't. Why would you think about things like that off in your fancy halls where all is well? We made you your weapons and your armor for your war, and then when the end was over, what use did you have for us? When have any of your kind set foot in our realm of their own accord since Ragnarok?"

He stepped back with the tap of a spear-end against the rock floor. "We haven't lowered ourselves to anything. The world we live in brought us low. We're just trying to claw our way back up. When it's that or watch your people die, I wonder if you'd really choose any differently. Take *that* back to Asgard, Blind One."

# 12

*Aria*

In that first early hour after I woke up, when Asgard was quiet and the sun just rising over the majestic buildings, I could almost forget we were on the verge of war. I stopped outside my hall, soaking in the dawn light. Then I spotted a golden falcon plummeting from the sky.

My heart lurched. That was Freya's falcon form. Had she been on the patrol just now—had she seen something?

I hurried over, reaching her just as her feet touched the tiles outside her own gleaming hall. She shook off the falcon cloak with a swish of the golden hair it matched and swiped her hand across her eyes. She looked tired. The impression didn't detract from her beautiful face at all, but it was unnerving to see all the same.

"What happened?" I asked. "Is Surt making another attack? Do we need to wake everyone up?"

Freya turned her blue eyes toward me, blinking for a second as if she'd forgotten that anyone else might be around. She rolled her shoulders with a twist of her mouth that didn't quite make it into a smile.

"No attack," she said. "No sign of Surt. I was out searching for Hnoss—for my daughter."

"Oh." From her expression, she hadn't found the younger goddess. I groped for something to say. "I guess there must be a lot of places to look."

"Yes," Freya agreed. "And I've been to all of the ones I can think of. It's been so long… It's hard to say how her tastes might have changed. I suppose I don't even know for sure she's there to be found."

Her voice wobbled, just slightly but enough to make my throat close up. What would I have done if Petey had been lost to me, not only mentally but completely?

"I'm sure you'll find her eventually," I said. "You'd know if something had happened to her, wouldn't you? You must have the same kind of connection to her that told you and Thor and the others that Odin was still alive."

"Yes," she said. "As vague as that is." Her jaw twitched. She smothered a yawn. Had she been out flying all night? "I'd appreciate that more if it would lead me to her."

"It's something," I said. What I wouldn't have given for a tie like that to Petey.

It seemed insensitive to say anything like that, but Freya's gaze turned knowing. The pain this conversation had stirred up in me must have shown on my face—or maybe she could sense it in other ways. She'd told me once that being the goddess of love didn't only mean the romantic kind but all sorts. And if I loved anyone, it was Petey.

"I'm sorry," she said. "I wasn't thinking of how hard it must be for you to be separated from your brother, with the things that have been happening on Midgard. You could look in on him, couldn't you?"

"Not on my own," I said. "That's how the dark elves found out about him in the first place." Even if I'd asked Loki to take me to watch Petey for a few moments hidden by his sly magic, I wasn't sure that would make anything easier. I couldn't stay to protect him. It would only distract me from what I needed to do here.

It'd be selfish, asking for that, taking that time and energy just to comfort myself for a minute or two. When we'd stopped Surt, when we knew he wasn't a threat anymore, then I could go without risking Petey more.

Freya lifted her head at the sound of footsteps. Odin was walking toward us, slow and steady, his posture a little less imperious than usual. When he reached us, he set his hand gently on the small of Freya's back and inclined his head toward her. "Wife."

"Husband," she said in a wry tone, the corner of her mouth curling up. I'd never quite wrapped my head around the idea that the two of them were a couple, but seeing that brief intimacy between them made it suddenly real.

I might have had a lot of beefs with Odin, but I could feel in that moment without even trying that he cared about his wife.

"We were just discussing little ones beyond our reach," Freya said. "Although I suppose it's a bit much to call Hnoss 'little' at this point. You haven't seen any sign of her in your glimpses from on high, have you?"

The Allfather shook his head. "I would tell you as soon as I did."

Would he? I wasn't sure I believed *that*, no matter how soft his gaze had become as he looked at her. Mostly because a flinty gleam came back into his eyes the second they shifted toward me.

To be fair, we hadn't exactly ended our last serious conversation on a positive note.

"You look in from time to time on Aria's brother, too, don't you?" Freya said.

Odin's gaze stayed on me. "Is that what's weighing on the valkyrie? Surt and his minions have not ventured near him."

Yeah, I definitely didn't trust him to tell me if I had something to worry about there. He wanted me practicing with the gods and honing our powers, not fretting about mortals. "Good to know," I said with forced cheer.

"If it would ease your mind," he went in on his impenetrable voice, "I could let you see for yourself."

I would have thought I was prepared for anything he could have said, but that offer left me speechless. Freya blinked at him with unmistakable surprise of her own.

"From—from your seat, up there?" I checked, waving my hand toward his hall at the end of the road.

"Where else?"

"I thought you didn't let anyone up there."

Odin smiled a thin and equally impenetrable smile. "You are a special case, are you not? A valkyrie I had no hand in creating, who was never prepared to venture onto a battlefield. And yet it's through you that my sons and blood-sworn brother have found an even greater strength. If it will keep you from distraction later when it matters most, making a small exception is very little price to pay."

He had made exceptions before, hadn't he? He'd brought Loki there for their secret meetings about Odin's dark plans. A fact which didn't exactly reassure me. But Freya was nodding now, her own smile growing, as if she thought his offer was a delightful idea.

"You can see him without Surt's fiends ever knowing," she said. "You deserve that, after everything you've given up for us."

I hadn't realized she'd considered how much I'd given up in any detail. Trading Midgard for Asgard must have seemed like a huge step up to her. But maybe all that time worrying about her daughter had gotten her thinking about the many different factors that went into making a place a real home.

Odin was watching me, waiting. What would he make of it if I said no? Was that even a reasonable choice? I *did* want to see Petey, with every fiber of my being.

"All right," I said. "Can we go now?"

The Allfather turned with a flap of his great cloak and a beckoning gesture. He strode back toward his hall without checking to see if I was following. I hurried after him, tempted to unfurl my wings and show I could make it there faster than him if I really wanted to.

We went through his hall, past the front room where the group of us had paid our respects before and on into the silent depths between the stone walls. Odin turned through a doorway into a small room that held nothing but a ladder with thick oak rungs. A circular panel covered the ceiling above it. He climbed the ladder, pressed a few points on the panel too quickly for me to follow the movement, and slid it aside. With a short huff of breath, he vanished through the opening.

My heart thumped faster as I clambered after him. I crawled out onto the hardwood floor of an unsettlingly familiar room. Tall windows loomed in a ring around me beneath a high peaked ceiling. A tall wooden chair stood in their midst—a larger and more worn version of the throne-like seat he had in his meeting room below. The whole space smelled like the ozone after a storm.

I was rather intimately familiar with that chair, or at least the construct of it Muninn had brought into being. I'd leaned against it while Loki's lips and tongue had sent waves of pleasure through my core. I'd perched on one of those broad wooden arms with Thor inside me. The memories sparked a tingle between my legs and brought a flush to my cheeks.

Odin couldn't know about any of *that*, I was pretty sure. He'd been stuck in a cage in a cave in Muspelheim when it had happened. And it hadn't really been this room or this chair. Better to put all that out of my mind.

"How does it work?" I asked, setting my hand on the side of the chair. The wood was surprisingly warm.

"Sit," Odin said, tipping his head. "Settle in. You'll see better if you're comfortable."

Ah, yeah, I was not going to feel super comfortable as long as I was in this room with the Allfather. But I gave it my best shot, scrambling onto the smooth seat and shoving myself so I could lean against the back of it. My feet would have dangled like a little kid's, so I tucked them into a cross-legged position instead. My hands came to rest instinctively on the arms of the chair.

"Each of the windows looks out onto a realm," Odin said beside me. "Can you tell which one is Midgard?"

I studied each of the ones I could see in turn. Symbols I hadn't noticed before were carved into the stone above each window. That one, like a flame, was obviously Muspelheim. My gaze settled on one at my other side, a tree-like symbol that tugged at me. I pointed. "There."

"Well done, valkyrie." Odin nudged the chair, and it glided around to face that window. The view beyond the frame was hazy. As I squinted at it, trying to bring something into focus, a rushing sensation crept over me, as if a sharp breeze were blowing under my skin instead of over it. My breath caught at the base of my throat.

"Let yourself go," the Allfather said in a low voice. "I'll help you find your way." He touched my shoulder, his fingers settling into place with a steadying grip.

My pulse hammered even harder, but I gave myself over to the rushing sensation. Petey was out there somewhere. This feeling would take me to him.

The landscape beyond the window spiraled with flashes of color. My sense of the room around me faded away as if the window had drawn me to it, though I could still feel the hard surface of the chair beneath me. Lakes and hills and buildings whipped by, until my stomach churned with dizziness. Then the view jerked to a halt looking down over a small backyard surrounded by an actual white picket fence.

A boy was sitting at a patio table on the low deck, the sun gleaming in his blond hair, his hand clutched around a spoon he was digging into his cereal bowl. Petey. A gasp escaped me. He was right there, and so real—

The woman sitting across from him—his foster mother—gave him a soft smile as he scooped up the last of his breakfast. "Would you like any more, honey?" she asked.

"No, thank you," Petey said in his shyly sweet voice, but he smiled back. His blue-gray eyes shifted to the cereal box. He reached out and grazed his fingers over an image there. I peered closer.

It was a photograph of one of the trading cards he collected. The kind I'd always been sneaking him packs of when I'd figured our mom wouldn't notice. His brow knit as he looked at it, and my gut twisted.

"We already got the prize out when we first opened the box. Remember?" His foster mother got up, taking his bowl, and ruffled his hair with clear affection. "There'll be another one in the next box."

"I know," Petey said, but his expression stayed pensive. Confused. How much could he even remember after Hod had wiped me and the rest of the people he'd known from his mind? Did he know he'd used to have a big set of them, fat enough that he'd needed two rubber bands to hold them in place? Did he have a sense that *someone* had pored over them with him and brought new ones for him to unwrap?

He got up and went down the deck's single step onto the trimmed lawn. A plastic tub of toys sat next to the step. He grabbed a couple of plastic dinosaur figurines and started them marching into the grass that came up to their bellies. After a minute, he paused, looking down the lawn as if he expected a playmate to come join him.

*This one's a triceratops, so we'll call her Sera. I think she's best friends with your stegosaurus.*

*Of course she is. My toys are always best friends with yours, Ari. They get lonely when you can't come and see us.*

*I know, kiddo. I know. Soon, you'll get to see me all the time. I promise.*

God, how many times had I made promises like that? Promises there was no way in hell I could keep now. Heat built up behind my eyes.

At the same moment, Petey's chin wobbled.

"Why did you leave me all alone?" he whispered to whatever vague shapes of memories he had of times before.

A sob choked me, and the scene in the backyard hurtled away. I slammed into the back of the chair so hard a jolt of pain shot up my spine. But it was nothing compared to the ache clutching my chest.

"Let me see him again," I sputtered. "I need to—I have to—"

"I think you've seen enough," Odin said, in a voice that wasn't quite gentle but wasn't accusing either. "He's safe. He's well looked-after. Isn't that what was important to you?"

My hands clenched against the arms of the chair. "Yes," I had to say. It was.

I'd also wanted him to be happy. He was away from Mom and her ranting and neglect. He was away from her boyfriends with their bruising hands.

But he'd looked so fucking *sad.*

# 13

*Aria*

The shakes started before I'd made it out of Odin's room with the ladder. I managed to hold myself stiffly in control as the Allfather showed me out of his hall. I couldn't tell what reaction he'd been looking for in me, but I'd be damned if he saw me break down.

I stepped out onto the marble tiles, and a tremor crept across my shoulders. I spun and hurried around Odin's hall, past the few smaller ones that were no longer occupied along the edge of the city, and into the narrow strip of forest that stretched between the city and the apple orchard that had once granted the gods their immortality.

When the trees had closed around me, I sank down to the ground with my back against a pine. A bird fluttered past through the soft warmth of the morning, and the scent of green growing things filled my lungs. None of it was enough to settle my nerves. I buried my face in my hands and breathed with a rasp, sucking air past my palms. My whole body shuddered.

*Get it together, Ari. You've been through worse. So much worse.*

But I couldn't erase Petey's thin voice from my memory. That plaintive question, that he couldn't even have known who he was asking. All he knew was *someone* had left him behind, without any ties to the life he'd had before.

*I'm sorry,* I thought at him, as if there was any chance he'd hear me. *I'm so fucking sorry.*

Even grappling with my tangled feelings, I didn't miss the crunch of footsteps approaching. My head jerked up, my body tensing. I forced it to relax as much as I could manage, grateful that no actual tears had slipped out to redden my eyes.

Loki ambled between the trees. He'd picked a deep purple tunic this morning, one that made his ivory skin look even paler and his hair flame even brighter. For about half a second I hoped he'd just been going for a stroll and he might not even notice me, but then he met my gaze so nonchalantly I knew he'd come out this way specifically to find me.

He meandered the rest of the way over and propped himself against the ash tree opposite my pine. "Ari," he said with a nod of greeting. His tone was light, but his eyes were searching.

"Loki," I replied. Despite my best efforts, my voice creaked a little. The strain of too much withheld emotion.

"You paid a visit to the Allfather, I noticed," he remarked.

My hackles rose instinctively. "I thought you said you weren't tracking my every move."

He gave me a baleful look. "Why do you assume I was monitoring *you*?"

Oh. He'd been keeping an eye on all of the comings and goings at Odin's hall? I couldn't really blame him for that, considering what the king of the gods had put him through.

"He offered to let me see Petey from his seat," I said. "I haven't, not for real, since we left him with the foster family. It was a way to check in on him without throwing off our plans or putting him in danger..."

I hadn't realized how tight Loki's expression was until it softened. "Oh, pixie," he said. "Of course you had to see." He cocked his head. "What happened? If he *had* been in danger, you'd already be halfway across Midgard to save him. But you hardly look pleased."

I rubbed my temples. "I don't know what I was expecting. Somehow I thought he could just move on from the blank slate we left him with. But he knows he's missing something. How could he not? We left a huge black hole in his memory. And it's weighing on him. I could see that."

"What did Odin make of all that?"

"I don't know." I threw my hands in the air. "What does he make of anything? He just told me that I should be glad Petey's safe and not to dwell on it or something. He didn't seem concerned, if that's what you mean."

"No. Of course he didn't." Loki let out a ragged laugh, and I realized his stance had gone rigid again. "That's how he always likes us," he went on in a distant voice that barely sounded as if it were directed at me. "Dangling over a precipice. Never quite on solid ground." His mouth closed with a snap. His amber eyes glimmered with a sudden spark. He held out his hand to me. "Come with me."

"What?" I said, easing myself onto my feet. "Where?"

"Just come." He grasped my fingers and tugged me into his arms. The next thing I knew, he'd taken off into the air with me braced against him, my head by his shoulder, my hip against his waist.

I had to loop my arm around the back of his neck to hold myself steady as the ground whipped by beneath us. "Loki! What are you doing?"

"Refusing to stand down," he muttered, whatever that was supposed to mean. The lean muscles in his arms were flexed hard where they were wrapped around me. His eyes were still blazing, his mouth set in a grim line as we soared onward, as much creating the wind as chasing it. The sharp heat of his fiery power seeped from his body into mine. I wasn't sure anything short of an incoming jumbo jet could have thrown him off course, and maybe not even that.

Sometimes I could almost forget I was dealing with gods. Not now. All I could do was cling on and see where we ended up.

We raced over the rainbow bridge and across the land below, passing over the terrain so quickly I couldn't make out more than a blur. It wasn't that long before Loki slowed. He came to an abrupt halt but landed with his usual grace on a rooftop on a residential street.

A familiar rooftop. A familiar street. I'd perched here with Hod to watch Loki and Baldur escort Petey into his new home: that two-story house with light blue clapboard I was staring at right now. He might still be playing with his dinosaurs in the backyard. It couldn't have been more than an hour since I'd seen him from Odin's high seat.

My stomach flipped over, and my legs wobbled under me as the trickster set me down. "Loki?"

"No one can see us," he said. "Not a single dark elf eye will make us out. But if you want, we can let your brother see you. You can tell him—whatever you like. Whatever you need to. Be there for him. Damn the rest."

My jaw dropped. I turned from Loki to the house, a queasy sensation uncoiling in my gut.

I'd thought about asking him to bring me here, concealed, so many times. I'd dreamed about walking back into Petey's life. The longing shot through my heart with a painful throb.

I took a step toward the edge of the roof, and my stomach churned harder. I swallowed thickly. The longing was there, but so were all the reasons I'd had to hesitate.

"I can't," I said. "I hate what we did to him, but I hate what could have happened to him if we hadn't even more. It's better... It's better that he be sad than be dead. He'll get past it. It's only been a week." He'd get past me, the me he couldn't remember, in time. A fresh lump rose in my throat. "I have to do what's best for him, and what's best for him is putting all my energy into stopping Surt."

Loki slid his arm around my shoulders. The almost manic urgency that had seemed to be driving him earlier had dissipated. I couldn't help leaning into him, letting him take some of my weight. My whole body abruptly felt very heavy.

"And they thought the valkyrie I'd bring them wouldn't be noble," he muttered.

I made a dismissive sound. "You picked someone like you, didn't you? How many times did you ignore what *you* wanted for what you thought was the greater good?"

That hoarse laugh escaped him again. "Maybe I was trying to rewrite a little of that history today." He stroked his thumb up and down the side of my arm. "Are you sure?"

The word caught in my throat for a second, but I knew what I had to say. "Yeah. I'm sure."

He bowed his head toward mine, his lips grazing my forehead. "Do you mind if I show you something else, while we're down here?"

"Of course not. What is it?"

"It'll be easier to explain when we're there."

I let him heft me up piggyback-style this time, now that I had more choice in the matter. The trickster god set off at a somewhat less frantic pace, but the city fell away behind us in the space of a few beats of my heart. Loki sped on, over fields and forests, towns and more cities, until a broad expanse of shimmering blue came into view ahead of us.

The trickster came to earth on a rocky beach. We were immediately buffeted by a wet salty wind. There was no one else in sight, just us and the gray stones and the paler gray of the ocean.

"You know I can change my shape," Loki said after a moment of silence.

"You demonstrated that very vividly the first day we met," I said, remembering the way he'd shifted his face to look like a woman's. Since then I'd also seen him transform into a wolf nearly big enough to rival the wargs we'd battled.

He nodded. "It seems because of that… when I have children, they don't always turn out quite as you'd expect."

I glanced at him. "How do they turn out?"

He gazed across the sea for a minute, his expression as serious as I'd ever seen him. "I had another wife, a giant wife, before my wife in Asgard—ages ago. She gave me three children. One of them, the girl, looked human enough, but deathly-dark all down one side. My sons came in the form of a wolf and a serpent. All of them as aware and intelligent as you or me, mind you."

I'd seen enough craziness in the last month to take that information in stride. "Where are they now?" I asked, thinking of Freya's quest to find her daughter.

"My daughter, you could say, was the lucky one," Loki said. "The gods couldn't stand the sight of her, so Odin cast her down to the realm of the dead, to oversee the souls who find themselves there."

He swiped his hand across his mouth, his voice going carefully flat. "My sons died in Ragnarok. Attacking the gods by my side. They weren't really monsters, you know. But that was how Asgard saw them, how Asgard treated them… They chained up Fenrir, the wolf, and kept him prisoner. And Jormungandr, the serpent, they hurled into this ocean on pain of death should he emerge. A promise Thor saw through when the time came."

I winced. "I'm sorry," I said. How much of his children's torments had Muninn taunted him with?

I turned to him, hugging him. Loki tipped my face up with a brush of his fingers over my jaw, and I welcomed his kiss. With the chilly wind whipping around us, for a moment it felt as if he were the only warmth in the whole world.

When I drew back, he was smiling. "It's all ancient history now, as they say," he said, his usual flippant tone returning. "I'm told it builds character to remind oneself of sacrifices made and pains endured."

No, he'd brought me out here for more than that. "Are you okay?" I asked.

He dismissed the question with a flick of his finger. "My dear Ari, when am I ever anything else? Come on now, I've had my fill of playing the maudlin for today. You want to defeat Surt? We'd best get back to our training before the others sound the alarm."

He scooped me onto his back easily, and I rested my head against his neck as he leapt up toward the sky. My gut was knotted tight. He'd snapped himself out of his melancholy, but I didn't believe for a second that the "ancient history" he'd talked about didn't haunt him.

If this was the message he'd wanted to convey to me, he could consider it received: It'd be over my dead body before Petey faced even a fragment of what Odin's scheming had done to Loki and his children.

# 14

*Baldur*

I was halfway to the practice field when my father's path converged with mine. I glanced at Odin as he fell into step beside me. His cloak looked even more faded than usual, the peak of his hat more crumpled, but his brown eye gleamed brightly.

"My son," he said with the warmth he always offered me. I'd never really thought before about the fact that he didn't use the same tone with everyone. Not even with my twin. But now, after the raw conversations Hod and I had been propelled into, the difference niggled at me. Why should I get that preferential treatment?

"Father," I replied with a dip of my head.

"How do you feel your training is coming along?" he asked. "This joint power the four of you have found, is it coalescing?"

"Five," I said automatically. "The five of us."

"The valkyrie. Yes. Although it seems she is more of a conduit than a force in herself."

I choked on a laugh. He wouldn't have said that if he'd ever seen

Aria in real action. "She might not have godly strength or magic," I said, "but she's a fighter to be reckoned with. She's had much less time than the rest of us to stretch her powers."

Odin hummed to himself. A skeptical sound. Part of me wanted to insist he give Aria her due respect, and another part balked. Deserved or not, I had my father's favor. Did I really want to find out what it might be like to lose it?

Of course, even with his favor, he'd let me die and linger for ages in that void, as part of the grand plan he'd never bothered to share with the rest of us. A ripple of shadow passed through me, bleeding tendrils from my fingertips. I swiped them away against my shirt, feeling the threads fray in their wake.

This wasn't the time for bringing up all that history. Not when the giant who'd once slaughtered so many of us meant to repeat the job. I brought my mind back to Odin's question.

"I think the cohesion between us is becoming more instinctive," I said. "For now we've been relying on one of us—usually Thor—giving our cue to move in unison, but the moments of natural harmony are coming more frequently. Freya has been providing some 'surprise' elements to keep us on our toes."

My father chuckled. "I can imagine she's enjoying that. From what I've gathered, you handled your last encounter with the dark elves well. Do you think you'd soon be ready to confront a larger foe?"

Our last encounter with the dark elves, when we'd sealed the second gate on Midgard, had felt far too easy. Less like a battle and more like an extermination. The shadows seeping from behind my ribs twitched. Every day, more of them wriggled free, searing through the light that normally filled my chest.

"It's difficult to say," I said. "Do you think we need to take the battle to Surt already? We've hindered his supply of draugar soldiers. I'm not sure it'd be wise to launch an offensive on his home ground until our combined powers are completely in sync." And perhaps not even then. The five of us—seven, if Freya and Odin joined the fight as well—against the giant of flames and his entire army in the realm he'd claimed as his own? Surely we needed more preparation before we attempted that.

"The longer he remains active, the greater the scourge," Odin murmured in his vague way. "Well, I will see your progress for myself, I think."

The others were already standing in the practice area where the field's grass was alternately trampled, gouged, and burnt from our previous efforts. Several physical targets stood at various points around our group, but after the number we'd destroyed, Freya had taken to conjuring the illusion of other attackers around those with her magic. "More fighting, less crafting," she'd said yesterday.

Odin halted at the edge of the field as I loped over to join my companions. Thor and Loki were talking, Thor letting out a bellow of laughter at something the trickster had said. Aria shot me a welcoming smile. My twin smiled too, but Hod's eyes stayed dark. I studied him, wondering if he looked grimmer than usual or if I'd simply become more affected by his moods now that I wasn't wrapping myself in a gauze of dreaminess to escape anything that might provoke distress.

"The gang's all here now," Freya called from the sidelines. "Shall we get started?"

The truth was that despite my hesitation with my father, the style of combat we'd been discovering between the five of us was becoming second nature. My gaze caught Thor's and then Loki's as Aria took her position in our midst. A tingle of connection passed over my skin from every direction. I felt as much as heard our breaths fall into rhythm with each other, our movements start to sync up without any conscious effort.

It was becoming natural here on the practice field where we'd worked on that harmony so much. How organically would we slide into these patterns with an army of draugar coming at us?

Hod came up beside me, and along with the sense of our unified connection, a shudder of tension wafted off of him. I frowned. Something was bothering him, clearly. He was trying to stand loosely, but that tension was wound through the muscles of his shoulders and down his back. Was it only having our father here watching us that had affected him? He might not be able to see Odin, but I had no doubt he'd picked up the Allfather's voice as we'd approached.

I could hardly ask him about that with Odin right there to overhear. Later I could offer my ear, if he wanted to talk. It was the least I could offer after how long I'd spent avoiding any of the conversations that might have given him a little more peace.

We arranged ourselves before the first target. Freya's conjured figures wavered into being around it, a swarm of filmy dark elves. Thor raised his hammer as our signal, and we all leapt forward.

I never knew quite how the light I cast out would twine with the others. Our magic seemed to find its way of its own accord. This time it collided with Loki's slash of fire, sparking the flames brighter and hotter. Thor's hammer flew through them, sending them even higher with a crackle of lightning and emerging with a glowing blaze to smash into the one solid target. The illusionary figures hissed out of existence in the wake of the flames.

Freya wasn't done yet. I'd only just registered our "victory" when several bolts of magic screamed down at us from above. We whipped around with a common heartbeat. A flash of lightning burst from Aria's hands, smaller than Thor's but still potent. I hurled a blazing glow upward in unison with the others and watched those beams spin around Hod's shadowy missile before both split apart to shatter through our "attackers."

The torn strands of Freya's magic dispelled as they cascaded harmlessly down. Thor let out a triumphant shout and raised his hand for a high five that Aria jumped up to return. From across the field, Odin applauded us with a slow clap.

"This is how we'll defeat those villains," he said in a pleased voice. "See how much farther you can hone that power."

He turned to meander off again, and Freya picked that moment to hurl a couple of the other straw targets our way. I flinched and spun at the rustling, the others jerking around in turn.

Thor's shout to direct us was more instinctive than calculated, but it served as a cue all the same. We blasted the targets together. Singed straw rained down over us.

"Villains," Hod repeated under his breath as he swiped at a few shreds of straw that had clung to his shirt. He turned his head the way Odin had gone, cocking it as if listening. Our father had already disappeared between the city's buildings.

"He's gone," Aria said. "What's bothering you?"

Hod's jaw set. He swiveled back to face the rest of us. "I went down to Nidavellir to talk to the dark elves this morning."

"What?" Thor exclaimed, and Aria's eyes widened.

Loki's eyebrows arched. "So, Mr. Doom and Gloom does have a few tricks up his sleeve."

Hod grimaced in the trickster's direction.

"What did you find out?" I asked, my chest tightening. It obviously wasn't anything *good*, from the way he was behaving.

"Oh, there's resentment there for sure," he said. "They didn't apologize for what they've been doing. But it didn't sound as if they were all that happy about the choices available to them either. The realms have become even more unstable than we might have thought. The caves of Nidavellir are crumbling. The dark elves barely able to grow enough food to sustain themselves. The situation for them is clearly 'Kill or die,' and I'm not sure I can blame them for taking the former route. Surt's the only one offering them any way out."

"Is there anything we *can* do?" Aria said.

Hod's head bowed. "I don't know. I don't know why the realms are failing at all. But if anyone does, it's Odin, and he's pretending he doesn't know a thing about it. He must have some idea. We brought the matter up with him directly, and he acted as if they had no reason other than spite."

He bit off the last word, his stance tensing even more. The darkness twisted through my innards spasmed.

My hands clenched against that chilling sensation. A fragment tumbled from my fingers anyway, dappling the grass at my feet with rot. My heart lurched, but everyone's attention was still fixed on Hod.

"If he knew—" Freya started.

Hod lifted his head toward her. "Do you honestly think there's any way he doesn't?"

Her voice faltered. She pulled her posture up straighter. "I'll speak to him. I don't need to tell him that you went behind his back. I can simply urge him to consider other possibilities, to dig deeper, to be open at least with me."

And we'd see how far that got us. A sudden sense of hopelessness pierced my chest. What could we accomplish when even the one who should be guiding us might be leading us astray?

"We should finish our training," I heard myself saying without having thought through the words. "We're all set up now, and we will still need to fight. Then—then we can discuss how to proceed."

"I'll agree with that," Thor said gruffly, which seemed to settle things. We shifted, a little more begrudgingly than before, toward the next target. Freya bit her lip and motioned with her arm to summon forth more of her magic. Not dark elves this time. draugar.

The sight of their bloated bodies, even hazy as the conjured forms were, dredged up a wrenching memory from Muninn's prison: that moment when Hod and I had knelt by my own slumped body, and it had risen like a draug itself, accusing my twin with every dark thought I'd tried to burn away.

Thor gave a shout. We all lunged forward. I whipped out a

scorching bolt of light—and the dark tendrils inside me wrenched out with it. The blaze stuck the target as I'd intended, but as it flew it flung the dark mass to the side. The tendrils smacked into Loki's calf with a searing hiss.

The trickster yelped and fell back on his ass as he pawed at the clotted energy clinging to him. Blood was already seeping through the leg of his slacks. My pulse stuttering, I threw myself to him, summoning healing light into my shaking hands.

"What in the nine realms was that about, Freya?" Loki sputtered. "*I'm* not the sodding target."

My shoulders stiffened, but I knew it was too late now. I couldn't hide this any longer.

"It wasn't Freya," I said as my magic melted away the trickster's wound and the vicious energy that had dealt it. "It was me. I didn't mean to—it slipped out before I could catch it."

Everyone was staring at me now, including Loki. "If you're covering for someone, that's a poor show," he said. "That shadowy thing didn't look like anything that could have come from you. It could have been your twin's doing, though."

"No." I tipped back on my heels. The darkness inside me writhed even more insistently than it had before. It took no effort at all, when I wasn't fighting to suppress it, to raise my hand and let the tendrils seep from my palms.

"Baldur," Aria murmured.

"In my death," I said, before anyone had to ask. "In the void. It was dark and cold and—after a time it clawed its way into me. I thought I left it behind when I was reborn, but I never let myself look all that carefully. I— After Muninn— I can overcome it. I just have to find the right way."

I couldn't quite bring myself to look at any of them, not even my twin. So many threats before us, and I'd brought one right into our midst inside me.

# 15

*Aria*

Baldur looked so torn up that my chest constricted. I went to him, setting my hand on his shoulder where he was crouched next to Loki. "We'll figure it out," I said.

"Yes," Loki said, pushing himself to his feet and brushing himself off. "Perhaps we should hold off on further practice sessions until you've gotten that little hitch under control." He glanced at Freya. "You could have that chat with your husband."

Freya's mouth tightened, but she nodded.

"Do you need anything from the rest of us?" Thor asked his younger brother. "If I can help somehow—"

"No," Baldur said quietly. His voice had lost almost all of its usual brightness. "But thank you. It's in me. I'll see what I can do to better contain it."

Loki clapped Thor on the back. "Why don't you come with me? I can think of a few other ways we might determine what's shaking up the realms. But people always seem to answer questions faster when you and your hammer are around."

There wasn't much humor in Thor's chuckle, but he followed Loki off the field. Hod knelt down at his twin's other side.

"What does it feel like?" he asked. "The darkness. Where is it coming from?"

"I'm not sure." Baldur touched the middle of his chest. "These cold strands of it just keep seeping out from somewhere inside me. They're too thick for my natural light to burn them away."

A thought struck me, so sudden and unnerving my throat closed up. "It isn't because—I encouraged you to explore other sides of yourself. To let yourself be wicked. Could that be why—"

Baldur was already shaking his head. He clasped my hand, lifting his bright blue eyes to meet my gaze. "This isn't your fault, Aria. Not at all. Whatever's in me, it's been there for a long time. I needed to face my past, and this is part of it. I just didn't realize there'd be so much of it, so deep, to overcome."

"And I doubt our father will be of much use," Hod muttered with a sharper edge than I usually heard from him. "For all we know, this is part of his great plan somehow."

The thrum of tension I'd felt from him earlier shivered over me. Baldur rubbed his forehead, his own expression taut. I groped for an idea to suggest, a course of action that gave me something to do other than walking away and leaving them to deal with this mess on their own.

"Maybe containing it isn't the right answer," I said, straightening up. "If you've got too much bottled up inside you, then why not let some out? You should be able to control it more if you're sending it out on purpose." I glanced over at the gleaming walls of Valhalla to the side of the field. "I get the feeling we might all enjoy blowing off some steam in a more concrete way."

Hod raised his eyebrows. "What did you have in mind, valkyrie?"

He'd used to call me that as if to distance himself from me.

Now, the way he said the word sounded like a caress. A compliment that reminded me of all the powers I had in this new life I'd been given.

"It seems to me there are an awful lot of weapons in the hall of warriors that've been so sadly neglected," I said, allowing myself a smile. "What do you say we hack a few things up with our hands instead of all this magic here and magic there?"

Hod still looked skeptical, but he got up too. He offered his hand to his twin, who took it and pushed himself to his feet. We tramped across the field to Valhalla.

The swords and spears hanging on the walls glinted as ominously as they always had. I looked them over and settled on a short sword with a slightly curved blade and a leather-bound grip. The muscles in my arm flexed with my experimental swing. The sword wasn't as comfortable as my familiar switchblade, but it had a satisfying heft to it. Maybe it was time I moved on to more powerful weaponry.

Baldur detached a sword of his own, longer than the one I'd picked with a silver sheen that suited his natural light. It sang through the air when he gave it a whirl. For the first time since I'd seen him this morning, a hint of a smile curved his lips.

"I'm not sure giving the blind man sharp weaponry is the wisest idea," Hod said dryly. He ran his fingers tentatively over the blades mounted on the wall.

"We'll give you plenty of space," I said. There was a clear area in front of the hall's main doors, a span of some twenty feet before the rows of tables started. "If you feel like you want to do some hacking too."

"The idea *is* appealing. I'm thinking short would be better in this particular case." He tugged off a dagger that was only the length of his forearm and took a careful jab at the air in front of him. "I can give us something to fight, too."

At a wave of his other hand, shadows slipped across the floor and rose into blank human-like forms in front of each of us. Mine sidestepped when I did, following my movements.

"It'll stay with you," Hod said. "So I don't have to keep track of where you are. Do whatever you like to it. It's only shadow—you can't hurt it."

I swiped my sword through the figure's arm, and a wisp of darkness sloughed off with a hiss. Nice. I caught Baldur's eye, and he raised his own sword. His posture went rigid for a moment. Then a stream of darkness trickled from his palm down the blade.

I couldn't help watching as he lunged at the shadowy target. Something flashed in his eyes, fearful but determined. He cut straight through the figure's torso, the darkness he'd expelled coursing across the blade's path. The form shuddered, bits of shadow scattering the floor, and reconstructed itself.

Baldur swung the sword again and again, carving up the shadowy form with glints of steel and wafts of his own darkness. His expression became fiercer with each heft of the blade. A sheen of sweat formed on his forehead, dampening his white-blond hair. The emotions radiating off him were so fraught my heart started to ache.

He'd spent so long bottling up *everything* that had ever bothered him. I suspected it terrified him, letting any of that turmoil out. But what mattered to him most was making sure he never hurt any of us again, even by accident.

I turned back to my own target and gritted my teeth. *Slash.* That was for Odin and his secrets and his condescending tone. *Slash.* That was for Surt plotting to slaughter us all. *Slash.* That was for Muninn and the awful memories she'd thrown in our faces. The growing burn in my muscles brought a rush of relief.

A grunt across the room drew my attention. Despite his hesitation, Hod was tackling his own target, his feet planted in place in the section of the room he'd taken, several feet from Baldur and me. In the moment, my gaze found him, his expression was nothing but smoldering rage. He stabbed and wrenched his dagger through the shadows he could only have felt, not seen. His chest heaved with ragged breaths.

The ache around my heart squeezed tighter. I lowered my sword and set it on the top of the nearest table. Circling the benches, I came around to Hod's side of the room.

I was worried about startling him, but he must have heard the pad of my feet. He jabbed at his target a couple more times and then turned toward me. His face was flushed, his dark green eyes glittering with silent emotion.

"Are you all right?" I asked. I hadn't realized *he* might need the release quite this much.

He rotated the grip of the dagger in his hand as his jaw worked. "I'm fine," he said. "I've lasted this long under the Allfather's rule. I… I just don't know if I can protect *you* from whatever he might lead us into."

The ache turned into a lump that rose to my throat. "Hod…"

"This was good, though," he went on in a more casual tone, before I had to figure out what to say. "Let it out, like you said. I do feel more grounded. Is the sparring helping you, brother?"

Baldur had come to a stop at our voices. He nodded, wiping at the sweat on his forehead. "I think some of the darkness really is gone. It's less tangled up inside me right now—less twisted." He paused, and the corner of his mouth slanted down. "I wish I knew that it wouldn't come back. That this is all there is, and once I'm rid of it, I'm done."

That comment sent a different sort of twinge through me. It wasn't very long ago that I'd admitted to Loki how scared I'd become of the shadows inside *me*, the ones that could reach out through my body to claim lives as a valkyrie was supposed to. I'd managed to find a sort of peace with that power, hadn't I?

"Would it really be so bad if you couldn't get rid of all of it?" I said. "It doesn't have to hurt anyone. Hod carries darkness with him, and he decides how it acts." His shadows had proven they could bring pleasure just as easily as they could pain. The memory of them gliding over my skin sent a warmer shiver to my core. "You don't think of him any less for having it, do you?"

Baldur set down his sword, his mouth twisting but his gaze fond as he looked at his twin. "Of course not. But that's in his nature. It's simply a part of him. In me…"

"It isn't that different." A new urge came over me, with the release of some of that frustration I'd been carrying. I touched Hod's arm first, leaned in to brush my lips against his shoulder. His skin tasted faintly smoky. "And it's not a burden, something meant to be hidden away. It can be beautiful too." The next words wrenched a little coming out, a nervous tremor passing through my body, but I clamped down on that fear. "I love Hod's darkness."

Hod's voice came out thick with feeling. "Ari."

He cupped my face, and I gave myself over to his kiss. To everything he felt, dark and light, even if the tenderness of his touch stirred up enough longing in me to scare me. Then I moved from him to Baldur.

"I could love the darkness in you too."

The glow that came into the light god's eyes was nothing but hungry in that moment. His hand came to rest on my waist as I stepped right up to him, his breath hitching faintly as I pressed my mouth to his.

I soaked in the heat of his body against mine, the ripple of his muscles as his other arm came around me to pull me even closer. He angled his head to deepen the kiss, his tongue teasing over mine.

Desire flared low in my belly. I kissed the light god harder, running my hands up under his shirt to trace the lines of those muscles skin to skin. A groan escaped him.

He tipped my head back, and his mouth found the sensitive skin at the crook of my neck. His hands eased up my sides, spreading a shimmer of pleasure everywhere they touched. With a hoarse breath, he yanked off my tank top. A flick of his thumb loosened my bra.

Baldur brought his hand to my breast, a glow lighting on his palm. I whimpered as it tingled over my skin. A flicker of shadow joined it, a brief jolt of cold amid the heat. My nipple pebbled at the contrasting sensations. I didn't jerk away, but pushed into his touch encouragingly.

With a needy sound, he ducked his head to suck the tip of my breast into the wet heat of his mouth. I arched into him, a gasp slipping from my lips. But at the same time, my exposed skin prickled with the desire to be touched even more. To be encircled on both sides by this affection I'd never have dreamed I could have deserved.

Baldur worked my nipple over with his tongue, and I clutched the nape of his neck. I reached my other hand toward Hod. "Please. I want you more than witnessing today."

He moved to us so quickly I guessed I probably hadn't needed the plea. The dark god's lips skimmed the side of my neck, his body pressing against me from behind. "Like this?" he murmured, his voice full of so much promise I all but quaked with longing.

"Yes. Oh!" His hand closed over my other breast, his thumb teasing the tip with another cool flicker of shadow. Baldur suckled me harder, and Hod turned my cheek so he could reach my mouth with his, and right then I was floating on nothing but pure bliss.

Bliss, and the burning for even more. Baldur's hand slipped down between my thighs. I cried out as he eased his fingers over my core through my jeans, spreading another warm glow flecked with chilly exhilaration in their wake. Hod released my mouth to kiss a path down my bare spine, and I tugged Baldur up to meet me for another kiss. My body rocked wantonly with the motion of his hand. My fingers trailed down his chest to the bulge behind the fly of his slacks.

He groaned again. I stroked him up and down, and a very specific wanting came over me.

I could do this. I wasn't a victim anymore. What I wanted, I could take—and give. The past didn't matter if I didn't let it.

My hand fumbled with the button and the zipper. Then I was tucking my fingers inside his loose boxers to circle the silky hard length of him. Baldur bucked into my grasp, his breath stuttering against my lips.

I pulled my mouth from his and wrenched up his shirt with my free hand. As I kept stroking him, I pressed kiss after kiss down the length of his torso. "Aria," he murmured when he must have realized where I was heading.

Hod sank onto his knees as I fell to mine. He fondled both of my breasts as he tested his teeth against my shoulder blade, right at the spot where my wings would have emerged.

A fresh wave of pleasure rolled through me. I swiped my tongue around Baldur's navel. Then I dipped my head and closed my lips around the head of his cock.

Baldur braced himself against the table behind him, his fingers tangling in my hair. I could feel him holding himself back from plunging deeper into my mouth. Every inch of him hummed with longing.

I slicked my tongue along the underside of his erection, drinking in the summer-sweet taste of him. As he shuddered, another hard length brushed my ass. Hod needed attention just as much as his brother. Hell, *I* was still burning to be filled between my legs as well as my mouth.

I shifted my ass back against him as I sucked Baldur down deeper. Hod nipped my back, and one hand dropped to the waist of my jeans. He trailed his fingers over my skin, tracing the hem of my panties, until I tugged his hand to my fly to show him I was all for this direction.

With a flutter of movement from his fingers and his shadows combined, he peeled my clothes down to my thighs. His fingertips circled my clit. I moaned around Baldur's cock, arching my back to give Hod better access.

He didn't need more of an invitation than that. With a rustle of his own clothes, his naked cock nudged between my legs. I gripped the base of Baldur's erection and gave him a firm pump as I edged my knees apart. Hod and I gasped together as he slid into me from behind.

Oh, Lord, yes, I loved this—being worshiped and worshiping in return. Hod moved inside me with smooth, steady thrusts, his mouth searing my neck, and I set a rhythm working my mouth and hand up and down Baldur's length. The light god's legs trembled as I took him even deeper.

"Fuck," he muttered, the first time I could remember hearing him swear. I took that as my cue to pick up the pace. His fingers tightened in my hair, holding me but not directing me. Letting me keep control the way I needed to. "Aria. I'm almost—I'm going to—"

He came with a rush of salty fluid and a wash of light that tingled from him through my entire body. As my lips clamped and swallowed, that energy seemed to burst between my thighs. Hod's thumb grazed over my clit, his cock filling me even more deeply, I tipped over the edge in turn, clutching Baldur's hip for balance.

My body clenched around Hod, and his movements turned jerky. He looped his arm around my waist, holding me to him as he spilled himself inside me. His mouth feathered kisses along my shoulder.

Baldur sank to the floor to kiss me on the mouth. I ended up tucked between the two of them, my head on Hod's shoulder and my hand on Baldur's thigh, as we lingered in the afterglow.

"Maybe you're right. A little darkness isn't a bad thing," Baldur murmured in a wry tone.

I laughed a little breathlessly. "No. Not at all." I squeezed his leg affectionately and snuggled closer to Hod's chest. In a minute or two, we'd have to break out of this joyful state and go back to reality, but I was going to enjoy this moment for as long as we could drag it out. "And three can definitely be more fun than two."

Hod snorted. "Suddenly I'm very glad there's only the four of us —unattached, anyway—in all of Asgard."

I swatted him. "I wouldn't want anyone else anyway. Four is more than enough, thank you very much."

His comment started my thoughts spinning in a totally different direction, though—to Freya, soaring home after her search for her daughter. To all those empty halls where Asgard's other inhabitants had once lived.

"The other gods who did used to live here," I said slowly. "Most of them are still around somewhere, right? They just took off to take an extended beach vacation or whatever?"

"As far as we know," Hod said. "Why, are you rethinking that 'four is more than enough' remark?"

I rolled my eyes. "No. I was just thinking that more gods would be helpful if we're supposed to be taking on a giant and his entire army. Shouldn't we go looking for the others? If Surt takes over the only stable realms left, it'll affect all of them too. This *is* still their original home."

Baldur shifted. "We could mention it to Odin."

Every nerve in my body balked. "No. Do you really think he'll say okay when he's shot down every other idea we've given him? He's too stuck on whatever he thinks is the right way for this to all go down."

"I won't argue with you there, valkyrie," Hod said. "But we do need him."

I tipped my head up to look at his face. "Do we really?"

That question hung in the air for the space of several heartbeats. A hint of a smile touched Hod's face. "All right," he said. "Supposing we don't… Shall we come up with a few plans of our own?"

# 16

*Aria*

The spray of the vast waterfall tickled over my face and bare arms. I swooped lower, but the only figures I could make out anywhere nearby were a couple of kids a little older than Petey who were splashing their feet in the lake at the base of the torrent.

Thor was shaking his head when I soared up to meet him at the edge of the rushing river. "I'm not sure where else to look," he said. "Njord ruled over the seas, so he has an affinity for water… If he's not hanging around any of his favorite spots, he could be anywhere along the coastlines or major lakes."

I motioned to the campsite we'd found, the stones around it marked with a few faded runes that Thor had said would have brought warmth overnight and repelled animal intrusions. "Do you have any idea how long it's been since he used that site?"

"The ashes from the firepit have been washed away by rain, and even the scorch marks on the rocks are worn down," Thor said. "I'd guess at least a few years."

I made a face. Thor and I had come down to Midgard to search out any of the gods who might be lingering there—Loki might have covered ground faster, but he'd pointed out that most of the gods wouldn't exactly welcome the sight of him. So far, the thunder god and I hadn't had much luck. This campsite was as close as we'd gotten to finding any of Asgard's former residents.

"At least we know he was still around that recently," I said, trying to look on the bright side. "You'd think they'd stop by their old home every now and then just to see how things are going."

"Ah, we didn't all part ways on the most favorable of terms," Thor said. "After our return from Ragnarok, a lot of things changed. Marriages broke apart, friendships turned sour. The war rubbed most of us caught up in it pretty raw."

"But not you?" I said with a lift of an eyebrow. I'd seen Thor conflicted now and then, but he'd never talked about that earlier war with the sort of horror I'd heard from the others.

He shrugged as he sent his lightning crackling over one of the stones with a message in case the sea god returned any time soon. *You're needed in Asgard.*

"I fought as well as I could," he said. "Our enemies were clear. I'd been in a lot more battles than any of the others except maybe Odin and Freya—and even they are just watching over the field as often as they're on it."

"You were in your element."

He chuckled. "Something like that. And also, my death was brief, since it happened right at the end. I can't begin to imagine how hard it was for those like Hod and Baldur who were left to linger in death so long."

Even though those words were serious, that comment brought back my interlude with the twins in Valhalla yesterday—the heat of Baldur's kisses, the caress of Hod's hands, the moments when it'd felt as if we existed only for each other.

"I think they're getting past that," I said.

Thor shot me a knowing grin. "A little help never hurts."

We set off over the landscape again, but our flight was more aimless now. I rubbed my arms as the wind buffeted my wings. "What do you think our chances are of just stumbling on any of them? Freya's been searching for her daughter for days with no luck."

"We're doing everything we can," Thor said. "At this point, we may have to rely on the messages we've left. I can't believe none of them ever return to their favorite haunts anymore."

"But they might not return before Surt decides to make his move." How long could we afford to wait before we took him on by ourselves? Not even Odin admitted to knowing how large his army might be already. Even if the giant would have preferred to wait another decade to grow it larger, he had to be aiming to start his invasion as soon as possible now that his plans had been exposed.

"Whatever happens, we'll put him down," Thor said, but he frowned after he'd spoken.

He thought of a couple more spots for us to check: a mountainside hut from which Heimdall the gatekeeper had apparently liked to survey the realm of humankind and a stretch of apple farms where Idunn might have taken comfort. Neither turned up any godly presence. Thor etched his message here and there, his frown deepening.

"It's getting late," he said. "I think *we* should be returning to Asgard now."

My body protested at the thought of giving up our search, but obviously we couldn't count on the other gods being the solution to our problems. With a sigh, I swiveled toward the rainbow bridge.

We passed Heimdall's former hall, an ivory structure that clung to the side of the cliff next to the bridge. "He used to spend all day sitting on his front step, watching who'd come and go," Thor told me. "His eyes were as sharp as Loki's. The two of them never got along all that well. Maybe because he always spotted what the trickster might be up to sooner than the rest of us."

"At least Loki usually got you out of any trouble he got you into, right?" I said. And the gods had brought plenty of trouble down on Loki, too, not that any of them seemed to think of that most of the time.

"He did, he did. We'd have been much worse off without him. I believed that even before, in spite of everything. It was never as simple as hero or villain with him."

Those words lingered with me after we'd reached the city. "Should we scrounge up some dinner?" Thor suggested, but my mind was already leaping ahead of me.

"I'll grab some food later," I said. "There's something I want to check first."

Thor studied me. "Do you need company?"

"There are a few things I can do without godly assistance," I said, jabbing a finger at him with a smile to show I wasn't offended. He laughed and waved me off.

I didn't think he'd have seen me off that easily if he'd known exactly what I was planning on checking. I soared over to Valhalla and tucked my wings close to my back as I hurried down the length of the room. The one table was still askew where Baldur had leaned against it yesterday. I tugged my gaze away. I was interested in memories right now, but not my own.

The empty space around Yggdrasil closed against my skin as I stepped onto the bark-covered path. Sometimes the still blackness around it unnerved me. Today, there was something steadying about it. All the places I'd seen with Thor today, all those disappointments—they fell away as I walked with smooth strides along the trunk toward the branch that would lead me to Muspelheim. I paused at the base of that branch, breathing in slow and deep until my heart beat in an even rhythm. Then I pushed myself through the gate into the realm of fire.

Dodging the watchful dragon came instinctively now. I flattened myself under the sheltering ridge, waited until it had settled, and slipped away through the shadows. The heat of the realm penetrated even those dark patches, bringing sweat to my skin in a minute.

I hadn't come here to spy this time, though. I wanted to be found—just not by any monsters with jagged teeth and talons.

When I'd left the dragon far enough behind, I ventured out onto the dry plain at the foot of the cliff. I kept my wings spread, providing me with a little shade. The silver-white glimmer would stand out against the dark gray rock. I ambled along, waiting for the prickle of that being-watched sensation.

I'd just reached the edge of one of those rivers of magma when the feeling came over me. I stopped, a thicker heat wafting up from the churning liquid with its pulsing red glow. Maybe I didn't want to be standing quite this close to a substance that could mean my instant death for this conversation. I backed up a few steps and turned slowly.

My watcher was nowhere to be seen, but I'd expected that.

"Muninn," I called out, loud enough for my voice to carry but not so loud I thought it would disturb the distant dragon. "I came to talk to you. Peacefully." I held out my arms, my hands open. No weapons except the switchblade always in my pocket, and I didn't think the raven woman was all that scared of it.

The seconds slipped by with the trickle of a bead of sweat down my back. Had she said everything she'd wanted to last time? Maybe she didn't like the idea of giving in when someone else was trying to call the shots.

I was debating my next moves when a black flutter appeared at the edge of my vision. My head jerked around.

Muninn landed as she transformed, her pale limbs steadying her on the ground with her usual awkward grace. She'd left several feet between us, as if she didn't totally trust me not to lunge at her even with just my hands as weapons. If this had been right after we'd escaped from her prison, that would have been a reasonable fear.

She cocked her head. "What brings you here looking for me, valkyrie? I thought you had no interest in talking."

I swallowed, my throat rough from the dry heat. "You told me things before that you wanted me to keep in mind. You were right. I was hoping you might know other information that you'd be willing to share."

Her expression didn't change, her dark eyes sharp, her lips curved with mild curiosity. "What sort of information?"

"You used to travel all over the realms with Odin and on your own, didn't you?" I said. "I want to find the gods who've left Asgard. Maybe you've seen places where they liked to spend time that the others wouldn't know about. Or you got ideas about where they might go from their memories."

Muninn grimaced. "I have no interest in adding to Asgard's numbers. If the gods wish to return, they can find their own way back."

"We'll have more options for setting things right if we have more of them on our side," I said. "Isn't that what you want?"

She shifted her weight from one foot to the other. "I don't know what you mean."

I had to stop myself from gritting my teeth. "Why did you tell me about the dark elves? Don't you want us to fix what's wrong with the other realms? How are we supposed to do that when we know Surt could be storming Asgard any day now?"

"I suppose that's for you to figure out."

"That's all you're going to say?"

Her near-black eyes stared back at me unwaveringly. My hands clenched. "I want to fix things. None of us wants to see the realms failing—well, I don't know how Odin feels, but the rest of us will do whatever we can."

A rasp of a laugh escaped her. "If Odin will let you, hmm?"

"He's not *my* master," I said, and she flinched.

"He isn't mine anymore either," she said, her shoulders shifting as if she were about to slide back into raven form. "If you want answers, he knows more than I do."

"You know it's not that simple." I let out a sound of frustration and forced my voice to soften. "Please. Do you really want to see Midgard and Asgard burned down? You're angry with Odin—I get it. I don't like him all that much either. But he's just one god."

"The ruler of Asgard," Muninn spat out. "The one whose orders you'll all follow in the end."

"No," I said. "We won't. Not if we have other ways. Are you looking to bring the realms back to how they're meant to be, to stop whatever problems he caused, or is this just about getting revenge on him? Because if it's the latter, you're not really any better than him, are you?"

Muninn bristled. "*You're* like him," she said. "You push everyone else to do what you want, and where will that leave us in the end? With him still lording over all of us. He could *never* pay us back. Never. He'll never admit or believe he's done anything wrong. Deal with him, and then I'll deal with you."

She spun around and darted into the air with a rippling of black feathers. After a few flaps of her wings, she was nothing but a dark speck against the flat gray sky.

# 17

*Loki*

As hard as it sometimes was to believe, certain areas of the realm of giants were actually rather peaceful. The snowy mountains to the far north, for example, had been one of my favorite places to escape to long ago, before I'd come to Asgard, when the company of my supposed kin had grated on me too much. And this pine forest to the west, deeper into it than the realms inhabitants usually ventured—perhaps it was a relief to escape here from my godly oath-sworn kin too.

The breeze carried a crisp chill and the pines' sharp scent. Fallen needles crinkled under my feet as I wandered the lonely landscape. To tell the truth, I'd been hoping to find it a little less lonely. The gods of Asgard might have disdained the company of giants, but they'd been more than happy to take advantage of Jotunheim's more isolated corners when nowhere in Midgard appealed to them in their current mood. It had become increasingly difficult to find any part of the human realm that mortals hadn't penetrated.

I found no sign of any recent passage here, though. The

only evidence I'd come across was proof that my former home was succumbing to the same decline that Hod had reported from Nidavellir. Many of the pines were stooping, their trunks weakened by some ailment I didn't recognize. The mountains, when I'd visited them earlier, had shaken once with an ominous tremor. I'd kept my distance from the towns and cities, but the dry earth and the constant chill despite it being summer made me wonder how well any crops were growing here.

It couldn't hurt to leave a few signs of my own, on the off-chance Bragi meandered this way in the following weeks to find inspiration for a poetic verse, or Skadi came seeking that wintry chill. They might not have been overjoyed if they'd seen me, but I didn't think they'd ignore an urgent call back to Asgard.

With a flick of my fingers, I inscribed a new message into the trunk of one of the wider pines. The tangy smoke tickled my nose. I turned to survey the forest, hesitating. I couldn't think of any other secret places the gods might have declined to tell their real kin they liked to travel to, but the thought of returning to Asgard empty-handed didn't sit well either.

No doubt Hod would have some snarky remark about where I might have gone. Or perhaps I'd find Thor had been searching for me again, wanting to make sure I hadn't gotten myself into any trouble. If only they'd spent a little more time focusing on the real source of so much of our troubles…

I pushed that thought aside and set off toward the gate that had brought me through to Jotunheim. I had a lot of ground to cover. And I couldn't say I enjoyed the thought of running into any of this realm's inhabitants.

The forest gave way to scruffy tundra at the edge of the giants' realm. Coarse tufts of grass sprouted here and there on the cracked earth, which was packed so hard my footsteps might have carried for miles if I'd let them touch the ground. Not that there was anyone around to hear my passage anyway. Or so I thought until a gravelly bellow called out to me.

"Sly One! I've been waiting for you."

I whirled around, propelling a burst of flame into my hand. There were few who'd be looking for me here who wouldn't be hoping for a fight, preferably one ending with my head on a pike.

The looming figure I found standing at the edge of the forest would have liked that, perhaps more than anyone.

Surt had always been a giant among giants. Even now, with the age that had finally started to catch up with him leaving his shoulders slightly hunched, he stood a few inches taller than my formidable height and nearly as broad as our Thunderer. His steel-gray hair hung lank above his glittering hazel eyes, his beard long and grizzled enough to rival Odin's.

He held himself in what should have been a casual stance, his arms loosely crossed and his weight leaned to one side. My gaze couldn't help catching on the broad sword he was gripping, though.

"Blazing One," I replied, encouraging the flames to rise from my palm with a twitch of my fingers. "Are you looking for a good scorching?"

Surt chuckled, a low rough sound. "Feel free to try me," he said. "My sword is always hungry for more."

Yes, it was that damned sword I had to be most wary of. A fiery gleam leapt along its length even now. Anything I threw at Surt, it could absorb and spew back at me, now or some later even more inopportune time. My chances of felling this giant alone were slim. But then, so were his of felling me. I could speed away from here in an instant on my shoes of flight.

"What do you want then?" I demanded. "Why would you wait for me *here* of all places?"

"I have underlings watching every gate at my disposal," Surt said. "One saw you emerge here from your realm. Your great tree won't let me through to speak to you in Asgard, and your companions didn't appear to take well to my attempt at a bridge. This seemed a better meeting spot."

"Well done," I said. "You've found me. I'm still waiting to hear the purpose of this 'meeting.'"

Surt's narrow eyes studied me for a long enough moment that my body tensed even further. "I think this meeting has been a long time coming," he said. "Don't you? Tell me, trickster, are you really all that satisfied with the choices you've made?"

"Perhaps you could be a little more specific," I suggested. "I'd estimate I make verging on a thousand choices every day. My breakfast this morning was quite satisfying, if that's what you're concerned about."

His expression didn't waver. He motioned to the landscape around us, his gaze still fixed on my face. "You left behind your home. Forsook your people for those shining ones of Asgard." His teeth gnashed on that last word, as if he could chew it up and spit it out. "And what have they ever given you? Chains and poison? What a poor puppet you are, slinking back to them after you'd brought them to their knees."

The "puppet" comment rankled. "It *was* my choice to remain there," I said. "Clearly you know nothing about my life. If all you came to do is rant about events from eons ago, I'll take my leave now."

I moved to turn on my heel.

"Loki," Surt said, straightening up. He stepped toward me, but his sword stayed down at his side. "You know we have more kinship than you share with any of those lordly beings up in their bright city. Have you forgotten where you began so quickly?"

"Oh, believe me, I remember quite well," I said. "In particular, I remember why I left it. Nothing I've seen since then has led me to regret that decision. I'll take the arrogant over the brutes, thank you."

"The brutes." Surt shook his head. "Come? I will show you something."

"And why should I want to see anything *you* would want to show me?"

His eyes glittered. "Because of all the beings in Asgard, you at least care to know everything you possibly can. Or have they finally taught you how to close your mind like they do theirs?"

He strode off along the line of trees, his sword swinging at his side. I grimaced at myself and followed after him, keeping a safe distance. Our greatest enemy stood before me. It would be foolhardy to ignore anything he might be willing to share. I gathered knowledge, yes—so I could use it to my advantage when I needed to. If wielded properly, a fact could be a sharper weapon than any blade.

Surt's powerful legs carried him swiftly even if he couldn't leave the ground. I had to walk briskly to keep up. We passed the span of forest where I'd done my searching and veered across the mostly barren ground toward what appeared to be a narrow valley carved into the hard-packed earth.

The giant stopped at the edge of the wide crevice. He swept his free hand toward it.

"This is what's become of our homeland. The ground itself will not hold. It splits and breaks as if wrenching itself apart."

I tipped my head to one side. "A bit of a hassle for one passing through, I suppose, but hardly a catastrophe."

Surt whirled toward me, a surge of fire hissing along his blade. "Do you think this is the only one? The only place? The earth opened beneath the capital a few years ago. It swallowed hundreds with their houses. And there were more before and since."

"Ah," I said, keeping my expression and my voice blank. I hadn't actually discovered that yet. I hadn't had all that much time for venturing around Jotunheim since our escape from Muninn's prison, and I'd had no access for decades before then. This was worse than I would have imagined.

Odin had known, hadn't he? How could he have failed to notice a crumpled city in his constant peering from his high seat?

"And do you intend to seal the earth back together through some magic you haven't shared with me yet?" I inquired. "How does your great plan to rip apart the realms that remain untouched help anyone, really, in the long run?"

"Do you know why the realms are falling apart?" Surt asked. "Why only Asgard and Midgard hold steady? Surely the great mind of Loki can put the pieces together."

Asgard was the realm of the gods, and Midgard lay at the center of it all. That was how we'd explained it when we'd discussed it between ourselves. But it wasn't really an answer, was it? What was so special about Midgard, really, other than it being a land far more appealing to myself and my companions than any other…

Or perhaps that was my answer right there.

"The gods used to visit all of the realms regularly," I said slowly. "Now we rarely venture beyond those two."

"And still you say 'we' as if they'll ever truly let you be one of them." Surt made a scoffing sound. "This is all their doing. My imprisonment in Muspelheim. The fracturing of the realms. They can't be bothered to act as the caretakers they take such pride in being. And you'd stand by them still?"

"As opposed to standing with you while you burn everything else to the ground?" I retorted.

"Oh, there *will* be burning," Surt said. "But only as long as it takes to claim the better lands we're owed. There's plenty of room in Asgard and Midgard to fit us, isn't there? The humans will adjust to a little extra servitude. Perhaps they'll be better off. And this time it'll be the gods who are chained. We'll bring them down to the realms, force them to lend their powers to healing these worlds, as they rightfully should."

He sliced his sword through the air, and the fire in it warbled. "I can do it faster and more cleanly with you alongside me, Loki. You're worthy of greater honors than they'll ever offer you. Stand with me and take what should be yours, and we'll divide the realms between us. Isn't it time they lost the upper hand? You can save the realms they always claimed you would destroy."

His words tugged at something deep inside me. The bitter anger in them stirred a matching emotion I'd so often buried. Suddenly I understood him so well I could have cringed and laughed at the same time. My fingers curled into my palms. Oh, I knew that anger, all right.

I'd seen Surt's brutality with my own eyes, all those centuries ago—but then, I'd also seen plenty of brutality from the gods. After all this time under their heels, kicked about like a dog they didn't want at the dinner table… The thought of taking the reins and putting them in their places did have a certain appeal. I could be a kinder jailer than they'd ever been to me.

A sickly satisfaction spread through me at the idea. How many times had I dreamed of a moment like this, all those ages ago? I could be brutal too, in my own ways, when the situation called for it. Could I really say I got no enjoyment from it at all?

Perhaps Surt was right. We were more alike than I'd wanted to consider.

I studied the giant, and resolve solidified in my chest. There *was* something to be gained here after all.

"I may entertain your offer," I said. "Perhaps we should discuss it further in your own kingdom, behind walls where Odin has no chance of overhearing?"

Surt grinned. "Come along then, and we'll see where we end up."

# 18

*Aria*

Evening had fallen as I sprawled on my stomach at the edge of the grassy cliff-edge where Asgard fell away into the sky. The rainbow bridge's surface still shimmered. When Loki came loping across its arc, glints of its color caught in his pale red hair and cast his paler skin in odd shades.

His gaze was distant, his expression unusually serious. I sat up, and it was only then that he seemed to notice I was there.

"Pixie," he said, coming to a stop at the foot of the bridge. "Playing watchdog?"

I wasn't completely sure what he meant, but it did probably look a little odd for me to be perched here.

"I was thinking about Heimdall watching the bridge all the time when he still lived here," I said. "Trying to figure out where someone like that would want to go if he *wasn't* here. So far it hasn't really helped, though."

I expected Loki to stroll over and join me, or else to beckon me to join him, but he just stood there, his stance a little stiff. A tickle of uneasiness ran down my back.

"We gave the search our best shot," he said. "At this point I assume if the other gods care to join us, they'll have to do it by their own steam."

I pushed myself to my feet. Loki didn't exactly pull away from me as I walked over to him, but he did start striding on toward the city as if it didn't matter to him all that much whether I reached him. The tickling niggled deeper.

"Hey," I said, jogging the last few steps to grab his elbow. "What's the hurry? Did something happen down there?"

He stopped and arched an eyebrow as he peered down at me. "Nothing of note. I'm merely tired of rushing to and fro searching for those who apparently care so little what happens to this place. There's leftover roast in my cold room I had a mind to eat, and a bed I'm looking forward to collapsing onto."

He was talking in his usual wry tone, but there was something distant about it too. I inhaled as I decided what to say next, and a whiff of a smoky chemical smell seeped into my nose, just barely perceptible to my heightened valkyrie senses. I leaned closer, and Loki eased away from me.

It had come from him. I knew that smell. It was the stink of Muspelheim.

Why would he have risked going there alone? And if he'd gone there, how could he have been coming back over the rainbow bridge? I'd been sitting by it since Thor and I had gotten back—I'd have known if Odin had directed it somewhere other than Midgard.

If Loki had been acting like normal, I'd have asked him directly, but the distance in his demeanor made me balk.

"Where did you search?" I asked, keeping my tone as casual as I could manage. "It seemed like Thor and I covered most of Midgard. But maybe you know different places than he does."

"Oh, here and there." The trickster waved his hand dismissively. "There's a lot of world to cover in that realm of yours." He gave me a smile that would have settled my nerves if I hadn't known he'd just lied to me.

My stomach twisted. I didn't know how to confront him on that lie. Loki could talk his way out of just about anything. If he didn't want to admit what he'd been up to, there was no chance in hell I'd pry the truth out of him.

"Okay," I said. "Well, go enjoy that roast of yours."

He tipped his head to me. For a second I thought he might lean in for a kiss. But he pulled himself back and hurried on toward his hall, leaving me with an ache that stretched from my gut to my heart.

Loki had been more tense than I remembered from our first few weeks together ever since we'd escaped from Muninn's prison, but that made sense. He'd been faced with horrors as traumatic as anything I'd been through, ones I was sure he'd buried to keep the peace with the other gods. And he'd obviously been frustrated that they weren't willing to force the issue of Odin's past actions with the Allfather yet.

This was something different, though. He'd never been so standoffish with *me*. I was his valkyrie, the one he'd chosen. If he didn't even think he could trust me with the truth of what he'd been doing…

I didn't know how to follow that thread to a logical conclusion. Or maybe I did, but none of the conclusions I could draw sat right with me. Biting my lip, I wandered into the city along the same path he'd taken.

Loki had already disappeared into his hall—assuming that was where he'd really been going. I paused partway down the road, unsure of where *I* wanted to go.

The door to Thor's huge hall eased open, and the thunder god came out onto the threshold.

"Is everything all right?" he asked. "You look a bit lost."

"I'm okay," I said. "I just…" I rubbed my face. I didn't know what to say about it either.

"Do you want to come in?"

Thor's tone was soft, but a thread of heat wove through it anyway. I paused, tugged by a totally different sort of emotion. I never had made good on the promise that he'd only have to wait a few more hours to enjoy each other's company after we'd been interrupted the other morning.

And I didn't really want to be alone right now, with this uneasiness creeping through me.

"I think I would," I said, and went to meet him in the doorway.

I hadn't paid a whole lot of attention to his hall when I'd snuck in here that night, other than to figure out where the bedroom was. In the clearer light of the evening, I was struck by just how vast the place really was. The ceiling loomed far enough over the central hall to have held two floors instead of just the one, and at least a couple dozen doors lined that hall.

"This is an awful lot of space for one guy," I said. "Even a guy as big as you." I knuckled Thor's arm affectionately.

He chuckled. "Well, it wasn't always only mine."

Oh, right. "You were married," I said. "Before."

"Before Ragnarok. Yes. Sif." He said her name easily and evenly, so I guessed that split hadn't been too painful. Or maybe it'd just happened so long ago that he'd had more than enough time to get over it. Curiosity pricked at me anyway.

"What happened?" I asked. "You said before that a lot of people went their separate ways afterward, everyone was so shook up. Was it just that?"

"That was some of it. She was definitely shaken." He rested his hand on my shoulder blade and ushered me down the hall. "She didn't want me to leave on any more adventuring, and she couldn't stand that Loki and I made peace with each other. She and him…"

He paused, the corner of his mouth quirking up. "I was furious at the time. She had the most gorgeous hair, even closer to gold than Freya's is, and one day he got it into his head to chop it all off when she was sleeping. He never did own up to why. Maybe it was part of that ruckus-raising Odin ordered him to do."

A shadow crossed the thunder god's face then. I slipped my hand around his and squeezed. "What happened?"

"Oh, I yelled at him some, and he promised me he'd only been making way for an even finer head of hair for her. Off he flew down to Nidavellir to have the dark elves craft some—out of actual gold. It really was the most lovely thing. *She* liked it, even though she didn't want to admit it. And I got Mjolnir out of that same bargain. As far as I'm concerned, all's well that ends well. Sif… Sif could hold quite a grudge."

He'd patted the hammer hanging from his belt when he mentioned it. My stomach knotted all over again. The story he was telling me—it was another side of the story that had ended with Loki's mouth sewn shut because the gods had judged against him on his bet.

That memory still stung Loki. Thor smiled when he talked about it, even though he'd seen the consequences the trickster god had faced.

Maybe it wasn't surprising that Loki sometimes retreated into himself, even from me. He'd had to hold so much in for so long. Keeping up that slyly cheerful front must have gotten exhausting.

That still didn't explain him outright lying about sneaking off to Muspelheim, though.

Thor motioned me into a side room where a cushioned bench squatted next to a low table. The table was laid with bread, various fruits, and a hunk of cheese.

"Already time for your second dinner?" I teased.

"Who says I ever finished my first one?" Thor replied with a grin.

The niggling doubts stayed with me as I sat on the bench next to him. I picked up a strawberry and bit into it, but the tart juice on my tongue wasn't enough to distract me.

"Loki hasn't gotten into any 'trouble' since then—since Ragnarok—has he?" I said. "It seems like all the stories I've heard are from before."

"Nothing extreme enough that I remember it," Thor said. "And from what I remember, he was very contrite when we first returned. He has his sly ways about him, for his own amusement, and he certainly enjoys prodding those he doesn't get along with on occasion, but… Well, even before, he was rarely actually cruel."

"There was no reason for him to be stirring up chaos anymore," I said.

"No. I suppose not." Thor shook his head. "If he'd been allowed to be completely on our side, I can't help wondering if we could have avoided Ragnarok altogether."

I blinked at him. "Odin seems to think it had to happen." None of the other gods, even Loki, had indicated they didn't agree with that one thing.

"And maybe he's right," the thunder god said. "He would know better than me. But with Loki's cleverness… I suppose Odin is the only person he could never quite outwit. If he'd put that mind to use fighting for us, I can only imagine how differently that final battle might have gone."

He looked at the cheese sandwich he'd been putting together as if he couldn't remember why he'd thought he was hungry. His forehead furrowed. "I suppose it's silly for me to think *I* could come up with some sort of scheme."

"Of course not," I said. "Just because he's clever doesn't mean he's got all the wits in Asgard. Why? Did you have a scheme?"

Thor waved me off. "It's nothing. The others made that clear."

"No, come on." I scooted closer to him, setting my hand on his arm. "*I* want to hear about it."

He was silent for a long moment. Then he set down the sandwich and ran his fingers through his thick hair. His gaze slid away from me as if he were afraid to watch my reaction while he spoke. There was something sweet about how nervous he was to share this part of himself.

"I've thought, the way the giants are—Surt's been apart from them for so long, and they always did squabble amongst themselves as it was—they're so easily tricked if they think something they want is in reach, or that they have to avenge themselves of some slight… Perhaps we could find a way to use them against Surt. Make them our army without them even realizing who they're fighting for." He ducked his head. "Just a vague idea."

"It sounds like a good idea to me," I said, imagining a horde of giants charging toward Surt's fortress. "Why don't you tell the others and figure out the rest with them?"

Thor made a pained expression. "I tried. They brushed me off and went on with their own planning. It's not as if I've been a fountain of wisdom in the past, you know. I'm the Thunderer."

"Hey." I poked him in the arm so he'd look at me. "That doesn't mean they shouldn't pay attention when you do have an idea. And anyway, you're not just thunder, are you? You've got lightning. Why focus only on the loud and strong side when you can be quick and sharp too?"

His mouth opened and closed again before he managed to answer. "That's a very good question," he said. "I've spent so much time thundering around, it's easy to forget how powerful even one bolt of electricity can be."

Even a small one. "I haven't forgotten," I said, thinking of the sparks that had danced from his fingertips over my body during that interlude in Muninn's prison. A sudden heat pooled low in my belly, urged on by the warmth of his body right next to mine. I lowered my eyelashes, trying out a little slyness myself. "I'm always happy to offer myself up as a test subject if you need a little practice to jog your memory."

Thor looked at me so intently that the temperature in the room seemed to rise by a few degrees. "Is that so?" he said, his already low voice even huskier than before.

I touched the side of his face, and he bent down to kiss me. His hot breath mingled with mine, with a twitch of his tongue against my lips that sent an electric tingle through me. Oh, yes, that'd been a good talk, but I was ready for more now.

I murmured encouragingly, gripping the front of his shirt. Thor kissed me again and again with more hunger each time. His hands started to trail up and down my sides. Each brush of his fingertips, even through the thin fabric of my tank top, sent a fresh burst of quivers over my skin.

When he slid his palm around to cup my breast, I pressed into his touch, kissing him harder. His thumb swiveled over the swell of flesh, and a spark danced over the tip. I whimpered as my nipple hardened in an instant.

He teased it for a minute longer through my top before moving his sizzling torture to the other side. Then he eased his hand under my shirt to caress me without interference. His fingers stroked and flicked, each point of pressure like a tiny jolt of lightning. I yanked him closer to me, moaning.

His hand dipped lower, to my jeans. A tremble of need ran through me as he tugged open my fly. He slid his fingers right inside my panties, his breath catching when he felt the dampness already gathered there. A zap of pleasure jolted over my clit, and my hips jerked. I gasped.

"Oh, God." Just like that, I was already so close to release. I groped down his body to pay him back in kind, but Thor eased back and caught my wrist. His other hand stayed between my thighs, his thumb slicking from my clit to my folds and back again.

"I want to watch you," he said thickly. His brown eyes

smoldered with longing. "I want to see just how good I can make you feel, no distractions."

I swallowed hard, my chest tightening with emotion. So much emotion, swelling inside me, that I didn't know what to do with.

I'd said I loved Hod's darkness. What could I say about Thor? I loved his strength. I loved his compassion—and his passion too. I could have said that, but it didn't feel like enough to encompass even half of the feelings surging through me.

Thor's fingers twitched with another electric tingle, and every other feeling was overwhelmed but the pleasure racing through me. I tipped my head back, bucking to meet his hand, giving myself over to everything he wanted to give me.

# 19

*Aria*

I might have slept a little longer that morning if an enormous but joyful bellow hadn't shaken the floor beneath my bed.

"Tyr!"

If Thor was that happy, whatever was going on couldn't be a bad thing. I sat up, rubbing my eyes, and went to see what the fuss was about.

Asgard's other current inhabitants were also gathering in the courtyard the shout had rung out from. At first I couldn't see anything except Thor's broad form. Then he stepped back from his embrace to reveal a lanky man with bronze-brown hair that fell to his shoulders. The new arrival looked older than my gods and younger than Odin, maybe late thirties or early forties if I could have judged by human standards, the corners of his eyes slightly crinkled. His face held the same divine attractiveness as every god I'd met so far.

He was also missing a hand. The base of his right arm, just

before where his wrist should have been, ended in a smooth stump, the edges only faintly rippled with scar tissue.

"Quite the welcoming party," he said in a warm bass voice. "Maybe I should have come back sooner."

"It's good to see you," Baldur said. "Where have you been?"

"Oh, mostly rambling around southern and eastern Europe," Tyr said. "All sorts of interesting developments in those areas recently."

"Tyr's domains are law and combat," Thor said, catching my eye. "And it's been at least a couple centuries since we last saw him." He clapped the other god on the back.

Another war god? I guessed between this guy, Odin, and Freya, they covered all the possible angles.

"Although interestingly, neither domain explains how he lost his hand," Loki said, his tone managing to sound both light and caustic at the same time. "It's such a shame it wasn't reborn with the rest of you, isn't it?"

Tyr gave the trickster a wary glance and seemed to decide to ignore him. "I gathered Asgard was in need," he said, turning back to Thor. "Although the message I came across was rather vague."

"Hmm," Odin said. I flinched—I hadn't heard the king of the gods approaching behind me. "There is a certain strength in numbers. Welcome home."

"Come," Thor said. "We'll explain everything we know so far. The most important part is that Surt has reappeared, and he means to make good on every threat he made in the past and more."

He motioned Tyr toward his hall. Baldur, Hod, and Freya moved to join them. Loki wavered, his jaw tight. Before I could decide whether to follow the others or go to him and find out what was bothering him, Odin's hand closed over my shoulder.

"Valkyrie," he said, the word holding no admiration when *he* said it. "I think we need to have a talk of our own."

Loki's gaze darted our way. "What business could you have with her?" he said, his eyes much darker than the mild curiosity in his voice warranted.

"Oh, it seems we have a great deal to discuss," Odin said. He tipped his head in the direction the other gods had gone. "Don't let that keep you from staying abreast of the plans being made."

They stared each other down for a moment, king and trickster, the tension prickling over my skin. Loki lifted one narrow shoulder in a careless shrug. "I'll see if there's anything I can add to Tyr's education," he said, and strode off. My stomach tightened as he passed out of view, leaving Odin and me alone.

Odin nudged me in the opposite direction toward his hall, and I went, my heart thumping uneasily. "What's this about?" I said.

"All in good time," the Allfather said in a tone that didn't offer any room for argument.

My back itched, my wings eager to break free and carry me away from Odin and his foreboding presence. It was hard to think this conversation was going to be an enjoyable one, even if I didn't have any idea what he wanted to talk about. But running away hadn't been a very successful strategy when it came to the gods. It wasn't as if I could avoid ever coming back.

Maybe he just wanted to check in and see how I was doing after looking in on Petey the other day. A little regal concern toward his subjects. Ha ha ha.

When we reached his hall, Odin stepped into the fore-room where the group of us had always met him before. I hesitated in the middle of the thick soft rug as he settled into his throne-like chair. There was nowhere for me to sit in here unless I wanted to grab one of the pillows along the wall. I was pretty sure he expected me to stay standing while he peered down at me like he was doing right now. My hackles rose at his grim expression before he even started to speak.

"I've gathered that you've been diverting my gods from the

course of action we decided on," he said. "As the sudden appearance of Tyr lends proof to."

"*Your* gods?" I repeated. "I'm pretty sure they belong to themselves. We're the ones who've been doing all the fighting while you've sat around back here making your plans."

"My plans that will ensure both our realm and your former one remain safe. Unless you've decided you no longer care about that cause."

I crossed my arms over my chest. "How exactly does finding more gods to join the fight hurt the cause?" Or finding out what was driving the dark elves, although if Odin didn't already know Hod had ventured into their realm, I wasn't going to spill the beans. "And why are you talking to *me* about this? We're all working together. I don't exactly call the shots."

He gave me a baleful look. "Do you truly believe it could have escaped me how much influence you've managed to gain over them? You've earned their loyalty through honest means, from what I've gathered. Let us not switch to dishonesty now."

How much had he seen, with all the spying he did from his high seat? I couldn't tell whether this was a bluff or he knew for sure I'd been the one to suggest we go searching for the other gods. He couldn't see through walls. How much had we discussed it outside?

"I'm not lying about anything," I said, which was technically true. Omissions didn't count, right? "I *honestly* believe that having more manpower makes it easier to win a war. I'd have thought that was common sense."

"This isn't a common war," Odin said, his voice rising to a rumble as he leaned forward in his chair. He glowered down at me for a moment, a fierce light in his brown eye, enough power emanating from his body that it took all my willpower not to cower. My arms went rigid at my sides.

"Fine," I said. "Nothing about this situation is normal to me. You want me to stop coming up with new plans? Tell me what the hell yours really *is*. Because you can't think that the six of us charging at Surt's fortress alone is going to win that war."

Odin leaned back in his chair slowly. He turned his head toward the window across from us, his gaze going distant.

"I see things, you know," he said. "Not just from my high seat. Not just with my eye." He tapped the scarred patch above his other cheek. "I gave this one up for knowledge beyond what we can grasp in front of us. It comes to me in whispers and fragments… but it comes."

A shiver ran down my back. "And you've seen something about the battle with Surt?"

His gaze returned to me. "I know this much: No matter how many reinforcements you summon, our victory comes down to you five and the power you hold between you. That is what we must depend on. That is where we must build our strength. The rest may not matter at all."

*You five and the power you hold.* The chill that had touched me a second ago tickled deeper. "What exactly did you 'see'?" I asked. "What are we going to do?"

Nothing shifted in his eyes, which were flatly dull now. "I know only the wisdom that reaches me. That is what I must use to guide me. But if the answer is the five of you, then the five of you must focus on your strengths. Build on your power. This running around across the realms only weakens us."

"So, that really is your whole plan?" I said. "We charge in there at Surt and hope that we manage to destroy him and his army?"

"How much you're able to destroy will be up to you," Odin said. "When you're ready, I hope it will be enough to cripple him. Perhaps you will have to give your all to see the battle through, but that would be a worthy sacrifice."

"Give our all?" I stared at him. "You mean you think we're going to go down in the fight. I guess it'd be hard not to, if it all comes down to the five of us trying to wreck everything we can reach. And you really think because of some 'whispers and fragments' that's the best way to go? You're fine sending your sons and your blood-brother off to be slaughtered?" I didn't expect him to care at all about me, but the others… My jaw clenched. They deserved better than this.

"Perhaps any that fall will be reborn again as they were before," Odin said evenly.

"And maybe they won't. You admitted yourself you don't know if that's a guarantee."

"It is a chance they'll willingly take to save our realm." His eyes narrowed. "Will you?"

How could I answer that? If I could die knowing Petey would be safe for the rest of his life, the rest of the realms would be a bonus. But I couldn't believe that was the only way, not when there was so much Odin was refusing to consider or even admit to.

I could feel, standing there before him, that he wasn't going to budge, not this morning. Possibly not ever. I raised my chin.

"I'll fight for Asgard, and I'll fight for Midgard, wherever that takes me, whatever the risks," I said, meaning it. I kept the rest of my thoughts to myself. I'd also keep looking for other ways to fight, no matter what Odin thought about that. If he wanted to stop us, let him go ahead and try. So far he'd been a lot of talk and not a whole lot of action.

"Good," Odin said. "Then you know where to aim your focus. Make me glad to have a valkyrie in Asgard again, Aria."

"I'll do my best," I said, and the weird part was, I meant that too. Just not in the way he'd have wanted.

I fled Odin's hall as quickly as I could manage without totally embarrassing myself. The other gods were standing far down the road outside Thor's hall in a cluster of conversation. I guessed they hadn't made it all the way inside before Tyr had insisted on getting some answers.

No head of pale-flame hair stood out among them, though. I

frowned, scanning the buildings around us, but Loki appeared to have vanished. Remembering how he'd spoken to Tyr and then Odin, the queasy feeling I'd had since he lied to me yesterday bubbled up again.

The trickster god was one of the five of us. Odin couldn't get mad at me for going looking for him, right?

I slipped away into the forest behind Odin's hall where Loki had found me the other day. No sign of him there, or in the orchard beyond it. I paused, listening, wishing that the bond between us that allowed him to track me worked both ways. If he'd been close, I could have sensed his presence like I'd found each of the gods in Muninn's prison, but he wasn't anywhere near here.

It'd be easier to track him down from above. I unfurled my wings and pushed off the ground. The air rushed over me as I swept myself higher and higher, until it seemed almost all of Asgard sprawled out beneath me. I soared over it, searching for a speck of red against the green landscape.

My gaze slid to the blue-gray line of the sea in the distance, almost the same stormy color as Petey's eyes. As I turned toward it, the faintest hint of salt met my tongue on the breeze. Like on the beach Loki had taken me to when he'd talked about his slaughtered children.

I flew toward the rocky span of shoreline. I didn't know how many miles I'd crossed before I made out a tall pale form standing there.

The flaps of my wings slowed. I glided closer, holding my breath. Would Loki want to be interrupted? I was thinking probably not, given that he'd gone this far to get away from the rest of us. What was he even doing out here?

Not much, from the looks of things. He was standing next to a large boulder. No, not standing—leaning against it with his forearms braced against it and his head bowed.

There was something so anguished in his posture that I

hesitated, hovering, torn between going to him and giving him the solitude he'd obviously been looking for.

What was that rock? Why *here*? I hugged myself, the certainty I'd felt when I'd faced down Odin faltering.

I could stand up to the Allfather. I could encourage *my* gods to make other plans, try other strategies. But watching Loki slumped against that rock right now, it couldn't have been more clear that our problems ran deeper than that. And I didn't have a clue how to solve this one.

# 20

*Thor*

The costume I'd assembled wasn't half as ridiculous as the one I'd once worn to trick the giants. But then, it would have been hard to top a wedding dress. I was lucky Freya had ever forgiven me for that coarse impersonation.

Today I wasn't attempting to look like anyone in particular. I just needed to *not* look like myself.

"What do you think?" I asked Baldur. He was the only one of my companions I'd mentioned my intentions too. It would be a lot more satisfying to return victorious and show them the results than to listen to their doubts ahead of time—if I even got a word in edgewise—and a lot less embarrassing if nothing came of this gamble.

My younger brother looked me over with his head tipped to one side. "You can't do much to hide your size," he said. "But bulk isn't that unusual in giants anyway. I'm not sure *I'd* recognize you without your usual ten-day shadow if I hadn't been here to watch you shave it off."

I mock-glowered at him. "Be glad it'll grow back. Does the glamour look natural enough?"

He nodded. "It just lightens your usual color, in your hair and your face, not adding anything. And it should hold until you return."

He'd used his powers to wash out my appearance. My normally dark reddish-brown hair was now so pale it looked almost blond; my ruddy skin had turned peachy. Between that, going clean-shaven, and the fact that I hadn't adventured in Jotunheim in quite a while, I didn't think anyone would peg me for the Thunderer unless I gave myself away.

"You're leaving the hammer, I assume," Baldur added.

My hand dropped to Mjolnir where it hung from my belt. The thought of walking into giant territory without my greatest weapon, not even knowing I was going to retrieve it there, made my skin tighten. But that hammer would be more of a tip-off to my true identity than anything else.

I detached it and set it by Valhalla's wall. Amid the swords and spears mounted there, I spotted an axe. "This will do. A suitably giant-ish weapon."

I smiled as I removed it. Its handle was thick enough to fit on my belt exactly where I usually hung Mjolnir. I brushed my hands over the plain tunic and pants I'd chosen, dragging in a breath. "I suppose I'm ready to go, then."

"Are you sure it's wise for you to go alone?" Baldur asked. "I could join you—as Father said, there's strength in numbers."

I shook my head. "I couldn't ask you—or any of the others. You're full-blooded Aesir. I at least have the giant heritage in my blood." Loki could pass, of course, and could shift himself into an even better disguise than I could ever manage, but this once, I wanted to make my way without the trickster smoothing the way. Let him see that I had some brains to go with my brawn.

"Good luck, then," Baldur said, squeezing my arm. "If you haven't returned by tomorrow, I'll have to sound the alarm."

"If I can't manage to do this by the end of the day, I deserve the shame of being subjected to a rescue," I said. "Don't worry yourself too much. How many times have I ventured into the realm of giants and returned as well as when I'd left?"

My brother smiled. "More than I can count."

Neither of us mentioned the fact that I'd never ventured there both without my hammer and completely alone.

"Should I be worrying about you?" I asked him as he accompanied me through the vast room to the hearth's entrance. "The darkness inside that you were struggling with—"

Baldur cut off my question with a gentle wave of his hand. "It seems I was fighting so hard against it I only made the pressure of it worse," he said. "I've started letting a little of it out here and there under my control, and I feel steadier every time I do. Nothing could quash my light."

"I never doubted that." I patted him on the back before stepping away from him to duck into the blackness of the hearth.

Yggdrasil's branch into Jotunheim brought me out nowhere all that near any of the major cities. It was the capital I was aiming for, where my ploy was most likely to reach the ears it needed to. Thankfully the isolated terrain where I emerged meant I could coast along with bursts of lightning-twined cloud until I reached one of the better-trafficked roads leading toward the realm's largest city.

A couple carting smoked meat in that direction gave me an uncertain look but agreed to let me ride in the back, as long as I helped them unload once they reached their shop in town. The only difficult part of the journey was restraining myself from sampling their merchandise, which I had to admit set my mouth watering. I could criticize giants for many things, but they did know how to eat well when they took a mind to do it right.

Perhaps that was where my great appetite came from. The

thought settled uneasily in my gut, but I grasped onto it, setting my jaw. I was here as a giant. I had to embrace every bit of me that my mother's line might have affected.

Who would have thought it might be my giant side and not my godly nature that would help me save Asgard?

Unloading the cart only took a few minutes, even though I played down my strength so I didn't draw outright stares. Then it was a simple matter of spotting the most popular drinking establishment in town—the one where figures of some influence among their giant peers would be inclined to enjoy themselves.

The streets were quieter than I remembered being usual, but then, I'd only entered this city a few times in the past, and those times many centuries ago. I assumed it was just a slower night until I turned a corner and found myself faced with a chasm that ran straight through the road. It gaped several feet wide, and the buildings on either side had crumbled into it, leaving only ruins that no one had yet attempted to reconstruct. A makeshift bridge of wooden boards weighted with stones spanned it near the spot where I stood.

What calamity had caused this? I approached the chasm cautiously and peered down into its depths, finding only darkness where the sides narrowed. The couple with the cart had made some mutterings about the "splittings of the earth," but I'd assumed they were talking about a minor earthquake or the like near their farm.

Was this happening a lot? My memory slipped back to Hod's comments about the cave-ins in Nidavellir. Could the realm of giants be cracking open just as the dark elves' home was collapsing?

I wasn't sure I quite felt *sorry* for the giants, given our history, but the possibility left my nerves creeping with even more uneasiness. At least the general sense that their home was under threat should help me convince whoever listened to the story I had to tell.

I backtracked, not entirely trusting the rudimentary bridge

under my substantial weight, and wandered farther through the streets. It wasn't long before a whiff of ale reached my nose. I followed it to a street lined with restaurants, shops, and taverns.

One particular tavern took up the space of two buildings on the edge of a cobblestone square, its windows bright and energetic voices already carrying through the open windows even though it was only mid-afternoon. That looked like a promising spot.

Girding myself, I pushed past the door into the dim light of the establishment. Giants sat around the many circular tables of heavy oak, most of them with tankards in hand. The barkeep behind the matching counter at the back of the place was just setting out several more frothing mugs for the patrons.

Several gazes turned my way at my entrance. This was where I had to find whatever cunning I had in me. I let my shoulders slump and lumbered over to the counter as if I had the weight of all nine realms resting on them.

"A glass of your best ale," I said, leaning against the counter. "Ah, no, make it two glasses. No doubt I'll need more than that before I'm through."

"Had a rough time of it?" the barkeep asked as he poured my drink.

"You could say that," I said. "But not as rough a time as we'll all have if something isn't done. Those bastards in Asgard! They've never missed the chance to lord it over us."

One of the giants sitting near me glanced over. "What's this about Asgard?" he asked, his face already flushing.

If there was one thing I knew about giants, it was that you didn't mention the highest realm unless you wanted to provoke some tempers.

I shook my head as if defeated. "There's no point in talking about it. Look at us. Look at this city. He's right. We're doomed."

A couple of the other giants nearby peered over at me. "What do you mean, doomed?" the first one demanded. "Speak plainly, will you? I'm not interested in guessing games."

I eyed him and the others looking our way, pretending to consider. My heart was thumping faster than if I'd been in the middle of a battle, or at least more anxiously.

I could do this. I could be sly—maybe not as well as Loki, but I'd watched him in action often enough, hadn't I?

Imagining the impressed shock on the trickster's face when he found out what I'd pulled off bolstered my confidence.

"Maybe you'll listen," I said. "The others I talked to were too slow to wrap their heads around it. But you—you seem to know what's what."

The giant drew himself up straighter. Another thing about giants: They were so easily manipulated by flattery. Especially when it came to the intelligence they were often accused, with good reason, of lacking. "I'll listen," he said.

Some of the others tugged their chairs closer. "What's going on?" a woman among them asked.

"I saw Surt today," I said. "I *spoke* to him."

A murmur passed through my audience. Even more heads turned my way. "Surt?" someone said. "I haven't heard talk of him in years. Wasn't he banished to Muspelheim for that failure of a war against the gods?"

Someone else snorted. "Some victory he brought us. Wipe them all out just for them to spring up again good as new."

"He was banished," I said, nodding. "But somehow he's sneaking back to our realm now and then. Maybe the gods are letting him. I have to think—the things he was saying—Odin must have done more than banish him. He must have Surt in his thrall."

"What are you talking about?" the first giant said.

I looked down at my hands as if it pained me to say this part. "He was ranting about how weak the jotun have become. How none of us deserve this realm. That the draugar he's been raising are better warriors than us. I think he means to take the realm by force. Why would he do that if the gods weren't behind him, urging him on through their awful powers?"

The murmur that rippled around me at that question sounded like agreement. I restrained the urge to smile. My ploy had worked. I'd hooked them.

"A draug fight better than a giant," the woman who'd spoken earlier muttered. "Any of us could take on ten."

"I tried to tell him that," I said. "But he just laughed. He said he's been building his army just to prove it to us. It was horrible, seeing him like that. I tried to tell the others I spoke to—we have to help him. Break him out of their spell. Or at least we have to *stop* him before he tears this realm apart even more than it's already been shaken."

"The latter would be simpler," the first giant said, with an uneven grin that told me I wouldn't need any more persuasion to send him on the path I wanted. "Surt thinks so highly of himself? I think he's lived far too long."

# 21

*Aria*

"Well," Tyr said, clapping his hands where he was standing at the edge of the practice field. "That was quite the show."

He sounded impressed but wry at the same time, as if he hadn't expected us to topple that set of targets, but he couldn't bring himself to find the act all that amazing either. I touched down on the grass, my feet braced against the earth and muscles still humming with adrenaline, trying to ignore the pinch of annoyance.

No one had insisted he stick around and watch our continued training to perfect our combined attacks. If he was bored with it, he could go jerk himself off with his one hand.

"Considering your areas of expertise," Loki said from behind me, "I'd expect you to know the difference between warfare and entertainment." His voice had the same edge I'd heard yesterday when he'd talked to Tyr. If anything, after a couple hours of performing with that additional spectator, the edge was even more prominent.

Also like yesterday, Tyr ignored him. "You do seem to run out of targets quickly," he remarked in Thor's general direction. Then he turned to Freya. "What part are we meant to play in the battle exactly while this bunch is demonstrating their flashy talents?"

"I'm sure we'll fight beside them as always," Freya said, her expression suggesting she wasn't incredibly fond of Tyr's attitude either. "We just need to make sure to give them room to work those talents. I've seen them in a real skirmish too. It really is incredible the way their magic merges."

"And if that doesn't suit you, we already know you make excellent bait," Loki tossed in.

Tyr did stiffen at that remark. He frowned at the group of us. "I came back because I understood my help was wanted. I'm here to protect Asgard. Is that a problem?"

"Of course not, of course not," Thor said, stepping forward.

"Come now," Loki said. "You know me. I always enjoy a good joke. Don't be so quick to draw arms." The tension in his posture told a different story. He bent to scoop up an apple that had inadvertently ended up in the jumble of targets we'd hauled out to the field, tossed it in his hand, and caught it. "Let me know when we're set up for another go. I feel the need to stretch my legs."

He sauntered off past the nearest halls without another word or a backward glance, still tossing the apple with sharp flicks of his wrist. My gaze caught Baldur's. He gave me a pained smile as if to say, *I suppose it could be worse?*

I wasn't really sure it could be, though. Every time I'd seen Loki in the last few days, he'd seemed more irritable and more distant at the same time.

"We could get carting those new targets over," Hod said.

He turned his face toward me, including me as well as his twin in the suggestion, but the tug in my gut pulled me toward the slim figure just vanishing beyond the gleaming buildings. "I think I'd better try to talk to him," I said.

Hod didn't need to ask me who. "Good luck," he said, not entirely sarcastically.

I hurried away from them in the direction Loki had gone, letting some of my valkyrie strength and speed flow through my legs. I'd never beat Loki in a race, but he wasn't walking that fast. I got the impression he hadn't expected anyone to bother following him.

"Does the great Tyr request my presence?" he asked when I caught up, his gaze still fixed on the forest he was heading toward.

"No," I said, abruptly annoyed with him. "What's with you lately? He's kind of a jerk, but he's not *that* bad."

"Perhaps he should be the one you're chatting with then."

I restrained a growl of frustration. As I strode faster to keep pace with him, a hint of scent drifted off his shirt. A tinge of that sulfuric smell I associated with Muspelheim. Had he gone back there again this morning?

My irritation washed away with a wave of hopelessness. I gritted my teeth against the sensation. Loki had given me a whole new life, had seen me as worthy of it when none of the other gods would have looked twice at me. I couldn't give up on him.

A spark of inspiration hit me with the leap of the apple up from his palm. I walked alongside him a few steps farther, and then I launched myself into the air just as he tossed the fruit. With a whip of my arm, my fingers had closed around its smooth skin.

"Pixie!" Loki said in protest.

I whirled around to face him, hovering a couple feet above the ground with a flutter of my wings, and tossed the apple like he had. "You want it back? Come and get it."

Even a grouchy Loki couldn't resist a little mischief. A gleam lit in his amber eyes. "Are you sure that's a dare you want to make?" he said in the sly tone I was more used to.

I arched an eyebrow at him. "Trying to talk me out of it because you're afraid I'll win?"

He sprang at me without warning, but not at full-speed—and I'd been waiting for a move like that anyway. With a sweep of my wings, I took off toward the forest. My fingers stayed clutched around the apple. It was an ordinary one, already bruised from being tumbled with the practice supplies, but right then it felt like something precious.

The breeze warbled as Loki dashed after me. I veered one way and swooped another, pushing my wings as fast as they would carry me. Once I was in the shelter of the forest, he'd have a harder time pouncing.

There. I shot between two trees on the fringes, jerking to the side an instant before his hand could close around my ankle. Indignant laughter escaped his lips. He wove back and forth through the brush, never more than a few feet behind me. Then, just as I reached the point where the wilder forest gave way to the apple orchard, he sprang so fast I didn't even feel him coming until his arm had already snagged my waist.

The sudden tug spun me around as we fell. My wings contracted into my back. Loki's arm jerked up, his hand cupping the back of my head to protect me from the worst of the impact as we crashed into the soft grass at the edge of the orchard. Which meant he landed over me, his heave of breath spilling hot against my cheek, his lips just inches from mine, his body braced above me.

Even though his arms had caught most of his weight, panic jolted through me at the impression of being pinned down by his body. My back tensed against Loki's protective embrace. His playful expression vanished.

He pushed himself backward, moving off me as he slid his arm free, and a different sort of panic flashed through me. I was about to lose him again, to lose the pleased light I'd just reignited in him.

My hand darted out to snag in the fabric of his tunic, halting him. "No."

Loki peered down at me, going completely still. "Ari?"

I inhaled shakily. Too many emotions were colliding inside me. The fact that it terrified me that I might lose him terrified me all over again in turn. When had anything or anyone other than Petey mattered to me even half this much?

If this scenario went wrong, where the hell would that leave me?

I didn't know, but I did know that it'd be even worse not to have Loki at all. I adjusted my grip on his shirt, willing my breaths to even out. One of his knees had brushed my inner thigh when he'd moved. My skin was already tingling from that contact.

He wouldn't hurt me. He wouldn't take anything other than what I offered him. I knew *that.*

"I want this," I said, holding his gaze. "I trust you."

Loki flinched. I couldn't have said what reaction I'd expected, but it definitely hadn't been that. My heart ached before he even spoke.

"You'd be the first, then," he said, and hesitated. "I don't want to stir up those memories, to make you think of… I'm not very good at handling fragile objects, pixie. I have a tendency of breaking them, even if I end up fixing them after."

The rawness in his voice made my heart beat even faster, but it was a heady drumming now. My initial panic was pulling back, bit by bit, in the wake of the warmth between our bodies.

"Maybe you just think you're not good with them because no one ever expected you to be before," I said.

Loki stared at me. "Ari," he said, and then didn't seem to know how to continue.

I tugged on his shirt. "Anyway, I don't break that easily."

A hoarse chuckle slipped from his lips. His head dipped down, his nose grazing mine. "No, you certainly don't."

I tipped my face, seeking out his mouth, and he closed that last short distance in an instant. His lips met mine with a flicker of heat that coursed straight down to my core. He kept himself braced over me, no part of us touching except our mouths and that knee resting just above my own.

That kiss bled into another and another, each one a little deeper, a little sweeter. The nerves still keeping my muscles tight started to loosen. My fingers stayed curled in the fabric of Loki's shirt, but the rest of me relaxed against the grassy ground. This was nothing at all like those memories he'd alluded to. It was something utterly different. Something new.

Loki eased a little closer, his hips pressing against mine ever so slightly, and my pulse hiccupped. But his tongue teased into my mouth at the same moment, and the fear was overshadowed by that fresh rush of heat.

Our tongues tangled like dancing flames. I dropped the apple I'd still been holding with my other hand and looped my arm behind Loki's neck to pull him even closer.

He shifted his weight onto one arm so he could stroke his fingers along the curve of my breast. A gentle stream of heat followed his touch. I arched toward him, kissing him harder, wanting more.

The trickster eased his lips away from mine to consider my tank top. His finger glided along the neckline, sparking pleasure across my collarbone.

"What should we do with this?" he murmured.

"Whatever you want," I said with a tickle of curiosity to see where he'd take that opening.

A grin curled his mouth. "Hmm. You do have a decent supply of clothing in that hall of yours, don't you?"

"Yes?" I said, giving him a questioning look. Freya and I had taken a brief trip down to their house in Midgard not long after we'd first arrived so I could collect some changes of clothes.

"Excellent. In that case..."

He traced a line down my breastbone, and literal flames leapt up in the wake of his finger. The magical sear of them soaked into my skin without burning. They spread across my top, consuming the fabric as they went, flooding me with more and more of that blissful heat. When they licked across my now-bare nipples, I gasped with a bolt of pleasure.

I yanked Loki's mouth back to mine. As he kissed me, the flames he'd lit continued their scorching path down—over my ribcage and across my belly, tickling my navel, then creeping along the waist of my jeans.

When they sizzled over my clit, my hips arched of their own accord. The flood of pleasure was so intense my whole body shook. A moan caught in my throat, and my teeth nicked Loki's lip. "Loki…"

"Right here, pixie," he murmured. "Whatever you need from me." His thumb flicked over the peak of my breast, drawing a whimper out of me.

I ran my hands down his lean chest. His flames hadn't even singed his own clothes. I grasped the hem and yanked it up. "Off."

He stripped off the tunic and tossed it to the side in the blink of an eye. I'd already reached lower to cup his rigid cock through his slacks. Loki groaned, and the flames he'd sent right down to my feet a few moments ago returned to lick across my core. The gentle but hot caress brought another moan to my lips. As he leaned in to reclaim my mouth, I felt as if I were being devoured in both places at once.

My hips bucked again, brushing the bulge of his arousal. I fumbled with his fly. There was no hesitation, no fear left in me, only a torrent of desire.

More flames sparked as Loki kicked off the rest of his clothes. They crackled across my nipples and nibbled my throat, blazed across my belly and lapped at my clit. Not a hint of pain came with the thrill they provoked.

The sensations coursed deeper when Loki teased the head of his cock along my opening. I made an insistent sound and raised my legs to embrace his hips. He slid into me with a surge of heat and pleasure. A sigh tumbled from my lips.

Loki eased in and out of me slowly, ecstasy swelling within me with each stroke of his cock, filling me with the most delicious burn. The magical flames tingling over every sensitive spot on my body had me writhing with just a few thrusts. One pinched my clit, and the dam inside me broke. I came, shuddering, on a wave of bliss.

"Oh, I think we can take you further than that," Loki said by my ear. He kissed me through the final tremors, and then he started moving again, his thrusts still measured but picking up speed. With each one he filled me deeper. That sizzling heat spread across my whole sex, pulsing against my clit, making my body flare hotter inside and out.

Another wave of pleasure built and built, until I was trembling for release. Whimpers escaped me with every panted breath. My fingers tangled in the silky hair at the back of Loki's head. He met my eyes, his amber eyes smoldering with a strange softness as he gazed down at me. We rocked together, every plunge of his cock bringing a bolt of bliss. His expression tensed with his own rising need.

"Come with me, Ari," he said, in the most tender voice I'd ever heard from him. The flames licked at me with a sharper prickling of pleasure, but it was that tone and the look in his eyes that sent my spirit flying.

I cried out, my head tipping back as my eyes rolled up, my back bowing to ride the explosion of my second release. Heat burst in my core and radiated through me. A ragged cry escaped Loki in turn. He thrust harder, gripping my thigh, and I spiraled even higher than before. For an instant, as his hips jerked and he followed me, my vision blurred with a white-hot glaze of ecstasy.

Loki swayed to a stop over me. He held there for several seconds as he caught his breath, and then he slipped his arm under me, flipping us in one smooth movement so he was on his back holding me against his chest.

I snuggled against him, still drifting back down from the heights of my orgasm. His fiery heat had seared the sweat from our bodies, but my skin was flushed everywhere it touched his.

The trickster's fingers brushed over my hair. I nuzzled his jaw and lifted my head for another kiss. His hand rose to cup my jaw, and the kiss lingered on and on until I was breathless again. My heart thumped so giddily that I couldn't think of what to say.

Loki tucked his head against mine. "No proclamations?" he said lightly, but I thought I caught a hint of longing in his tone.

I swallowed thickly, breathing in the spicy scent of his skin. "Did you have one to make?

"You know, I think I just might."

I wasn't prepared for the rush of emotion that hit me, even though he hadn't actually said anything yet: an answering affection —and a jolt of fear at what might happen when this moment ended and we were faced with all the horrible complications of real life again. I wrapped my arm around his chest, hugging him tight. The words slipped out before I could catch them.

"Don't leave."

"Whoever said I was going to?" Loki replied, but his muscles had tensed against me, just slightly.

"You've been going down to Muspelheim," I said to his chest. "I can smell it on you. But you didn't tell the rest of us about it. You've been talking to Surt?"

He really tensed then, his body shifting as if to propel himself upright and push me back from him. "If you think for one second I'd align myself with that wretched excuse for a—"

"No!" I caught his shoulder, drawing back far enough to hold his gaze. "That's not what I meant. I know you. I know you wouldn't turn your back on us because you wanted to. I was just worried that Odin was sending you off on some new scheme.

Forcing you to play one of his games. He pushed you so far before…" My grip on Loki's shoulder tightened, as if I could hold him with me, away from the Allfather and his manipulations, just with that one hand.

Loki's expression softened in an instant. He did sit up, but only to collect me against him, hugging me on his lap. "Oh, pixie. You don't need to worry about that. My blood oath with Odin still connects us, but any compulsion to obey his orders dissolved with our first deaths. I don't intend to follow his instructions into villainy ever again."

"Then what *have* you been doing down there? You've seemed… upset, the last few days. And the way you've been going at Tyr—"

"Tyr is a different story," Loki muttered. "Do you know how he lost his hand?"

I hesitated, suddenly not sure I wanted to know. "I don't."

"I told you they chained up my wolfish son. He was a smart one. He could tell they weren't just playing games like they told him, testing his strength. When they brought the dark elf-made chain, he wouldn't let them put it on him unless one of the gods was willing to offer his hand in Fenrir's mouth as a show of good faith." Loki let out a humorless chuckle. "Tyr was the one 'brave' enough to offer. Without any faith. And so he lost his hand, and my son lost his freedom for the rest of his life."

"Oh. No wonder you don't like him."

He sighed. "I suppose I should be over those grudges by now. It's just been the last week, so many memories stirred up…"

"I know," I said gently.

He tucked my head under his, his embrace tightening. "About the rest—my little jaunts down to Muspelheim… Surt came to me offering an alliance. I played along for a little while to see what I could find out about his plans and resources."

"And you went with him into his realm to discuss all that?" I leaned into him to ease the prickling of fear. "What if he'd tried to cage you like he did with Odin?"

Loki made a dismissive sound. "Do you really think any regular giant could outwit me? I stayed on my guard. Unfortunately, *he* didn't trust me particularly, although I suppose in this case that caution was warranted. I was hoping to have more to report before I spoke to the rest of you. I'm not sure anything I gleaned will be all that useful."

"Are you going back?"

"It would appear not. This morning he insisted that we'd done enough talking, that I commit myself to his cause in unshakeable fashion. I don't think he was very pleased when I told him I wasn't satisfied with my end of the theoretical bargain." His next chuckle sounded more like his usual self.

"You've been grouchy since before Tyr showed up," I said. "Were you just frustrated that you hadn't been able to find out more from Surt?"

"Well, yes. That, and..." Loki paused, his chest rising and falling with a slow breath. "Talking with him, it reminded me too much of certain feelings that used to be all too much a part of my life. Feelings that had been creeping back into my mind, in ways I hadn't totally acknowledged."

"What do you mean?"

"I have many real grievances with the gods of Asgard, pixie, but—I didn't have to agree to Odin's terms. I didn't have to keep his secrets. There were parts of me that enjoyed seeing the gods get their comeuppance at my hands. Who's to say whether I might have fit in more smoothly over time if it wasn't for that?" He sighed. "Perhaps I'm not the monster they liked to see me as, but I'm not a hero by any stretch of the imagination either."

My chest squeezed. I buried my face in the crook of his neck. "You're you," I said. "Who's a hero all of the time anyway?"

I certainly wasn't. But I'd be damned if anyone, king of the gods or giant with flaming sword or army of draugar, took the joys and peace I'd found in my new life away from me.

"I'm honored by your devotion," Loki said. His tone was dry, but his embrace tightened around me for a moment before he eased back. "I suppose if we want to get on with the heroic side of things, we should find out what the others have gotten up to. Back to that bloody training."

I got up, looking around as he pulled his slacks back on. "Um," I said, crossing my arms over my bare chest. "I do have plenty of clothes back in my hall. I don't suppose you had a plan for how I'd make it *back* to my hall to get them, now that you've turned what I had on into ash?"

Loki laughed and tossed his tunic to me. "Wear this. I can protect your modesty as well as the rest of you."

The shirt was long even on Loki's tall frame. On me it fell nearly to my knees. I stuck my tongue out at him as we set off for the city.

"How do you know it won't be *me* protecting you, huh?"

He grinned, his hand dipping down to close around mine. "I'll be perfectly happy either way."

## 22

*Aria*

"Are we sure this is the best course of action, after everything we've learned?" Hod said as the group of us came down off the rainbow bridge.

The humid air in the part of Midgard that Loki had directed us to closed in around us. The dark god turned his head, presumably taking in the sounds and feel of the terrain around us just like I was taking in the look of it. Jungle-like vegetation grew tangled along one side of the road. A cluster of small houses on stilts stood in the distance in the other direction.

"We don't need to decide how to *act* yet," Loki said, brushing his hands together. "At this point, we're simply investigating. One of the draugar I convinced Surt to show me had a shirt with a very specific logo. It's almost certain that victim was picked up around here, which means there must be another gateway in this area, whether the dark elves are still delivering bodies through it or not."

I stretched out my wings behind me. "Let's go find out. We

can't help them fix their realm until they've stopped hurting all kinds of innocent people."

"If we catch them in the act…" Thor muttered, hefting his hammer as we started walking. He didn't need to finish that threat.

Baldur came up beside me. "Can you sense their energy nearby?" he asked.

I'd already pushed my awareness forward across the terrain. "I might need to go up in the air to get a wider impression—oh." A shimmering clot of that oily energy brushed my valkyrie senses from what felt like not far at all to our right. "There are dark elves that way," I said, pointing into the jungle. "Four or five of them, I think."

"Into the wilds it is, then," Loki said with a spring in his step. Our encounter by the orchard seemed to have released him from the bad mood that'd been gripping him for so long.

Thor bashed a path with his hammer for a couple paces until the trickster pointed out that "it might be preferable if they didn't hear us coming from miles away." After that, we picked our way across the damp ground, around tree trunks choked with vines, much more slowly. But we'd only been heading that way for a few minutes when a figure appeared amid the brush in front of us: a dark elf, short and stout like most of them were, with the usual black hair and sallow skin. He held up a white cloth just a few shades lighter than his hand like a gesture of surrender.

We halted, studying him. "You've been stealing people from the towns near here," Thor rumbled. "We need to—"

"We don't want to continue those crimes," the elf broke in. "Not if there are other ways. We've had delegations waiting at our remaining gateways, watching for you to come for us again. There's no way for us to reach out to you in Asgard on our own."

"A delegation?" Hod asked, his tone wary but not harsh.

"Three of my superiors would return with you to Asgard to speak with Odin," the man said. "Between them they have authority over several sectors of Nidavellir, and they could persuade the other leaders too if they feel it's in our interests. We would rather this conflict didn't turn to outright war."

The five of us exchanged a glance. A delegation wanting to discuss peace with Odin—that sounded promising. It was kind of hard to take them completely at face value after everything we'd already seen, though.

"Have these 'superiors' come out," Loki suggested with a beckoning motion. "We'll want to look them over. If we're to trust them, we need to see no weapons and none of your war-like contraptions."

The dark elf bobbed his head and shuffled away through the dense vegetation. Less than a minute later, he returned with three companions—two men and a woman, all of them similar in stature and coloring but wearing embroidered tunics in a deep blue that I guessed reflected their status among the elves.

"I can look them over," Hod volunteered with a wry smile. He lifted his hand, and his shadows stirred around him. They seeped through the bushes around us to coil around the dark elves, testing their pockets and any bagginess in their clothes for hidden items.

"We don't want to fight," the woman said. "We're only trying to do right by our people."

"You lost the benefit of the doubt when you started slaughtering a whole raft of other people to do that," Loki retorted. "Give us a moment to confer."

Wc took a couple of steps back, and Loki swept his arm with a tingle of magic that must have concealed us the way he'd hidden me when we'd gone to watch over Petey.

"From what I could sense of their motives, they're mostly anxious about the future and a little desperate for this attempt to work out," Baldur said softly. "There was hope in them, and regret for the past. I think they honestly want to bargain with us. I felt no sense of deception."

"That's the same impression I got from them," I said. "That doesn't mean we shouldn't keep a close watch. But this could be the way we beat Surt for good, if we bring the dark elves over to our side, couldn't it?"

Thor was frowning. "I'm not sure how far I'd trust the dirt-eaters to follow through on any agreement after everything they've already done. We may not need them."

"It certainly can't hurt to *have* them," Loki put in. "In my opinion, we may as well hear what they have to say before we go dismissing it."

"I agree," Hod said. "They've done horrible things, but they were in a horrible situation. And what could the three of them hope to do to us or Odin that they couldn't have when they had him captured for all those years?"

Thor lowered his head. "All right," he said. "But I'm keeping Mjolnir ready."

"As well you should, my friend," Loki said, clapping him on the arm. He waved away the magic he'd drawn around us and raised his voice so it would carry to the dark elves. "All right, come along. Let's see this through quickly."

The three elves trudged through the jungle with us quietly, their expressions stoic. Were those prickles of shame I felt from them for the harm they'd done or also for having to turn to the gods for help at all? I couldn't tell. As long as it was mostly the former, I guessed it didn't matter.

Loki led the way up the rainbow bridge, Baldur beside him and Thor, Hod, and me bringing up the rear behind our "guests." Freya and Tyr had stayed behind in Asgard to continue discussing strategy and catching up, but they were waiting by the top of the bridge. Freya took one look at the dark elves in our midst, and her eyebrows shot up. Her hand leapt to her sword.

"Why are you bringing *them* here?" she demanded.

"A delegation to speak with Odin," Loki said with a sweep of his arm toward our company. "We'll take them straight to him, if you don't mind."

Tyr's expression was skeptical, but he didn't argue. Freya fell into step beside us as we headed down Valhalla's main road. "Are you sure this is quite—"

"What is this?" a low voice demanded, rolling through the air. Odin had emerged from his hall and was striding toward us faster than I'd have thought that stately body was capable of.

Loki stepped to the side as if he felt the dark elves might as well state their own case. The woman bowed her head to the approaching Allfather. "Great Odin," she said, her shoulders tensed. "We know we have done you and the people of Midgard wrong. If you would give us the chance—"

"Begone!" he said, as thunderous as I'd ever heard Thor, coming to a stop in front of them. "Begone from my sight. Begone from my realm."

Hod stiffened where he'd also eased to the side. "Father, I think we should at least hear them out."

"There is nothing a dark elf could say that would be of any interest to me," Odin said. "No deals can be made with those who act like vermin." He waved them off with a sweep of his cloak. His spear gleamed as he smacked the base of it against the marble tiles. "Off with you. *Now.* Before I decide to send you off in a much more painful fashion."

"Odin," I protested, but the dark elves were already cringing in the wake of his anger. They turned and hustled for the rainbow bridge.

"I really think—" Loki began.

Odin swiveled away from him, toward his hall. "I'm not interested in your thoughts on this matter."

He barreled back to his hall as quickly as he'd come at us, his cloak flapping behind him.

My jaw clenched. No. He was not going to ruin what could be

our best chance at winning this war—and getting through it *alive*—because he refused to consider anyone's position other than his own.

I darted after him, lifting into the air for the speed my wings could lend me. Odin marched into his hall and flung the door shut behind him with a dull thud. I wrenched it open with a heave of my valkyrie strength and followed.

"Stop!" I said. "We've got to call them back. You've got to talk with them. If we had them on our side—"

He spun back to face me, his single eye so furious my words caught in my throat. "They mean nothing," he said with a jab of his finger. "Did you not hear a single thing I said to you yesterday? We will not suffer the excuses of traitors or lift them up when they will play no part in our victory or failure."

"You don't know they won't," I protested. The door rasped over the floor behind me, footsteps tapping against the floor as at least a couple of the other gods came in behind me. "All you know is we're important. They could make some difference still, couldn't they? The difference between it being an easy victory or a hard one. A difference between whether your own *sons* live or die."

"They held me in a *cage* for years," Odin retorted. "I will not bargain with them."

"*Surt* held you in a cage," I said. "They were following his orders because they didn't know what else to do."

"Because you abandoned them," Loki spoke up, appearing at my left, his arms folded against his chest. He glanced back at the others who'd followed us. "We all did. The realms are failing because of our neglect. So who can say where the fault lies first?"

"This is the hand we've been dealt," Odin said. "I've seen how it plays out. I've seen all I need to know. For ages I have led you, and Asgard has prospered."

"The other realms matter too," Hod said quietly, coming up at my right.

Odin's eye flashed. "Things will be as they are. We act where we can. There isn't—"

I was so tired of arguing with him. So tired of it going nowhere. All that frustration tore through me at once, and before I'd thought it through, my body was moving. I threw myself at him.

Odin was a god of war, but he wasn't the warrior Thor was—and he hadn't fought anyone in all those years. His spear hand swung around fast enough, but my reflexes reacted faster. I shoved the pole away with my heel and whipped around behind the Allfather before his other snatching hand could catch hold of my limbs. My switchblade leapt into my hand at a tug of my fingers. I grasped Odin's grizzled hair and slammed the knife straight toward his remaining eye.

My hand jerked to a stop less than an inch from piercing the brown iris. Odin had gone rigid. The hall around us was silent. When I didn't follow through with the blow, he shifted to shake me from his shoulders, but I was already springing off him. I landed on the floor right in front of him, glaring up at him, the switchblade still gleaming in my grip.

"If I'd wanted things to turn out that way, you'd have no eyes now," I said. "You'd see nothing except for those 'whispers and fragments' in your head. Did they warn you about that? Did you see me coming? Or is it possible there's a thing or two that you miss?"

Odin stared down at me, his jaw working. A light touch fell on my shoulder. To my surprise, it was Baldur's clear voice that rang out.

"She's right, father. You don't know everything. We all should have a say in how we fight this war—in everything we do from here on."

Odin blinked at him. "My son."

Baldur swallowed audibly, but he didn't back down. "You've ruled us well. I love you. But I will not stand beside you if you push every other opportunity we have away. The rest of us have lived almost as long as you now. We've seen almost as much—we've seen things you haven't. These are our lives, maybe the last we'll ever get. We should have as much of a say in how we use them as you do."

I looked up at the light god, startled by the vehemence in his voice. Baldur's sparkling gaze was fixed on Odin, his stance firm. With the murmur of other footsteps, I felt four other figures come to stand around us.

"You've done enough," Hod said. "No more lies, no more schemes behind our backs. We deserve that much respect."

"We *all* have ideas we can contribute," Thor said. "We can't get anywhere if you won't listen to anyone but yourself. If you're hiding things from us."

Odin's gaze slid to someone now just behind me. "You told them," he said hollowly.

"I showed them," Loki said in a low voice. "The circumstances demanded it. And don't you think it was time?"

"It was." Freya walked up to her husband, setting her hand on his arm. "Share the burden with us, love. Let us construct this new path together. The rest… The rest we can discuss when the catastrophe is averted."

Odin's shoulders sagged slightly. He exhaled in a rush. "I know what I have seen," he said, but his tone faltered more than it had before.

We had to press this advantage while we had it. "We can call back the dark elves," I said. "Or—if you don't want to deal with them, let one of your sons talk to them. You…" The answer came to me as soon as I started to put it to words. "You need to make your peace with Muninn. She doesn't like Surt. She doesn't want his war either. But whatever happened between the two of you, she can't get past it, not without some offering from you. She was one of your closest companions for centuries, wasn't she? There has to be some way you can win her back."

Odin grimaced, and I expected him to argue. Then he lowered his head and ran his hand over his beard.

"I may know a way to reach out to her," he said. "But you must bring her to me first. I will not meet her on Surt's ground while he still rules."

# 23

*Hod*

"They might be angry after the way Odin chased their three leaders off," Ari said as we crossed the field toward Valhalla. The grass was getting taller, the soft spears hissing against our feet. I dragged in a deep lungful of its warm near-sweet scent, as if it could last me the entire time I was in the dark elves' caves.

"We already know Muninn has more than enough anger toward Odin and the rest of us," I pointed out. "I'm not sure your request will be any more welcome."

"Mostly Odin," Ari muttered. "And there's only one of her."

"And she trapped us in a nearly inescapable prison for longer than I care to remember." I reached out with enough sense of her presence to rumple the waves of her hair. "I think we should just say that both of us are heading into a fair bit of danger. There's no winning the contest of who should be most concerned, valkyrie."

"Maybe not. I'm still going to worry, though." She was silent for a moment. Then, so quickly I almost stumbled, she turned and wrapped her arms around me, stopping me with her embrace.

"Ari?" I said, surprised even if I was pleased at the same time. Norns knew our valkyrie could be tender, but I wouldn't have expected this much affection out of the blue.

My arms came around her, hugging her to me. I couldn't deny I'd have preferred to never let her go, for neither of us to have needed to venture off into uncertain realms.

"I just… You know how much you mean to me, don't you?" she said. "You and the others… You mean so much to me that it scares me. But I told myself, I *promised* myself, that I wasn't going to let myself back down out of fear anymore. You have to know—in the last ten years, no one's mattered as much to me except Petey, and you've seen how much I care about him."

"I have," I said, my voice becoming hoarse. "You don't need to say anything, Ari. I'm not waiting for something you haven't given me. The way you are, right now—that's all I want. I swear it. All right?"

She nodded against my shoulder, but she was still holding onto me so tightly it made my stomach knot—for her, for how hard she tried to do right by everyone, for how hard it was for her to accept that she might be loved as she was. I didn't think I could have loved her more, and those feelings had nothing to do with what she said or didn't say.

I brought my hand to the side of her face and eased her into a kiss. She might not have initiated it, but the moment my lips brushed hers, she claimed my mouth, pouring so much passion into our linked bodies that a bolt of desire shot through my chest to my groin.

Later. When this was over, when Surt was conquered, we'd have all the time in the realms to explore each other further than we already had.

The walk through Valhalla was becoming increasingly familiar. I only needed a few brief tendrils of shadow to make my steady way between the rows of tables now. A hint of a chill emanated from the hearth, the doorway beyond it at odds with its normal purpose. Ari stepped through onto Yggdrasil's path first and waited for me to join her.

"Let's see who can make it back first," she said, sounding more relaxed as we started across the trunk.

"I'm not sure this is the right time to have a race," I said.

"Okay, maybe not. Just—be careful with them, all right? We don't know how much we can trust them."

"The same to you with Muninn."

"Oh, believe me, I'll be watching my step around her for a long time, no matter how this pans out." She stopped at the branching that emitted the acrid smell of Muspelheim and squeezed my hand. "I'll see you soon."

Somehow that casual promise released a little of my distress at knowing she was venturing off into Surt's realm yet again. "And I'll see you," I said.

She kissed me quickly, and then she was darting down the branch.

I didn't have to walk much farther to reach the route I needed to take. I squared my shoulders and strode along the branch to the gate that would take me to Nidavellir.

The air that washed over me on the other side was as damp and chilly as before. I tested my footing on the rocky floor and turned my head to where the guards had been waiting last time. I doubted they changed up their preferred post much.

"I come from Odin with an urgent need to speak to any of your leaders."

The guards murmured amongst themselves without even bothering to address me this time. It sounded as though they were having something of a disagreement, but I couldn't make out enough words to put together the content of it. I waited it out, shifting from one foot to the other and hoping my discomfort wasn't apparent.

Finally, one of them moved toward me, a shift in the dank air. "You can follow me? Come on, then. I can't promise how much he'll want to see you, though."

"Whatever you can do," I said with a grateful dip of my head.

My shadows helped me trace the path of my dark elf guide with only an occasional stubbed toe on the uneven patches in the cave floor. I hadn't been through here often enough to have formed much of a mental map, but I had the impression we were going the same way as before. That impression was reinforced when I stepped out into a larger room that felt the same as the one where I'd met the local commander on my first visit.

"Wait here," the dark elf instructed.

For the first few minutes, I wondered why he'd left me unguarded. Then a soft scuffing sound down the tunnel behind me told me that wasn't the case—he simply hadn't drawn my attention to my sentinel.

It seemed like longer than the last time that I waited. Perhaps the commander didn't want to be bothered with me this time. When footsteps finally scraped against the stone floor to meet me, there was a sharpness to them I didn't remember.

His voice was sharp too. "Blind One. So you return. What is it this time? I've already had word that your Allfather ran a peaceful delegation out of Asgard this morning. I don't see what's to gain from talking now."

"I understand that," I said quickly. "And I apologize for the way your comrades were treated. Odin is still recovering from his imprisonment, and I hope you can understand why he wouldn't have the most pleasant associations with the dark elves right now. But the rest of us believe we should at least attempt a treaty. He's come to agree with that stance. That's why I'm here."

"Am I supposed to just take your word for it that the Allfather has changed his mind so quickly?"

I dipped my hand into my pocket and held out a carved stone token. "He gave me this as proof that I'm here in his stead, speaking for him."

One of the commander's underlings, I suspected, slunk forward and snatched the stone from my fingers. There was a minute of silence as the commander considered it.

Odin didn't give out those signs of his favor easily. He imbued the runes on them with a temporary magical glow that only he could create, that should tell anyone who saw it that it had come from the Allfather himself, and recently. Of course, that didn't mean the dark elves had to accept it as proof.

"Your delegation was waiting for us," I said. "They had something specific they wanted to offer. I'll hear that offer now, if you'll let me. I can negotiate on Odin's behalf. We don't want to see this realm fail, I can promise you that."

A rough breath escaped the commander. He flicked the token back at me—it struck my arm and tapped to the ground. I bent to pick it up, my heart sinking at the same time.

"What if we no longer believe in anything you'd promise?" the commander said.

I hesitated, and it occurred to me that talking might not be enough. It hadn't been enough to break through to Odin. How could it be to shatter the centuries of animosity that must have built up as we'd ignored the outer realms?

"I can show you," I said, hoping I was right. "You can see me make good on that promise right before your eyes. Take me to one of the caves that's starting to crumble."

The commander exchanged a few words with his underlings. Then he sighed. "All right. Come along then."

He didn't slow his pace for me or offer any assistance, but that was fine. I kept up well enough as they led me deeper into the warren of caves. A mild claustrophobia prickled over my skin, but I pushed aside my uneasiness. How much worse was it to live in this place all the time and not know when the ceiling might fall on your head?

"Here," the commander said, drawing to a halt. One of his underlings grasped my sleeve and tugged me forward.

My hand came to rest on the edge of an entrance where another cave split off from the wider passage we were standing in. Even in that brief touch, a shiver ran over my palm. This rock was shifting, thinning—minutely but enough to make anyone wary.

"So? What great godly magic will you work?"

I ignored the skepticism in the commander's voice, training all my attention on the cave ahead of me. My shadows flowed from my body along the floor, walls and ceiling, relaying information back to me about every dip and crack. And there were several cracks, spidering along the ceiling and the upper walls. I set my jaw and bowed my head.

All this dark rock, this cold mass all around us—it resonated with part of my nature, deep down. I focused on the cracks I could feel almost as clearly as if I were grazing my fingertips over them, pouring more and more shadow into them. Letting that shadow flow on up into the solid rock. Trickling through every gap, every unsteady space. Hardening, solidifying, as cold and firm as mid-winter's ice.

Pouring all that cool energy through me left my lungs clenching. I sucked in a breath and propelled more forward. I had to do everything I could. I had to ensure not one pebble dropped from this ceiling in the following days, or everything I'd attempted here would be for naught.

I wasn't sure how much time had passed before sending forth more shadows sent a splinter of pain through my chest. I eased back, letting the last few wafts of darkness test my handiwork.

The rock all along the narrow passage was smooth now, every

crevice sealed. It held firm against my resting hand. I turned back to the commander.

He brushed past me, the closest he'd dared to come to me so far, and stalked into the cave. His feet stilled. He turned, stopped, and turned again. His fingers whispered over the stone surface.

"This isn't an illusion?" he said, but his voice was already awed. "It'll hold?"

"Better than any rock you've ever dealt with," I said.

"It's not enough to fix all our troubles. Not by far."

"I know." I inhaled deeply into my aching lungs. "I would come back. Once a week, until such a time as we decided a different arrangement would be better. I'd stay long enough to stabilize another passage like this, or to help clear new caves, or simply to hear your news and pass on any I have myself."

The commander returned to the mouth of the passage. "You must have conditions of your own, from Odin."

"You will cut off all relations with Surt," I said. "Barricade any gateways to his realm—I can help you with that. Pass on what information you know of his army and his schemes. You didn't really want to be his lackeys anyway, did you?"

"If we do that now, how can we trust that you'll follow through on your end? You might defeat Surt tomorrow, and where does that leave us if you renege?"

I held up my hand, my heart starting to thud. I'd come down here knowing I might need to take things this far. I'd been prepared for it. But my body still balked for a moment before I could force out the words.

"I'll take a blood oath. Like the one that bound Odin and Loki for all of their first lives. Neither I nor the one who swears with me will be able to back down from that."

A hush fell over the dark elves gathered around me that felt more startled than before. The commander swallowed audibly. "A blood oath with a dark elf?"

"We failed you too long," I said. "I think you're owed this much."

"Well… Come with me, then. It isn't me you should be swearing to. I'll tell them what I saw. If you're truly willing to go through with this—you'll have our loyalty, however much of it you require."

# 24

*Aria*

I perched on the edge of the table, my feet braced against the bench as I resisted the urge to swing them impatiently. The faded mead smell of Valhalla seemed thicker than usual today, although maybe that was just because Odin was sitting on his golden throne where I'd first pictured him, before I'd known the real god.

"She said she would come," I said, pressing my hands against the varnished wood to stop them from fidgeting too. "But she couldn't just hop back here the way I can. She would have had to get to the portal in Surt's fortress." My gaze shot to the Allfather. "You *did* make sure Yggdrasil's magic would open to her, didn't you?"

He inclined his head, his eye glinting at my skepticism. "As I promised. I never closed it to her. A being of Asgard stays a being of Asgard."

That was one small relief. I didn't think Muninn had tried to return in however long it'd been since she and Odin had first gone their separate ways.

She'd been watching for me, or for anyone from Asgard, like before. I hadn't gone far from the gate I'd entered Muspelheim through this time—just giving myself enough distance from the guarding dragon that I hadn't been too worried it'd swoop down on me. Then I'd simply sat at the base of the cliff and spread out the cloth I'd brought on the dark rock. White silk, courtesy of Freya—a request for a truce, like the dark elves had shown us.

It had taken about half an hour for Muninn to notice, but she had come. And even though she'd grimaced when I'd told her Odin wanted to speak with her, to make amends, she'd stayed and listened.

"How do I know this isn't a trap?" she'd demanded when I'd finished my plea. "All of you planning revenge for the hand I had in your capture?"

"I guess you can't know for sure," I'd said. "But how can we know you won't pull some kind of memory trick on us either? We're trusting you to come in good faith. I hope you can find a little trust for us too. If you don't like the look of things, you can just leave."

She'd hummed to herself and ruffled her dress, and then she'd said that she would give the Allfather a minute or two, no promises of more. "The gate to Asgard from here is with the others in the back of Surt's fortress," she'd said. "He's given me free access to them, but I may need to wait until there's no one around to see which I take."

"Of course," I'd said. "We'll be waiting."

And now here we were.

"Even if she doesn't come, we can win this battle without her," Hod said from where he was sitting on the bench next to me. He rested a reassuring hand on my calf. "The dark elves have given us a good starting point. Thor is seeing what he can make of his scheme with the giants."

"Thor the Schemer," Loki murmured from where he'd propped himself against the next table over. "I never thought I'd see that day."

"You can't claim *all* the wits in Asgard, trickster," Freya said teasingly. She was standing on the other side of the throne from the hearth, looking as if she thought she might need to defend her husband from his former servant.

Loki grinned. "And I suppose I should be thankful for that."

"How easily can we guard against these illusions of hers?" Tyr asked. He'd taken a sword off the walls, but he let it dangle at his side in a relaxed pose.

"She can't work them on me," Odin said. "I doubt she'd try with me here, but if she did, I'd break you free of them."

"I'll be paying attention to her emotional state," Baldur said. He leaned back against the table where he was sitting next to Loki, his gaze on the hearth. "If I sense any malice, I'll give warning."

"What are you going to say to her?" I asked Odin. Frankly, I was more worried about him screwing this up than anything else. Muninn's feelings about him ran so raw I could see the hurt and rage in her eyes whenever I so much as said his name. If he brought even a hint of his know-it-all arrogance to this conversation, we could kiss any hope of making peace goodbye.

"You'll hear it when I say it to her," the Allfather said evenly, which didn't really comfort me. I shifted my weight, the squirming impulse wriggling deeper through my nerves.

A ripple of energy washed over us from the hearth like a faint breeze. My head jerked up. Odin shifted forward.

"A guest has arrived."

He pulled himself to his feet and considered his spear. After a moment's thought, he leaned it against his throne rather than keeping it in his hand. I guessed even he could figure out that facing Muninn unarmed was going to go over better. Something in his expression softened, more than I'd have thought was possible. Maybe he was really ready for this conversation after all.

A rustling caught my ears, so muted I wasn't sure anyone else except Loki would have caught it. Then a small black shape burst from the hearth and soared toward the ceiling with a fluttering of feathers.

The raven circled beneath the rafters, peering down at us. When she'd glided over our heads a few times—enough to decide we didn't have a bird cage at the ready to toss her into, presumably—she swooped down to land in front of the hearth. She stood up in her human form with the ashy opening at her back. It'd give her a quick escape route if she didn't like what she heard in that minute or two she'd offered us.

"Odin," she said in her softly hoarse voice, her shoulders slightly hunched in a defensive stance. Her large dark eyes shone starkly from her pale face. They didn't leave him for an instant. The rest of us might as well not have been in the room.

"Muninn," Odin said with a respectful dip of his grizzled head. "Thank you for coming. It's been a long time since I saw you here."

"And far too long before that," she shot back.

"Yes." He kept his head low, rubbing his mouth. "I failed to consider that you might want a life of your own beyond what you had serving me. It was an oversight unworthy of me, and I apologize for that."

Muninn blinked, looking startled. Then her mouth tensed again. "And did you only just realize this oversight?"

"It's only recently I've realized just how angry with me you were," Odin said with a hint of irony. "But did you think I forgot about you the moment you set off on your own path? I have looked in on you over the years."

She bristled. "You *spied* on me."

"No!" He raised his hand. "You know my seat doesn't allow me to peer through walls. I didn't invade your privacy. I only caught a glimpse, now and then, when I wanted to be sure of how you were faring. But that was enough to catch a fragment or two of certain types of conversations."

The raven woman was still tensed. Odin let out his breath. "For a long while, I saw you as little more than an extension of myself, and that was wrong. That doesn't mean I wasn't concerned at all with your well-being."

"You had strange ways of showing that concern," she shot back.

A knowing gleam came into his eye. "I never asked anything of you I wasn't completely sure you were capable of handling."

"It's not just me. You've neglected so many of the realms—so many of the people in them—"

"I know," he said. "I have many apologies to make. But we have already started to reach out. We'll bring the strength of the gods back to all the realms."

"I just spoke with the dark elves this morning," Hod put in. He held up his hand, the one marked by a still-raw scratch of a knife that he hadn't let his twin heal. "We'll put things as right as we can. We all should have realized sooner."

Muninn shifted on her feet. She looked from Hod to Odin. "Well, what now? You can't give me back what was lost. How could you possibly make up for all the centuries I was under your thumb?"

The gleam in Odin's eye shone brighter. "I can't make up for them—I acknowledge that. But I *can* give you a little more time with what you most recently lost, and I promise you may make a home for yourself in Asgard or call on us as you need us like any of the gods, without any expectation of your service, from here on."

"What I most recently lost?" the raven woman repeated.

He gave her a smile that looked almost gentle. "I may have missed some very obvious things, but I don't think there's any way I could miss this. I can't summon a spirit for long after this much time detached from the world of the living, but Valhalla has enough power to grant them a brief additional respite."

He lowered his tall frame into his throne, his hands gripping the golden arms. His eye closed. Muninn stared at him, her body rigid.

A faint hum carried through the hall. The hair on the back of my neck rose. I gripped the edge of the table, suppressing a shiver.

There, in front of the throne, three figures started to form. At first they were no more than shadowy impressions, but as Odin's forehead furrowed and the hum rose to a higher pitch, their bodies sharpened. All three were men, one with the coloring of a dark elf but at least half a foot taller than any I'd seen before, one a burly guy with a sweep of light brown hair and soft features that contrasted with his square jaw, and one…

The last one, I recognized. His blond hair had been white when I'd seen him in what I'd assumed was one of Muninn's memories, his face much more lined, but there was no mistaking the scar that cut jaggedly across the left side of his lean face.

In the moment I'd seen, they'd been cuddled together like lovers.

Muninn's eyes had widened. Her hands clenched and opened again at her sides. When the three men had completely solidified, they seemed to come to life. They looked down at themselves and around, the big guy gaping, the dark elf letting out an amused chuckle. Their gazes all settled on the raven woman.

"Svend," she said. "Gunnar. Jerrik. I—"

She cut herself off and simply threw herself at them. In an instant, they'd enveloped her in a joint embrace. My skin prickled with the feeling that us being here at all was a huge invasion of privacy.

For once, Odin was clearly thinking along the same lines as I was. "We'll give you this time to yourselves," he said quietly, and moved from his throne. All of us who'd assembled there filtered out of the hall of warriors as quickly as our feet would take us.

"How long will those temporary manifestations last?" Loki asked the Allfather when we'd come to a stop on the field outside.

Odin sighed. "Several minutes at least, I hope. It's difficult to summon spirits that long dead back to life, however worthy they may have been. Valhalla's power can only accomplish so much."

"It looked to me as though she was glad to have them at all," Freya said. A soft smile played across the goddess's lips, reminding me that she presided over love as well as war.

A lump had filled my throat. "I think that was the right thing," I said. "To show her—to show her you understood, and that you want her to be happy."

Odin's gaze settled on me for a long moment—long enough that it started to weigh on me. "Perhaps I have needed some reminding to extend the same courtesy to you, my patchwork valkyrie," he said. "I should apologize for that as well."

The apology took me by surprise, but not so much that I forgot myself. "And maybe to your sons and the other gods here as well," I suggested.

He sputtered a chuckle. "You aren't one to back down, are you? We will see how the confrontations ahead of us play out. There will be time enough for more discussions once Surt has been put down. But I am ready to have those discussions."

He glanced at Loki, whose jaw tightened. The trickster god offered a nod of acknowledgment.

It was closer to an hour before Muninn emerged from Valhalla, so I guessed Odin's and the hall's magic had worked better than he'd expected. Or maybe the raven woman had taken some time to herself before rejoining us. A hint of redness lined her eyes and her cheeks were flushed, but her posture was more relaxed than I'd ever seen her before.

"Let's set the realms right," she said. "If you're going to stop

Surt from wrecking even more havoc, you need to strike tomorrow afternoon."

# 25

*Aria*

The mountainside Muninn had us stop on gave a direct view of Surt's fortress from a distance. She peered at the roughly carved landscape around us and nodded.

"I don't think any of the patrols should catch you here. This isn't along any of their routes. You can wait without any interference until you're ready to jump in."

"Are you sure he's gone?" Hod asked. "The dark elves I spoke with said they'd never seen him leave the fortress. He always seemed to be on guard, watching for a fight."

Muninn's thin lips curled. "For a couple of hours every other afternoon, that Surt is an illusion drawn from their memories. I created a construct of him as part of our arrangement, so that he could go surveying the territories in Midgard where he might begin his invasion. He wanted to give the *appearance* of being constantly on guard."

"There are still guards," I pointed out. Even from across the wide plain between us and the uneven walls, I could make out the figures perched along it and stationed outside the buildings beyond the walls.

The raven woman shrugged. "You're never going to find it *un*guarded. But most of those 'soldiers' have plenty of training and no real battle experience. They'll look to him first before they realize they need to come up with their own plan of defense. If you can sow the destruction you're planning as quickly as you say, you should be able to take out the draugar before they've called many of them up—or started much of any counterattack, really."

"The giants will distract them first," Thor said. "We rush in while they're busy fending off that horde."

"If they show up," Loki said with an arch of his eyebrow.

Thor glowered at him good-naturedly. "They're coming. You should have seen how stirred up they were by the time I was done with my call to action." A little of the light glamor Baldur had cast on him still shone in his hair. I'd never seen him look quite so relieved as when he'd strapped Mjolnir back onto his belt, though.

"We have seven target spots," I said. "Should we look over the map again, now that you all have the fortress to compare?"

"It can't hurt to be as prepared as possible," Baldur said.

Hod pulled out the folded paper he'd been carrying. The dark elves had given it to him: a sketch of the fortress layout with markings to indicate the support walls of the caves they'd helped dig out and expand beneath the surface. They'd confirmed that was where Surt had been stashing his army of the undead—thousands of them now, in vast rows of caverns. If we broke through in just the right spots, we could bring the rocky ceiling toppling down on them all, leaving them as sitting ducks.

Freya and Tyr studied the map again too, even though their job was going to be protecting our backs while the five of us did the heavy work with our combined powers. Odin hadn't been *wrong*, not really. If this worked, it'd be mainly because of the five of us. He just hadn't been completely right either. It might not work at all if it hadn't been for the other ways we'd contributed. If Hod hadn't reached out to the dark elves. If Thor hadn't riled up the giants.

The ledge we were standing on trembled beneath my feet. I tensed where I was crouched. Thor smiled.

"Here they come."

A moment later, the first charge of the giants moved into my line of sight on the plain below. They rushed forward, their heavy feet thundering over the ground, hollering and brandishing their weapons.

Loki rolled his eyes. "You'd think over the ages they might have finally picked up a tiny bit of subtlety."

"The guards are moving," I said. "What if they start bringing the draugar out?"

"Then we send those ones crackling back into the peace of death on the surface," the trickster said.

"We just need all their attention on the giants," Freya said. "The ones by the buildings are heading to the walls now. They're gathering together at the front to watch the approach, just as we expected. Let's go! We can come at them first from the side—they won't know what's hit them until we're already halfway through."

She didn't need to say more than that. We were already pushing off the ledge. Only Muninn hung back, her pale face tight with anxiety for a second before she shifted into her raven form. She flew higher up the mountain, where we'd decided she'd stay and watch to report back to Odin as needed. "Just like old times," she'd said when we'd discussed it, but without too much bitterness.

If this went well, we'd *all* be returning to report to Odin on our success. My pulse thrummed faster as we glided around the edge of the plain and soared toward the fortress's flank. The guards along the wall were shouting at the giants, who'd nearly reached the steaming moat of magma. They *were* bringing up the draugar—several lurching figures had already emerged from a hollow beside one of the buildings. My heart stuttered.

"Hurry," I said. "They're summoning the army."

I flapped my wings even harder than before. Thor surged ahead of us, raising his hammer. We threw ourselves over the stinging heat of the moat, and he let out his battle cry.

I moved automatically now, swinging the short sword I'd grabbed from Valhalla. It might not have the history of my switchblade, but for this battle, I was going in fully armed. Around me, my other gods whipped their magic at the first of our targets, a patch of earth just a few feet from the corner of what looked like barracks.

Fire and light and shadow twined and caught hold of Mjolnir, which smashed into that spot with the force of four gods—and whatever a valkyrie could provide. The ground lurched, and cracks spread across the rocky terrain.

A shout came from the front wall. They knew there was more trouble now. I veered to the right, my wings straining with the effort, and my companions moved with me. We hurtled toward our next target.

With another blast of magic and hammer, the rocky ground all across that side of the fortress's yard shattered inward. The building beside us sagged as the cracks spread beneath its foundations. Gritty dust burst upward with the collapse. I swiped at my eyes, yanking myself around.

"This way!" Freya called, her sword gleaming as she jabbed it ahead of her.

As we sped around the building toward the back of the fortress grounds, pounding footsteps approached. I dodged the shriek of a crossbow bolt and ducked beneath a searing flame flung from one of Surt's magicked blades. The top of my wing stung where the magic grazed it. Thor shouted again, and we propelled our united force at the motley crew of guards who'd left the giants to tackle us.

The smack of the gods' magic sent them toppling. We wheeled around to aim another blast at the ground. More cracks spidered across the stone surface. A faint groaning reached my ears—the draugar, realizing they were doomed?

They'd been human once, but Surt had turned them into monsters. I steeled myself for the next strike and the next, letting out a cheer as more of the dark rock crumbled down into the hollow depths beneath it. Loki motioned to us, and he and Baldur lashed out together, sending a flood of glittering flame through the caved in terrain. The few boulders that had been shifting went still, scorched black.

Just two more spots to hit—around the front, where the giants were roaring even louder now. We hadn't seen Surt yet, which seemed to show what Muninn had said was true. He wasn't here to rally his troops or to fight us off himself.

Surt's surface level guards were stepping one way and another, nearly colliding with each other, not sure which threat to deal with first. A growing horde of draugar shuffling up from the caves nearby milled around them. A few of the giants had managed to hurdle over the magma moat and were wrenching at the drawbridge. The creak of its hinges told me it wasn't going to hold much longer.

"Push them back, push them back!" Loki cried with a gleeful grin, pointing the guards toward the giants as if he and the other gods really were allied with Surt's side. The giants who spotted him let out bellows of rage. We didn't want to still be here when they broke through.

Thor shook his head at the trickster, but he was smiling too as he shouted for our next blast.

The ground gave way under the feet of the guards who'd been rushing at us. They and a bunch of the draugar above toppled down into the caverns. Other guards charged at us from the opposite direction, but Freya and Tyr were there with their swords to fend them off. We hurled one last missile of power at the final spot the dark elves had marked for us.

A pit opened in the ground at the foot of the great tower of

Surt, in the middle of his fortress. The tall structure teetered forward. My breath hitched as its front wall started to spill down into the pit like an architectural landslide.

Thor raised his hammer again, and I moved into battle position, even though I couldn't really help with this part. Another wave of flame crackled over and between the rubble.

We'd done it. We'd battered Surt's hall and torched his army.

Or had we? As I spun around, ready to find the gate to Asgard that must lie in the wreckage of that tower, a faint scraping sound reached my ears through the din. My gaze leapt to the cliff just behind the fortress walls.

There was an opening there. An opening that led to another cavern? The dark elves hadn't mentioned anywhere else Surt had stashed his undead soldiers, but they might not have known—or they might have been hedging their bets.

Loki darted over beside me. His ears, even sharper than mine, must have caught the noise too. "Burn and smash it?" he suggested.

"You read my mind," I said.

At his gesture, the others swept over the back wall with us. Loki led the attack this time. "Incinerate them!" he shouted with a slash of his hand, and we all launched ourselves at the cliff face as one.

A wave of fiery flickering light seared across the landscape and into the opening. Something hissed and crackled on the other side. From the swell of light, the flames had burst into an inferno within.

Thor had thrown his hammer at the same moment. It slammed into the cliff just above the entrance, and a real landslide poured down. With a thunder befitting the thunder god, a shower of boulders and smaller rocks piled over the opening.

"The gate," Baldur said, turning toward the ruin of the tower. "I can feel it—all of them. They're this way."

"We haven't dealt with Surt," Thor grumbled, smacking his hammer against his broad palm.

"That was the whole idea," Loki said. "We've devastated the

army he spent decades building. We can hunt him down and skewer him in good time."

A giant's triumphant bellow and the crash of the drawbridge told us *we* might be skewered soon if we stuck around here any longer. "Come on," I said. "Let's go home."

# 26

*Aria*

Asgard really could be a lovely place when you weren't spending every spare moment preparing for a zombie invasion. I squirmed deeper into the soft grass, my head resting on Thor's thigh, my feet tucked under Baldur's arms where they were both sprawled in the field with me. A warm summer breeze drifted over us, and no sound interrupted my relaxation other than the chirping of a few birds gliding by.

Why had I ever found the idea of feeling this close to my gods scary? This was exactly where I was meant to be. I could feel *that* with every particle of my valkyrie being.

"Okay," I said. "It's decided. I think I'll just stay in this position forever."

Thor chuckled and brushed his hand over my hair. A short distance away, Loki perked up, shaking off his thoughtful reverie.

"But there are so many positions we haven't had the chance to try yet, pixie," he said in his smooth sly voice.

I rolled my eyes at him as well as I could while I was lying down. "Just let me enjoy the moment, okay?"

Soon, we were going to have to get back to work tracking down Surt. The war might be over, but there was nothing stopping the giant from gearing up for another attack while he was still on the loose. Baldur had suggested it might lighten all our spirits to take a day to recuperate before we started on that next quest, and I wasn't going to argue with that. Even if I wasn't sure my spirit could ever be totally "lightened" while the giant who'd meant to tear apart this world and my former one was still free somewhere, probably fuming at us.

A black form swooped by overhead—a bird that wasn't just a bird. Muninn had been reacquainting herself with Asgard, switching back and forth between her forms at random, as far as I could tell. She'd admitted to me this morning that she'd never experienced the realm of the gods as anything but a raven before now.

"You know what we could really use?" Hod said from his spot behind me. "Some of that fine mead, the kind we saved for the celebratory feasts."

Loki shot him an amused look. "You are not who I'd have expected to hear that suggestion from, Dark One."

"I can appreciate a good beverage," Hod said, matching Loki's playful tone. "Shouldn't you be able to figure out where we can get some, Sly One?"

Thor stirred. "We *do* have an excellent reason to celebrate."

I waved them all off. "You can have the mead. Just bring me a beer while you're at it. Or a rum and Coke if that's on offer."

Baldur squeezed my foot affectionately. "You might not say that after you've tried proper Asgardian mead."

I grimaced. "After the amount of time I've spent in Valhalla in the last couple weeks, I think I've gotten my fill through osmosis. Don't you drink *anything* other than—"

A crackling sound broke through our banter. I stiffened, my head jerking up.

A torrent of fire was coursing against the sky, over the trees at the edge of the field.

My pulse hiccupped. I scrambled to my feet alongside the others. “Odin!” Tyr hollered.

The torrent arced and descended toward us, a bridge of flames. And standing at its crest was a burly man with a gray beard and a sword dancing with its own fire.

“Hello, Asgard,” Surt roared. “I’ve finally come to finish what I started.”

# Waking the Gods

## Their Dark Valkyrie - Book 4

# 1

*Aria*

To some people, a bad day was when it was raining, and their heel broke, and then they were late for work. Those people had never had a bloodthirsty giant appear out of nowhere on a flaming bridge ready to slaughter them and everyone they cared about.

Right now, as the giant Surt descended toward me and my gods, swinging his fire-laced sword with a vicious grin, I wished I were one of those people with their blissfully mundane lives.

"Hello, Asgard," he bellowed. "I've finally come to finish what I started."

The flames of his bridge arced down to singe the grass in the field where I'd just been having my first really peaceful day in Asgard. Heat wafted over my skin, and the thin smoke coated my nose and mouth. With a twitch of my shoulders, I urged out my valkyrie wings. They'd been a part of me for so long now that their weight as they sprouted from my back felt more like a comfort than a burden. I grabbed my old switchblade from my pocket, wishing I had a larger weapon on hand.

Thor and Baldur, who'd been sprawled in the grass enjoying the peace with me, braced themselves at my sides. Thor hefted his magical hammer, his square jaw clenched and his normally warm brown eyes now blazing with fury. Baldur's hands beamed with the supernatural glow he could turn into a weapon of his own. His normally bright boyish face had shadowed.

Loki sped over on his shoes of flight to join us. "Lovely to see you," he hollered to Surt. "You've saved us the trouble of tracking you down. We'll finish this war, all right, but not with the outcome I think you'd prefer."

He'd grabbed a sword of his own. His other lithe hand held a crackling ball of fire, the same pale red as his hair.

Surt chuckled, low and rolling, as he strode down the blazing bridge. The flames shuddered under his brawny form. He was nearly as big as Thor, and his magic made him a formidable foe—but there were a bunch of us and only one of him.

At least, that's what it looked like in that first moment. Then a rush of shambling bodies poured over the peak of the bridge's arc after him.

My heart seized at the sight of their deathly pale faces. The smell of damp rot reached my nose an instant later. They were draugar—the undead figures Surt had been collecting into an army.

But we'd *destroyed* his army. Just yesterday, we'd smashed his hidden caverns to bury the creatures and then burned them to ash. Where had this mob of soldiers come from?

Something gleamed on their skin and in their hair. Streaks of water, I realized—melted water. Here and there, flecks of ice and snow still clung to their clothes, disintegrating with the bridge's heat as they marched down toward us.

Somewhere behind me, Hod cursed. Even if he couldn't see the threat we faced, the god of darkness must have caught enough from scents and sounds to understand the gist of it.

"Not so confident all of a sudden?" Surt rumbled. "Did you really think I'd keep all my eggs in one basket? Underestimating your enemies has always been your downfall, Asgardians."

"So, you carted most of your army off to Niflheim," Loki said, his tone acidic. "How very clever. You're lucky they thawed."

Niflheim was a frozen realm that the gods had mentioned in passing. I'd never been there. It was the last place we'd have thought to check for the army of a giant who was so keen on fire, that was for sure. Especially when we'd had every reason to believe we'd already decimated that army.

My heart thumped faster. Had our victory yesterday meant anything at all? We must have taken out at least part of his forces. But he might have gathered more draugar than we'd ever suspected.

"We destroyed the army you left behind in Muspelheim, and we'll destroy the one you've brought here," Thor said. "No giant takes Asgard!"

He raised his hammer, and the other three gods converged around me. After all the battles behind us, we moved instinctively, following the sense of connection that had bound us together ever since the four of them had combined their talents to bring me back from the dead as a valkyrie.

As I sprang forward, I saw Freya arrive beside us, her golden hair streaming behind her. She swung her sword with a bolt of magic.

"This will be your end, cur," a sharp voice shouted. Tyr came charging up, swinging a dagger with his remaining hand. I guessed the war god could still put up a good fight even missing part of one limb.

Just like every other time I'd fought beside the four gods I was bound to, my awareness expanded with a sense of their pulses thudding in time with mine, the energy surging through their bodies as they launched their attacks. And just like before, their powers merged as they threw them forward. Flares of light and darkness searing with a fiery intensity swirled around Thor's hurled hammer, straight toward Surt.

At the same moment, the giant jerked his hand, and the bridge lurched. It tossed him in an epic leap over our heads and sent the rest of his army spilling down toward us even faster. Thor's hammer and the blaze of magic around it toppled a dozen draugar, but there were hundreds of them, maybe thousands.

The thunder god spun around as Mjolnir flew back to his hand. Loki, Hod, and Baldur drew closer in a circle around me. We had the giant at one side of us and the draugar behind us now.

Surt left us no time to regroup. He was already lunging at us, fire streaming from his sword. We flung ourselves out of the way of the lashes of fire. Loki toppled the first line of draugar with a wave of his own flames, but others raised shields that propelled the heat back toward us. His scorching magic wasn't much use when these soldiers had been equipped by an enemy with his own affinity for fire.

Odin appeared at the edge of the field, striding toward us with his silver spear. Tyr and Freya darted along the sides of the horde. They were trying to surround the giant in turn, I suspected, but Surt hurtled forward again—toward us and then around us as he whipped his sword through the air.

Thor yanked me to the side, but one of those tongues of flame sliced across my calf, sizzling straight through my jeans and, it felt, down to the bone. A stabbing pain radiated up my leg.

"Little valkyrie," Surt said, not even stopping for breath before he charged again. "So small and frail among the gods. Yet somehow you broke my raven's prison. I don't think you can escape *me*."

Thor squeezed my shoulder, I gave a quick nod, and the five of us moved together to meet the giant's attack. Somewhere to my left, a draug let out a groaning sound as one of the other gods must have crushed the life from it. Thor and Loki pushed ahead of me, Baldur's light blazing over Thor's hammer and Hod's darkness twining around Loki's sword.

But Surt cut his charge short. He planted his feet with a thud that shook the ground and slashed out with his blade. Some of the flames that spilled from it shattered as Loki's sword cut through them. Others smashed into nothingness with the impact of Thor's hammer. One thick hissing current shot straight at me.

I tried to dodge, but my wounded leg wobbled under me with a fresh spear of pain. With a flap of my wings and a hiss through my teeth, I threw myself to the side, but I wasn't fast enough. The streak of fire slammed into my arm and torso, throwing me to the ground.

I really cried out then. A thousand burning needles might as well have jabbed into my skin.

An instant later, a cool blanket of shadow dropped over me, smothering the flames. "Ari!" Hod said hoarsely.

Surt bellowed. I shoved myself upright, stumbled, gasped, and clenched my teeth against the pain. We had to keep fighting. The gods needed me. Even if half my body felt as if it were still on fire.

A thicker smoky scent prickled my nose. Some of the draugar had barreled past us to reach the halls of Asgard. The enchanted weapons they carried had set fire to the thatched roofs and anything flammable inside. Sparks blew from the windows in a flurry like glowing snow.

*No.* This was my home now, as much a home as I had. I hadn't fought all the battles I'd been through already to lose this place to some asshole giant.

"Keep at him," I choked out. "We can take him."

But the draugar were swarming all around us too. Blazing knives and pikes stabbed at us from every angle, and Surt sprang at us with another roar.

Thor moved to hurl his hammer, and a draug's blade sliced into his forearm deep enough to spill blood. Surt aimed his blast straight at me.

He'd called me out for a reason. That thought hit me with stark clarity in the instant as his fireball whipped toward me. I was his main target. Because I was weaker than the gods, and because I had strengths he didn't understand.

He wanted to destroy *me* more than anyone—or at least to destroy me first.

This time I threw myself upward, into the air as fast as I could sweep my wings. The fireball crashed into my thighs and propelled me several agonizing feet through the air. My wings shuddered with the pain. I dropped to the ground and rolled, barely conscious of anything except the vicious throbbing crackle and the need to make it stop somehow.

I ended up facedown in the grass, smoke penetrating the earthy smell of the field, every muscle in my body knotted. Just the movement of the air against my raw skin made me suck in a sob. I wanted to push myself up, to move, to do *something*, but my limbs refused.

Shouts and the clang of weapons echoed around me. A groan that sounded more godly than zombie reverberated through the air. More thuds. More warbles of magical fire. I flinched at the sound.

Someone crouched down beside me. "Keep going," I said, my voice coming out a rasp. "Keep fighting. Don't worry. I—"

"That's enough talking, pixie," Loki said, wry but strained at the same time. "We're getting you out of here."

Out of the field? But Surt—the draugar—

He lifted me, even his gentlest embrace turning my body into a maelstrom of pain. Tears trickled down my face and stung my scraped cheeks. I wasn't sure I could feel anything below my ribs anymore. Not anything except that vicious searing.

"Let's go!" Loki called out, and then he started to run, cradling me against him to shelter me from the wind that stirred when he sped across the landscape. I managed to focus on the world around me for long enough to realize that we weren't just heading for shelter in the city. He was racing past Asgard's buildings, past the stone-tiled streets, toward the edge of the realm, where Odin could call out a bridge of his own that shimmered like a rainbow.

He was taking me out of Asgard.

"No," I murmured. If we left, then Surt would have won. We couldn't lose the realm of the gods to him and his zombies.

"It'll be fine, Ari," Loki said in his breezy way. "We'll patch you right up and then put that charcoal-brained kin of mine back in his place. Where is the damned Allfather?"

He wasn't able to keep the urgency completely out of his voice with that last question. It occurred to me then, through the haze of pain, that maybe we weren't letting Surt win by leaving. Maybe he'd already won.

# 2

*Thor*

With every fall of my feet as I rushed after Loki past our city, I felt as if I were leaving part of myself behind. My teeth gritted against the rage surging inside me.

We'd been complacent. We'd assumed our victory before it had been truly ours. And now Surt and his army had all but overpowered us. The halls of Asgard were burning. Our *valkyrie* had been burning.

I could barely make out Ari's slim form in the trickster's arms, but a few strands of her blond hair flew out with the breeze. The ends were singed black. I hadn't heard her say a word since Loki had picked her up.

"As soon as we have somewhere to take shelter, I should be able to heal her," Baldur said, racing along on a beam of light beside me. Despite my brother's words, his face was grim. Healing Ari would depend on her still being alive when we made it to somewhere Surt couldn't blast her again.

"He went right at her," Hod muttered from just behind us. "He wanted to take her down first."

"Because he knows how strong she is—how strong she makes us," I said. A burst of pride penetrated the fury in my chest for a second as I remembered how Ari had leapt up to fight the giant and his army without the slightest hesitation.

But her strength had revealed our own weaknesses when we'd lost her. We gods had battled Surt and an army alongside him before, during Ragnarok, but there'd been dozens more in Asgard then. The seven of us remaining hadn't had much hope of pushing back both him and his mass of undead that he'd armed with blazing blades and shields.

Our main hope had been the heightened power the four of us had discovered together—the power that linked us through Ari. Without her, our weapons and magic wouldn't merge and amplify. From the first moment she'd stumbled, I'd felt that connection waver. When Surt's last blast had left her slumped and charred, our attempts to halt him and his draugar had faltered completely.

I'd managed to clip his shoulder with Mjolnir, but he'd barely seemed to feel it. And at the same time, one of his undead soldiers had stabbed a brutal wound just below my ribs. If I'd dodged any slower, I might have lost my liver. The cut made my hasty breaths burn. With the blood that was dripping down my side, I really was leaving part of myself behind here.

We'd be back. We'd be back, and we'd reclaim it *all*.

Freya whipped around us with her falcon cloak and hurled a bolt of her magic toward the attackers on our heels. Her lovely face was tight with pain. A burn streaked across her other forearm all the way to the hand she held her sword with.

I couldn't let her and the others behind me do all the fighting. As we reached the stone tiles of the courtyard that stretched almost all the way to the point where the rainbow bridge would form, I sprang around and landed with a thump of my feet that would have made the clouds thunder over Midgard beneath us.

In a split-second, swift as lightning, I took in the scene we were fleeing. Freya had dipped down to cover Odin as he slashed his spear through the line of draugar that had nearly caught up with him. Hod paused for just long enough to heave a wave of shadow that caught a few of the undead figures before the others sliced it apart with their fiery weapons. Tyr had lost his dagger somewhere in the fray, but he was making use of what he could. His warrior arm flung a stone hard enough to smash a draug's skull.

Hundreds of draugar were still charging toward us, Surt near the fore of their crowd. More were pouring through our city, setting fire to whatever they could reach. My hands clenched at my sides. Smoke coated my mouth and clouded the sky. How *dare* he degrade our home this way?

If we could just topple Surt—if we could take him down, his whole assault would crumble. The draugar had no stake here beyond what he'd ordered them to do.

I flipped my hammer in my hand and pitched it toward the giant with every ounce of strength and fury I had in me.

Mjolnir's shining surface shimmered through the air, but even with the speed I'd given it, Surt saw it coming. He snatched up the body of a hulking draug in front of him and threw it toward my hammer to shield himself while he dodged to the side.

The draug exploded in a hail of undead flesh that its companions barely appeared to notice. Mjolnir whipped onward, fast enough to make Surt's beard twitch—but it smashed through a line of draugar just beside him instead. His harsh laugh ripped through the air as my hammer flew back to my hand. A growl of frustration reverberated in my throat.

Just by stopping for those few seconds, I'd let his army gain several feet on us. I hadn't destroyed enough of them to make any real difference. I caught Mjolnir, meaning to throw myself after

Loki toward the edge of the realm. But Surt lunged forward right then with a swipe of his sword.

That eerie fire it carried coursed off its gleaming surface and hissed toward us like a raging forest fire. Hod tossed another wave of shadow at the flames, and Freya cast out a waft of magic that chilled my skin as it rushed past me.

Most of the flames sputtered out. One small lick scorched across the tiles to where Tyr had been standing and heaved him into the air.

Surt had used his fire magic that way at the start of the battle, when he'd made his bridge launch him over us right into Asgard. Now he had it hurl my fellow god all the way to his flaming blade. Tyr tumbled onto the ground in front of the giant. Even as I jerked back my hammer, Surt sliced his sword down on the war god's neck.

The blade severed clean through Tyr's neck, leaving behind a smoking stump. I lost sight of his head in an instant as it rolled into the horde of draugar.

"One god down, just a few more to go," Surt hollered with a vicious grin. He spun his sword in the air. "Your people rose once. Let's see if he will again—or if that blessing ended with his second chance."

My gut lurched. As I hustled backward, away from the draugar's continuing charge, my gaze shot to the field where we'd all risen after Ragnarok—the field that was now a scorched ruin. Surt snatched a spear from one of his soldiers and stabbed it into Tyr's chest. He hefted the limp headless body in the air and brandished it like some kind of trophy.

Our former bodies, mangled by Ragnarok's battle, hadn't lingered when we'd returned. They'd vanished with our resurrection. I watched Surt's display for several thuds of my heart, willing Tyr's form to disappear, to reform whole and well in the distance.

The warrior god's blackened legs dangled lifelessly. His body stayed solid—solid and dead.

Surt left out another bellow of a laugh. He flung the spear with Tyr's body at the nearest hall, so hard the weapon dug into the stone. My comrade's body hung there from the building's wall. Not just a trophy. A warning.

We hadn't known for sure whether Asgard's gift of rebirth could touch us again, whether we were fully immortal or merely graced with endless life as long as we protected that life. Now the question was answered with gruesome certainty.

It wasn't only Ari who could die in this battle. It could be any of us.

Surt picked up speed, running at us with a wave of his arm to urge the draugar faster too. I wrenched my gaze from Tyr's far-too-mortal body and spun on my heel.

Loki had reached the edge of the realm. Odin, just catching up, thumped the end of his spear against the ground. Bifrost arced out through the air and down into the clouds, its rainbow glow the most welcome sight I'd ever seen. Ari's body huddled in Loki's arms looked nearly as limp as Tyr's did. My rage sputtered out beneath the chill of my fear for her.

"That's right," Surt bellowed. "Turn tail like the cowards you really are. Asgard is mine!"

Every particle of my being roared in defiance of that statement, but I couldn't see any way to defeat him now. I dashed for the bridge with the others. Hod's shadows snaked past me over the tiles, helping guide his way.

He and I reached the bridge last. I grabbed his elbow, hurrying him onto the rainbow's gleaming surface. Loki was already racing down into the clouds. As I hustled on after him, Bifrost's surface faded behind me.

"I won't let him follow us," my father said, his low voice sounding even more hollow than usual. One of Surt's attacks had burned part of the broad brim of his hat to a crisp. Ash dappled his shoulder over his dark blue traveling cloak. "Neither he nor his fiends will set foot on my bridge."

I wasn't sure the giant even meant to try. Surt's laughter carried after us as we fled down toward the world of humankind, but it sounded distant now, as if he'd halted his chase.

He *would* follow us down to Midgard before long, though, wouldn't he? From what we'd understood, his plan was to take control over both of the remaining stable realms among the nine. It made sense that he'd started with Asgard—smaller, and easier to catch us in a vulnerable state by surprising us there. But the vast and wonderful realm of humanity would be his next target.

Tension wound around my lungs, sharpened by the still-seeping wound on my side and the other on my arm, and by the sight of Midgard's forests and towns below the clouds. I was meant to be the protector of humanity, more than any of the other gods. This realm was my responsibility. I hadn't managed to protect my own realm from the invader. I had to do better by the mortals here, who were so much less equipped to fight back than we'd been.

First, though, I needed to know that my recently human companion had made it through.

I pushed myself faster, but even my well-muscled legs couldn't beat Loki's enchanted shoes. He'd already reached the ground. Odin had set Bifrost down by a barn that, from its sagging roof, hadn't been used in some time.

The trickster carried Ari into the barn. Baldur flew after him. When I reached the doorway, Loki had lain Ari on the straw-strewn floor. The musty smell that reached my nose must have been why he was wrinkling his, but his amber eyes were fixed on the valkyrie.

Her wings had contracted into her back, making her look as if she were fully human still. Her face had escaped the worst of the damage from Surt's attacks, but her eyes were shut, her lips parted and jaw slack. The rest of her was a mess of charred fabric and skin mottled black and red. My fingers clamped around Mjolnir's handle so tightly my knuckles ached.

Ari wasn't just a fighting companion and a friend. She'd seen parts of me even I'd almost forgotten existed and helped me recover them. She'd shown me tenderness and affection I'd never thought I'd find again.

I'd started to think I'd get to spend the rest of my days with her by my side—and if the trickster and the twins shared her affections too, that didn't diminish what she and I had, only showed the capacity of her heart. She captured *my* heart, with a depth I hadn't entirely known until right now, watching Baldur bend over her ravaged body, feeling that pounding vessel inside me nearly tear itself apart.

"Is there anything I can do?" I asked, every muscle in my body clamoring to be put to use.

The god of light shook his head without glancing up. He rested his hands gently on Ari's chest. A glow began to seep from them through her body.

"Her heart is still beating," he said, his voice ragged with relief. "She's breathing, just barely. It'll take some time, but I can save her."

Loki stood up, his mouth twisting. He'd managed to pull his lips into one of his usual sly smiles by the time he met my eyes.

"Let's give the healer room to work his magic without distraction, Thunderer."

Reluctantly, I stepped back from the doorway. Hod stayed turned toward his twin, his stance tense, but the blind god couldn't speed up Ari's recovery any more than I could.

Odin had sunk down by the weathered fence along the dirt road that divided the farmland from the forest. Freya was crouched next to him. Where she'd moved aside his cloak, his trousers were darkly damp with blood. One or more of Surt's soldiers had gotten to my father too.

Baldur was going to have his work cut out for him, patching up the lot of us.

A fresh surge of fury gripped me. I stalked toward the road, tossing Mjolnir in my hand. With a satisfying heave, I hurled the hammer at one of the nearest trees.

The trunk burst like the one draug's body had, splinters pattering against the neighboring trees. The top of the pine crashed down into the forest. My momentary pleasure drained away. This wasn't accomplishing anything. It was senseless destruction.

"You're leaking," Loki said lightly, nodding to my wound. "I might not be able to magic it better, but I could cauterize it for the time being."

"I'm fine," I grumbled, which might not have been the most sensible response either, but the thought of dealing with my injuries when Ari was still unconscious from hers made my spine stiffen.

I prowled along the line of the fence all the way around the abandoned farm, telling myself I was keeping guard. As long as I was in motion, my worries and aggravations could only nip at my heels, not gnaw right into me. I'd just finished my eighth circuit when a thin but clear voice carried through the barn doorway.

"Where are we?"

My heart leapt. I barged through the doorway, only managing to make it there ahead of Loki and Hod because I'd been closer to begin with.

Ari was sitting up against the wall. Her cheek was smudged with ash and her clothes still hung in burnt tatters on her small frame, but her limbs were only mottled pink now instead of the raw horror they'd been before.

Baldur was gripping her shoulder as he explained where we'd ended up. His white-blond hair clung to his forehead, damp with sweat from all the energy he'd expended.

Ari's gaze leapt from him to the rest of us as we came in. A smile lit her face all the way to her blue-gray eyes. "All right," she said. "So, how are we getting Asgard back?"

Here she was, just restored from the verge of death and already eager to leap right back into battle. A laugh of joy tickled up my throat. But the sound had hardly fallen from my lips when my chest tightened all over again.

How *were* we getting Asgard back? I didn't have the faintest idea where to start.

# 3

*Aria*

The gods set up their little council in the barn, mainly so that I didn't have to try to walk anywhere yet, I suspected. I wasn't keen on being carried around, but my body still throbbed enough just sitting propped against the rough boards of the wall that I didn't trust my legs to hold me up yet. Baldur might have had magic hands, but even divine magic had its limits.

That truth of that thought hit home even harder when I glanced around the circle of figures that had hunkered down around me and noticed we were one short.

"Where's Tyr?" I said, my stomach already clenching with dread in anticipation of the answer. Somehow I had the feeling he hadn't just gone for a stroll.

The gods all glanced at each other as if hoping someone else would take on the task of replying. Odin sighed, adjusting his grip on his spear, which he'd leaned against his shoulder as he sat on an old crate.

"Tyr fell in the battle as we retreated," he said. "A worthy companion lost."

"Lost," I repeated. "So he didn't—he isn't going to— You weren't sure whether any of you *could* really die or not."

"Now we're sure," Loki said, his tone arch but a little subdued by his standards. "No more do-overs. We fall and we're gone."

I sucked in a deep breath full of the dry smells of straw and dust. The possibility that the gods might die had hung over us in every battle we'd found ourselves in, but now, looking at them in the beams of dwindling sunlight that were streaking through the gaps in the barn walls, it felt as real and solid as my hands. Because it was a fact now and not a possibility. Because for the first time we'd faced an enemy strong enough that he'd sent the gods on the run from their home.

Of course, maybe they wouldn't have needed to run at all if they hadn't been trying to save me. My hand dropped to my knee to rub an achy spot there. The outer marks of Surt's attacks were fading, but I could still trace the lines his magical fire had carved into me.

"He took us by surprise," I said. "When we're ready and properly equipped—when we can take *him* by surprise—no one else will have to fall on our side. Right? So what's the plan?"

"I'd imagine the most difficult part will be getting back into Asgard without walking straight into an ambush," Hod said, his dark green eyes instinctively moving over the faces around our circle even though he couldn't see any of us. I knew he had a clear enough picture of where we all were from every small sound of our movements, our breaths. His boyish face had always looked harder than his gentle twin's, but now his expression was outright strained.

"Surt knows where Bifrost connects to Asgard," the dark god went on. "He knows the only other entrance into Asgard is through the paths along Yggdrasil. He'll have both the head of the bridge and the base of the great tree surrounded by his draugar. We won't take him by surprise that way."

"Are there really no other ways in?" I asked. "Surt managed to show up right where he wanted with his fire magic. Aren't there any gods who can do something like that?" I looked to Odin. "Can you make your rainbow touch down in some other spot?"

Odin shook his head, his silvered brown beard swaying. "Bifrost is born from Asgard. I call it forth from the place of its origin. It's only the other end I can aim at my whim." From what the gods had told me, the abandoned farm he'd set us down in today was somewhere in the middle of the French countryside.

"But there might be other ways of creating a bridge," Loki said. "The five of us know we aren't any use for that—we gave it a shot when you were missing, Allfather—but if we could track down one of the gods with a closer affinity." He snapped his fingers. "Heimdall."

"He was the bridge's guardian," Thor said. "Nothing to do with creating it."

Loki waved his hand dismissively. "He rules over connections and the binding of one thing to another. That sounds bridge-like enough to me."

"It only helps us if we can find Heimdall," Hod put in. "We did spend a good chunk of the last couple weeks searching for the other gods, and Tyr is the only one we turned up."

"We didn't have Muninn with us then," I said. "She might have spotted one of them in her travels around Midgard." My pulse stuttered. "Where's the raven?"

Odin's former raven of memory had become a part of our group so recently and been an enemy of sorts for so long before that, I hadn't immediately been thrown by her absence. Had she been caught or even killed by Surt and his draugar too?

"We don't know," Freya said, with a slight edge. I suspected it was going to take her a while to completely forgive the raven woman for imprisoning her husband and allowing Surt to torment him.

"None of us saw her during the battle," Baldur said, his voice as clear and melodic as ever. "I wouldn't blame her if she fled from the start. She isn't a warrior."

My shoulders tensed. "If Surt catches her, he might kill her. He's got to know by now that she betrayed him to us in the end."

Thor tipped his head toward the doorway. "Baldur laid out a bit of a light display that she should recognize if she's searching for us. If the giant has her, we'll just have to hope we make it back to Asgard before he takes his full revenge."

Back to Asgard. An idea jarred loose in my still pretty muddled head. "I can jump straight back to Valhalla," I said. "Obviously I can't fight Surt and his army on my own, but I could at least take the lay of the land, see where the guards are…"

Anything else I might have said caught in my throat at the darkening of Hod's face. "No," he said. "We *know* there'll be guards in Valhalla, lots of them, watching the entrance to Yggdrasil, remember? They might even be on guard specifically for you to appear if Surt's aware of that valkyrie skill. He's not going to give you any opening. He'd just take the opportunity to kill *you*."

It was strange to think that a month ago, Hod hadn't even wanted me around. Now, his anguish at the close call I'd already met at Surt's hands threaded through his words. My connection with each of the four gods who'd summoned me had deepened in all sorts of ways, many of them very enjoyable, since I'd found myself with them, but Hod had opened up the most. He'd offered me his heart, his love, whether I could bring myself to say the same to him or not.

I hadn't managed to repeat that sentiment to any of my gods yet. Love wasn't an emotion I had a whole lot of experience with after years of my mother's abuse and worse at the hands of her boyfriends. I tried to show them how much they meant to me in other ways, though. In that moment, I wished I could put my arms around Hod and show him how much I really was still here, alive and unbroken. That might not be a very productive move for getting on with this meeting, though.

"But Surt's guards might *not* be watching for me," I said. "They could be all at the end of the hall by the hearth. I think I can control, at least a little, which part of the room I appear in. If I landed between the tables, they might not even notice me sneaking by."

All of the gods were frowning, even Freya. Loki reached out and squeezed my arm. His touch sent tingling warmth over my skin without any magic involved. "For once in my existence, I agree with Mr. Doom and Gloom. It's not worth the risk. We have time to attempt other strategies."

Not worth the risk. Just like it hadn't been worth the risk of continuing to fight when I'd been wounded? A lump rose in my throat.

"Yggdrasil may be the key, nonetheless," Freya said. "They can guard the entrance, but no one but those of Asgard can open it. If we found one of the gateways from the other realms, and we assembled enough of a force, we could possibly take whatever draugar he's stationed in Valhalla by surprise and slaughter them before they can raise the alarm. We'd just need to be ready to strike directly at him right after that." The goddess of love and war set her mouth in a firm line.

"Do we know where the gateway from Midgard is?" I asked.

"There isn't one," Thor said. "It was closed at this end ages ago, after it became too likely some human would stumble on it and get himself into trouble." He glanced at Hod. "But we do know where at least one gate to Nidavellir is, and the location of their gate to Asgard."

Hod nodded slowly. "I could go and plead our case to the dark elves. I think it would shatter all the good will we've managed to restore with them if we simply demanded the right to barge through their home at our convenience."

Not that long ago, the dark elves had been helping Surt, but for understandable reasons. Nidavellir, their home of underground caves, had started to fall apart after centuries of the gods' unthinking neglect. Surt had promised them a place in one of the realms that was still stable if they helped him claim those realms. Hod had managed to regain their trust by going to help restore their home, but it was a tentative truce so far.

"If we're asking the dirt-eaters for help, perhaps you could put in a request for some of their creative weaponry as well," Loki said with a grin.

I perked up. I hadn't thought of that. The dark elves had constructed most of the gods' greatest weapons, from Thor's hammer to Odin's spear.

"I'll see what I can do," Hod said. "They aren't all that happy with us, remember. Just a few weeks ago, they were trying to *kill* us."

"A grave misunderstanding now rectified. But I take your point."

"In the meantime, the rest of us could set out more messages in places the other gods seem likely to visit," Thor suggested. "That did work to bring Tyr back to us."

Only Tyr, after days of searching. I nibbled at my lower lip. "How long do you think we have before Surt starts his attack on Midgard?"

"He'll wait until he's confident in his defenses around Asgard," Freya said. "That might not take more than a day or two, though. After that… We can hope that he'll enjoy his victory for some time before attempting to extend it, but I don't think we'd be wise to count on a delay. And there's no way of telling where or how he'll even begin his assault on this realm."

"If he arrives in Midgard via that flaming bridge of his, I should sense that magic." Loki wiggled his fingers. "It makes my own turn prickly."

At a fluttering sound outside, all our mouths snapped shut, our gazes jerking to the doorway. A second later, a raven swooped inside. It banked over our heads and dropped to the ground just inside the barn, shifting into the form of a skinny knobby-limbed woman at the same time.

Muninn crossed her arms over her chest and peered at us with her dark eyes. From her stance, she was considering whether she'd need to bolt back out that door.

None of us had exactly been on friendly terms with the raven woman until even more recently than our dark elf alliance. Once Odin's servant as the guardian of memory, she'd let out however many centuries of pent-up rage by agreeing to help Surt capture the Allfather and then tormenting us with awful moments from our personal histories in a prison she'd created.

She'd given us a tip to help us destroy Surt's fortress. Suddenly I couldn't help wondering how much she'd known about his decision to move most of his army to a different realm. Had she still been playing both sides?

"I found you as quickly as I could," she said, with a bird-like cock of her head. "By the time I realized you were leaving Asgard, Bifrost was already retracting."

"How did you end up here, then?" Thor said. His tone was even enough, but his hand had dropped to his hammer where it rested at his side.

"I flew straight to Yggdrasil, before Surt had time to notice." Muninn shuddered. "He would not be pleased to see me."

My valkyrie senses were designed to read emotion and motivations—to help me decide who lived and died on a battlefield, if I'd been a proper valkyrie with the old guard. Picking up impressions from divine beings was always a trickier business than with mortals, but her horror felt genuine to me. I relaxed against the wall.

"What did you see before you left?" Freya asked.

"Little you wouldn't have, I'd imagine," the raven woman said. "I was only a few minutes behind you. Lots of burning, lots of smoke. Surt shouting about how wonderful he is." She cut her gaze toward Odin. "In case I didn't make it clear enough before, I never *liked* him. Our agreement was a matter of necessity."

Odin dipped his head in acknowledgment. I knew the two of them must have talked more than I'd been a witness to. He didn't look especially troubled, but then, it was hard to tell with the Allfather. You might say he had kind of odd reactions to things. Or you could just say he was batshit crazy.

"We were just talking about looking for the other gods who left Asgard," I said. "I was thinking you might have seen them in the time you spent here. It sounded like you've done a lot more roaming around than these guys did when they visited."

Muninn paused. She shifted her weight from one foot to the other. "You were thinking I could take you to them, you mean."

"You're under no obligation to help us," Odin said.

Thor let out a guffaw. "I'd say she is. If it wasn't for her helping Surt, the giant might never have raised enough of an army to challenge Asgard in the first place."

Muninn's shoulders twitched in a motion that brought to mind ruffled feathers. "I had my reasons. And I serve no one now." She eased back a step toward the doorway.

"Ah, let's not bicker," Loki said. "We've got plenty of draugar skulls to bash without turning on our own, don't we?"

"And she is our own," Baldur put in quietly. "She's of Asgard, even if she was turned against us for a time."

I caught the raven woman's eye. "Don't go. Everyone's just… riled up, after what happened up there."

Muninn's jaw worked. She didn't move forward again, but she stayed where she was, at least.

"The other gods," she said. "I may have an idea or two."

# 4

*Aria*

A gust of snow stung my face as I glided down to land on an icy ledge next to Muninn and Freya. I dug my feet deeper into the fur-lined boots Loki had procured for me and tugged the coat he'd doctored to allow room for my wings even more tightly around me. My valkyrie strength protected me from the cold some, but not completely. And the chill was waking up all the aches that hadn't quite healed after yesterday's encounter with Surt.

I wasn't going to mention that to anyone, though. The gods had fussed enough about me joining in on this undertaking. As if I wanted to sit around cooped up in some dusty barn while a mad giant planned to destroy this entire world. My heightened senses might help us spot the goddess we were searching for if she tried to take off on us. I *had* agreed to getting a night's rest first, and that should be enough for them.

Muninn and Freya seemed impervious to the weather in both their forms. There on the ledge, they transformed from raven and falcon so that we could talk with each other, Muninn wearing her usual loose black dress and Freya in an elegant blouse and slacks with her feathered cloak still slung over her shoulders. I tucked my wings closer to my body, the wind tickling over their silver-white feathers.

"You two should stay here while I fly closer to the usual spots on my own," Muninn said. "She might slip away if she sees a whole brigade approaching before we know exactly where we're going." The corner of her mouth curved up. "The gods are not always as observant as they like to think. They rarely noticed me coasting by."

"Come for us as soon as you've found her," Freya said, tossing back her golden waves. She set her hand on the hilt of her sword and scanned the snowy mountainside as if she expected Surt might appear even here.

Muninn leapt up into her raven form and flapped deeper into the valley we were perched on the edge of. She'd said she'd seen Skadi, the goddess of the hunt and of winter, in this range enough times to think she'd made a home here. A hunter sounded like a decent ally to have on our side.

"How easy do you think it'll be to convince Skadi to come back with us?" I asked.

Freya shrugged. "Skadi was always something of a loner, but she was loyal to Asgard. She won't want to see it or this realm fall to Surt."

"Do you think she's more likely to listen to you than the others? I have to think…" Suddenly I wondered if I should be bringing up this subject at all. But I'd already started, so I barreled onward. "You must want to keep searching for your daughter."

She'd mentioned her regrets over her falling out with the younger goddess, whom I'd gathered she hadn't seen in at least a couple centuries, after we'd started searching for all the other former inhabitants of Asgard a week ago.

"I wouldn't be sure where else to try with Hnoss," Freya said. "And I know Skadi better than any of the louts we're with. She was married to my father for some time—and she did truly care for him. They just wanted lives that were too different from what suited the other."

A hint of melancholy had crossed her face. How much because she was thinking of Odin, who was constantly wandering off without her on his rambling journeys, and how much for the daughter she hadn't seen in hundreds of years—partly because Hnoss had disliked her new stepfather?

I wasn't any stranger to fucked-up family dynamics. I knew what it was like to hate the new guy your mother had brought around, to know he was up to no good. Of course, at least Odin had thought he was doing the right thing, even if he'd encouraged his realm toward destruction and forced Loki to play the villain for that purpose. My mother's boyfriends—the one of them in particular—

I shoved that thought aside. I wasn't letting Trevor affect me anymore. I'd risen above everything he'd done to me, all the pain he'd caused and the ways he'd torn us apart. *My* mom didn't give a shit what had happened to me—that fact she'd made abundantly clear. There was a lot more hope for Freya and her daughter. Freya cared.

The icy chill was starting to penetrate my boots. I shuffled my feet to encourage the blood flow through them, and a sharp twinge ran through my hip. No, this body was definitely not in fully working order yet.

"Are you all right?" Freya asked, her blue eyes as keen as in her falcon form.

"Just a little cold," I lied.

It didn't matter if I wasn't totally recovered from my wounds. I had to do whatever I could to help finish this war with Surt, not just to support the gods I'd started to consider family but to protect the one part of my original family I still cared about.

My little brother Petey was off with the foster family we'd

arranged for him. I'd thought he'd be safe there from everyone who'd threatened him. If Surt claimed Midgard too—or if he found out I had a brother he could use to hurt me—I didn't want to think through what would happen to that sweet kid. He didn't deserve any of this.

Petey deserved better from *me*. Hod had wiped his memories so he couldn't accidentally slip up and give away anything about our real mother. If the agency found out who he was and where he'd come from, they'd have to send him back. Back to her and her latest lover who'd left fingerprints on his neck.

A black shape soared back toward us, stark against the white snow. Muninn dropped to join us. She was smiling when she shifted into a woman.

"She's here," she said. "There's a cabin just over that slope. I think Skadi's been living there. She's farther down the valley, hunting hares. I don't think we can completely surprise her, but if we arrive quickly enough, she'll see it's you and hopefully stay to chat."

Freya nodded and drew her cloak over her head. In an instant, she was a golden falcon, darting up toward the sky.

Before Muninn could transform too, I grasped her arm. I hadn't had much chance to talk to her alone until now.

"Before," I said, "when you were working with Surt… Did you ever tell him about my brother?" I knew she was aware of Petey's existence. She'd used him to torment me in that prison of memories she'd trapped us in.

The raven woman shook her head. "I never had any reason to. You've seen how Surt is. With an 'ally' like that, you're best off keeping everything you can close to your chest in case you need it later."

I guessed that comment was a little comforting, other than the implication that she probably would have told him if she'd thought it would get her out of a jam.

"Did you hear any of the dark elves mention it to him?" I asked. They'd threatened Petey to try to get me to back down too, although Hod had wiped their minds of all memory of my brother as well as he could after. I didn't know how many specifics of their plans they might have shared with Surt.

Muninn's gaze held mine with a gleam that looked almost curious. "To the best of my knowledge, Surt has no information about your brother. He didn't even think much about *you* until you broke out of my prison. Even if one of the dirt-eaters did say something, they couldn't know where your brother is, could they?"

"No." She only did because of the memories she'd peeked at in my head and Hod's. I let out my breath. "Okay. I'm sorry. I just needed to know."

"I'm glad I could help," she said, with a strange note in her voice, as if she were a little surprised by that gladness.

Freya's falcon wheeled in the air overhead, letting out a faint cry of impatience. I waved to her and sprang off the ledge with a flap of my wings.

My knees throbbed for a moment from the jump, but my newest appendages had escaped the worst of Surt's blows. It was a relief to glide through the air with the wind buffeting them, the rest of my body barely needing to move. Freya swept up toward the top of the slope Muninn had indicated, and I pushed myself faster, speeding after her. The raven streaked into view alongside me.

We whipped up over the slope and plunged down the other side. A log cabin, the roof blanketed with snow like everything else around here, stood about a mile down the mountainside. My sharpened valkyrie eyesight picked up a smattering of footsteps between the door and a heap of chopped firewood leaning against the cabin's side. A hint of pine smoke reached my nose from a fire that must have been put out no more than a few hours ago.

More footprints headed off to a small shed a few feet away on the other side. From there, long slivers of tracks sliced through the snow, heading downward. Skadi was on skis, I realized after staring for a moment.

Freya was hurtling down the slope. I caught a gust of wind that propelled me after her. A few seconds later, I spotted a figure with a trim jacket and a white wool hat pulled over her dark brown hair. She was braced on her skis, her arms lifted to pull back a bowstring, the arrow aimed at something I couldn't make out amid the trees across from her.

She let the arrow fly. Freya emerged from her cloak, keeping it unfurled behind her. "Skadi!" she called in her bright but firm voice.

The other goddess's head snapped around, her bow slipping in her hands. I hung back as Freya moved to greet Skadi. Muninn swooped around and flew back toward the cabin. I wondered if she planned to reveal herself to the goddess of the hunt at all.

"Freya," Skadi said, shielding her eyes from the sun as she stared. She shook her head in disbelief. Her smile was tight. "It's been a long time. What are you doing all the way out here?"

"It has been," Freya said, smoothly but quickly. "And I know you've wanted your peace from the politics of Asgard. I wouldn't have disturbed that peace if it weren't an incredibly urgent situation." She sucked in a breath. "Surt has returned. He's taken Asgard—the entire realm."

Skadi's eyebrows shot up, and her eyes flashed. "We can't have that."

"Exactly," Freya said, her own smile relieved.

"Come back to my cabin where we can sit properly, and you can tell me the whole thing while I pack," Skadi said. Her gaze slid to me. She looked me up and down where I was still hovering in the air. A thread of disdain came into her voice. "What did you bring a valkyrie for?"

Freya hesitated. "We didn't think it wise for any of us to travel alone," she said, which I guessed was the answer she thought Skadi would most easily accept.

"As if you need the protection of one of Odin's warrior dolls. Well, come on."

My mouth refused to stay shut. "I'm not a doll," I said. "And I have very good hearing, by the way."

Skadi rolled her eyes at me. "You're created for the gods' purposes, and you'll break much easier than any of us. Sounds like a doll to me. Just try to keep up, all right."

I bit my tongue against several barbed comments I'd have liked to make in return. Freya gave me a pleading glance and then turned back to Skadi. "Aria has proven herself well. I don't think you've any reason to worry that she'll slow us down."

Of course I'd be able to keep up with them. I had my wings, and Skadi was skiing uphill.

But then, it turned out I'd underestimated the goddess's strength. Skadi whipped up the mountainside with shoves of her powerful thighs, each push carrying her at least a tenth of a mile. I managed to keep pace, but by the time we reached her cabin, the tendons in my wings were starting to throb too.

Skadi shed her skis and stalked into the cabin, leaving Freya to hold the door for me. Muninn stayed perched on the roof.

Inside the single-room home, the pine smoke smell was sharper, but the goddess of the hunt didn't bother lighting the logs again, as much as I'd have enjoyed a little relief from the constant chill. She opened up a chest at the foot of her simple wood-frame bed.

"Tell me what happened," she said. "Just the important parts."

"Well," Freya said, sinking into the room's single chair, "it seems Surt was planning this invasion for a rather long time. As in, as far as he's concerned, he's wrapping up unfinished business from Ragnarok."

She summed up the events of the last several decades faster than I'd have been able to: How she and the five gods who'd remained in

Asgard had come down to Midgard for one of their regular visits, and not long after Odin had set off on his own usual wanderings. How he hadn't returned for tens of years, longer than ever before, until they'd started to worry about him. How the other four gods had summoned me, and how I'd ended up managing to lead them to Odin in Surt's grasp, from which we'd freed him.

Freya breezed over the details of the prison we'd been trapped in, our efforts to make peace with the dark elves, and our attempt at destroying Surt's army. I guessed that made sense. The only thing Skadi really needed to know was that Surt had arrived in Asgard with most of that army and proceeded to batter us.

"We weren't prepared for the attack," Freya finished. "And there were only the seven of us—well, and Ari."

I tried not to tense at being an afterthought. How much had I added to their defense anyway? How much had I held them back with the weaknesses Skadi had pointed out so briskly?

She wasn't completely wrong. The gods had made me, and I was a lot more fragile than their nearly immortal selves were.

"So you're gathering as many of the old guard as you can," Skadi filled in. She'd stuffed a bundle of arrows and a few pieces of armor into a pack she now slung over her shoulders. She hooked another bow, larger and gleaming with a golden sheen, onto its strap. "Of course I'll help. And I can do one better—or maybe two. I know where Njord settled down in this realm."

An amused glint lit in Freya's eyes. "You never could completely stay away from each other, could you?"

Njord must be Freya's father—Skadi's former husband whom she'd mentioned before. A slight flush colored Skadi's cheeks before she shrugged with a jerk of her shoulders. "I know where he is, is all I'm saying. And I think he still meets with your brother from time to time. We may be able to gather them both. It sounds as though time is of the essence. Are you ready for a longer journey?"

She aimed the question at Freya but then shot a pointed look my way. Freya didn't miss it. Before I could bristle, she stood up and rested a soothing hand on my back. "We're ready. You're right—the faster we can gather everyone, the better."

And they weren't leaving me behind. I was starting to wish we could leave *Skadi* behind. But she clearly knew her way around that bow, and she was tough enough to battle Surt. It wasn't as if I'd never met a blunt-talker before in my life.

I'd just usually been stronger than that talker—or in a position to head elsewhere if they annoyed me.

Outside, Skadi strapped on her skis with a few firm jerks of her hands. "Quickest way down the mountain," she said when she caught me watching. There was a challenge in her voice. *There's no way a mere valkyrie could outrace me.*

Freya lifted into the air in her falcon form, and Skadi started to push off. I was already getting left behind. I moved to leap after them, and my foot slipped on the slick snow. My other calf jarred as I caught my balance. A spear of pain pierced through my muscles from ankle to hip, and I couldn't swallow the gasp that flew up my throat.

Skadi swiveled to the side to peer back at me where I'd come to a stop, half-crouched and panting. "Are you coming?" she said.

I clenched my jaw. Squeezing my hands against the pain, I straightened up and rose from the ground with a sweep of my wings. It wasn't a grand departure, but the slow ascent allowed me to avoid putting any more weight on my sore leg.

"I'm right behind you," I said, knowing I hadn't quite erased the strain from my voice. Skadi gave a little sniff and sped off. I'd just proven everything she'd been thinking about valkyries, and we still had who knew how many miles to cross.

There was nothing I could do but flap these wings and hurry after her.

# 5

*Hod*

The cold rock trembled against my palms, but as I pushed more shadows into its rough surface, it steadied. With my mind's eye, I could see the miniscule cracks that had been forming all through this underground passage filling in and solidifying.

The effort sent a prickling through the muscles of my shoulder and back. I set my jaw and compelled more of my dark energy into the cave around me.

This rock would never have weakened in the first place if we gods hadn't neglected all the realms except our own and Midgard. The dark elves of Nidavellir had needed us, and we'd ignored them for hundreds of years, too caught up in our preferred pastimes. When the ceilings of their home had started collapsing on them, I wasn't sure we could really blame them for buying into Surt's promise that he could conquer a new home for them if they helped him gather his army.

If I wanted them to help *us* now, I had to show just how committed we were to making up for those past mistakes. If I'd had the power to seal the stone through the entire realm all at once, I would have. I'd learned that one length of cave was enough to leave me sweating and breathless, though.

When I felt my magic smooth over the end of the passage, I let myself ease back. The space around me was quiet other than the faint rasp of my companion's breaths.

The commander of this clan of dark elves had insisted on staying to watch my work. The gate we knew of into Nidavellir from Midgard was at a different end of their realm from the one I'd mainly been arriving through from Asgard, and I'd never spoken to this man before. Any other inhabitants of this section of cave, he'd told me, had been evacuated a few days ago when a few chunks of the ceiling had started to fall.

"It'll be stable now," I said, turning my face toward him as closely as I could estimate his position. "I can return again soon to work on another passage."

His steps padded past me into the cave. The cool air shifted against my damp skin. I swiped the back of my hand over my forehead, wishing I'd thought to bring a warmer shirt. It was summer where we were staying in Midgard, but nowhere in Nidavellir ever got all that warm.

A rapping echoed from within the cave as the commander prodded the walls with what sounded like a metal cane. He strode back to me.

"It appears as you say. I'd heard the Blind One of Asgard had been restoring parts of our realm, but it was difficult to believe without seeing it."

"We've stayed apart from your people for too long," I said, with a respectful dip of my head. "I'm doing my best to make amends. We want all the realms to be safe and secure for their people."

I'd gone so far as to swear a blood oath with the local commander near the Asgard gate committing to my continued help. I'd shown this dark elf the scar on my palm when I'd arrived here.

"We appreciate your efforts," the commander said, but his tone still sounded guarded.

I had to broach the other reason for my visit sometime. "I want you to know that what I did here today—what I'll keep doing—is solely part of those amends. I don't expect any repayment for it, and I'll continue doing it regardless of how you respond to what I say next. We— Have you heard of the recent attack on Asgard?"

"Ah." The commander shifted his weight. From that one syllable, I could tell that he had and that he'd already guessed my intent. "Your attempt to eliminate Surt and his army was not as successful as you'd hoped."

That was one way of putting it. "He has taken over Asgard," I said. "That's why I could only reach your realm through the gate from Midgard. We need to regain our realm—and to protect the realm of humans, which he's indicated he means to conquer as well. We won't ask you to fight on our behalf, of course, but if you'd give us permission to reach Asgard through your realm, if we decide that's our best option for launching a return attack, it could make all the difference."

"Yggdrasil's root reaches us many sectors from here," the commander said. "You'd want us to host an army of gods as you travel that distance?"

"It's not likely to be a very large army," I had to admit. "And we'd simply be passing through." But tramping through miles of caves could be plenty of disturbance on its own, especially when the dark elves were already crowded into the more stable areas of their home after so many cave-ins. I wet my lips. "We'd follow whatever requirements you set out."

"And that's all you'd ask?"

I hesitated, but if I didn't ask for the rest, the others would no doubt press for me to pursue the subject next time, and then the dark elf leader would feel I'd lied.

"If you had any weapons to spare, or could forge a few that might assist us in taking back our realm—we would repay you in every way we could."

"If you actually win back Asgard, where all your riches are," the commander said.

"We will," I said firmly. We had other riches, bank accounts and stores of cash in Midgard that we'd used for our visits there, but that wouldn't appeal to the dark elves. They'd want gold. We might be able to buy some bars of the stuff in the realm of humans, though. "And I can see if we can offer some in advance—just a portion of the full reward."

The commander hummed to himself. He still sounded skeptical. My fingers twitched with the urge to ball into my palm, but I forced them to relax. By Asgard, if only I had Loki's quick tongue. He'd always been able to charm just about anything out of the elves, sometimes without any payment at all. Sweet-talking wasn't exactly a skill of mine.

"Surt will know we were involved," the commander said after a moment. "If you fail, he'll punish our people as well as yours."

"We won't fail," I said, as if I could guarantee that. "Having your support will make that even more sure."

"Nevertheless… I will need to discuss it with some of the other sector leaders. I certainly can't make a decision like this for all of us on my own."

"Of course," I said, even though my heart had sunk. I believed he'd bring forward our request, but I had the suspicion he wasn't going to put a positive spin on it. "I'll return within a day or two, as soon as I'm able to, and you can let me know if you happen to have an answer then. Either way, I'll see to another of your caves."

"Then we will welcome you." The commander motioned, and

one of his guards approached with heavy footsteps. "Please escort our guest back to the gate."

I'd paid enough attention to the turns and the shifts in the air that I probably could have navigated back to the gate on my own. We hadn't come that far. But having a guide gave me room to confirm my impressions of this area. It seemed I might be venturing down to this part of Nidavellir rather frequently in the next several days.

When I stepped out on the other side of the gate, a hot humid breeze washed over me with tart smells of vegetation. I conjured a sheet of shadow to lift me off the ground and glided up over the treetops where I could soar along freely. I knew from the taste of the wind and the rippling of my strands of dark magic across the ground below which way to go to find my way back to the others.

Last night, we'd moved from the musty barn to the farmhouse down the lane, which was equally abandoned. With a touch of magic, we'd make sure it stayed that way as far as the locals were concerned for as long as we needed it.

And it was a good thing we'd put wards in place to hide our activities from any outsiders, because as soon as I directed my swath of shadow down toward the farm, the sounds of spirited conversation reached my ears, loud enough to draw attention.

Three voices I hadn't heard in quite some time had joined those more familiar.

"My goodness, Thor, I think you've managed to bulk up even more since I last saw you." That slightly husky alto belonged to Skadi.

"Baldur, it's good to see you looking so well." That deep, almost creaky bass was Njord.

"We really mustn't let it take a war to bring us back together next time." That spritely tenor was Freyr.

Freya and Ari's mission had been successful, then, even more so than they'd expected. Muninn hadn't led them astray. The newcomers and our original group had gathered in the yard outside the house. From the comments I'd overheard, I had the impression these three had only just arrived.

I bade my magic to set me down at the edge of the yard.

"Well, and here's Hod," Njord said. My ears were too practiced to miss the flattening of his tone compared to how he'd spoken to my twin. Baldur had always been the popular one. After all, who wouldn't prefer basking in sunny light over a wintry chill?

"So, he managed to escape even your hammer?" Skadi was saying to my left, and Thor let out a self-deprecating chuckle.

Odin stirred by my right with a rustle of his cloak, and everyone went still. "We'll need all of Asgard in this trying time," he said. "I commend you for your swift arrival."

"How could we do anything else, Allfather?" Freyr said, a respectful lilt in his warm voice. Most of our fellow gods had drifted away from Asgard because they hadn't enjoyed living under Odin's watchful eye, but they recognized his authority all the same. "As soon as Freya gave her horrific account of Surt's assault, we knew there should be no delaying. Surt will fall, swift and hard."

"What bright plans have you been coming up with, hmm?" Njord said, with a soft thump as if he'd given Baldur a friendly slap on the back.

"Oh, I think it's best I leave the planning mainly to the gods of war," my twin said with a smile in his voice.

"But you'll be there to light our way. Don't sell yourself short." Skadi tsked her tongue.

They were slipping back into the usual patterns, as if they'd never left. Where had Loki gotten to? Probably slinking around somewhere on the fringes, waiting to see where he could get a jab in. There was a reason most of the gods had never been all that keen to keep his company, even if they'd forgiven him for his role in Ragnarok.

And there was a reason they'd barely given me a greeting. I

hadn't really played an active role in Asgard's community when it'd been more full—not beyond furtive favors done in the shadows. The darkness I carried with me had always seemed to put a damper on the joys of those around me. I'd almost forgotten what it was like, hanging back on the fringes myself, taking it all in but rarely putting myself forward.

When it had only been the six of us, the balance had seemed equal enough. I'd been a necessary part of the whole. But that would change as more and more of our former companions joined us.

An ache ran through me for my study full of scientific and philosophical texts in our usual house in Midgard. For the even larger library in my hall above, if Surt hadn't burned every page in it. If this were a normal situation, if I'd had access to either, I'd have holed up with my books and lost myself in their words rather than make an awkward attempt at socializing.

I wet my lips, and the one voice I would always be happy to hear reached me. Unfortunately, it came with the question I was the least looking forward to answering.

"Hod's come back from Nidavellir," Ari said, with a hint of annoyance in her tone. "If we want to stop Surt, let's give him a chance to share what they said."

I felt all the gods' attention turn to me. I shot a quick smile toward our valkyrie, but my stomach had twisted. Sticking to the sidelines had been my choice as much as anyone else's. What did I have to offer even now other than more gloom?

"The dark elves were unwilling to commit to allowing us to move through their realm or to supplying us with any equipment for our attack," I had to admit. "The commander I spoke to said he'd discuss it with some of the others, but… I think we'd do best not to count on them."

# 6

*Aria*

The big table in the farmhouse's dining room didn't have any chairs, but that didn't stop the gods from using it for their conference. With the nine of them squeezed around the worn oak surface someone had wiped the dust from yesterday, there wasn't much room for me. Loki had caught my eye and motioned me over when we'd first come in, but I'd waved him off. The truth was I only trusted my legs to hold me up when I had a wall to lean against.

I could hear just fine from where I was standing anyway. And the truth was there wasn't a whole lot I could add to the discussion they were having right now.

"I haven't spoken with Heimdall in at least a hundred years, maybe more," said Njord, the sea god with a long weathered face and twinkling blue eyes that matched his daughter's. "I got the sense he roamed around quite a bit."

"Yes, I agree it'd be useful to have him on board, but I'm not sure where we're likely to find him," agreed Freyr, Freya's brother and Njord's son. His golden waves fell only to the tops of his ears, and a golden sheen of a beard colored his narrow jaw as well. "I'd imagine you'll have already looked anywhere I'd have thought of."

"Frigg would be useful in a battle with that magic of hers," Skadi said. "But you'd know her inclinations better than any of us, Allfather."

Odin frowned at the mention of the goddess I'd gathered was his first wife. "I can think of a place or two we may not have investigated yet," he allowed. "I doubt she'll be eager to see this face at her door, though."

"I can go speak to her if we find her," Baldur offered, and everyone around the table nodded. The story of the bright god's death came back to me. Frigg was his mother—she was the one who'd gotten every object in the world to swear it would never hurt him… except the mistletoe.

I didn't want to linger in the memories that thought brought back. Muninn had re-enacted Baldur's death for us in agonizing detail. I'd had to watch him fall, speared through by a throw from Hod's hand, with Loki's guidance and Odin's implicit approval.

The three newer gods didn't know about that last part. Which was probably why they were saving their wary glances for the god of darkness and the trickster while hanging off the Allfather's every word.

Skadi cut a glance toward Loki right now, her eyes narrowing for a second before she said, "What about Vidar? He could nearly rival Thor in a fight."

"Hey, now," the thunder god said in mock dismay.

The goddess of the hunt rolled her eyes at him. "I did say *nearly*. But he proved himself well during Ragnarok."

Everyone's eyes seemed to twitch toward Loki then. I wasn't sure if it was just because of the role he'd played there or if there was something more about this Vidar guy. From the bits and pieces I'd heard about Ragnarok since joining the gods, I knew it was

Heimdall who'd killed Loki during that battle, so it couldn't be that. But there'd been plenty of anguish going around, clearly.

Loki raised his chin, but Odin spoke before he might have. "Yes. It would be good to see another of my sons again, as well."

"You know," Freyr said, tapping his chin, "I think I can guess the general area where he might be. We crossed paths once a few decades ago, near the coast of Tanzania, and he said he was headed inward to the savanna. That sort of terrain does seem to suit his temperament. Whether he's stayed there, who can say, but it would be worth a try."

"A few of us should head over there to check at once," Freya said, straightening up.

I pushed myself off the wall, drawing myself up straight too. I might not have any clue about the temperaments of the rest of the gods we could be looking for, but once I got pointed in the right direction, I could pitch in with my valkyrie eyes and ears. "I'll go."

Njord gave me a quizzical look. "The valkyrie? I expect he'll react better to a familiar face. The right familiar face."

He wasn't as disdainful as Skadi had been, but his dismissal pricked at me anyway. "I've got supernaturally sharp eyesight and hearing," I said. "I'd be useful for covering more ground, for looking for signs of where he might have been. I'm happy to let someone else do the talking."

"Ari has been a great help many times before," Thor put in, with a slightly threatening rumble that dared anyone to argue.

"Should she really be flying off around the world when she's not even recovered from that first battle?" Skadi said. "She took a bit of a tumble when Freya came for me."

"What?" Hod swiveled toward me. "You didn't say anything."

"I'm *fine*," I insisted, but when I moved to demonstrate my fully functional body, my traitor leg chose that moment to twitch with another jab of pain. My balance wavered, and my jaw clenched.

"My legs are just a little sore still," I added quickly. "I can fly perfectly fine."

Hod had already moved to my side. He touched the side of my face. "Baldur should look at you again," he said, and lowered his voice. "Surt hit you harder than any of us. It's nothing to be ashamed of."

Had the giant hit me harder, though, or had I simply taken the hit harder than the gods would have? I grimaced.

Loki spoke up in his flippant way. "We really wouldn't want any additional harm to come to those lovely legs of yours."

I glowered at him, and the trickster grinned back at me. Hod grasped my arm, bending closer. Baldur had already stepped back from the table.

"I'd be okay," I told the dark god.

"Of course you would," he said, his blind eyes aimed straight at mine. "But you'll be more okay if Baldur heals you wherever the pain is lingering. Don't make me carry you out of the room, valkyrie."

I made a face, which didn't do me any good because he couldn't see that either, but I knew he'd do it. And maybe I should see if a little more healing would help, so I'd be able to defend myself when I really needed to.

"All right," I grumbled. Then, because I could, because I knew it'd stop him from looking so worried, and maybe a little because it was the only other way I could think of to show the new gods that I had a place here beyond just "the valkyrie," I tipped my head up to catch his lips for a quick kiss.

Hod returned the kiss with a brush of eager warmth. His mouth curved into a soft smile when I eased away. I'd probably left him with a bunch of questions to answer from the others, but he didn't look as if he minded at all.

Baldur rested his hand on my back as he walked with me into the hall. A sitting room a couple doors down held a few armchairs and a sofa. Baldur sent a gust of light through it that washed the dust from the furniture. He motioned for me to sit on the sofa with my legs sprawled out, closed the door behind us, and tugged over one of the chairs so he could sit next to me.

"Where does it hurt?" he asked.

"It's just my right leg. Sometimes in my hip, and sometimes my knee, and sometimes my ankle… Kind of everywhere," I admitted. "But the pain will probably get better on its own. It's only been a day."

"It won't heal on its own if you're running all over the place," Baldur said, raising his eyebrows at me with a pointed look. He set his hand on my calf, and the heat of his hand seeped straight through my jeans. "There may be new tears in the muscles I can heal."

"Fine, if it'll make you and Hod feel better."

Baldur smiled, with a clarity in his bright blue eyes that I hadn't seen until a couple weeks ago. Back when I'd first met him, he'd hardly seemed to ever totally focus on me through his dreamy haze. He definitely wouldn't have been alert enough to tease me. "I think the point is to make *you* feel better."

He started at my right ankle, his fingers circling the joint. A glowing sensation tingled through my skin and down to the muscles and tendons. I let myself relax against the cushioned arm of the sofa.

"You light him up, you know," Baldur said after a moment.

I blinked. "What? Who?"

"Hod." His hand slid up to my calf, trailing his shimmering warmth in its wake. "I've known him my whole life—and his, obviously—and I don't think I've ever seen anyone bring that much joy out in him. He worries about you because he doesn't want to lose you." He paused, his thumb tracing a gentle arc over my shinbone, and raised his gaze to meet mine again. "None of us do. You're one of us now, Aria."

None of the four—my four—who'd brought me into their world wanted to lose me, he meant. "I'm planning on sticking around," I said, but his words had sent a flutter through my chest. I'd spent a lot of my life not caring about anyone other than Petey, but I *wanted* to matter to them now. I wanted to be someone who made their lives better, in every possible way.

"If I bring out the light in him, do I bring out the darkness in you?" I had to ask. "How… How have you been coping?" Shadows had seeped inside the light god while he'd been trapped in his temporary death. As he'd woken from his peaceful daze, the darkness that had lodged inside him had seemed to wake up too. He'd found it hard to control, at least at first.

"You help me accept the darkness in me, Aria," Baldur said, his voice softening in a way that had me tingling all the way up my leg. "I've been releasing it, here and there, as I can. But I know it doesn't have to diminish my light."

"A little darkness can be very useful," I said, unable to stop myself from thinking of when we'd come together in Valhalla—the way he'd mingled heat and cold in his touch to spark all kinds of sensations through my body. As his hand moved to my knee now, fresh heat pooled between my thighs.

If I'd changed the gods, they'd changed me at least as much in turn. Before them, I hadn't realized I had the capacity to care this much for anyone other than my brother and myself. They'd given me a second chance at living, offered me new strengths and led me to uncover others I'd buried deep, made me want to brave and move beyond the horrors of my past.

The gods might have resurrected me for their own goals, but because of them this life was fully *mine* now, in a way my first one hadn't really been, not from the first moment that asshole boyfriend of my mother's had crept into my childhood bedroom.

These four gods were mine, and I was theirs, no matter what any of their cohorts thought about it.

Baldur's fingers skimmed up my thigh. The remaining tension in the muscle there melted away—and a bolt of longing shot straight through my core. My breath hitched.

Baldur stopped, peering into my eyes. "Did I hurt you?"

"No," I said, my cheeks flushing. "Um. The opposite."

He looked confused for a second before understanding dawned on his face. It brought with it the slightly wicked smile I loved so much. Oh yes, a little darkness mixed with Baldur's light extremely well.

"I'd take advantage of that fact," he said. "But I do have a whole other leg I should check over just in case, don't I?"

He reached for my left ankle. This time, as he eased his hand over my limb, he stroked me through my jeans in a way his healing efforts hadn't required before. Each graze of his fingertips stoked the heat inside me higher. The longing that had risen up inside me earlier knotted into need.

Baldur leaned forward as his hand caressed my thigh. His natural glow washed over me with an even headier tingle, leaving me a little breathless. His thumb worked along the inside of my leg, closer and closer to the spot that was throbbing in a pleasurably torturous way for his touch.

"All healed up," he murmured. "If you're not in any hurry to get back to the others…"

"Fuck them. No, better idea—fuck *me*." I tangled my fingers in his soft hair to yank his mouth to mine.

Baldur's kiss was as bright as the rest of him, like a beam of sunlight racing through my nerves. He met my urgency with equal passion. His tongue parted my lips and swept past them to tease over mine. He slid off the chair, bracing his knees against the edge of the sofa.

His hand slipped up my body, skipping over the place where I'd wanted it most, but it was hard to regret that omission when a moment later his fingers grazed my breast. I arched into his touch with a whimper. A shimmer shot over my skin, chased by a flicker of cooler darkness that licked over my nipple. I nearly bit his lip trying to hold in a moan. If we got too loud, if the other gods left their conference, someone might hear us.

But then, why should I care what they thought? Three of them could join in if they wanted. The others would judge us however they decided to no matter what I did.

I wanted to absorb Baldur's brilliance, to be lit up from the inside out with a shine so stark no one could ever get close enough to hurt me—not Surt, not snarky remarks, not any of it.

The god of light nudged up my shirt so he could caress me skin to skin, and I raised my arms so he could strip the top right off me. He tugged his own shirt off in turn.

"I want to feel you," he murmured. "All of you, right against me."

My pulse skipped a beat. Baldur didn't often talk about what *he* wanted, he was so busy trying to keep the rest of us in harmony. If he was asking something of me, I'd do whatever I could to give it. I expected I'd enjoy this request as much as he did.

He knelt over me on the sofa. My heart stuttered again, with a jolt of anxiety this time, but I focused on the brilliance and the warmth and the flecks of darkness that brought a gasp to my lips with their giddy contrast. This was Baldur, the kindest gentlest man—the kindest gentlest *being*—I'd ever met. If I could trust Loki, trusting the bright god was nothing. Not a single particle in me doubted that he'd sooner sacrifice his own life than do me harm.

Baldur lowered his head to my breast. I sucked in a breath as he slicked his mouth over the tip, heat and cold twining together with the swivel of his tongue. His hand dropped to the waist of my jeans, and I arched to meet him, offering myself up to him. With a careful tug, he undid the fly.

When he tilted forward to claim my lips again, I fumbled with his slacks. A moment later, we were both groping and kicking our way out of our pants and underwear. My body trembled with need everywhere his fingertips so much as grazed. But I remembered what he'd said about wanting to feel me against him.

I looped one arm around his back, the other across his shoulders, and drew him to me. Baldur let me pull him close with a faint groan. He kissed me harder as our bodies fit together, our legs intertwining, his heart beating over mine through his chest.

I was engulfed. I was embraced. Every movement of his mouth told me I was treasured.

The firm length of his cock by my hip confirmed he was definitely interested in more than just cuddling. I squirmed to bring his hardness right against my core and couldn't bite back a moan. Baldur nuzzled my cheek and nibbled along my jaw.

"What do you want now?" I asked, my voice thick.

He flicked his tongue against the crook of my neck, provoking another shiver of pleasure. "To be inside you. To feel you in every possible way. To make love to you like a fucking symphony."

Hearing a swear word drop from his lips always got me twice as turned on. I clutched his shoulder, my hips already starting to rock in encouragement. "I'm ready when you are."

He chuckled softly and tucked his hand under my ass to find the right angle. A little cry broke from my throat as he eased his cock inside me. He filled me with heat, but it wasn't the same as Loki's fire or Thor's crackles of lightning. Baldur's heat was a steady beaming glow that radiated through every nerve, leaving them somehow soothed yet quivering with bliss at the same time.

He adjusted his position again, stroking my hair with the hand he'd braced near my head to carry some of his weight. His next kiss was sweet as melted caramel. He pulled a little back and then thrust deeper, and deeper.

A little pulse started to beat over my breasts in time with his rhythm—a patter of bright warmth and a lick of cool shadow, teasing my nipples even harder with a melody of pleasure. I gasped and arched into the sensation. The song he was playing on my body and the smooth hot skin of his chest made me giddy with bliss.

As he increased his tempo, the pulsing slipped down over my belly, flowing and condensing, until it reached my clit. It hummed against that sensitive spot over and over, faster and faster in harmony with his movements. With each flutter of warmth and cold, my nerves sparked from my core all through the rest of my body, brighter and brighter.

"Do you like that?" Baldur asked, almost shyly.

"Oh, God, yes," I said, and then I was lost. Lost in the pulsing glow against my clit and the sweetness of his mouth and the gleaming heft of each thrust inside me.

Light started to glitter at the edges of my vision. It whirled around me, surrounding me with pleasure. Bliss flooded every inch of me and Baldur was everywhere, and I let go of any last shred of hesitation inside me. Just let go and let the ecstasy of the moment carry me wherever it and he wanted to take me.

My orgasm rushed through me like a solar flare. My head tipped back with a sob of pleasure. For a few seconds, I lost track of my limbs, of the beginnings and ends of my skin, of everything except that bliss and the choked breath as my lover joined me in it.

# 7

*Aria*

I dozed for a while with Baldur tucked against me on the sofa. There wasn't really a whole lot of room for both of us, though, which is probably why when I woke up some hours later from what must have turned into a deeper sleep, he was gone. He'd left a blanket wrapped around me, imbued with his sunny warmth. I snuggled deeper into it for a few minutes before I convinced myself to go back out and see where the gods' discussion had taken us.

When I stepped into the hall, voices reached me from the dining room. It sounded like the conference was still in progress. Maybe I hadn't slept as long as I'd thought.

My stomach grumbled, announcing that it had been at least long enough for me to have missed a meal. I ambled into the kitchen at the back of the house to sort through the groceries someone had picked up while Freya and I were off in the snowy mountains. Mostly for my benefit, since the gods didn't require food quite the same way, as much as Thor enjoyed sating his expansive appetite.

The farmhouse had no electricity, so the offerings were all non-perishable stuff that required no cooking. My nose wrinkled as I poked through the bags. I was about to rip open a bag of sour-cream-and-onion potato chips—not the healthiest meal I'd ever eaten, but not the worst either, to be fair—when a shape passing by the kitchen window caught my eye.

It was Odin's broad-brimmed hat, a little less broad after some of Surt's fiery magic must have caught it. And it was sitting where it usually did, on Odin's head.

The Allfather strode by the window and out into the backyard, his spear in hand like a walking stick and his cloak wafting out behind him, giving no indication at all that he planned on stopping any time soon.

I craned my neck toward the window, but I couldn't see anyone else out there with him. Why was he heading off alone while the others were still deep in conversation?

There were plenty of possibilities, but something about his silent departure sent a prickle down my spine. I dropped the bag of chips and went to the back door.

The hinges squealed as I opened it. Odin had already reached the broken chain-link fence that surrounded the yard. He swung his leg over the crumpled metal, and I darted down the back steps.

"Hey!" I said. "Where are you going?"

Odin paused and peered over his shoulder at me. For a second, I thought he might decide I wasn't worth the effort of an answer. His single eye was as inscrutable as always, and the ridged scar where its partner had been told me even less.

I loosed my wings, both because I thought I might need them and as a sort of threat—if he kept going, I planned on following. The Allfather studied me a moment longer and then turned to face me. I tucked my wings close to my back as I hurried across the patchy grass of the yard, but I didn't retract them. If I'd learned anything since we'd retrieved Odin, it was not to trust the king of the gods any farther than I could throw him, even if he had made a few amends recently.

A cloud had passed over the summer sun, cutting the worst of its glare, but the muggy air stuck to my skin. At least my legs held me up without even a twinge as I hustled over, thanks to Baldur's ministrations. The additional sleep had probably helped too.

I stopped a few paces from Odin and folded my arms over my chest. "Where are you going?" I repeated.

"I mean to wander in search of a vision," the Allfather said in his measured voice.

Sure, that sounded like a typically Odin thing to do. And also an answer typically short on the details. "For how long?" I asked.

"Until the vision I need finds me."

My back prickled again. The last time he'd gone wandering, hadn't the gods lost track of him for *decades*?

"You're leaving," I said. "You're taking off on us. Did you even tell the others that you're going? You look like you're sneaking away."

Odin's expression didn't shift. "They know my ways. It is best, when I am seeking answers, that I am not distracted by the concerns of the rest of the world."

The slight sharpening of his tone suggested that he didn't appreciate the distraction I was creating here either. Well, he could bite me. Maybe slinking off into the unknown without a word was what his wife, sons, and friends were used to, but it was time *someone* put their foot down. It'd also become very clear in the last couple weeks that Odin had gotten away with an awful lot of bullshit for way too long.

"What the hell good is a vision going to do us if you're not here when we have to get everyone together to take on Surt?" I said. "You're needed *here*."

He blinked slowly. "There was a time when you appeared not to appreciate my guidance."

I shook my head. "No, you're not getting away with playing that card. Just because I don't want you calling *all* the shots without listening to anyone else doesn't mean I think it's perfectly fine for you to abandon us to fight your battles for you. You know how to use that spear as more than a walking stick."

"Seeking visions is the best advantage I can lend to those battles," Odin said. "They bring insight from beyond the nine realms. They may lead us to the gods we need to turn the tide or to some other course of action we might not otherwise have considered."

Wasn't it those craptastic visions that had convinced him to prop Loki up as a villain and speed on the end of the world way back when? Maybe it was better if we left the courses of action they prompted unconsidered.

I didn't think Odin would see it that way, though. He might have made apologies for a few of his past acts, but he hadn't shown any sign of doubt over Ragnarok. I guessed you had to be pretty committed when you were planning for the destruction of your home and everyone in it.

"Are you sure that's the best you can do?" I said instead. "Or is it just the advantage you can offer that lets you not be around when the flames are flying? What makes you think a vision is going to come soon enough to help? Surt could start his invasion in five minutes."

"The giant waited centuries before he made his first attack," Odin said evenly. "I expect he'll take his time carrying out his intentions."

"You can't *know* that."

Odin thumped the end of his spear against the ground. "You have been part of this world for barely a heartbeat compared to our lifetimes, valkyrie. I can judge what is right. And I will find no visions standing here discussing the matter with you."

With a whirl of his cloak, he swung back toward the fence. He stepped over the sagging part and marched off, his steps even brisker than before.

I wavered on my feet, wanting to fly after him, unsure it'd do me any good. If he got frustrated enough, would he stab me with that spear? I wouldn't put it past him.

In his mind, as in Skadi's and, it seemed, Njord's, "valkyrie" didn't mean much at all. If some of the other gods would have been upset about my death, there was no reason to think that mattered to Odin. He hadn't seemed to care much about their feelings when he'd let Loki guide Hod into killing Baldur.

A small dark form swooped down beside me. Muninn transformed from raven to woman as she landed. I held back a flinch. I hadn't been sure she'd stuck around after she'd guided us to Skadi. She must have been hanging around outside the house in her bird form.

She'd obviously overheard my conversation with the Allfather. She glanced toward Odin's swiftly retreating back and then at me.

"He knows what paths to travel," she said.

I stared at her. "Are you okay with this? Shouldn't you be more upset than anyone that he's leaving us in the lurch?"

She gave a twitch of a shrug. "I didn't like that he ordered me around, sent me to do his bidding without concern. I had no problem with him choosing what he did with himself. Why shouldn't he follow his own will?"

"Because his visions are a load of crap and the real planning is happening in there?" I gestured toward the house.

"He has seen a great deal," Muninn said. "Some of it more telling than you could imagine. He'll return with knowledge of value—he always has."

It was hard to stay angry when the woman who'd raged at Odin in the past was taking his departure so calmly. "So, we just stand around and wait for him, then?" I said.

She gave me a piercing look. "I believe there's more the rest of you are capable of than that. Why are you out here instead of in there helping to make those plans?"

"Well, I— He—" I let my protest go with a sputter of frustration. She wasn't completely wrong. "Are *you* going to come in and join the conversation?"

She shuddered beneath her loose dress. "Too many fraught memories crowded into one space," she said. "I'll join the fray as I'm needed."

She hopped up into the air again, shifting into her raven form in a blink. A few flaps of her wings carried her to the house's chimney, where she dropped down to perch.

Fine. I guessed I'd go inside and see if the gods had figured out any way *I* could be needed. They must be discussing something interesting if they still hadn't noticed Odin's disappearance.

Thor's deep voice rang down the hall as I approached the room. "We shouldn't part ways for more than a day at a time. We already know we have trouble tackling Surt with smaller numbers."

"Which is why it's more important that we take all the time we can to search for our comrades, isn't it?" Freyr answered. "How much could the giant possibly manage to destroy in a few days? Midgard's a large realm."

My hackles rose automatically. The thunder god obviously didn't like that answer either. His normally ruddy face was flushed an even deeper red than usual when I peeked into the room.

"And the people of this realm depend on us to protect them from threats like that. There may be thousands of cities, but that doesn't make it all right for the giant to level ten of them."

"Brother," Baldur said from the spot where he'd rejoined them around the table. "Freyr. I'm sure we can reach a compromise that accomplishes all our goals."

"Or we could just go and stop with all the talking about it," Skadi put in, but her voice sounded more weary than anything else.

Freya was rubbing her forehead as if she had a headache. Loki had stepped back from the table completely to lean against the wall, his arms crossed and his eyes narrowed. I might not be able to read the gods' emotions very clearly, but I didn't need any special sensitivity to pick up on the vibe in the room. Everyone was worried and worn down by uncertainty.

The gods had never really lost Asgard before, had they? Even during Ragnarok, they'd simply been reborn right back into their home. They were on unfamiliar ground as much as I was. And they were a whole lot less used to having to cope with situations they couldn't simply overpower.

My stomach grumbled again. Loki glanced over with an arch of an eyebrow, but I wondered if my body's signals might be a sign of what everyone here needed.

"Maybe before any more talk or traveling, we should all have a proper dinner," I said, pitching my voice loud enough to fill the room. "I know you don't *need* three meals a day, but we haven't had much since yesterday morning—it can't hurt, anyway, right?"

Loki pushed off the wall with a clap of his hands. I wasn't sure if he actually thought eating was a good idea or he was just happy for an excuse to end the conversation. "Excellent thought, pixie." He made a grabby motion toward Thor. "Come on, Thunderer. I know where we can find ourselves some decent food, but if you want enough to fill that gut, you'd better be the one to carry it."

Thor guffawed, but he followed him. Baldur aimed one of his brilliant smiles at me.

"We could make a bonfire in the yard," he said. "Skadi, if I remember right, you'd be the best of us to set up a spit."

The aloof goddess couldn't seem to resist a compliment to her skills. Soon we'd all tramped out into the backyard. Skadi sent Freya and Freyr into the nearby forest to gather some firewood with strict instructions and set to work constructing a roasting platform. By the time Loki and Thor made it back carrying several skinned chickens, fresh cobs of corn, and apples from a farmers market, flames were dancing against the growing dark.

Hod came to stand beside me as the smell of roasting chicken filled the air. "Better?" he asked softly.

"Yes," I said. In more ways than one. Baldur's second round of healing had erased the last of my body's aches, and our encounter afterward had soothed some of the ache in my heart. No matter what the new gods thought of me, my four saw me as an equal.

I reached out and slipped my hand around Hod's. He twined his fingers with mine, a smile curving his lips. Then Njord looked around.

"Where's Odin gotten to?" the older god asked.

My back tensed. The worst part of having seen him leave was that now I had to deliver the news.

"He took off," I said. "I saw him going. He said he was going to look for a vision that would give us some more ideas of what to do."

I'd been braced for raised tempers, but the closest I got was the tightening of Hod's hand around mine. Loki rolled his eyes. Njord simply chuckled and said, "Well, that's the Allfather's way, isn't it?" and everyone went back to debating whether the first chickens were totally done, as if the Allfather's absence really mattered that little. Well, they had to be a lot more used to Odin's wanderings that I was. Who was I to point out that this might not have been the best time for it?

The tense vibe I'd sensed in the dining room faded away as the gods dug into their meal. I had to admit the fire-roasted chicken leg I devoured was just about the best thing I'd ever tasted.

As I licked the last bits of grease from my fingers, wondering if I had room for another cob of corn, Loki's head jerked up on the other side of the fire.

"Quiet!" he snapped.

We all stared, the other gods' voices falling away. The trickster closed his eyes and drew in a slow breath through his mouth. His shoulders had gone rigid.

"What is it, Sly One?" Skadi asked after a moment, managing to sound both skeptical and nervous.

Loki's eyes opened. The amber in them glowed with the firelight. His mouth twisted for a second before he said, "I can taste his fire. Surt has arrived in Midgard."

# 8

*Aria*

In the first moment after Loki's declaration, we all stood frozen in shocked silence. Then Freya blurted out, "Where?"

The trickster's head swiveled to the right. He opened his mouth again, drinking in the air. I couldn't taste anything except the chicken juices going sour on my tongue, couldn't smell anything except the thin smoke of our own fire, but I'd gotten my honed senses from Loki. His were even sharper than mine—and he was tied to Surt by both his giant ancestry and his fiery talents.

"East," he said. "I'll be able to narrow it down as we get closer."

"Are we ready to challenge him?" Njord said.

He wasn't really suggesting we just stayed here enjoying the rest of our dinner while Surt ravaged communities some other place, was he?

Hod squeezed my hand. "We'd better be," he said. "We'll have the advantage of being prepared to get into a fight this time."

Thor already had his hammer in hand. "That giant will regret ever setting foot on this realm or ours," he said in a growl.

Freya held out her hands. The fierceness of her war goddess nature shone through her beautiful face. "We can't just rush in. If we want to defeat him, or at least push him back, we need strategy as well as strength. Gather whatever weapons you brought with you, and Loki will lead us to him. We'll hang back and take a lay of the land before we plan our defense."

Whether she had enough authority as Odin's wife or as a warrior in her own right, the new gods nodded at her words. They hustled into the house where they'd left their belongings, Freya alongside them. Loki hadn't removed his sword from his belt since we'd left Asgard, and the twins fought with magic rather than weapons.

My hand dropped to the pocket of my jeans where I kept the switchblade my older brother had given me a couple years before his death. It'd gotten me through plenty of mundane jams in my first life, and I always felt a little more secure carrying it, but it wasn't going to get me far against a giant.

"I still don't have a proper weapon," I said.

"Don't worry yourself about that, pixie," Loki said, his voice still taut despite his light tone. "Considering the grudge Surt appears to have against you, I expect you're better off not trying to engage in any hand-to-hand combat. You move with us, create that connection, and then let us tackle the brute."

That was mostly how we'd fought as a unit before. Even with a sword and my valkyrie powers, I couldn't pack anywhere near as much punch as a god. But I'd always put up at least a bit of a real fight before rather than simply going through the motions. My stomach knotted.

"I could at least— Do you think the draugar have life energy I could tear away?" As a valkyrie, I had the ability to snuff out lives with a touch—the shadowy power Hod had contributed to my formation—but I'd never tried it on a creature that wasn't exactly alive anymore to begin with.

Hod frowned. He should know better than anyone else. “It’s magic that animates the draugar, not any natural energy,” he said. “No true life there for you to claim. The only way to stop them is to destroy them or destroy the one controlling them.”

Great. Well, at least if I had something bigger than a pocketknife, I could behead a few or something.

The other gods were already hustling back from the house, Freya with her sword, Freyr with one of his own, Skadi with her golden bow and a bulging sheath of arrows, and Njord with a trident in his hand and a hooked blade dangling at his side. My gaze caught on a glint of metal in the shed beside the house. I dashed over, snatched up the hatchet the farm’s former owners had left behind there, and ran back to join the others feeling a little more confident with its weight in my hand.

Loki took off into the sky. His shoes of flight could carry him miles with every stride if he didn’t hold himself in check. The rest of us couldn’t manage to soar quite that fast by our various means. I swept my wings through the cooling summer air, grateful for the nap I’d taken. My nerves buzzed, and my pulse thumped with anticipation, my mind starkly alert.

I didn’t know if there was any chance we could end this war now, but we could at the very least prevent Surt from taking any more ground. Maybe we could wound him enough to make the battle to regain Asgard easier.

We were flying away from the sinking sun, into total night. Within a few minutes, we’d left the last glow of dusk behind completely. The lights of human civilization gleamed by beneath us: cars and trucks weaving along winding highways, little towns and vast cities glittering with their lesser and greater nightlife.

Loki paused and swerved to the left once, then again, and then a tad to the right as he must have been orienting himself with his awareness of Surt’s magic. I still couldn’t sense it at all. Then I didn’t need his fiery affinity to track the giant’s location, because a streak of flames came into view over the distant horizon, streaking down from the sky into the center of a sprawling city. A hint of acrid smoke prickled in my nose.

My heart lurched. Lights dotted skyscrapers and shorter buildings for what looked like several miles in every direction. There had to be millions of people living in that city. Millions that Surt and his army were probably slaughtering without hesitation right now.

I flapped my wings harder. A fresh strain spread through the muscles in my shoulders, but every second until we reached the city could mean dozens more lives lost. The people who lived there were just ordinary human beings who'd never had any idea that gods and giants might fight over their home. Ordinary men and women, innocent kids...

My fingers clenched around the handle of the hatchet. I'd take *Surt's* head off if I could. Let's see how he liked the same treatment he'd given Tyr.

The flaming bridge arced down into what appeared to be the downtown core, in the middle of some of the tallest buildings. Even as we soared over the suburbs, we couldn't make out what might be happening on the ground. The hiss of the flames reached my ears first. Then a distant booming like a series of sharp explosions.

We swooped between the skyscrapers. Freya darted into the lead and held out her hand to slow us. Take the lay of the land first, she'd said. I guessed that made sense, even if every muscle in my body was itching to dive in there and chop up any draug or giant I could.

At the goddess's gestures, we glided down onto the edge one of the lower rooftops and walked along it in silence to the far end that overlooked the foot of Surt's bridge. There was no need to worry about the locals noticing us, because our natural magic kept us invisible to humans unless we consciously decided to reveal ourselves, but one glance told me they wouldn't have been paying attention anyway.

The flaming arc touched down in the middle of a wide road. A car unlucky enough to have been driving past that spot at exactly the wrong moment was now a mass of melting metal. The asphalt bubbled with a liquid gleam.

draugar lumbered all across the road, hacking at the other cars that had pulled off at awkward angles, breaking down the doors of the shops and restaurants that lined the street. Bleeding bodies scattered the sidewalks. Shrieks and gasps carried up to us as more locals fled down the side-streets. Fire was crawling up the faces of several of the buildings the draugar had already trashed.

Surt stood in the center of it all on the top of an abandoned SUV, brandishing his sword and letting flames leap from its polished surface. "You see what I can do," he roared. "Obey me! Bring your leaders to me, or I'll raze this city to the ground."

"What does he want with their leaders?" I asked with a shudder. I didn't think any mayor would be in a hurry to offer himself up to that sword.

"It'd hardly be efficient for Surt to take over all of Midgard one city at a time," Loki said, his tone as sharp as it was wry. "He must think he can negotiate control over the entire country."

Oh. Maybe he could manage that. Anyone here who wasn't already desperate to end the carnage would be soon. These people didn't know how to fend off a monster like him.

But we did.

"There'll be no negotiation tonight," Thor rumbled, swinging his hammer. "Let's take him. If we go at him now and fast, we might get a fatal strike in before he even realizes we've arrived."

That sounded like a perfectly good plan to me. Freya hesitated and then nodded. "You four and the valkyrie work your special connection. The rest of us will slip around to the other side to surround him. Wait until you see the flash of my cloak."

The other three gods followed her as she darted across the roof and vanished over the side. Thor leaned his brawny arms against the railing at the edge of the roof, studying the scene below us with a grim expression.

"Loki, since you can't bring your fire to bear directly against Surt, perhaps you should switch positions in our usual formation with Baldur," he said. "And Ari… You can stay behind all of us instead of in the center. That'll give Surt a harder time if he tries to target you again."

I wasn't going to use my gods like a shield. "I'll be fine," I started. "I'll be even more on guard this time."

Hod turned his head toward me with a pained grimace, and I realized I didn't really want to have this argument. I didn't want them worrying about me because I'd insisted on being closer to the front lines than I had to be. That would only distract them from the important thing here, which was pummeling Surt into a pulp.

"But I'll be fine at the back of the formation too," I amended. "You focus on Surt, and I'll be there to cover you if the draugar get feisty."

Loki snorted at the same time as he tousled my hair affectionately. "They'll be sorry they ever met you, pixie."

"Get ready," Thor said. "We need to move the moment we see Freya's signal."

We gathered around him at the edge of the roof. Doing my best to ignore the bloodbath on the street, I searched the shadows around the building across from us, a bank office with mirrored windows.

I'd just caught a flash of golden feathers when Loki, who must have spotted it a split-second sooner, said, "Let's go!"

We moved together so well now that we didn't need any more cue than that. The gods sprang over the railing straight into our formation as they swooped down toward Surt; I fell in behind them with a flap of my wings. I braced my legs and raised my axe, and that common pulse flowed through us all as the gods launched their attacks.

Unfortunately, as soon as we'd left the shelter of the building, the element of surprise was gone. Surt's head snapped around at the motion from above or maybe the sound of Mjolnir whipping toward him. With a gnash of his teeth, he threw himself down and to the side of the SUV.

Thor's hammer clipped him across the shoulder all the same, making him lurch. He still slashed his sword up to deflect the bolt of scorching darkness Hod and Loki must have produced in tandem. Then he ripped the blade through the air, sending out a roaring wave of flames.

He'd marked my presence, even here at the back. The flames dipped and leapt and twisted, a few streaks of them racing around the magical shields the gods threw up. Those streaks raced straight toward me.

My body flinched in memory of yesterday's pain. My wings heaved me upward, but the rippling lines of magical fire shot after me. I dodged to the side, and hands grasped my shoulders, yanking me down.

I hit the street cushioned by a swath of shadow. Hod braced himself over me, Surt's flames sizzling against the dark shell he'd called up around us. The blind god's chest pinned me to the ground, his breath spilling with a rasp against my cheek. I might have been able to enjoy the feeling of him lying over me now if I hadn't known we had a battle to get back to.

"I was getting out of the way," I said.

"Ari," Hod said, his voice ragged, "I could hear the fire. You were almost cinders."

He shoved himself onto his feet and offered his hand to help me up. I didn't even have time to thank him before Thor let out a war cry. We dashed back into the chaos.

Freya's contingent had launched an attack from the other side of the street and then scattered in the wake of Surt's flames. Our group came at him again, but the gods shifted closer together, their movements more defensive than offensive. Trying to protect me.

Guilt jabbed at my gut. I'd been the one who'd deepened their connection with each other, and now I was holding them back.

We swiveled around Surt as one, searching for an opening. The crackle of gunfire echoed down the street. My gaze jerked up.

A mass of human soldiers in army fatigues was pouring onto the road, rifles raised. The gods lurched out of the way as the squadron opened fire on Surt. The giant whirled his sword in the air, sending the bullets ricocheting away with a wheel of fire. He laughed and waved his draugar army forward.

One of the soldiers hollered. With an eerie whine, a land missile hurtled toward the giant.

I thought I saw Surt's eyes widen. He lurched backward, but the projectile came too fast. It tore through the side of his thigh, shredding the flesh almost to the bone.

His draugar gouged open the chests of several of the soldiers, but the human army smashed a whole bunch of their skulls in turn. Surt scrambled around the SUV, blood gushing down his leg. He slapped his sword against the wound to seal the flesh with a stomach-turning hiss. He looked as if he were gnashing his teeth.

"It'll have been a long time since he tangoed with any humans who weren't already dead," Loki murmured beside me. "I do believe our fiery giant has underestimated their resilience. And their weaponry." He motioned to the other three. "I can fend off the bullets with my fire. We can take him down while he's dealing with the bazookas."

But before the trickster had even finished speaking, Surt had heaved himself onto the base of his flaming bridge. "You'll all die!" he roared. "Gods, humans, all of you pathetic things."

He jabbed his sword into the bridge. The flames flooded the street, bowling over the nearest soldiers, licking under the horde of draugar. Then, carrying Surt's army and the giant himself, it retracted back into the sky toward Asgard like an elastic band recoiling.

Thor grasped my arm with one hand and Hod's with the other, dragging us away from the road. "He's not doing any more damage here tonight. We'd better regroup before he does."

# 9

*Loki*

"Surt was stronger than I expected," Freyr admitted with a dramatic shake of his head. The god of plenty had always enjoyed making much of his opinions. "And the draugar, with the weapons he's given them—they were formidable too."

"The *humans* were the ones that forced him back in the end, not us," Skadi said with a note of disgust. Her lip curled disdainfully.

We were gathered around the farmhouse's dining room table again, a little fresher after a night's rest but far from at ease. Ari was pacing along the edges of the room around us, her eyes bright with what looked like an equal mix of panic and ferocity. Her shoulders twitched at the huntress's remark.

"There were a few hundred more of those human soldiers than there were of us," I pointed out. "And I think we can claim a partial victory. If Surt hadn't needed to contend with us as well as the humans with guns, he might very well have managed to level them —and then the rest of the city."

"But we need to be moving into offense efforts, not constantly defending against him," Freya said. "He's still dictating the battlegrounds."

"If we're going to have any hope of confronting him in Asgard now that he's entrenched there, we'll need greater numbers of our own," Skadi said. "There has to be a faster way of tracking down the rest of the gods."

"Whoever's still left," Hod said quietly. The blind god had seen a few of the lesser Aesir off to their final ends. I didn't think those petulant souls would have contributed much to our cause anyway.

"Vidar may have seen some of the others," Njord suggested. "If his brothers manage to bring him back, Freyr and I could search the coastal lands with Freyr's boat. We'd cover a lot of ground that way."

"But that would leave us without the two of you for several days at least, through any other attacks Surt launches on Midgard," I said. "I'd imagine Thor would have my head if I approved of that plan in his absence." Our valkyrie wouldn't be terribly pleased about it either.

Njord scowled at me, but he couldn't exactly argue with my statement. The Thunderer had made his feelings about prioritizing the safety of Midgard very clear yesterday. I doubted the sea god would have mentioned the idea at all if Thor and Baldur hadn't set off on Freyr's directions to see if they could bring their hard-hitting brother back to us.

Freyr raised his head at a haughty angle. "Do you have a plan, Trickster? Isn't plotting supposed to be your area of expertise? Or have you lost your touch for scheming?"

It was hard to tell from his tone whether he'd have preferred I'd gone dull over the centuries or not. I offered him a sharp smile. "I do have a thought, actually. In consideration of… How many of the gods we haven't yet collected are even warriors? There's little point in gathering those with no relevant skills to offer. We ought to accept that we're not going to build up an entire army of our own—not one large enough to simply barge into Asgard and toss Surt and all his undead minions out."

"You're not saying we should leave the realm of the gods to a *giant*," Skadi said, with just enough edge to her horrified voice to tell me she remembered very well that I had been born kin to Surt myself.

Through an epic effort of self-restraint that I wouldn't get any credit for, I managed not to glower in her direction. "Of course not," I said. "I'm simply suggesting that *we* choose the grounds of our final battle. We can't do that in Asgard where he's already laid claim to all the ground. We already know he's prepared to act on Midgard. *He* knows we're here and doing our best to get in his way. It shouldn't be too difficult a thing to lure him into an ambush."

"An ambush," Njord repeated, as if it were the first time that word had entered his vocabulary.

"Yes. We lead him to believe we'll be up to something—gathering weapons for the battle, meeting with potential allies, something else he wouldn't like—in a specific spot. He'll charge down to slaughter us, but we'll be waiting for his arrival. Before he can get his bearings, we end him."

"Do you think he's really worried enough about our interference to bother?" Freya asked.

That was a reasonable question. "Perhaps we need to offer more incentive than that," I said. "We could use a human city as part of the lure, make him think it'd be an ideal target because of worldly influence or what have you. Two birds with one stone—very tempting."

Ari halted in her pacing. "Then you'd be tempting him to come down and kill a whole bunch of defenseless people."

I offered her a mollifying look. "The intent would be that we'd kill him before he had the chance. I don't want to see more bleeding bodies in the streets if I don't have to either."

Njord muttered something under his breath even my excellent hearing didn't quite catch—something along the lines of he'd have thought I'd have enjoyed a scene like that. I kept my hands braced against the table, my smile in place.

There was nothing strange about his attitude toward me—or Skadi's or Freyr's. Not long ago, any of my usual companions might have made the same sorts of remarks. If Hod was expressing himself more moderately now, it was only because of how his eyes had been opened, figuratively speaking, to the fuller truth of our shared history. After those revelations about their own father's insistence on my supposed duplicities and after discovering the connection we'd forged through our valkyrie, I thought he and Baldur and Thor might be finally setting the old wariness and prejudices aside.

But now we were calling the rest of Asgard back to us, and I could hardly replicate the exact same experiences to transform their opinions of me. I wasn't certain I'd even want to go through all that turmoil again.

No, the truth was that if we settled back into Asgard as a larger community again, it would be as it always was before. I would be the interloping traitorous giant only allowed a place thanks to Odin's possibly misguided good will, every comment I made would be viewed by nearly everyone around me with suspicion, and every tragedy would immediately result in at least a few fingers pointed my way.

Perhaps the last several weeks had changed *me* more than I'd realized too, because even as that realization settled over me, my usual ire didn't stir. What of it? I'd lived that way for centuries before. *I* knew who I was, possibly better than I ever had. This time, at least, I had a few companions I might hope would speak up in my defense without prodding. The opinions of those four were the only ones that mattered to me.

It really would have been too much to hope we'd all live together in Baldur's dream of perfect harmony for more than a few hours, hadn't it? I was more practical than that. If I felt a pinch of loss, surely it wasn't for that hogwash. It was for the frown that crossed Ari's face as her gaze jerked toward Njord too.

She might very well have heard him. The newly returned gods would do their best to make her regret her associations with me, no doubt. And what happened to her… that mattered to me more than nearly anything else I could think of.

I had faith in her affections. After the way she'd gazed into my eyes and told me she trusted me with her in every possible way, how could I not trust her? She wasn't the type to waver because of someone else's snarky remarks. But she shouldn't have needed to bear those remarks in the first place.

She deserved to take pride in every man or god she chose to stand beside.

"How would we pass on word to Surt without him realizing we wanted him to arrive?" Freya asked, drawing my mind back to the current topic of debate.

"Perhaps Muninn could go to him as if to make amends," I started.

Ari shook her head. "She expects him to try to kill her if he sees her again. She might not have the chance to say anything if we sent her to Asgard—if she'd even agree to take the risk."

I couldn't fault the raven for looking after her own feathered hide. I tapped my lips, considering our alternatives, and the house's front door thumped open.

"Look who we dredged up," Thor called in a jovial tone. He and Baldur ushered our newest arrival into the dining room.

Vidar might as well have been created by throwing those two of his brothers into a blender. He stood just an inch or two shy of Thor's massive height, his shoulders and chest nearly as broad. His short-trimmed hair and neat beard gleamed a reddish gold. His expression, though, was almost as solemn as Hod's so often was. So perhaps all three of his brothers had ended up in that blender.

I wondered if that was the face he'd made when he'd kicked open my wolfish son's jaws and stabbed a sword down Fenrir's throat. It was hard to say, since whenever I'd seen him speak of that moment during Ragnarok, he'd always smiled with the telling.

"Brother," he said, with a tip of his head to Hod. "It is unfortunate that these are the circumstances under which all of us have come back together. I understand we have a rampaging giant to put down."

"We were just discussing our next steps," Skadi said. "The trickster, naturally, thinks we should trick Surt into an ambush. Laying a whole city out as bait."

She hadn't seemed to care all that much about human cities when she was complaining about the effectiveness of their soldiers.

Vidar's gaze slid to me. "Surely there is a more honorable tactic we can employ?"

I managed not to roll my eyes. I didn't even hold any particular animosity against Vidar—he had killed my son avenging my son's devouring of his father, so really, who was I to criticize?—but his strengths were clearly not in his head.

"Surt has shown no indication of honor," I said. "We can't expect him to comply with any rules we lay down for fair combat. It seems to me the most honorable thing is to prevent him for destroying any more innocent lives as swiftly as we can by whatever means necessary. Any other definition of honor may give him room to destroy dozens more cities while we dress up our war in silks."

"I agree with Loki," Ari said, catching my gaze for a second before meeting Vidar's eyes. "I don't like putting more people in Midgard at risk, but it does seem like they're in more danger otherwise. And that's speaking as the only person here who was ever human herself."

Even as I saw a few pairs of eyes narrow at her, I couldn't completely suppress my smile. Our valkyrie certainly provided plenty of reasons to be proud of *her*. She wasn't going to be cowed by any god.

Hod shifted by the corner of the table. "I agree with Loki too," he said, and I was still capable of being a little surprised he'd admit as much. "Surt has been preparing for this war for decades, maybe centuries. How can we compete with that unless we find some way to even the odds in our favor?"

"He's certainly made use of everything and everyone he could," Freya muttered, and my mind lit on just the idea.

"Not just Muninn," I said. "The dark elves as well. One of *them* could manage to pass on word of some city we're especially trying to preserve. Send someone injured by one of their cave-ins—he'll believe they'd still want to claim Midgard alongside him. Can you get them to agree to that, Dark One?"

Hod's mouth tightened. "I'm not sure. It would be a much smaller act than giving all of us permission to carry on our war efforts through their caves or handing over weaponry..." He hesitated as if he weren't sure of his next words. "Maybe they'd be more easily persuaded if you came along to lay out how well this plan of yours ought to work."

The god who was recently my most obstinate critic was inviting me along to meddle with his alliance? I blinked as I recovered my tongue. We really had come a long way, hadn't we?

"If you think it would make the proposal go down more smoothly, I am entirely at your disposal," I said with a mock bow. The corner of Hod's lips curled with what might have been a hint of a smile.

"Hold on," Vidar said, as if he'd been leading this discussion rather than arriving toward the end of it. "We'd better hammer out the details of that proposal first before we go setting the pieces in motion."

"I completely agree," I said, and snapped my fingers to call up a tracing of flames on the tabletop in the shape of Midgard's continents. "First let us pick a city."

As the other gods leaned forward in consideration, a small spark of satisfaction leapt in my chest. Whatever they thought of me, they couldn't deny the worth of my insight. But all the same, the victory rang a bit hollow.

This plan was more trickery, as Skadi had said. Sly schemes were how I worked best. Would there ever be more than that I could offer and have accepted?

# 10

*Aria*

"He may be reluctant to show himself," Vidar said in his knowing voice as Muninn and I prepared to leave. He'd insisted on walking us to the front door and then out, adding a few last-minute bits of advice that just rehashed what he'd already told us. "I'm lucky I saw Heimdall recently at all. The second I moved toward him and he noticed me, he pushed me backward with his magic and had already hurried off when I recovered myself."

"Got it," I said. We'd heard all about that encounter before we'd started making plans. Heimdall's apparent hesitation to deal with any of the gods was the whole reason Muninn and I were making the trip alone. But I wouldn't be surprised to find out Vidar had forgotten I'd even been in the room when that discussion had taken place. He wasn't overtly condescending like some of the newer gods, but every now and then he shot a puzzled glance my way as if he couldn't figure out why I was in the room.

Muninn tugged impatiently at her dress. The wind rippled over the long grass in the yard outside the country home we'd managed to find not far from Beijing, the city the gods had chosen for their lure and ambush. We had a long flight ahead of us, much of it over the Pacific Ocean. Vidar had spotted Heimdall in a town on the outskirts of the Canadian north, dressed like an outdoorsman.

Vidar sucked in a breath as if he were about to give us some other repeated insight, and I jumped in before he could. "Ready?" I said to Muninn. She gave me a brisk nod, I offered Vidar a quick wave, and the raven and I leapt into the air together.

Muninn's wings might have been smaller, but with only her compact bird body to propel forward, she could match my speed no problem. We soared over the great sprawling city Loki expected would tempt Surt into appearing and across the plains beyond, dotted with innumerable towns. The Yellow Sea glittered up ahead.

With our supernatural speed, we hoped to be back within a day. The ambush was planned for the day after tomorrow—a supposed meeting at noon with representatives of the Chinese government to form a god-human alliance. Skadi had snorted at the idea and Freyr had chuckled, but it seemed like something Surt might believe and want to prevent. What we'd actually do was gather around the park where the fake negotiations were meant to take place an hour early, poised to spring on Surt before his flaming bridge even touched the ground.

Flying with Muninn was a lonely business, I discovered. Not that I wanted to be constantly chattering, but she couldn't say anything at all in her bird form. At least Freya could shrug her cloak back and still fly with it just covering her arms if she wanted to. For a while, there was nothing but salty wind whipping my hair, warbling waves below me, and that small black form flapping steadily on just a few feet away. The sun peaked over us and then started to dip behind us.

Well, at least I was doing something useful. Loki thought

Heimdall's magic might give us the advantage we needed to take back Asgard. If the ambush plan failed, he might be our only hope.

My wings were just starting to prickle with fatigue when the coastline came into view up ahead. Muninn glanced over at me, her beady eyes gleaming. I thought I could read the same thing I was thinking in the tilt of her head.

"We'll take a moment to catch our breath?" I said.

Her head bobbed. When we reached the land, we dipped down onto a wild stretch that was all wet rock and brambly bushes. I sank onto a boulder and massaged the base of my wings where they met my shoulder blades.

Muninn shifted into human form and leaned over, touching her toes and stretching her back. The knobs of her spine pressed against her thin dress. We were still on the summer side of the hemisphere, but the evening breeze off the ocean had a cool edge to it that she didn't appear to feel.

I couldn't help glancing toward the dimming sky to the southeast. If my sense of direction was right, we weren't that far from Petey's new home. The idea tugged at my gut. I could have made a small detour and checked in on him… but what if Surt or a lackey we didn't know about managed to track my movements there somehow?

Every part of me ached to see my little brother again, but that was a selfish longing. The right thing to do was to stay far away for as long as I might still put him in danger.

"You're thinking about him," Muninn said. "The little boy."

My gaze jerked back to her. "My brother," I said.

She nodded as if it were all the same to her. "What you're thinking of affects the memories that drift off you," she said, which I guessed was how she'd known. She paused. "He means a lot to you."

"He's the most important thing in the world to me. Can't you see that from my memories?"

"There's not much sense of relative emotion… Caring about someone in that sort of way, as a child, isn't something I have much personal experience with to compare."

She didn't have siblings, presumably. Could the raven woman even *have* kids, in either of her forms? It seemed rude to ask something that private. I shuffled my feet, and then said, "You cared a lot about those three guys Odin brought back for you."

"Yes." Her voice dropped to a murmur. "They're the only beings I've ever really cared about. Loved. They woke up something in me I hadn't known I was capable of feeling. Serving Odin meant something to me, but as a matter of pride, not…" She shook herself. "But that is in the past now."

She hadn't quite managed to dislodge the haunted look that had come over her face. My chest tightened. How long ago had she lost her three lovers? And all the time since then, she'd been tangled up in mourning them and raging at Odin.

After we ended this war, she'd have a chance to find some kind of love again. Not that it seemed at all polite to mention that either.

"I'm sorry he couldn't bring them back for longer," I said instead. Odin had summoned the spirits of Muninn's three lovers as a sort of apology—to show he understood what she was mourning, I guessed—but they were so long dead he hadn't been able to sustain that magic for much time.

Muninn gave me a small tight smile. "As am I. Are you rested enough? Shall we track down our watchful god? We may need to cover a lot more ground."

Heimdall might not even still be in this part of the world. But the sooner we figured that out, the better. "Let's go," I said.

We flew across thick evergreen forests and rolling green hills that led up to snow-topped mountains. I stayed high so I could scan as much ground as possible, peering through the thinning daylight and then dipping closer to reach out my senses for any hint of the warmly radiant godly energy all of the Aesir gave off. I wasn't sure even straining my hardest if I'd be able to pick it up at any kind of distance, but that talent had helped us find the dark elves before. It couldn't hurt to try.

In the end, it wasn't any supernatural vibe that caught my attention. It was a path of flat stones just above the rushing surface of a wide river. They wove slightly as they marked a course across the water, but they were too close together and too consistent for me to believe they'd ended up there by chance. But we'd seen no sign of anyone living nearby for miles.

Maybe the god who'd once guarded the world's greatest bridge had found himself making new ones?

I swooped along the forested slope beside the river, my search focused on the water now. Several miles farther along the river's course, another line of stones had been set out. Were they for his own use? Just out of habit? I couldn't imagine any god *needed* stepping stones to cross a river.

A thin stream of smoke trickled up against the purpling sky to the north. I slowed, and Muninn did the same. If Heimdall was living out here, we had to go cautiously as we came close. I might not be a god, but he'd know I'd come from Asgard easily enough. He might even recognize Muninn as more than a simple raven. The gods had said his vision was even sharper than Loki's.

Of course, he'd only know I was from Asgard if he saw my wings. The rest of me looked human enough. Human enough that plenty of the gods couldn't seem to forget that I was more than that now.

When the first hint of the smoky smell reached my nose, I decided it was time to switch to walking. I glided down between the pines and drew my wings into my body. The ache of their muscles melted into my back.

Muninn flew on between the trees as I picked my way over logs and past low needley branches out to the riverbank. The pebbles there rattled under my sneakers. Hiking boots would be more appropriate for this terrain, but I hadn't needed to think about footwear too much lately. They'd have to do.

I still had my valkyrie reflexes, which let me set my feet down quietly when I wanted to. With careful control over my balance, I marched silently along the rough slabs of rock that bordered the river. Here and there, the uneven surface had gathered pockets of dirt where grass and little wildflowers sprouted. The river rushed on with a steady warbling.

We must have traveled at least a few miles more when I caught a brief movement up ahead. I froze, training my eyes on that spot farther up the river.

A tall man with shaggy sandy-brown hair was crouched next to the bank. He dipped his hands into the water, and the deer standing next to him lowered her head to drink. A fawn stood on wobbly legs next to her.

The man raised a slow hand, and a stone like the ones I'd seen before rose to the surface of the water. Then another, then another. When they formed a line all the way across the river, he eased upright and swept his arm as if to say to the deer, *There you go.*

The deer and her fawn gambled across the rocks with hesitant steps and then darted into the brush on the other side. The man I had to assume was Heimdall waved his hand, and the stones sank. I guessed he didn't think that bridge would get much use. But he'd raised it with his powers just so those two animals could reach new ground.

He was the god of connections, and he liked to help creatures weaker than himself. It might be a good thing I'd arrived in my sneakers after all.

I let my feet come down carelessly as I walked on, not minding if the pebbles rattled. The breeze tousled my hair, and I let the dark blond strands hang tangled beside my face. The air was mild but not especially warm—a regular human would have been cold in this shirt. I rubbed my arms for effect. A rock rolled under my heel, and I even let myself stumble.

When I looked up again, I was close enough that even regular human eyes could have made out Heimdall. He was standing where I'd seen him before, watching me. I stopped, hugging myself as if scared by the sight. This gambit would work even better if I could get him to come to me.

And he did. With even strides just a smidgen too quick to be of this realm, he came up to me.

"Are you all right?" he said in a brisk voice. "What are you doing all the way out here dressed like that?"

I gazed up at him, opening my eyes wide. "I was looking for you," I said. "Are you Heimdall?"

His shoulders stiffened under his sheepskin jacket. His foot shifted as if to back up, and my hand shot out pleadingly.

"Don't go! You have no idea how far I've come… Don't make me go back with nothing."

"Go back where?" he asked, outright brusque now.

I ignored that question. He was listening well enough that I could get the important part out now. "Surt has taken over Asgard and driven out everyone who was living there. He's trying to destroy all of Midgard too so he can use it for him and his allies. He's already killed so many people."

Heimdall stared at me. "Who are you?" he demanded. "*What* are you?"

"A messenger," I said. "Someone who used to belong to this world and doesn't want to see it going up in flames. You care about this place, don't you? I don't know what problems you have with any of the gods, but you know what Surt is capable of."

"Odin wouldn't want *me*," Heimdall said, his face hardening. "You've come for the wrong god."

He turned, and Muninn landed where he was now looking, transforming while he watched.

"I wouldn't be here if that were true," she said.

"The powers you have might be the key to saving this realm and Asgard," I said. "Even if they're not, we need all the help we can get against Surt's army. You'll have to face him eventually, even if you try to hide away."

"Why would he bother with the wilderness up here?" Heimdall said.

"Why would he let you keep roaming around? He wants to destroy you all. He's going to bring the giants and the dark elves and who knows who else to take over this place. They're not going to care about preserving the forests or the deer." I gestured toward the river.

"I was angry at Odin once," Muninn added. She raised his chin. "I helped Surt capture him and keep him in a cage—I was *that* angry. But I realized, after a time… He truly doesn't intend cruelty, even when that is the result he produces. Whatever he did to wound you, he did it because he thought it was right for Asgard. That's always what he thinks of first. It's a little sad, really. It's his loss, not ours."

Heimdall grimaced at her. "Why are you telling me that?"

"Because letting your anger direct you is like holding a grudge against the river for flowing downstream. Because the Heimdall I knew who watched me come and go so often wouldn't have been able to bear to see the realms shattered by war."

Heimdall's jaw worked. I grasped onto one last appeal I could make.

"Please," I said. "I'm not asking you for them or even for me. I have a little brother. If Surt carries out his plan, he'll end up dead or worse. He's six years old. This realm should be his."

Tension squeezed around my heart as I waited. Heimdall sighed and shoved his hands in the pockets of his jacket.

"You drive a hard bargain," he said, sounding not at all happy about it. "All right. I'll talk with them. That's the most I can promise."

# 11

*Aria*

The dining room in our new residence was a little larger than the last one, which was a good thing, because even this one was getting crowded. A couple delegations of gods had managed to turn up three more former Asgardians who'd joined the conversation along with Heimdall. There was constant shifting around the table as one or another made room for someone else to speak.

I hung back in the corner. No one asked what I thought about anything, and maybe I didn't have as much to contribute as the actual gods, but I wanted to at least keep track of what was going on.

Other than a jovial "Good work!" from Thor when I'd walked in with Heimdall a few hours ago, no one had even acknowledged what I *had* contributed. As if they figured it'd been as easy as walking over to the watchful god and just asking him to take a trip with me. Or maybe the newer ones figured it'd been all Muninn.

"That first step is done," Hod was saying, at the head of the table for now. He'd just returned from another visit to Nidavellir. "One of the dark elves will pass on the supposedly secret information about our meeting in the park tomorrow. Their leaders are still hesitating to help us in any more concrete ways, though."

"Do the dirt-eaters really want that giant ruling over them?" Skadi muttered.

"Easy for them to ignore destruction that hasn't yet touched their realm," Vidar said.

Hadn't anyone told him that destruction *had* touched the dark elves—because of the gods' neglect? Why would they jump to put their necks that far on the line when they'd already been burned? From the tensing of Hod's mouth, I suspected he was thinking the same thing.

Before the dark god could say anything like that, Njord pushed up to the table, bumping Hod to the side. "We should expect Surt to arrive tomorrow, then," he said. "What do we still need to get in place for this ambush?"

Several gazes turned toward Loki, I guessed since he was the one who'd come up with the plan. He snapped his fingers. "Who has that map? We'll want to pick our positions carefully."

"Force from all sides," Freya said, squeezing over beside him. When one of the others tossed the map of the park we'd gotten onto the table, she grasped it and took charge of the discussion. "We can't give Surt enough time to deflect all of us. In that first charge, one of us must strike a fatal blow. We won't get half as good a chance once we've lost the element of surprise."

All sides. I perked up with a spark of an idea. "Could we cut straight through the bridge with magic and attack him through it too?" I said, pitching my voice loud enough to carry through the room. "Maybe Hod's shadows could snuff some of the flames?"

"Is that the valkyrie?" one of the newest arrivals asked, craning her neck.

Freyr waved his hand dismissively. "Save the strategizing to those with the experience. For an attack this important, we can't be depending on an unpracticed skill." He turned back to the table, leaning in beside his sister, as if his godly talents had anything to do with war. "Now, it seems to me—"

I stepped back to the wall, my jaw tight, but apparently I wasn't the only one irked by the god of plenty's brisk brush-off. Thor set his heavy hand down on the table.

"Hold on," he said in his rumble of a voice. "Ari has had *more* recent experience with Surt and his minions than most of the rest of you. Her ideas have gotten us far before. We shouldn't ignore them out of hand."

"You have nearly three times as many godly minds at your disposal than you did in recent weeks," Freyr said. "And little time to spare for exploring wild imaginings."

"Aria's suggestion didn't sound all that wild to me," Baldur put in, gentle but firm. "It's not as if we couldn't generate fire of our own to practice with."

"But we don't know exactly how Surt's magic works," one of the other new arrivals said. "If we want to end him quickly, we should stick to what we know."

Njord nodded. "I agree. Valkyries have their place—in Valhalla. This is a totally different matter."

"You wouldn't say that if you'd been around for half of the battles we've already fought," Loki said with an edge in his lilting voice. "Perhaps it's been too long since you fought any battles."

"Perhaps we've already fought too many of them, thanks to you and your kind," Heimdall snapped from where he'd been standing stiffly by the far corner of the table.

Thor's hand clenched against the table. Loki grinned with a baring of teeth, a hard glint in his eyes that I didn't think would lead anywhere good. My stomach knotted. I stepped forward, touching their arms.

"It's okay," I said. "I don't have the same kind of experience. I don't have the knowledge. Whatever the rest of you decide, I'll pitch in wherever you need me."

We weren't going to win any battles if we started fighting each other. Up until now, I'd been the one who bound the gods together. The last thing I wanted was to be the cause of some kind of schism between my gods and those we'd managed to gather. Stopping Surt was more important than what any of them thought of me.

I could decide how to earn their respect, if I even bothered to, when there wasn't a mad giant trying to end the world as we knew it.

"Pixie," Loki said, with a look that suggested he'd been looking forward to roasting a few of his companions.

I squeezed his forearm. "No. Keep working out the plan. I need to stretch my legs a bit."

Hod turned his head my way as I slipped out of the room, but I didn't wait to see if anyone would follow. I didn't want them to. I hurried along the tiled floor and ducked out onto the covered porch.

The stretch of my wings as I unfolded them over my head was a sort of relief. After the hard flight yesterday and overnight, the muscles were starting to cramp staying compressed inside my human body. I gave them a few tentative flaps, stretching them out with an enjoyable burn, and then lifted off into the air.

I'd thought maybe Muninn would like some company. We could commiserate about not being entirely welcome among the gods or something. But when I glided up to the house's curved tiled rooftop, there was no sign of the raven. She must have gone off to patrol or to chase down some other lead.

I ended up circling in wider and wider sweeps over the house's grounds. A little stream ran through the property at the north end by a wrought-iron fence. To the west, in a small clearing inside a clump of forest, a gazebo stood, its faded blue paint flaking off the wood. South was the narrow road that led into the nearest town, and east was the rise of a hill dotted with little purple flowers. Their delicate scent reached my nose even from high above.

The warm wind caught my wings and let me coast for a while. I didn't really want to go back down. What the hell *did* I know about fighting giants? I'd developed my chops in minor skirmishes on Philly's streets, with guys who only stayed tough until you kneed them in the balls—and the guys too tough for that, I'd kept my head low around and skipped any need to fight.

I'd drifted out past the gazebo again when Thor's voice reached me. "Ari?"

He was standing by the structure's narrow steps. I wheeled and dropped down into the clearing to meet him.

It was amazing how the fierce warrior who battered our enemies without restraint could also look at me with a gaze so soft and set his broad hand on my shoulder with a touch so careful. "Are you okay?" he asked.

"Sure," I said. "Are the plans all worked out? What's our position for tomorrow?" The one thing I knew for sure was that my four gods and I would be coming at Surt together, even if they kept me at the back again.

"We worked out a solid strategy," the thunder god said. "But that's not what I wanted to talk about. I want you to know I'd have liked to bowl over most of those knuckleheads with Mjolnir, the way they were talking about you."

The corner of my mouth twitched upward. "I appreciate the sentiment," I said, "but I've got a pretty thick skin by now. I've heard a hell of a lot worse from people who owed me a hell of a lot more." My mother, my supposed father figures, teachers and kids I'd grown up with…

Thor made a growling sound. "Which is exactly why you shouldn't have to put up with that from anyone here. The other gods… We Asgardians can become somewhat stuck in our ways. You shook up our little group, jostled loose some new ideas, but the others are still wrapping their heads around the fact that we've lost our entire realm. They're not looking deeply enough to see everything you have to offer right now, but they will. Even if it requires a hammer to the head to make sure of it."

His vehemence tugged at my heart. Not that long ago, he'd been struggling with the feeling that the other gods in our little group were dismissing *his* ideas, seeing him as nothing more than the brawn with no brains worth listening to. I'd encouraged him to believe he could be more than they saw. Now he was returning the favor.

Our situations weren't quite the same, though. "Hopefully that won't be necessary," I said. "Especially since in some ways they're right. I might be stronger than the average human, but I'm weaker than any of you, by a lot. Both physically and when it comes to any kind of magical powers. It's not like I came into the strength I have on my own either. I'm basically something the four of you made—a human turned into a patchwork valkyrie, powers borrowed and wings pasted on."

I waggled my wingtips and started to retract them into my back. Thor's hand shot out, but his fingers were gentle when they brushed the feathered surface.

"No," he said, his voice so thick and his body so close that I tingled right down to my toes. "Leave them out."

I let them completely open again. Thor skimmed his hand over the bony frame that arced from my shoulder blades through their length and then teased his fingertips down over the thinner flesh that made up most of their surface. Everywhere he touched, a quiver of electricity shot through my nerves.

I'd rarely had anyone touch my wings at all except to slash at them in combat. Definitely no one had ever explored that new part of my body anywhere near this tenderly.

"You're so much more than a patchwork valkyrie, Ari," Thor said. His head bowed next to mine as he traced the arc of my wing again, and my pulse kicked up a notch in anticipation. "You were *you* before we ever found you. All we did was build on the strength you already had so much of. That's why you're here and not the other valkyries we summoned."

"Or maybe I just got lucky?"

He snorted. His warm breath caressed the side of my face. "Not a chance. I've watched you in action. I've fought alongside you. I've seen how fierce you can be. Ask any of the gods in there who the strongest of us is, and they'd point to me. You can bring me to my knees."

A tendril of desire unfurled through my belly, trailing lower. "Oh, really?" I murmured. "You seem to be standing just fine right now."

Thor's hand fell to my side. He tipped his head to tease his lips across my cheek. He kissed the corner of my jaw, the side of my neck, with a more literal electricity, slipping from his caress in blissful little sparks. My breath caught as he started to sink in front of me.

His kisses crossed my collarbone and marked a heated path down the front of my shirt. My nipples pebbled as his head dipped between them, but his stubbled jaw only brushed my breasts briefly. His knees hit the grassy ground, as promised. He pressed his lips just above my bellybutton. His thumbs hooked over the waist of my jeans. He looked up at me, his brown eyes dark with wanting, waiting for my permission.

A tremor ran through me, but it was all eagerness. "Please," I breathed, resting my hand on his dark auburn hair. A few thick strands slipped loose of his short ponytail as he leaned even closer.

He kissed my belly where my shirt rode up just slightly over my jeans. Then the line of my fly, until the pressure of his mouth settled right over my core. Even with two layers of fabric between us, a whimper escaped me.

"Not good enough," he muttered. With a yank of his hands, he wrenched my jeans and panties to my knees. In an instant, his hot lips pressed against me skin to skin.

I whimpered as his tongue flicked over my clit and then delved lower. More sparks raced over my core. My legs wobbled with the rush of pleasure. Thor gripped my thighs firmly, holding me up while he devoured me. My fingers tangled in his hair. I held on tight, riding each wave of sensation as the strokes of his mouth and the wash of his breath sent me higher and higher.

He teased his tongue over my opening over and over, curling up inside so I gasped, before returning to my clit. The edges of his teeth just barely grazed it. He swiveled the tip of his tongue around that nub, making me cry out. I rocked into his mouth, so close, so close.

He suckled me even harder with a blissfully sharp jolt of his powers, and pleasure burst through my body. I came shaking against his lips, drooping over him as my body turned to jelly. He kept working me over, holding me up with those big hands, until the aftershock subsided.

When he started to get up, I'd recovered my wits enough to push him back down. "Oh, no. We're not finished here."

Thor grinned as I nudged him back so he could lean against the base of the gazebo. The old wood creaked faintly at his weight. I trailed my hand down his torso to the hard hot length of his cock. He groaned when I palmed him.

We were *definitely* not finished. I kicked my jeans all the way off and tugged his down in turn. As I climbed onto his lap, our mouths met for the first time. I could taste my own tang on his lips and the thicker salty essence that was all him.

Thor pulled me right up against his chest, cupping my breast, claiming my lips even more thoroughly. I rubbed my core against his erection from head to base and back again.

"Fucking hell, Ari," he said hoarsely. "When I've got you like this, I could stay on my knees for the rest of my life."

"No need for that," I said by his ear. "I like variety."

His chuckle was lost in my mouth as I kissed him again, hard. I sank lower, taking his thick length inside me, and another groan reverberated in his chest. I moaned in turn as he stretched me like no one else ever could.

His hands slid down to my ass. We set a rhythm together, bucking into each other as our mouths mashed and parted with gasps and collided again. His godly strength rippled through his muscles all around me, but right then, I didn't feel weak at all. I matched him pulse for pulse, a fresh surge of pleasure racing through my body with every breathtaking shiver of his electric magic.

He nudged me a little forward, and his cock impaled me even more deeply. Bliss burned through my core. If I split apart, it would be the most beautiful breaking of my life. The wall of the gazebo shuddered as if it might break from the power of our fucking too.

"Ari," Thor said, his voice so ragged with need that it tipped me over the edge. My second orgasm knocked the breath from my lungs and the voice from my throat with a punch of ecstasy. My thighs clenched around Thor's hips, and he surged up into me with a rough sound. The heat of his release filled me even more than I already had been.

I sagged into his embrace, my nerves humming with pleasure. Thor hugged me to him with his chin beside my forehead. The power and the gentleness twined together through his body brought an ache into my chest. I swallowed hard.

How was it that every time I thought my heart couldn't get fuller, it expanded even more? And how could it still feel so impossible to tell this god who'd given me new life and held me up like something sacred even half of what he meant to me?

# 12

*Baldur*

The near-noon sun beamed down from a brilliantly blue sky, and the wizened red pines that were giving the five of us some cover gave off a delicate woody perfume. Birds twittered as they jumped from one branch to another. It might have been a lovely day to stroll through the park if we hadn't been waiting for a murderous giant to descend from high above.

No voices disturbed the peace, because Skadi had set down a magical aura to discourage any humans from venturing close to this spot. "It'll make them feel like prey evading a hunter," she'd said, looking more amused than was comforting. At least she hadn't argued about the need to protect the innocent lives of any mortals who passed by.

Aria shifted her weight, peering between the pine branches toward the pagoda where we were supposedly meeting with the government officials to plan our alliance. She'd been more relaxed when she'd returned to the house with Thor yesterday afternoon, for reasons I could guess with a bright hot ripple of memory, but uneasiness prickled all through her aura now.

"I guess there's no way to be sure which direction he'll bring the bridge down from, right?" she murmured. Her silver-white wings were already released, folded close to her back but tensed in anticipation.

"Surt isn't much for preambles," Loki said, propping himself against the trunk of a taller tree with his arms folded over his chest. The trickster could manage to look relaxed in almost any scenario, but we'd fought together enough times in just the last few weeks that I could recognize from the alertness in his eyes and the coiled strength in his stance that he was braced just as much as Aria was. "We can assume he'll touch down close to the pagoda. We won't have far to dash in any case."

Thor tested the flat of his hammer against his palm with a faint thump. One wouldn't need to have spent any time with him at all to notice the fierce light of a battle fury dancing in his eyes. "I still say we should be the ones going for the kill. The Vanir are skilled and all, but..."

"But you'd rather *you* were the one who got to bash that villain's head in," Loki said. "I don't think it'll diminish your status as official giant killer if you let this one pass, Thunderer. Freya *is* a war goddess—I expect she'll handle herself."

"And the others were right," Hod said. My dark twin didn't sound particularly happy about that fact, but then, a certain amount of gloominess was just his nature. "Surt's powers can at least partly deflect our magic, and your hammer isn't the most accurate weapon, no matter how powerful it is. We have a better chance this way, throwing everything at him for him to dodge while Freya and Freyr slip in there with their swords. One or the other of them has to reach him."

He was frowning, though, his head cocked to one side as he took in the sounds of the park. It wouldn't be the blazing light of

Surt's bridge but the crackle of those flames that told him when it was time to act.

"I suppose," Thor muttered, but his grumbling was half-hearted.

Loki grinned. "The entire plan was my idea, let's remember. If we topple Surt today, I'll happily share that victory with the rest of you."

"So generous of you, Sly One," my twin said, but I thought his mouth might have twitched with a start of a smile.

"We are a team now, aren't we?" the trickster said with a sweep of his hand.

Sometimes I'd felt as if that bond were slipping away as more and more of our fellow gods joined our semblance of an army, contrasting personalities and energies bumping up against each other and turning the harmonious vibe I'd gotten used to off-key. But here with the four of them, the connection hummed between us just as strong as before. We might have been an odd team, but I couldn't deny that we were one. I wouldn't have wanted to.

That bond was the only thing that kept me certain we *would* see Surt fall, now or another day.

"I don't need any glory," Aria said. "I just want him gone. Those five or so minutes when we thought we could chill out in Asgard for a while were really nice."

The day she was talking about had been clear and sunny just like this one. With a pang in my chest, I remembered lying sprawled in the field with her and the others. It had been the first day since Ragnarok when I'd been able to sit back and simply enjoying being present with my mind unclouded. I'd spent far too long hiding away from darkness inside and out behind the bright haze I'd wrapped around myself.

"They were nice," I agreed. Aria shot me a smile, warm as the sun. What would it be like to have not just minutes but days, weeks, years to soak up her company?

I was looking forward to finding out.

But even thoughts as pleasant as those didn't ease the unsettled sensation in my own stomach. When I looked back toward the pagoda, my nerves crawled under my skin. Something here was off-kilter.

Maybe it was only Surt's destructive intentions preceding him, marring the natural harmony of this space. Just the thought of him destroying the carefully crafted structure before us nagged at me. The pagoda was three stories of curved slate-tiled roofs with intricate carvings all along the edges and around the windows. Every surface was painted in rich greens and reds. It was a work of art, an aria of architecture.

Well, if we moved quickly enough, he might not even touch it.

I directed a soft calming glow over us and around the pagoda to where our companions were staked out for their part in the ambush. Stay sure, stay focused, let no worries distract us. We of Asgard might have drifted apart over the centuries, but we all still had that one common tie of the realm we'd once shared. We could unite to save our home.

The sun hit its peak overhead. It was noon now, the time Surt had expected our meeting. Hod's frown came back as we waited. I supposed it made sense that the giant would wait at least a few minutes to be sure everyone who'd meant to gather here had arrived. He'd want to catch us absorbed in our negotiations.

Another tremor of discord rippled down my spine. Had I sensed it from Surt? My gaze scanned the sky, but no fiery red glinted against the blue yet.

Loki pushed himself off his tree with a jerk. He stood there, his amber eyes turned oddly vacant, his tall slim body still and stiff. Then he bit out a curse.

"He isn't here," he snapped. "He isn't coming. He's brought his bridge down—somewhere. That way. Nowhere near here. Norns only know what he's doing while he thinks we're too distracted to come. Bloody giant. Come on! Whatever he's up to, it can't be good."

A jolt of panic raced through my chest. I hadn't been wrong to worry, then.

"Asgardians!" Thor bellowed as we rushed out of the shelter of the trees. "Surt has arrived elsewhere. The ambush is off. Loki will help us find the giant—follow as quickly as you can."

Murmurs of confusion and indignation reached my ears, but my heart was thumping too quickly for me to focus on them. The uneasiness I'd felt before niggled right down to my bones. Something in this realm was *very* wrong. We had to reach Surt before he saw his current mission through.

A flick of my hand summoned a bolt of light to carry me up over the landscape. Loki was already sprinting off to the east, Aria flying after him as fast as her wings could flap.

"What do you think happened?" she said, her voice taut and breathless. "Why didn't Surt take the bait about the meeting?"

"He might not have trusted the tip from the dark elf," Hod said, soaring up beside me on his swath of shadow. "He's a lot of things, but he's proven he isn't stupid. He was cautious enough to move his army before."

"Or he may have believed the tip but figured that whatever he's trying to accomplish now would get him closer to his goals than stopping our meeting," I said.

"Or he didn't really think he could take on all of us now that we're on guard and growing our numbers," Thor muttered behind us. "I've never met a giant that didn't turn coward when the odds seemed against him."

Loki made a sputtered sound of protest, and the thunder god coughed. "Ah, present company excluded, I should say."

"In that case, I agree with you," the trickster said archly. "But let's save our breath for this flight. I suspect reaching Surt quickly matters more than debating the exact reasons he ignored the lure."

"Right." Aria's hands balled into fists. The sun shone over her silvery wings and the mussed waves of her blond hair as she pushed herself faster.

I rested my hands against the streak of light that was carrying me, urging more energy down into it. It quivered against my palms. A glance behind me showed that our whole host was rushing after us by their various means.

We raced over the foaming waters of the ocean, a faint salt tang tickling my nose. The sun sank toward the horizon behind us as we left it behind. Surt had come to do his dirty business on the other side of the world under the cover of night.

By the time we approached the far coast, it was merely a glittering of electric lights against a darkened shore. Loki adjusted his direction more to the south. We swept past cities and towns and streams of lamps winding along the roads in between. The jitter of nervous energy that had disturbed me before reached a higher peak. We were close, and Surt was wreaking more havoc than ever before.

He really had picked a spot almost exactly half the world away. My energy wasn't close to spent, but Aria's wings were starting to falter. I cast a wash of soothing light toward her and heard her suck in a grateful breath.

The first flicker of fire against the darkness caught my eye, and my heart thudded even faster. All of us hurtled toward it, the wind licking over our clothes.

Flames were dancing on the ground beside the spot where the bridge had touched down. An eerie glow shifted across the walls and roof of a boxy building, long and squat with two stout towers jutting beside it. A broad river flowed by beyond its concrete yard. The glow caught on several shuffling draugar bodies there, but nowhere near the swarm Surt had brought down before.

There was no sign of Surt himself, but a shock of energy hit me as we descended, rattling my nerves. Something was shifting inside those buildings. Building, colliding…

"Shit!" Ari said, peering down at a sign on the compound's fence with her sharp valkyrie vision. "It's a nuclear power plant."

Loki's face turned even paler than its usual tone. "He must be trying to make it explode. He'll be inside. We've got to stop him before—"

Another wave of shuddering energy washed over us, streaked with a burning heat that felt like a condensed echo of the sunlight we'd been basking in just a few hours ago. My gut lurched. The giant had already done it. The bright hot energy inside that building was quaking and erupting, a chain reaction swelling in every direction faster than we could fly, faster than we could speak.

Instinctively, I raised my hands in front of me. Unstable or not, the energy stirring was the same radiant power as daylight. The same power that thrummed through my body when I called on it. That power gave life all over the realms. It shouldn't sear and destroy. If I could just fold it back into the shape it should have kept—

I sent a surge of my own light toward the building with a flash like a thunderclap. The surge had barely left my palms when I felt my mistake.

My light burst against the energy flaring inside the building and sent it shooting even higher, even faster. In that instant, I could already feel how the chaotic heat would flay flesh down to the bone and scorch those bones to dust. That light, that twisted twin to the light in me, was the most vicious threat I'd ever sensed.

And I couldn't stop it. I could only hasten its destruction of everything around it.

# 13

*Aria*

The air shook with an ear-splitting *boom.* Loki dove at me. He yanked me to the side and spun me around so his body shielded me, hollering over his shoulder in a voice so hoarse and frantic it barely sounded like him at all.

"Stop the explosion! Hold it all in—however you can—just *do* something!"

More shouts whipped past my ringing ears. Clutching me to him, Loki started to race away, the wind whistling as he leaned into the full power of his shoes of flight.

"Loki!" I gripped his shoulders and shoved myself back far enough that I could look into his eyes. "Stop. We can't just leave."

"My fire and my sword aren't going to do a damned thing against a nuclear explosion, pixie," he said. "And neither will your powers. Getting you out of range is the only thing I *can* do."

I shook my head and pushed at him again. "No. Surt's still there—we could still catch him before he goes back to Asgard. If we don't, he'll just do something like this again."

The trickster sighed, but his steps slowed. He glanced behind us. The warbling echo of the explosion had faded, but I didn't know how much that was due to the distance. Surt's bridge still blazed against the night sky. A sharp metallic-smelling smoke prickled in my nose.

"Well," Loki said, "it looks like they managed to pull a solution out of their asses after all. For now. If we start to lose control over the situation, I'm hauling you out of there again."

I made a face at him. "Shouldn't I get some say about when I get hauled?"

He gave me a crooked smile. "You're my valkyrie, Ari. I picked you; I helped bring you into our world. I'm not watching you get killed all over again barely a month later."

"I'm sure your reputation would survive the failure," I grumbled as he swiveled around and darted back the way we'd come.

"My dear pixie, when have you ever seen me give a damn about my reputation?"

His arm around my waist loosened as we reached the ring of gods gathered around the power plant. At least, the spot where I assumed the power plant had been. I couldn't see it anymore—couldn't see anything on the ground below us now. An area at least half a mile across was cloaked in a thick layer of shadow, darker even than the night.

My pulse stuttered. My gaze darted across the assembled gods and caught on the one I'd been searching for, a head of black hair over a pale face tipped forward.

Hod had dropped down to the road outside the plant. His arms were braced ahead of him, his hands set as if they were resting on that shadowy dome.

They weren't resting, though. It was the opposite. He was conjuring up that massive shell of magic to contain all the radioactive light and heat that had been going to sear through us and half the countryside.

His muscles stood out like chords in his lean arms. The tendons in his hands bulged. As I watched, a quiver ran through his shoulders. It was taking all his strength to hold that shield in place.

The other gods were all hovering above with bewildered expressions. I slipped out of Loki's hold and whirled around.

"Why isn't anyone helping him?" I demanded. "He can't do this on his own."

"I think he's going to have to," Freya said in a thin voice. "The darkness and the cold he can generate are the only things that can push back the energy from that explosion."

Baldur's head jerked up. He blinked as if snapping out of a daze. "I can try to help keep him going. Soothe his body as it tires out." He dropped down to join his twin on the road.

What about Hod's mind? His spirit? I knew what it felt like using the small bit of dark magic I had in me. Those shadows affected a lot more than just my body.

Thor glanced down at his hammer dangling useless in his hand. His mouth twisted. Mjolnir could destroy all kinds of things, but not nuclear fallout.

Before my eyes, the dome of shadow contracted about a foot. I flinched in surprise, but then my breath caught as I understood. Hod wasn't just holding back the explosion. He was defusing it—cooling its heat, darkening its radiance—and shrinking it bit by bit.

"Some of us can at least help solidify the barrier," one of the newest goddesses said. "We may not be able to generate the same kind of darkness, but we can help hold what's there together."

Freya nodded, her eyes and her golden waves wild. Another few seconds, and every god here might have died.

Maybe this was the first time some of them had really believed that might happen.

The surface of the shadowy shield twitched again, but this time the movement came with a shudder and a hiss from Hod below. At the same instant, a figure burst through the shield at the far side near the flaming bridge.

It was Surt. With a gasp, Hod heaved more shadow up to seal the hole where the giant had broken through. A few of the gods leapt to propel the darkness faster over the breach.

Our enemy sprang straight for his bridge. An unsettling glow wavered over his skin, as if he'd absorbed some of the explosion's toxins. But it didn't look as if they were hurting him. Before any of us even had time to charge after him, he'd already landed on the bridge and started up.

"Surt!" Loki yelled, darting over the top of the shield toward the giant. Thor followed at his heels. "A realm's no good to you if you poison the place into a wasteland."

Surt chuckled as the fiery arc of his bridge retracted, whipping him up toward the sky. "I get along with all sorts of fire," he said, his voice fading as he ascended. "Humans are too much hassle to rule. Better to wipe them out. My comrades can have this place when the poison fades."

His last words barely reached my ears before he disappeared, heading back to the realm of the gods. I shuddered. *Better to wipe them out.*

He saw every living being in Midgard as some kind of vermin rather than as people—and, hell, animals and plants—that had as much right to life as he did. It shouldn't have surprised me after the way he'd built his army of murdered people magicked into zombies, but I'd never imagined he'd go this far. That we'd be defending every inhabitant of my former home not just from attacks but outright annihilation.

I wheeled in the air. The ache in my chest was almost as sharp as the one spreading through my wings after so long in flight. I didn't think the darkness in me could add to Hod's shield—I'd never been able to compel it to do anything other than swallow lives in the middle of a fight—and Surt was out of reach. What the hell was I even here for if I didn't offer something? Maybe there was some way I could pitch in that I hadn't thought of.

I glided down onto the grassy shoulder of the road. My wings twinged with gratitude when I folded them against my back.

Hod was just pushing another step closer to the power plant, contracting his dome of shadow a little tighter. Baldur stood next to him, a thin glow emanating from his hands into his twin's chest. I wavered on my feet, abruptly uncertain.

"Is there anything I can do to help?" I asked, looking at Baldur. "If there's something I could bring, or ask the others to do, or—"

"Ari," Hod snapped in a ragged voice, interrupting me. Of course, he couldn't see who I'd been directing the question at—in that moment, I wasn't even sure he was aware of Baldur there helping him. "I've got this. Get out of here."

Baldur winced, but he tipped his head to me with a quick glance as if to say he agreed with the gist, if not the tone, of Hod's request.

The ache around my heart squeezed tighter. I backed up a step, and another, and then launched myself up into the air, because I couldn't think of where else to go.

Hod had this situation under control, but he was barely holding all that explosive power in. If Surt set off another meltdown before the dark god managed to recover—if he set off more than one—

Could the giant even manage that much destruction all at once? How much had it taken out of Surt to set off the explosion here?

There was no way to know, but if he found a way, Midgard was doomed.

The other gods had split apart, the few of them with magic that could support Hod's shield circling the dome, shoring it up as well as they could, and the others hovering in a cluster looking about as bewildered as before. Bewildered and weary. Seeing the fatigue on their faces brought my own exhaustion rushing to the front of my mind.

Loki obviously saw the same thing. He clapped his hands, his voice brisk. "All right. All of us who are useless here, we'd better find some new accommodations. Those who *are* working are going to need somewhere to recover afterward."

Beside him, Thor nodded. "After that journey, we all need rest and something to eat. And we should start planning our next course of action right away."

Skadi set off in the lead, using her huntress skills to seek out a building where we wouldn't be disturbed. We ended up at a sprawling structure that looked like it might once have been a school, with grass overtaking the parking lot around the side and collapsed rusted goal posts on the overgrown field beyond the lot.

A few of the gods rushed off again to get supplies. At Thor and Loki's urging, I found myself bundled in a sleeping bag on the linoleum floor of a small room that must have once been a teacher's office.

The gods' voices echoed faintly down the wide hall outside, but I couldn't summon the energy to strain my ears to listen, let alone join in the conversation. Three cross-Pacific flights in the same number of days was obviously my limit. My eyelids dropped shut like they had weights attached to them, and a second later I was out cold.

---

When I woke up, the whole building was quiet. Sun streaked through the room's grimy window, filling the space with a faint warmth. It didn't look as if the world had ended just yet. I sat up and rested my head in my hands. A renewed pang filled my chest.

I'd flown all this way, crossed continents and oceans—for what? To be a distraction again, to stand by helplessly while Midgard almost burned?

I had to be better than this. I'd tackled dark elves and draugar and a prison of memories. And this new fight was mine more than any of the others had been. Hell, based on the sign outside the power plant, we weren't more than a few hours by human speeds from the city where I'd grown up. A city that could have been leveled in the explosion or fried with radiation if Hod hadn't acted fast enough.

Not that there were a whole lot of people I'd known in that city who I cared that much about saving. Other than my acid-tongued mother and her string of asshole boyfriends, there were the wannabe and actual gangsters I'd worked as a courier for, the jerks from my schools who'd turned their nose up at my dirty clothes and hacked haircuts when I'd had to rely on Mom's parental skills…

But there were plenty of totally decent people there, too, I was sure. The kind of people I might have watched enviously while grabbing a cup of coffee or jetting through a park. Once or twice I'd wondered what it was like to have a life where you had people you could just relax and have a laugh with, enjoying each other's company without needing to be on your guard.

That was the kind of life I might actually have been experiencing right now with my gods, in a weird sort of way, if Surt hadn't decided to crash into Asgard.

My mind slipped from those memories to the ones of when he'd blasted into that first human city afterward. All at once, my breath caught.

It hadn't even been the gods who'd pushed Surt back there, at least not alone. The human soldiers with their guns and missiles had helped send him running. With the right weapons, the people here could kick plenty of giant ass.

We'd spent all this time searching out one or two gods at a time when I could have recruited us an entire squadron of fighters in one go.

I didn't give myself a chance to second-guess the burst of inspiration. I couldn't imagine more desperate times than these, so desperate measures it was. No way were the gods—the new ones, anyway—going to approve of this plan, so I'd just have to go get it done, and when I had the results, I didn't think they'd reject them.

I scrambled to my feet and eased open the door. The dim hallway was empty. A snore I recognized as Thor's drifted from somewhere farther down. Hoping Loki and his excellent hearing were similarly out of commission, I dashed for the front entrance.

The door squeaked when I pushed it open, but no one stirred behind me. With a ragged breath, I leapt up into the air and set off toward Philadelphia.

I had some old colleagues to catch up with. Let's hope they were happy to see me.

# 14

*Aria*

It might have felt as if I'd left Philly a lifetime ago, but the truth was it'd only been a matter of weeks. The crooks I'd worked for wouldn't have changed their ways particularly.

Back then, most of our business had been done with someone from one gang or another texting me a pick-up spot and a time, followed by a hand-off at that spot that included my delivery instructions. But I'd worked for the city's underworld long enough that I had a decent idea of where to find the second in command of the largest criminal network that operated here.

I landed in an alley beside the pub and pulled in my wings. It was going to take a concentrated effort to make my body visible to mortal eyes. I dragged in a breath, willing energy over my skin. Then I strode out of the alley and into the pub.

The place was pretty dead at this time of day, just a few particularly devoted regulars picking at the sparse brunch offerings around the varnished wooden tables that filled one side of the room and a couple of guys playing pool on the other side of the bar who looked like they probably should have been in school. The balls clattered after one of them took a break shot.

Even before anyone had started much drinking for the day, the whole place smelled like malt whiskey. I marched straight across the thin green carpet. The bartender, an older guy with slicked-back gray hair who'd been the one to pass me a payment several times, glanced up. His whole body went rigid, his eyes widening.

I guessed word had gotten around about my death by junkie jeep. I smiled and gave him a little wave as I stopped by the bar counter. "Hey, Steve. I need to talk to Harrison."

The bartender stared at me for another beat before he recovered himself. "Ari? I thought—we all heard—"

"Funny how these rumors can get out of hand, isn't it?" I said. I was counting on Mom not having bothered with a funeral or anything similarly public. There couldn't have been many eye witnesses. "I get knocked over by some asshole and decide to take a break while I'm recovering, and suddenly everyone's talking like I've passed over to the great beyond."

He laughed, a little hoarsely at first, but then his stance loosened. "That Gene," he said. "The dope. I'm surprised he manages to get his shirt on right way around most days."

"No kidding," I said with a grin. Just like old times. I almost could slip right back into my old life, couldn't I? Maybe I wouldn't be stuck living out the rest of my days in Asgard when this was over after all. Not that I wanted to pick up exactly where I'd left off or spend that much time with this bunch, but it could be nice change to play human with the old crowd now and then.

"What do you need to see Harrison about?" Steve asked.

That was the complicated part of this pitch. "There's a big deal on offer that I thought he and the boss would want to hear about right away. Kind of confidential, though, so I didn't want to just pass the message on."

Steve nodded and set aside the washcloth he'd been holding.

"I'll check with him. We don't usually see a lot of action this early in the day, so I'd imagine he can give you a few minutes."

I was hoping he'd give us a whole lot more than that, but a few minutes would do for a start.

The bartender ducked into the back room. I rubbed my finger on the counter, which was so polished my skin squeaked against it. Steve emerged a moment later.

"Go on back," he said with a jerk of his thumb.

If I'd been one of the guys, Harrison would probably have sent out a tough to pat me down, but I'd never taken sides in the various intra-gang squabbles before, and it wasn't as if there were many places I could have been hiding a weapon while I was wearing fitted jeans and a light tank top. These guys had no idea that I could now do more damage with a brush of my hand than any gun could.

The doorway to the back room had just a heavy curtain over it, so Harrison could hear if any trouble started in the main bar area. The rings clinked as I eased it aside to step past it.

Harrison Malloy's office-slash-meeting room was nothing fancy. The card table and the chairs around it were a metal folding set, the black paint on them worn down around the edges. Cabinets and shelving units of similar construction and in an assortment of muted colors stood along the walls. The desk he was currently leaning against was a table that had been scavenged from the bar after some idiot had scorched a line in the varnish with a cigar, based on the width of the mark. The liveliest thing in the room was the tall broad-leaved rubber plant that loomed nearly as high as the doorframe.

The whiskey smell faded in here, replaced by a whiff of pot. Not Harrison's, I had to guess. I'd never seen him anything but totally sober.

The man himself wouldn't have turned any heads, in interest or in fear. He had sort of a faded hipster look: his pale gray-streaked hair floppy, his eyes shielded by rectangular glasses, and a thick moustache adorning his narrow and kind of lumpy face. But the eyes behind those glasses were sharp as a steel edge, and the forearms he often rolled the sleeves of his checkered shirt up over were roped with muscle.

You didn't have to be around him much to figure out he wasn't someone to mess with.

"Ari," he said, with a smile that was the business version of warm. "I'm glad to see the stories of your untimely demise were greatly exaggerated."

I returned the smile. "If I'd known I was supposed to be a ghost, maybe I'd have had a little more fun with the visit."

"A missed opportunity. But not the opportunity you came to see me about." He motioned to the chairs in case I wanted to sit down. "Tell me about this deal."

I stayed standing, wetting my lips. "You and your people have weapons connections, right? You could collect some pretty heavy firepower if you wanted to?"

Harrison's eyebrows jumped up. "Have you got a line to a customer looking to stock up their arsenal?"

"Not exactly," I said. I was going to have to feel this part out carefully. "They'd need your people handling those weapons. They'd pay well—really well." Loki had mentioned the extensive financial resources the gods had set up on Midgard. They had to be able to afford to hire a squad of mercenaries at a very good wage.

The gang commander's eyebrows rose even higher. "And who would we be aiming those weapons at? We wouldn't be interested in inserting ourselves into someone else's turf war."

"It's nothing like that," I said quickly, even though on a broad scale it kind of was. "It's—look, you must have heard about the disaster overseas? Fire and destruction and all kinds of people killed?"

The amusement in Harrison's face dimmed. "They're saying some guy basically dropped out of the sky and started whipping fire around. I've heard people mention *zombies*. Whoever the hell staged that terrorist attack, they had way too much time on their hands setting up their special effects. What does that have to do with your deal?"

I decided I could let the special effects assumption slide. His people would see how real Surt's magic was when they confronted him. No point in trying to argue about it when I couldn't prove it anyway.

"The asshole who did that, he's who my people are trying to take down," I said. "But there aren't enough of us. We want to hire help—help that can supply their own firepower. Ten, twenty, thirty—however many you can get together and arm who are willing to take the job. The more people who join in, the more you get paid. Simple."

Harrison looked as if he had no idea what to make of this story. "Why would you have hooked up with some people fighting terrorists?" he said. "What the hell is this really about, Ari?"

"It's a long story," I said. "But it's about exactly what I said. The guy who brought down all that fire, who ordered all those people killed, plans on hurting people here too. Just last night—look up the Peach Bottom power plant. He destroyed it. Tried to nuke the whole country."

"What!?"

"Look it up," I said again, pointing to the laptop lying on his desk.

The expression Harrison gave me was completely disbelieving, but he grabbed his laptop anyway. There had to be something in the news about the plant by now.

He typed and scrolled, and the color drained from his face. "Shit," he said. "They leveled the place."

Were there photographs, then? That meant Hod must have finished defusing the explosive surge. Otherwise the news stories would be talking about a big shadowy dome.

The urge tugged at my gut to get back to my dark god, to confirm he was okay, even though I wasn't sure he wanted a whole lot of company immediately after that ordeal.

"You're saying this meltdown was caused by the same people who orchestrated the attack in Moscow?" Harrison said. "How do you even know? There's nothing in the news—it sounds like they have no idea what happened."

"I know it was the same people," I said, "because I was there. Trying to stop the guy. We didn't manage it, and he's going to strike again. Maybe next time we won't even manage to prevent the destruction he's trying to cause. That's why I'm coming to you. I thought of all the people I've worked with, and I figured if anyone had the means to turn the tide, it was you."

Flattery could be a very effective tool. I saw Harrison waver for a second with a hint of pride glinting in his eyes. Then he shut the laptop with a snap, and his expression shuttered too.

"No," he said. "This whole thing sounds too crazy. I don't know what you've gotten yourself mixed up in, Ari, but I think we're better off keeping out of it."

Fuck. I scrambled for some other way to persuade him. "You could at least come out and meet with the rest of my, ah, colleagues, or send someone out. Hear everything they have to say."

Harrison was already shaking his head. "This isn't our area. We can't go jumping into some arena we know nothing about."

"If you don't, this whole city could be leveled tomorrow," I said with a sweep of my arm. My voice was rising, but I couldn't rein it in. "This isn't just about business, Harrison, even if we would throw a lot of money at you. It's about saving the fucking world."

"Okay, okay," he said, holding up his hands. "Obviously you're very caught up in this mess. I'm sorry, Ari. Go to the FBI or the army or whoever. I don't know exactly what's real here, but either way it's a hell of a lot bigger than us."

"I can't go to the FBI or the army," I said. "I don't know them."

They wouldn't listen to me. I couldn't simply offer their agents or soldiers a wad of cash to do whatever the gods told them to do. And by the time Surt struck somewhere and we could call the authorities in with evidence, it'd be too late when they got there.

But Harrison wasn't listening either. He'd already shut the conversation down. He was pushing himself off his desk now, ready to show me out.

My stomach twisted. He didn't believe me because he thought it all sounded too crazy. Maybe I shouldn't have been downplaying the craziness. Maybe I should prove to him just how real all that stuff was.

My heart thumped hard at the thought. I'd never shown what I'd become to anyone who hadn't already understood what I was, anyone from my old life. If I did this, there was no coming back again. No pretending normal. No slipping back into the life that'd once been mine.

How much had I really wanted that life anymore? I wouldn't have thought it was that big a sacrifice, but cutting the cord completely suddenly made my lungs clench up in resistance.

I didn't have any choice. It was make the last move I had, or I slunk back to the gods with nothing to show for my gamble.

"Harrison," I said, "we need you because we need people who know how to change the rules and make up their own, because this *is* a completely new arena, and we can't take on our enemies with the usual methods. There's nothing usual about this at all."

I flexed the muscles in my back, and my wings sprang from my flesh. Harrison stumbled to a stop halfway across the room. He gaped at me as I spread my wings to their full span, the tips brushing the walls on either side of me. His mouth closed and opened and closed again.

"The people I'm with now are gods," I said, with a dramatic flutter of my feathers. "They'll pay you a divine amount of cash. But we need people who can get a job done, fast and right, to make sure the entire world doesn't end. Which, as far as I can tell, benefits you as much as anyone. Am I getting through to you yet?"

He walked from one side of the room to the other and then edged a little closer. I turned obligingly so he could see the spot where the wings met my back.

"How…" he muttered. "They couldn't have just come from—where the hell could you have been hiding them?"

"It's called magic," I said. "You start to get used to it when you've been hanging out with a bunch of gods."

He shook his head as if to clear it. "It can't be—this has got to be some kind of stunt—"

Oh, for fuck's sake. I tucked my wings closer to my body and held out my hand. "What do you need for me to prove it to you? Give me something there's no way I could possibly bend or break—if I'm just a regular human being. Come on. Let's get this over with."

Harrison started at me and then groped around. He shoved one of the metal folding chairs toward me.

Well, fine, if he didn't care whether this survived…

I picked it up by one of the metal bars, gripped it with both hands, and bent the back and then the seat at the middle. Then I snapped one of the legs in half, through the solid steel, with a heave of my valkyrie strength. Thor could have crumpled the thing into a ball, but this display would have to do.

Harrison still didn't appear to know how to respond. I let out a huff of breath and stalked to the rubber plant. "I can do more than that. Do you want to see my freakiest power?"

I rested my hand on one of the waxy leaves. A tickle of the plant's living energy grazed my palm. With a silent apology, I unlocked the dark rippling in my chest that was drawn to that light like a shark to blood.

The shadows inside me latched on to the plant's energy and

sucked it down. The leaf shriveled, and then its neighbors did too, the stem sagging over—

"Stop!" Harrison said raggedly.

I jerked my hand back. The gang commander took off his glasses, rubbed them on the hem of his shirt, and replaced them. I didn't imagine the cleaning had changed the view very much. His face wasn't just pale but a faint sickly green now.

"What are you?" he said finally, in a quiet voice that was equal parts awed and horrified.

I guessed it couldn't hurt to tell him that after everything I'd already shown him. "They say I'm a valkyrie," I said. "I really did die, and then I got resurrected. It's been interesting."

"Interesting," he repeated with a rough chuckle. He walked up to his withered plant and touched one of the leaves I'd drained. Only the top half had crumpled. "Can you bring it back?"

I swallowed hard. "No," I said. "Not a plant. Not like that. I'm sorry." Maybe some beings I could have blessed as worthy and sent them up to Asgard to claim a new life there, but I was pretty sure plants couldn't be warriors. And also that a plant resurrected in Asgard wasn't what Harrison was hoping for. Besides the fact that I had no idea if a patchwork valkyrie like me was even capable of that kind of resurrection for anyone. I hadn't had any opportunities to try.

"Well, you did make your point." Harrison stared at the rubber plant for a few seconds longer. His gaze slid to me. His jaw worked. "You're serious. These 'enemies' you were talking about—they're trying to destroy the whole world."

"The main one wants to exterminate all humankind," I said. "He nearly got a good start on that last night. We were just in time. I don't want us cutting it that close again. I think we can stop him the next time if we've got your strength to add to ours. There aren't that many of us—and the gods aren't going to pick up guns."

Harrison let out another chuckle, but this one sounded almost exhilarated. My spirits started to life.

"All right," he said. "I'll come out and speak to your gods. I can't promise anything, but I can't just walk away from a deal like that."

# 15

*Thor*

Loki had scrounged up a computer somewhere, and now, to my astonishment, Bragi, our god of poetry, was typing away at it as if he'd been using one of those human contraptions his entire expansive life.

"You have to understand the internet as a writer in this realm these days," he said when he noticed the many stares he was getting. "I may appreciate classic styling, but I keep up with the times as well."

"We're not composing verses right now," Vidar said tersely, peering down at the large world map we'd spread on the hard packed dirt of the yard. It was easier to see out here in the sunlight compared to the shadowy halls inside the old building, where the electricity appeared to have been off for quite some time. "Tell us where the other nuclear power plants are."

"Well, it appears there are rather a lot of them…" Bragi frowned with a purse of his lips. "Let's start with the largest ones, shall we? There's a sensibility to that."

Heimdall, who was standing just behind me, muttered something under his breath that Loki probably would have been able to hear. I could at least make out that it didn't sound complimentary of Bragi's sensibilities. I supposed it would be easier to appreciate the poet after the catastrophe was over when we could bask in his finely worded accounts of our glorious victories.

The trouble was we had to accomplish that victory first.

"All right," Bragi went on. "Simply going by plants still operational... There's one in Canada, near a town called Kincardine, in Bruce County, Ontario. Is that on the map?"

"Canada, Ontario..." Vidar bent down, and everyone else gathered around as he cast about with his hand holding a red pen.

I raised my head at the rumble of an engine. It shouldn't matter if any humans drove past this abandoned place, since they wouldn't see us unless we let them anyway, but I'd only heard a couple of vehicles pass by on that little highway since we'd gotten here. The place Skadi had found was certainly out of the way, even if I couldn't say a whole lot else in its favor.

The SUV that was driving toward us didn't simply cruise by like the other two vehicles had, though. It slowed—and then it pulled into the lane to the building's parking lot. Everyone else's heads jerked up then too.

"What in Hel's name do these people think they're—" Freyr started.

Before he could finish his sentence, the SUV jerked to a halt and the passenger door popped open. A familiar slight figure with a head of mussed blond waves jumped out.

For a second, I could only stare dumbly at Ari. I'd assumed she was still sleeping off the strain of the previous day in the room we'd found her for some privacy. Apparently she'd been up before any of us. Up and off on some quest I couldn't quite comprehend.

Three more people got out of the SUV: two men, one middle-aged with a bushy moustache and the other younger with a crewcut, and a well-muscled woman who looked a little older than Ari. All of them were regular humans. They aimed blank looks across the yard before giving Ari a puzzled glance. She was allowing the mortals to see her, but they couldn't see us any more than the previous passersby had.

"What in the nine realms is going on?" Heimdall demanded, pitching his voice to carry across the yard. He wasn't the tallest of the gods or the broadest—both of those honors belonged to me—but he could have a very imposing presence when he chose to. It was a gatekeeper thing, presumably.

"Wait here for a minute," Ari said to her companions. She jogged over to meet us and stopped at the edge of the yard, setting her hands on her hips.

"I brought help," she said simply, her defiant gaze daring us to complain.

"Those *humans* are your 'help'?" Skadi said before our valkyrie could go on. "What have you told them? What were you thinking?" She turned toward the rest of us. "I knew we shouldn't have kept her along."

Ari's eyes flashed at that aside, and suddenly I understood why she'd struck out on her own. She'd gone to her former people like I'd gone to the giants not long ago, determined to use the advantages I had even if my comrades had been skeptical.

We'd tried to defend our valkyrie's worth to the gods who'd more recently joined us, but the valkyries in the past had never been more than servants to the gods and attendants to the risen warriors. This bunch hadn't known Ari long enough to understand how much more than that she was. And it wasn't as if she hadn't heard all their dismissive remarks.

"I was *thinking*," she said in a tart voice, "about how quickly Surt turned tail and ran when those human soldiers opened fire on him during his first attack on Midgard. I know these people. They can get us weapons as good as those. We can double or even triple our firepower just like that."

"You expect us to fight with guns?" Vidar said with a note of disgust, his hand coming to rest on the sword hanging from his belt.

Ari looked as if she'd just barely restrained an eye roll. "No," she said. "You've got your ways of fighting already. Why mess with that? They've got people who'll fight alongside us, their way. An extra little army for us. If we pay them."

"Pay them?" Freyr sputtered. "A rabble of humans with—"

"We have plenty of money," Loki broke in before the other god could say anything more insulting. "That's no issue. Why shouldn't we make use of them if they're willing? It is their realm they'd be fighting for."

"As far as the money goes, we'd be asking them to risk their lives going up against Surt," Ari said. "We owe them something for that, considering it's mainly *your* fault he's here at all. Now can you make yourselves visible to them already? Without all the grumbling about humans? They're going to decide I'm batshit insane and leave in another minute."

Most of the gods looked as though they were absolutely fine with that possibility.

"We can't show ourselves to humans without proper precautions," Njord said. "These days, the way they think—"

"It's just not wise," Heimdall filled in. "They're too unpredictable."

"Oh, for Asgard's sake," Loki said, and stepped away from the group of us toward the figures waiting by the SUV. A brief flaring of light ran over his body.

The humans' jaws dropped as to their eyes he must have appeared as if out of nowhere. Grinning, he sauntered on over to them.

Why had I been waiting around for permission? Ari wouldn't

have brought these people here if she hadn't believed this was a good idea, and I trusted her judgment. I focused for a second on the texture of the air, the dusty scent of the yard, willing my body to be fully present in the realm. There. I wiped my hands together and gave our guests a grin of my own.

They appeared to be having some trouble forming words. Baldur ambled over to join Loki with a faint smile, the sun shimmering off his skin. I skirted the cluster of gods around the map to stand beside the two of them. The humans glanced from one of us to the other.

The older man, the one with the moustache, swiped a hand across his chin. "Well," he said. "Look at that."

"I did mention my colleagues were *gods*, right?" Ari said, her tone amused now that her sanity was no longer in question. "There's more of them here. They're just being shy. Apparently you're very scary."

Loki chuckled at that. The remark must have niggled at a few of my comrades' pride, because a moment later Vidar, Skadi, and Freyr came up beside us.

"We understand you can bring weapons, and you're willing to fight on our behalf," Vidar said, folding his arms over his chest. "What exactly can you provide?"

"Hold on a second," the older guy said. "I told Ari we'd come out here to talk. I'm not committing to anything until I'm clear about the whole situation. What we're fighting. What you need from us. And what you're providing to us in return."

"Payment will be no issue," Loki said with a wave of his hand. "Weapons—covered. You want a hundred thousand a day to be on our retainer, each? We can do that. Is the money your only hesitation?"

"There is the whole thing about fighting some kind of war with gods," the woman piped up. Her stance was still rigid.

"You wouldn't be fighting gods," Baldur said in his mild voice.

"We're all on the same side." Loki seemed to cover a snort at that remark, but he let it stand. My brother went on. "It's a giant we need to stop—a giant and the army he's raised of the undead."

"Zombies," the younger guy said. "Holy hell. They weren't just making that shit up."

"Yeah," the older guy said. "That's the stuff I'm talking about. I'm going to need to hear some more about how we go about fighting these… giants and undead and so on before I'm on board with bringing any of my people into this conflict."

Skadi grimaced. "Or you could just—"

"Come with me," I said quickly, before she could suggest they take off. I hadn't been planning on making the offer, but as soon as the words came out of my mouth, they felt right.

I was the champion of this realm, the protector of humankind. When was the last time I'd really talked to a human—someone fully human, not our summoned valkyries?

In the olden days, when I'd often adventured across this realm, sometimes with Loki at my side, I'd taken a human assistant more than once. There'd been something satisfying about watching them rise to the occasion. Humans had so much resilience in their short mortal lives.

I'd been a decent judge of human character back then. These three wanted to evaluate us, and I could evaluate them in turn. And if it looked like an alliance would work in both our favor, then who better to add to our forces?

The humans balked at my beckoning gesture, but after a moment's hesitation, the older guy, who seemed to be the leader of the three, headed toward me. The others fell into step behind him.

"Thor," Vidar said like a warning.

I shot him a look. "I can handle this. Midgard is my domain."

They couldn't argue with that fact. Ari hung back as I led the humans around to the field behind the building, probably figuring she needed to do a little more smoothing over and explaining before she had everyone's agreement. I suspected those instincts were right. At least I could take these three through the paces without constant skeptical commentary.

I stopped amid the overgrown grass where we couldn't see or hear the other gods anymore. The younger man and woman looked around, the guy toeing the rusted post that had fallen over. The older guy fixed his gaze on my face.

"Thor?" he said, half disbelieving, half… hopeful?

"That's me," I said with a smile, and offered him my hand, which dwarfed his lean one. He managed a firm enough shake all the same. "Pleased to make your acquaintance."

"Harrison," he said in return.

"You're *the* Thor?" the younger guy said, outright gawking now. "Like…"

"Thunder god, very strong, fond of bashing giants' skulls," I supplied. "Sorry you haven't seen much of me in a while. I've been distracted with other concerns—and, well, you've all seemed pretty caught up in your new modern world."

Harrison let out a sputter of a laugh. "I can't believe this," he said, shaking his head. "First Ari's got wings, and now I'm talking to a fucking Norse god."

"You are," I said. "And I've got my hammer and only a certain amount of patience." I lifted Mjolnir from its spot at my side, flipped it in my hand, and tossed it without even that much vigor toward the goal post still standing at the opposite end of the field.

The hammer gleamed through the air and smacked into the post with a metallic *thunk* that buckled the steel. The structure toppled over as my weapon flew back into my hand. I brushed its end against my pant leg and hung it back on my belt. "So let's be straight-forward with each other, all right?"

The younger guy's eyes had lit up. "I want to see what else you can do with that thing."

Harrison waved him quiet. There was something new in his

expression now, guarded but peeking through his internal defenses. I thought it was respect.

This might be one of the criminals from Ari's past, but I could see why she'd picked him to go to. I could already tell he wasn't a man who'd give his word lightly. If he signed on to our war, he'd see his end of the deal through all the way to the end.

"Tell me more about this giant and these zombies," he said.

I tipped my head. "The giant is the main problem—Surt. He uses fire magic, and he's strong. He's equipped his undead army with enhanced weapons and shields too. So, basically, a lot of trouble. But if we take him down, his army will fall apart." Possibly in a literal bodily way.

"And he's trying to destroy the whole world."

"He wants to claim Midgard—your realm here—for himself and anyone he likes," I said. "And he doesn't like humans particularly. After that first skirmish with some of your soldiers, he decided he'd rather annihilate the entire species than try to push you under his thumb. He'd have made quite a start of that effort if we hadn't caught him in time last night."

Harrison's jaw tightened, but he didn't look surprised. No matter how Ari had pitched his involvement to the other gods, he wasn't here just for the money. She must have made it clear to him it was about his very survival and that of the rest of the human race as well.

"Well, thank you for that save," he said. "Now, what exactly kind of weaponry would you be needing us to bring to the mix?"

I rubbed my hands together. Now we were talking.

"I'm not sure your average gun would do us a lot of good, but Surt really didn't like those—what are they called?—missiles that got launched at him..."

# 16

*Aria*

"This should get you off to a good start," Loki said, handing the wad of cash he'd retrieved to Harrison.

The gang commander made a show of rifling through the bills to confirm the amount, but his expression told me he was already sold. Whatever Thor had said to him and his lackeys, it had gotten through.

"I'll report back within twenty-four hours," he said, with a nod to me. I'd picked up a prepaid cell phone while I was in the city, since my old one had gone kaput with the rest of my former body. It felt weird carrying it on me now, but I needed some way to communicate with my former associates.

"I'll be waiting," I said.

The three of them got into their car and drove off. The second the SUV disappeared from view amid the trees down the road, Vidar swung his brawny body toward me. "Just to be clear, I still say you shouldn't have gone running off—especially to *humans*—

without putting the plan to us first. Exposing ourselves to mortals is a serious matter."

"Oh, please," I said. I'd already heard enough criticism in the last hour to last me a few centuries. "Without them, we all might be nothing more than nuclear waste in another day or two. What will it matter what they know then?"

"I'm not convinced a bunch of humans is going to make that much difference."

"It's not the humans so much as what they'll be carrying. You weren't there in Moscow." I motioned to the gods who had been there for that first battle in Midgard. "The missile really hurt Surt, didn't it? That's what sent him running."

"It's true," Thor said.

Even Skadi was nodding for once. "These advanced human weapons can have some impact. On the level of some elf-made contraptions." She cut her gaze toward me, just in case I'd thought she was letting me off easy. "But I agree with Vidar that you had no business arranging this without our input."

I gritted my teeth. "I had an idea. You were all sleeping. I went and got it done. We don't know how much time we have before Surt makes his next attempt."

"You can't make decisions for all of us as if you're in charge," Freyr said haughtily.

"Who *is* in charge?" I said, throwing my hands in the air. "Odin's been gone for days now. He didn't appoint anyone in his place, as far as I can tell. So we're muddling along together. I didn't make any decisions for you. I barely told them anything—nothing more than I had to for them to listen to me. You all had a chance to talk with them and discuss the idea. Can we move on?"

Freyr looked as if he were going to snap something back at me, but Freya caught her brother's arm. "Is this arguing really necessary?" she said, her voice sweet but firm. "Don't we have enough enemies right now without turning each other into them too?"

Freyr's gaze flicked briefly toward Loki. Baldur cleared his throat. He'd stood up with the others to greet Harrison and his people, but something in his face made my stomach knot. He looked as if he hadn't gotten enough sleep or as if something unpleasant were lingering in the back of his mind—a hint of shadow dimming his usual light.

He'd probably just worn himself out supporting Hod. His voice sounded clear and steady enough.

"Isn't the most important thing determining what Surt's next target might be?" he said. "We'd gotten started on that question when our visitors arrived."

Vidar grimaced, but he turned back to the map. "Bragi, you were going over that list you found on the… computer contraption. The largest power stations?"

As the other god mentioned the location of a nuclear plant, I stepped closer to Baldur. "How are you doing after last night?" I asked quietly.

He rested his hand on my shoulder and gave it a gentle squeeze. "I'm fine now that I've rested. Hod is still recovering. We set him up in one of the rooms inside where he wouldn't be disturbed. Containing and cooling that blast took a lot out of him."

"I could see that." I hoped the dark god hadn't strained himself too much. The thought of Hod in pain made my stomach clench even tighter. None of the other gods seemed all that concerned about him even though he'd just saved all our hides.

A black shape wheeled against the sky over our heads. I peered up at it. "It looks like the raven managed to find us again. I wonder what she's been up to." I hadn't seen Muninn since our mad dash from the park in Beijing to the nuclear plant.

"She might have observed something useful." Baldur raised his hand to beckon her down.

Muninn glided in another slow circle as if deciding whether to take that invitation and then swooped down to land beside us. A couple of the newer gods gave her a curious glance, but most of them were focused on Vidar and his marking of the map.

"You came a long way from where you'd planned," the raven said. "I couldn't find you until I saw a report about the disaster on the front of a newspaper."

"Well, if you weren't flying off to do your own thing all the time, you'd have been with us when we left," I reminded her. "Where did you go?"

"I was checking the other gates I'm aware of between Midgard and the other realms." The corners of her mouth creased with a frown. "Surt must realize we can sense when he's brought down his bridge. I worried he might start to diversify his strategies."

I hadn't thought of that. "Did you see anything that looked like a problem?" I asked.

"Not exactly. There were a couple of jotun who had come through their gate into Midgard, but they weren't disturbing anyone. They were acting more like tourists. I didn't like that they'd come here at all, though. The fewer giants, the better."

"Absolutely." A chill trickled through me. "One giant is more than enough."

"I'd prefer none," Muninn muttered, with a ruffle of her dress.

Vidar stepped back from the map, dropping the pen beside it. He rubbed his jaw. "All right," he said. "These are all the largest nuclear power stations in Midgard." His marks were spread out across the map. "I'm not sure how we can predict which one Surt will target. Has there been any pattern to his targets so far?"

"I can't think of any," Thor said. "But we've got no reason to think he'll stay near here."

"He attacked a large city the first time," Freya put in. "And the plant last night isn't far from another one. He appears to be aiming for maximum destruction. Does that help narrow it down?"

Vidar squinted at the map. "We could eliminate a few possibilities, but not many."

"Who's to say he'll follow the same logic that we are at all?" one of the other goddesses put in. "Would Surt even know how to find out which sites are the most powerful? He might be going by some other measure completely."

That was true. It'd hardly looked as if Surt's fortress in Muspelheim had been set up with internet access. Even the gods who'd been living here among humans for the better part of a few centuries looked at Bragi's laptop as if it were some kind of alien device. Where would the giant be getting his information—and how skewed would it be?

"Wherever he decides to attack next, it took him a long time to get the meltdown going yesterday," I said. "And he can't make us fly much farther than we had to then, considering we crossed half the world to get here."

Njord crossed his arms with a dark expression. "He'll have learned from that first attempt. We can't count on having anywhere near as much time when he strikes again."

Muninn eased forward to peer at the map. "And if he succeeds with this nuclear detonation he wants, what will be the result?" she asked me.

"Millions dead," I said. "Maybe more, depending on how big he can amp the explosion up. Not even bodies left, anyone who's close by—just ash. It'd be awful."

Her chin set. She stepped right into the middle of the crowd.

"I can go," she said. "To Asgard. I should be able to make it from here to Muspelheim and from there to Yggdrasil. I'm small and quick. I'll make sure the guards don't see me, and I'll listen in on Surt's planning."

The tension coiled through her body showed she wasn't making this offer lightly. She was putting her own life on the line.

Skadi gave the raven woman a narrow look. "Weren't you involved in helping Surt capture Odin in the first place?"

"That's right," Njord said. "How do we know you won't fall in with him again or lead *us* into a trap?"

"I made my peace with Odin," Muninn said. "That should be good enough for any of you. If I'd known Surt was going to carry out a plan like this, I wouldn't have helped him in the first place, no matter how angry I was."

"Easy to say that now," Freyr muttered.

"Hey," I said. "I've got as much or more reason to be wary of Muninn as anyone here. I had to live through her torture. But I believe she wants to help now. We could be so much better prepared if she can spy on Surt."

Vidar gave me a look that seemed to say my opinion wasn't worth any more than Muninn's was, but Thor spoke up then. "I'd say the same. Muninn has proven her allegiances. She made her original contract with Surt to save her life, not because she agreed with him. As I understand it, Odin was the one who forced her to put her life at risk in the first place. We can't judge from that situation."

"The wrongdoings of others are not always as they seem," Loki said with a crooked smile. "I say we let her go and see what comes of it."

The others glanced around at each other. I sensed another argument on the horizon. Then a low dry voice swept into our midst.

"I'll support the raven's suggestion."

We all jerked around. Odin had arrived in the yard as we'd been talking. His head was bowed a little lower than usual, his charred hat looking particularly depressed. Grit clung to his traveling cloak. But his grip on his spear was firm and his single eye glinted at us from beneath his hat's brim.

"Father!" Baldur said, rushing to Odin's side.

"I'm all right," the Allfather said, briskly but not unkindly. "I went looking, and pieces have come to me, but it seemed time to rejoin you all." His gaze slid over the assembled gods. "There are more of you here than there were before. It has been too long. I wish we were having a less fraught reunion."

Heimdall let out a rough chuckle but didn't say anything. Some of the other gods bobbed their heads in acknowledgment. Odin turned his attention to Muninn.

"Fly, dear raven," he said. "Be our eyes and ears where we cannot see or hear. And thank you."

Muninn gave him a flicker of a smile and contracted into her bird form. In an instant, she was flitting off through the air.

"You said you found 'pieces'," Thor said, approaching his father. "Pieces of the answer? What came to you?"

Odin sighed, planting the end of his spear on the ground in front of him. "The visions never come easily. I must see what I can and make what I can of that. What I sensed, from my walking…" He closed his eye. "The light of day can burn before a fire. But only the highest water can put out all the flames."

Ah. So, super useful advice then. I managed not to sputter a giggle, but it was a near thing.

"Excellent," Loki said. "Let us hope the rest of the pieces to make sense of that foresight find us sooner rather than later."

No one else seemed to know what to say about Odin's prophesying. Maybe that was for the best. With a sharp breath, Vidar turned back to the map.

"Whatever happens, wherever Surt appears, it'd be good to have as many Asgardians gathered to fight him as we can," he said. "Can we reach out to any of the others?"

Heimdall stirred where he'd been standing on the fringes. "I may have ideas for a couple. And I also—I was given to understand that through me we might bring the battle back to Surt instead of waiting around for him here. It seems like it's time I attempted to stretch my powers, perhaps in coordination with a few of you, the way Thor and the others have found their synchronicity around the valkyrie." He glanced at the thunder god rather than me. "If you could demonstrate—I haven't yet gotten to see how your powers merge in action."

Thor perked up at the prospect of getting to play out at least a fake battle and deflated a moment later. "We can't," he said. "Not without Hod. I don't think we should rouse him yet."

"Ah. Well… why don't you come along, then, and talk me through it, and—Skadi, your skills might be of use, and Njord, and Idunn."

The gods he'd called meandered away from the group with him. Loki had drifted away too, so stealthily I hadn't noticed him leaving.

Freya bent over the map again, and Odin moved to join her. Bragi turned back to his computer. Vidar dashed after Heimdall. "Before you get started—you mentioned there might be others you could point us too."

I rubbed my arms, my skin creeping with an uncomfortable sensation. Our group had gotten bigger, but it felt so scattered now. Not like a bunch of people with the same goal working together. How were we going to stop Surt if we were running off in every direction, arguing over every offer of help?

I didn't want to just stand here with those thoughts, and it was obvious no one out here had much use for me. I touched the phone in my pocket to confirm it was still there and turned toward the house. "I'll check on Hod."

# 17

*Aria*

Just past the school building's main entrance, I spotted a stack of bags in the room that had once been the front office. Someone had bought us a new stash of food. When Hod woke up, he'd probably need all the nourishment he could get.

I went over and crouched down to paw through the bags for whatever looked at least somewhat substantial. After a few minutes, I'd come up with a loaf of bread, a jar of peanut butter and a knife for spreading it, and a couple cartons of grape juice, which seemed like a safer bet for a god on the mend than the bottles of wine that had dominated the beverage selection. Doctors had people drink juice after they gave blood. Maybe the same principle would work for divine beings who'd given a whole bunch of their energy to saving the world.

I hadn't known for sure which room the gods had set up Hod in, but I didn't need to spend much time searching. Voices traveled down the hall from a door standing ajar about halfway down. I knew before I reached it that I'd found my trickster too.

"So that's the long and the short of it," Loki was saying in his languid voice. "Since half of those dopes forget that anything exists beyond what they can see in front of them, I thought I'd better take it upon myself to see if you had any suggestions to make about our current activities."

"I can't say I'm thrilled about the raven going off to Surt, but if the others felt she was genuine..." Hod spoke with a faint rasp, his tone wary but not hostile. I couldn't remember if I'd ever seen the two of them talking one-on-one at all before. For most of the time I'd known the dark god and the trickster, their conversations had mainly consisted of sniping at each other. I guessed they were actually coming to terms with the horrors of their shared past and the revelations of the last few weeks.

"I'm not sure there's anything else I can offer," Hod went on. "Other than we'd better catch Surt quickly if he tries that tactic again. There was so much power in that blast." His voice trailed off again as I slipped past the door.

Sunlight was streaming from a single large window into the classroom-sized space on the other side. It left patches of brightness on the white walls and floor. The other gods had set Hod up on a real bed—well, maybe it was more of a cot—with a folded blanket as a pillow and another tucked over his trim frame. Loki was leaning against the empty bookcase near the door. He gave me a nod. He'd probably heard me coming from the moment I walked into the building.

From the looks of it, this room must have been the school nurse's office. Appropriate for its current use.

Hod had propped his shoulders up on the makeshift pillow at the head of the bed, positioning himself halfway between lying down and sitting. He turned his head toward me at the squeak of my sneakers on the old linoleum.

Had his face gotten thinner since yesterday? The shadows beneath his high cheekbones looked starker, or maybe that was just my imagination, seeing him laid up like that. His short black hair was sticking up at various angles exactly like it would on any normal person who'd just been sleeping for hours. My fingers itched to smooth over it, to touch his pale cheek.

"Ari?" he said, only slightly a question. I guessed any of the gods would have had significantly heavier footsteps.

"I thought you might be hungry," I said. "Or thirsty. I brought a few things… How are you feeling?"

"Better," Hod said, pushing himself higher on the bed. A small smile touched his face, softening the hollows that had worried me a moment ago. "I've already eaten—someone left a plate for me to find when I woke up."

I noticed the plate in question and a nearly drained water bottle on the little table at the side of the bed. My cargo felt suddenly awkward in my hands. I went over and set the bread and the rest on the floor beside the table. "Well, if you get hungry again later…"

"Thank you."

I stood there for a few seconds, torn between a longing to wrap him in a hug and nervousness that I might hurt him somehow if I so much as touched him. A furrow formed in Hod's brow. He reached out to me and slid his fingers lightly around my arm.

"Hey," he said. "I'm sorry I snapped at you last night. I wasn't angry at you or anything like that—it was just such an overwhelming situation—"

Was he worrying about that? A lump rose in my throat. I eased my arm up to take his hand and sat down carefully on the edge of the bed. "I know. Of course you were on edge. What you did was amazing. I'm just sorry if I made it at all harder."

He let out a dismissive snort. "Not possible. Come here, then, valkyrie. Shouldn't temporary invalid status earn me a little coddling?"

My heart swelled. I leaned into his embrace, tucking my head against his shoulder, hugging him as tightly as I dared. His body still held all the lean strength I was used to and that familiar salty smoky smell.

He was okay. He was really okay.

The lump in my throat rose even higher, and tears formed behind my closed eyelids. I willed them back. I'd done enough crying in front of Hod for a lifetime, and the last thing he needed right now was even more reasons to worry about me.

I wouldn't let myself think about what would happen if Surt struck again before Hod had fully recuperated. Wouldn't let myself think about how another blast might seep through his shadows and sear him away from me. He was here now, solid and real. I had to focus on that fact.

"I'm glad you're all right," I murmured. "And I meant it—the way you stopped that blast and neutralized it was absolutely fucking amazing. We'd all have been fried if it wasn't for you. You can have all the coddling you want."

He chuckled, leaning in to kiss my temple. "I'm sure it won't go to my head. I should be back on my feet in an hour or two, and everyone can go back to not bothering to consult with me right in front of me instead of at a distance."

"I personally think most of the gods in that bunch have very bad taste in who they listen to," Loki said. "I supposed we should have expected as much, given that they gave up our excellent company for so long."

"We need them," Hod said. But even though his tone before had been wry, his muscles had tensed as he'd spoken. He'd told me before how the gods had treated him after Ragnarok: mostly avoiding him, only coming to him when they had a distasteful task he could handle that they barely wanted to acknowledge. And even before, everyone had always looked to Baldur the bright one over him.

Thinking back over the last few days, I couldn't remember

anyone seeking out his opinions. He'd been sidelined almost as much as I had.

Hod's fingertips caressed down my back, warm through the thin silk of my tank top. An eager tingle ran through me at his touch. Suddenly I was remembering how Thor had reminded me how much I mattered to at least a few of the gods here when I'd been feeling out of sorts. That was exactly the sort of generosity I was more than happy to pass on.

I eased back and set my hand against Hod's face. "They need *you*," I said, "even if they're too stuck-up to admit it. *I* need you. Would you like me to demonstrate how much?"

He pushed himself forward as I leaned in, catching my mouth an instant before I'd meant my lips to brush his. My pulse skipped. His arm looped tighter around my waist and his other hand was teasing into my hair, and just like that, his kiss felt as necessary as air.

I cupped his jaw and kissed him harder. Hod pulled me onto his lap, parting my lips with his tongue. His thumb eased up my side to trace the underside of my breast, and a pleased murmur escaped me.

Loki cleared his throat. "Well, seeing as *I'm* hardly needed here any longer, I'll leave you to your recovery."

The amused lilt of his voice washed over me like a caress in itself. I couldn't suppress the shiver of longing that passed through me at the thought of that second pair of sly hands moving over my body in tandem with Hod's.

Hod stilled beneath me. He pulled back with one last brush of his lips against mine and said, "You don't have to leave."

My heart hiccupped. I glanced over my shoulder. Loki had frozen with his hand on the door, staring back at us.

"What are you saying?" he asked in a measured tone.

Hod's thumb stroked higher on my breast, just below the peak. I couldn't help pressing into his touch, encouraging it to continue its climb. His blind gaze was fixed on my face, but his expression was relaxed. Almost pleased.

"I'm saying our valkyrie could be enjoying this moment even more if you wanted to contribute."

"Hod," I said, choking up. Forgetting his hand and its tempting ascent, I bent my head so my forehead grazed his. "You're enough."

"I know," he said, so easily I believed him. "But why stop there? You think I don't want to hear how you could gasp a little sharper, feel how you could tremble a little harder?"

I did tremble then, with a wave of emotion that was a lot more than just lust.

"Fuck," Loki murmured, with a click as he kicked shut the door. He crossed the room like a blazing wind. Hod tugged my mouth back to his, palming my breast, and the trickster leaned over me, pressing a kiss to my spine through my top as his hand came to rest on my hip. Every nerve in my body lit up with the promise of what was to come.

All that emotion still pulsed in my chest, even as I whimpered at the swivel of Hod's fingers across my nipple. That was how much I meant to him—so much that he got more from my increased pleasure than he lost by sharing this interlude with a companion he'd only just made a tentative peace with after centuries of animosity.

That was how well he knew me, that he could read my desires in an instant.

Loki stroked my hip as he drew up my shirt, kissing bare skin now. Every press of his lips came with a flicker of fiery heat. A softly cool sensation I recognized as Hod's shadows licked over my belly. Without breaking our kiss, I shifted my legs to straddle him. A different sort of need rose up inside me with a pinch of pain. He'd told me, shown me, over and over, how much I meant to him. But he might not realize he meant just as much to me.

In another minute, I'd be too lost in bliss to find the words. Or too lost for him to believe them. My throat tightened. I raised my head just slightly, my nose resting against Hod's, gazing into his dark green eyes that knew exactly where to find mine even if he couldn't have told me their color or their shape. My beautiful haunted dark god.

"I love you," I said. It came out in a whisper, buried under the rush of emotion that had propelled the words out, but he heard me. His lips parted with a startled breath.

Loki hesitated between kisses, his fingers halting with a jerk against my thigh. Did it bother him that I'd said it—that I'd said it to Hod? We'd made kind of a deal, the trickster and me, of no commitments and no grand declarations, and it wasn't as if he'd ever broken from that.

His reaction only lasted a second, and then he lowered his mouth to my back again as if nothing had changed. Hod trailed his fingers down the side of my face and skimmed my lips with his thumb.

"I love you too," he said hoarsely.

Our lips collided as if pulled together by an unstoppable force, and maybe that wasn't entirely untrue. A giddy tingling rushed through my chest, as if holding in that short statement had bottled up this huge anxious space inside me that was now opened up.

I loved him. I did. I loved all of them, didn't I? Loki and his quick humor covering the wounds that ran deep, Thor with his mix of gentleness and ferocity, Baldur and the harmony he could summon from just about anything. But right now I wanted to pour all that feeling into the god beneath me. He gave so much to all of us.

My mouth slipped to Hod's jaw. I kissed a path down his throat as I tugged the blanket away from between us. Loki unclasped my bra, Hod drew my top up over my head, and then the trickster was tracing my ribs with sizzles of flame while the dark god fondled my breasts. I almost forgot where I was going. But only almost.

I scooted farther down the bed and grasped the fly of Hod's jeans. He inhaled sharply. "Ari..."

"Lie back," I said, and licked up the trace of salt at the base of his belly. "Relax. You think I don't want to feel *you* enjoy the moment? I'm pretty sure you're still supposed to be resting. I can take care of you."

I swept my palm over the bulge of his erection, and he groaned. His body loosened, his hand coming to rest on my head. His fingers laced through the strands of my hair to caress my scalp as I yanked the zipper down.

His cock sprang free from his boxers with barely any encouragement needed from me. I nuzzled its silky firmness with a flick of my tongue, smiling at the way it twitched at my attentions. All Hod managed at that was a strangled sound. I swiped my tongue all up his pale length to the head and took him right into my mouth.

The sharp smokiness of him filled my mouth. His fingers tightened against my head. He bucked up with a ragged breath as I took him deeper. I worked him over carefully, gripping the base of his cock, applying the pressure of my tongue here, a teasing of teeth there, exploring. Discovering what I could do to make this man come completely undone in the most enjoyable possible way.

Loki had adjusted his position when I had. Now he leaned over me, gliding his hands up over my torso to cup the breasts Hod had relinquished. His thumbs darted over my nipples with flares of heat that sent a ripple of pleasure through me. He kissed my shoulder, the crook of my neck, and murmured with a scorching breath by my ear, "Oh, my valkyrie, you are glorious when you take control."

His voice provoked the same eager shiver it had before. I bobbed my head over Hod's cock, sucking hard, and he rocked to meet me, while the trickster sent his blissful flames licking down over my skin.

A whisper like cool velvet brushed my belly, and I knew Hod's shadows had rejoined Loki's flames. As I swiveled my tongue around what seemed to be the most sensitive spot on his cock, that shadowy sensation slipped lower. Under my jeans and my panties, tickling my clit with just enough pressure to make me whimper, and then nudging against my sex. All at once it felt like a solid thing probing my folds, as hard and taut as the cock in my mouth.

I couldn't hold back a gasp. Hod's hand stilled against my hair.

"Too much?" he rasped.

"No," I mumbled. "Fuck. Don't stop."

His next breath had the shape of a smile. That corded length of shadow pressed into me, stretching me, hitting every hungry place inside me. A needy sigh slipped from my lips. I arched to urge Hod's magic deeper and eased down over him again.

Loki chuckled with another wash of flickering heat. He ran his hands back down to my hips and tucked one between my thighs to massage the tingling bud at my core. Hod's shadowy instrument drove into me again and again, and Loki's flames laved over my clit.

With each plunge of that solid darkness inside me, it found new points of pleasure. I moaned over his cock, rocking instinctively with the rhythm he'd set. Bliss rang all through my body.

Hod's magic thrust harder. I started to shake. I was so close to that edge, but I meant to bring the dark god with me.

I pumped my hand over his now-slick cock, caressing my lips over the head in time with my movements. Hod's hips jerked. "Ari," he said, clenching my hair.

The salty spurt of his release flooded my mouth. His shadow bucked into me at a pace to match the stuttering of his breath. Loki bit down on my bare side, and I came with a lurch of my heart, feeling as if the rush of ecstasy would toss me head over heels. I clutched Hod's thighs as I cried out. My arms and legs gave, and I sagged down over him.

Hod tugged my shoulder and eased me up to cuddle against his still clothed but heated chest. I raised my head, and he met me with a kiss. It carried on and on until my heart ached with all the love I hadn't found more words for yet.

But I'd said the most important part. No matter what happened next, he knew.

Loki hunkered down next to the cot. My hand reached out of its own accord to trail over his neck and come to rest on his shoulder. He set his own hand over it.

"I never thought I'd be learning new tricks from you, Dark One," he said, sounding amused. "I'll have to put my own spin on that technique sometime."

I started to tense in anticipation of Hod's reaction, but the dark god just laughed. He kissed my forehead. "I have excellent inspiration to experiment. Perhaps sometime we should make a combined effort of it, if our valkyrie would like that. Our powers do seem to reach extra heights in combination."

"Mmmm," Loki hummed in what sounded like agreement, sending the ache in my chest straight to my core.

"Your valkyrie gives that plan two thumbs up," I said.

Hod laughed again and ducked his head next to mine. Loki's thumb traced a soft pattern over my knuckles. We relaxed there for a while, the last three any of the other gods would have bothered to come looking for, the three they didn't entirely want around. Right then, that antipathy didn't feel like an insult. It felt like its own little realm of freedom.

A shout of excitement filtered through the wall from outside. Loki sighed. "I suppose at some point we should see what the others have gotten themselves wrapped up in now."

He let go of my hand and started to stand. I eased myself up over Hod just in time to see the trickster freeze with one hand on the side of the bed, his back still bent. Hod's head snapped up.

"Surt?" he said.

"The bloody bastard," Loki muttered. "I don't think he's far this time. Let's see if we can melt *him* down first."

# 18

*Hod*

I'd jerked my clothes into place and was just swinging my legs over the side of the bed when Ari caught my arm. The trickster had already dashed out of the room.

"Are you sure you should come?" Ari said. "You already pushed yourself so hard last night—you weren't even planning on walking for a while yet."

If my sense of my body still felt a tad off-kilter, it was hard to say whether I could blame that on last night's efforts or the way Ari had just set me alight with pleasure. I touched her face, pulling her close enough that I could feel her breath.

"I know my limitations. The Trickster says it isn't far. And you were right. You—all of you—might need me again."

That, and there was no way in the nine realms I was letting her race off to battle Surt while I lounged around back here, especially not after the intimacy we'd just shared.

"Okay," she said quietly, in almost the same voice she'd used to tell me she loved me. The memory gave me a fresh thrill in spite of everything. It couldn't have been easy for her to say that, but she had, for me.

She slipped her fingers along my jaw to kiss me quickly, and then we hustled into the hall together.

"Let's go, let's go!" Thor was bellowing outside. I guessed Loki had passed on word first to his old adventuring companion. If there was anyone here the other gods were likely to rally around when it came to fighting giants, it was my older brother.

I'd used a strand of shadow to feel out any obstacles in the hall. The second we'd burst out the door, Ari unleashed her wings with a feathery hiss and I stretched my shadow into my usual ride. Up in the air, over this unfamiliar terrain, all I had to do was keep track of the others and assume they were going in the right direction.

It must have been around the middle of the afternoon. The sun beamed hot against the right side of my face as we set off in a direction I knew instinctively was south. The brisk wind raised by our flight cut through the worst of the summer heat. Some of the others were still shouting back and forth, debating strategy, but I tuned out everything except the rustling with each flap of Ari's wings and the faint murmur of Loki's enchanted shoes pushing off through the air.

He knew where we were going, and I knew there was only one strategy I'd need when we got there. If Surt was aiming to spark a second nuclear explosion, I'd just have to smother it with another wave of shadow.

Maybe if we got there earlier in the process this time, it wouldn't require every shred of strength I had in me.

It didn't exactly take a lot of physical effort to fly like this. All I had to do was stay balanced on the relatively wide strip of shadow. But within several minutes, a prickling sensation formed around my bent knees and my hips, the base of my neck, my hands braced against my conveyance.

All right, so I hadn't fully recovered my strength yet. It wouldn't matter if we reached Surt soon enough. Whatever he was doing now, I'd give everything I had to stop him.

I shifted my weight, adjusting my position by increments as new aches formed. The miles fell away beneath us.

"There," Loki said. The faint crackling of the flaming bridge reached my ears. The trickster sped forward even faster, and I pushed my shadow to follow with a thump of my pulse. Then Loki halted abruptly. The crackle vanished.

The Sly One let out a huff as I drew up nearby. "He's already gone. What in Hel's name was he doing *here*?"

I couldn't sense any explosive energy in the air, not even a hint of it on the verge of bursting. Our valkyrie glided over to join me. "It looks like a residential neighborhood," she said. "Some suburb —all wide streets lined with houses with big lawns. Nice place to live." Her tone was a bit dry. "No power plants. Nothing else destructive. Weird."

"We have to find exactly where he touched down," Loki was muttering. He edged forward again, one extended stride and then another. The rest of us moved after him.

"There's the mark!" Heimdall called, with more energy than I'd heard from him since he'd first arrived. Maybe he just liked that he'd beat the Trickster to our goal. "That yard is scorched from the bridge. He came down there."

I followed the others down to earth, noting the whispering leaves of a tree—birch, from the smell of it—and the sun-baked patio stones my feet landed on. Another impression, not quite a smell, not quite a feeling, quivered through my senses. It tugged at the deepest darkness inside me.

"Someone's died here," I said. "Recently. The body—" I gestured in the direction that quavering chill emanated from.

"I've found him," Freya said. Her voice was tight. "A dark elf. His throat's been burned through. But it looks like he was beat up plenty before the kill. He's got marks all over him—he's missing a couple of fingers—I think his knee is crushed."

"Surt tortured him," Thor said in a fierce rumble. "He must have needed the elf to tell him something or do something for him that he wasn't getting any other way. This house doesn't belong to the dirt-eaters, though, does it?"

We treaded cautiously around the building. A fresh quivering reached me from a different direction. I gritted my teeth. "The elf isn't the only one dead."

Broken glass crunched under our feet. We stepped through what I gathered was the shattered remains of a sliding door into the house. More glass rasped against the hardwood floor. My shadows helped me skirt a piano and an armchair. I stopped at an open door.

"That's the woman in the photos there," Baldur said softly. "This must be her home."

A few of the gods brushed past me to examine the body.

"She had a Ph.D. in nuclear engineering," Ari said. "Assuming that's her name on the certificate."

"Surt was trying to get an edge," Vidar muttered. "I wonder what information he got out of her."

I eased into the room, staying close to the walls. Whatever Surt had done to the woman, my powers were no use here. I could take life, but I couldn't offer it. There was nothing I could do for someone who'd already succumbed to the final darkness.

My hands encountered wooden shelves. Shelves full of books. I skimmed my fingers over the spines—most of them arced and creased, suggesting they'd been read fairly thoroughly.

I reached to pull one volume out and hesitated with my hand poised. That's exactly what the others would expect of me, wasn't it? Hod the dark loner, going straight to the books. I could remember the bemused murmurs as I'd added to my collection of texts in my hall with volumes gathered on earth. *Where does he think all that human rambling is going to get him?*

But it was human ramblings that had produced the inspirations to create the technology that had nearly destroyed *us* last night. It was human ramblings Surt had come here to learn about, presumably. Humans took the time to think about a lot of subjects the gods never bothered with, which did them credit.

What did I care what anyone here thought of me? No one that mattered to me would scoff. I wanted to know more about the woman Surt had killed, and what was on her shelves would tell me as clearly as anything.

I pulled out the book I'd already started to grasp and flipped it open to the first page. With a flick of my fingers, my magic darted across the paper, whispering the printed words into my ear.

It was a physics text, something about thermodynamics. Nothing very enlightening there. I picked another at random and another—a volume on organic chemistry and a memoir of a political figure I'd never heard of—and then I explored the shelves more thoughtfully. Which books here had held the most meaning for this woman?

"I can't get into her computer," Bragi was saying. "It's password protected."

"None of the papers on her desk look like anything Surt would have been interested in," Freyr said. "Just bills and ordinary things."

My fingers found a leather cover, stiff with age but solid and uncracked as though a lot of care had been taken with it. Hmm. I eased it out and opened it.

The first whisper that wound through my ear was an inscription. "To Dr. Carmen, Because you brightened our days and helped keep our boys safe. General Yancy & Sergeant Ramirez."

I stilled my fingers. "Are there any signs about the work she did?"

"Nuclear engineering, obviously," Freyr said.

"No, I mean who she worked *for*." I set down the book, cover open, on the desk. "I think she might have been a military scientist."

Someone snatched up the book less gently than I suspected Dr. Carmen would have approved of if she'd been alive to mind. Hinges squeaked, and the contents of desk drawers clinked. Ari came over to the shelves next to me.

"There's a plaque here," she said. "Some kind of commendation, it says. It looks like a military thing."

"We can't make too many assumptions from just those two things," Njord said, but he sounded doubtful of his own words.

"Oh, I don't know," Loki said, a thread of uneasiness running through his smooth voice. "I think we can put together a pretty convincing picture from what we've got. Surt wasn't content with the blast a power plant could offer. He's looking to get his hands on a bomb or two now."

My stomach flipped over. "Some of the bombs humans have developed—they have enough power to essentially end the world in one shot."

And there was no way I'd ever be able to contain that much fiery rage.

---

While the others gathered outside the building we'd taken shelter in to concoct some sort of dinner, I lingered in the invalid room they'd given me before, paging through one of the books I'd borrowed from Dr. Carmen's study. I figured she wouldn't mind. She probably had friends and family still living who she'd have been happy to know her personal library had helped save.

If we were going to save them at all. So far what I was reading was only confirming my worst fears.

Weapons weren't exactly my topic of choice when it came to

scientific treatises. I had enough death in my life as it was. So my standing knowledge of nuclear explosives was relatively limited. After I'd made my claim in Dr. Carmen's study, the other gods, even Thor, had laughed off the idea that humans could have constructed any weapon quite as destructive as I'd said. Loki's reminders not to underestimate humankind had been waved off as well.

It was true, though. The most powerful bombs humans had built could essentially wipe out all life on this realm. Maybe not all at once, but once the aftereffects spread…

I raised my fingers from the page and shut the book. I was already feeling queasy.

My renewed understanding had at least given me a shred of hope as well. I got up from the bed and headed down the hall, feeling for a familiar presence that was bright even to me. I'd always been able to pick my twin out of a crowd.

To my surprise, I didn't find him with the crowd this time. He'd wandered off a short ways into the field behind the building. It was a cool night coming on, and his innate warmth bled out into the air as if he were a miniature sun himself.

"Hod," he said, moving toward me before I'd reached him. "What is it? Did you find something?"

He'd helped me carry some of those books.

"Nothing that gives us any less reason to worry," I said. "If Surt manages to get his hands on those missiles or bombs, even one of them… Humanity may very well be doomed."

I didn't think my twin could help himself from looking at the bright side. "We don't know for sure that Surt even knew about the scientist's military connections. It could just be a coincidence, and he was looking for information on more effectively using the plants for his purposes."

Which would hardly be a good thing either, but I didn't think either of us wanted to count on it.

"Maybe," I said. "But without knowing, we have to be prepared for the worst. And I think… I think you'd be the key to stopping him, if it comes to that."

I felt the movement of air as Baldur's head jerked up. "*Me*?" he said. "You're the one who tamped down on that energy with your darkness before."

"I know," I said. "But it was hard enough at the power plant. With an actual bomb… I wouldn't stand a chance, Baldur. I can admit that."

"And you think I would?"

My mouth twisted as I said the only thing I could that was true. "I think if Surt detonates one of those bombs, we're all cinders. But their impact relies on a chain reaction that requires all the parts to be in just the right state. You could use your powers to melt down the elements inside—slowly—fusing them together. Even if you only managed to get to a small portion in time, it might be enough to stop the reaction and the deadliest part of the explosion completely."

"I don't know," Baldur said. "If it's not— Let me think about it."

He turned away from me. His voice had gone short. He was clamming up—maybe not into the dreamy haze he'd spent so much time in since we'd been reborn, but retreating from me all the same.

My instinct was to retreat in turn. There'd been a long time when I'd backed away from any uncomfortable topic between us. Whatever I could do to keep the darkness away from his light.

But he'd had darkness in him all along anyway. Darkness I could have helped him grapple with sooner if I'd let those conversations happen. I dragged in a breath and stood my ground.

"What's wrong, brother?" I said. "Tell me about it even if you don't want to talk to them." I tipped my head toward the gods gathered near the parking lot.

Baldur was silent a moment longer. He rubbed his smooth jaw. "I… Last night. When we reached the power station. I felt the explosion about to happen, and I tried to interfere, but my light—it only made the effect stronger. It *fed* the explosion. My power, the brightness in me, it was almost the same as that… that energy that almost killed us all. The energy you're talking about that could bring the entire realm to ruin in a matter of minutes."

"Light has always been able to burn," I said. "We'd enjoy the sun a lot less if we were standing right next to it."

"I know," Baldur said. "I just never thought I had that side of it in me." A brief laugh hitched out of him. "I was so worried about the darkness I'd absorbed, when really it's the affinity that's most a part of me that the rest of you should be frightened of."

"Hey." I clapped my twin on the shoulder, my gut clenching at the horror in his words. Horror at *himself* of all people. "No one's going to be frightened of you, because we know you control that power. You use it to bring life, not to take it away. You accidentally encouraged the explosion because you didn't know what to expect. Now you do know."

"And you want me to meddle with any bombs Surt collects."

Ah. I could see now why he'd balked. "Before the explosion is set off," I said. "To fuse them, under your control. Using your energy to act on the components before Surt can use them for his ends."

"If it really is that simple," Baldur said.

"I think it is," I said. "I think it's the best chance we'd have if we're faced with that situation. Better to take that risk than to know for sure he's going to annihilate us, right?"

Baldur's shoulders rose and fell with a long breath. His posture started to straighten. "How do you do it?" he asked, his voice a little less strained now. "Keep going, knowing there's something deadly inside you? Something that's what makes you *you*."

"I haven't had much choice," I said frankly. "I… I serve a purpose. I bring balance. As much as I can, I use my power to take away pain rather than to deal it out. We all have to make choices like that."

"I suppose that's what makes us gods," Baldur said. He let out another laugh, looser this time. "Thank you—for listening. And for the plan. I'll be prepared, if it comes to that."

He moved to amble over to the others, slowly enough that I could tell he expected—and wanted—me to join him. I fell into step beside him.

With our home stolen and Surt posing threats we'd never had to consider, maybe all of us Asgardians had been feeling a little adrift. A little apart from our comrades. But the darkness in those gaps between us didn't need to be empty. I could fill it with something more.

# 19

*Aria*

The ring of the phone brought me flailing out of my sleeping bag, my heart thudding and my eyes bleary from a night that had involved more waiting in tensed anticipation for a call to arms than actual rest. It took my panicking body a second to remember that if Loki had sensed Surt's arrival in this world, he wouldn't have been telling me over the phone.

I'd only given this number to one person. My pulse started to thump all over again as I fumbled for the answer button.

"Harrison?" I said, blinking myself into sharper alertness.

"There you are, Ari," the gang commander replied. "I was starting to think you'd gone and ascended to the heavens or something."

I made a face. "I answered as fast as I could. What's the news?"

"We got it."

I sat up straighter, my fingers tightening around the phone. "All of it?"

"Everything your people said they wanted. The cash was more

than enough to cover the equipment. Maybe I should consider switching bosses." His tone was dryly amused.

"I don't think 'my people' are going to be hiring after the whole saving the world thing is over with," I said. "But that's great. Can you get the whole arsenal out here, along with enough people to handle it, ASAP?"

"I figured that'd be the next step," Harrison said. "I'm just rounding up our little army right now. Unless we run into an unexpected hiccup, we'll be seeing you in a few hours."

"Perfect," I said. "Same spot as before. And thank you."

"Hey, I'm raking in dough and saving my own hide at the same time. Generosity didn't even figure into the equation. Hang tight or whatever valkyries do until I get there."

From the light streaming through the narrow window, my restless sleep had ended with me sleeping in. I'd kept my regular clothes on in case of a late-night emergency, so I jogged straight into the hall, running my fingers through the tangled waves of my hair as I went. The rooms I passed where the other gods had been sleeping were empty.

Heimdall was in the front office where we'd been stashing our food, poking at the offerings with a dissatisfied expression. No, I wasn't telling him the news first. Better to start with the gods who'd actually be happy about it. They could discuss it with the others. It wasn't as if most of the other gods gave me the time of day in the first place.

Thor and Baldur were standing not far from each other in a cluster of gods talking together in the yard outside. I caught Thor's eye and jerked my chin to the side. He tipped his head and grasped his brother's shoulder. I spotted Hod sitting with his back against the worn bricks down near the back of the school, his fingers skimming over the pages of a book he was vaguely staring at. Thor and Baldur followed me over there.

"Hey," I said as I reached Hod and the other two caught up.

"Has anyone seen Loki?" It made me edgy all over again not seeing him around. I couldn't imagine him going far when he was our only way of tracking Surt's movements, though. Last night we'd had a brief scare when he'd sensed Surt's fiery magic, but we'd only just set off when the impression had vanished again.

The giant couldn't have gotten much done in the ten or so minutes he'd been in Midgard, but he'd been doing *something*, and the fact that we didn't know what gnawed at me.

Before anyone had a chance to answer, the trickster himself slipped into view from behind the building. "You called?" he said with his sly grin, but the good humor in it didn't quite reach his amber eyes. He was wound tight too. "Good to see you're finally out of bed, pixie."

"Not that you can really call it a 'bed'," I muttered. "I had a call from Harrison. He's gotten the weapons together, and now he's just rounding up his people. They're aiming to get out here in a few hours."

Thor's face brightened. "Rocket launchers and machine guns?"

Loki chuckled. "Are you considering trading in Mjolnir, old friend?"

"Of course not." The thunder god patted his ever-present hammer affectionately. "But I can't say I'm not curious what it'd be like to give some of this human technology a whirl."

"I think we'd better all stick to our strengths," I said. "At least those of us whose strengths already work against Surt. Maybe I should get a few lessons in machine gun usage, if there's time for that. It'd stop you from having to worry so much about me, anyway."

Hod had stood up. He reached to tug a lock of my hair, grazing my cheek with his knuckles as he did. "I don't expect there's anything you could be armed with that'd stop us worrying, valkyrie. Unless you're going to tell me you don't worry about us too."

I elbowed him lightly. "Somehow I think there's a *little* more worry going one way than the other. But never mind that. We're going to need to come up with a plan for what we do with these guys—and girls, maybe—when they get here." I glanced at Loki. "You haven't gotten any closer to figuring out what Surt was up to last night?"

The trickster shook his head. "I haven't gotten a hint of him since then. It might have been nothing more than a feint, intended to confuse us. I'm not sure he realizes that I can't trace the point where the bridge came down after he's removed it. He may not even have worked out how we're finding him at all. He might be reasonably clever as giants go, but with giants, that isn't saying a whole lot. With myself being the obvious exception."

"Obviously," Hod said with an arch of his eyebrow, but he sounded more amused than anything else.

"He's appeared in North America three times in succession, as far as we can tell, hasn't he?" Baldur said in his soothingly serene way. "We can probably—"

He stopped, his gaze sliding to something beyond my shoulder. Some*one* beyond my shoulder, I determined from the scrap of boots over the dusty earth. I turned to see the other gods who'd been conversing together heading our way, Vidar in the lead.

"What's this private conference you've got going on over here?" the muscular god asked. His tone wasn't quite accusing yet, but his eyes had a hard glint to them. "If you're making plans, shouldn't we all be involved? I believe that's what we agreed on yesterday."

By which he meant, he and some of the others had agreed, and they'd assumed I had to follow whatever they told me.

"Brother," Thor said, giving the side of Vidar's arm a playful cuff. "We were just determining whether we had a plan to present to the rest of you before we got to the presenting part."

"That tends to be the most productive order," Loki added helpfully.

"They've got their own little clique here," Skadi said, coming up beside Vidar with her arms folded over her chest. "Around their little valkyrie."

I managed not to bristle other than the terse smile that sprang to my face. Baldur set a reassuring hand on the small of my back.

"The four of us had a lot of time with just each other over the last few centuries," he said. "I think it's normal that we gravitate toward each other even with so many of you here now. And Ari knows us far better than she knows anyone else here. It was only a conversation."

"We're seeing a lot of these separate conversations happening between the bunch of you," Freyr put in. "After all the work you put into gathering us, you give off an awfully strong impression that you don't feel you really need our input."

"Now, hold on," Thor said, still trying to keep his voice warm. "We weren't making any decisions, and we certainly don't consider ourselves in charge. That's the Allfather's role, and I wouldn't want it if he offered it to me. You're here now. Let's talk. Unless you'd rather fight with us than with the draugar."

Vidar glowered at him. "I say you should—"

A shout went up farther across the yard. A glimmering white figure glided down by the side of the road, with two companions flanking her: an elderly man and a young woman who didn't look like she could have been older than me. It was Idunn, the goddess of regeneration who'd joined us in the last wave of newcomers, and two more gods she'd managed to find, I guessed with Heimdall's directions.

Thor sucked in his breath, a sound that wasn't all that pleased.

"What?" I said, peering at him.

"That girl," he said, nodding to the young woman, who was winding a lock of her golden hair around one finger as she made her cautious approach. "That's Hnoss. Freya's daughter."

---

Knowing the family connection, it was impossible not to see the echo of Freya's face and frame in Hnoss's—even when they were at opposite ends of the yard.

I fiddled with my switchblade in my pocket as I looked from one to the other. Hnoss was talking with several of the other newer gods, her stance still tensed after a couple hours in our presence. She'd angled herself away from her mother. Freya had drawn closer to Odin, who seemed to be consulting with Njord about something right now, but her gaze kept darting toward the younger goddess.

After all the anguish I'd seen Freya express over her separation from her daughter, their reunion had been a flop. Maybe the reasons for that anguish were why it'd been a flop. The goddess of love and war had come dashing out of the old school building when someone must have passed on word to her. Hnoss had looked up at the squeal of the door. Their eyes had met, Hnoss's jaw had clenched as she'd turned away, and Freya had stopped in her tracks, her arms sagging at her sides.

"But that's the thing," Bragi was saying over on Hnoss's side of the yard now. "We can't be sure what understanding Surt is working with, so we can't predict his next moves, not even with a pattern in the past."

We'd spent most of the time since the two new arrivals had reached us catching them up and then discussing the dilemma of what to do next. Thor had managed to break the news that Harrison's men and their weapons were on the way, but most of the others had looked uncomfortable even starting to discuss that. I guessed we'd get down to that part of our strategy when there were a few dozen living breathing human beings here in front of them that they'd find much harder to ignore.

"We can still make a reasonable guess," Vidar said, motioning to the map. Before he could continue, the Allfather strode over to that larger group, Freya and Njord trailing behind him.

"I feel we are moving swiftly toward the critical junction," Odin said in his low but resonant voice. It sent an uneasy shiver down my back. "The visions I brought back may hold the key. We should do our best to decipher them before we proceed."

"I'd imagine your insights about those visions would be the most accurate, father," Baldur said. "You have the full context."

"But perhaps I don't." The Allfather trailed the end of his spear across the packed earth. "The context is Surt and these battles and all of you."

"'The light of day can burn before a fire, but only the highest water can put out all the flames'," Loki intoned. "That was it, wasn't it?"

Baldur glanced toward his twin. "The first part—the light of day—that could refer to my powers. I'll be on watch for chances to use them to hold off Surt's fire."

Which the bright god would have been doing anyway. I wasn't sure how Odin's ramblings had helped us there. The other gods stirred, a restless energy moving through the group.

"The highest water could mean some sort of mountain spring," Idunn ventured. "What is the highest peak in Midgard?"

Freya stepped to the map, and Heimdall let out a sharp sound. "Is this really what we're going to do?" he said. "Run all around the world looking for mountain water instead of focusing on the next battle?"

Odin swept his arm. "The water of my visions, if found, could end the entire—"

"Enough!" Heimdall interrupted. "You're the Allfather and you led us well for a long while, but we need a real leader right now, not an old man's dreaming. Do you even listen to yourself anymore? 'Light of day' and 'highest water'—this isn't one of Bragi's poems, it's an actual *war*, and it's happening right now."

"Not that you'd know," Vidar tossed out. "Since you haven't been here."

I shifted my weight, hugging myself instinctively. The shift in the tone of this conversation left my nerves prickling. I wasn't Odin's biggest fan, but this didn't seem like a good time to hash out all the gods' personal complaints about his past leadership.

"Now, hold on," Freya said, holding up her hand. "Odin's words, even when vague, have often set us on the right course—"

"Have they?" Hnoss's clear voice, as sweet as her mother's even when there was an edge to it, rang out. She stepped closer to the front, looking at Freya rather than Odin. "They led us straight into Ragnarok, didn't they? Not that he'd ever admit any fault there. What does he care about the rest of us over preserving his high position?"

Thor's eyes flashed. "Whatever else you can say about my father, he's always done his best for all of Asgard."

Hnoss glared at the thunder god. "Then his best fell far short of what we were owed."

"Hnoss," Freya started.

Her daughter's head snapped back around. "Don't even start. You know how I feel. It obviously never changed anything for you."

Loki clapped his hands with a fiery crackle. For a second, even the uneasy murmurs in the crowd fell silent.

"My good people," the trickster said jauntily, "you all know I am never one to shy from offering criticism. But even if there may be elements of Odin's methods I've disagreed with, I believe his visions were always accurate, once the meaning became clear. I don't say we should dash off in search of mountain springs, but we could spend a few minutes discussing the possibilities before moving on?"

"Why would we follow *your* advice, Trickster?" Freyr sneered. "You've led us into more ruin than anyone."

I winced on Loki's behalf. The trickster simply gazed back at Freya's brother balefully.

"Exactly," Hnoss said. "If the Sly One says we should listen to Odin, that's all the more reason we shouldn't. He's never been anything but treachery."

A protest rose in my throat, but I wasn't sure if I'd be helping the situation or only adding more fuel to the fire by saying what I knew. If even Loki didn't seem to think it was wise to get into the full accounting of blame—

"No!" The single syllable rolled across the yard like a thunderclap, in time with the smack of Odin's spear against the ground. His knuckles had whitened where he was gripping the staff. His single eye glowed with a fierceness nearly as bright as Baldur's magic.

"You want an admission of fault?" the Allfather said to Hnoss. "I will make it. The Trickster has been the most loyal of any of Asgard's citizens. He carried out my instructions as I expected him to, often against his own wishes, in deference to the blood oath we'd taken. Ragnarok was looming over us. I needed everything in order, to take us through it in the smoothest possible way. We required chaos to come through to peace; we required a villain; I put that responsibility on his shoulders."

He paused, and his voice turned a little ragged. His gaze swept over all the assembled gods. "I may not have judged everything correctly. I may have caused you more pain than was necessary. And perhaps I could have spared some of the pain that had to come by revealing more. I regret that, and I regret that it has taken me so long to say as much to you."

For a few seconds, no one seemed to know how to respond. The angry vibe that had been swelling amid the gods had petered out. I guessed it was hard to stay furious with someone who'd just accepted all that anger and acknowledged it was fair.

Loki was staring at Odin. From the shock on his face, he'd never had the slightest expectation that the Allfather would ever volunteer the truth about their association. He wet his lips and raised his chin.

"Our king may overstate the case," he said, managing to keep his usual light tone. "I'm sure I took more than a few digs on my own behalf. You're welcome to continue hating me if you'll rest easier that way."

"Odin," Njord said, his eyes wide. He didn't seem to know how to continue.

The Allfather bowed his head. "We can speak on this matter more if you wish. But I will defer to Vidar and Heimdall now. We have a battle that must be fought. My visions will clarify themselves when the time comes. All I ask is you remember them and act if you see your chance."

"Well," Vidar said. He looked at the map and back up at his father, his jaw working. "I suppose..."

Engines rumbled in the distance. My heart leapt. A familiar SUV, a small transport truck, and a few vans were making their way along the road toward us. Harrison and his reinforcements had arrived.

# 20

*Aria*

The gang's vehicles pulled into the parking lot one after the other. A shiver of energy raced through the air as several of the gods must have willed themselves visible to mortal eyes. I did the same with a fresh gust of the hot summer breeze over my skin.

The engines cut out, and people started hopping out. Harrison headed over to us first while his team hung back. He nodded to me and considered the gods, his eyes sharp as ever behind those rectangular glasses. I wondered if he could pick up on the fact that they'd just been arguing.

"I brought all the weapons you asked for and the people to wield them," he said. "Do you want to look them all over?"

Thor strode forward before anyone had a chance to express hesitation. I jogged to catch up with him, and a bunch of the others trailed along behind us. Harrison gestured to the guy who'd gone to stand at the rear of the truck, and the younger man opened the back with a jerk. We peered into the dark space. A cloying metallic smell filled my nose.

Harrison hopped in along with the young guy and shoved some of the crates closer to the sunlight. He snapped the lid open on one to show us a pretty impressive bazooka, and then another to display a few machine guns. "We're well-stocked for ammo too," he said. "If bullets and missiles can take this giant down, he's going down, absolutely."

Vidar had come up beside us. His back stiffened as he eyed the truck's contents. "This is not how gods fight," he muttered.

Harrison gave the warrior god a puzzled look. "That's why my people are here too. I understood we'd be handling the guns."

"That's the idea," I said quickly. I turned to Vidar. Maybe he'd be less critical if I made him feel like he was more in charge of the situation. Odin had pretty much offered that role to him anyway. "We could have groups of them stationed at each of the most likely targets, just so we'll have back-up on hand right away wherever Surt shows up. Which did you think were the key places? Should we stick to this region, since he's mostly appeared here?"

Vidar's expression was still wary, but he stepped back from the truck and glanced toward the map still spread on the ground. "That would be my suggestion, at least for local allies." He touched the side of the truck. "How quickly could these get into place?"

"We drive fast," Harrison said with a smile. "You tell us where to go, and we'll be on it."

"Don't take off with all of these," Loki said, leaning in to run his fingers over the bazooka. "Lovely. Let's see how Surt feels about *this* kind of fire." He turned and beckoned the rest of the gods closer. "Come on, who here isn't much of a fighter? With fancy contraptions like these, you'll be out-blasting even Thor!"

Thor grumbled quietly in protest, but a grin stretched across his face as a few of his fellow gods made their way over to consider the weapons on offer.

"Wait," Vidar said. "We battle with our own powers and the weapons we know. That was what we decided."

"I don't think we came to any final decisions, brother," Thor said. He hefted a machine gun and offered it to Bragi, who cradled it as if he were afraid it might explode in his hands if he jostled it. "Why shouldn't we all fight to our fullest, even those of us whose powers don't lean that way?"

"I can't see anything good coming of this," Freyr muttered. "How much can we trust these human inventions anyway? They might blast us instead."

"I can assure you that we're careful in picking our suppliers," Harrison said. "It's *our* world we're trying to keep in one piece, remember. We're not going to cut any corners."

"To the best of their judgment," Skadi said from where she was pacing near the back of the bunch. "However much that's worth."

My teeth set on edge. "Hey," I said. "We've got one more way to take down Surt. As long as you all have good enough judgment not to aim the guns the wrong way around, you should manage not to blow yourselves up with them."

Bragi adjusted the gun in his grip, testing his hold with growing confidence. Vidar watched him, and his jaw clenched. He shook his head.

"I know what we discussed before," the warrior god said. "But Thor, you bowled the rest of us over insisting on it. This isn't what we need. Not humans, and not human weapons. I know you've got a soft spot for your valkyrie, but look at this. We need the best of our own weapons, not… that." He made a dismissive gesture toward Bragi's machine gun.

Oh, for fuck's sake, couldn't we get through any situation without an argument? I was starting to see why the gods had gone their separate ways before. But they'd rallied against all kinds of threats, before Ragnarok, hadn't they? If they'd worked together then, they should be able to now.

"Any weapons you don't have on you are back in Asgard," Loki said dryly. "Which I shouldn't have to remind you is under the control of the giant we are looking to blow up. Unless you have some grand plan for retrieving them that for some reason you've failed to share up until now..."

"Then we go to the dark elves and *insist* they craft us something suitable."

Hod tensed where he was standing near the edge of the crowd. "Our peace with them is fragile enough as it is," he said. "Try to bully them, and they'll take Surt's side all over again."

"Not while Surt is searing their throats through," Heimdall remarked.

Harrison raised his hands. "Maybe I got my wires crossed here. What I heard was that you wanted these weapons and my people to fight for you. It was your money I spent to get them. No skin off my back if you don't use them. But I know my guys. We'll keep up with you. You can't say we didn't come through."

"'Keep up'," Vidar said under his breath. "'Come through.' You barely even comprehend what we're up against. This is just..." He spun to face the largest part of the crowd, the gods still hesitating, and snatched the wrist of Harrison's young lackey who was standing nearby. "Look at them? Is this what we want to throw at Surt—mortals? *Humans*? We'll be tripping over them. He'll take one look at this 'army' and laugh, and then—"

He waggled the guy's arm, making the guy's whole body shudder. I wasn't sure what exactly Vidar had hoped to demonstrate, but I could already see this wasn't going to end well. I pushed toward him. "Let him—"

The crack of a breaking bone cut through the air. The guy cried out and muffled a curse with his free hand. Vidar blinked, staring down at the figure he'd been shaking with his godly strength, at the arm now bent where it shouldn't have, and then dropped the guy's wrist as if it had burned him.

Whatever he'd been going for, it obviously hadn't been *that*.

"What the hell?" Harrison demanded, rushing to the guy's side.

He wrenched off his checkered shirt to tie it into a makeshift sling as his lackey braced himself with a hiss through his teeth. The gang commander swiveled toward Vidar, his eyes blazing with anger but his stance defensive.

My stomach flipped over. I'd used fear to get Harrison involved—fear of what would happen to all of us if we didn't stop Surt. Now he was afraid of the gods too.

"You don't want us here," the gang commander bit out. "We can take a hint. I think we'll take these weapons too, since you don't seem to want them either, and we'll keep our own eyes out. Maybe we'll take down this giant without any help from you."

Vidar's horror fell away as he bristled at the suggestion. "Now look here—"

"Stop." Thor grasped his brother's shoulder. "If anyone can right this, it's not you, not now." He turned to Harrison. "I am so sorry for my brother's reckless behavior. Baldur can heal your man's arm—which doesn't make up for the injury caused, but at least it'll fix the injury?"

The bright god had already moved to the lackey's side. He offered a small smile. Harrison looked from him to Thor and then to me, familiar compared to the divine beings around us even with all the supernatural features I'd gained since we'd known each other.

"Baldur's healed me from worse than that," I said. "Better than any of our doctors could." I didn't know what to say about Vidar's actions.

The young guy's body went rigid when Baldur offered his hand, but after a moment he nodded. A glow seeped from the bright god's palm through the makeshift sling, and the lines of pain in the guy's face fell away almost immediately. Harrison wavered on his feet, his shoulders up and movements tight, like a wild animal unsure whether it could simply flee without having to claw its way free.

Freya tugged Vidar to the side to snap something at him under her breath.

"You'd better put that back where it came from," Skadi said to Bragi, and the poet god's grip tightened on the machine gun.

Odin eased into the middle of the crowd. "If we could all take a step back to give our human allies some space, perhaps there is still room for a calm discussion."

Whether that was true and how that discussion would have gone, I never got to find out. Because an instant later, a black shape dove out of the sky like a streak of lightning.

Muninn hit the ground so hard she stumbled as she transformed. Odin caught her arm to steady her. She swept her hair from her eyes and spun to take us all in with a panicked expression. A burn that hadn't been visible in her raven form formed a dark streak across her cheek.

"We have to go," she said. "Now. Surt's settled on his next destination. He's organizing his army and giving them their instructions. We might be able to get there before him—"

"Where?" Thor broke in, his voice rough. "Where is he going?"

"Albuquerque," she said. "New Mexico. He was talking about some kind of weapons storage facility there—he grabbed a human, and he's been torturing the man for information, I think that's how he settled on it—but I didn't hear any details until just now. One of the guards in Valhalla almost sliced my head off as I was leaving. Surt might know by now that I was there."

Weapons storage. Thor caught my eye, his expression as anguished as I felt. "They must be nuclear weapons. He's going for the bombs."

Loki swore. He started to speak and then looked to Odin. "Allfather?" he said, like a request.

Would the gods gathered here even listen to their king? Odin cleared his throat and motioned to the crowd. "We must go, quickly, every one of us with all the power we can summon. The survival of this realm may depend on reaching this facility before Surt."

"What about—" My gaze slid to Harrison. The gang commander was standing there stunned. He stared as several of the gods dashed for their weapons or leapt into the air to start their flight.

But some of those gods still didn't have weapons. We couldn't know if the powers we had would be enough to stop Surt and his army even if we did make it there first.

I stepped up to Harrison and waited until his eyes met mine. "Please," I said. "This monster is aiming to get his hands on a crapload of nuclear weapons. We're all goners if he does. I know some of the gods are assholes, but a broken arm vs. total annihilation…"

Harrison swiped his hand over his mouth. He glanced toward his lackey, who was flexing his once-broken arm with an awed expression. "How do we know we won't all end up killed by one side or the other?" he said.

I swallowed hard. "I guess you don't," I said. "But if Surt wins, you know for sure we're all dead. You came out here ready to do this. Don't let one jerk on a power trip cancel out all the reasons you signed on in the first place."

He drew in a ragged breath and turned toward his people standing around the vehicles. "I'm not going to order you," he said. "I told you from the beginning this was a special job and a risky one. If anyone wants out…"

"If you say we're good, then we're good, boss," said a woman who was leaning her arm out the window of one of the vans. The others nodded.

"Yeah," a guy said. "Let's show that motherfucker what we're made off."

Given how these gangs worked, I would have been surprised if none of them had ever been roughed up by their own comrades or superiors before. The broken arm might have shocked the other gods more than it had them.

Harrison faced me again. "I might not trust your colleagues, but I'm going to trust you, Ari. Now how the hell are we getting us and our equipment all the way to New Mexico as fast as you need us there?"

I hadn't even thought that far yet. No way could any vehicle drive that far that fast. I hesitated, and Loki swooped in with a hand on my shoulder.

"We can take care of that," he said with a tight smile, and motioned to Hod, who'd lifted into the air on his shadowy flying carpet but waited for me. "Dark One, I think we'd better work together sooner than anticipated."

Hod's mouth twisted, but all he said was, "What do you need, Sly One?"

"Conjure me up a chariot out of those shadows of yours—like Thor's old one, but larger?"

"Large enough to carry the humans and their weapons," Hod filled in. "I don't think I can manage to drag all that as fast as we need to go."

Loki's smile widened and tightened at the same time. "You won't need to pull it," he said. "I'll take care of that."

With a loose shrug, he hunched over. His body rippled and expanded in an instant. One second I was looking at the god, and the next an enormous stallion stood in his place, mane and body a pale roan almost the same shade as the trickster's hair.

"Fuck me," one of the gang lackeys muttered. Several of Harrison's people were gaping. If they hadn't been totally convinced this wasn't all some elaborate prank before, they knew for sure it was real now.

Hod was already whipping up a structure of solid darkness. It lashed around Loki's stallion body and stretched out behind him, half was wide as the parking lot.

"You can handle that?" the dark god called down, and Loki tossed his head as if to say, *Don't you dare doubt me.*

Harrison sprang into action. "All right, all right, everybody grab a crate and get on there. Hang back if this has gotten too crazy—but if you're not coming, you don't get a share of the cash."

Five minutes later, the chariot was packed. Loki tossed his head again and hurtled forward, his hooves striking the ground and then rising off it, his shoes of flight speeding him on even in this unusual form. I took off after him, Hod right beside me, and we bolted for the south.

*Oh, please*, I prayed to I didn't know whom, *let us get there in time.*

# 21

*Loki*

Even hauling our little human army and their weapons supply, I'd outpaced the rest of the gods by the time our destination came into view. For a place that could lead to the end of all Midgard, the site looked rather drab and unimpressive. At the southern edge of the sprawling city, just before shrub-dotted red-brown plains rose into a ridge of hills, several rows of low buildings squatted in a yard cut through with a few narrow roads.

A car was puttering along one of those roads. A few human figures crossed the paved ground from one of the smaller buildings to a larger one with a pale spotted roof. I hadn't had time to think while I'd been conveying our mortal allies here about the mortals who would already be on hand. They didn't look ready to fend off a sudden invasion of draugar.

I cantered in a circle over the base as the other gods caught up. The mad dash in horse form had actually been invigorating. Now I was itching to set down to earth and grab one of those very tempting-looking rocket launchers for myself. Let Surt bring on his army and his flames. We were ready for him now, no more chasing at his heels.

"Stay above until the bridge appears," Thor was yelling. "Humans, get your weapons ready. We'll tackle him here above."

Well, I supposed that was a reasonable strategy too, even if it left me as nothing more than a carthorse for the battle. I let out a snort and kicked my heels a little faster for good measure. Ari soared past me, exchanging a few words with the leader of her former colleagues. She veered close enough to me to brush her fingers against my neck. I turned toward her—

And the sky split with a streak of fire that raced toward the ground like a bolt of lightning.

Surt had upped his game. The gods shouted and sprang forward, and the rattle of machine gun fire sounded behind me, but the flaming bridge had shot Surt past us in the blink of an eye. He leapt off its base into the yard and charged toward the nearest building.

So much for an ambush. I dove down at a gallop. The second Hod's chariot of shadows touched the ground, I shook off my animal form and leapt toward the weaponry. With a wave of my hand, I cast a swath of concealing magic over the humans there. The soldiers from the base were already yelling to each other. We hardly needed them shooting at our allies. All they'd see was the results of the chaos, not the cause.

The bridge had brought a surge of draugar with it too. Dozens spilled across the asphalt yard as more poured down from above.

Thor's hammer slammed through the nearest contingent. Vidar, Heimdall, Freya, and Freyr raced in with their swords. Blazing light and burning shadows seared past me. A missile whined through the air and blew apart at least twenty of those undead bodies just as they barged off the bridge.

I snatched up one of the bazookas and swung around to where I'd last seen Surt. He was just bashing through the doorway of the building he'd run for. Thor and Vidar raced after him with matching roars.

I couldn't get a clear shot without blasting straight through the gods. Damn it. I swung around and let loose one of my missiles into the swarm of draugar instead.

The undead figures swung out with their fire-enhanced swords and hid behind their shields, but taking on this many gods and our human allies was a far more balanced fight than when they'd descended on the six of us and our valkyrie in Asgard a few days ago. Even our raven was diving into the fray now, clawing at the face of a draug that had been barreling toward Odin. The putrid forms tumbled left and right, sliced through, shattered, or burnt to a crisp.

I set aside the human gun to whip a blaze over a line of draugar. They shrieked as if in pain, but it was all part of the horrific magic that had animated their bodies. We were putting those poor bodies out of the misery of their slavery.

"Where's Surt?" Ari called out where she was wheeling just above our heads. She'd grabbed a machine gun of her own, looking like some kind of unholy avenging angel with her silvery wings outstretched and that cold black shape in her hands. I could have sat back and simply admired her all day if we hadn't had more draugar—and that bloody giant—still to deal with.

Thor stumbled toward us. Blood seeped down his shirt from a wound across his belly that was burnt black along the edges but raw red through the middle. Surt had caught him with his damned fiery sword.

Ari's face paled. "Baldur!" she cried, searching the crowd.

"I'll survive," the Thunderer said raggedly. "Surt's gone below. Vidar chased after him. We have to follow. If the weapons are down there…"

"The destruction will spread farther if he ignites them

aboveground," Hod said grimly. "He'll come back up to us. Let's be ready for him."

We converged on the building. My pulse thrummed in my veins. It hadn't felt fully real before, being on this side of the battle. The right side, Asgard's side—the side I wanted to be on. There might have been gods around me I'd sooner piss on than do a favor for, but I still liked them far better than the brute who'd instigated this conflict.

Maybe no one would remember this battle over that first one, but being here, fighting where I wanted to be, was enough in itself.

"Where do you need us now?" the leader of our human allies hollered.

Thor waved Ari's former colleagues out of the chariot and around our blockade. Despite the Thunderer's protests, Baldur had already reached his side, sealing the wound with the glow of his magic.

Near me, Hod toppled another few draugar with a slash of his dark magic. Between the gods and the human guns, we'd slaughtered most of them. The base's soldiers were picking them off too even as they gaped, bewildered, at the scene they could only see part of.

"Should we try to break through the ground to go after Surt?" Ari asked, landing between Hod and me. "If we used our combined powers, like we did at his fortress, we might be able to break straight through."

"We knew exactly where to strike there," Hod said. "I'm not sure—we don't know exactly where the weapons are, or how our magic might affect them. The last thing we want is to help Surt's plan along."

"He's not getting away from us," Thor rumbled. "We really have destroyed his army now, and—"

A chorus of battle cries resonated through the air. We spun

around to face a horde of giants that had appeared over the crest of the bridge.

I had battled innumerable giants in my time, most often with the Thunderer by my side as he was now. I'd lived among them for the first sorry span of my life. Nevertheless, seeing that swarm of them careening down toward us over the flames of Surt's bridge made the bottom of my stomach drop out.

While we'd been accumulating allies, Surt had been gathering more of his own as well.

Ari's former colleagues opened fire. A missile struck one giant in the shoulder as he leapt off the bridge, sending him crashing to the ground, but two more heaved themselves into the midst of the humans at the same time. The slam of their arms and the slash of the blades they carried cracked skulls and splattered blood.

Ari let out a pained sound and lunged forward as if she meant to challenge a hundred giants all on her own. My pulse stuttered. I dashed faster than she could, catching her by the elbow.

"We fight them together, pixie," I said. "We need you with us."

"They're all going to die," she mumbled. "I asked them to come, and now they're going to be slaughtered."

"Not on our watch," I said firmly, catching Thor's and Baldur's eyes. Hod was already skimming toward us on one of his shadows. I swept my arm toward the giants, and we charged. The other gods barrelled forward around us.

Unfortunately, a fair number of our human allies were beyond saving. The giants flung their lifeless bodies toward us and crushed this gun and that rocket launcher with heaves of their bulging arms. Flecks of blood and what might have been bits of brain matter dabbled my cheek. I grimaced and thrust my arms forward with all the searing magic I could summon.

The other four of our quintet moved at the same time. That bizarre cohesion we'd developed between us around our valkyrie crackled through my nerves. My fire blazed over Thor's hammer and tangled with Hod's shadows and Baldur's knife-edged wave of light.

We'd mainly used our combined powers against dark elves and draugar before now. Several of the giants toppled with the onslaught, but a few of them immediately started shoving back to their feet, burnt and bleeding but not conquered. More of their kin streamed around us.

Blades flashed, and teeth gnashed. Even as we whirled to try to push back another lot of them, I saw a giant catching Njord with a sword through his back. The old sea god collapsed with a gush of blood. Somewhere in the fray, a voice I knew must be Skadi's shrieked.

Even as our next attack left a dozen giants sprawling, another wave charged in to fill the gap. The asphalt around the base of the bridge was melting, sticking to my shoes and filling the air with a tarry tang. Bragi aimed the machine gun he'd retrieved at our foes, but as the bullets tore through two of their chests, another giant hurled himself at the poet. Bragi's skull collapsed under the bash of the brute's spiked club.

I wrenched my eyes away from the sight and dragged in a painful breath. We could still do this. The giants were battering us, but we were battering them in turn. Maybe we'd lose a few more of our number before the battle was done, but they couldn't overcome all of us. I was certain of that much.

Then a bellow of victory reached my ears, and I realized overcoming the giants eventually might not be enough.

Across the yard, Surt had emerged from the building he'd vanished into. He had a sort of metal net slung against his back with a haul of at least ten shiny white missiles, each nearly as tall as he was and as thick as his thigh. His leg arm and his side were stained with blood, but he stood steadily enough, brandishing his sword. His loot clattered as he dropped it on the ground. He reached for the nearest nuclear warhead with a fiery gleam in his eyes.

"Look at what he's doing!" Ari shouted at the other giants as they closed in around us, barricading us gods from the giant who meant to end this world. "If he sets off that bomb, it's going to kill all of you too! Don't you care? Don't *you* want to live?"

Oh, my darling valkyrie. My dearest Ari, who'd once expressed so much fear at the darkness inside her, was trying to get through to the damned giants as if they might listen to reason and save themselves. She never gave up on anyone, did she?

The thought brought a strange tightness to my throat. Ahead of me, Thor shoved toward Surt, but the giant's comrades had managed to surround us completely. Thor's hammer shattered a raised shield without displacing the giant behind it and flew back into his hand.

Baldur's blazing light tossed a few giants back into the wall of bodies behind them, and their fellows shoved them back upright. Freya's and her brother's swords clanged against blazing blades raised to meet theirs.

We'd break our way through eventually, yes, with many more of them falling than of us, but it might not be in time to stop Surt's intended wave of destruction. If we were going to blast a quick path through his allies to him, we'd need both speed and distraction.

Two elements no one here was better equipped to supply than me.

I saw how it would play out in a flash, perhaps the same way Odin's visions came to him. I saw every move I could make; I saw the way the crowd would sway; I glimpsed the inevitable end. And even though my stomach clenched, a larger part of me felt suddenly freed, light as a breeze.

This was my moment, as surely as if it'd been laid out for me. I'd be a villain if I didn't take it.

I wasn't quite so selfless to spring into that opening without a second thought. My gaze snagged on Ari's face, so beautiful in its frantic fierceness, and my heart squeezed in that way I was only just starting to get used to.

I couldn't give her a chance to interfere, but after all the ways she'd trusted me, after all the pain I might bring no matter how much I'd have liked to spare her, I could make one small offering of truth for her to hold on to when I was gone.

Bodies pushed and swiveled around me. I caught my valkyrie's hand and tugged her close enough that my lips brushed her cheek.

"I love you," I said, quiet but clear. Not really a proclamation, just a simple statement of fact.

She sucked in a startled breath, and I was already propelling myself away from her, toward the wall of giants around us.

My shoes of flight launched me through the air so swiftly that I raced between the swings of swords and over the swipe of a spear. Flames blazed from my palms. I threw fire out on every side, lighting up the space around me in stark relief, so bright no giant could fail to see me.

I didn't run toward Surt. That direction contained so much glory if I succeeded, but too much risk if I didn't. I slammed my heels into the heads of several giants at that end of their ring, and grasping hands nearly snagged my ankles. Spinning away with a mocking jeer, I dashed in the opposite direction.

The crowd surged around me as the giants started to give chase. I could have darted higher, but they wouldn't follow if they knew there was no chance of catching me. Besides, this way I could batter a few more giant heads along the way. I kicked a forehead here, hurled fire into a face there. Let them fall, let them fall, let them—

Not one of the gods could have run fast or nimbly enough to outpace the horde like this forever. I darted on for as long as any of us could have. Too many hands snatched after me at once, and one closed around my foot with a yank that nearly dislocated my knee. I whipped around, slicing out with lashes of flame. Giants stumbled back with groans and grunts, the grip on my foot loosened—and a club slammed into my ribs with a piercing *crack.*

I jerked my head up for one last look. Most of the giants had rushed after me, and the other gods were shoving past the few left behind toward Surt. A smile crossed my face.

Then a fist pummeled my skull. One last gush of fire exploded from my hands just before a searing pain gouged into my chest. I fell away into darkness.

# 22

*Aria*

It happened so quickly I barely had time to think: Loki's whisper by my ear, his blazing dash across the giants' heads, the sea of them parting as they took up chase, and the gods around me surging forward toward the one giant we had to stop more than any other.

My heart tugged after Loki, but I threw myself forward with the other gods. Surt's head snapped up where he was bent over his haul of warheads. His teeth gritted, and his hand shot toward his sword.

Thor tore through the last few giants between us and Surt, his hammer splitting flesh and shattering bones. He hurled Mjolnir ahead of him. Surt managed to deflect the hammer with a smack of his sword, dodging twin blasts of light and shadow at the same time. He braced himself to fling a wave of his own fire toward us.

Before he had a chance to, a *boom* rattled my eardrums right beside me. A bazooka missile screamed through the air and ripped straight through the giant's shoulder.

Harrison let out a hoarse breath where he'd planted his feet to make the shot. The missile launcher wobbled in his grasp. His hair was damp with sweat and blood, and the side of his face was scraped raw, but he'd survived the slaughter.

Surt let out a roar that sounded as much like agony as rage. His sword arm dangled uselessly at his side. Thor and the others barreled on toward him. With a snarled curse, the giant wrenched his netted heap of warheads off the ground with his good arm and threw himself toward his bridge.

The flaming arch licked up to catch his leap. With a hiss of heat, he vanished into the sky with his bounty—alone.

Some of the giant companions he'd abandoned on the ground were hurtling toward us from behind. We spun around, Thor's hammer flying, Odin's spear slashing, swords flashing as they sliced open our enemies' bodies. I'd lost the gun I'd grabbed somewhere in the fray. I launched myself off the ground and at the giants with the most innate weapon I had.

My fingers grazed the top of one giant's head. The void of darkness inside me opened at my beckoning, and I yanked his life into that hollow place. The waft of energy came, stickier and thicker than the dark elf lives I'd wrenched away before.

As he collapsed, I barely heaved myself out of the way before another giant swung her dagger right where my neck had been. I whirled around—and my gaze caught on a tall slim form sprawled amid the other bodies with so little grace that my mind jarred against recognition.

But it *was* Loki. It was my slyly defiant trickster, trampled and bludgeoned, a ragged gash in his chest where it looked as if the giants had torn his heart right out.

My own heart flipped over. Vomit seared the base of my throat. I choked, sputtered, and pushed myself forward, willing my eyes to be wrong.

I could hardly see by the time I reached the trickster's body, my vision was so blurred with tears. I sucked back a sob and raised a shaking hand to his pale red hair, streaked scarlet now with his blood. His jaw slanted at an unnatural angle. One of his perfect sharp cheekbones had been pummeled flat. Another surge of nausea rolled over me.

Loki had known what he was doing. He'd known he'd have to give the giants a chance to catch him if he was going to draw enough of them away. Why else would he have said those three words to me before he'd taken off?

He hadn't thought he'd get another chance.

And he wouldn't. He was lying here without a hint of life in his body. As much as I wanted to believe he'd suddenly drag in a breath, sit up, and smirk at me as if my tears were ridiculous, every moment I crouched there beside his prone form confirmed what we'd learned with Tyr, what the maimed bodies of the other gods who'd fallen today proved. They'd already gotten their second chance. They wouldn't rise again.

Unless…

My chest clenched. I stared at my hand hovering over the trickster's face. My small trembling *valkyrie* hand.

That hand had stolen the life out of a giant just a minute ago. It was supposed to be able to restore lives too—to summon them up to Valhalla. I'd never tried—I didn't know if I could—

Every second I hesitated, Loki's spirit might be slipping farther away from me.

My pulse rattled in my ears as I leaned over him, setting both of my hands on his chest while avoiding the bloody wound at its center. My eyes slipped shut. I reached down into the depths of my being to the place where that killing darkness lurked. At the same time, I drew up every memory of why this spirit was deserving.

The weight of responsibility Loki had carried leading up to Ragnarok. The insults and sneers he'd so often shrugged off with a simple glib remark. The way he'd been able to see worth even in me, and the lengths he'd gone to in order to convince me of it—so many words of admiration my heart swelled thinking of them. The passion with which he'd leapt into every battle I'd fought with him. His haste to track down Surt no matter the time or situation.

Just now, hurling insults and flinging flames as he raced to his doom to clear the way for us to save my realm.

He'd told me not that long ago that while he wasn't a villain, he wasn't much of a hero either. I couldn't imagine many people meeting his definition if it didn't include him.

Beneath the coiled darkness in my gut, a spark flared. Its heat spread through my torso and out into my limbs, raising the hairs on my arms and the back of my neck. The air in my lungs shimmered. I focused all my strength into that sensation.

*Him. Him. Let him rise.*

"Let me claim him for Valhalla," I said, the last plea slipping from my throat.

The spark cracked open with a blaze of light that blinded me from the inside out.

In that searing white, I tasted the spicy sweet flavor that always lingered on Loki's skin. My hands clasped around a quiver of an even brighter light. It thrummed in my grasp with an energy that felt almost like a sly grin. Gasping, I tossed it upward with all my power, up to the vast hall of Valhalla with its walls of glinting blades, away from this mortal realm.

The spirit flitted up toward Asgard away from me, and my stomach cramped with a pang of loss. My awareness was tumbling back to earth.

No. I had to be there—I had to make sure my gambit worked, that Surt's guards didn't sever Loki's life all over again.

I heaved myself off the asphalt with my mind trained on that image of Valhalla. The smell of stale mead trickled through my senses. I willed myself there with all my being.

The air shuddered, and I stumbled amid the long oak tables beneath the high vaulted ceiling.

There was a rasp and a grunt somewhere near me. The giants poised near the hearth and Odin's throne at the far end of the hall were already spinning around.

A strange exhilaration raced through me. My hand snatched my switchblade from my pocket faster than I'd ever moved before. I whipped it straight and hard between one guard's eyes while I hurtled toward another with a swift flap of my wings.

My hand brushed the guard's forehead as he swung at me, yanking out his life by the roots. I wheeled out of reach of a third giant's sword—

And that one erupted into flames.

My gaze snapped down the hall in time to see a tall slim figure with hair like a lick of flame hurling another fiery bolt at the guards. Loki snatched two daggers off the wall, one in each hand, and flung them simultaneously at the two giants still standing. The blades slammed into the guards' hearts. They collapsed together with a resounding thud.

Loki swiped his palms together with a sharp satisfied smile. "Well, that takes care of our most immediate problem." He glanced around the hall and then down at himself.

He'd appeared in the same clothes he'd been wearing moments ago in Midgard, a typical green tunic and gray slacks, but the cloth was whole and unbloodied, not at all like it had looked those few moments ago. A hint of confusion crossed his face. "Maybe you can enlighten me on how exactly we ended up here, pixie, because I seem to have a disturbing blank in my memory."

Seeing him so vibrant and real and *alive* knocked the breath out of me. I'd done it. I'd actually done it. With a thrill that shot straight through my wings, I dove to meet him. I caught him, my arms wrapping tight around his waist, my face pressed to his chest, drinking in his spicy sweet scent.

"You got yourself *killed*," I said. "That's what happened."

His arms settled around my shoulders. He ducked his head, his lips brushing my hair. "I remember that part," he said, quietly but lightly. "Apparently it didn't play out quite as I expected it to."

"Because you're lucky enough to have a valkyrie on your side," I grumbled into his shirt.

"So, you—" He let out a laugh, all amused awe. "You resurrected me to the hall of warriors."

"I had to try." I clutched him harder, revelling in how warm and whole his body was against mine, and then pulled back to look him in the eyes. My throat closed up for an instant, but this second time was easier. The words still tumbled together as they rushed out. "I love you too. You didn't have to pull a stunt like that to get me to say it back, you lunatic."

Loki laughed again, short and breathless, and then he was kissing me with so much heat my nerves ignited. I wanted to melt right into him, to lose myself in the joy of his survival, but this wasn't the best time or place for that.

As Loki knew as well. He kissed me once more, tenderly, with a graze of his fingertips down the side of my face. Then he eased back and glanced around.

"What happened on Midgard after my untimely end?" he asked. "Did Surt..."

"We reached him before he could detonate any of the warheads," I said. "But he got away with them, back up here. One of my guys took a good shot at him with a bazooka. He's hurt. Not sure how much that'll slow him down."

"I suppose we're in an ideal position to find that out." The trickster glanced toward the main door with a grin. "We can gather some of those weapons Vidar was moaning about missing while we're at it. Let's see if my powers of concealment survived my second resurrection, shall we?"

"Hold on." I strode over to the first giant I'd killed and wrenched my switchblade from his skull. I wiped it on his shirt before jamming it back into my pocket. Then I tugged a short sword I liked the look of off the wall. Its narrow blade gleamed menacingly. "Okay, now I'm ready."

Loki's grin widened. "My valkyrie."

I waggled the sword at him, my own lips twitching upward. "Oh, no, I'm not your valkyrie anymore. You're *my* raised hero."

Loki blinked at me. The smile that crossed his face next was nothing but light, beaming bright as the sun outside.

"So I am," he said, the same brilliance sparkling through his voice. "Come along then, and we'll discover what heroics lie ahead of me."

He tucked his hand around mine, and we stepped together toward the door.

# 23

*Aria*

As the trickster and I reached Valhalla's entrance, my earlier sense of exhilaration kept tingling through my veins.

I'd used the greatest power a valkyrie had. I'd brought back a life instead of just taking them.

I wanted to do it all over again.

We could have had a much larger army if Valhalla were full again. Did Odin need to be in the hall if he wanted to summon more valkyries? I guessed that possibility might have gone off the table as soon as Surt had conquered Asgard. But if there'd been more of us, and we'd all summoned heroes from Midgard…

Loki made a sweeping motion with his hand around us, and the light shimmered for a second before settling down. "We won't be noticeable as long as we steer clear of any direct interaction with Surt and his minions," he said. "Don't go stabbing anyone, and we should get past them just fine."

"I think I can manage that," I said.

He raised an eyebrow. "I know you must be looking forward to trying out that sword."

When he eased open the door, I realized that avoiding any kind of interaction with our enemies might be a little more difficult than I'd assumed. Surt clearly hadn't brought his whole army down to the weapons facility. At least a hundred draugar were shuffling around the courtyard and along the divine city's streets—between the halls now blackened and in places bashed right open.

A couple of giants appeared to be delighting in smashing the statue in the middle of the courtyard's fountain. Several other of their kind stood clustered not far from Valhalla, muttering to themselves. It was a good thing we'd dispatched the guards in the hall before they'd had time to raise the alarm, or we'd have been toast.

The sight of the wandering undead dampened my giddiness. All those haggard vacant human faces… What Surt had done wasn't at all like what I'd done for Loki. I'd brought the trickster back fully to life, with all his thoughts and free will. But at the same time, the idea of raising an army of fallen human warriors to do our bidding suddenly turned my stomach.

Maybe it was better that we hadn't had the option. Using that tactic would have been like stooping to Surt's level. I'd known Loki—known he would want to live on if he could—and it wasn't as if I really had any power over him. To resurrect strangers and send them off to battle giants and draugar without them having any real say in it… In some ways, that might be even worse. These zombies, at least, were mindless. Risen warriors would know they were being used.

I remembered too well how I'd felt when my gods had told me how they'd summoned me. They'd given me a choice, but dying all over again hadn't felt like much of an alternative. I was happy with the hand I'd been dealt now, but, no, I didn't think I'd be calling up a host of formerly dead human beings any time soon.

Loki slunk out into the city, and I followed just behind him. "Thor has quite a stash of weapons, many of them dark-elf made," the trickster said under his breath. "That seems like a reasonable place to start our collection."

We crossed the courtyard and started up the tiled road, veering around giants and draugar alike. They ambled on by without so much as a glance at us. My skin prickled passing so close to our enemies. I might not have planned on stabbing anyone, but I kept my hand tight around the hilt of the sword I'd grabbed and my wings unfurled over my back.

More giants were standing around Thor's hall. A few seconds later, I understood why. Surt's ragged voice bellowed through the walls.

"You will tell me how to work these weapons. Don't tell me you can't."

A yelp pierced the air—one that sounded distinctly human. My shoulders tensed.

"Muninn said Surt had grabbed another human from Midgard," I said. "That must be what he was doing that brief visit we couldn't track. Another nuclear scientist, maybe?"

"He's trying to fill in the blanks in his knowledge," Loki said. "I might allow myself to be slightly impressed by his resourcefulness if it wasn't leading toward the destruction of everything we hold dear. It sounds as though he hasn't gotten very far, as a consolation."

It also sounded as if he was torturing the man trying to get what he wanted. My muscles itched to fly at the door, to rush in and haul the poor guy away from the giant, but that would blow our cover completely. If I even made it far enough to help the man. Coming closer, I could see that giant guards surrounded the whole hall, swords and axes gleaming in their hands. Surt was keeping himself well-protected.

"It figures he'd set himself up in the Thunderer's home," Loki muttered. "He wishes he were even half the warrior Thor is. But perhaps we'd best give that stash a miss. I know other treasures we can lay our hands on more easily."

He stalked on up the road. I dodged splatters of blood that darkened the pale gray tiles. Surt had still been bleeding from that missile wound when he'd made it back up here. Had Harrison managed to ruin his sword arm for good?

Not that his sword was what we really needed to worry about right now while the giant was carting around a dozen or so nuclear warheads.

Loki's hall had taken an especially brutal beating. One whole side of the building was charred all the way across the roof. Several chunks of the thatching had fallen in.

We ducked inside to sunlight streaming through the holes in the ceiling. The trickster sighed and kicked aside fallen cinders as he headed down the front hall. "I have to say I don't much care for Surt's interior decorating tastes."

His death and resurrection obviously hadn't affected his sense of humor. I jogged to keep up. He stopped at a locked door, applied his finger to the keyhole, and pushed it open.

The room on the other side smelled like machine oil. Crates and sacks were heaped along the walls. Loki tugged open one and then another while I stood there looking around.

"What is all this stuff?" I asked.

"I'm in the habit of collecting a few things here and there myself," the trickster said. "Not around quite as combat-focused a theme as the Thunderer's loot, naturally, but I should have a few things that could be of use… Ah." He tucked something small into his slacks pocket. A few moments later, he slung an entire sack over his shoulder. He stuffed a box about the size of a textbook in to join whatever contents the sack already held. Finally, from a box in the corner, he retrieved a sleek dagger with a leather-wrapped hilt that shone like a moonbeam when he offered it to me.

"I think you'll find this serves you even better than that lovely piece you picked up, pixie," he said. "The magic on the blade will allow it to cut through any material you have the will to pierce."

Oh, I had the will to slash up quite a few things. I took the dagger carefully, my fingers closing around the grip as if it'd been made for them. I gave the air an experimental slash, and a shiver of power ran up my arm.

I smiled. Now *this* was a real weapon. I just hoped I had the chance to apply it to Surt sooner rather than later.

After leaving Loki's hall, we slipped into Freya's. Loki turned up his nose at most of her weapons collection—"functional but not exceptional," he remarked—but he did scoop up the polished sword in its scabbard near the doorway.

"She didn't have time to go back for her favorite blade when Surt attacked," he said. "I think she'll appreciate having this the next time we do battle."

Farther down the road, the trickster inclined his head toward a tall building with bronzed thatching that had been lightly scorched. "Vidar's hall," he said. "I noticed he isn't wearing his famous shoes. If they were good enough to break my son's jaws, they should be good enough for tackling Surt."

"Famous shoes?" I repeated, hurrying after him. "Like yours?"

"Does Vidar seem like the type to have similar interests to mine?" Loki asked. "Swiftness and flight weren't important to him. He found himself the strongest and sturdiest shoes in existence. That really is how he killed Fenrir. They kept his toes intact when he kicked my son's mouth open to shove a sword down his throat."

He found the shoes in question in the back of a cabinet and tossed them into his sack too. When we returned to the road, he set off straight toward the forest beyond the city's main buildings, not even glancing at any of the other halls.

"Where are we going now?" I asked.

Another bellow echoed through the air from behind us. Surt

sounded even angrier than before. “That isn’t enough! I don’t care about your people’s ‘policies’!”

“We’re almost done,” Loki said. “There’s one last thing—I’m not even entirely sure it’ll be there. But I’ve heard rumors, and the Norns aren’t around anymore to dissuade a little prying.”

“Rumors about what?”

We passed into the woods, Loki’s steps speeding up to a supernatural pace. I lifted off the ground and flew after him so he didn’t leave me behind.

“Have you ever heard the story of Freyr’s sword?” he said.

I shook my head. “I don’t know anything about Freyr except he’s Freya’s brother.”

“I suppose it doesn’t make the most exciting telling,” the trickster said. “My and Thor’s exploits are much more entertaining. Well. One of Freyr’s prized possessions was a sword that could fight on its own, with barely any guidance from its owner. It’d guide your hand, know exactly how to hit the mark… Some say that if Freyr had kept it for Ragnarok, he might have defeated Surt then. So it stands to reason it’d be helpful to have it against the brute now in place of the lesser one he’s been using.”

“He didn’t have that sword for Ragnarok?” I said. “Why not?”

“Oh, that ridiculous affliction called love.” Loki shot me a crooked smile over his shoulder. “An emotion that can provoke wondrous acts, to be sure, but also rather idiotic ones at times. Freyr got it into his head that he absolutely had to marry a particular giantess. My former people demanded his sword before they’d allow her to consider it. He was smitten enough that he agreed. So, if you look at it from a certain angle, *he’s* really the one who caused Asgard’s fall, not me.”

I made a face. “Somehow I have a feeling Odin had a hand in that story somewhere too.”

“I wouldn’t be surprised, but the Allfather never mentioned it to me. In any case, the rumor I heard was that one of the giant kings brought the sword to the Norns while they were still sharing their visions of past and future. He had some important matter he wanted them to weigh in on, and that was the most valuable item he could offer in payment. It seems likely they would have accepted it. The only questions are whether that story is true at all, and if it is, where they'd have hidden it."

He drew to a stop in a clearing I recognized from my travels through the warped version of Asgard we'd explored in Muninn's prison. The arc of a huge tree root jutted from the ground—part of Yggdrasil, the great tree that connected the realms, from what Freya had told me then. A stone well stood next to it. Otherwise the clearing was empty, no sign anyone had been through here in ages.

"What happened to the Norns?" I asked as Loki prowled around the well.

"None of us are entirely sure," Loki said. "They became rather faded over the years since Ragnarok. I think perhaps as the gods turned to them less and less, and other realms began to forget they even existed, their ties to the present faded. They never were quite beings of a concrete nature the way we are. I wouldn't be surprised if they reappear someday just for the pleasure of keeping us on our toes."

We searched all around the clearing, testing the stones on the sides of the well, the ground all around it, and the trunks on the trees edging the open space. Finally, Loki stopped and crossed his arms with a defeated huff.

"Perhaps they took the damned thing with them. I supposed the one sword can't matter that much. If it'd been the key to defeating Surt, I'd have expected something to have turned up in Odin's visions about blades or steel or…"

He trailed off, his eyes narrowing as he considered the well.

"What?" I said.

"I'm thinking about what Odin visions *did* offer us. 'The highest water.' Asgard is the highest of the realms. The Norns' well was held up as sacred. You might say it could burn through the haze of what was and what has yet to be. It could be his visions meant this."

I gave the well a skeptical look. "You really think that water could stop Surt?"

Loki shrugged. "We're here now. It can't hurt to take some."

He dropped the bucket down to a distant splash. As he hauled it back up with one arm, he drew a couple of small pouches from his sack with his other hand.

The water in the bucket glinted with an unearthly energy that made my skin prickle. Maybe it did have the power to make a difference. Loki dipped in one pouch, slipped it into his pocket, and then offered the other he filled to me.

"Just in case," he said, his crooked grin coming back. "I have managed to get myself killed once."

I jabbed him in the chest with my finger as I took the pouch. "It'd better be the last time you do that. Now what?"

Loki frowned. "We don't want to give Surt a chance to detonate those bombs back on Midgard. Let's take a look at how heavily he has Bifrost's gate guarded right now. You can find your way to Odin quickly through Valhalla's doors. If we can clear the way, you could bring our findings down and tell them to get up here and fight."

I suspected Surt would have the place where the rainbow bridge could form nearly as heavily guarded as his chosen hall. Maybe we could draw some of his allies away with Loki's trickery if we couldn't brute force the issue?

We hustled back through the woods and into the city. We'd just passed the first of the halls when a cry rang out from up ahead that wasn't furious or pained at all, which somehow made it even more awful.

"Yes! I can feel it. That's the key. Come on, come on, we have to move. Midgard will belong to me before the end of the hour."

Surt burst from Thor's hall with a stream of giants behind him.

His shout brought the wandering draugar hustling his way. His sword arm still dangling limp at his side, his shoulder packed with a thick bandage that was already mottled with blood, but his other arm moved without a hitch as he swept it through the air. The flames of his bridge arced off the ground. He sprang onto it, his net of warheads slung against his broad back.

My heart stuttered. "He's going now. Down to Midgard somewhere with the bombs." And from the sound of that joyful cry, he was sure he knew how to set them off now. "We have to follow him—we have to stop him."

Dozens of giants and draugar were rushing onto the flaming surface after their leader. Loki's mouth twisted. "Even I'm not arrogant enough to think the two of us can take down his whole army alone."

Inspiration hit me like a smack to the face. "We won't have to be alone," I said. I sprang off the ground, soaring as quickly as I could toward Valhalla.

# 24

*Baldur*

"They'll find their way back," I said to Hod as he paced the stretch of New Mexico desert we'd retreated to. "You know Loki can find his way out of anything. And Aria—"

And Aria fell out of the sky.

She hit the dry ground in a crouch, her wings spread to slow her fall and soften the impact. We'd barely turned when she was springing upright. She dashed not to us but to Odin.

"You have to open the bridge to Asgard," she said, grabbing the edge of his cloak. "*Now*. Surt is about to detonate the bombs—it's the only way we can get to him in time—"

"Wait a moment, valkyrie," the Allfather said in his distant way.

Aria let out a noise of frustration before he could say anything else. "No. There's no time to wait. This is what we have to do. I've just been up there in Asgard—I know what's happening. Can you just trust me?"

All of us gathered there—all the gods we'd found except the three who'd fallen in that last battle, as well as Aria's human colleague and a handful of his underlings—fell silent as we watched Odin. He stared at Aria for a second. Then, to my surprised relief, he raised his hands.

"I think perhaps this is where we must part ways," he said to the leader of the humans. "We must go quickly, and the one who carried you before is no longer with us."

The man who'd shot Surt stared at the expanse of shimmering color rising up into the sky and let out a choked laugh. "I'll have to trust your judgment. Take that asshole down for us, all right?"

Thor hurried up beside our valkyrie as we started up the bridge. He brushed his broad hand over her hair. "Loki?" he asked.

"I summoned him up to Valhalla," she said with a little smile, managing to look just a shade pleased despite the tension still tightening her face. "He's distracting the guards who were watching for the bridge. There aren't that many. Surt was getting low on lackeys. He brought most of them with him—to wherever he's going." She touched his side gently. "Are you okay?"

He patted the spot where I'd sealed up his wound as well as I could. I could tell from the slight hitch in his steps that he was still hurt. I'd stretched my energy thin as it was, healing all of us I could heal. And I might need more power yet before the end of the hour. I gazed up toward Asgard as I loped faster over Bifrost's gleaming surface, my stomach knotting.

I couldn't deny what Hod had said about my affinity for light. I'd been shaken by the burning energy in the nuclear plant that had harmonized with mine before nearly wiping us out, but if I found the right way to use it, to control it…

The words were right there in the vision Odin had related to us. *The light of day can burn before a fire.* Burn up all the explosive power those bombs might have unleashed?

The streaks of color flew by beneath my feet. Muninn soared over our heads, and the other gods raced on alongside me. Some of their breaths had already turned ragged. Surt was injured from that last battle, but we'd taken plenty of hits too, and we were tired. The allies he'd brought with him were those he'd left stationed in Asgard, fresh for this fight.

We'd lost a lot. Njord. Bragi. Vidar, somewhere in the depths of the facility where he'd tried to chase after Surt. So many of those human allies Aria had brought to us. Nearly Loki. How many more would be gone, beyond my or her ability to save, before we ended this war? Would any of us survive?

I pushed my strides faster, speeding my feet along with bolts of light. Hod glided along beside me, relying on his shadows, his expression taut with determination. Thor barrelled on at the front of our charge despite his small limp. Mjolnir flashed in his hand.

No matter what might lie ahead, we were not backing down.

We burst out through the clouds. My heart ached at the sight of Asgard before me, so welcome and yet so horrifying with the halls blackened and the fountain smashed.

A few giants were standing at the edge of the realm, braced as they watched the bridge. Thor leapt forward to hurl his hammer, and I moved at the same time instinctively, whipping a spear of light. Aria slashed her glowing dagger through the air, Hod threw a surge of shadow—and our trickster dashed into view around the side of the nearest hall, tossing a ball of fire as if he'd known this was the time to meet us. Which perhaps he had.

Our powers whirled around the giants and slammed them together with a shower of sparks. Mjolnir bashed right through all three of their skulls before flying back to Thor's hand. He nodded to Loki with a wide grin.

"Sly One. You managed to slip even death."

"Only Ari can take the credit there," the trickster said. "I thought it had me through and through this time. And it may yet if you don't all light a fire under your feet. Literally. Let's go!"

He waved his arm, and my gaze followed his gesture. Surt's

bridge of flames seared up across the realm from the road beyond the courtyard.

Aria darted forward, her wings flapping with a whisper of feathers. The rest of us ran on alongside her. The heat of the bridge prickled over my face as we drew close. A black patch was spreading across the marble tiles it had sprung up from.

But the giants and the draugar had survived walking on that surface. I braced myself and rushed onward.

"Freya," Loki said. "I thought you might appreciate this." He tossed a sword to the goddess, who threw her lesser blade aside and snatched the new one up with a smile. The trickster glanced around as we ran on. His expression darkened. "Did Vidar fall?"

"We lost him somewhere in those tunnels beneath the buildings," Thor said. "We called for him, tried to reach him, but he didn't answer, and the human army was pouring in to secure the base as well as they could… He may make it still." The thunder god couldn't summon much hope into his tone. He might not want to admit what he knew, but I'd felt our brother's passing like a slice across my gut as the same wrenching crossed Hod's face.

Loki passed a few more items from the sack he carried to the other gods. The flames of the bridge hissed as our feet trampled over them. A thicker heat washed over my body. My skin felt as if it were baking, but I could survive that.

Much like Bifrost's shape, Surt's bridge arched up and then plummeted down toward Midgard. Sparks sizzled through the clouds it had parted. A smell like hot iron clogged my lungs.

As we half-raced, half-tumbled down the bridge's steep slope, the fiery giant and his remaining army came into view on the ground below. He'd set down on the top of a grassy hill. Nothing stirred there except for him and his minions, but just a few miles away, the suburbs of a massive city sprawled toward the glinting skyscrapers of its downtown.

Surt wanted to make sure he destroyed as many humans as possible with that first blast.

Not now. Not ever, if we had any say in it.

We hurtled downward, Thor splitting the air with his battle cry. Surt was waving his working hand toward us, urging his army into motion.

"Whatever it takes, whatever we have to do," Aria called out to us. "If he ignites even one of those warheads, we've lost everything."

She pointed her dagger toward Surt, diving faster. Heimdall brought his battle horn to his lips and blared it like a warning and a call to arms all at once.

"All of us together," I shouted, determination blazing through me. Every god still with us threw themselves forward with their magic and their weapons, but only five of us moved in perfect unison.

Many times now, I'd felt a connection with my brothers and Loki around our valkyrie while we fought. In that moment, the sensation hummed through me more potent than ever before. I could feel Hod's sharp inhalation, the twinge in Thor's abdomen, the gritting of the trickster's teeth as we launched our attacks together.

We weren't just ourselves in that moment but part of a larger whole, a larger harmony.

Our mingling wave of magic laced around Mjolnir and toppled the first row of attackers careening toward us. Freya swooped by, slashing with her sword. Odin sprang from the flaming bridge with an agility I hadn't known my father still possessed and stabbed his spear through the chest of a giant. Freyr dove in with his own sword singing through the air.

Surt's army swarmed to meet us, to blockade us off from the giant we needed to stop as they had before. Our greatest enemy was hunched over his stack of cylindrical bombs, his good hand braced against the metal surface. From the clenching of his jaw, he was exerting some sort of magical energy on it to bend it to his will. To force it to explode.

My pulse hiccupped. In that instant, focusing on him and the weapon beneath his palm, an impression of all the caustic energy that shell contained radiated through me like a thousand searing needles. A thousand searing needles that quivered in tune with the glow of power inside me. Nausea swelled in my gut.

I didn't want to touch those weapons, not even from this far away with only my magic. I wanted to put all the distance I could between my being and that awful devastating potential.

But I couldn't outrun the destruction. My absence wouldn't prevent it. It wasn't a question of whether I made those devices explode or not. It was only a matter of whether I could stop the explosion or whether I didn't risk trying.

I glanced over at my twin. Hod was braced behind a shield of shadow, hurling lashes of darkness into the fray. I couldn't imagine how he must experience a battle like this with no vision to orient him, only the shouts and grunts and clangs, the smells of metal and blood. He didn't hold back. He took the darkness inside him and shaped it to his will to save as many as he could. He'd carried so much responsibility on his shoulders for so very long.

If he could stand up under all that weight, Asgard help me if I didn't too.

I sucked in a breath and sent another draug crumpling with a bolt of magic. Then I backed up to the foot of the bridge, climbing a few paces so I could see Surt and his stockpile clearly.

Training all my attention on his weapons, I sent out a stream of light, so thin he shouldn't notice it with the sun beaming down over him. My magic licked over the bomb he was working on and through the metal shell.

There. This was the substance tremoring and ready to cascade into the chain reaction Hod had talked about.

I closed my fingers toward my palms, willing more heat into my stream of light. Slowly, carefully, I fused particle by particle, easing back when they started to quiver harder. I melded this one to this one to this one, on and on, until I could feel the material settling like a massive weight condensed in the casing—inert and unshakeable.

Sweat trickled down my back. I shifted my feet to steady my weight and focused on the next of the bombs. Confidence started to ripple through me, but I didn't let it hurry me. What I'd done had only worked because I'd kept such a tight leash on my powers.

Another clump of matter hardened inside the metal shell, large enough to block the reaction. Swallowing thickly, I started on the next, and then the next. The heat of the bridge thickened around me, searing into my lungs, but I tuned it out. If I could just reach them all—if I could disable every one of those missiles…

I'd made it to the sixth when Surt slammed his hands against the one he'd been working on with a curse. He heaved it off the stack and reached for the one underneath, which I hadn't targeted yet. I snapped my attention to that one as swiftly as I dared. Melt it down, fuse it solid, before he could spark the sharper flame.

Whatever technique he'd been using to feel out the weapon, the giant was getting more confident too. After just a minute, he frowned and shoved that bomb away too. The next one I'd already tackled. I started on the eighth, but this time it was only a few seconds before Surt leapt to his feet with a roar.

I wasn't looking directly at him, but my skin still flared when his gaze found me. I clenched my hands, willing more energy into the bomb. Just a few more left. Just a few more and at least this one crisis would have been averted.

"The bright one," Surt hollered with a jab of his hand. "On the bridge. He's interfering somehow. Get him!"

Giants and draugar charged around the cluster of gods to challenge me. I shifted my stream of energy to the ninth bomb and whipped a scorching line of light around me toward my attackers at the same time.

A few fell back, but the others converged around me. I tried to dodge, my exhausted legs wobbled, and a giant barrelled straight into me, tackling me to the ground. He slammed his club down on my head at the same time as my skull smacked the dirt, and my focus snapped.

# 25

*Aria*

A cry caught in my throat as the giant crashed into Baldur. I heaved my wings even faster and jabbed my dagger into the back of the brute's head.

The giant's club struck Baldur across the forehead, and they both sprawled in the grass. Baldur's face was pale, blood streaking from the gash the club had opened. I couldn't tell if he was breathing.

"Idunn!" I shouted. My chest was clenching achingly tight around my lungs, but I didn't have time to make sure the light god was okay—that he was even alive. The rest of the gods hadn't managed to break through Surt's forces to get to him yet. It might take every one of us to make sure any of us survived.

With a wisp of relief, I caught sight of the skinny shimmering goddess slipping through the fray to Baldur. I threw myself back to the fringes of the battle.

As long as I wasn't in any of my gods' eyeline, I didn't have to worry they'd hesitate in their fighting to protect me. I'd been skirting the crowd, picking off draugar and the occasional giant that tried to come at the gods from behind. I just hadn't been quite fast enough to dispatch the bunch of attackers that had all run at Baldur at once.

Surt had ordered that charge—the light god must have been doing something to foil his plans. It hadn't looked like he'd finished yet. Panic had flashed across his face right before he'd fallen. The giant was still grappling with his warheads.

Surt hadn't paid much attention to me during this battle, either because I'd kept out of view or because he was too occupied with his new arsenal. I bashed my heel into a draug's skull, slashed the dagger Loki had given me through a giant's throat as if her flesh were butter, and peered at Surt through the milling bodies. He'd already tossed a couple of the warheads aside. Because Baldur had ruined them somehow?

As I watched, the fiery giant cursed and heaved another one out of the way. Muninn flung herself over the heads of his minions toward him, raven claws outstretched, and he paused just long enough to swipe his sword in her direction. She dodged, but the stream of fire veered after her. It smacked her head over heels, sending her tumbling to the ground. I winced. Let Idunn get to her in time too.

The swarm of attackers between our forces and the fiery giant pressed harder with sweeps of their own flaming blades, as if they meant to herd us right back up the bridge. Not a chance. I knocked two more draugar aside and found myself next to Heimdall.

The watchful god was breathing hard, his muscles rippling through his arms as he slammed his sword right through a draug's chest. "Wouldn't this be a good time for you and your devotees to work some of that valkyrie-merged magic?" he hollered at me.

I propelled myself up to smack my palm against a nearby giant's head and ripped the life energy from his body. "We can't," I snapped as the giant fell. "Baldur's down. The connection needs all five of us together. So, unless you want to finally give it a try with *your* magic…"

Heimdall's jaw clenched. He dispatched another draug. I was scanning the fray again, looking to see where I was needed and not really expecting him to answer, when he exhaled in a rush.

"Maybe I should."

Even as my gaze jerked to him with a startled stare, he was tapping Freyr's shoulder next to him, calling out to all the other gods around us. "We started to see some effect when we worked together before," he said. "Push forward on my word, moving at the same time, and I'll connect our efforts as well as I can. Ready? Now!"

He whipped his sword and swept his other arm through the air to signal their attack. The gods hurtled forward around him. A hum of energy rippled through the air, and Freya's bright magic leapt from blade to blade to Odin's spear. A streak of Hod's searing darkness caught around one of Skadi's arrows.

The effect wasn't quite as explosive as what my four gods had managed to produce before, but it added an extra punch that sent several of the giants stumbling backward. More draugar fell with their eerie groans. The gods pressed the momentary advantage they'd gained, slicing and blazing a path through our attackers toward the crest of the hill where Surt still held the highest ground.

My gaze found the giant, and my stomach flipped. He'd cast aside several of the warheads, but he was gripping a new one now, and a pleased smile was stretching across his gnarled bearded face. He leaned closer, sliding his hands over the metal casing, and bellowed at his army. "Hold them, slaughter them, make them pay!"

The words seemed to rally the draugar. They flung themselves at us even more ferociously, with no concern for themselves at all, as far as I could see. They existed for nothing except to serve the master who'd raised them.

The giants in the swarm roared, launching themselves at the nearest gods. I flapped my wings to lift out of reach of a stabbing sword and saw Loki leaping from the ground too—but four giants barged at him from all around, yanking him back. One of them burst into flames, and he slashed out at another.

The casing beneath Surt's hands started to glow.

The fiery giant's chuckle carried over the cries and clatter of the battle. My pulse hiccupped. In that instant, my awareness narrowed down to one simple fact: I had a straight line to the giant, and no one else did.

My throat closed up, and my fingers tightened around the handle of my dagger, but at the same time, Odin's words about acting if we saw our chance rose up in the back of my mind.

Maybe I was only a valkyrie and not a god, maybe this body could break much easier than any of those below me, but this was my realm. I would defend it with every ounce of my being, whether that was enough or not.

I threw myself forward, dagger raised, my other hand shooting to the pouch of well water Loki had given me. *Only the highest water can put out all the flames.* This had better be that water.

The wind shrieked in my ears. Surt's head jerked up, his lips parting in a triumphant snarl. His arm swung up to heave me back, but I wasn't aiming at him.

I slammed the dagger into the warhead's casing with all the strength and will in my body. The blade drove straight down through the metal. I splashed the contents of my pouch over the opening.

The glow that had infused the shell crackled away. Surt made a strangled sound and swung his fist at me. The first bash clocked me across the temple and sent me sprawling on the grass, my ears ringing. The giant lunged at me, a ball of hissing fire forming around his clenched hand—

—and the gods burst through his army.

The flames had only just seared my cheek when Thor hauled Surt back. A blast of shadow smacked into the giant's face. Surt fumbled for his sword, swiping at the darkness clinging to his eyes, but he couldn't get his bearings fast enough.

Odin loomed over the giant. With a bellow, the Allfather plunged the tip of his spear right through Surt's throat.

The giant's body went slack and crumpled to the ground between the useless shells of his warheads. His flaming bridge sizzled and snuffed out, leaving only the taint of smoke in the air. I stared at Surt's prone body, my own body tensed, half-expecting him to stir and rise.

Freya strode up to him, her eyes glinting fiercely and her golden hair flowing out behind her. She lifted her sword and swung it down to sever the giant's neck. His head rolled to the side, thumping into one of his missiles, eyes glazed and beard soaked through with blood.

My heart thudded for several beats before the reality of the moment hit me. He was done. Gone. We'd finally beaten him.

A slightly hysterical giggle bubbled in my chest. Loki dropped down from the sky next to me, touching the battered side of my head with a grimace. As I struggled to my feet through a wave of dizziness, the rest of the gods spun to take on the remains of Surt's army.

The draugar had frozen in place as their master died. They sagged as if as one, their bodies folding in on themselves, some of them—the older ones, I guessed—crumbling into dust. The couple dozen giants still standing gaped at the fallen draugar and their slain leader. They took in the flash of the gods' blades and the flare of their magic. And then they scattered, fleeing down the hill.

"Baldur?" I croaked. "Where is he? Is he all right?" If Surt's minions had killed him, I had to get to him in time to work my valkyrie magic. Even if my own head felt about ready to pop off my shoulders, the way it was throbbing.

Loki tucked a gentle arm around my waist and walked me over to the place where the bright god had fallen. Baldur was sitting up, his forehead bruised but his blue eyes alert as Idunn straightened up over him. She'd managed to heal him. The air rushed from my lungs in relief.

"I think this one could use a little of your magic," Loki said, ruffling my hair gingerly. I grasped the side of his tunic as my relief merged into another rush of dizziness.

"Muninn needs healing too," I said raggedly.

A hoarse voice carried across the field. "I can wait. See to the valkyrie first." The raven woman was sitting up on the grass in her human form, hunched with one seared arm cradled in front of her but in good enough spirits to manage a tight smile.

Idunn nodded and moved to me. I sank down next to Baldur and let the goddess attend to my head.

"The warheads," I said to the bright god. "You did something to them so they wouldn't explode?"

"Most of them," Baldur said. "I couldn't quite— I used my light to melt the cores so they couldn't… shatter apart."

"You got enough of them to slow Surt down until we could reach him," I said, and paused. "Your light. The light of day?" The giggle I'd been suppressing broke from my throat. "Odin's visions came true."

Hod had come up behind us. He set a gentle hand on my head. "They always seem to," he said. "Like a light in the darkness, giving direction if not certainty. There's a reason he's led Asgard for so long, regardless of the complaints any of us might raise."

The other gods gathered around. When Idunn had healed me well enough that my skull didn't feel ready to crack open, she moved to Muninn.

Skadi meandered closer to us, her elbow pressed to her side where I'd seen her take a heavy blow. Baldur pushed himself to his feet to offer his own healing powers. The goddess of the hunt glanced down at me, her eyes gleaming sharp as ever. But her voice was hesitantly warm.

"You did all right out there, valkyrie. My respects."

A grin tugged at my lips. "Thank you."

Freya turned to her daughter, who had a raw scrape across her cheek. Hnoss stiffened, but she didn't back away when her mother set a cautious hand on her shoulder. No one seemed to know quite what else to say.

"What do we do now?" I said finally, to break the silence. "We're safe now, aren't we?"

"The giant of flames is felled," Odin said. "Midgard is saved, and Asgard belongs to the gods again."

"And he's left us with quite the reconstruction job up there," Loki said. "I foresee a great deal of scrubbing and stone-laying in our future."

"All of our futures?" Thor said. He glanced around at his fellow gods. "Will you come back to Asgard with us?"

The gods we'd gathered for our fight hesitated. Freyr swiped his hand across his mouth.

"I suppose now that we've reclaimed it, we might as well revisit the old realm," he said. "It was probably about time I stopped by and reinvigorated my powers."

"I don't expect I'll stay very long," Skadi put in.

"We wouldn't put demands on anyone," Freya said. "But you *are* all welcome. It's your home as much as it is ours. We can return and make what repairs we need to, and then we'll see how we all feel. None of us could have planned for this… but perhaps the one good thing that's come of Surt's uprising is that it's given us a chance to find each other again." She gave her daughter a tentative smile. "To make long-needed amends."

"Then let us ascend," Odin said. With a thump of his spear and a sweep of his arm, he ushered forth the arc of his rainbow bridge.

# 26

*Aria*

The glittering ground shimmered brighter as Baldur poured more of his magic into it. The hollow patches that had formed in the crystal-like surface filled back in. The stretch of trees to our left seemed to shudder, their leaves glinting a richer green.

The god of light leaned back on his heels with a pleased smile. A week after our final battle with Surt, a faint pink mark still showed on his forehead where the one giant had bashed him. He'd told me he'd rather let it heal the rest of the way on its own. *Some things are better solved without rushing.*

"That's all there is to it," he said now, motioning to the shining landscape around us.

Alfheim, the realm of the light elves, lived up to its people's name, especially once Baldur had worked his restorative power. Everything glinted or gleamed, from the grass poking through the soil to the tops of the distant mountains.

"I'll come once every few days, like Hod has been doing for the dark elves, until the realm is stable again," Baldur went on. "And after that we'll have to make sure to come by and touch base with the light elves regularly, so that things don't start to run down again."

"They've been welcoming?" I asked.

He nodded. "Distant but appreciative. As the light elves tend to be." The corner of his mouth curled up. "I expect Thor's reception in Jotunheim will be much less friendly."

The thunder god was planning on dropping in on the land of giants after a little more time had passed. Approaching them too soon after the battles seemed more likely to stir up new conflicts than heal old wounds.

"They'd better appreciate him," I muttered. "They should be begging our forgiveness."

"The giants are as they are," Baldur said. "For all the troubles we've had with them, we've also mingled with them enough. Maybe if we hadn't neglected them so long as we did the other realms, Surt wouldn't have riled them up against us so easily."

And no one really wanted any of the nine realms to fall apart. Freya and Freyr had gone together to check in on their original home, Vanaheim, and to bring the news of their father's death. Skadi had offered to help as much as she could in Niflheim, the realm of constant winter, and Loki was lending some fire to Muspelheim, as much as it already seemed to have. *There's always a balance to be kept, pixie*, he'd told me with a smirk when I'd commented on that.

Odin himself had traveled at least once to the lowest realm, the land of the dead, where Loki's daughter, Hel, apparently still ruled. The Allfather hadn't said much on his return, but at least he *had* returned, so I guessed the visit couldn't have gone too horribly wrong.

There wasn't much I could contribute to healing the realms, but I'd been curious to see at least one of the gods at work. Maybe in part because it was about time I healed something that felt much more fragile.

Baldur glanced at me as he ambled closer to the trees. "Aren't you supposed to be taking that trip to Midgard soon?"

I dragged in a breath. "Yeah. I should probably be getting back. I told Hod I'd find him after he finished with the dark elves today."

I should have been relieved that this day had arrived, even excited, but instead my nerves were jumping, poking at my gut. Baldur stopped and touched the side of my face. "Whatever you decide to say, it'll be right. You know him better than anyone."

"I know," I said. "I just… He matters to me more than anyone."

"And you'll be there for him, just like you were meant to be." The god of light stroked his thumb over my cheek, and I bobbed up for a kiss. A little of his brightness flared through me, settling my nerves.

"Okay," I said. "I'm doing this. I'll see you tonight."

I slipped away through the trees to the gate that would lead me back to Asgard. The jolt through blackness that came with passing through was starting to feel familiar. I emerged onto Yggdrasil's branch and hurried along its trunk to the hearth entrance into Valhalla.

It wasn't hard to find Hod, because the dark god was already in the hall waiting for me. He turned at the sound of my steps over the hardwood floor. A smile crossed his face, so much more relaxed than the ones he'd been able to offer most of the time I'd known him. That fond expression made him so handsome my heart still skipped a beat, even though I'd been surrounded by divinely attractive gods for weeks now.

I'd talked to Baldur as if I were ready for what Hod and I had planned, but seeing him there, prepared to go, made my chest clench up all over again. I walked to him and wrapped my arms around him, escaping for a moment into his solid embrace.

"Hey," the dark god said, leaning his head next to mine. "You can take more time. We don't have to do this now."

"We do," I said. "I wish I hadn't left it as long as I already have. I just—what if it goes wrong?"

Memories from Muninn's prison flitted through my head—false ones of events she'd invented, but horrible all the same.

"That's why I'm coming," Hod said. "My magic can help smooth things over."

"Right." I breathed in his faintly smoky smell and found the determination to step back. "Odin didn't have any objections?"

"He seemed to like the idea, actually," Hod said. "He should be waiting for us at the edge of the courtyard now. I think you've managed to win him over with all that tough love, valkyrie."

I elbowed him in mock-offense, and he chuckled as we headed out of the hall of warriors.

The Allfather was indeed already standing at the far end of the main courtyard. At the sight of us, he swept out his arm, and the rainbow bridge leapt from the land's edge toward the realm below. His ability to direct Bifrost to any end point he wanted was going to make this a much shorter trip than if we'd had to find our way from Yggdrasil's gate.

"Go well and return at peace," Odin intoned as if delivering a prophecy. I'd be happy to take those words as one.

"Thank you," I said, and he tipped his broad-brimmed hat to us—a new one that was no longer burnt but somehow just as rumpled as the old one had been.

I extended my wings so I could take the trip over the bridge faster. Now that we were going, I didn't want to drag out the journey. Hod glided along beside me on a patch of shadow, and we followed the curve of the rainbow bridge down into the clouds.

We came out over a residential neighborhood, all pastels and steepled roofs, quiet in the middle of the night. My heart thumped faster as we made our way toward the house I'd stared at for so long in the past and in my memories.

"Take your time, and let me know if you need anything else from me," Hod said. "I'll stay out of the way and follow the plan we discussed."

We came to a stop by the bedroom window at the back of the house. The light was still on, a pale yellow glow filling the room. My little brother sat cross-legged on his foster home's bed, a chapter book open on his lap, a dragon-shaped pillow tucked under one of his skinny arms. Not quite as skinny as it had been a few weeks ago when we'd whisked him away from my mother's house. That sight gave me a little burst of confidence.

Leaving him had been hard and had caused us both some pain, but it'd been better than the alternatives. And now I could make amends.

I came to rest on the window ledge and readied myself. Then I willed myself visible and knocked lightly on the wooden frame.

Petey glanced up. His blue-gray eyes widened when he saw me —all of me, wings included. He blinked as if he thought I might disappear if he cleared his gaze.

"Hey," I said softly through the screen. "Petey. May I come in?"

Petey's mouth opened and closed and opened again. He didn't look frightened so much as startled and uncertain. I could handle that.

"Who are you?" he said. "How do you know my name?"

"Don't you remember me?" I said with a quick glance toward Hod, who was hovering beside me invisibly. "It's Ari. Your imaginary friend."

Hod made a delicate motion with his hand. He was the one who'd shadowed most of Petey's memories in the first place. Now he was lifting that veil just a little, just enough for some of my brother's memories of me to seep through, without the full context of who I was or where we'd known each other.

"Ari," Petey murmured, and recognition lit in his eyes. The smile that sprang to his face was so bright it brought tears to my eyes. I swiped them away quickly as he darted over to the window.

"So, can I come in, buddy?" I asked.

"Of course," he said, still staring at me. I detached the screen carefully with a nudge of my valkyrie strength and set it on the floor inside next to the window. Then I climbed in, keeping my wings close to my back.

I hadn't been sure how much my brother would trust me, coming to him like this, with his memories still so fractured. I hadn't wanted to push for more than he was comfortable with. But the second my feet hit the floor, Petey flung his arms around my waist, squeezing me tight. He pressed his face to my chest.

"I was scared," he said in a ragged voice. "I thought—I couldn't remember anything from before. I didn't know anything. Why haven't you come in so long? What happened?"

I knelt down in front of him, blinking hard to hold back any further tears, and set my hands on his shoulders as I held his gaze.

"You were in danger," I said. I'd practiced my explanation so many times the words came automatically. "There were people who wanted to hurt you. Now they're gone, but they—they wanted you to forget everything."

It was easier to blame his clouded mind on our enemies than to try to explain why I'd needed to do it. I wouldn't have needed to take that step if it hadn't been for Surt and his minions anyway—and I still needed to protect Petey from our mother and the men she'd let shove him around.

"I had to make sure they were completely beaten before I came to see you again," I added. "But now they are. You're totally safe. You're happy here, aren't you?"

"Yeah," Petey said. "Brenda and Stuart—they say I can call them Mom and Dad if I feel like it, but I don't know yet—they're really nice. But I knew there was someone I was missing. I knew there had to be." His hands closed around my arms. "You don't feel imaginary."

"Well, I'll tell you a little secret." I dropped my voice. "I'm only imaginary to everyone else. To you, I'm totally real. You're the only one I want to let see me, because you're special."

He looked up at my wings, open down above my back, and knit his brow. "Did you always have wings?"

I swallowed a laugh. Those wouldn't have figured into any of his memories. "I did. I just wasn't sure if you'd think they were too strange. But you don't mind them, do you?"

"No," he said with an awed expression. "I think they're awesome. Can I grow wings too?"

I did laugh out loud then. "No, kiddo. But you don't need them. They come with the whole imaginary friend thing." I brushed my fingers down the side of his pale face, my heart aching. I wanted to just hold him for an hour, but there were certain boundaries I had to keep. He needed to stay focused on his real life. I needed to accept that I was never going to be as much a part of that real life as I'd used to be.

But I could still be a part of it, even if only a small one.

"I can't stay much longer," I told him. "I just wanted to let you know that I'm still here. I've looked out for you since the day you were born, Petey, and I'll be here for you all through the rest of your life. I'll come talk to you now and then, but if you ever need me right away, stick something red over your windowsill, okay? I'll come as soon as I see it."

Petey nodded. "Okay. You don't have to leave *right* now, do you?"

I swallowed the lump in my throat. "No. Not quite yet. Come here?"

He nestled into my arms again, and I did hold him, even if it was only for five minutes instead of the hour I'd have preferred. Then I kissed his forehead and stood up.

"I'll see you soon," I said. "You'd better get to bed. Remember, no matter what happens, you'll always have me."

"Thank you, Ari," he said, beaming.

It took all my self-control to walk back to the window and clamber out. Hod pulled me straight into a hug. I ducked my head into the crook of his neck and let out a sob Petey could no longer hear.

"That was perfect," the dark god said, stroking his hand over my hair. "You gave him everything he needed."

I wanted to protest. If I'd led the life I'd meant to before I died, I'd have given Petey a home myself, been everything he needed in a parent. But he did have everything he needed here too. And the fact was that if I hadn't died and gotten swept up into this godly mess, maybe Surt would have conquered Midgard after all.

It was hard to have any real regrets, knowing that.

"Time to head back?" Hod asked when I'd gotten a grip on my emotions.

"Actually," I said, "there was one other thing I wanted to do first. It'll just be a little detour."

---

We arrived back in Asgard with both of us laden down with bulging takeout bags. The smells wafting out of them already had my mouth watering. Hod grinned at me as we carted our loads over to the hall that was now mine.

Loki was standing outside his own hall with a few of the other gods who'd lingered on in Asgard at least for a little while. Freyr was laughing at something the trickster had said, clapping him on the shoulder with amusement that looked genuine. Hnoss made a wild gesture that got Idunn giggling too, and Loki waved her off with mock-horror that quickly broke with a chuckle. His eyes gleamed so eagerly I almost choked up all over again.

They were treating him like an equal. Like a friend—like someone who belonged here in Asgard. I could tell from the tension that lingered in his posture that the trickster wasn't quite sure whether to relax into their acceptance yet. After all that time when they'd shunned him, it'd probably take a while before he could completely believe they weren't going to change their minds all over again. But those last few battles, the truths Odin had shared, and the sacrifice Loki had made to save the rest of us had shifted the balance between him and the gods in a way I suspected would last.

He caught sight of us and left the others after giving Freyr a playful nudge. His eyebrows arched with curiosity as he sauntered over. "You've brought back quite the haul."

"I brought back dinner," I said. "A real Midgard dinner, not a bunch of convenience store junk. Can you find Thor and Baldur and remind them we were supposed to eat together?"

"I doubt the Thunderer will have forgotten where he's getting his next meal," Loki said with a wink, and sped off on his enchanted shoes.

By the time the trickster returned with the other two gods in tow, I'd spread out our feast along with bottles of mead on the hall's ridiculously large dining table. I could have seated all the current inhabitants of Asgard around it, but I wanted to share tonight just with my four.

Thor strode in and immediately caught me by the waist with an epic hug. "What do we have here?" he asked, bending over me.

"Chinese takeout," I announced. "From my favorite restaurant in Philly. I got three roast ducks just for you."

Thor let out a rumble of a laugh and tipped my chin up for a kiss. "A woman after my own heart."

My pulse leapt at the brush of his lips against mine and the thought of things I'd meant to say tonight. But maybe I'd save that until after we'd eaten. "I thought this heart was already mine," I teased, poking his chest when he released me.

"You know it is, Ari," he murmured, his voice so low my knees wobbled.

"Was the rest of your trip a success?" Loki asked as we grabbed plastic forks and dug in. He kept his usual light tone, but he was watching me carefully. He knew how much my visit to Petey had meant to me.

"I think so," I said. "He accepted the story once he had whatever memories Hod brought back. He's got that reassurance now—that someone from his past life is still around and looking after him. I think it's the best way I could have stayed in his life given…" I waved to my wings before pulling them into my back.

"Here's to you and your brother, then," the trickster said, lifting his glass of mead. "And to Hod, for his deft magic. Ah, why not to his brothers too? I'm sure you two are good for something or other." He smirked good-naturedly.

Hod shook his head with a wry smile and jostled Loki on purpose as he moved past him to grab the chow mein.

Baldur swallowed a mouthful of lemon chicken with a blissful expression and gazed around the table at us. "I think this is really it," he said. "We've found our peace. No more attacks, no more enemies known or unknown."

"You never know," Loki said, waggling a finger. "The raven may change her mind and challenge Odin for rule of Asgard yet."

I laughed. "I think ruling anywhere is the last thing Muninn wants." The raven woman had looked about as content as I'd ever seen her the few times she'd dropped in on us in human form in the past week, but mostly she seemed to be reveling in her freedom, out from under every thumb that had ever pinned her down.

"It is good," Thor said, slinging his arm around the bright god. "We deserve a little peace after all that strife. And I mean it when I say there's no one other than the four of you I'd rather enjoy that peace with."

"Although we do have another couple guests arriving," Hod

remarked, his head coming up at a sound from down the hall. He turned to me. "I hope you don't mind. We told Odin he could stop by—he wanted to speak with you after you returned from Midgard. I don't think he expects any of the dinner."

"Oh," I said. "Okay." I *had* wanted this to be just the five of us, but if Odin wasn't going to stay long, I guessed it didn't matter.

What did the Allfather want with me now? I might not have been as irritated with him as I had been during the first period in which I'd known him, but we weren't exactly chummy.

I set down my fork as Odin and Freya appeared in the dining room doorway. The Allfather's singular gaze settled on me at once. "Aria," he said. "Thank you for receiving us. I was hoping we could have a word." He motioned me over to him.

My legs balked for a second. I made myself walk over. What could be wrong? Freya wouldn't be smiling like that if they'd come with bad news, I didn't think.

I stopped in front of Odin, feeling suddenly awkward, aware of the four gazes behind me directed my way, including the blind one. Odin peered down at me, his deep brown eye as penetrating as always.

"The patchwork valkyrie," he said, leaning a little of his weight onto his spear. "I've given the matter of your existence a lot of thought in the time since we ended Surt's rebellion. The truth of it is, there's a reason I dismissed those who lived in Valhalla quite some time ago. Well, several reasons. But the most relevant one at this moment is, I don't have much need for a valkyrie. There is no one in Valhalla to serve, and I have no interest in beginning a new collection of risen warriors."

"All right," I said. My spine had stiffened. Why was he saying all this? He wasn't going to send me off to make my own way through the realms, was he?

"Dear one," Freya said, squeezing her husband's arm. "Less rambling, more getting to the important part? You're worrying her."

Odin made a face that looked almost apologetic. "My point is that I'm hoping you can contribute more than the valkyries of old used to. You already intend to return to Midgard regularly to check in on your brother. I would like, if you would accept the responsibility—and the honor—to name you the official overseer of that realm."

I stared at him. "I—what?"

"It would be your duty to check in on all the areas of Midgard as you have time to," Odin said. "Seeing as you can come and go as you please via Valhalla, there is no one better suited. And you understand that realm in its current state better than any of us, even the gods who've been living there but at a distance from humans for ages. You would simply watch over humanity and let us know if you saw any trouble with which you felt we should intervene."

An eager shiver ran through me. I wouldn't just be a hanger-on in Asgard, living among the gods but without any real role. I'd be working alongside them to oversee the realms like an equal. For the second time in as many hours, tears started to prickle at the backs of my eyes.

"Of course I'll take that responsibility," I said. "And the honor. It is one. Overseer of Midgard." I couldn't help grinning. "It's perfect."

Odin brushed his fingertips over my forehead. "Then consider it done. I expect you will do Asgard credit. Now I will leave the five of you to your feasting."

He swept back down the hall. Freya blew me a kiss and followed. I turned, a little dazed, and found all four of my gods beaming at me in kind of a knowing way. A suspicion wriggled through my mind.

"This was your idea," I said. "You suggested it to him."

Loki shrugged. "I will neither confirm nor deny. Whoever's idea it may have been, it was an excellent one, don't you agree?"

"We wouldn't want you getting bored of Asgard—and of us," Hod said.

"As if *that* could ever happen," I said, rolling my eyes. "I just never thought…"

"Never thought what?" Baldur asked gently.

My voice snagged in my throat for a moment before I could force the words out. "I never thought I'd ever do anything that would really make a difference."

A wave of the emotion I'd been trying to hold in rushed over me. I dropped my face into my hands. My gods were around me in an instant, their arms encircling me, their heads bowed together toward mine.

"You've already made a difference," Hod said, rubbing my arm. "A huge one. You know that, don't you, Ari?"

All I could do was nod. I twined my arms with theirs, leaning into Thor's brawny chest, absorbing their mingling scents. Right then, I could have believed almost anything.

The words I thought I might struggle with tumbled out of me as if I'd said them a dozen times already. Which maybe I had, silently, in my head. "I love you. All of you. *You* know that, don't you?"

I looked up at Thor, gripped his hand. "I love you." I met Baldur's eyes next, cupped his jaw. "I love you." I let my hand come to rest on Loki's tunic over the heart that still beat because of my powers. "I love you." I turned to Hod, leaning close enough to brush a kiss against his cheek. "I love you."

"I think the bond between all of us runs deep enough that I can say without a doubt that we all love you," Baldur said. "Our valkyrie."

My smile came back. "My gods."

Thor dipped his head to nip the crook of my neck. "Worth saying all the same. I love you."

Loki teased a flicker of flame along my waist with his lithe hand. "I love you."

Hod trailed his fingers across my shoulder, nudging the strap of my tank top down my arm. "I love you."

Baldur eased a step closer. "I love you," he murmured, his mouth grazing mine. Then he was kissing me, his light washing over all of us, twining with Thor's sparks and Loki's fire and Hod's shadows. All the elements that had made me who I was now.

I tugged them all closer, wanting to feel them around me in every possible way.

I'd found my freedom too. The freedom to shed all the scars of the past that had held me back so long. The freedom to enjoy love given and to offer it back in return. The freedom to construct a new life out of the gifts I'd been given, one that could change the very course of the world toward something better.

I would do myself proud—myself and the gods I loved.

# LIVING WITH GODS

## A THEIR DARK VALKYRIE BONUS EPILOGUE

*Aria*

As my wings held me aloft in the courtyard between the apartment buildings, I squinted, cocked my head, and flapped a little closer. None of that changed what I thought I'd seen: a lone red sock hanging from the balcony railing.

Dusk was falling over the city, but it wasn't dark enough yet to dilute that unmistakable bright crimson. And the sock had clearly been fixed there intentionally, since the calf-length fabric was tied around the steel bar. My pulse kicked up a notch, the sort of adrenaline trickling through my veins that these days I usually associated with battles.

I drifted to the side to consider the apartment windows. The blinds were drawn, no light glowing through them. At this time in the evening, that probably meant the inhabitants had gone out for dinner.

I hovered there for a few minutes longer, barely registering the cooling late-spring air or the rumble of traffic beyond the courtyard. My stomach twisted and balled until it'd formed a knot a

Boy Scout would have admired. I didn't know what to do about this unexpected development, and lingering here thinking about it wasn't getting me any closer to a solution. What I needed was a second opinion.

Closing my eyes, I focused on the vast interior of Valhalla, Asgard's hall of fallen warriors: the gleams of gold all around, the swords and spears mounted all across the walls, the scent of mead and aged wood lacing the air. I pulled my sense of myself inward and hurled myself toward those impressions—

And with a lurch and a gust of wind, my feet landed on the polished floorboards. I dragged the mead tang into my lungs and glanced around me.

Valhalla still looked as lonely as it had when I'd first been propelled into the building two decades ago. The only fallen warrior who'd graced this space in centuries was the godly giant I'd raised from the dead, who had plenty of better things to do than hang around in here. Neither Odin nor the other gods had seen the need to conjure any valkyries besides me.

But while it'd felt haunted back then, now the expansive silence gave me a sense of peace. I stretched my arms, soaking in the atmosphere and letting the tension in my stomach release as much as I could convince it to. Then I headed out into Asgard.

None of the gods ever bothered locking their doors. I barged right into the god of darkness's hall to hear voices carrying from one of the rooms—both Hod's and Loki's.

"All I know is your schemes have gotten us *into* trouble about as often as they've gotten us out of it, Sly One," Hod was saying, his tone dry but not caustic. He and the trickster hadn't been at each other's throats since the war with Surt, which meant now they had about as close to a friendly relationship as anyone could really hope for.

"And then I get us right out of that trouble," Loki replied in his breezy way. "Although I assure you *this* scheme will be nothing but joyfully received. Do you still have no trust in me, Dark One?"

Hod made a sound like a *harrumph.* Before he could answer that teasing question, I reached the doorway to the library where he was sitting in an armchair with a book, Loki ambling along the shelves behind him.

Both men's heads snapped towards me, Loki's amber gaze nearly as bright as his fiery hair, Hod's dark green eyes centering on me by sound alone. He knew me so well I would have believed he was actually seeing me if I hadn't been aware of his blindness.

I raised my eyebrows at Loki. "What are you plotting now?"

"Ah, don't worry about that, pixie. You'll find out when the time is right." The trickster swept over and stole a kiss I didn't mind giving up, the heated press of his mouth offering a passionate promise of good things to come. He drew back with a sly grin. "You know I wouldn't pull off any of my best plans without you."

I poked him in the chest. "A little advance notice would be nice this time."

"But surprises are so much fun." He winked at me and walked jauntily off.

I glanced toward Hod, who shook his head, predicting my question before I could ask it. "I hate to think how he'll eviscerate me if I go spilling his secrets. It might not amount to anything anyway. How was your foray to Midgard?"

I found I was too wound up still to want to confine myself to a chair. I nudged a book over and hopped up to perch on the edge of a side table instead, my legs swinging restlessly. If the god of darkness minded me misusing his furniture, he didn't show it.

"I caught yet another giant roaming around in a national park," I said. "It definitely looks like a bunch of them came through from some passage and decided to see how much preying on humanity they could get away with. Luckily they haven't had the brains to stick together, and picking them off one by one isn't too hard."

All it took was a few swift dodges and a smack of my palm to the top of the brute's head to drag his life from his body. Any twinge of guilt I might still have felt at using *that* one of my valkyrie powers had vanished the moment I'd seen him stalking a family with a couple of little kids.

"You know you can call on any of us if you do need backup," Hod said.

"Of course. But there's no need to drag you down there when I can handle it myself—better to take care of the jerks before they can do any more damage than they already have." I looked down at the floor and then back at Hod with his steady unseeing gaze. "There was something else, though. I—I went by Petey's apartment."

Hod barely moved, but his posture jerked just a tiny bit straighter with a tension that showed he recognized how important this subject was to me. "Was everything all right?"

"I think so. As far as I know. It didn't look like he and his girlfriend were home." I rubbed my face. "But there was a sock on the balcony."

Hod's reaction softened enough for him to offer a hint of a smile. "So, you're worried that his feet may be cold?"

"It's a *red* sock. That was our signal, way back when. He'd leave something red on his windowsill when he wanted me to come visit him."

Hod blinked. "Right. I'd almost forgotten." He paused and added in a careful tone, "How long has it been since he last reached out to you that way?"

"Long. It's got to be almost fifteen years now." I stared down at my hands again where they'd clasped together over my knees. "It's ridiculous. I'm an immortal supernatural being with powers over life and death. But… I don't know what to do."

Hod didn't ask why I'd come to him. My bond with my little brother, the guilt I'd felt after I'd been forced to leave him and the responsibilities I hadn't been willing to give up, were parts of my life the dark god had always understood better than anyone else. He'd been the one who'd followed me to my mother's house after I'd first been resurrected, the one who'd clouded over Petey's memories so we could place him safely with an adoptive family far from my mother and the mythic enemies who'd been threatening him. The one who'd come with me when I'd revealed my new form to my brother with as much truth as I'd felt I could offer.

He'd had plenty of his own guilt and sense of responsibility as a sibling hanging over him for much longer than I had.

"Are you sure it's a signal?" he asked. "It couldn't be a simple coincidence?"

"It looked pretty deliberate. The sock was tied right to the railing. It's not like it was laid out there to dry or something. And there was only the one. And red socks aren't exactly super common anyway."

"Remind me how you left things with him when the visits stopped."

I dragged in a breath. "It's been almost fifteen years. He was getting older—eleven, twelve. Asking more questions I couldn't answer, trying to figure out how it was even possible I was there. Seeming kind of agitated about it. Then he stopped signaling me at all. I was still coming by pretty frequently then, just in case, watching to make sure he was okay. One time he had some friends over, and I heard him laughing with them about the imaginary friend he'd made up when he was younger, like it was so absurd... He stopped believing I could be real. I heard him joke about it a couple more times over the next few years and after that he didn't mention it at all."

When I looked up, Hod's attention was still fixed on me. "You'd expected that to happen. That there'd probably be a point where he'd grow out of relying on 'imaginary friends'."

"Yeah. It was hard not being able to interact with him anymore, but I understood. After a while I cut down how often I checked on him, but I've kept popping by a couple of times a month just to see. I don't know how long that sock has even been out there. He could have tied it to the railing days and days ago."

And left it there all that time, waiting on me, even though I hadn't shown myself yet.

"So why are you hesitating now?" Hod asked.

"Well, I…" I grimaced. "I guess I'm afraid that showing myself after so long would be the wrong thing to do. He's all grown up. He's older than I was when I died. I *want* to see him, to finally talk to him again, but what if he freaks out that I actually appear? He might decide he's crazy or something. It's not like twenty-something-year-old men usually chat with childhood imaginary friends. Even if I told him what I really am, that wouldn't sound any less bonkers to him."

"He must be at least somewhat prepared to see you if he's requesting your presence."

"Maybe he's just looking for some final confirmation that I really was imaginary." I kicked my legs harder as if I could punt the problem all the way out of the nine realms. "I just don't know."

Hod got up and walked over to me. I held my legs in place so I didn't kick *him*. As he grazed his fingers over my hair, tipped my head into his touch. He hadn't called his shadows out to play, but his nearness always brought a soothing sort of quiet over me, profounder than what Valhalla offered, as if I was wrapped in the deepest night. Gazing up into his boyishly stunning face, so young and eons old at the same time, still took my breath away.

He was a god, yes, but more than that—he was the first man who'd ever loved me. The first man I'd ever loved back. I loved all four of the divine men who'd created a home for me here in Asgard, but Hod was the one who'd opened that door and made it feel possible.

He stroked his hand down the side of my face, lingering by my jaw. "You said you want to talk to your brother. You can list all the horrible things that could result from it, but there could be negative consequences from failing your promise to him too. I think… you can't know what would be best for him. So all you can go by is what would feel best to you."

A pang formed in my heart. I set my hand over Hod's and kissed his palm like I had years ago while we watched Petey discover *his* new home.

"Okay. That makes sense."

"Do you want me to come with you? I can tell you if I sense any reason for you to hold back."

I smiled against his skin, letting him feel the gesture. "Yes. That would—I'd appreciate it."

"Well then, I'm sure I can find the time in my incredibly busy schedule."

I did kick him then, but only gently. Smiling back at me in a way I'd never seen until after all the trouble with Surt and the rest had been over, he took my hand as I hopped off the side table and walked with me out toward the edge of Asgard's grand city of looming stone halls.

I could come and go from Asgard via Valhalla, one of the few skills in my supernatural arsenal that none of the gods shared. The city's other residents had generally relied on Odin's conjured rainbow bridge to make their way down to Midgard or back again. But several years back, Odin had gotten restless to go wandering again as I'd gathered he made a habit of doing pretty regularly and didn't want to risk the others ending up trapped if he was gone longer than usual.

After some trial and error, he'd determined that his son—Hod's twin—Baldur could master the magic if he worked in unison with the bridge's original overseer, Heimdall. I guessed it made sense, since Baldur's powers came from light as Hod's did from darkness, and what was a rainbow other than light made visible?

The god of light came out on a daily basis to practice the magic so he'd stay strong in it, and he was out there at the far end of the courtyard today, though not alone. Heimdall lurked in his tower that jutted from the edge of the realm well beyond speaking distance, but Hnoss, Freya's daughter and about as gorgeous as you'd expect from a woman born of the goddess of love, was leaning against a column chatting with Baldur.

I might have felt a tiny twinge of concern or jealousy if it hadn't been for the way Baldur beamed at me the second he saw me, as if a sun had lit within him. It was an expression twice as bright and fond as I'd ever seen him aim at anyone else.

Hnoss didn't look offended by the shift in his attention. She dipped her head to us in acknowledgment.

"Want a chance to show off your skills?" I asked Baldur. "We need to head down to Sacramento."

"I think I can manage that," he said. "Happy to make some real use of the magic." A flicker of concern passed through his expression. "Do you want more of a hand down there? If you're having trouble with the giants—"

I waved off his offer before he could go on. "It's not that. And for this particular situation, I need someone who'll be pessimistic about it." I bumped Hod with my elbow playfully and grinned at his twin. "But thank you. Maybe when I get back, I'll drop in on you."

Baldur beamed even wider at both of us. "You both can if you'd like."

Now that was an invitation it'd be hard to turn down. There was nothing like being wrapped in light and dark together.

Baldur turned to the edge of Asgard's land and stretched his hands toward the haze of clouds where the earth fell away. His face tensed with concentration. The act clearly didn't come as easily to him as it did the Allfather, but within seconds, a colorful shimmer streamed through the air. It expanded and thickened until the full expanse of the rainbow bridge stretched out ahead of us before veering down through the clouds.

Hnoss clapped her hands in appreciation. I leaned in to give Baldur a quick kiss. "Thank you," I said again, and unfurled my wings. The rainbow bridge might lead us down into Midgard, but that didn't mean I had to literally walk on it.

Hod took a similar tactic, conjuring his typical flying carpet of shadow to soar alongside me. It still awed me how well he could navigate with the use of his magic and his senses beyond sight. He kept pace with me down through the clouds and into the deepening night that had fallen over the human city my brother had moved to after graduating college.

I knew the route to Petey's apartment so well *I* could probably have found it blind. As we came up on it, my chest constricted, part of me expecting to find the sock gone as if it'd been a figment of my own imagination. But there it was, wrapped around the railing, the light seeping through the thin curtains over the balcony doors catching on its vibrant color.

Petey and his girlfriend were home now. I could make out the vague silhouette of Michelle with her wavy ponytail sitting in the bedroom, swaying slightly to the beat of a pop song that filtered through the window. Another form moved in the living room beyond the curtains. I recognized my brother from that motion alone.

I landed on the railing and crouched there, my heart thumping as fast as it had before. For now, unless I decided to let myself become visible, mortal eyes couldn't see me at all. But it was time to make my final decision.

Hod glided up beside me. "Having second thoughts?"

My fingers curled around the cool metal of the railing. "I just don't want to mess this up. I don't want to mess *him* up. All I've ever wanted is to make sure he's safe and happy."

As I glanced toward Hod, a movement in the shadows of the

courtyard beyond him made me tense up instinctively. Was someone watching us by the edge of the neighboring building?

But no human should be able to see us right now anyway. I peered into the thicker patch of darkness, frowning—and an alley cat leapt down from a window ledge and trotted away.

I shook my head at myself. Maybe I was just looking for excuses to avoid taking that final step forward.

Hod had probably noticed my momentary alarm but chalked it up to my worries about Petey. "You know him better than anyone," he pointed out. "Do you honestly think he'd ask for this meeting if he wasn't prepared for it to be real?"

"I don't know," I had to admit. "I don't think I do know him better than anyone at this point. For the last fourteen or so years I've really just been watching from the sidelines, only getting snippets of what he's thinking and doing." I looked back at the wavering form beyond the curtains. "We're not on the same page anymore. Not just him—everyone I used to know. They're all moving forward with their lives, and I'm staying the same, not aging, not changing…"

I was the one with the supernatural powers and an understanding of the universe far greater than nearly any human being, but I really didn't know what it was like to be Petey right now—to have graduated college, be building a career, making whatever plans he was for a family, and all that mortal stuff.

Hod's voice went oddly quiet. "That might be true, but it doesn't make you any less his sister."

"I know." I inhaled, exhaled, and squared my shoulders. "I promised him I'd always be there for him. I can't go back on that, not out of nervousness. If—if it goes horribly wrong, if it messes him up seeing me, you could wipe that memory away, couldn't you?"

Hod tips his head. "It'll be harder with one specific thing, but I should at least be able to reduce any distress he feels."

That would have to be good enough. Better I let Petey face the truth than have him think I'd abandoned him. Whatever he wanted out of this call to me, he'd have a chance to get it now.

I hopped down from the railing onto the concrete floor of the balcony and retracted my wings. Looking reasonably human in my razorback tank top and jeans, if possibly a little windblown and not arriving by the typical route, I knocked lightly on the sliding door.

The silhouette I knew was Petey froze. When he stayed motionless, maybe wondering if he'd heard right, I knocked again, only a little louder. If his girlfriend noticed and came to see what was going on, that would make this whole situation ten times more complicated.

He moved toward the doors. I stepped back, my pulse hitching, and gripped the back of one of the patio chairs. For one fleeting second, the panic that I'd made the wrong choice pealed through me. Then my brother tugged aside the curtain.

A thin stream of the living room's light fell across my face. Petey stared out at me through the glass, blinking, his lips parting in shock.

I hadn't encountered him this close-up in years. Even in his gob-smacked state, I could see the traces of the little boy I'd once watched over in those blue eyes, the rumpled blond hair, the few freckles dotting his nose, amid all the ways his face had matured into a man's.

In that first moment, I half-expected him to yank the curtain back into place and walk away, convincing himself it'd never happened. But then he recovered himself enough to reel in his jaw—and his mouth stretched into a smile with all the delight six-year-old Petey would have expressed when gifted with his favorite chocolate bar.

He grasped the handle on the sliding door—he was coming outside. My heart lurched. I didn't know what to do with myself, what to say. I hadn't really thought past the first moment when he'd either be pleased or horrified to see me.

At least the answer to that question seemed to be pleased. As he stepped onto the balcony, I stayed where I was, my grip on the chair tightening. Hod remained silent and invisible to my brother's eyes on his floating swath of shadow.

Petey closed the door behind him and then stared at me again for a long moment. I decided it was better to let him decide how to start this conversation.

"You really came," he said finally, his voice a lower version of the childish one I used to hear, rough with emotion. "I wasn't sure —it seemed so unbelievable…"

"I keep my promises." My own voice came out thicker than I liked. I cleared my throat. "It's been a long time. I haven't been checking as often. I'm sorry if I left you waiting very long."

He shook his head, his awed gaze still fixed on me. "No. It's only been a few days. I still can't—" He sucked in a sharp breath and appeared to gather himself. "Will you tell me the truth?"

Now that was a loaded question. "About what?" I hedged.

He made a vague gesture with one hand. "I did one of those genetic tests for finding family connections a little while back. I thought—Michelle and I are getting married soon, and we've talked about kids—I wanted to see if I could find out about any health problems I could be a carrier for, or if I have relatives around I didn't realize."

My lungs clenched. He couldn't have reached out to our mother. I'd checked up on her a few times over the past couple of decades. About five years back, she'd died—not at the hands of one of her psychotic boyfriends or in a bar fight or anything else I might have guessed, but from liver cancer of all things. That didn't mean her legacy couldn't have scarred him in some way she hadn't managed to once I'd freed him from her clutches. And I had no idea how his dad's family might have reacted to him if he'd tracked them down.

"Did that… go okay?" I asked tentatively.

"Yeah. Well, I didn't find out a whole lot. There weren't many people who showed up as blood relatives who were even still alive. I talked to a second-cousin a little who seems nice enough." Petey paused, his expression turning even more intense. "But I was able to figure out my original last name, and some of that family tree, and following that trail there were more names, pictures… You're my sister, aren't you? Half-sister, at least. I recognized your face the second I stumbled on the yearbook photo."

My mouth dropped open, but no sound came out. I closed it again, struggling to find words. I'd prepared myself for this moment as well as I could, but I hadn't expected this.

He'd asked me for the truth. Didn't I owe it to him?

"Yeah," I said hoarsely. "I am."

He knit his brow, studying me. "You died when I was six. I don't remember any of that. That was right before I ended up with my foster family. Are you… are you a ghost, or an angel, or…?"

A weak laugh tumbled out of me. "Something like all of the above. It's complicated, and some of the story isn't really mine to tell. I died, and then I got to come back, but in a way that means I couldn't return to my old life. But I could still watch over you. That was always the most important thing to me."

"You were there, right from the start, when I ended up with Brenda and Stuart. Do you know—no one's ever been able to explain why I'd lost all my memories—"

My mouth twisted. "I'm sorry, Pe—Peter." I knew from my observations that he'd dropped the childhood nickname a long time ago, even if I had trouble calling him anything other than Petey in my mind. "That was the only way I could figure out to protect you. Our mother… I don't know if you've found out anything about her, but she never looked after us right. And the men she'd bring to the house would shove you around. I was going to take you in with me as soon as my situation was secure enough, but then the whole dying thing happened. I had to get you out of there and make sure you didn't go back to her."

Petey nodded slowly. "I read and heard a few things. I don't suppose there's any way I can get those memories back? I'd just—it's unnerving, having that blank spot in my mind."

I glanced toward Hod automatically. Petey followed my gaze, the furrow in his brow deepening since he couldn't see who I was checking with.

The dark god shrugged as if to say it was my call. I turned back to my brother. "Some of those memories aren't very pleasant. But if you really want them—they're yours. I didn't want to take them away in the first place."

The corner of his mouth curved upward. "You're in them too, right? So they can't be all bad. I'd like them."

I motioned to Hod, and the god leaned forward, his expression intent.

Petey's face twitched. He swayed for a second, his eyes widening. Then his gaze caught mine again. "Oh. Wow. That was…" He swallowed audibly. "Thank you. For letting me have those back, and for making sure I didn't keep living like that."

He moved forward abruptly and pulled me into a hug. After my first jolt of surprise, I hugged him back. The worry that had been wound through my chest cracked and fell away.

He was still Petey. Still my little brother, even if he looked older now, even if he was nearly a foot taller than me at this point. I hadn't lost him.

"I'm sorry I pushed you away for such a long time," he said, still squeezing me tight. "It was just so hard to believe that you could be real. I had no idea you could be anything other than a strange friend I imagined out of nothing."

"Well, I am pretty strange."

He laughed and eased back. "I only meant—the wings. You do still have them? I didn't make that part up?"

"Nope." With a nudge of my mind, I released those extra limbs from my back. Their feathered span stretched across the width of the balcony, their weight comfortably familiar.

"*Wow*," he said more emphatically, and swiped his hand across his mouth. "When Michelle sees this—"

I tucked my wings closer to my shoulders. "When *what*?"

Petey made a jerky gesture toward the apartment behind him. "It was her idea to reach out to you. I told her about my old 'imaginary' friend and what I'd found out about my sister, how I wasn't sure whether you might have been real somehow after all, and she encouraged me to try. You have to meet her. She's amazing, really. I mean, I wouldn't be going to marry her otherwise." His smile turned shy with so much affection it resonated into me.

Still, I couldn't help hesitating. "Are you sure— I mean, you've known about me your whole life, even when you didn't know who I was. She probably figured nothing would happen and you'd be able to put the idea aside. What if she freaks out that I'm really here?" I was a hell of a lot less certain of her reaction than I'd been of his. I'd seen a little of Michelle over the past few years, but not enough to know much more than that she made Petey happy.

Petey raised his chin. "I'm going to share my life with her. I can't pretend this never happened now that I know. If—If she can't handle it, then she isn't the right person for me after all. But I think she'll get it."

Well, I'd come this far, and Hod wasn't raising any objections. I combed a quick hand through my windblown hair. "All right. I guess it's about time she met what she can of the family."

He sputtered another laugh, looking like he still didn't quite believe this was happening himself, and pushed open the door. "Come in. I'll go get her—I'll explain. Maybe keep your wings out, so it's obvious you're… something else."

Something other than human. Fair enough. I wouldn't want her wondering if I was just some random girl who'd climbed up to their balcony.

I followed him into his living room. The space was reassuringly cozy, with a comfy looking sofa and a rug thick enough that my feet sank into it, the light fixture overhead casting a warm glow over everything. Michelle's music filtered through the wall from the bedroom. Petey headed over to get her.

The music shut off. Voices followed, most of them too muted for me to make out the words, but there was one, "You're kidding me!" that reached my ears. At least she sounded more amazed than panicked.

A minute later, Petey walked back out hand-in-hand with his girlfriend—no, his fiancée. I hadn't been paying close enough attention during my past visits to pick up on the subtle but elegant diamond ring that now adorned her left hand. Her fawn-brown hair was still up in its ponytail, her athletic arms hugging herself nervously. She stopped just a couple of steps into the room, her jaw slack. Her gaze roved over my wings and then back to my face.

"Oh my God," she said.

My lips twitched with amusement. "Not a god. Just a big sister who wasn't willing to let death stop her from watching out for her little brother."

"So you really— Oh my God."

I adjusted my stance, my wings stretching and contracting, and her eyes bulged even more. "They *move*," she said.

"Yep. Hard to fly if they don't."

She gawked for a few seconds longer. Then an undeniably delighted giggle spilled from her mouth. "This is amazing." She gave Petey a light punch to the arm. "You must be even more special than I thought to have an actual guardian angel."

Her excited response and her fond teasing relaxed the rest of my doubts. Yeah, he'd found the right girl.

At my brother's urging, I recounted the story of my time with Petey in fairly vague terms, cutting off any questions that would have opened too much of a can of worms. Michelle didn't ask much anyway, too impressed by the fact that I existed at all to push for more. When I wasn't sure I had anything more I could tell, I figured it was my turn to ask some questions, now that I finally could again.

I motioned to her ring. "When's the wedding?"

"July 7," Petey answered. "You know—you should come! You can put the wings away, right? It'd be weird if I suddenly had a sister, but you could tell people you're a distant cousin or whatever. It'd be wonderful to have you there. You *should* be there."

He glanced at Michelle, and she nodded enthusiastically. "Yes, you should."

How could I refuse the chance to see my little brother setting off into a new life of his own with a woman he obviously loved? A smile split my face. "I'd love to. I'm sure you've already got the catering and everything set up—you don't need to worry about a meal. I could drop in just for the reception. I'd love to."

I paused, thinking of the man I'd left outside, the others back in Asgard. "Would it… be okay if I brought a few friends with me? From the place where I live now? They're important to me. I'd love for you to meet them too. I promise they wouldn't be a distraction or anything." If we weren't eating anything, it wasn't too horrible to ask for a plus four, was it?

"The more the merrier," Michelle said with an extravagant sweep of her arm. "It'll be at the pavilion on Osprey Lake."

They chattered more about their wedding plans, finishing each other's sentences and being so generally adorable that a weird sort of ache formed in my gut. I was so incredibly happy for Petey, so incredibly happy I could share that joy with him openly, but at the same time it was a reminder of how different my life was from his.

When I headed out onto the balcony after a round of hugs and requests that I come visit again, I shoved that sensation down as far as it'd go. Hod was waiting for me, patient as always.

"I got us a wedding invitation," I told him. "July $7^{th}$ at Osprey Lake."

He chuckled softly. "You never cease to amaze me, Ari. Let's go let the others know. They may need all the preparation they can get."

---

Thor twisted his neck as if he'd be able to see me past his square jaw where I was leaning close to fiddle with his tie. "I'm just not sure I'm a suit and dress shirt sort of man."

I smacked his massive bicep. "You'd better be after how much work it took to get this custom made." No chance of any suit off the rack fitting the thunder god.

With one last tug on the tie's knot, I stepped back to examine my efforts. Thor might have been more at home in casual tunics and trousers, but he filled out the deep gray suit and linen shirt damned impressively. I let out a low whistle of appreciation that brought a hint of a flush to his already ruddy face.

He swiped a hand over his dark auburn hair and peered down at himself. "It turned out all right?"

"You're lucky I don't want to have to go through the trouble of squeezing you back into that thing or I'd be peeling it off right now." I fluttered my eyelashes at him with a grin. "You look absolutely delicious."

Thor let out a low rumble of a laugh, but his own broad smile showed how pleased he was with the compliment. He rumpled my hair, his powerful hands always gentle when they touched me. "And after I join you for this event, will you finally bring me along on your giant-hunting? It's been a while since I had any skulls to bash."

I knuckled his chest. "And we should be glad about that. I never know for sure that I'm going to run into one until I do. You could end up bored if you tag along."

A fond glint lit in his dark brown eyes. "I'm sure I could find other ways of staying entertained. Especially with you by my side."

Before he could take that flirtatious line of thinking any further, Loki poked his head through the doorway. "Is the great lunk ready to go yet? I swear you preen more than our goddess of beauty does."

Thor guffawed. "I think I'm fit for a wedding reception now."

"Excellent. Because I certainly am." The trickster sauntered in with a jaunty tug of the lapels of his suit—which fit his tall, slimly muscled frame perfectly, and was also a lurid purple that seared my eyeballs and made his light red hair look even more fiery. The fabric gleamed with a satiny shine.

I coughed, just about choking on my tongue. Loki raised his eyebrows at me. "So stunning I've struck you speechless?"

Hod and Baldur trailed in behind him in suits identical in cut but contrasting in color, which fit their specialties while being more typical formal hues: midnight-blue for Hod and a pale dove-gray for Baldur.

The dark god rolled his eyes skyward. "I don't even need to see you to know this has to be said: We're supposed to be trying to blend in, not stick out like sore thumbs."

Loki patted his suit with a vaguely disappointed air and let out a huff. "Fine, fine. Suppress my vibrant spirit, will you?" With a shake of his shoulders, the jacket and slacks darkened into a shade that was nearly black, only a hint of indigo showing where the light hit it most strongly.

"Better," I said, patting his arm apologetically, but he'd already moved his attention elsewhere. Specifically, on me.

"*You're* not ready yet, pixie. Where's that dress Freya scrounged up for you?"

I restrained a grimace. "Back at my place. I'll go get it on now. It shouldn't take long."

I expected him to make some comment about how happy he'd be to help with that effort, but the trickster immediately spun to face the twins. "And are you all prepared?" he said in a vaguely meaningful voice.

"We have everything we need," Baldur replied, and smiled at me innocently when I gave him a questioning look.

I wagged a finger at Loki. "No mischief-making at the reception. We *are* supposed to be keeping a low profile."

He pressed a hand to his chest in mock-offense. "I can behave."

"Yeah, but you don't always want to. And I know what your sense of humor is like."

He tapped my chin, letting his hand linger there just long enough to spark a flare of warmth, but his expression turned momentarily serious. "I know how important this is to you, Ari. I promise I'll be on my best behavior." His somberness dissolved with a cheeky wink. "That doesn't mean I can't show you a good time, though. *I* know how much you like to dance."

"Hmm," I said, unable to deny that, and swatted him out of the way, because I really did need to get that dress on if we were going to make our appearance at the wedding in a timely fashion.

I hustled across the stone-tiled path to the hall that was now mine, as absurdly grand as it seemed for one once-mortal valkyrie to occupy on my own. I spent more than half my nights in the bedrooms of my lovers' homes anyway. But it was nice to have a space that belonged just to me, as if that confirmed I really belonged here in Asgard.

When I reached my bedroom, where I'd left the dress laid out on the bed, I balked like I had before I'd gone over to check on Thor.

I trusted that Freya had judged the sizing right. She was the goddess of beauty—among other things—that Loki had referred to, after all. The fabric was a gorgeous blue-gray silk with a subtle mottled pattern that made it look like rippling water, nearly the exact same color as my eyes.

It just looked way too fancy for someone like me to wear. My typical uniform was jeans and tank tops and maybe a hoodie if I was going someplace particularly chilly. The last time I'd worn a dress in my mortal life…

The last time had been the scratchy black smock Mom had tossed onto me for Francis's funeral when I was twelve. I'd been so numb with grief and guilt watching my older brother lowered into the ground that I hadn't cared that it didn't fit right.

So maybe it was appropriate that the next occasion I wore a dress while I played mortal was to celebrate how far my younger brother had come in his life.

I girded myself and reached for the soft fabric.

The gown did fit perfectly, its simple design hugging my slender curves but not overemphasizing them, the flowing skirt stopping just above my ankles. Freya had managed to find a design that looked elegant but still sported my preferred razorback straps so that I could free my wings without ripping anything. And she'd kindly paired it with strappy silver sandals that had only a slight heel so I wouldn't be wobbling all over the place.

I swept my fingers back through my hair, peering at myself in the mirror, and decided that was good enough. I didn't own any makeup or mousse, and I didn't think Petey cared whether I fancied up my face. I was his dead sister come back to life—that was pretty spectacular in itself.

I headed back outside to find my four plus-ones waiting for me on the pathway outside. Their gazes all shot to me the moment I reached the doorway. Loki's typical smirk stretched wider and turned softer at the same time. Baldur's bright blue eyes shone with undeniable admiration. Thor let out a cheer and clapped his hands, which brought a flush to my cheeks like his had reddened not long ago.

Hod couldn't observe the dress, but I guessed he could hear the shape of it from the whispers of the silk against my skin. He offered his elbow to me and leaned in as we set off toward the rainbow bridge. "I don't need to see *you* to know you look utterly beautiful."

"Flattery will get you everywhere," I informed him, squeezing his arm, and tried to focus on the handsome quartet of godly men around me and not on my first public family appearance in two decades.

We timed our arrival well. Bifrost set us down just shy of the lake, and when we reached the pavilion—a white domed structure with windows glowing with light—the dinner tables were all being pushed to the sides of the room to clear the floor. We made ourselves visible and slipped inside to join the crowd of guests just as Petey and Michelle stepped out for their first dance.

It was hard to imagine my little brother was the rather dapper-looking young man in the tuxedo swaying with his wife in her ivory tea dress to a song too recent for me to be familiar with. But he was still every inch Petey, from his now carefully combed hair turned blond again under the bright chandeliers to the wide smile stretching across his face. I wasn't sure I'd ever seen him so happy.

Then, as that first song ended, he glanced around the room and caught sight of me, and his smile grew. My heart ached with so much love I didn't know what to do with it.

As the guests swarmed onto the dance floor, Petey wove through them to reach me, Michelle close at his heels. He grabbed me in a hug just as tight as the other night at his apartment and then looked me over. I couldn't tell if he was having trouble adjusting to the idea of me in fancy clothes or checking to make sure I hadn't left any supernatural features showing.

"You came," he said, still grinning.

I reveled in the fact that I had him looking at me at all; that I was standing this close to him, that I could talk to him like a normal person. "I had to. Congratulations! You both look wonderful. The whole place does."

Petey's gaze slid past me to the four men clustered around me. "And these are…?"

"The people who made sure I'd still be around both back when you were a kid and today," I filled in. He didn't need to know all the intimate particulars of our shared relationship. Definitely TMI for little brothers, even little brothers who were now technically older than I'd ever been.

It occurred to me that I should probably introduce them a little more specifically, though. And also that using their actual names would give away more than I'd like to. I worried at my lip for a second and then motioned to the gods in turn. "This is Tom. Lukas. Barry. And, um—"

"Harry," Loki supplied helpfully with a twinkle dancing in his eyes. "Twins—you know how it goes."

Hod managed not to glower at the trickster before offering his hand to Petey. "It's a pleasure to meet you. We've heard a lot about you from Ari."

If my brother had any memory of the god who'd stolen most of his memories all those years ago, he didn't show it. He shook each of their hands in turn, and then Michelle offered us all a little curtsey, her smile a bit giddy. I braced myself for her to pepper the gods with questions to try to figure out more about their supernatural status, but thankfully she wasn't about to get *that* distracted from her own wedding celebration.

"It's great—really great—that you could make it tonight," she said. "Enjoy yourselves! There can't be too much dancing."

"We'll definitely get in plenty of that." Loki grasped my hand.

After another few seconds just grinning at me, my brother was drawn away by other guests wanting to give their blessings. I let the trickster tug me onto the dance floor. The reception didn't have a whole lot in common with the clubs I'd been inclined to frequent when I got the itch before, and I definitely didn't want to make a spectacle out of our presence, but we could still have a little fun in the celebratory atmosphere.

True to his promise, Loki stayed on good behavior. He spun me around and dipped me with a playful flourish, but mostly stuck to the basic bopping most of the crowd was comfortable with. After a couple of songs, Baldur stepped in and took me for a whirl himself. Then Loki shoved Thor toward me insistently. The thunder god trod gingerly among the mortals, careful of his bulk.

Through it all, Hod hung back by the sidelines, but he appeared content there. Too bad for him, *I* wasn't content leaving him there. After my boogey with Thor, I went over to pull the dark god into the throng.

"Is this really necessary?" he asked, but the corner of his lips had curled up with a hint of amusement.

I interlocked my hands behind his neck. "No one gets to sit the celebrations out. I don't think anyone here's going to judge your prowess."

He hummed. "I think I can keep up with the current pace all right."

We swayed together in silence for several moments before he turned his blind gaze on me in the way that told me I had his full attention even if he wasn't actually studying me with sight. "You're enjoying yourself."

Was he surprised by that? "I am," I agreed.

Hod paused. "Do you miss having a life like this?"

What a question. The ache I'd felt watching Petey earlier sank lower in my chest, growing heavier as it did. But as I took in the festivities around us, the weight of the idea faded away.

"I never would have had a life like this. I wasn't that kind of girl."

"You don't know how things might have turned out."

"I know enough." I eased a little closer to him. "I know I'm happier with what I have now than I ever was with my life before. No regrets here."

He drew in a breath as if he were about to say something else, but before he found the words, a sudden noise reverberated in from outside.

It sounded like—like a roar. A roar loud enough to break through the music and rattle the crystal in the chandeliers. My blood turned cold.

As I spun in the direction the roar had seemed to come from, another bellow split the air, this one with words.

"Where are you, valkyrie? How many mortals will I need to pummel before I find you?"

The voice was faint, carrying across some distance, but still far too close for comfort. The lights overhead flickered. I froze, exchanging frantic glances with the gods.

"Giant," Hod murmured, his hand firm against my back.

The other guests glanced around with confused expressions. I wasn't sure how much of the giant's words they'd made out with their less-keen mortal ears, but witnessing any of this at all was too much.

Somehow, one of the giants who'd barged into Midgard had found me here. Probably with a few bones to pick about the comrades I'd taken down over the past couple of months. And from the sound of the booming roar that echoed through the pavilion next, he was getting closer.

We couldn't let the brute ruin Petey's wedding. If he thought I was going to cower while he stomped around here, he could forget about that.

I touched Hod's arm and made a subtle gesture to the three gods nearby. The others nodded, Thor already heading for the door.

My gaze darted through the room and snagged on Petey's. My brother had frozen too, his mouth tight. As his eyes searched mine,

I gave a slight tip of my head I hoped he could take to mean, *I'll take care of this.*

Once more for old times' sake, I was going to protect my little brother and do whatever I could to ensure his happiness.

The five of us hurried out of the pavilion as quickly as we could without raising more alarm—or provoking questions I didn't want Petey and Michelle to have to answer. Outside, the breeze licked over my skin, warm with July heat even in the darkness. Stars glittered in the sky over the lake. And a shape larger than any human being lumbered by the scattered trees about a half a mile along the shore.

No, *three* shapes lumbered there. The giants had finally caught on that there was strength in numbers.

No problem. I had plenty of company too.

As we strode toward them, Hod summoned a thick cloud of shadow to stretch across the landscape behind us.

Loki nodded in approval. "Better not to let any prying eyes observe what we're about to get up to."

Thor cracked his knuckles, grinning way broader than anyone had a right to when being faced with enormous blood-thirsty fiends. "Just like old times?"

Baldur offered a little smile of his own. "I think we all know our roles by now."

One of the giants' mutterings reached my ears. "She *said* she was going to be at Osprey Lake tonight. Where is— Ah, ha."

He'd caught sight of us. My skin prickled with anticipation and irritation. Something other than a cat must have been lurking in the courtyard near Petey's apartment the other night—something that had passed on word of my whereabouts to the giants. The smaller creatures of the mythic realms could roam more freely than these brutes, and not all of them were friendly to those of Asgard.

Oh, well. This bunch would regret following up on that tip soon enough.

The three giants let out a chorus of roars and charged our way. One swung a massive sword; another brandished a club studded with jagged bits of metal. They each stood as tall as Loki and as burly as Thor, and aggression radiated from every movement they made.

They didn't stand a chance.

We hadn't needed to fight together anywhere near as often in the past several years as in those first weeks after the gods had resurrected me, but our powers resonated with one another as naturally as if we'd kept doing this every day. I shot into the air to swoop over the giant in the middle. Loki's flames tangled with a glare of Baldur's golden light, shooting toward the giant on the left. Hod and Thor cast a shadow-tinged bolt of lightning toward the one on the right.

The air thrummed with the heft of all that magic. The giants had just an instant to realize what was coming for them. They clearly hadn't counted on facing off against not just a valkyrie but four gods as well. They all stumbled to a stop and might have backpedaled if our attacks hadn't struck in the next moment.

The glowing blaze of fire burned the one giant's head down to a charred coal. As his body crashed to the ground, his companion's chest seared open with the passage of the ominous lightning.

The giant I'd sprung at was slightly nimbler than the others. I swiped at the patchy hair sprouting from his scalp, meaning to yank the life energy from his body, but he whipped to the side at the last second. His fist flew up, thick fingers snatching at the skirt of my dress and hauling me back toward him.

Lovely as the gown was, it definitely didn't make an ideal combat costume. I heaved away from him with a forceful flap of my wings and a hiss of ripping silk that made me wince. The giant roared, and a whirlwind of his own unexpected magic blasted around us. Flecks of sharpened air sliced across my arms and face.

"Duck!" Baldur hollered, just as Thor let out a battle cry of his own. I flung myself toward the ground.

A thunderclap rang out with a sizzle of scorching flame. Heat coursed through the air just above my shoulders. I slammed into the grass with my arms out to protect my face from the impact and rolled to the side.

My attacker swayed in the thin light from the starry sky above us. His gigantic body had turned into one immense cinder. With a creak, that cinder teetered over and hit the ground a few feet away from me. It burst into a flurry of ash.

Loki snapped his fingers, and both of the other giant bodies went up in flames. Within a few seconds, they'd burned away in a whoosh of heat. Nothing left but three blackened spots to show where our enemies had been.

As I picked myself off the grass, Thor reached me first. "Are you all right?"

I gave him a puzzled look. "Yeah, of course. They didn't put up that much of a…"

I glanced downward, and my voice faded out. Oh—*that* was why he was asking.

The lovely dress Freya had brought me was singed and torn and possibly even grass stained by the knees. I had a feeling my hair didn't look much better. And the giant's last spell had left thin scratches on my arms and, from the stinging sensation creeping into my awareness, my cheeks.

Baldur touched my elbow. A glow formed around his hand and washed over me. The stinging subsided; my skin sealed. My dress, however, still looked just as much a wreck.

I groaned. "I can't go back to the wedding like this."

Loki hummed, wiping his hands together in satisfaction with the job we'd done. "I'd imagine they'll be wrapping up before too long anyway. We had a good run of it. If you'd like me to return and give my condolences to your brother…?"

And get up to who knew what mischief while he was there without me keeping an eye on things? I cocked my head at him. "We should probably let him know we survived, but I think I'll let Baldur handle that job. Smoothing things over is his specialty, as he just demonstrated."

The light god pressed a quick kiss to my temple and set off toward the pavilion, vanishing through Hod's wall of shadow. His twin stepped between two of the smears of ash, his nose wrinkling. I expected him to suggest we head back to Asgard now, but instead he just tugged his wall a little farther along the lake, leaving the remains of the battle behind.

The filmy shadows blanked out all of our surroundings other than a grassy stretch of about twenty feet and, with a parting of the dark mist, the view of the lake. The water lapped gently at the bank. It was actually kind of a peaceful scene after the violence we'd just taken part in.

I flopped down on the grass, tucking my hands behind my head and gazing up at the stars in their frame of conjured shadow. It was suddenly hard to believe I'd really been at Petey's wedding at all.

"Now we have our own little bubble on Midgard," I said. "It makes things look more like a dream than real life. But I guess that's how most of my life is now."

Loki sat next to me and teased his deft fingers over my hair. "A good dream, I hope? Not one you keep hoping to wake up from?"

"Well, I could do without the periodic giant attacks…" But something in his tone demanded a more serious answer than that. Was there something in the air tonight? His question echoed Hod's from while we were dancing.

I glanced up at the trickster and then past him to Thor and Hod, and Baldur just returning. Emotion swelled in my chest.

I lifted my hand to rest it over Loki's, but when I spoke it was to all of them. "It's a better dream than I could have imagined asking for. Maybe there are a few things I wish could have happened differently, but it's pretty damn close to perfect. And I'd never want to wake up and find myself without the four of you. I love you, in case I haven't mentioned that enough recently."

Loki's mouth twitched into a smile. "Excellent. And while we're on the subject… Tonight's activities provided a perfect segue into an endeavor I've been considering for some time. I had intended this for after the main event—but I suppose we've made it to 'after' now if not by the expected route. What would you say to making this odd bond we share as real as it can be?"

"What do you mean?"

"My darling Ari." He slipped his fingers around mine and lifted my hand to kiss my knuckles, his eyes gleaming with something much deeper than mischief. "We dragged you into our lives without any idea how you'd inspire us to be so much more than we already were. Our existence had become rather hollow, and you've been the spark to fill that emptiness with vitality. I'd get down on bended knee if you weren't already sprawled on your back, which makes the pose rather awkward. Will you marry us?"

My mouth fell open. It stayed that way, with no sound coming out, for several beats of my heart before I managed to snap it shut again.

My gaze darted from the trickster to the others again: Thor, his arms crossed over his brawny chest and his expression so eager it made my heart outright skip; Baldur, with a faint glow of joy broken out all over his form as he waited for my answer; and Hod, shifting on his feet, awkward and yet wrenchingly hopeful in the way his dark eyes found mine, knowing exactly where I was without the need for sight.

I pushed myself up so I was sitting. "You're serious," I said, which maybe wasn't the response they'd have been looking for right off the bat, but I felt the need to confirm.

Loki chuckled. "I'm rarely completely serious in anything, but I wouldn't suggest this if I didn't absolutely mean it—and know my motley companions are equally on board."

"How—how exactly would we do it?"

He shrugged. "There are various traditions we can draw on. But seeing as we have three gods among our number, just about the highest authority you could call on, I feel safe in saying we can make our own damn ceremony up however we like and call it official."

The emotion that had welled up inside me before expanded, sweeping from my chest through my limbs with a giddiness so bright I wouldn't have been surprised to discover I was glowing like Baldur. If you'd asked me a few minutes ago what could have made me happiest, I'd never have thought to ask for this, but now that it'd been offered to me—

"Yes," I said, finding myself breathless. "Yes, let's do this."

Loki tugged me to my feet. The other three gathered closer around me. The trickster clapped his hands. "First let's have some decorations to make our little shadow pavilion appropriately festive."

Hod smiled crookedly and waved toward the shadowy veil around us. It drew closer, hazing the view of the lake without disguising it completely, arcing over us to blot out the stars. But in their place, with a motion from Thor's and Baldur's raised hands, warmer lights sprang into being against the darkness: sizzling lightning bolts streaking back and forth overhead, little glittering fireworks twinkling where they were frozen in mid-bloom.

"Now, naturally we need an officiant. I think I can shape myself to that role easily enough." Loki flicked his hand past his face and down his body. With that gesture, the hue in his hair leached away to leave it a silvery gray, his normally smooth face formed enough wrinkles to give it an aged authority, and his suit shifted to include a clerical collar. He drew himself up with a solemn expression that was undermined by the amusement dancing in his bright green eyes. "Shall we begin?"

"A Christian priest doesn't seem like the most Asgardian way of going about this," I had to point out.

The trickster waved me off. "We're blending traditions. If you want I could make myself look like the man who conducted my first marriage ceremony, but I'm not sure anyone wants to be looking at Odin's dour mug during this."

Yeah, no. I'd become more at ease with the Allfather's unpredictable moods and tendency to make sudden ominous declarations, but that didn't mean I wanted even a pretend version of him presiding over what was supposed to be a romantic occasion.

At my silence, Loki smirked and spread his arms. "Who gets the honor of wedding our blushing bride first?"

I hadn't been blushing before he said that, but when Thor stepped up at that question, my cheeks heated despite myself. The thunder god gazed down at me with adoration smoldering in his dark brown gaze.

It was all happening so fast, but staring up at him, I didn't feel a trace of hesitation. I'd already committed myself to these four men in ways far beyond anything I'd ever offered anyone else. I couldn't imagine my existence without them. The only part I had a little trouble wrapping my head around was that they'd want to commit so formally to me. But Thor left no doubt about his enthusiasm.

His voice came out in a low, warm rumble. "I don't have the same way with words that my sly friend does, but I can say there's no one I'd rather be conquering giants with. I hope to crush many more enemies with you by my side."

As I laughed at his framing of the sentiment, he pulled a short sword I hadn't realized he was carrying from within the jacket of his suit. He held it out to me, turning it so the leather-bound hilt faced me. A single black gem gleamed in the pommel.

I grasped the hilt instinctively, giving him a puzzled look.

Before I had to ask, Loki piped up. "Rings are for wimps. Our tradition is to exchange swords on the wedding day."

Another laugh tumbled out of me. "Of course it is." And blades made an awfully fitting symbol for our relationship considering how much bloodshed there'd been while we came to trust and love each other. But— "I don't have anything to give back." Even my precious switchblade, the one Francis had given me, was back in my hall, since I hadn't brought anything to carry it in.

The trickster shrugged. "No matter. Technically, Valhalla belongs to you, which means all the weapons on its walls do too. You can pick whichever you like to return the favor when we return." He motioned to the two of us. "Do you agree to honor each other, defend each other, and remain faithful to each other—within obvious acceptable bounds—for as long as this marriage holds, etc. etc.?"

I rolled my eyes at his casual approach to the vows and beamed at Thor, needing to respond to his statement of devotion first. "There's no one I'd rather turn to when there are foes to crush. Thank you for never doubting my strength, even when I did. I do."

"I do as well," Thor said with a matching grin. Without waiting for our faux priest's go ahead, he scooped me up in his arms and planted a kiss on me that sent tingles straight to my core. When the thunder god set me down, I was smiling even wider.

"Very good, very good," Loki said. "Who's next to claim our fair maiden?"

Balder was already moving to take Thor's place in front of me. He held a thin dagger that gleamed pale as the moonlight. "You helped me trust my light again and stood with me while I confronted my darkness. Nothing else in this world makes me shine as bright as you do, Aria."

I closed my fingers around the dagger's hilt and said the truest words that came to me. "Being with you lights *me* up like nothing else. But I'll always love every part of you, including your darkness."

As Loki asked for our vows in the same breezy tone as before, I laid the dagger on the grass beside me with Thor's short sword. I was certainly going to be well-armed by the time I'd become a wife four times over.

"I do," I promised, meeting Baldur's eyes again.

"And so do I," he said, and leaned in to kiss me. The familiar glow that his presence provoked filled my chest.

Other than the trickster conducting the ceremony, only one of my lovers remained. Hod approached me without prompting, his dark eyes even more intense than usual in his pale, handsome face. The ache that had closed around my heart earlier returned. Maybe I shouldn't need to ask this, but I found I couldn't stop myself.

"This is what you were arguing with Loki about the day you came with me to see Petey, isn't it? Are you sure—"

Hod cut off the question with a hand at my cheek, his head bowing over mine. "Any qualms I had were never about my feelings for you," he said, his voice soft but rough. "I was only concerned about whether you'd welcome the idea or find it too much of an imposition."

"Ye of so little faith," Loki muttered without any real rancor.

I clasped Hod's wrist with a reassuring squeeze. "Are you convinced now?"

The dark god offered the gentle smile I'd only seen him make for me. "It won't be the first time I've misjudged a situation—or you—and clearly I'll never hear the end of it. But if putting up with the trickster's 'I told you so' means I have you by my side until whatever end we eventually meet, I can't say I mind. I'm at home in the darkness, but I'd let it consume too much of me before I met you, Ari. You showed me a way out, and every day that's passed since, the gladder I've become to be here, to be happy—with you, and with my brothers and, most of the time, even this one." He tipped his head toward Loki, who snorted.

"You deserve every bit of that happiness," I told him. "I feel lucky that I get to share it with you. Even though you can't literally *see* me, you see me in other ways no one else ever did before."

Loki made a broad flourish with his hand. "Oh, you already know what I'm going to say. You obviously do."

I slid Hod's hand closer to my mouth so he could feel the curve of my smile. "Yes, I do."

"I do," he murmured back, and kissed me long and hard. When he released me, he fumbled in his jacket and produced a sleek curved knife. "I almost forgot."

"Right. It definitely wouldn't be official if you hadn't offered me an instrument of destruction." I took the knife from him and added it to my growing collection of blades. Then I turned to our self-proclaimed officiant. "How is this part going to work? I assume you're planning on participating as a groom too?"

Loki grinned. "You should know by now I'm nothing if not adaptable." He formed his clerical face into a somber mask. "Will the fourth husband to be please present himself?"

He side-stepped with a sweep of his arm into an extravagant bow, and when he straightened up he looked like himself again, smooth-faced and red-haired in his dark purple suit. His amber eyes gleamed with both mirth and a deep affection that echoed through to my bones.

He caught my hand and ran his thumb over the backs of my fingers, his gaze holding mine. "Ari, my pixie. I picked you because you weren't an angel, and somehow you proved I wasn't a devil after all. You believed in my goodness even when I couldn't. I suppose it's fitting that we brought each other back from the dead into a different sort of life. I enjoy being your risen hero far more than I ever reveled in playing the villain."

The trickster said it all in his usual glib tone, but I knew him well enough to recognize the current of truth underneath. I set my other hand over his, choking up for a second before I found my words.

"You believed in me enough to make me everything I am now. Even when you thought you were a villain, you proved over and over again that you'd be there for me no matter what came. When we first got together, you made a point of asking for no commitments, and I was relieved at the time because I was too scared of letting anyone near my heart. Tonight, I'm just overjoyed that we both changed our minds."

Shockingly, the man I'd never known to be lost for words looked as though he might be a tad choked up himself. He recovered quickly with a squeeze of my hand and brandished a full sword with ruddy stones glinting across the hilt. "For when a puny dagger isn't good enough."

Thor let out a soft guffaw. "You can never pass up the chance to one-up, can you, old friend?"

Loki spun the sword in his hand with an unnerving sort of grace and shot his frequent adventuring partner a grin. "There are some benefits to being the one orchestrating the schemes." He extended the sword to me hilt first. It swung in my grasp easily enough for me to suspect some magic had gone into its construction.

As I set the weapon with the others, Loki stepped back into his original position with a quick transformation into priest form. He glanced to the spot where he'd been standing beside me and then to me with an air to total importance. "Do you agree to honor each other, defend each other, and remain faithful to each other for as long as this marriage holds, and all the best of other things as well?"

With a twitch, he was across from me in his regular appearance again. He tipped his head to me. "I certainly do."

"I do," I said, and grabbed the lapel of his suit, bobbing up on my toes to claim the kiss I knew was coming. Loki made it hot and fierce, his fingers tangling in my hair.

When he released me, he spun me to face the others, holding up my hand as if I were the winner in a boxing match. Thor let out a cheer as loud as his battle cry had been. "The best wedding I've ever attended, except for one thing. You can't celebrate properly without mead."

"*You* can't, maybe," Loki teased.

"There's plenty of that back home," Baldur pointed out, and paused, his lips curving into the rare wicked grin that sent an eager shiver through me before he even spoke. "But perhaps there are a few other ways we might want to celebrate the occasion while we have total privacy here."

"Hmm." Loki rested his chin on the top of my head, his fingers trailing down the side of my neck to my shoulder to delightful effect. "You've become impressively corrupted, Light One. I like it."

Even Hod looked amused. "It *is* already the wedding night, conveniently enough." Not to be dissuaded by the trickster's pose so close to me, he moved in to collect another kiss.

I'd had twenty years to get used to the benefits of having four lovers who were willing to share, but the feel of more than one set of hands on me at the same time, more than one pair of lips against my skin, still gave me the headiest of thrills. I kissed the dark god back, cupping his jaw, and leaned into Loki's embrace as he slid his arms around my waist and pressed his mouth to the crook of my neck.

Not just lovers now. My husbands. That thought came with a thrill even more electrifying.

These divine men were mine, and I intended to show them just how glad of that I was.

Another hand found me—Thor's broad one against my hip, his mouth descending to my shoulder. Then, finishing our quintet of joy, Baldur nipped my earlobe before skimming his fingers down my torso and, as he sank to his knees, around my thigh.

Thor traced a path upward at the same time until he was stroking the curve of my breast. His thumb flicked over my nipple with a tickle of electricity, and I made a breathless sound against

Hod's mouth. The dark god kissed me once more, hard enough to make my knees go weak, and then nibbled his mouth along my jaw.

I turned my head, grasping Thor's suit jacket, and pulled the thunder god to me. His mouth collided with mine, his touch coaxing my nipple to a sharper peak through the silk with more little jolts of his electric magic. Quivers of pleasure radiated through me with each caress.

Loki hitched up the torn skirt of my dress to offer Baldur better access. The bright god simply breathed against my thigh, stroking the sensitive skin there, and a warm glow coursed all across my leg up to my core. His fingers glided upward and traced my mound to spot where my panties were already dampening.

My hips swayed toward him encouragingly. When his thumb found my clit through the fabric, I moaned.

Thor swallowed the sound with a sweep of his tongue delving between my lips. Baldur took the encouragement to tug my panties down and press his mouth to my sex. Bliss flooded me with the lap of his own tongue and the glow he cast all through my body.

I grasped his hair, urging him on, and the solid length of Loki's erection brushed against my back. When I ground into it in invitation, he groaned and grasped my hip. A moment later, with the hiss of a zipper, he was pressing against me from behind, the head of his cock gliding against the slickness of my slit.

Baldur suckled me harder, and the trickster slid right into me. I shuddered with the pleasure radiating through every part of me, my head lolling back against Loki's shoulder. Thor was still kissing me, Hod bringing his mouth to my unattended breast now, the five of us a mass of sexual satisfaction.

Adrift on the swelling of ecstasy, I found the wherewithal to tuck my hand into Thor's slacks. As my fingers curled around his thick erection, his breath stuttered. He pushed into my hold, matching the rhythm of Loki pumping into me, of the flick of

Baldur's tongue over my clit. Hod teased my nipple between his teeth, Loki thrust deep enough to hit the sweet spot inside me, a flare of fiery heat tingling through me at the same moment, and I shattered between them all with a gasp.

My hand clenched around Thor's cock, stroking him harder, faster. "Oh, Ari," he groaned, his voice ragged. He released my lips to kiss my cheek, my temple, with a growing wildness. Hod leaned in to reclaim my mouth.

Loki didn't slow his pace, rocking in and out of me with delighted abandon. Each pulse of his cock against that giddy spot inside sent me flying higher again. As he sped up his strokes, I did the same with Thor.

The thunder god's arm caught me in a crushing embrace. He jerked and sighed with the spurt of his release across my hand. The trickster tensed against me in the same moment, spilling himself inside me with a last few frenetic bucks of his hips.

I hadn't quite reached my second peak—and I had two more husbands I wanted to bring to the same heights. As Thor and Loki eased back, each dappling my shoulders with a few final kisses, I sank to my knees, nudging Baldur onto his back. As I yanked down his slacks, he caressed my arms, my breasts, lingering on every place that made my breath catch.

"You too," I said to his twin, tugging at Hod's pants. The dark god let out a pleased chuckle and freed himself just as I did the same to his brother.

The thunder god and the fiery trickster weren't done with me yet. As I positioned myself over Baldur's rigid cock, rocking back and forth over the head with a friction that made us both moan, ripples of mingled flame and electricity tingled across my torso. I felt as if I melted as much as lowered myself, taking the bright god's length into me.

A brilliant warmth whirled over my skin to join the crackling flames. Then Hod stroked his hand over my head, and cooler shadows spilled down over me, creating a blissful contrast of sensations. I drew him closer and licked the length of his cock, and his fingers tightened in my hair.

"You're a wonder, Ari," he murmured.

"I feel pretty damn wonderful," I said, my voice breaking with the cant of Baldur's hips as he pushed farther inside me.

I closed my mouth around Hod's erection, gripping his thigh with one hand and Baldur's shoulder with the other as the bright god hefted himself up to better meet me. A familiar darkly musky flavor filled my mouth. I bucked over Baldur, urging him even deeper, and swirled my tongue around Hod's length.

The rush of the combined streams of magic shivered and blazed all across my body. That was what we were together: magic, of a sort not even the gods had experienced before. And I wanted to soak up every particle of it for as long as my immortal life might last.

Hod came first, with a sharp sound and a twitch of his fingertips across my scalp. As his salty cum surged into my mouth, Baldur thrust inside me with renewed intensity. His glow washed through me, pooling between my legs and blazing with a golden pleasure so intense my vision blanked.

The final burst of ecstasy tossed me up and over, soaring in a way my wings could never have matched. Baldur's chest hitched, and he followed me, a thicker heat welling inside me.

As I came back to earth, the light god sat all the way up, tucking me against him but not shielding me from the other three men who clustered to form a ring around us.

Loki tipped his head against my back. Thor ran his fingers idly over my thigh, apparently in no hurry to get to his mead after all. Hod kissed my shoulder and tucked his arm around my waist. I nestled my head against Baldur's neck, surrounded by blissful warmth and something even better. Something I'd never believed I could have before these four divine men had dragged me into their lives.

"I love you," I said, my voice coming out quiet but clear.

Each of my husbands pulled a little closer, until I felt as if I were collected in the fondest of embraces.

"To our wife," Baldur said.

"To many adventures to come," Thor added.

Loki nuzzled the nape of my neck. "To happiness and hopefully a minimum of necessary heroics."

Hod gave a soft laugh and kissed my cheek. "To our dark valkyrie, and all the light she's sparked from this realm to every other."

# ABOUT THE AUTHOR

Eva Chase lives in Canada with her family. She loves stories both swoony and supernatural, and strong women and the men who appreciate them. Along with the Their Dark Valkyrie series, she is the author of the Bound to the Fae series, the Flirting with Monsters series, the Cursed Studies trilogy, the Royals of Villain Academy series, the Moriarty's Men series, the Looking Glass Curse trilogy, the Witch's Consorts series, the Dragon Shifter's Mates series, the Demons of Fame Romance series, the Legends Reborn trilogy, and the Alpha Project Psychic Romance series.

*Connect with Eva online:*
www.evachase.com
eva@evachase.com

www.ingramcontent.com/pod-product-compliance
Lightning Source LLC
Chambersburg PA
CBHW020345310726
48979CB00015B/2511/J
*9781989096949*